The White Goddess:
An Encounter

The White Goddess:
An Encounter

Simon Gough

GALLEY BEGGAR BRITAIN

First published in 2012
by Galley Beggar Press Limited
The Book Hive, 53 London Street,
Norwich, NR2 1HL

Typeset by Galley Beggar Press Ltd
Printed in the UK by TJ International, Padstow,
PL28 8RW

A CIP record for this book
is available from the British Library

ISBN 9780 9571 8530 2

For Sharon,

our four barking children,

and for theirs—

and for my mother, her beloved family

and mine.

GLOSSARY

Juan:	Joo-an
Lucia:	Loosia
Ruthven:	Riven
Teix:	Tesh
Soller:	Sol-yair
Puig:	Puj
Pa amb oli:	pambolly
Fornalutx:	Fornalooch

FOREWORD

This is a fragment of autobiography written in narrative form in an attempt to breathe new life into a remarkable story which occurred over fifty years ago.

It is the first of two books concerning The White Goddess; the second, the aftermath, has yet to be finished. When I first began writing them, in a bid to save my own life, I called them *Auto-bi-fantasies* – *Auto* because they were unavoidably about my part in them, *fantasies* because who, after so many years, could possibly describe every conversation and event of so long ago, and *bi-fantasies* because the story is told, entirely subjectively, from the viewpoint of a middle-aged man using his memories, and his collection of contemporary letters and manuscripts as stepping-stones to reach back to the instantaneity of his youth, and undo the harm that was to lie in wait for him in years to come.

Unlike a professional biographer, I feel under no constraint to be bound by precise dates and times, and for that reason I have emphatically avoided every reference in any biography of my grand-uncle which covers the early 1960s. My memories of those times are mine alone, and I was determined that they should not be distorted or contaminated in any way by the memories or opinions of others. To me, the narrative itself is far more important than whether or not an event or conversation happened on such-and-such a day. I want to tell my story as simply and fluently as I can, in the order I remember it. The atmosphere it evokes – and the reader – are all that concern me.

Novels are necessarily contrived; the truth – even the recovered truth – is not negotiable, and yet if I should inadvertently hurt any of the people I have portrayed, I apologise with all my heart; it was never my intention to do so. I am grateful to them for all the extraordinary parts they played in my life, and have tried with all my might to do justice to my memories of them.

29 February, 2012

BEWARE, MADAM!

Beware, madam, of the witty devil,
The arch intriguer who walks disguised
In a poet's cloak, his gay tongue oozing evil.

Would you be a Muse? He will so declare you,
Pledging his blind allegiance,
Yet remain secret and uncommitted.

Poets are men: are single-hearted lovers
Who adore and trust beyond all reason,
Who die honourably at the gates of hell.

The Muse alone is licensed to do murder
And to betray: weeping with honest tears
She thrones each victim in her paradise.

But from this Muse the devil borrows an art
That ill becomes a man. Beware, madam:
He plots to strip you bare of woman-pride.

He is capable of seducing your twin-sister
On the same pillow, and neither she nor you
Will suspect the act, so close a glamour he sheds.

Alas, being honourably single-hearted,
You admire and trust beyond all reason,
Being no more a Muse than he a poet.

Robert Graves

[1989]

CHAOS

It was late one evening in September, soon after I'd come out of hospital with a brand new lymphoma diploma certifying that I had only five years left to live (seven if I was lucky), when the phone rang. I should have suspected something at once; the telephone's ring had sounded different somehow – rustier – and my whole world tilted sharply to the right as I picked up the receiver. But by then it was too late; I was already drawn back into a past from which I'd long thought myself free.

'Simon? Hi! This is Foster Grunfeld. I'm calling you from New York. You remember – Foster? Fred Grunfeld's son? From Deya—?'

Who—?

'Yes, of course! Foster! How are you?'

I ransacked the Pandora's Box of my memory in the hope… Grunfeld…? Wait, just give me a moment—

—not Foster: 'Hey, listen, I was speaking to your great-aunt Beryl in Deya a few days ago. She said you sell old books now, which is why I'm calling you. Fred died suddenly – you know—?'

'No, I didn't, I'm sorry—'

'Yeah… it was quite a blow I can tell you, but the thing is, he was a historian – art and music – very respected – and he's left behind his library…' (he could hardly have taken it with him, I thought unkindly) 'and we have to sell it because it takes up half the house. Now, you know Max Reed—'

I tripped headlong over Max's sudden staring grin. He was the one-armed bandit of all time, with three lemons for a heart and a pip for the jackpot (if you could find it on the floor). He knew

1

more about books on art than any punter who'd ever pulled his handle. 'I know Max—'

'Ring him! He's just been over and bought a handful of art books. Fred used to buy from him, so he had first pick, and he mentioned you too. Hey – just come to Deya and look at them. What's to lose?'

'Foster—'

'Simon, listen!' His tone hardened dramatically; was someone with him—? 'Are you in or out?'

I strangled the phone against my ear, willing him to die. He breathed on noisily, unaware. I could hardly turn him down; this was the kind of offer that booksellers dreamed of. But Deya... A sickening sense of vertigo overwhelmed me as I clutched the phone— 'All right.'

'All right what?' he demanded.

'I'm in,' I grated, visualising his chubby, bespectacled smile of triumph. Foster had begun to seep like gas under the door of my memory. I recalled that I hadn't much liked him. In fact, now I came to think of it, I could remember ambushing him with Juan, throwing dried donkey droppings and fir cones at him from the top of the giant elephant rocks that guarded the entrance to the *cala*, the narrow stony beach at Deya. He'd been wheeling and dealing even then – usually beyond our means. And yet I couldn't help admiring his staying power; to sound unchanged after so many years—

'I'll be back in Deya next week,' he was shouting, 'so come out Thursday or Friday! Hey, it'll be great to see you again! Fond memories! Adios, amigo!'

Fond memories? His must be more forgiving than mine.

I slowly replaced the receiver while the implications began to sink in, my lips numb, a faint cold sweat on my face as I stared across the study at an old blown up black-and-white photograph pinned to the far wall – of Deya at sunset, a photograph taken from the garden at Canellun, looking past the Norfolk Island pine towards the two mountain buttresses which towered high above the village. In the deepening darkness of my room the shadows the tree cast seemed to move slightly, as though stirred by a draught—

This was ridiculous! What was I frightened of?

Of memories. Of the past—

Of going back.

I'd returned to boyhood haunts before; it was like returning as the conscience of another time to a place which had long since buried all trace of your existence. The locals stared straight through you on the streets, or worse, recognised something about you and averted their eyes – even the people who had once looked after you and your family. If you were brave enough, you might re-introduce yourself, to expressions of pained or feigned surprise, 'How you've changed, sir!' (or *M'sieu*, or *Signore*—)

I hadn't changed! Aged, yes, but not changed; childhood was unchangeable, the last playground of conviction; everyone and everything remained the same the moment you passed through it, as though touched by the Snow Queen's wand and set in breathless memory. As a child, you were given a bag of gold which was soon squandered, and I realised that only more gold would have bought back their loyalty. If I'd known as a child that a single bag of gold was all you got, perhaps I would have spent it... better?

Differently, at least.

I rang Max Reed.

'Ah, Goughie!' I could visualise his terrible staring grin. 'So you're going back to Deya!'

'Am I?'

'Of course you are! It's nine or ten tons of books – twenty or thirty thousand volumes. I'm too old for that malarky – I drove down to Majorca last week and took what I wanted. Hardly a boot-full, and Foster nailed me to the cross. Don't pay too much! No one else would be mad enough to go. The one bright spot was seeing your great-aunt Beryl – she's extraordinary – laughing and joking about Robert, and yet still missing him! How long since you've been back?'

I thought for a moment. 'Twenty-five years—?' Longer...

'Didn't you go to his funeral?'

'They bury people the same day out there – there wasn't time—' Not strictly the truth—

'Well, I got the impression from Beryl that it was high time you went back. Hang on,' he muttered urgently, 'I think one of my customers is about to faint – is it the beauty of the book, I ask myself, or has he seen the price? I'd better catch him. Good luck!'

Before I could think of another excuse for not going, I rang a travel agent and booked a flight to Palma for the following Thursday, with an open return.

The next few days were spent in the same state of pre-medication as I'd gone through before my biopsy. Responses became automatic and unimportant, while time passed like a cloud, painlessly and swiftly, as I wondered what it would be like to go back, letting my remote imagination stray through scenarios of possible encounters while at the same time trying to re-remember the secret ways between houses and villages and seemingly inaccessible coves.

I began to feel like some ageing *agent provocateur* pulled out of retirement to infiltrate the country of his childhood. This spectre of a middle-aged man preparing to advance upon his youth would have seemed ridiculous if I'd caught a glimpse of myself in the all-pervasive mirrors that littered the house, but I avoided them, shaving by touch, dressing carelessly.

There remained the very real problem, aggravated by my complete inability to make a decision, of where I would stay in Deya once I arrived. Much as I loved my cousins, who still lived there in their own houses, I felt that it might be awkward for them to have to offer hospitality to someone they hadn't seen in years, and might no longer wish to see.

The person I most wanted to stay with was Beryl, whose understanding of things, though seldom voiced, was augural, but whose reactions, for the same reason, could be harsh. I'd probably left things for too long, though – beyond good manners, certainly; beyond even great-nephewly bad manners.

The compass point to which I clung now was that it had been Beryl who'd insisted that Foster should get in touch with me. Was it a signal, I wondered, sent in that curious way she had of putting messages into bottles and letting them either sink to the bottom with a shrug, or drift off into the human current which restlessly and forever swept past the narrow cove at Deya?

Right or wrong, I decided it was, and made the telephone call that would finally decide whether I would see it through, or pull myself out of a vortex which seemed already to be turning with a slow, inexorable momentum.

'*Diga me!*'

'Beryl?'

'Yes?'

'It's Simon. Simon Gough.'

'*Simon.*' No exclamation mark, just the certainty of my name – as certain, it seemed, from the lack of surprise in her voice, as her conviction that I would telephone; and at once I was a child again and she'd unerringly found my latest hiding place: '*—there* you are—' leaving no room for doubt in either of our minds.

Was I going to come to Deya and look at Fred Grunfeld's books? She thought I *should*. Did I need a bed at Canellun? Would I like to use her car? I was welcome to both. She couldn't drive any more – her eyesight had got so bad that she no longer even recognised the people she knocked down—

I found it almost impossible to hold a normal conversation while being choked by emotion at hearing the sound of her voice again. By the time I'd replaced the receiver I was shaking and sweating.

Memory — so innocent and naive in itself, so potentially fatal when stirred, like the coiled snake that it was in its pluperfect lair. The past was not to be trifled with; while the present and future moved at their own irrevocable speeds, the past was time spent, time-without-energy, which could be moulded or stretched into infinite versions of remembered truth—

My sight had become too heavy and dazed to focus on anything except the cavalcade of violent remembered beauty within, knowing that I would at last reveal it, had to reveal it. I had a story to tell — a love story; a true love story. No one else would tell it now. Once I was dead, the story would die with me.

My past had haunted me for so long that if I didn't attempt to return to it now — lay bare the ruins which had become the foundations of the rest of my life, I'd not only have denied its existence, but denied my own. And yet, as ego-archaeologist, I'd have to be very sure of my reasons for disturbing not only the catacombs of my own life, but the sacred tombs of others, whose lives, however fleetingly, had changed my own.

Admittedly, Robert was dead now, and beyond harm. As for Beryl, I could simply ask her permission. If she agreed, then I'd write the story for her, for my family — and for Margot and Alastair — at worst an explanation, at best an apology. But above all, I suppose I'd write it for myself, not to be free of it (since my responsibility to it would only increase as I wrote it down), but out of a compulsion to re-live it, to draw out my once familiar self from this now stranger's dying body, like entrails, poring over them in search of reasons and omens for my continued existence.

To most people, the past was hallowed ground, never to be disturbed; the last memory before dying. Now, perhaps too late, I'd come to realise that it was a place to take by storm, that somehow I had to smash my way back into that maze and wreak havoc among the classical allusions to inviolable monsters, because the past, as surely as it was, once, paradise, could as easily become the womb for monstrous chimeras if left unchallenged.

As always, Beryl held the key to everything, if only in her head now. It was she, apparently, who had behaved most honourably of all. By burning her diaries, which she'd kept up night after night since first meeting Robert, she'd not only protected his memory but declared an amnesty to everyone who had ever behaved... not quite as they should have.

As for Robert, if I were to reveal anything of my grand-uncle it would be a glimpse of the dark side of his moon, that unexplored face of his personality which was often turned away from his biographers. Who, after all, apart from Beryl and those closest to him at the time, could put a date to an expression, to a bad mood, to euphoria, to a smashed bowl whose destruction stained and littered with regret an entire day's work? Or to the moment when the beginning of a poem materialised in a mind which a split second before had been utterly engrossed in the ripeness of a loquat?

On that fateful Thursday morning I found myself sitting at the back of a Boeing jet on the tarmac, looking through the small, rain-spotted window the drab fifties council estate of London Airport which seemed no more than a denser part of the grey gloom that hung over it. I was astonished at how little it seemed to have changed since I was a child, when it had been the newest airport in the world, and yet had already outlived the imagination of those times.

One by one, after an audible click, the jet engines were switched on and began to climb the scale of whining until they merged together into a banshee scream, the plastic cabin creaking and shaking in protest at the din.

Tail-first, we were pulled from our mother terminal like a piglet from a sow's teat, juddering with fury.

Interminable minutes later we drew to a lurching, rubbery halt at the beginning of the runway and the plane's temper took a turn for the worse, the fuselage shaking with repressed fury as the turbines surged to a deafening, intolerable pitch. Cramming my fingers into my ears, I hunched forward, eyes screwed up. This was the first time I'd been in a jet, and quite apart from the absence of propellers, I found the shattering noise unnerving. But it was September, and the plane was half empty, with no one in the seat next to me to witness my growing fear.

I cast about wildly in my mind for something to distract me—

I should have left it blank. My stick disturbed it, and from out of its lair the serpent struck.

I hardly felt a thing—

PART ONE

FROM GENESIS—

[1953]

THE STORY STARTS IN EDEN

Rain lashed the window beside me as the aircraft clawed its way upwards. Beneath me, London at last looked as I'd always imagined it would from the air – like Lilliput, a child's plaything, tiny, embraceable – and was gone as the Elizabethan burrowed into low cloud.

A new door of awareness opened briefly in my ten-year-old mind: *there is more; more than power, more than fear, more than* me—

The aircraft, so huge on the ground, became suddenly dwarfed by the cloud engulfing us, yawing from side to side, propellers driving us ever higher—

'Hello, you must be Simon! We've been told this is your first time in an aeroplane—'

I tore my frantic, excited gaze from the porthole as a stewardess, neat and perfect in her tailored suit, slipped into the seat opposite me on the other side of the table and buckled herself into her safety belt, smiling, calm—

How on earth did she know my name?

'I'm Sonja, with a "j". Captain Andrews asked me to look after you. It's not as bad as it seems, I promise. We'll be above it soon—'

I stared at her dumbly, still trying to work out how she knew me. *Audrey – that must be it!* Once I'd been through customs and could no longer be seen by my new nanny (whom I already hated), I'd carefully removed every label that she'd tied to me as she worked systematically from a list of final instructions left behind by my mother: 'Simon Gough, c/o Graves, Canellun, Deya, Majorca, Bally Aric Islands, Spain. Flight B.E.A. 146', all written on brown luggage labels and tied through the buttonholes of my jacket, through the beltloops of my shorts, and one even sewn into the lining of my school cap—

Sonja smiled brightly at me. 'Was that your mother at the airport?'

NO BLOODY FEAR!

'Er – no – she's in Majorca—'

'A friend, then?'

'Not really.'

'Ah,' she nodded wisely. 'She just sort of sees you off—'

'Yes.' I smiled back at her gratefully—

The floor dropped away beneath me, and I fell like a stone – *Our Father which art in heaven!* – my eyes flying drunkenly back to Sonja, imploring her—

'Don't worry, it's only an air pocket!'

I felt my hands begin to shrink painfully, and looked down to see that she was clasping them across the table.

'Shall I come and sit next to you?'

'It's all right, thank you—'

'You're taking it awfully well. But I promise you're safe—' Someone was noisily sick further down the aisle. 'Oh dear.' She withdrew her hands and anxiously craned across the empty seat next to her. 'Thank goodness, Sally's looking after him—'

Her eyes suddenly flew back to me, as mine had to hers only moments before. 'Do *you* feel sick?'

'No,' I grinned. 'It's like the Big Dipper!'

And we became friends, miles above the earth.

Just as she'd promised, we finally broke through the clouds and into the most dazzling sunlight and the deepest, bluest sky I'd ever seen. It was the colour of pure lapis lazuli, that polished stone which had been brought back to Beachborough by Saleem

Kassum. It had been sent to him by his uncle in Zanzibar who had bought it from his brother in India who had bought it from an explorer in Afghanistan who had then been eaten by a tiger. It was the impossible colour of heaven, and I craved it with a yearning so poisonous and all-consuming that to possess it was the only antidote. One summer's evening, strictly against school rules, I laid out, in order of suspense, my entire wealth on the thin grey blanket which covered my bed and which protected even my pillow from 'dust'. Against the dreariness of the blanket my tube of Life Savers, pocket money and fountain pen glowed, my penknife, given to me (I'd had to swear on the Bible in my locker) by Stanley Baker, glinted wickedly in the sunset which I'd carefully staged for the swap. Kassum stood at the end of my bed shaking his head slowly, a curious, sickly grin on his lips, his liquid brown eyes nervously watching my face.

Kassum was a Muslim, and I remembered something my grandfather had told me never to do to Muslims. With my heart in my mouth, I asked him to bring out the polished shard of lapis lazuli from the pocket of his shorts, where I knew it to be. 'How beautiful it is!' I exclaimed in my best imitation of a sultan. 'How it reminds me of the eyes of my dear mother! How I wish I could give her such a precious reminder of my love for her!' At which point Kassum was supposed, by Arab lore, to give me not only the piece of lapis but the entire contents of his tuckbox and the hospitality of his house forever. But in a faint cloud of acrid spices he vanished, leaving me painfully alone.

Sonja had gone off to help prepare lunch for the passengers.

I searched the sky again, desperate for something to distract me from where I knew my thoughts were heading. I was going 'abroad'! I didn't *want* to think about school – it was as bad as thinking about death, and last term at Beachborough had been bad – the worst yet, the worst that I could remember of all the schools I'd been to. It wasn't just the feeling of imprisonment, but the endless dread of punishments, of black marks and stripes, of daily 'worksheets' which had to be filled in by the master at the end of each class; if 'poor' or 'bad' outweighed the 'fair' or 'good' you were beaten every night until you conformed.

Like most of my fellow boarders I'd already endured seven years at school and a further two and a half years in boarding 'homes', first to escape the bombing in London, and then because my parents were both actors, which made it impossible for me to be at home with them except when one of them was out of work and could look after me. But whenever my mother was out of work she became ill – *'fat lot of good to you'* she would write in her letters – and what with that and my father's increasing success in films, she assured me there wasn't much of a home to come home to anyway.

Beachborough itself was as beautiful as any boy could wish, with a dense wood, a lake, a swimming pool, and a wide, slow river bordering the grounds at the foot of the sloping Great Lawn. If the school had been grim and ugly, like those in Dickens' books, then the discipline and violence within would have made more sense, but as it was, the contrast was baffling, especially when nightmares became reality, when the door of the dormitory was suddenly flung open after lights out—

'*Gough – dressing gown! My study—!*'

'Simon—?'

I was jerked out of my day-mare by Sonja bringing a tray of lunch, a meal made even more exciting by the thought that I was eating it thousands of feet above the earth, with nothing between me and certain death but a few inches of steel.

I discovered that flying was the most natural thing imaginable, that whatever fear was attached to it seemed only to heighten the excitement as I looked down through my window, like God, onto the hills and valleys and rivers of France, and then onto the highest snow-capped peaks of the Pyrenees before passing slowly over the Mediterranean, the darkest, bluest sea I'd ever seen, the 'wine dark sea' of Homer, which I'd read about at school but had never quite been able to visualise until now. The further we flew over it, the deeper blue it became, until I felt that if the aeroplane were to turn turtle I'd have found it difficult to tell the sea from the sky, the feathery wake of boats so far below from the feathers of cloud so high above. I was utterly and perfectly suspended between the two, in a state of such harmony with both that I could have sworn my heart stopped beating for a time – or beat so slowly that I could have lived for a thousand years. It was as though I were suspended not only in space, but in time.

I gazed, transfixed, as a new range of mountains slowly took shape out of the ether ahead, at the very edge of the horizon. Even the monotonous roar of the engines changed, rose, as if in recognition—

'Do you know where that is?' Sonja's voice fleetingly over my shoulder as she stared out through my window at the approaching mountains. 'It's Majorca!'

'Gosh!' I gasped, staring down as the island expanded towards me. So this was going to be 'abroad'!

The sudden sense of escape filled me to the brim. Perhaps I could stay here forever—

GRAND-UNCLE ROBERT

My ears began to ache. The lower we descended, the more they ached. I swallowed hard, then held my nose and pursed my lips and blew through my ears, as Sonja had told me to do. The pain grew worse. I could no longer look out of the window, although I wanted to so badly, but sat pressed into the back of my seat staring straight ahead, my hands clasped to my ears in an effort to soften the pain.

Sonja came back, recognised my problem at once, and took a boiled sweet from a pocket so immaculate that there seemed no room for one inside it. 'Suck that, Simon – it should help. It's only the cabin pressure. You'll be fine once we land,' she smiled reassuringly as she strapped me into my seat, and then strapped herself into the one opposite.

The plane, from being a magical cocoon slipping through space, became clumsy and hesitant, rocking from side to side, rising and falling as if it couldn't make up its mind what to do. The engines throttled back, increasing the terrible din in my ears. We didn't belong on Earth—

'Is your mother meeting you?'

The question came as such a shock that I almost forgot the pain. Of course she would! Unless she had asthma or bronchitis or something, I'd see her in a few minutes – oh, God, please make the pain go away so that she needn't know. She'd make a fuss, get tired, cross—

Sonja touched my arm and pointed through the window.

I gasped. Only feet away, rushing past me, was a windmill – then another, and another, faster and faster, strange white windmills with little canvas sails stretched over frames on the ends of long poles, motionless in the breathless sunlight—

A jolt and screech of wheels bouncing onto the runway, then another, the turbines roaring, my ears bellowing back, the aircraft braking and braking until I felt as though I were being dragged through my seat backwards – then suddenly released as the engines relaxed at last and we began to taxi, bouncing and bumping over what looked like endlessly repaired tarmac.

Sonja ruffled my hair and smiled at me. 'I'll let everyone else off first, so you can get used to normal pressure again.' She glanced out of the window. 'Is your mother here? Can you see her?'

I looked out at the shacks and prefabs of the tiny aerodrome. It had obviously been raining hard; a small group of people was waiting on the tarmac, standing knee deep in shimmering water – which began to vanish as we approached – a mirage! The biggest I'd ever seen—

In the front of the group were two soldiers in green uniforms with rifles slung over their shoulders, wearing the oddest shiny black hats with the brims turned up at the back, as though they'd been leaning against walls all their lives. Between them, a small man in a suit and dark glasses was sitting at a desk.

And then I saw her, as I'd never seen her before: even more frightening, with a scarf tied under her chin, a straw hat clutched to the top of her head, her blood-red lips fixed in a smile made all the more sinister by a pair of gleaming, expressionless dark glasses. With her other hand she was waving at the aeroplane as we turned broadside-on to the knot of people and came to a halt.

And then she seemed to actually see me, her smile becoming suddenly real, her waving frantic, and I let out a gasp of relief which I must have held in since I first saw her. She was happy! I waved back.

The noise of the engines died away, and the other passengers began to rise to their feet, talking excitedly into the sudden silence as they pulled small bags from the string racks above their heads. The door of the fuselage was opened and daylight and a hot draught suddenly filled the compartment.

I pulled back out of sight, so that my mother could let go of me, although I went on watching her from the shadows. She was talking to the people on either side of her, to a man in a flat black Spanish hat who dwarfed everyone else, and a lady with dark hair chopped off short against her neck, clutching a shiny white handbag. The man seemed somehow familiar as he looked around impatiently, exchanging the odd word with other people in the welcoming group. His pale linen suit was creased and shapeless, but he wore a colourful waistcoat and a red handkerchief round his neck. All at once he raised his hat to a lady who had just reached the bottom of the gangway, and I could see his face properly. His hair was greying and curly, his nose like a Roman emperor's – perhaps this was Great-Uncle Robert... *yes!* He looked just like Great-Uncle John and Great-Uncle Charles, but bigger – *more—*

'*Simon—?*' Sonja was gesturing to me from the end of the almost empty aisle where the Captain and crew were waiting in line to say goodbye to the passengers. I hurried towards them, apologising, shaking hands, until I got to Sonja, whose hand I shook very firmly. 'Thank you very much! It was amazing! I do hope...'

She threw me the most perfect smile. 'So do I. Goodbye, Simon.'

I stepped unsuspectingly out of the plane and onto the gangway—

The heat hit me with such a blow that it sucked the air from my lungs and I had to cling to the rail for a moment, stunned, trying to shade my eyes from the dazzling sun.

By the time I got to the foot of the steps, the pain had grown again in my ears as I was gathered into my mother's embrace, into her dark, familiar scent of perfume and illness. 'Darling, I was so frightened—'

Still dazed by heat and strangeness, I was told to show my passport to the man seated at the desk, who stamped my visa violently and gave it back, just as I was introduced to my great-aunt Beryl, who didn't look like a great-aunt at all, but appeared to be about the same age as my mother. She looked down at me with enthusiastic curiosity. 'Just call me Beryl, it's so much easier—'

'And you remember your great-uncle—'

'*Grand*-uncle!' he protested at once, grasping my by the shoulders and leaning down to give me a stubbly kiss on both cheeks. '*Great* is for steamships and railway lines, don't you think? *Grand* is for fathers and uncles – and Russian dukes, of course! You probably don't remember, but we last met in your pram—'

'Oh, *Robert*!' exclaimed Beryl. 'He doesn't want to be reminded of his dratted *pram*!'

'Nonsense! Queen Anne kissed me in mine—' He fixed me with his startling blue eyes. 'Not literally, of course, but in direct line, if you see what I mean – you must read my autobiography one day. I only wish I'd met you before, so I could have put you in it. I say, you look awfully hot. Did you fly too close to the sun?' He laughed and poked me in the ribs. 'Who am I talking about?'

'Icarus, sir,' I said at once, grinning up at his surprise. School had its uses after all. 'But I think they got the story wrong,' I went on intrepidly, in spite of my mother's sudden frown. 'The wax couldn't have melted, because the higher you go, the colder it gets – the pilot said so—'

'Bravo!' he exclaimed, thumping me on the back. 'I say, I do believe we're going to get on! But don't call me "sir" – you're *family* – so you can call me Robert, if you like, or Uncle Robert, or grand-uncle – take your pick. Now let's get your jacket and tie off – we're very informal here, and all this looks horribly like school uniform to me. Chuck it all away!' He made a curious gesture over my head, then threw whatever he'd found invisibly over his right shoulder. '*Ego te absolvo*,' he intoned, 'I hereby declare you to be purged of the sin of wearing school clothes on holiday!'

'Well, *that's* all right, then,' said Beryl in a matter-of-fact sort of voice as she and my mother gathered up the layers of my peeled-off clothes – my mother with slight murmurings of impatience. But I was still squinting up and smiling into the face of my grand-uncle as I undressed, into the face of this magician who was reading my thoughts as they occurred to me. It was wonderful to be understood without having to explain oneself.

'Shoes and socks?' he suggested, his face alive with wide-eyed daring. 'No, on second thoughts, the porters spit on the tarmac – wait till we get to the car.' He led the way to a dusty Land Rover standing, like himself, head and shoulders above the crowd of cars next to the control tower. He turned back to me, eyebrows raised in surprise. 'My friend Ricardo Sicré lent us this, just to come and get you!' And again he forged on ahead of us.

My eyes widened with every step he took. At the bottom of his trousers he was wearing not shoes, but black slippers on his bare feet. 'Why's he wearing slippers?' I whispered urgently to my mother, who '*Sssh'd*' me as Beryl burst out laughing.

'Those aren't *slippers*! They're called alper garters. *Alpargatas* in Spanish. They have rope soles so that you don't bruise your feet on the rocks. We'll get you some. Now, I expect you're thirsty—' So they could *both* read my mind! 'I thought we'd stop in Palma and have a cold drink and an ice cream. It's quite a drive through the mountains to Deya, but it'll be dark by then, and you can sleep if you like. I dare say your mother could do with a drink, too – eh, Diana?'

'I should jolly well think I could!' gasped my mother, and for some reason they both laughed.

On the way out of the aerodrome I became aware of the strangest thing: Beryl was driving. It wasn't that I'd never been driven by a woman before, but the steering wheel was on the lady's side, and the sensation was... odd. Robert sat next to her, fidgeting but apparently unaffected, lost in thought, his eyes staring inwardly around him, while my mother and I sat behind them both, her arm around me, asking all the questions that grown-ups ask and none of the questions that they don't but *should* if they were as clever as they made out. So I was ready for anything, and could let my eyes and my imagination run wild as I answered her on automatic pilot (or 'George', as Captain Andrews had called it when he'd invited me into the cockpit) – until she asked the one question I dreaded: 'Have you seen your father?'

'No. But he sent me ten shillings! He's making a film in Ireland with a ferret. I mean, he has a tame ferret in the film.' I reached into the inside pocket of my jacket which lay next to me. 'And he sent me a letter to give you—'

Instead of opening it, she took it quickly, almost secretively, unclipping her handbag, and stuffing it inside before she leaned towards me and pulled at my head. I thought she meant to kiss me, and gave her my cheek, but she pushed it away and whispered into my still raw ear. 'Did you bring me the money?'

'Yes!' I whispered, drawing back. 'I went to see Mr Hill at Drummond's, and he gave it to me in a sealed envelope. It's in my suitcase. He said I wasn't to put it in my pocket in case I was kidnapped!'

She squeezed me to her. 'Clever Mr Hill! He always knows the best wheeze. And did you bring your school report, darling?'

'Er – Audrey packed it, I'm sure—' which was perfectly truthful – but later I'd slipped it out of my case and flung it as far as I could under my mother's huge double bed. If I was lucky, she'd be ninety before she found it. Under-the-bed gave her asthma.

I stared past her, at the darkening blue of the Mediterranean with its playful fringe of white surf tickling the drowsy ochre sand. On the horizon, an enormous blood-orange sun was coming to rest on the rim of the sea, wobbling like a water-filled balloon before, to my chagrin, it began to sink with the loss of all hands, including me. I'd always dreaded sunset and the onset of night.

The stifling heat clung on and on into the growing darkness.

I was awfully thin! I was awfully hot! Did I have a headache? I looked pale—

Again, Beryl said everything that I couldn't: 'Diana, stop *fussing*! He's perfectly all right, he just needs a good holiday. You won't recognise him after a month in Deya!'

Robert, huge in the gathering darkness, turned round in his seat and told her that his mother used to faint at the sight of him when he came home from Charterhouse. 'It takes an awful lot to kill an English schoolboy – I know people who've been trying for years!'

As we approached Palma the crescendo of new experiences seemed to grow and grow, to the point where I couldn't absorb any more. The jolting road, the din of the narrow streets, the neon lights, the heat which seemed to expand inside my throbbing ears, and my mother's constant, anxious stares. Unlike Beryl, she simply couldn't understand the hugeness of the meal I was trying to digest – a meal which was beginning to sicken me with its dark richness, its noise and smells and its sheer strangeness. And above all – the heaving icing on an increasingly blurred cake – the desperate need *not* to be sick, to be polite, to not let her down – for *my* sake.

Finally we drew up on the corner of a wide, dimly lit avenue lined with palm trees, and got out of the Land Rover. Once my feet were on the ground again I began to feel less sick, and after a moment I felt all right enough to dutifully walk round to my mother's door. She'd taken the envelope I'd given her out of her handbag and was opening it just as I came up to her window. Some instinct made me wait in silence as she unfolded the sheet of paper and searched impatiently for enough light to read it by. But there were only a couple of lines of writing.

'*Bah!*' she spat, and crushed the letter in her hand.

I opened the door to a face that was suddenly tired and ravaged. Quickly, she turned away from me, stuffing the letter and her despair back in her bag. I heard her take a high-pitched, stifled breath before suddenly turning to me again, a ghastly smile fixed on her face. 'There!' she whispered triumphantly – *all better!*

Grudgingly, I admired her. My father had obviously sent her no money.

'This street is called the *Borné,*' said Beryl. 'Well, actually, it's now called the Avenida Generalisimo Franco, but I wouldn't worry about *that*! Nobody else does. It's the main street of Palma, and *this*—' as we turned the corner, 'is the Bar Formentor. We come here whenever we're in town. It's our *meeting place*—' I darted a quick look at my mother, but she seemed to have recovered herself, 'so if you're ever lost in Palma, you must ask for the Bar Formentor and tell them you belong to us. Don't say Graves, though, say *Grah-vés*. Can you say that?'

'*Grah-vés,*' I said gravely.

'From Deyà.'

'From Deyà. *Grah-vés* from Deyà.'

'Good! *Very* good. Now, the reason we come here isn't because it's the smartest bar in Palma, but because it has the best ice cream!'

Which it did. And the best orange juice I'd tasted since my war ration vitamin C, though not quite as good, even though Robert said it was made with fresh oranges and couldn't be better if it tried.

The bar was certainly very smart, with its concealed neon lights and green leather upholstery, and the hundreds of extra things they brought to the table when all we'd asked for was ice cream and some drinks. The people sitting around us were equally smart, the men in double-breasted suits with macassar oil on their hair, the women with hard, expressionless faces under pale pink face powder, touching their jewellery in sudden jerks, as though afraid it might have been stolen while they talked. Everyone kept staring at us, as smart people did, even though they went on with their conversations. I thought them quite rude until it dawned on me that I must look a bit odd, half undressed in a smart bar, and Robert in his alper garters with no elastic in them. I shifted my chair a little to shield his feet from their gaze, and caught him watching me with an odd expression on his face. I smiled quickly and looked away. It was one of those private expressions which were too risky to work out. He must have looked away, too, because suddenly one of the men at another table caught his eye and they both leapt to their feet and began shouting at each other across the room, exchanging Spanish like machine gun fire, though Robert's accent was exactly the same as when he spoke English. I was pointed out—

'Stand up, darling, and smile!' came my mother's harsh whisper.

I stared at her in astonishment. 'But he's rude! He's arguing with Uncle Robert!'

Beryl choked on her drink. 'No! It's all right, they're *friends*! It's Joàn Miró, a local painter. They've been friends for years. He's pretending to be offended that Robert didn't recognise him. Robert's telling him that God cursed him by making him too tall, and that he doesn't notice anything under two meters high—' She started to laugh silently. 'It's just the *language* – Spanish always sounds as if people are having terrible fights, when all they're talking about is the weather. You'll soon pick it up—'

'*Stand up and smile when I tell you!*'

I stood up and turned towards them, but the conversation had passed me by, and I was ignored.

Once we'd finished our drinks and ice creams, Beryl took my mother off to the loo. As she walked away, my pain and nausea seemed to follow her, as though it was attached to her rather than to me.

My relief was short-lived, though, because when I turned back to my grand-uncle I realised, with sudden alarm, that we were alone together. I shot him a fleeting, wary look and saw that although he appeared to be staring at me, in fact he was looking straight through me, with such concentration that I turned round to see if something had happened in the street.

All at once he towered to his feet and began pacing restlessly up and down in front of the windows, staring unseeingly through them in the same way that he'd been staring at me. Then he suddenly turned back and smiled a courteous, sweet smile. 'I expect you're tired—'

'No, I'm all right – really!'

'It's odd, I was just thinking, watching you seeing things here for the first time – things that I first saw – what? – nearly a quarter of a century ago. The island's changed so much, you see, but because I live here I don't really notice. One gets used to anything, I suppose, if it just steals up on you. Even to unhappiness. Don't you find? The trick is to change your viewpoint, never to let yourself get stale. Or unhappy. Then even those things you're most used to appear beautiful again, and things you're frightened of become familiar, so they become less frightening. D'you follow?'

'Yes—' But to be spoken to as his equal had left me tongue-tied. It was as if, somewhere among the foliage of his words was concealed a gate into an awareness to which I had no key as yet. Even when my mother returned, smiling now, I was still trying to reach into his world. Had he meant himself, or my mother? Or me?

Beryl must have defended me in the ladies, because when we left the Bar Formentor and went back to the Land Rover, it was my mother who climbed into the back and arranged the rugs and pillows for me before getting out and helping me in. 'I'm very proud of you,' she whispered, kissing me.

My great-aunt was clearly someone to be reckoned with!

I got in and lay down on top of the blankets as we set off again. It was still too hot to pull them over me, and I couldn't sleep. The earth itself, this strange new earth, seemed to speak to me through the whining hum of the tyres and through the jolting and bumping of a road that got worse with every mile we travelled. After a while, when we started to climb, I heard it even more clearly when Beryl double de-clutched at the approach to each bend. I might not understand a word of what the earth was saying yet, but I swore to myself, and to the earth, that I would somehow learn its language – and my grand-uncle's.

Every now and then, at the beginning of the journey, my mother would look over the back of her seat to make sure I was asleep. By listening for her movements I could be ready for her, and close my eyes. I badly needed to be alone, to lie next to my other, older self and absorb, between us, the breathtaking events of the day which had sometimes threatened to drown me in the wake of their passing.

As we left the lights of Palma behind and drove into the darkness, I became aware of a growing brightness through the skylight in the roof: a rising moon surging up the sky, silent and remote, spilling silver light and coal-black shadows onto my face and clothes.

I sat up soundlessly, as ghostly as the light itself, and looked out through the side window.

Walls of rock enclosed us on either side. I lurched to my feet, stretching out my hands against the inside of the roof to steady myself, and looked up through the skylight. Far above, the rocks turned into crags, and then into silent mountain tops, so distant and yet so clear that I gasped in awe.

Beryl's voice shouted back at me above the noise of the engine. 'Are you all right, Simon?'

Guiltily, I turned and met her eyes in the driver's mirror.

'*Darling*—' My mother's shocked voice.

'But it's so beautiful—'

Beryl laughed, leaning forward and banging her forehead lightly against the steering wheel, then shaking her head. In the moonlight I saw her teeth gleam in a smile as she repeated my words to Robert. His voice floated back to me. 'Well, it is! He's no fool—'

'Darling, lie down, it's dangerous,' murmured my mother.

Still precariously clutching the roof, I looked down into her silver, bloodless face.

'But it's beautiful,' I whispered fiercely, staring out again. But not as beautiful as before she'd spoken.

'Lie down! You're blocking Beryl's view in the mirror.'

Clutching the seat on either side of me for balance, I lay back on my makeshift bed, stewing with resentment.

The air became cooler as we climbed. Pulling one of the rugs over me, I turned onto my side, drawing my knees into my chest, gradually becoming aware again of the droning chant of the earth speaking to me through the tyres, rumbling and echoing around the cab of the Land Rover, and thought I could at last make out the sound of the word

home...

I had come home...

Or was I simply grasping with one hand for what I'd just lost from the other?

I didn't remember being put to bed that night – I didn't remember much else about that night at all, apart from arriving at Canellun and toppling disjointedly out of sweaty sleep and the Land Rover into a tropical moonscape by Gauguin. There were huge plants everywhere, exotic smells, an immense palm tree curving over the drive, and a Norfolk Island pine which I recognised at once from the drive at Beachborough, which delighted Robert. His surprise at my knowledge was enough to overcome my reluctance to follow him up the drive towards a shadowy and rather forbidding stone house, its shutters drawn tight against the mosquitoes which my mother started to warn me about even as they began to bite me. Suddenly I stopped dead in my tracks while she went on up the drive towards a weak light hanging over the porch.

I held my breath and listened, staring up at the silver terraces of olive trees that gently rose behind the house towards a distant fan-shaped mountain top, pale and haunting in the moonlight.

'What's that noise?' I called out. The strangest high-pitched chirring noise surrounded me, growing louder, undulating, and all among it a flat clonking sound, like saucepans being clunked together.

'Come in quickly, darling, or you'll get bitten!'

'I already have. But what's that—'

'They're sickarders—'

'What are they sick of?'

'No, C-i-c-a-d-a,' she spelt, 'like crickets. Come on! Everyone's waiting to meet you—'

I started to move slowly towards her. 'But what's that clonking sound?'

'*What?* Oh – sheep bells! Hurry! You won't even hear them after a couple of days.'

But I wanted to hear them! I liked them—

Slapping at another bite, I looked up into the immense velvet sky, its nap, like moleskin, stroked by moonlight to a silver-greyness, dimming the stars.

'*Simon—*'

Despite the size of the house, the rooms were quite small and seemed to be packed with people who had gathered for a welcoming supper, almost all of them taller than me, lit by naked bulbs whose light ebbed and flowed dimly. Robert and Beryl and my mother shepherded me round, introducing me to their friends and to my relations, including a tall, dark-haired girl called Lucia, who was my cousin, and obviously wished she weren't.

As if in a nightmare, I craned my neck up into face after sweating face looking down at me, eyes like gleaming fried eggs, white smiles in dark faces like the bones of the lamb cutlets that my mother picked clean with her teeth and piled up on the side of her plate like a vulture—

Desperately, I looked round in search of a companion of my own—

Now standing in front of me, with white-blonde hair, wild eyes magnified behind National Health spectacles, mouth open wide with mock delight at meeting me—

'Hello, I'm your cousin Juan! I'm nine! I've got diarrhoea and you're sleeping in *my room!*'

JUAN

Nothing I had ever been taught, at school or at home, could have prepared me for Juan.

If he wanted to be bad, he was bad. It was as simple as that. No one could stop him because no one could catch him. He slithered like an eel, ran like a hare, and if he put on so much as a pair of shorts then it had to be Sunday. He thought his penis was the funniest thing since the wife of the Mayor of Deya had apparently choked on the body of Christ at Mass and spat her false teeth into the Communion cup.

Within moments of our waking up the next morning he had burst every pillow in the room – *his room!* – over my head. The place looked like a massacre in a henhouse, with feathers muffling every inch of the floor, the books and pictures, clinging to the ceiling, while he and I, our bodies sweating even at this early hour, were covered in white and orange down from head to foot. As Juan flung open the shutters onto a blazing morning, his elder sister Lucia flung open the door to see what was going on, the sudden draught sending thousands of feathers bursting out through the window to rain like soft manna onto the terrace below, where Robert and Beryl and my mother were sitting at breakfast. In the pandemonium that followed, Juan simply vanished.

Moments later I was pinned to the wall by my mother's flaying tongue. My shouted explanation that we'd both had nightmares that we'd been the Princes in the Tower and that our pillows had tried to smother us, was dismissed out of hand. Even Lucia's surprising attempts to pacify my mother with stories of Juan's previous outrages

31

were ignored. It wasn't until Beryl arrived that calm was restored and feathers began to float back down from the ceiling.

Then began the 'Hunt for Juan', with Beryl offering a reward of a *duro*, five pesetas, for his capture, Lucia offering to bring him back, dead, for nothing, and Beryl turning away from us with the oddest expression on her face. Lucia must have upset her. She tried to call out Juan's name, but her voice quivered so much that she couldn't get it out. Speechless, she signed to Lucia to call him. Lucia leant against the wall of the passage, tears of laughter streaming down her face. Beryl's temper seemed to snap. Running down the passage to her room, she slammed the door behind her. But then I was amazed to hear wails of laughter floating back to us, which only made Lucia worse. She sank to the floor, all legs and knickers, banging her head with her fists and screeching about 'demented chickens in a snowstorm!' Even my mother laughed, until Juan's baby brother, Tomás, began to cry in his nursery next to the bathroom, and they both hurried down the passage to comfort him.

I slipped back into Juan's room, to find him standing in the middle of the floor, grinning, naked except for his tiny pants, in a halo of blazing sunlight and feathers, trying to cram his specs against his nose and eyes, even as they were being pierced by the sharp little quills.

To see him helpless for the first time, defiant yet poised for flight, and blind as a bat, at once aroused my instincts for fair play. With a deftness and practice learned from a lifetime of emergencies at school, I slammed the door soundlessly, scooped up yesterday's vest and pulled him to the 'blind' side of his 'L'-shaped room, where he wouldn't be seen if anyone came in. Whipping off his specs, I thrust the vest into his hands and pushed it against his face to wipe away the feathers while I cleaned his specs on my pyjama trousers.

'Where were you hiding?' I whispered incredulously.

'At the end of my bed, where the sheet's pulled back! I can make myself as flat as a *tortilla*—!' He started to laugh his wild, crazy laugh, and I '*Sssh'd*' him urgently as I gave him back his specs.

From downstairs came the sound of Robert's voice calling up: 'What's going on up there?'

And again, as my eyes darted fearfully towards the door, Juan simply disappeared, so swiftly and suddenly that when I looked back a second later, he'd gone.

Frantic whisperings echoed in the tiled passageway as I heard Beryl's door opening again.

'It's all right, Robert!' she called down unsteadily. 'One of the boys' pillows burst. It was very old. Diana's coming down—'

My mother the actress now, as she went down the stairs, apologising for the burst pillow and offering to send a dozen new ones from Derry & Toms the moment she got back to London. Her voice (and my wavering trust in her) faded to a murmur. I leant my head against the cool wall, remembering her 'Rules For House Guests' (which we always were – no one ever came and stayed with us): '*Never blame your Host or the Children or Servants of your Host, but blame everything on Yourself, your Children, Servants...*'

'*Is it safe?*' An urgent whisper.

Determined to pay him back, I tiptoed over to his bed and tore away the crumpled sheet from the end. Nothing! I fell to the floor, suddenly, to frighten him, and stared under the bed. Nothing. I searched his cupboard, under his school desk, stared up at the ceiling—

He rose from under the sheet at the bottom of *my* bed, screaming with laughter, pointing at my astonished face, when through the door like a daemon flew Lucia, slapping him so hard that his specs flew across the room before she disappeared in a blur of laughter down the passage.

By the time Juan and I came down for breakfast, it had been cleared away. Beryl was standing in the gloom of the shaded kitchen surrounded by squabbling cats and a pair of pale poodles called

Joté and Ygrec who were so hypnotised by a huge saucepan she was lifting onto the table that they hardly glanced at us as we walked in. 'Ah, there you are! At last!' She had the funniest way of speaking, emphasising certain words as if they were vital. She looked at me and smiled. 'Lucia claimed the reward, I'm afraid, so I've sent her off to the village with Diana, to buy some sweets. Now Simon – what would you like for breakfast?' She reached into the huge saucepan and pulled out the dripping skinned head of a sheep. 'There's a nice sheep's head, and some chickens' claws—' She casually split the sheep's skull in half with a cleaver, then in half again, and offered the pieces to the dogs, saying excitedly *'There! The sheep's head!'* as they each took the grisly offal daintily in their jaws and pranced out of the kitchen – followed, a split second later by a yowling mob of jealous, spitting cats – followed, a split second after that by Juan, swept up in the drama, flailing his arms, barking and yowling – followed, at a run, by Beryl, shouting at him to be quiet or he'd disturb 'Father'—

Followed, as though in a trance, by me.

The fly screen that separated Canellun from the outside world, although made of nothing more than spiral strands of crewcut hemp weighted with lead, seemed to act as a powerful divide between two magically different worlds. As I stepped through it that morning I stepped from the cool shaded Englishness of the house, from a world of familiar people and language into a silent, baking world more ancient than anything I'd ever seen, into a landscape which seemed to draw in its breath as I stared at it.

Behind the house, from as far to my left to as far to my distant right, a massive wall of grey and yellow and orange mountains, flecked with red, cut us off completely from the world beyond. Groves of silver-green olive trees rose in stone terraces to the last possible inch of foothills before the sheer cliffs defeated them. To my right, but lower, I could just make out the distant roofs of the village, while ahead of me, as I walked slowly out onto the wide terrace beside the house, a tree-filled gorge fell away to a wedge of twinkling sea. Distantly, I could hear Beryl still calling for Juan, her voice wafting up to me among the pungent smells from the garden, of fruits and flowers and the smell of the heat itself. Letting out a huge breath at last, I stretched out my arms to embrace this paradise and had a fit of such happiness that I began to do an ecstatic, silent war dance, stamping my feet, punching the air to smithereens—

'I say, are you all right?'

The fright he gave me turned my legs to rubber.

'Yes, sir!' Dizzily I focussed on the huge figure of my grand-uncle who had appeared round the corner of the house.

'No, don't be frightened—' he gave me a casual wave and wandered over to the edge of the terrace, as if to look at the sea. 'I just came to see what all that racket was about. I suppose it was Juan again?'

I said nothing.

'Were you dancing a particular dance,' he wondered politely, 'or can I join in?' He ambled over and started to shuffle round me, swaying rather oddly, as though his joints had suddenly turned to rubber. 'And don't call me "sir", I told you before. I'm not a schoolmaster – although I was once, for a bit. My brother Dick – your grandfather – got me a job teaching English in Cairo after the war. Do you know who my brightest pupil was?'

'No,' I said curiously.

'Gamal Abdul Nasser! The chap who's giving us all this trouble in Suez.'

'Crikey!'

He looked as surprised as I was. 'To tell you the truth,' he said confidentially, 'I rather liked him, though I suppose it's unpatriotic of me to say so. Tell me,' he asked in a casual sort of way, 'do you get on with your grandfather?'

'Yes!'

'Oh, *good*! So do I!' I felt that I'd been passing tests without actually sitting an exam. 'Now, about this dance – I take it that you were doing a Red Indian war dance, which isn't really a war dance at all. In fact, it's a rain dance – sort of down and up? In a circle?' I nodded. 'Well, the point is that "up" is to the clouds, praying for rain, and 'down' is showing the rain where to fall – onto the crops, so that the tribe won't have to be forced on by drought. So your hands have to really reach up to the clouds, because that's the praying part—'

When I next looked up from our dance, which had gradually worked itself up to its original savagery, it was to see Beryl sitting on the low terrace wall, bent over double.

'It's Beryl,' I whispered breathlessly to Robert, 'I think she's got a stitch—'

He stopped and beamed at her, gasping for breath but not in the least put out. 'Hello, darling!' he cried. 'We were just doing a rain dance—'

'Thank *goodness!*' she gasped, and I realised that she'd been laughing. 'The *deposito's* almost empty. Perhaps you could show Simon a *breakfast* dance, too, because he hasn't had much of *that*, either.'

Beryl hadn't found Juan, so she sat and talked to me while I ate – or at least she tried to talk to me, but Robert kept coming in and out of the kitchen, fiddling with things, taking corners of toast from my plate and crunching them absentmindedly before wandering off, only to return a few minutes later to open and close cupboards or to rearrange plates in the rack before helping himself to another piece of toast.

Beryl lost patience with him. 'For heaven's sake, Robert, go and do some *work!*'

He stood in the middle of the kitchen, looking lost. 'I can't seem to settle down.' He snorted, pressing his huge fingers to his cheeks. 'I think I've got catarrh coming on.'

Beryl's hand flew to her forehead. 'Oh not *catarrh!*' she looked at me pityingly. 'Poor *Simon!*'

'What is it?' I asked anxiously. 'What's happened?'

'Your grand-uncle had his nose broken very *badly*, when he boxed for his regiment in the First War, which is why he looks so peculiar. Ever since, he's had terrible sinus and *catarrh*, and now and then he has to sing about it—'

'I knocked the other chap out, though!' he said proudly, before suddenly bursting into song—

> 'Oh Jean-Baptiste *pourquoi?*
> Oh Jean-Baptiste *pourquoi?*
> Oh, Jean-Baptiste, *pourquoi* do you grease
> Your little dog's nose
> wiz tar?
>
> *Mon chien* 'as bad catarrh!
> *Mon chien* 'as bad catarrh!
> And zat is ze reason why I keep on greasin'
> My little dog's nose wiz tar!'

The song, and the expression on his face as he sang it were both so ludicrous that I burst out laughing. I'd never heard anything so silly coming out of someone so supposedly grown-up.

Beryl seemed to agree. 'I don't know why it still gets to me – it's so *stupid*, I suppose. And his expression is so *stupid!*'

Robert was still beaming into my face. 'Shall I teach it to you?' he asked.

'Yes, please!'

'Help me with the compost, then. I want to talk to you, anyway. You can learn it as we go.'

He flung open the heavy olive wood doors under the sink, exposing two evil-smelling pails. 'Bring me your breakfast plate and

I'll show you how it works.' I did as he asked, but in fact, everything on my plate ended up in his mouth. Grinning at me, he pointed to the brimming pail on the right. 'This is the *compost meantis*,' he explained, 'by which I mean that it's *meant* for the compost heap – old fruit and vegetables and things like that. The other pail is *non-compost meantis* – in other words, for rubbish and leftover meat and fish, or for anything which might encourage the rats. We burn that lot. Now, if you'd bring the *compost meantis* pail—'

Repeating after him the words of '*Jean-Baptiste*' I stumbled manfully in his massive wake down the stone steps that wound through the garden to a darker, wilder part, where two ominous-looking mounds lay shrouded under old army groundsheets. The gloom here, I realised, was caused by two trees which overshadowed the ground. A child's swing hung from one of their branches, moving slightly, as though a ghost were sitting on it.

Robert reached down and carelessly threw back one of the groundsheets, to the sudden furious buzzing of bloated flies, then plunged his hands, like two great bunches of bananas, into the pail of refuse I was carrying. The weight of his hands alone almost caused me to drop the bucket. Drawing out fistfuls of slimy muck, he carefully distributed it among the hollows in the mound, then grabbed the pail from me and tipped out what was left, spreading the slop with his fingers.

'Pass me that fork, will you?'

With difficulty I wrenched the tines of a garden fork from the hard red earth between the roots of the second tree and dragged it to him. He seemed to transform it. In his hands the fork became a trident, which he stabbed into the mound with all his might, then twisted, as though he could see something I couldn't. He stabbed again and again, until finally he stopped and drew back, panting.

Fearfully, I stared down at the grave. 'Is it dead?'

He snorted as he threw me an astonished smile. 'On the contrary, I'm breathing new life into it! Piercing allows oxygen to be drawn

in, which speeds up the decomposition. Now we just add water—'
He took the pail and filled it at a small sump that formed part of a
network of dry irrigation channels that wound through the garden.

'There. That'll keep it nice and humid. By autumn there'll be
a wonderful compost which we'll spread all over the garden, and
next Spring, after the rains, we'll have ambrosial vegetables. I hope
you'll come back and help us eat them. Give me a hand to put the
cover back on, would you?'

I took a corner of the tarpaulin and we began to drag it back
over the mound. 'Gardens are a bit like children,' he gasped, still
slightly out of breath. 'You pour all your efforts into them, making
the finest compost you can with what's available—' he pulled a face
'—usually money – but if the rain doesn't come in the form of luck,
then everything wilts…' he stared around at the parched garden
with a wry expression. 'Like now. We've had drought for nearly
two months—' he looked back at me suddenly, directly, opening his
eyes wide. 'Children need a bit of watering, too, when they're run
down or they've had a shock.' He raised his eyebrows, as though in
query, but again I didn't quite follow the question they were asking.
He grunted and paced past me, pressing his dirty fingertips to the
front of his cheeks as he sniffed through each nostril in turn. 'Now,
this divorce between your mother and father—' He swung round
and came towards me, staring at thoughts over the top of my head.

Oh… that…

Was that what he'd been trying to talk about in the Bar
Formentor last night—?

'The trouble with divorce is that people don't just divorce their
wives or husbands, they divorce their children, too. Or at least the
children think they do. I mean, your father's "all right",' he made
quotation marks on either side of his head with his huge fingers, 'I've
always got on with him. And I'm very fond of your mother – favourite
niece and all that – and Beryl loves her, too, which is always a good
sign. The thing is, I don't blame your parents for what's happened,

and you mustn't, either. Nor must you blame yourself—' He fixed me with a forbidding stare. 'That's very important—'

Blame myself? I felt a moment of panic. It had never occurred to me—

For the first time, my grand-uncle misread my thoughts. 'You really mustn't! It's not your fault. If anything's to blame, it's their profession. The theatre's not the real world, as I'm sure you know, but actors get taken in by the parts they play, so that when the curtain comes down, all that's left is reality – which can be pretty grim. And if they're married to each other it's even more dangerous. D'you follow?'

I stared up at him, shading my eyes from the sun. 'I think so,' I said uncertainly.

'Well, go on, then, say it back to me. I need to know that you've understood—'

But I'd been listening too closely, remembering scenes at home, when I'd been woken by muffled shouts from the drawing room below, by cries so sudden and desperate as one of them opened the door to go to the kitchen, leaving half sentences of hatred, like ghosts, to haunt the stairwell—

'I'm sorry—' I stumbled—

Wake up, Gough! The past participle of pugnare! *Quickly!*

'—I was listening, honestly—' I wouldn't be able to bear it if I let him down—

My heart sank as his attention wandered off, his restless eye caught by something in the tree above me. He reached up, pulling and snapping.

'Here – have an *algarroba!*' he said with a grin, giving me a curious dried-up fruit like a huge French bean, the colour of polished mahogany. 'Break it in half and chew it. It's rather pleasant. Good for the memory—'

The fruit was dry and strong smelling, and tasted slightly sweet, like a very old date.

Having given me a few moments to recover while he looked round absently, he turned back to me. 'Well? Has it worked?'

'—You said it wasn't their fault, that they weren't divorcing me, that the theatre is make-believe—' Relief flooded through me.

'Well done!' He laughed as he tapped my head painfully with his knuckle. 'I *thought* there was someone at home. Here, give me the other half and I'll try and remember why I'm saying all this.'

I did as he asked, and he chewed on it for a moment, spitting out the dry skin. I copied him thankfully, spitting out the whole lot.

'Your mother – that's it! The thing is, this whole business has knocked her back rather. She isn't well, and I think she's very depressed – feels it's all her fault, which is quite natural. And of course she's worried about *you*. So what we need to do is to get her better and at the same time make sure you have a nice time as well. Now, do you think you'll like it here? I know you haven't had much of a chance to get to know it yet – or us – but you seem to be getting the feel of the place—'

'Yes! Thank you—'

'Good! And you're all right with Juan? He's a bit wild, I know, and he gets into scrapes...' His voice trailed off. 'I want you to try and calm him down a bit—'

The tree next to the *algarroba* suddenly came alive, the dense foliage shaking with outrage.

'*But I don't want to be calm down, Father!*' cried Juan in his curious pidgin English.

Within the thick stone walls of the house, Juan's behaviour was more or less contained under the watchful eyes of Robert and Beryl and Lucia – at least while he was asleep. Once he'd broken out into the garden, though, it was as if he'd scented the strange wildness of the mountains that rose above the house, whose roots flexed through the earth beneath it. Beryl had told me mournfully that

41

her endless attempts to turn the land into an English garden, with flower beds and orchards and a shaded lawn were almost always foiled by drought, so that the true nature of the landscape showed through her threadbare efforts like unbreakable bones.

To Juan, though, the garden was a magic cage – *his* cage – and he moved through it like a monkey, shinning up trees at the slightest hint of danger, flying from rock to rock or from terrace to terrace so agilely that the stones could hardly have felt his weight. There were even moments, I could have sworn, when he would bounce off an invisible mesh that surrounded the grounds of Canellun, his feet kicking against the sky as he changed course in mid-air to avoid a sudden summons from the house. He was dazzling to watch. I only wished that he'd just let me sit back and envy him, as I might envy a wild animal – not in a wicked or jealous way, but in fascination. For a boy to have such freedom, to be able to refuse point blank to be stifled by people or clothes or manners, struck me as the most incredible luck and awakened in me a longing to know what it must feel like.

But for Juan to be forced to share his idyllic playground with a mere cousin who was not only revoltingly polite and obedient but a year older than him, was more than he could bear at first. I was an interloper whose very presence was a threat to him, if only by comparison: I was 'good', he was 'bad', I was polite, he was rude; if he could make me as bad and as rude as him, I'd no longer be a threat. And the more he tried, the more I cursed my 'bringings up' as Robert called them, and longed for the courage to express my naked self.

At first, I was puzzled by my grand-uncle's strangely aloof and detached attitude to Juan's behaviour – until it dawned on me that this was how Beryl wanted it. Juan was *hers*. Robert was always there if she needed him – a Last Resort – but Beryl was in charge. Juan was a force of nature, quite unlike her other children, apparently. My mother, with a shudder, called him 'that feral fiend', and it was true that he seemed more animal than human sometimes. But then, Beryl loved animals. In her book, they had a right to freedom, even when they were caged. I just wished I wasn't in the same cage.

I was ambushed, attacked, 'denounced', as he called it, and lied about from one day's end to the next, and I was powerless to do anything about it. Never having been to school in England, Juan had no conception of fair play or honour or even of cricket. To have sneaked on him in turn, though, was unthinkable, so I had to grin and bear it.

Finally, exasperated by both of us, Beryl took us out into the garden one evening and spoke to us severely, telling us that things were getting out of hand, and that Robert's Slipper would have to be summoned. It was size fourteen and made of hard leather, and it hurt *very badly*, no matter whose bottom it landed on! And it could find naughty boys, even in the dark—

'It's true!' Juan stared at me with wide-eyed apprehension as he stuck his hands down the back of his pants.

So Beryl thought that we'd better stop quarrelling and become friends. It was only when we'd shaken hands, though, that I was reminded, by a funny smell, of where Juan's hand had just been.

Within a week of my arrival (and of his influence), it was as though I'd ransacked my school trunk for all the bad habits I'd learned there – deceit and cunning and disobedience – and applied them to my life here, hiding yet another useless straw hat that my mother insisted I wore against certain sunstroke, stuffing my blue Aertex shirt into its crown until I retrieved them both before returning to Canellun for supper; working out how to make my escape from Juan's room through a 'secret' passage that led under the roof into her bedroom next door to ours; how to avoid the dreaded 'lunchtime' and its hated last course of an enforced siesta; how to terrorise the half wild sheep until the olive groves echoed with the cacophonous symphony of their clunking bells. In other words I began to throw in my lot with him, to live like the savage I'd always longed to become, revelling in the heat of a sun which was already turning my skin to the colour of the earth, blending me into it like a chameleon and at the same time filling me with the new sense of power that I'd felt when I'd lain in the back of the Land Rover that night.

The number of people who called at Canellun, whether by appointment or on the off-chance that Robert would see them, was extraordinary. Some of them were apparently famous, but this cut no ice with Juan and me. If they were remotely patronising they were left to fend for themselves, or were redirected to Soller, five miles of hairpin bends away. The gates (kept shut to prevent the dogs from being run over) were constantly screeching and clanking their warning of new arrivals, and as if that weren't enough, Isabella-the-Donkey, who lived in a sort of porter's lodge next to the gates, under an *algarroba* tree, behaved like a French concièrge, hee-haawing belligerently at everyone's comings and goings. If Juan was in earshot when she brayed, he would take to the tree and bombard the unfortunate visitors with *algarrobas* the size of boomerangs. His favourite targets were elderly German tourists, shy and diffident, who had come to pay their respects to 'Ze Great Man'.

'He lives on the *cala*,' he would shout, 'and he eats *caca!*'

One afternoon, after we'd been told that my mother felt much better at last and had decided to give a tea party, we both shinned up the tree which overhung the stable and lay in wait for the guests. The mutual pax which Beryl had forced on us had begun to turn into a grudging friendship, although we would both have denied it hotly if anyone had remarked on it, and we whiled away the time with a farting competition. Ever since I'd told him that a boy at school had broken the record by doing it ninety-nine times in a row without disgracing himself, he'd been determined to beat him.

After a quarter of an hour of absolutely nobody arriving (and pathetically little leaving Juan in the way of wind), there suddenly came to the gate an apparition so wondrous that I could only stare down at it in awe.

A tall, thin negro, beautifully dressed in a tropical suit, dark glasses, and a wide-brimmed hat, stood in the road, looking from side to side as he minutely examined the rock wall and the gate. Then he slowly raised his head and called up the drive. 'Hello?'

Juan nudged me excitedly in the ribs. 'It's Alston! He's a poet!' he hissed, as Isabella stuck her head out through the upper half of her stable door and began to bray an alarm.

The negro politely tipped his hat to her. 'Good afternoon. I can't seem to find the bell—' An *American* Negro!

'There isn't one!' yelled Juan.

The man leapt back in shock. 'Jesus, it talks!'

Juan and I became so helpless with laughter that we lost our hold on the branch and fell out of the tree onto Isabella's roof, panicking her into a fit of braying and kicking which only made Juan worse. With a scream, he flung himself off the roof into a huge pile of her old droppings.

Somehow I made it to the gate with only a few scratches, and dragged back the bolt.

Alston was now standing on the far side of the road, leaning nonchalantly against the wall, looking back towards the village, to where a number of people were trailing towards the house.

'Would you like to come in, sir?' I asked as I pushed the gate open.

He pretended to be startled by my question, then stared at me intently through narrowed eyes. 'I'll bet you thought that I thought the donkey could talk, huh?'

'Yes!'

From behind the stable there was a fresh wail from Juan. The man sniffed contemptuously and looked slowly up and down the road again, as if afraid of being overheard. 'Well, I did!'

I thought Juan was going to choke himself to death.

'My name's Alston Anderson. I have a formal invitation to tea with Miss Graves at five o'clock, so I thought I'd better ring the bell. Seems there's no bell, though, and the help's no help at all. Can't even open his own gate—'

'Hers,' I corrected him quickly. 'Isabella's a lady.'

A high pitched screech from Juan whistled through the air like a firework. Ignoring it, the stranger pushed himself away from the wall and advanced towards me, raising his hat again. 'Well, I'm sure I beg her pardon,' he drawled, then raised an eyebrow at me. 'And who might you be, may I ask?'

'I'm Miss Graves's son,' I began, before realising that Lucia and my mother were both Miss Graves, and there might be some confusion. 'The one who invited you's... son,' I blundered on. 'Simon.'

He held out his hand. 'How do you do, Simon?' We shook hands. 'And who's the hyena? Not Juan, by any chance?'

'I'm afraid so—' A grim thought suddenly occurred to me: 'Please – you won't tell anyone—?'

He glared down at me. 'Are you kidding? You think I'm going to sit there at tea and tell them you saw me talking to a donkey?' He strode off up the drive.

It took several seconds for the sense of what he'd said to seep into my brain. Then relief gave me wings and I ran happily up the drive in his exotic, scented wake.

My mother's health had truly taken a turn for the better by that teatime, as it usually did when there was a performance to be given. Her mane of black hair waved and tossed, her skin gleamed as pale as moonlight, and her painted lips were turned up mischievously at the corners in a glittering smile which somehow included everyone, even though it was aimed at you alone. In her bright summer frock, with its full skirt swaying elegantly around her calves, she walked across the terrace as though it were the stage of Drury Lane, sweeping up her audience with her wit and beauty.

Bill Waldren (an American) and Frank Hodgkinson (an Australian), a pair of bearded, rugged-looking artists, showed all the usual sickening symptoms of being smitten by her, and were soon arguing over which of them was going to paint her portrait. On being consulted, though, Beryl told her that they were both abstract painters, and that if she wanted her portrait done in sand and stones and bits of old cork, that was her affair.

The tea party was at its height when Beryl's low cry of 'Oh, *Juan!*' brought everything to an unexpected full stop. Filling the sudden silence – even deepening it – was the sight of Juan, half naked and covered from head to toe in donkey droppings and wet straw.

I flushed with guilt. I'd left him on the dung heap swapping kicks with Isabella, and forgotten about him in the excitement of getting ready.

His wild gaze suddenly found mine, his eyebrows rising and his mouth falling open in sarcastic amazement at my neat appearance (I'd rushed upstairs earlier to put on a clean shirt and shorts). His look told me that I'd betrayed him – crossed the no-man's-land between childhood and the 'enemy'.

Instantly, without a word spoken, Beryl grasped the potential for a war of words, if not of actual fisticuffs, and quickly turned to the gathering. 'It's all right, everyone, just carry on! This has nothing to do with you!' As people tactfully began to turn their backs, she beckoned to me urgently. Taut with apprehension, I went over to where Juan was stamping his foot and complaining bitterly.

'Mother, he—'

'Yes, well, never mind *that*, Juan! Whatever happened, I'm sure Simon didn't *mean* it—' Her eyes flew past me. 'Diana—'

My mother had broken away from the others and was approaching with a dangerous look on her face, as though already scenting that I was in some way responsible for *something*. Beryl was brilliant, distracting her in an urgent stage whisper: 'Diana, I've just seen a you-know-what crawling under Tania's chair!' (Tania Jepson was so terrified of spiders that she either screamed or fainted if anyone even said the word.) 'Quick! Go and warn Robert! *Quick!*' If she hadn't been holding onto Juan for grim death and gagging his mouth with her hand, he would have rushed into the throng and shouted '*spider!*' at the top of his voice. As my mother hurried away, Beryl shook him. 'Juan, there *isn't* a spider! I just wanted to distract Diana for a moment. Now *listen!*' She shook him again to get his attention, 'Tomorrow we're going to have two treats. We're all going to have lunch at the *cala*—'

'*Arroz con pescado!*' shouted Juan, his eyes suddenly lighting up.

'*Yes!*' She laughed and turned to me to explain. 'It's fish soup—'

'—the best fish soup on the whole island! You'll love it!' exclaimed Juan. 'Even though I hope the bones and fish heads stick in your throat and make you sick all over the table!'

'That's *enough*, Juan! And the second treat is that in the evening we're all going to the *fiesta* in Soller, and you've been asked to dance in the *paseo* with your school friends—'

'*NO!* I absolutely are *NOT!* No, No, *NO!*'

And he was gone, his brown body bent backwards almost in half with fury as he ran down the drive, hands clasped to his ears, screaming up at the sky.

'Oh dear…' Beryl made a rueful face at me. 'I've been trying to find a good moment to tell him… Never mind—' She threw me a huge smile. 'So you're going to the *cala* at last. About time.'

'Am I really allowed to?' I asked anxiously.

'Of *course* you are! We've told your mother not to be so silly – you can't come all the way to Majorca and not be allowed to swim. Just try to be as good as you can – until we get there, at least.'

We'd hardly turned back to the party when there was a shout of *'Grenade!'* from the garden below, and a lump of rotten wood sailed through the air and hit the terrace. Three huge, bewildered spiders scuttled off it and headed towards the shadows cast by the guests.

AT THE *CALA*

The procession which set out from Canellun the next day at one o'clock precisely (in order to reach the *cala* for lunch at two), would have astonished my friends at school, and given my enemies enough ammunition to rag me mercilessly.

In all, there were eighteen of us, strung out in a long line, with Robert at the head of the cavalcade leading a temperamental Isabella wearing one of his old straw hats with holes cut out for her ears. Sitting astride her, with her own wide-brimmed straw hat tied down with a silk scarf and wearing her dark glasses, was my mother, in a sleeveless white blouse, a wide black patent leather belt and a flared white skirt with huge black polka dots. Over her shoulder she twirled a parasol which Beryl had lent her. On either side of her were two friends of Robert's, each ready to catch her if she showed the slightest sign of falling off. The smaller man, on her left, panting, bespectacled, and already sweating, was Ruthven Todd, a writer. The tall man on her right, shambling along, laughing and talking, was Alastair Reid, a journalist and a friend of my mother's in London, who had come over from Fornalutx to spend the day with us. Behind the donkey, clutching a child's painted bucket and a tiny spade, came Alston (or '*Compost Dementis*' as Robert had christened him that day, since it was his job to pick up any pearls of wisdom that Isabella might scatter behind her and preserve them for the garden). Lucia had chosen to stay behind and look after Tomás, so Beryl walked with the Jepsons. Selwyn, who had been a colonel in the S.O.E., was apparently Very Important to Robert, though I wasn't quite sure why except that he advised him about a great many secret things, including money. His father had been Edgar Jepson, a successful thriller writer whose red-backed books lined the bookcase in the upstairs passage at Canellun. The Jepsons were followed at a respectful distance by Robert's small, slightly sinister secretary, Karl Gay, and his wife Irene (or Reenee as he called her), and their very pretty little blonde daughter, Diana. At an even more respectful distance from them came a jolly bunch of writers and painters from the village, led by Waldren and Hodgkinson. Juan and I were the rearguard, acting as lookouts for landslides and bandits and for an army of man-eating scorpions which Beryl said were rumoured to be in the area.

I'd spent all morning in a fever of excitement at the thought of swimming at last, but even though she was coming with us to witness it with her own eyes, my mother was still infuriatingly uncertain about allowing me to go out of my depth.

'But I'm a Yellow!' I'd shouted at her in her bedroom.

She sighed with relief. '*I'm* afraid of water, too. You mustn't be ashamed – it's probably hereditary.'

I smashed the side of my head with my fist. 'Not yellow *frightened*—' I howled at her, '*A* Yellow! The second best swimmers in the school!' None of the boys was allowed to wear his own bathing costume, but had to wear school swimming 'slips' whose colour was determined by the difficulty of the tests we had to pass. The slips themselves were made out of old pillowcases by the matron's staff, and then dyed. They were little more than cotton loincloths with a single tie at the side, which left one feeling wonderfully naked, but were embarrassing to wear after a beating. To have won yellow before the age of ten was unusual, and I was incensed by her ignorance. If she'd come to our swimming displays, she might know more about my achievements. Somehow I needed to convince her that I could survive in all four Elements created by God and conquered by Man. I was safe on Land, I was safe in the Sky, with Fire from the homemade explosives I experimented with at school, and if she'd only let me, I'd prove to her that I was safe in Water, too. Once she'd accepted that, she might relax at last and leave me alone!

My excitement seemed to be shared by everyone in that strange procession, with talk and laughter becoming more and more infectious in spite of the heat. Even the respectful distance between the prickly Karl and the gaily dressed Deya contingent began to narrow, and when he turned round occasionally to say something to them, I saw that he was smiling like someone on holiday. He was the strangest looking man, very small, wearing a neat white shirt, but with his bottom half swamped in a huge pair of American Levi jeans. He'd rolled up the legs over and over again, and yet the turn-ups still completely covered his feet and dragged in the dust. My mother had told me that his real name was Goldschmidt, a German Jew whom Robert had rescued from a Fate Worse Than Death during the war, refusing to leave Majorca on the last British destroyer unless Karl could accompany him as his secretary. As if unable to forget those days, his mouth was always turned downwards in a cynical twist, which seemed to keep people at arm's length.

Once we'd left the road, we followed an old winding track down through the olive groves, planted in shallow terraces here, quite different from the steep, high terraces behind Canellun. The dense heat, and the almost mystical patterns of the terrace walls that weaved among each other until they became an infinite blur, seemed to combine softly and invisibly to overpower conversation. One by one we fell silent, until only the Americans' voices could be heard...

Until at last there were only the cicadas and the muffled sound of tramping feet as everyone stared about them, lost in their own confusion or understanding of what they saw and felt.

My understanding, I knew instinctively, was the right one – something had happened here; we were walking through a somehow sacred place.

And yet no one remarked on it. It was 'understood', and I liked that.

A little later, the atmosphere began to change again, as though a two minute silence had been observed and now everything could get back to normal.

The olive groves gave way to huge flat rocks, with tortured-looking pine trees growing out of the fissures between them, their warm, resinous smell engulfing us. I was breathing it in fiercely when Juan grabbed my arm suddenly. 'Come!' he whispered excitedly. 'I want to show you something!'

Unnoticed, we moved out from behind the column as it began to descend into a sloping tunnel of pine trees, with Robert and my mother already entering the dappled shade it cast over the path, as if they were entering a dream.

Then I saw, through the trees on our left, a small square stone tower which Juan was running towards as he beckoned me, skidding happily on the smooth pine needles. The tower appeared to be deserted, its broken shutters nailed shut. All at once, Juan stopped and waited until I caught up. 'Be careful,' he whispered, wide-eyed, 'it's haunted here!'

On one side of the tower was a flying staircase, like a buttress, which led to the roof, and it was to the foot of this, under the stone arch of the staircase, that Juan led me by the wrist, quite unselfconsciously, perhaps more to give himself courage than to guide me, but once we'd reached the jumble of rocks and rubble and old branches which were piled against the crumbling wall, he became his old self again. Motioning me to help him, he squatted down and started to clear away the rocks and stones from the farthest end of the pile, slowly at first, then more frantically, as if someone were buried alive beneath it. Infected by his haste, I squatted down next to him, scrabbling at the stones and bits of wood, my eyes unblinking, wary of giant scorpions, not sure what we were looking for—

Suddenly he stopped what he was doing and fixed me with a wild glare. 'This is a *secret!*' he hissed. 'If you tell anyone, the ghosts here will tear out your tongue, and *caca* will come out of your eyes, and Dito and Mito will tie you up and piss on you—'

'I won't say anything, Juan! I promise,' I promised.

'Swear!'

'I swear!' I swore. 'Cross my heart—' I crossed it fervently.

'All right. You can look—'

He pulled a few more rocks away, scattering some frightened centipedes, then stared at me, his eyes wild with suspense. 'There!'

I craned forward excitedly, my eyes on stalks. But all I could see was more rubble—

A faint chorus of '*Juuu-an! Siii-mon!*' drifted towards us through the trees.

I stared into his crazed eyes. 'But there's nothing there!'

'*Exactly!*' he screamed triumphantly. 'I've shown you *nothing!* And you've sworn not to tell anyone—'

Yelling with laughter, he made off, with me in hot pursuit, skidding across the needle-strewn rocks and through the tunnel of pine trees towards where the column had come to an untidy halt. Juan shouted '*Pax, pax!*' and we both slowed down, each of us changing back, with every step, into what was expected of us.

Beryl and Selwyn were already walking back up the column. 'Ah, *there* you are,' she called. 'What have you two been up to? *Eh?*'

'Nothing—' I called back.

'*You promised not to tell anyone!*' screamed Juan.

Angrily, Selwyn broke in. 'Be quiet, please! Simon, your mother's decided it's too dangerous to go down to the *cala* on Isabella, so Robert's gone on ahead with her – with Isabella, I mean – so he can have a bathe before lunch. Your mother wants you to be her walking stick, and she's getting impatient, so I should cut along if I were you—'

With my heart sinking, both at the schoolmasterly tone of Selwyn's voice and at the task ahead, I ran down the column of people who began to cheer me on, clapping and calling out to me as I passed, so that by the time I reached my mother I was smiling unstoppably.

Even her impatience, apparent to me at once from the sun's deeply etched shadows on her face as I approached, had no chance against the high spirits of the others, still less against my obvious happiness, and it was a wonderful sight to see her mouth lift into a smile, at first grudging, then overwhelming, like the sun bursting out from behind a dark cloud. She even laughed as I came up to her.

'Bloody boy! Where were you? I'm bruised to within an inch of my life! Give me your shoulder to lean on. Alastair, darling, hold my other hand. I intend to shut my eyes until I'm at sea level.'

'Shouldn't Simon have a quick look at where he's going first?' suggested Alastair in his gravelly, faintly Scottish accent.

'Oh, of course, he hasn't seen the *cala* yet! *You* take him, Alastair darling. The very thought of looking down—'

Alastair took my hand and led me away from her. 'Keep your eyes on the ground until I tell you,' he murmured.

Out of the corner of my eye I could see the donkey steps leading downwards to my left, but we went straight on for a moment, until his grip tightened on my shoulder.

'You can look now.'

Raising my head, I found that I was looking over a terrifying precipice and instinctively clutched at his arm.

Far below – so far as to belong to another world and to another century – lay a pirates' cove that I might have dreamed; secret, and timelessly still. At its narrow beginning, directly beneath me, was a wild, boulder-strewn beach, with a huddle of fishing huts and boat houses clinging to the huge rocks. Steep slipways of bleached pine logs ran down to a sea so incredibly blue and clear that I could make out every stone and boulder that lay beneath it, down to the sudden blackness of underwater caverns. On either side of the narrow bay, sheer cliffs tumbled straight into the water, with spindly pine trees reaching out along the far point towards a widening sea streaked with restless currents which seemed to guard the entrance to this perfect sanctuary. At the very end of the farthest spit of land I could make out the turret of a Martello tower staring out above the pine trees, with cannons still sticking out through the battlements—

'Gosh—' I whispered.

'What?'

I tore my gaze away and looked up into his granite face, afraid he might have heard me, and we both broke into a smile at the same moment.

'It's beautiful,' I said more loudly, though not so loudly that anyone else could hear.

My mother was waiting for us impatiently. Ruthven, who had tried to keep her amused, had apparently failed. 'I asked him to tell me the saddest story he knew, and he told me about a goldfish with no tail!'

'I'm no good at tales,' muttered Ruthven abysmally, 'but I *have* written books about goldfish—'

'*Bah!*' My mother withered him with a glance.

It was torment having to descend so slowly when everything inside me was begging to be set free, to slip her leash and run headlong down the steep path and fling myself into the sea, particularly when I saw Robert, far below on Isabella, turn and wave Beryl's parasol at us as they reached the bottom. And yet my mother managed to distract everyone from the slowness of her descent. Not one of them had taken advantage of our halt at the top to push on ahead. She made them laugh, and they liked her.

Alastair and I didn't last long as a pair of crutches, and Ruthven simply couldn't cope with the weight of responsibility. If anyone should have been carried down, it was him. Drenched with sweat, he still managed to beam at my mother whenever he glanced round to see if she was about to fall on top of him, but every time he turned back to look where he was going he either stumbled or went crashing off into the undergrowth, or toppled down the steps, causing my mother to whinny nervously.

In the end, Alastair decided that the only way he would get my mother to the bottom before teatime was to give her a piggyback. This childishly simple solution soon, childishly, swept like a craze through the whole column, with only Selwyn and Karl refusing to carry their partners, and Beryl politely refusing to be carried by anyone. Juan, of course, with a wild yell, leapt onto my back, and the two of us fairly galloped down the donkey steps, pursued by shouts of encouragement from the others and distraught cries from my mother, but we no longer cared – we had more right than them to behave like children.

We were still whooping and tally-ho-ing as I staggered round the last shoulder of rock and onto the beach, Juan now barely clinging to my back as I crashed headlong into the plate glass door of beauty itself – no longer distant and detached, but real now, expanding every sense – my eyes from the sheer beauty of the little bay and the sight of Robert waving as he swam towards us, my nostrils from the heavy scent of pine needles and wood smoke, my taste buds from cooking smells wafting down from the café, my ears from the throbbing shrill of crickets and the quiet lapping of the tiny waves against the rocks; and touch – feel – the most parched of all my senses, muffled, smothered by the very clothes that I was tearing off – that Juan was tearing off – as we danced over the smooth hot boulders, faster and faster, toppling, plunging into the sea, the warm–cool salt blue water as it sucked me down, deafeningly, then gripped and threw me upwards again through a rising scale of noise until I surfaced under the blazing sky, punching and splashing and raging with happiness. I was *here* – at last—

'*Simon*—'

I watched, bewildered, as Robert swam powerfully towards me, fixing me with the concentrated stare of a lifesaver.

'Grand-uncle—' I spluttered.

'*I'm coming – stay still*—'

'—this is Paradise!'

He frowned uncertainly and slowed down, until he was treading water beside me. 'I'm sorry, I thought you were drowning!' He smiled, as though recognising me suddenly. 'Of course it's paradise! That's why I came here in the first place—'

'—and because the fish were only five *centimos* a kilo in 1929 – the cheapest on the island.'

'Cheapskate!' my mother burst out, laying an apologetic hand on his arm as she wheezed with delight. A moment later the others caught on and the dreadful pun did the rounds, its retelling marked by little outbreaks of laughter.

The long table, covered in oilcloth, stretched the entire length of the café terrace under the shade of rustling palm fronds tied to slender driftwood poles. Apart from a kitchen, hidden somewhere among the rocks, there was nothing more to the café than that.

Robert sat at the head of the table, with Selwyn and my mother beside him, then Tania and Beryl, Alastair, Alston, Ruthven, Juan and myself, with the others sitting next to us in order of their seniority in Robert's affections. I had quickly discovered that being part of his family was one thing, and sacred in itself, but that his friendship was something that had to be earned.

Karl sat at the foot of the table, as a sop to the least-loved and as a Prefect to their behaviour. When my mother's feeble joke finally reached him he smirked dryly, staring towards her almost with affection. You, too, I thought. When he caught me watching him, I expected his look to change, but to my surprise, it didn't. I smiled back, and looked quickly away.

So far, all we'd been given by the two young fishermen and their wives who ran the café, were some loaves of coarse bread, some olives, and half a dozen sweating bottles of the cold, almost black local wine. Beryl, my champion, insisted that I be allowed to drink it '*mig-y-mig*', mixed half and half with water. I watched it turn a deep cherry colour in the glass, and raised it to my lips, conscious that everyone was watching me.

'Just sip it, darling,' said my mother warningly.

I took a cautious sip, to make sure it tasted as good as it looked, then knocked back half a glass.

Everyone laughed. 'He takes after you, Diana,' joked Alastair.

She wasn't amused, but didn't want to make a scene. 'He's disobedient—' she muttered.

He leaned across the table and took her hand. 'All boys are disobedient at his age,' he reassured her quietly, 'believe me—'

'How would you know?' she demanded sharply, 'you have no children—'

'Not yet,' he agreed quietly, 'but believe it or not, I was a boy myself once.'

After half an hour of just sitting and talking (instead of eating), Selwyn's patience snapped. 'Where's lunch?' he demanded crossly. 'Tania's hungry! It's almost half past two, for heavens' sake.'

'Well, have some more bread,' said Beryl tartly. 'Personally, I like waiting. I mean, there's nothing you can *do* about it. The Majorcans eat lunch later than us, never mind what time you order it for, and it's their country, after all.' She sighed at Selwyn's stony expression. 'Oh, all right – Juan, take Simon and go round to the kitchen and ask Maria if she's got some *gusanos* or something – anything for a bit of *peace*—'

Juan beckoned to me urgently, and I followed him round behind the chairs, past curious scraps of conversation towards the smoky murk at the back of the café, where he disappeared through a blanket-covered entrance in the rocks.

I followed him automatically – into a scene from hell.

Intense heat and swirling oily smoke filled the dark cave. On the far side, a long cooking fire blazed under the overhang of a massive, blackened boulder which swelled towards us like the gleaming stomach of some nightmarish giant before vanishing through the roof. The flickering tongues of flame beneath it made it look as if the giant's legs had already melted into the cooking pots that hung over the fire below, and that the stomach above them was writhing in agony. A sudden burst of flame lit up a vertical fault in the rock which acted as a natural chimney.

Against this inferno, the dark silhouettes of two girls, barefoot, in long, full skirts, moved swiftly between cauldrons hung on chains from the rock-face and the blackened pots that were half buried in the flames below.

'Hola, Juán!' they cried as we entered. '*Qué tal?*'

The girls and Juan exchanged a rapid fire of Majorcan while I stood back and hungrily inhaled the thick, stinging smell of their cooking and watched them, fascinated, as they stooped and stirred and ladled, their gold earrings glinting in the firelight against the blackness of their hair, gleaming dark faces turning back to Juan now and then, eyes wild, teeth flashing enticingly. He asked one of them something in a surprisingly respectful voice, and she laughed as she deftly snatched up an earthenware bowl and ladled some smoking, plopping liquid into it before holding it out to him in a gesture so graceful that it became etched in my memory.

Cupping the bowl in both hands, Juan beckoned me to hold back the blanket for him, and it was only then, as we were about to leave the sweltering cave, that I saw the fishermen. They were watching us, motionless, from a table in the darkest corner, their eyes glittering like bandits'. They gave me such a jump that I let go of the curtain for a moment, almost knocking the bowl out of Juan's hands. The girl called Maria laughed, and shouted '*Cinc minuts!*'

Slowly, still muttering curses at me, Juan made his way down the length of the table to a growing chorus of discontented murmurs from the hungry gathering, which turned into a roar of outrage as he carefully, with shaking hands, placed the steaming bowl in front of Selwyn. Revelling in his exclusiveness, Selwyn dismissed the uproar with a haughty gesture and made a great show of inhaling the obviously wonderful smell from the bowl while his poor wife just sat there, looking rather cross. A sudden silence fell as he dipped his spoon into the soup and carried it to his mouth, his eyes darting smugly round the table as he blew on his intended mouthful. At the last moment he glanced at the curious 'thing' that wobbled in his spoon surrounded by steaming liquid. 'What's this?' he asked casually.

Beryl had gone very still. '*Gusanos*,' she said lightly. 'They're considered a great delicacy in Majorca. If you don't want them, perhaps Tania might like them.'

Robert was fidgeting, impatient for this exchange to be over so that he could continue his interrupted conversation. 'They're sea slugs,' he said, just as the quivering disgustingness was halfway into Selwyn's mouth.

All hell broke loose as spoon and sea slug hit the table, the sea slug slithering along the oilcloth to be stabbed at greedily by the forks of everyone it passed. But it seemed to have come alive again, bouncing away like a slimy rubber ball from all attempts to spear it. People started screaming and rising in their seats until there was a sudden crash as Robert slammed his fist down on the table. 'Stop that!' he bellowed. 'Food isn't funny!'

There was an embarrassed silence as everyone sat down again, avoiding his eye.

A few minutes later the conversation was still subdued when Selwyn slyly nudged my mother and gestured at Robert.

'*Uncle Robert!*' she gasped, loudly enough for everyone to turn to the head of the table.

The last sea slug was just disappearing into Robert's mouth, his mouth closing, his eyebrows raised in innocent enquiry as he dropped his empty spoon into the empty bowl and turned his artless blue eyes on Juan and me. A second later his jaws leapt into action, quickly pulverising the last evidence of his skulduggery.

We were so lost in admiration at his stylish sleight-of-hand that we started to clap him, at which the whole table began to applaud. 'Waste not, want not!' he cried primly.

And suddenly, in all the commotion, I had one of those flashes of insight which I half dreaded almost as much as I longed for them – because nothing was ever quite the same afterwards. All at once I saw Robert through 'their' eyes, sitting in the place of honour like a god, basking in the attentions of these mere mortals who surrounded him.

I blinked hurriedly, so that I could see him as my grand-uncle again, but something about him had already changed, grown, although perhaps it was nothing more than my own image of him. But as I looked at everyone looking at him against the backdrop of this wild landscape, cut off from the world, I realised that he was their King, and Beryl was their Queen, however reluctant. As for the others, they were no more than courtiers, even my mother. Her beauty and wit might have raised her to the position of Favourite Niece and Court Jester, but she could rise no higher than that. And as the son of the Court Jester I was little more than the bell on her cap of office, to be shaken at will – at *her* will – unless I could prove myself to be a person in my own right. Only a dwindling part of me was still a part of her, after all—

My trance was violently interrupted by a sudden clamour of spoons being banged on the table as the food finally arrived.

And what food! The *arroz con pescado* wasn't merely delicious, it was the finest thing I'd ever eaten, and in spite of Juan's attempts to make me sick by waving whole fish heads and octopus legs at me and secretly gouging sea snails from their shells and stuffing them up his nose, I ate and drank the soup until I was awash, almost capsizing on my chair. The dish was so full of saffron that every face was smeared with gold by the time we'd had seconds and thirds. Hardly a word was spoken as we ate, only grunts and groans and slurps until every last grain of yellow rice and every drop of the salty yellow liquid had been guzzled, and every fish scale picked clean.

After we'd eaten, conversation soared again for a while, my mother's wit fairly crackling under the seats of those around her, making some of them wriggle uncomfortably. She had a knack of prizing open egos and tweaking the little nerves of self-esteem before they had time to retract, then soothing them with a laugh or a light touch of her fingers, or by instantly turning the same knife on herself. And yet she appeared always to be forgiven by those she teased. Selwyn, who was as wily as a fox and realised that the barbed circle of her wit was beginning to close in on him, quickly turned to Robert and began to talk about birthdays. Robert's fifty-seventh had taken place some ten days before, but Lucia whispered to me that he'd been so depressed by a scandal over the ownership of his land that he'd felt ill, so the day had passed quietly. 'It lacked its promised variety, I admit,' he joked.

In the middle of laughing, my mother slapped her hand dramatically over her mouth in a gesture that always made my skin crawl with apprehension. 'Dear God!' she gasped, her eyes bursting with feigned horror as she looked round at me. 'It's Simon's birthday on the fifteenth—'

There was a friendly cheer from around the table.

I froze with embarrassment at being singled out by her, and gazed down into my bowl, at the sudden graveyard of my wonderful lunch. Discarded skeletons lay in its crater, smeared with mustard gas and surrounded by the ruts and pools of spilt food which had gathered in the creases of the oilcloth, the huge crusts of half eaten bread lying among them like the rusting hulks of tanks.

I became aware of Ruthven fixing me determinedly with his wobbling gaze. We'd never really spoken to each other before. 'How old shall you be?' he asked carefully. At first I wasn't even sure that he was speaking to me, his eyes seemed to stagger so – one moment against me, then against my bowl, then weaving to the left and right of my head, and I suddenly realised that he was as embarrassed as I was, not on his own account, but on mine.

'Eleven,' I said hurriedly.

'Ah! An important age! I remember being eleven—' But he couldn't bring himself to meet my eyes this time, and I knew that he remembered no such thing. 'Double-one, side by side – *wickets*! signifying the true beginning of your life. "*From this point I will make my stand*"—'

'The end of childhood—' murmured Alastair, and my mother gave a sickening little cry and pressed her hand to her heart.

'Quite!' Ruthven beamed at him, 'but not as something to be mourned – on the contrary, something to be celebrated. We must celebrate his birthday!'

'Of course we must,' said Robert, as though we already had.

'No, I mean *really* celebrate it!' Ruthven began to work himself up. 'Give him a send off! Mark the occasion—' Pulling a grubby spotted handkerchief from his pocket, he mopped at his dripping neck while he shakily poured himself another glass of wine. 'And I do so love a party!' he gasped.

Beryl leaned across to him, eyes alight with inspiration. 'I know – let's do a play! We haven't done one for ages—'

'A *play*!' In his excitement, Ruthven's head jerked towards her in a spasm, dislodging his spectacles. Unfortunately, he tried to catch them with the hand which was clasping his wine glass, and he threw the entire contents all over himself.

'Oh, *bugger* – I mean, I beg your pardon, but – *Christ*—'

Laughter exploded all around him. Juan at once became uncontrollable, mimicking Ruthven by throwing glass after glass of anything he could find over his own head and down his front.

'*Juan, stop that!*' shouted Robert over the din. 'If you can't behave properly, then you'll have to leave the table! Go on—'

'Oh, Robert, for heaven's sake,' protested Beryl as she mopped at Ruthven's shirt with a handkerchief. 'It's only high spirits – and it's mostly water—!'

'There's a drought!' retorted Robert as Juan skulked away from the table – until something on the beach caught his eye and he began to bray like a donkey. Isabella brayed back, and with a bloodcurdling howl, Juan vanished down the steps.

Ruthven laid his hand gently over Beryl's. 'Actually, it's quite refreshing,' he murmured, 'no – no, really… where were we…? A play! That's it – Simon's birthday play. What shall we do?'

'Why not do a combined birthday play?' suggested Selwyn. 'Robert hasn't celebrated his fifty-seventh yet, not properly, and it would lend a certain *gravitas* – if you'll forgive me?' He looked round at me brusquely as though daring me to do anything else. 'I don't mean to diminish your importance in any way, but perhaps a Pride of Leos would attract a wider audience…?'

I caught Robert's eye, and we grinned at each other, both knowing that we'd been checkmated. 'Would you allow me to share your birthday?' he asked, puffing on a cigar. 'I'd be ever so 'umbly grateful!' he added in a dreadful imitation of a cockney accent.

'And Si would be ever so deeply honoured, guv'nor,' said my mother, effortlessly correcting his accent. 'Wouldn't you, darling?'

Si would ever so dearly have loved the earth to open up and swallow her whole—

Selwyn was my unexpected champion. 'Let the boy answer for himself, Diana,' he said testily.

To be offered such sudden largesse from such a tight purse at least gave me the courage to answer, even if the words were secondhand.

'I'd be deeply honoured,' I said, smiling.

'Spoken like a gentleman!' Robert declared. 'What play would you like performed, Sir, and what part would you like to play in it?'

Quick! Who did I like? Shakespeare, Fry, Ustinov, Morgan, Ibsen—? (School holidays spent in the wings of theatres watching my parents and godparents performing into the dusty motes of golden beams of light—) Something of the confusion I felt must have shown in my face. Ruthven, who seemed to recognise desperation when he saw it, leaned across the table so that he could fix Robert with his wobbling eyes. 'If I might suggest—?'

A general hush fell on the table as all eyes turned to him. 'A *new* play,' he went on, 'written by Mr Alastair Reid and myself – a morality play, to cleanse Simon's mind of impure thoughts and to arm him against the Wiles of Women, who will soon be lying in wait for him.'

There was a sudden outburst of feminine protest and male approval as Robert clapped his hands for silence. 'What fun!' he cried excitedly. 'I know – we could do an allegory on the Book of Genesis – the Garden of Eden – Adam and Eve, good and evil – ! It has all the ingredients, after all. Will you accept a commission? A guinea, say? A birthday present from me to my grand-nephew?'

Ruthven gave the offer a moment's deep consideration. 'Would you excuse me while I confer with my unsuspecting fellow author?' He leaned towards Alastair's left ear and whispered into it with such force that Alastair had to jam his finger inside it. After a moment he leant towards Ruthven and did exactly the same to him. Then they both looked at Robert, like hear-no-evil, with their fingers still in their ears. '*How* much?' demanded Alastair. 'I'm sorry, we appear to be deaf.'

Once the contract had been drawn up on the tail of Ruthven's shirt (the only dry bit left), and was duly signed by all interested parties, a kind of torpor gradually descended over the table. The sun had crept closer to the surface of the sea, casting up reflections which were too dazzling to look at now. The air had become breathless, the screech of cicadas so frenzied that it was almost unbearable. Everyone appeared to have had enough for the time being, content to doze off under the shade of the dry palm fronds as they occasionally stirred and rustled, promising breezes that never came.

Beryl made up a rough couch for Robert, scattering old canvas cushions along a stone bench that ran along the rock face, while the others put chairs together for her and my mother, then made themselves as comfortable as they could.

It was as though a spell had been cast under which, one by one, the Court and courtiers fell asleep. The cove itself had become becalmed. Nothing stirred in the heat...

Until I was the last one left awake.

I would go on watch, I decided – pretend that the terrace was the deck of a ship. If I were an enemy, after all, this would be the time to strike! Perhaps something out of the Greek Myths that Robert was writing at the moment might come bursting out of the sea, or crash through the rocks to take revenge on him for telling their secrets to the world—

I looked around for Juan, but he still hadn't returned from his banishment. I imagined him lying in ambush for me somewhere, angry that I hadn't followed him out. Or perhaps he, too, had fallen asleep under the spell—

Easing myself out of my chair, I'd begun to tiptoe towards the steps when my eyes suddenly met Alastair's, and I froze. He was sitting at the table, quite still, his chin cupped in his hands, staring into nothingness. Gingerly, I edged forward, but his eyes didn't move at all. Perhaps he was sleep-watching.

As I finally stepped out of the deep shadows cast by the palm frond roof, it wasn't Juan, but the sun who lay in ambush, smiting me a blow of such blinding heat that at first I was stunned. But then some instinct, stronger even than self-preservation, made me stay where I was and not retreat back into the shade, and the power which had at first seemed almost violent began to soften, like an embrace, as it absorbed itself into my body which in turn seemed to expand to make room for it. Stretching my arms upwards, I threw my head back so that my face and brain could soak up this silent power, so molten and dazzling even on my closed eyelids. Like a lunatic, I slowly forced my eyes open and stared back into the sun until the pain and blindingness became unbearable and my head exploded into rocks—

It was Alastair who caught me as I fell, my palms pressed against my eyes, hands trying desperately to contain the avalanche that threatened to burst my head open.

'What the hell are you doing?' he whispered angrily.

'I don't know,' I moaned, 'it hurts!'

'*Sssh*! Come away, quickly – give me your hand—'

I groped for him and he took my wrist, pulling me, whispering directions as we went. 'Three steps up... left... right a bit... mind the blanket...'

The darkness inside the kitchen was like aspirin, soothing the pain—

'It's all right, there's no one here,' murmured Alastair, 'they've gone for their siestas. Lie down.' I lay down on the earth floor. 'What were you doing?' he demanded. 'Were you staring into the sun?'

'Yes,' I whined.

'Quiet! Do you want your mother to hear? Shall I go and wake her—?'

'No! Please—'

'I didn't mean it as a threat,' he frowned, 'you know what I meant, for Christ's sake. If you want her, I'll get her – if you don't, I won't.'

'No, thank you,' I said more calmly.

'Try opening you eyes. What can you see?'

'The sun,' I whimpered, jamming my palms over my eyes. I would have to become a blind matchseller – no! Too boring! A blind musician, then – a cellist! I like the cello!

'Were you deliberately trying to blind yourself?'

'No!'

'Sssh! Are you sure? It's just that some children hurt themselves on purpose to draw attention to themselves—'

How could he be so stupid? '*No!*' I whispered fiercely. 'I didn't know anyone was watching. The sun was staring at me, and I just wanted to stare back—'

He laughed suddenly, and I became rigid with frustration. I wouldn't tell him the rest—

'Try and sleep for a bit,' he said, patting my shoulder. 'It should wear off. I'll come back in a while and see how you are.'

For a big man he moved almost noiselessly. I only sensed that he'd left when the kitchen grew lighter for a moment as he pulled back the blanket over the entrance. At least I could recognise light and darkness. I tried opening my eyes again. The ball of fire was still blindingly there, but the pain was fading, and if I twisted my head back I could just make out the doorway at the edge of my vision. Anything I looked at directly, though, was still consumed by a writhing halo of fire.

I wished I could have turned that look on myself.

After a while I must have dozed off, only to be woken by the shock of having fallen asleep. But at least my vision had recovered enough for me to creep out of the gloom of the kitchen, just as the spell of the siesta was suddenly broken by the sound of someone plunging into the sea from the café terrace. Soon, everyone except Beryl and my mother had either dived or flung themselves over the edge, shouting and laughing and splashing each other as they refreshed themselves for the *fiesta* which was still to come.

Nobody noticed the curious sideways angle of my head as I ran down the steps to the sea. I still had difficulty seeing anything head-on through my sunstruck eyes, and didn't realise that it was Alastair who was pulling himself out of the water in front of me until I heard his voice.

'There you are,' he said quietly. 'I was creating a diversion before coming to wake you. Are you better?'

'Yes – thank you—'

Suddenly we heard my mother's voice anxiously calling my name. 'He's with me, Diana!' he called back. 'We'll swim round – he wants to show you his crawl!'

'Side stroke!' I whispered desperately as I pulled off my shorts. 'I can't do the crawl.'

'*Side stroke!*' he shouted.

Word must have gone round to everyone in the water that I was having problems convincing my mother that I could swim, because whatever I managed to do, however badly, they did it worse. She sat on the edge of the terrace like an empress, looking down at us with what appeared to be a broad smile, which after five minutes or so gave the impression of being tied to her ears. Even Juan, who had appeared out of nowhere, was either sporting enough or blind enough to allow me to beat him in a race to the huge diving rock on the far side of the *cala*.

Eventually Karl called out my name and pointed urgently to where my mother was beckoning to me. I broke away from the others, swimming across to her and pulling myself out of a sea that seemed unwilling to let go of me. Scrambling back up the rocks to the terrace, I stood before her, breathless and dripping and as happy as a sand boy. All I needed now was the stamp of her approval, like the visa on my passport, and I'd be free to move among all the Elements—

71

She turned her weird, fixed smile on me, and I saw that it wasn't a smile at all but a grimace of pure terror. Beryl, who had a hand on her shoulder, leaned over the wooden rail and called out to Robert, who waved and swam towards us.

'No, don't!' my mother begged her.

'It's all right,' said Beryl soothingly, 'I'm just going to get him to talk to you.'

'What's wrong?' I asked, bewildered.

'It's just me, darling – your silly mama—'

'What is it, Beryl?' Robert shouted as he held onto the rocks below and trod water.

'Diana's convinced that Simon's going to *drown!*' Beryl called down quietly.

I stamped my foot in fury. Beryl glanced at me and tried not to laugh. '*Wait*, Simon! It'll be all right—' She called down to Robert again, 'I've told her she's silly, and Alastair's told her she's silly, and even *she's* told me she's silly. What she needs is some avuncular *advice!*'

Robert had closed his eyes briefly, eyebrows raised, visibly marshalling a list of answers in the order of their probable effectiveness. 'Darling niece,' he called up at last, 'not only is half your son's blood from counties Cork and Limerick, but he floats like the former and swims like a doggerel! He can even beat Juan – without his specs, I admit – but he can still beat him, and the only thing that might ever drown him is your worrying about him, which could muddle him fatally at the wrong moment—'

'Yes, but dearest uncle, he's all I have—' Although she spoke lightly, to my horror I saw tears begin to run down her cheeks. 'If anything were to happen – oh, I'm so *stupid*—'

As far as I was concerned, I no longer existed. The shell of the boy who stood beside his mother, head bowed to detach himself as a witness to this scene, was someone else's son. My spirit had fled up into the pine trees above the café, where I could get some peace while I tried to sort out the battle raging in my head.

I hadn't realised that she felt so alone. On the other hand, I hadn't imagined that she would go so far to expose her feelings. And in public, too. Mothers just didn't cry in public, and were the first to tell their children not to. She had shamed me – but she probably hadn't meant to. She was being honest. Or was she? Or was she merely playing to the gallery again? Or was she, in fact, having a 'breakdown'? I'd been warned about them just before I'd left England; a well-meaning but meddling great-aunt had offered me one, with a selection of cakes, at Gunter's in Curzon Street, when she'd heard about my difficulties at school: '*You may have a breakdown, like your great-uncle Robert,*' she'd said, as though giving me permission. '*You may do lots of silly things like cry and steal and want to hurt people,*' she smiled, '*or you may have a slice of Battenberg for being a good boy and not giving in to vulgar impulses—*'

At once I was determined to do all these things, since of all the cakes, and of all my great-aunts, I disliked Battenberg and her the most.

That must be it – my mother was having a 'breakdown'! My father belonged to the Automobile Association who attended breakdowns on motorcycles with a sort of coffin attached to them where the sidecar should be—

My spirit leapt back down the cliff and into my body and raised my head: 'It's all right,' I smiled, 'I shan't swim if you don't want me to.'

It was inspired.

She turned to me, her eyes refilling with tears. 'Oh, darling, how *sweet* of you!' she gasped. 'But of *course* you must swim! It's only me being selfish and silly. Uncle Robert has promised to look after you with his life, so I'll just go for a walk with Beryl, and then I won't have to look.' She leant down and kissed me, like Christ kissing Judas, on top of my nasty little head.

So she walked, and I swam, digging with all my might into the warm and uncomplaining sea, swimming with all my strength into an ever-growing resistance which I believed would strip me of my past and leave it, like the useless husk that it was, floating in my wake.

The atmosphere of the procession that made its way back up the cliffs from the *cala* that evening had changed, just as the landscape around us had silently, almost mystically changed from when we had passed through it on our way down that morning.

Although the people were the same, travelling the same path but in the opposite direction, everything had somehow shifted in a way that was more than the passing of time. There was a feeling of loss in the heavy air, as if none of us would ever return to that golden day.

The feeling was so unsettling that I kept looking around, trying to understand what had altered so powerfully, yet so privately that no one mentioned it.

Then I realised, with the same feeling which had revealed Robert to me in a different light, that it was the lengthening, deepening shadows that had altered not only the entire landscape, but its effect on everyone in it. Whereas at midday the world had looked thin and sharp, drained of colour by the bleaching heat, with people and objects standing in little pools of almost non-existent shadow, every one of us now dragged behind them a burden longer than ourselves. The distant olive groves had become stark ladders of light and darkness scaling the foothills; the mountains beyond, so remote and hazy at noon, were now almost threatening in their nearness.

Motes of golden dust swirled with insects in the lengthening rays of the sun as we slowly, broodingly climbed the endless donkey steps back to the top.

Isabella, who was finally performing her only real task that day (to carry my mother up from the beach), did so with bad grace, continually stopping to inspect and dislike the way a particular stone lay in her path, or to protest at the flouting of her right-of-way by a sunstruck and indifferent bee. Only the combined force of Robert pulling on her lead rein and Alastair throwing his weight behind her and twisting her tail, kept her moving at all.

'Blasted creature!' cursed Robert. 'She's bad at the best of times, but when she's like this I'd swap her for a pot of glue!'

'No, no, Uncle Robert!' cried my mother theatrically. 'Don't say such a thing – at least not until I've got off at the top, when I'll cheerfully help you throw her into the cauldron!'

'I don't know what's got into her,' cried Robert, exasperated.

We soon found out. From the near darkness of the valley below came the sudden, primeval braying of another donkey.

Isabella jolted to a halt, took several panting breaths, and then HEEE-HAAAWWWWED so shatteringly in reply that Robert dropped the rein, my mother screamed in panic, and Alastair was blown backwards by a fart so violent and putrid that Juan and I, following behind, were gassed in our tracks and fell to the ground shrieking with delight. And when Isabella then proceeded, in her excitement, to empty the contents of her bowels onto the path in a spattering rush, our laughter rose up the scale of sound until it was completely silent as we clung to each other, kicking and struggling for breath.

'*Get up!*' bellowed Robert, towering over us, his face contorted with fury. '*Stop this at once and get up!*' He grabbed Alastair's arm, angrily pulling him to his feet as he, too, wept with hysteria.

Beryl came hurrying up to us. 'It's all *right*, Robert! They're only *laughing!*' She saw the look of fear on my face and tried to smile reassuringly. 'It's the *noise*, Simon,' she went on, 'your grand-uncle can't stand sudden noises and *screams*, that's all – it's just leftover shell-shock from the First War. Isabella, you *brute*—'

My mother had told me about Robert's shell-shock, but I'd always presumed it was caused by shells exploding, not by laughter.

He looked down at me and must have seen (or recognised) something of the fear which petrifies a schoolboy when confronted with the tearing edge of a master's rage as we both – he first – began to pull ourselves out of the horrors of our pasts.

'No, I'm sorry Simon – don't be hurt—' he looked around wildly, 'Isabella's fault, not yours. Beryl's quite right – I can't bear loud noises—'

'Robert, have you got a hanky?' Beryl interrupted urgently. 'Diana's lost hers – *quickly!*'

He delved into the pockets of his baggy khaki shorts, but all he found was a crushed cigarette, which he stuck between his lips.

Alastair produced a handkerchief and took it over to my mother. As he handed it up, though, and she turned and looked down at him, I saw that they were both wearing expressions of such suppressed and explosive mirth, like a pair of puce pressure cookers, that they had to look frantically away from each other. Then my mother let the cat out of the bag by blowing her nose so messily into the handkerchief and at the same time letting out a terrible raucous cackle, that their hysteria, as uncontrollable as being sick, suddenly erupted again. She tried to stuff the handkerchief into her mouth as tears and mascara poured down her face, Alastair burying his face in her skirts to help muffle his cries, drawing the material round his head as though trying to make himself invisible.

I darted an anxious glance back at Robert, but he just grinned at me. 'They're all *med*, as my dear mother used to say.' He sniffed dismissively through his cigarette. 'I say, have you got a light?'

FIESTA

'*Si, darling, come here and let me look at you before we go——!*'

My mother's call brought me racing down the passage to her bedroom, tucking in and smarming down and licking furiously at bits that never seemed to pass inspection. Skidding against the doorway, I rebounded into her room like a well-aimed billiard ball, when the sight of her brought me up short of the pocket of her expected embrace. 'Crikey!' I gasped.

She could have been in her dressing room in London, before a first night, sitting in front of her mirror in a haze of scent and face powder as she applied the last touches to her lipstick. She looked beautiful, in a black cocktail dress with long sparkling earrings, her pale, slightly drawn face strikingly stark against the blackness of her hair and the material of her gown, dark eyebrows plucked to within a millimetre of their lives and curving like drawn bows above pale blue eyes whose colour and intensity seemed to change with every thought she had. Staring fixedly at herself in the looking glass, she carefully smeared her painted lips together before releasing them in a little pout, their finely etched shape now perfectly and precisely covered by her lipstick. I was always entranced by this miracle of deftness. A tiny smile played at the corners of her mouth.

She was so absorbed in her face that she seemed completely unaware of my presence as she leaned forward slightly into the mirror, her eyes widening, changing, as though she were answering a question which only she could hear. Suddenly she stumbled across my own stare, unconsciously reflecting hers, and at once I felt like an intruder as her pupils contracted in shock. To my relief, though, she smiled, first at me and then, pulling a wry face, back into her own reflection.

'It's all I've got,' she murmured with an odd, distasteful little shrug, 'and you, of course—' She glanced at me fondly. 'And one day there'll just be you.' Her eyes slid back to the mirror. 'How long will my face last, do you think? And if you say 'forever', I may strike you!'

'Always, then,' I grinned.

'Ha! You're learning some wit! One golden rule, though: never say something funny twice, even if you think no one heard it the first time; they always have, and if they didn't laugh then, they're even less likely to laugh if you repeat it.' She looked me up and down and smiled. 'You look very smart, darling.' Her eyes slipped back to her own reflection, as though for reassurance. She fiddled with her hair. 'You won't let me down tonight, will you? We may be very late. Perhaps you should stay here—'

'No, of *course* not – I'll be *fine!*' I protested, panic-stricken. Even at this last moment she might refuse to let me go— 'Juan's going, and I'm older than him! And Lucia – and I'm nearly the same age as her and she's a *girl!* And anyway, Beryl said I could come—'

The oddly detached conversation we'd been having into the mirror was shattered as my real mother turned on me, like a portrait that my cousin Ben had once drawn for me to try and explain cubism, every side of her anger suddenly rushing towards me out of her painted face. 'Beryl is not your mother,' she hissed, 'I am! And don't argue with me. It isn't as if you haven't already let me down today—'

'*How*—?'

'You went swimming before lunch when I expressly forbade you to go into the water unless I was there – you gulped your wine when I told you to sip it—'

In spite of her temper (or perhaps because of it), my eye was drawn, as though by the force of something unfinished, back into the mirror where I stared at her profile staring down at me in another dimension. I looked away from her reflection into my own reflected eyes, afraid that by staring into her unguarded face I might join up forever the magic circle of her anger, as endlessly and infinitely as our echoed reflections—

'—and *look at me* when I'm speaking to you!'

'I *am*,' I protested honestly, 'in the mirror!'

'Don't be insolent!'

'I'm *not*—'

'Now then, now then,' Beryl's calm voice echoing down the tiled passage. 'What's all *this*?' Her face appeared round the half open door, smiling. 'Hello! May I come in?'

My mother took a huge pull at herself and smiled back frozenly. 'Of course, dear Beryl—'

'Diana, you mustn't allow yourself to get so worked up. You know what the doctor said – *tranquillidad*! A few little jaunts, but back to bed the moment it gets too much. And no *excitements*! You have *nervous debillitations*, after all.'

They both started to laugh, my mother rather shakily as she pointed a trembling finger at me.

'It's this bloody boy! He's too precocious! He answers back, disobeys—'

'Yes, well, I wouldn't know about *that,* but I'm sure he doesn't *mean* to, eh, Simon?' I shook my head emphatically. 'It's just high spirits, which are perfectly natural in a boy his age. Now come along! Let's all go to the *fiesta* and have a lovely time.'

Leaving the room with Beryl, I couldn't help feeling resentful of my mother. As an only child I'd been told that I was precocious before, which I hadn't liked the sound of at all, since I'd mistaken the word for 'precious' at first, but once I understood it, I thought it was hardly surprising. Any boy who was brought up (during the school holidays at least) entirely by grown ups – and notoriously bright grown-ups at that – was

bound to have a wit and a vocabulary that were beyond his
age—

'Beryl, is it actually *bad* to be precocious?' I asked her on the
stairs.

'*Very* bad!' she said firmly. 'You could end up like your grand-
uncle!'

We set off as night fell, in a convoy of cars and shooting brakes
along the dark and twisting road to Soller, our headlamps conjuring
the vivid greens of tropical plants out of the warm darkness as they
tumbled in motionless landslides towards the road, their heavy,
night-scented odour blown back to us by the draught of the car
in front.

Juan and I were crammed into the back seat of Beryl's car,
between my mother and Ruthven, who twitched whenever he
was spoken to, slamming his specs back up his nose with his thumb
and clearing his throat noisily before each reply. As we climbed
towards the pass at Son Bleda, he started to wriggle disjointedly
while trying to appear not to wriggle, his right hand, pressed up
against the door, groping for something in his pocket. Squeezed
against his other side, I peered round at him. Beads of sweat
were trickling down the sides of his face. He caught my eye and
grimaced horribly, putting a finger to his lips and motioning me to
give him some more room. Obediently, I budged up against Juan,
who looked round in protest. I quickly put my finger to my lips
and rolled my eyes towards Ruthven. Juan, suddenly alive with
curiosity, edged forward in his seat to look round me. Ruthven
was frozen comically in the same attitude, his finger still pressed
to his lips. Then he slowly toppled towards my lap. A bead of
sweat dripped onto my bare leg, and I wiped it away in disgust
as his right hand snaked into his freed pocket, and with a loud
and revolting throat-clearing noise he tugged something out of

it, jammed it between his legs and straightened up in the same movement, beaming sweatily down at us. Again his finger went to his lips before his hand dropped shakily to his lap. Juan's mouth hung open in anticipation. I think he thought Ruthven was about to expose himself, and I started to giggle helplessly until Ruthven jabbed me in the ribs with his left elbow and started to fiddle with whatever it was he'd stuffed between his legs. Then he raised his left hand and held it to the side of his face, shielding it from us as his other hand came up, holding something that gleamed dully, like a mouth organ. In the lights of the car behind I could just make out that he was putting it to his lips. Brilliant! I thought, he's going to play something—

He swallowed convulsively. And then swallowed again—

'*Ruthven!*' shouted Juan.

There was a spluttering, stifled cough, and suddenly we were both sprayed with drink as Ruthven collapsed in a choking fit, dropping his metal flask, fumbling for it as it fell, then knocking it, gurgling, into my lap, which made me leap into the air with a cry, causing Beryl to veer across the road in alarm as Robert shouted '*Puncture*—' and my mother screamed as Juan drummed his feet hysterically on the floor.

'We have *not* got a puncture!' shouted Beryl. 'Ruthven's *choking!* Somebody bang him on the back! That's *enough*, Juan—'

As she pulled in with a screech of brakes I knelt on the seat and started to thump Ruthven on the back with my fist. Robert leapt out, threw open our door and dragged the helpless Ruthven onto the verge before pulling him to his feet and thumping him so hard on the back that he fell to the ground and was noisily sick. Behind us, the other cars had pulled in, their occupants running towards us with cries of 'It's a fight!' 'Don't hit him, Robert!' and some idiot even crying 'Bully!'

At that moment a group of flickering torches came towards us from the direction of the pass. Three civil guards, in their strange black *papier maché* hats, materialised in the headlights, their rifles unslung and pointing at us nervously.

'Oh, no – *guardias*!' groaned Beryl. 'They'll think we're smugglers!'

It took forever to convince them that we weren't – and that Ruthven wasn't being murdered. The 'poor brutes', as Beryl called the *guardias*, had been forced to miss the *fiesta* as a result of minor lapses in discipline, and instead of joining in the fun down in Soller they'd been sent up to the pass to lie in wait for *contrabandistas* – when any fool knew that every *contrabandista* in Majorca would be at the *fiesta*. To emphasise their point, they insisted on shepherding us to their vantage point at the top of the pass, where on the one hand they could look out over the empty, starlit sea for the smugglers' boats, and on the other they could look straight down, enviously, into the black velvet purse of the valley below them, where the lights of Soller lay scattered like diamonds a thousand feet below. The heat of the day was still rising from the town, carrying up with it occasional faint snatches of music.

'Come along, everyone!' Beryl called impatiently. 'The *fiesta*'s started and Juan's got to join his school for their folk dance. They're number fourteen—'

'*Mother!*' Juan's scream of outrage stopped everyone in their tracks. 'You promised you wouldn't tell anyone!'

'Oh dear – well, I forgot because we're late. I'm sorry—'

Robert ambled past him distractedly, on his way to the car. 'Anyway, Mother didn't tell *anyone*, she told *everyone*, so that's all right!'

'That's *cheating!*'

On the dangerous descent down the narrow hairpin bends to Soller, with only the occasional low dry stone wall to mark the boundary between the road and certain death, Beryl had to promise an apoplectic Juan that she would take everyone into a bar and close the doors while he was dancing.

'I don't want *anyone* to see me! Or *everyone*, neither, especially you, Father!' he yelled. 'Except Simon,' he added more quietly, turning round to me. 'Will you come?'

'If you want,' I said, surprised, and glanced at my mother who looked as if she was on the verge of hitting him.

Soller was stifling and strange. The little tree-lined *avenidas* on the outskirts were promising, but the streets soon got narrower and narrower and more and more claustrophobic, as though the builders of the town had buckled under the pressure of the prison-like wall of mountains which surrounded it. The nearer we drove towards the centre, the more people thronged the streets, all in their Sunday best, all staring down at us in our car, their expressions unchanged as they went on talking to each other.

'They don't look very friendly,' said my mother anxiously. She'd been doling out smiles through the car window like Maundy money, but the crowd either didn't realise their value, or were too proud to accept them.

'It's just their way,' said Beryl. 'Most of them come from the mountains and have never seen foreigners before. And they're Majorcans!' she added, as though that explained everything. 'I'm going to park here – we'll walk the rest of the way.'

As we got out, my mother, still disgusted by Ruthven's behaviour, decided to wait for Alastair as he pulled up in the car behind. Ruthven, still smelling of sick, waited beside her sheepishly as Beryl told Juan and me to stay with her and follow Robert. It wasn't long before Robert became impatient with our slow progress, though, and said he was going on ahead to see if he could find Judith.

'Who's Judith?' I asked Beryl as he barged politely into the back of the crowd, head and shoulders taller than everyone, eyes searching, his mind already elsewhere, I'd heard Judith's name spoken occasionally, but had paid no attention.

'She was your grand-uncle's *muse*,' she said. 'Until last year, at least, when things went a bit wrong. Her mother still lives in Soller, and Robert thinks she may turn up tonight. Of course, she won't—'

'What's a "muse"?' I asked curiously.

'Someone who inspires poets to write – usually a woman. They're very important—'

'*I want one!*' shouted Juan, just as my mother called me back to help her through the crowd. Alastair and Ruthven were chatting away behind her, and she was clearly miffed. Still wondering about Judith, I asked her to tell me about muses in an attempt to distract her.

'*Bah!*' she spat. 'They're just an excuse for poets to have mistresses!' A moment later she dug her nails into my shoulder. 'You're not to say I said so, though. Do you understand?' I nodded obediently. 'Uncle Robert's extraordinary, but in some ways he's a bloody fool. I don't know how Beryl puts up with it. Now that's enough—'

The nearer we got to the centre of town, the louder grew the sound of music and clapping. The mood of the crowds in front of us suddenly began to change as their pace quickened and they turned and actually smiled at each other in anticipation, calling out excitedly as we were all squeezed like toothpaste round the last narrow bend and burst into the seething, dazzling town square. Alastair and Ruthven now flanked my mother for protection, so I ran on ahead to be with Beryl and Juan.

Hundreds of naked lightbulbs were slung on cables between the wilting plane trees, where clusters of loudspeakers relayed blaring music from a crude stage, like a boxing ring, which had been set up against the massive wall of the church. Beryl had been absolutely right – the band looked as if it was made up of every desperado on the coast, all playing under the protection of a man who looked like the corrupt Chief of Police, chainsmoking contraband cigarettes on a bursting old sofa below. He was surrounded by pretty women and expressionless young men in dark glasses. (I learned later that in fact this was the local football team and their manager.)

'Oh *dear!* We seem to have lost the others already!' shouted Beryl in the crush. 'Hold hands, you two—'

'No!' screamed Juan.

'Well, hold *mine* then, both of you!'

Obediently we each took one of her hands, Juan and I blindly helping to push Beryl to wherever she was leading us.

Moments later we were shoving our way up a flight of stone steps to the highest point in the square, a broad terrace surrounded by more plane trees, filled with café tables packed with shouting and laughing townspeople, the younger ones already the worse for wear.

'Hold tight!' yelled Beryl above the noise.

We fought our way through towards one of the biggest cafés, with '*Sollerense F.C.*' in huge steel letters over the facade, and once inside, in the unbelievable din, we continued to barge our way through the neonlit pandemonium by the bar to the lounge, almost equally filled, where we were greeted with cries of relief by Robert and my mother and the rest of the Deya contingent. I was introduced to several people I'd never met before including, to my surprise, Alastair's wife, called something like Suzy. I hadn't realised he was married. She was dark and pretty, but seemed strangely ill-at-ease.

Beryl shouted to my mother that she was going to take me back to the square so that I could watch 'you-know-who' do his 'you-know-what' on the stage. Predictably, my mother turned pale, but Juan simply grabbed my hand before she could protest and began to force his way back out of the room. When I dared to glance back at her, I saw that she was being supported on all sides by her friends, pressing their drinks on her—

And I was free! Free to be myself at last among all this noise and heat and swirling chaos. My mother really *could* be overruled by Robert and Beryl. She was completely in awe of their certainty about everything. It was as if I'd been sucked into the middle of a magic circle which was stronger than hers, where it seemed that no harm could ever come to me—

'*This is wonderful!*' I shouted at Juan.

'What is?' He turned his head to look back at me.

'*All this*—' We grinned stupidly at each other, our sweaty hands still clutched together.

The sight of Juan dancing with his class on the stage took me completely by surprise. Specs gleaming under the electric lights, he banged his tambourine in perfect time as he weaved gracefully in and out of his classmates in a Majorcan folk dance that looked more complicated than any Scottish reel. He wasn't remotely self-conscious, even when he saw Dito and Mito and the older members of his gang, who weren't dancing themselves, cheering him on from below the stage. He scarcely seemed to notice them, his whole attention wrapped up in the complicated movements he had to perform, with just the faintest trance-like smile fixed on his lips. By the end of the dance it was obvious that it was he who was stage managing the whole performance, calling out sharp directions to the others, avoiding collisions with a nudge here and a push there, yet never once losing the rhythm or missing a step. Roars of approval and wild applause from the crowd greeted their finale, and yet he didn't even wait to take his bow, but leapt off the stage and into the arms of his friends with a huge grin on his face.

Like a local hero he was surrounded by a phalanx of children and rushed through the throng to where Beryl and I were watching on the terrace.

'Don't say *anything!*' he screamed as he approached.

'All right, we won't,' Beryl called down, 'but it was *very good*! I'll go and tell father and the others that they can come out now. You two stick together while I'm gone. Don't move from here!'

No sooner had she turned her back than Juan climbed up onto the terrace and grabbed my sleeve, cupping my ear to his mouth.

'I'm just going to go and have a Coke with Dito and Mito!' he shouted. Then he put his sticky hand under my chin and forced my head back gently. 'Look up between the trees! Above the lights—'

I looked up, beyond the glare of the lights, and could just make out what looked like strings of sausages slung between the trees.

'Fireworks!' yelled Juan. 'Just wait – they're unbelievable! Don't move from this place!' And he dived back among his friends who closed round him again and carried him off up one of the side streets as another band took to the stage and began blasting away.

'Where's Juan?' asked Beryl anxiously when she returned.

'He's gone off with Dito and Mito!' I shouted back. 'He said there'd be fireworks later—'

'Not until midnight, I'm afraid, and we'll have to miss them anyway. Robert can't stand them – they remind him of the war—'

'Was he ever wounded?' I asked.

'*Yes* – very *badly*! In fact *The Times* reported him Killed in Action!'

My mind flew back to school, to the shelf of huge bound volumes of *The Graphic* and *The Illustrated London News* covering the First World War. They were the most pored over books in the library with their grisly pictures of pitched battles, of dead horses and bayonetted Germans. 'Was it a particular battle?' I asked, determined to look it up when I got back.

'Mametz Wood was the worst,' she shouted back. 'He lost his lung there—'

I was astonished. 'But how can he breathe?'

'He's got two, silly!' she laughed. 'Or at least, he *had*. Now he's just got one and a bit.'

A little later we were all offered a table on the terrace by some Majorcans from Deya who were leaving to join their friends in another bar.

I was almost too happy, thrilled to still be up at ten o'clock at night, sitting where I was between Robert and Alastair, listening gravely to their conversation about the power of something called Mescalin, and yet in spite of the intensity of their conversation, Robert's eyes still restlessly searched the square.

Alastair suddenly broke off the conversation. 'She's not here, Robert,' he murmured. 'Honestly, I'd have heard—'

'No, I know—' Robert flung himself back in his chair. 'I just hoped that perhaps her mother—'

'If she'd wanted to see you, she'd have found you. You stick out like a sore thumb—'

There was the sudden distant crackle of gunfire. We all froze, staring at each other in disbelief – and excitement on my part—

'Smugglers!' I shouted. 'The *guardias* are shooting them—'

'It's not *smugglers*,' cried Beryl grimly, 'it's *fireworks!* Robert, *quick!* Some *brute* must have set them off early! Everyone! Get him inside—'

A strangely haggard look flitted over Robert's face. 'Oh, blast!' he said, then shrugged. 'Oh, well, call me when it's over—'

Just as Juan had been surrounded and carried through the crowd by his friends, so Robert's friends leapt to their feet and closed ranks around him, forcing their way urgently through the crowds and back into the café. He strode among them in the middle, like Caesar, staring up distractedly at the strings of still silent fireworks among the trees.

Beryl stayed with me, looking around anxiously as the sound of the bangers drew nearer and nearer down one of the side streets before suddenly bursting into the square like hooligans, the flashes and explosions racing through the trees as fast and as loud as machine gun fire. Although the young people in the crowd cheered and waved their arms over their heads, the older inhabitants looked at their watches and shouted angrily at each other.

Beryl and I were hunched together with our fingers in our ears, eyes tight shut. These weren't anything like English bangers – these were like sticks of dynamite exploding in rapid succession, as if they'd never stop, and I understood why Robert couldn't stand it.

Then at last, as quickly as it had come, the noise began to fade down a street on the opposite side of the square, and people began to laugh and yell as the band struck up again.

Beryl slowly sat up in her chair again. 'Thank goodness *that's* over!' She looked at me with an odd expression on her face, and then took hold of both my shoulders. 'Can you hear me, Simon?' she shouted. I nodded. 'Where's Juan? *Eh?* Where did he go—?'

'I told you – he went off with Dito and Mito and the gang. It's all right, he said he'd come back.'

'What were they doing? Do you know?'

'No!' I scented danger. 'I think they were just going to have a Coke,' I said feebly.

'You promise you know nothing else?'

I nodded even more vigorously. 'Do you think something's happened to him?' I asked anxiously.

'It's what's *going* to happen to him, that's the *point*! Come on—'

'But what's he *done*?' I asked.

'Never mind! I suppose I could be wrong... I suppose pigs *might* fly...'

In spite of myself, I darted a quick look up at the sky, just on the off chance—

There was still no sign of Juan at eleven o'clock when Robert decided that it was time to go home. In desperation, Beryl took Karl's little daughter Diana aside and quietly told her to slip out into the square and spread the word among the children that if Juan wasn't by the cars in fifteen minutes he'd be left behind to rot in a Spanish jail for the night.

Diana's long blonde hair (the envy of every dark-haired girl on the island) gleamed with self-importance as she ran down into the square. I watched as she stopped small groups of children in their tracks and rattled off her message in Majorcan, and then the groups exploding like grenades, flying into the crowd with shrapnel urgency.

As we walked back to the cars, Robert forging on ahead again, I puzzled over Beryl's anxious questioning of me. There was only one logical explanation for what Juan had been doing, and yet it was unthinkable – completely impossible! That Juan could play a joke *on the whole town!*

Robert had already reached the car as we turned into the street. '*It's all right, Beryl!*' he shouted. '*Juan's asleep on the back seat—*'

'I very much doubt he's *asleep*, Robert, not with you shouting like that!' Beryl called back, and then, under her breath, 'in fact, I very much doubt whether he's asleep at all!'

I was told to sit between Juan and Alastair, whose wife had left the café early complaining of a headache, and had gone back to Fornalutx. Alastair had some work to do with Robert the next day, so he was coming with us. I climbed into the back seat, where Juan lay sprawled, and tried to ease him along. One of his eyes flew open and glared at me.

'Come on, Juan,' I whispered crossly, 'budge up a bit—'

'I can't budge up!' he shouted. 'I'm asleep! Father said so!'

Beryl's hand snaked in through his open window and dealt him a stinger on his bare thigh.

'*Ow!*' he yelled, skidding into his corner. '*What for?*'

'*You know very well what for!*' hissed Beryl angrily. 'I'd go on being asleep, if I were you, or there might be *more* fireworks!' She opened her door and got into the front seat.

Juan, who was sitting slumped over now, suddenly looked round at me with a manic grin on his face, and pointed wildly at himself.

MORE PERCUSSIONS

Half past two in the afternoon, lying on my back on a towel (the coarse grass of the lawn parched and prickly, not at all like English grass) under the shade of the palm tree that hung over the drive, trying to think of a hundred words that meant 'hot', until it was too hot to go on – too hot to think...

Occasionally, the palm fronds high above me stirred and rustled slightly, and unbearable shards of sunlight slashed at my eyes, reminding me of the *cala* and of Alastair.

It had felt odd, last night, being picked up by a man who was not my father and being carried to bed and undressed, tucked in. A bit like love, I supposed, in a way... although different from that, really. My mother had been there, and yet she'd made no move to help him—

I suddenly remembered her scathing remarks about Robert's muse. All right, she'd been in a bad mood, but what was wrong with having a muse? Keats had his nightingale, and his *Belle Dame Sans Merci*, and Shelley had whoever-she-was – surely poets should be granted whatever they needed to inspire them. Christians had the Virgin Mary after all...

I let my head fall sideways, away from the glare of the sun, and found myself staring at Juan's empty towel beside me. He'd been gone for ages. Why had he been so mysterious? Usually secrets just burst out of him like popcorn – though not so sweet. We'd been trapped into having lunch at Canellun, and then into having a rest because we'd come back so late from the *fiesta* in Soller. My mother had told us to stay in the shade until three o'clock. Why hadn't *she* undressed me when Alastair had carried me up to bed? She'd been with him; I remembered her scent, and her whispered goodnight—

'Simon—'

No, not like that. She hadn't said 'Simon', she'd said 'Darling' (except she always said 'Duhlling').

'*Simon!*'

Instantly I scrambled for cover behind the palm tree. It had been Juan, half shouting my name, and I expected a shower of *algarrobas*, or even stones to come clattering through the trees.

'*Simon!*'

I peered out cautiously, in the direction of his hoarse cry.

'*Over here! In the torrent!*'

The grounds of Canellun were divided by a deep torrent which passed through the property on its way down from the *Teix* to the sea far below – except that it was bone dry at the moment. On one side of the torrent was Canellun land, and on the other side was Ca'n Torrent, where Karl and his family lived. A little humpbacked bridge linked the two properties.

For Juan to be in the torrent was unnatural. He and Karl hardly ever saw eye to eye – they didn't see each other for dust if they could help it – and even though Karl's land belonged to Robert, it was out of bounds to us unless we were invited.

Expecting a trap, I darted out from behind the palm tree and raced across the naked, burning drive into the shelter of the new lemon grove. Flitting from tree to tree, I finally peered down into the torrent. It was as empty as ever, baked dry by the sun.

'*Here—!*'

I looked downstream to where it disappeared under the road. A blinding glint of sunlight reflected from one of the lenses of Juan's specs as he emerged slightly from the darkness of the tunnel, his white–blonde hair gleaming.

'*Come!*' he beckoned to me urgently, before retreating back into the deep shadows. '*Quickly!*'

Climbing down, I hurried to the mouth of the tunnel and into a darkness so impenetrable that I blundered into him. He giggled as I reached out for the wall to prevent myself from falling.

'Be careful, stupid! You'll break the bomb!'

I was making such a racket that I misheard him. 'What? What are you doing, Juan? I can't see yet—'

He giggled again. 'I've made a bomb,' he drawled slowly. 'Look—'

The darkness itself seemed to shrink back as my eyes expanded urgently to piece him together as he shook a box of matches under my nose, warningly, like the tail of a rattlesnake, and then struck one awkwardly, away from his body. In the sudden flare his face burst open before me, grinning. Why was he wearing a shirt? He almost never wore a shirt except in the evening. And why was it bulging out over his shorts? Had he found an animal?

Still holding a lighted match in one hand, Juan reached into the open neck of his shirt and began to pull out a gleaming, snake-like coil. I drew back in fear.

Laughing, he held the match closer, until I saw that what he held was as frightening as any snake – the twisted end of what must have been a yard or more of the Spanish firecrackers that he'd pointed out to me in Soller the night before, like a string of sausages but filled with gunpowder instead of meat, tightly enclosed in waxy brown paper.

'For Christ's sake be careful, Juan!' I gasped. 'And anyway, we mustn't—'

'Why not?' He sounded outraged. 'What's the point of having a bomb if it doesn't explode?'

'We might hurt someone!'

'Good!' he said cheerfully. 'I want to give Lucia back something!'

'Don't talk nonsense,' I said sharply.

'Or I know – maybe we could get one of the dogs to eat it – Ygrec! She bit me last week – make her pretend it's sausages, and when it and it starts coming out of her bottom, we could set fire to her tail!'

We both burst into nervous giggles, but in the darkness of the echoing tunnel the laughter sounded slightly mad and frightening, and we stopped.

'If you don't help me do it, you're a coward!' he said at last.

Not again!

'Oh, all right,' I gave in as usual. 'Where?'

He thought for a moment. 'I don't know until I've decided.'

Having crawled out of the torrent, we ran across the lemon grove and into the garage where we collected some old newspapers and matchwood, then raced silently up the drive, flying past the dark mouth of the kitchen doorway, the fly-curtain moving slightly, as though someone were waiting behind it to pounce.

Juan suddenly swerved into the courtyard beyond.

'*Here!*' he whispered decisively, looking quickly around.

I could see his point. The courtyard was three-sided, facing towards the mountains, with only small windows overlooking it – the larder, the upstairs lavatory, and the one in the passage on the way to our bedroom. On the ground floor a pair of French windows stood open into the hall, providing a perfect escape route. Otherwise, the only opening in the stone walls of the courtyard was a closed door which looked as though it had never been opened.

Juan was already squatting down on the yellow tiles, pulling his shirt out of his shorts and letting the newspaper and matchwood and the sweaty serpent of fire crackers tumble out. I hurriedly gave him my collection of twigs and helped him build a small fire. On the top, with shaking fingers, he laid the waxy coil of fireworks, then took the box of matches from the breast pocket of his shirt and got ready to strike one.

Our eyes caught as we stared across the pyre, our excitement daring and double-daring each other to make the first move. But we seemed paralysed for a moment, freeze-framed like an old piece of jammed film, hearts clattering, motionless.

A door slammed – the washroom door? – and a girl's voice, high and pretty, started singing. *Lucia*—!

Trembling with fright, Juan struck a match and flung it into the pile of twigs and shavings, but it went out. Panic-stricken, he struck another, which snapped in half. Snatching the box from him, I pinched half a dozen matches together, struck them, and held them to the shavings until they caught.

We'd hardly made it through the open French windows and hidden under the stairs before a series of almighty explosions shattered our eardrums and every pane of glass in the windows – shattered our very lives, it seemed, shaking the foundations of the house, of our world, echoing and re-echoing endlessly between the thick stone walls and the mountainside beyond.

Somewhere in the dense smoke Lucia was screaming, the closed door into the courtyard suddenly bursting open and the terrifying figure of Robert rushing out, dazed and mad-looking—

Frantically he began to trample and kick away what was left of the fire, bellowing something that became confused with the echoes of the explosion. A last fire cracker exploded behind him. There was another scream—

As the smoke cleared, I could see Lucia kneeling on the far side of the courtyard, rocking forwards and backwards, clutching her music case to her chest, and it was the sight of her that finally galvanized us both into action, racing through the smashed French windows with cries of remorse, apology, repentance, tears flying behind us as we ran towards her.

'*Sorry – so sorry! We didn't mean—*'

But none of us could hear each other properly.

I saw Lucia's eyes grow huge with disbelief as she started to scream again, and an instant later the towering figure of my grand-uncle was among us in a whirl of smoke, more dangerous even than the bomb.

'*What?*' he bellowed. '*What?* Was it you two? Christ, I can't hear—'

But one look at our terrified faces was enough. In the split second before he went for us, Juan grabbed my wrist and started to pull me after him, just as Lucia went for my legs, toppling me out of reach of a blow from Robert that would have knocked me cold if it had landed.

With Juan still pulling me frantically away, and my stricken conscience still trying to dig its heels into the stony drive, we were past the garage and leaping over the closed iron gates before I even realised that we'd actually fled.

Dashing across the road, we leapt the stone wall opposite, tumbled into the dry bed of the torrent below the far side of the tunnel, dancing over logs and tree stumps that the winter storms had failed to wash away, then shinned up the broken bough of an olive tree and into the maze of terraces below the house. I was still too terrified to look back, knowing from my rising hackles that Robert's outstretched hand and smoking breath were within an inch of my collar. I could smell him, feel him, hear his footsteps thundering after me—

Whimpering like an animal, I finally stumbled and fell, crashing headlong into the red earth, sobbing, hands clasped behind my head to ward off the blows—

Which failed to fall. Juan ran back and hauled me to my feet by the back of my shirt. 'There's no one!' he gasped. 'Quick! I know a place we can hide!'

Moments later I was sliding down into the hollow bole of an ancient olive tree which had been struck by lightning, while Juan climbed into another one further along the grove.

All I longed for now was the power to leave myself, to leave behind the corpse of a possible murderer who had probably driven his favourite grand-uncle mad with shock, and perhaps killed his cousin, and had then run away like the coward he'd always thought he was not—

'*Simon*—'

There was a single chink in the bole of the olive tree, and when I pressed my eye to it I could look back along the grove towards the torrent. It was uncanny – as if we no longer existed. There wasn't a single clue to show where we were hidden; just one of the trees talking, that was all—

'*Simon!*'

'What?' I answered irritably, my voice echoing strangely inside the hollow tree.

'I'm hungry.'

'Juan, if we go back we'll be beaten! I'll probably be banished—'

'I don't care, I want something to eat. And anyway, you were the one who lit the bomb!'

Silence. I imagined scorpions scuttling around my feet in the darkness, but I no longer cared. 'We'd better be quiet, Juan, or they'll find us. Try and sleep for a bit…'

We must have dozed off, because when I next peered through the chink it was dusk, and someone was moving around outside.

Had Juan given up? Or had they found us—?

'*Hello?*'

Beryl! Thank God! I should have known that if Juan knew a hiding place, then she was certain to know it, too.

Silence. I couldn't be the first to betray our presence. It was up to Juan.

'Mother...' as if he were expecting her, 'I'm hungry...'

'*There* you are!' her voice completely calm. 'Well, I'm not *surprised* you're hungry. Invisible children always starve to death in the end because no one knows where to put their *food!*' There was a muffled scream from Juan. 'Is Simon with you?'

'Yes, Beryl!' I called out, startled by the loudness of my voice. 'I'm in here!'

She made an odd, strangled sort of noise. 'I don't mind telling you, this all feels very *peculiar.*' She made the noise again, and I realised that she was laughing – or trying not to, rather. 'Do you think you'd both like to come out now? Someone else is bound to turn up in a minute, and I don't want to be sent to a lunatic asylum for talking to trees!'

Juan was already on the ground when I finally emerged into the branches.

'Is Lucia—?' I began.

Beryl looked up at me, smiling. 'Lucia's perfectly *all right,* thank you for asking. She just had a *shock.* It was much worse for your grand-uncle, though – he thought another war had broken out. And I'm not *stupid,* Juan. I know it was you who got hold of those fireworks last night, and that you were the *ringleader.*'

I tried to distract her. 'Does my mother know?' I asked urgently.

'I told her that you just happened to be passing when the bomb went off, and that Juan *kidnapped* you, for company. I'm not sure she believed me,' she laughed quietly, 'but she seemed to want to, and there wasn't any point in making things worse. Anyway, Juan,' she said severely, 'Father says you're to go to bed without any supper, and I daresay Simon will do the decent thing and go with you—'

'Yes, of course—'

'NO! I'm *hungry*—'

'—but once you're *in* bed, I daresay you'll each find a tray underneath, although I wouldn't know anything about *that!*'

News of what had happened spread like laughter through the foreign community in the village. The Majorcans, though, found it far from funny, and the size of Juan's local gang was halved as smacks and blows fell around the village like a castanet concerto.

REPERCUSSIONS

Next day, my ashen-faced apology to Robert, made in the kitchen at a moment carefully chosen by Beryl (while my mother was resting), was greeted with an instant apology from him for having frightened me. Bewildered, I was caught up like a fish in the net of his verbal wake and dragged by it, without realising quite where we were going, into his study.

Even so, as he shut the narrow double doors firmly behind us like a schoolmaster, I was filled with a sense of dread, the blood thundering through my ears so loudly that it was almost impossible to understand what he was saying at first. Then it slowly dawned on me, as he chatted away, that I wasn't going to get a beating after all. Slowly, I looked up and stared around his study in growing wonder as he went on talking. Even within the world of Canellun, this was another country entirely. Although it wasn't at all big, his room was so full of his desk and chairs and of hundreds of books and piles of work, of pictures and objects, knick-knacks, boxes, statues, sticks, spears, drums, that it seemed as though the room *had* to be enormous simply to fit everything into it.

He went on talking as I sat in the chair opposite him, about shellshock and shattered nerves and inflamed brains, but I'd already heard most of it, and didn't pay much attention. Then he suddenly changed course. 'No, the only thing you have to apologise for is failing to keep an eye on Juan, as I asked you to. You can see now that he sometimes goes too far—'

'Yes, but—'

He raised his eyes enquiringly. 'Go on—'

'He's my friend—' I began, staring at him desperately in an attempt to hypnotise him into understanding.

'And we're not?' he asked irritably, his eyebrows raised. 'Sometimes, I admit, you have to make a choice between two evils, but then you must choose the lesser of the two – the one with the most good in it. And in this case you should have chosen mine because it was *entirely* good – and because your loyalty was to me when you agreed to watch out for Juan. You really should have stopped him. You've let me down quite badly you know. I expected more from you… I say, are you still there?'

By this time my head hung so low in shame that from where he was sitting I must have disappeared completely behind the row of books that lined the front of his desk.

'Yes.' I tried to look up, but couldn't.

I heard his chair scrape back suddenly, and then his appalled voice: 'I say, don't cry!'

'*I'm not*—'

I was as appalled as he was.

He strode round the table and thumped me well-meaningly on the back, which made me choke in surprise. 'There! All's well! No real harm done! A few broken windows – you can pay me back in kind. Juan, too, of course. We'll think up something.'

The door leading from his study into the courtyard (the door that he had burst through after the explosion) opened suddenly, and Karl came in with a sheaf of papers, his eyes still looking down as he counted them between his fingers.

'—twelve pages, Robert; a hundred and fifty words to a page – you're still three hundred words over—' He broke off as I scrambled to my feet. 'I'm sorry, I didn't realise you were busy—'

'Nonsense! Simon and I were just having a chat—' he took the sheets of typescript. 'Couldn't we just let *them* do the editing? I mean, wouldn't they rather have too much than too little? Let them feel they've got their money's worth?'

'Robert, if you leave the editing to them, they'll muck it up. If you do it, and send them precisely what they commissioned, they'll print it verbatim, and there'll be no misunderstandings.'

I was fascinated by his rolling French 'r's and by the way his down-drawn mouth seemed to be so full of words, and yet they came out in such a slow, precise drawl. Here was Juan's Public Enemy No. 1, a German spy if Juan was to be believed, and yet he was giving my grand-uncle advice that was almost an order – and what was more, Robert was listening to him.

'Oh, all right, I'll revise it in a minute. Meanwhile, and more importantly, we're trying to think of a task that Simon and Juan could do, as a punishment—'

A sardonic grimace drew down the left hand corner of Karl's mouth even more, in what I'd come to recognise as his upside down smile. 'Five years hard labour!' he suggested promptly. 'The explosion made Renee drop one of our best coffee cups. And may I suggest ten years for Juan?'

Robert snorted. 'That's a bit stiff! What if I offered to replace the cup?'

'It's irreplaceable. It was part of a set that Tom Mathews sent us from America. Now, is there anything else? If not, I was going to take Renee to the pictures in Palma this evening—'

'Yes, wait, there *was* something!' Robert began to rummage through the papers on his desk. 'I saw Ruthven in the *estanco* this morning. He said that he and Alastair were overcome with inspiration at the *fiesta*, and he gave me a rough draft of the play for Simon's birthday—' He stopped dead, and I think we all froze at the same thought. *That* could be the punishment – no play!

Robert put his fingers to his mouth and tugged fiercely at his lower lip. 'Not doing it would save me a guinea! How many pesetas is that?'

'About two hundred and fifty,' said Karl with an actual grin on his face at last.

'I'd make a profit! Castor quoted me fifteen *duros* to mend all the windows! And then there's all the wine for the party afterwards... which I wouldn't have to buy... at two pesetas a bottle...' He started calculating on his fingers.

I watched him, dumbstruck, and obviously looking very foolish because when he next glanced at me he burst out laughing. 'I'm only teasing! Of course we'll do the play! Not that I've read it yet—' he picked it up and looked at the title page. 'Am I my Brother's Keeper? That's it! Sounds fun—' he gave me a piercing look, 'and very appropriate!' He handed the thin script to Karl. 'Tomorrow will do, though. No hurry. Apparently we'll need twelve copies—'

Karl took the script absentmindedly. 'I've just thought what Simon and Juan could do as a punishment. They could clean out the grotto, ready for rehearsals. It's in a shocking mess.'

Robert's face lit up like a lamp. 'Wonderful idea!' He suddenly stared out of the window, frowning abstractedly: 'Where's it gone, by the way? The grotto—?'

Karl closed his eyes wearily. 'Don't be ridiculous, Robert, you know perfectly well! It was Diana – your Diana. She was worried that Simon would fall down the steps, and she asked me to cover them up, so I got Castor to make a plywood lid. From the way Diana talked about him, I thought Simon was going to be a toddler, not a ten-year-old boy.' He shrugged. 'But I suppose it will be useful when Tomás starts crawling...'

'Oh, well, as long as it's still there,' said Robert. 'I'd have missed it if it had gone!' He grinned at me. 'It's where we do all the plays, you see,' he explained. 'It's very beautiful, but because it's out of sight, it's out of mind, and gets neglected. Will you do that for me? Clean it out?'

Before going to bed that evening, I went in search of the grotto. I'd vaguely noticed some old plywood boards lying on the ground in the furthermost and wildest corner of the garden, weighted with rocks which I heaved aside, revealing a stone staircase spiralling down into the gloom. With my heart in my mouth, and my eyes peeled for scorpions, I made my way down the steps and through a cave-like opening into such an unexpected and magical world that I gasped in amazement.

A dramatic overhang of rock, covered in thick roots and vegetation, vaulted thirty or forty feet above me, half covering a simple theatre: a stone stage at one end and a long, narrow auditorium of packed earth, with a low wall separating it from the olive grove beyond. A young fruit tree was growing out of the middle of the auditorium. My eye was drawn to the sound of trickling water, to a stone trough filled by a spring to overflowing before the water disappeared into the rich undergrowth. It must have been from this constant trickle, even in times of drought, that all the plants and roots fed themselves, allowing them to smother the huge rocks above us and bind them together like a living net. I was on the point of exploring further when I either felt or saw something moving in the thickest part of the undergrowth on my left – a woman-shaped darkness denser than the rest, turning towards me—

With a low cry of fear, I fled.

Once back in the house and surrounded by familiar things, I calmed down a bit and went to look for Beryl, who was in the Press Room. I asked her if there was a hermit in the grotto – a lady hermit—

'A *lady* hermit!' She looked astonished. 'No, I don't think so—'

I told her what I'd seen, and she puzzled over it for a moment before telling me that Robert was always seeing things that weren't there. Perhaps it was one of them – or a trick of the light, perhaps. Whatever it was, though, it was probably best not to tell my mother.

The next morning, Juan and I set to, clearing out the grotto with a will – or rather, I set to with a will, and Juan with an emphatic 'Won't!'

No sooner had we arrived for work than he stuck his broom in the trough and soaked me with freezing water. Stupidly, I started to chase him, which only made him abandon his broom altogether and leap into the overhanging tree roots, scrambling up them and then hanging upside down over my head in a way that made me sick to look at him. '*Please*, Juan! If you fall, we'll only get into *more* trouble—!'

'*You'll* get into trouble!' he shouted. 'You'll have to go home! *I* won't! I live here!'

It was said carelessly, but it hurt – because it was the truth, I supposed. Juan had said out loud what I didn't even like to admit to myself. I *was* only a guest here. Robert and Beryl could ask me to leave, or not invite me to come back to this magical place that was growing around me and into me as surely as the roots that Juan was climbing. The thought of having to leave anyway, in ten days—

My silence only angered Juan. 'I can *make* it that you go! I can just say "I don't like Simon any more", and you'll have to go back to your horrid boarding school in England and be beaten till you bleed!'

I couldn't even find the energy to argue with him. Dropping my broom, I made for the little wicket gate which led out into the olive grove.

'No, wait, Simon!' he yelled. '*Wait*! I won't say anything if you watch me climb!'

He was already swinging himself up into the overhang. 'I hope you fall and break both your legs,' I shouted up at him, 'and that the stumps go into your *culo* and come out covered in *mierda*—!'

Screaming with laughter, Juan continued his climb. I watched with my heart in my mouth as he occasionally missed his grip and had to cling to the bare rock with one hand while he groped around for a root with the other. He looked so small compared with the hugeness of the cliff face, and there were moments when I seemed to lose him completely, when his nut-brown body became part of the roots themselves and his sun-bleached hair reflected the colour of the foliage. At last, with a final heave, he was over the top, laughing triumphantly as he danced along the brink, half-naked, beating his chest—

'*Juan!*' Lucia's voice cut through the air like an arrow from somewhere behind him.

The effect on Juan was comical, as if the arrow had gone straight through him, his knees buckling with fright. For an awful moment I thought he was going to jump straight over the precipice into the grotto, but then he turned and bolted, pursued by her scolding voice. '*Father said you were to help Simon clear out the grotto, Juan – it's a punishment!*'

I rushed over to grab my broom as Juan burst like a bat through the entrance to the grotto and fell to his knees, scrabbling at the dead leaves around him.

We both of us held our breath (my fear was as healthy as Juan's) as we heard Lucia's careful footsteps coming down the stairwell. The suspense was unbearable. At last her feet appeared on the steps, in neatly-buckled shoes and ankle socks, then her long calves and the hem of her dress, and then the reason for her coming down so slowly – she had Tomás in her arms. He greeted us cheerfully, squeaking and waving his baby arms and grinning from under his wonky sunhat.

'Hello, Tomás!' I called.

'He can't actually *see* you yet,' said Lucia knowledgeably, 'he's just having a nice day! You'll have to come closer if you want to talk to him.'

Juan and I approached cautiously, Juan instantly feeling Tomás's nappy. 'He's done a pee-pee!'

'I *know,* Juan! I was just going to change him—'

But of course once Juan had started he couldn't stop. He lifted up the front of the nappy and peered underneath. Without disturbing

Tomás in the slightest, Lucia dealt him a stinging slap on the arm. 'Don't be disgusting, Juan!' she hissed.

'I only want to see if it's grown!' Juan clutched his arm in outrage.

Lucia glared at him through narrowed eyes. 'You've been climbing the grotto wall, haven't you? You know it's forbidden! Look at you – like a savage! Couldn't you even have put some shorts on?'

'I forgot,' said Juan forlornly, then stretched up and blew a huge raspberry into Tomás's tummy, making him gurgle with delight.

Lucia smiled in spite of herself. 'This must be his first time in the grotto! I'll just introduce him.'

She looked so pretty as she carried him round, showing him everything. Her thick, straight black hair was cropped quite short, exposing the back of her slender neck. When she stretched up to show him a flower, her gesture was very graceful. She went to ballet school in Palma once a week. I wished she liked me more.

She might almost have heard me. 'Mother said you saw a ghost here last night, Simon,' she said brightly. 'I overheard her telling Father—'

'A ghost?' yelled Juan. 'I'm off!' And with a quivering scream he shot straight through the wicket gate and into the olive grove, and was gone.

Lucia stamped her foot. 'Oh, he's so stupid!' she gasped. 'Now he'll never finish clearing up!'

'It doesn't matter,' I shrugged. 'I like it down here—'

'*I* wouldn't work down here alone if I'd seen a ghost.'

I felt uncomfortable under her wide-eyed gaze. 'It was probably just a trick of the light,' I mumbled, remembering Beryl's words.

'Father sees ghosts! There's one at the top of the cellar stairs, but he doesn't call them ghosts, he calls them pre-somethings—' She frowned, trying to remember. She was very particular; things were either right or wrong, and anything in between made her cross.

'*Pre-cog*-somethings… Blast! It'll come in a minute… —*nition!*' she sneezed.

'Bless you,' I said automatically.

'No – precog*nitions*! They're the spirits of people who have yet to come, rather than ghosts, which are the spirits of people who've already *been*.' She looked directly at me. 'If that helps?'

I was taken aback. 'Yes! I mean, if they still haven't been, then they can't hurt you yet, can they?'

'Exactly!' She gave a little laugh of triumph. Tomás joined in. 'Do you like babies?' she asked.

I hurriedly searched my memory, but couldn't find any. 'I like Tomás,' I said lamely. I wished I could think of something intelligent to say—

'My brother William goes to a school called Oundle. He says it's quite tough. Do you know it?'

'Yes!' – relieved that at least I knew *something* – 'Quite a few of our chaps go there. It's a public school—' But I didn't want to think about that. 'You're awfully pretty,' I said instead, without thinking.

She froze for a second, clutching Tomás, then spun round on her heel and walked straight back up the steps.

AM I MY BROTHER'S KEEPER?

It came to be known as The Miracle Play. By the end of the first rehearsal I began to see why.

Things had started so well at the read-through, with everyone except Ruthven turning up more or less on time and taking their seats in the grotto. Karl passed among us with freshly-typed scripts while Beryl kept everyone topped up with freshly-made *sangría*. But I think she must have misread the recipe, or somehow misjudged the quantity of brandy she put in, because by the end of the read-through most of the cast was blotto.

Am I My Brother's Keeper? had ended up as a retelling of the first four and a half chapters of the Book of Genesis, up to Cain's murder of Abel, with Lucia opening the show by dancing The Creation of the World accompanied on the guitar by Juan, who refused to do anything of the sort at the top of his voice, and had to be sent out. But the real fun started once the coal-black Adam (Alston) and the deathly pale Eve (my mother) had bitten into the fruit of the Tree of Knowledge (Karl). No sooner had their teeth sunk into it than The Serpent (me) turned into the landlord of a sleazy nightclub called *The Twice Shy* in Deya, with Adam as the bartender and Eve as his moll. The smugglers and riff-raff from the surrounding countryside (Waldron, Hodgkinson, and an eccentric Spaniard called Estéban Francés, who had designed sets for Diaghilev and had even worse sinus problems than Robert) came to the club with their wives and girlfriends, where they swapped gossip about the odd people who lived in the village (Madame Coll, the tightfisted, moustachioed grocer, came out of it very badly). The villagers, meanwhile, were attempting to bribe God to remove the Serpent from their midst, since he put so much temptation their way that none of them could get any work done – and besides, they were sick of eating lotuses and pandering to foreigners. The two brothers, Abel (Robert), who kept sheep, and Cain (Alastair), who owned the land on which Abel's flock grazed, would meet at *The Twice Shy* to drink and flirt with a group of expat girls from the village led by a dancer called Jessie, and her 'Jessie-Belles'.

The climax to the play came when Cain and Abel both fell in love with the same muse, a dark, rather beautiful girl tourist who had chosen to stay on in Deya. I hadn't realised that farmers could have muses, too, but Robert said they might have been the earliest poets in biblical history, and as always I stretched my imagination to fit into his. In the fight-to-the-death that followed, Cain killed Abel, God demanded to know why, Cain demanded to know if he was his brother's keeper, God shouted 'Yes!' and all the foreigners in the nightclub were destroyed, leaving Deya to the Majorcans, with Madame Coll as their triumphant, bearded King. The script was almost entirely made up of terrible puns and scandalous village gossip, so that by the time the read-through was over and Beryl's *sangría* had been drunk dry, the cast was already hysterical, with everyone trying to add their own jokes to the script.

I soon discovered that one person's strong views could curdle even the happiest atmosphere when Selwyn, who had read the absent Ruthven's part (God), as well as his own, announced in his high-pitched, rather bossy voice, that he thought he was better cut out to play God than Ruthven. Everyone groaned and told him to shut up; God was to be played by Ruthven, and Selwyn was to play the Cherubim with the Fiery Sword and that was that. Then Karl mutinied, saying that if he'd known he was going to play the Tree of Knowledge, he'd never have typed the bloody play! Robert had insisted that the fruit of the tree hadn't been apples at all, but sacred mushrooms which grew around the tree and gave visions and wisdom to those who ate them. It made perfect sense to me; no amount of apple eating had ever left me a jot the wiser. But Karl, even as a non-practicing Jew, took exception to the idea – and to his costume; he would look utterly ridiculous standing in the middle of the stage dressed as a tree, with mushrooms growing out of his feet.

'But Karl, that's the whole point!' cried Robert, exasperated. 'We're all made to look stupid and coarse. We could give you a mask if you like, but the thing is, you look perfect for the Tree of Knowledge, which is why you're playing it – your face is so… lugubrious and… and—' his eyes almost popped out of his head as he groped for a flattering word.

'—Wise! Lived-in—' interrupted my mother desperately. But Karl was no more taken in than the rest of us. He looked at her as though she'd stabbed him in the back, and turned away. 'I think it's pathetic,' he sneered.

Alastair turned on him. 'You think it's what?'

'Pathetic! Most people here are stupid enough already without having to exaggerate—'

A full-blown 'scene' was only prevented by a startled cry and a sudden commotion as the absent Ruthven came crashing down the grotto steps at an impossible speed, still desperately trying to keep his balance as he staggered across the auditorium and hit the wall opposite with a startling sound of breaking glass. In the stunned silence that followed, Juan's screams of laughter floated down to us, so infectious that not even the sight of blood pouring from Ruthven's jacket could stop us joining in.

'It's all right, it's all right!' Ruthven was shouting as everyone rushed to help him to his feet. 'For Christ's sake, it's not blood, it's Syrup of Figs! I'm just egg-bound, that's all. And I am not drunk, Selwyn – how dare you! I was just talking to Juan and forgot there was a staircase—'

By the time it came to the night of the performance, most people had swapped roles so many times, and then swapped back, that it was a wonder anyone could remember their lines. Then my mother complained of a sore throat and suddenly began to lose her voice.

Two hours before the performance I slipped off, alone, into the grotto. The evening was hot and still, the sky already turning a luminous darkening blue with the approach of night. Beryl, who had allowed me to be in charge of the lighting, had supplied me with hurricane lamps, candles, and almost her entire stock of Price's nightlights, which meant that Tomás might have to sleep in the dark forever if more supplies weren't brought over from England.

With every lamp I lit, the olive grove beyond the wall retreated deeper into the twilight, like an expectant audience. Tray after tray of candles-in-jam-jars had been brought down to be used as footlights, and to light the way across the garden to the stairwell down into the grotto. The nightlights I hid carefully among the roots and niches of the overhang, spreading them out like a spider's web of light, as high as I could get with the help of Castor's ladder, lighting them as I went.

When everything was lit, I walked with my head down to the back of the auditorium and closed my eyes tightly for a full minute. Then I turned round and let them spring open—

The grotto had become a glittering faery cave, growing brighter and brighter as the eye travelled towards the stage at the far end, while the nightlights in the foliage seemed to rise into the sky – and beyond, as one by one the stars began to appear. If I'd created nothing else but this – if everyone forgot their lines – if the world exploded! – it would be enough.

The invited audience came from all over the island, entering the grotto at first in twos and threes, then in groups, and finally in a flood as the time approached for the performance to begin. I counted some seventy people before I slipped up onto the stage with the other actors to change behind the two screens that had been set up at the back. On the men's side, everyone was sweating with heat and nerves, especially Ruthven, who was toppling around with his flask jammed to his lips. It was a relief to lie on the ground and struggle into my snake's costume – a sheet which had been sewn into a tapering tube, like a wind-sock at the aerodrome, and then painted with scales and vivid zigzags and magic symbols. As soon as I'd tied it under my arms, I hopped to the edge of the screen and peered round.

The auditorium was packed to bursting now, with people even sitting on the stairs, the roar of conversation rising into the foliage above and setting the nightlights flickering and dancing. Everyone had brought down bottles and glasses and their own cushions to sit on, until the atmosphere was like one of my mother's cocktail parties in London.

When the hubbub was at its height, Robert went out onto the stage, dressed in his most colourful waistcoat and his black sombrero, and appealed to everyone for quiet.

'Stick close to me, Simon,' whispered Alastair behind me. 'I think he might call you out.'

'No!' I found myself crying hoarsely, just as Juan might have done. 'I don't *want* to be called out!' I wasn't Simon any more, I was the Serpent!

He gripped my shoulder as I tried to turn away. 'Do as you're told, there's a good chap!'

'Before we start,' Robert was shouting, 'I'd just like to say that we're here to celebrate a certain Serpent's birthday, as well – rather belatedly – as my own—' (respectful applause and cheers from the crowd) 'Thank you—' he gestured for silence again. 'So I want to summon before you that certain Serpent, who is not only the excuse for these celebrations, but is the architect of the transformation you see around you; he's turned what I've always thought of as a charming old cave into a faery grotto fit for Titania – and as his *oberon-kel,* if you'll forgive the Teutonic pun, I wish to make a public presentation. Simon!'

With a shove, Alastair sent me tottering from behind the screen onto the stage. Out of the corner of my eye I could see my mother peeping out from behind the screen of the ladies changing room, her eyes swimming, hands clasped to her mouth. Staring fixedly ahead, I did the fastest sack-race to Robert's side that I could manage in my costume, while the audience shouted and clapped.

'On thy belly shalt thou go in a moment!' continued Robert as he pulled a small box from his trouser pocket, 'but meanwhile I present you, O snake in my bosom, with this Napoleonic medal with the head of Bonaparte on it, because you and he share the same birthday – August the fifteenth. Did you know that?' I shook my head. 'Well, you do now. It's made of solid something, so don't lose it. The point being that you obviously share some of his traits, and this reminder of his fate may prevent you from sharing that as well – or at least from trying to blow me up again, for which I now publicly forgive you!'

As we squinted at each other, I up at him against the darkness of the sky and he down at me, smiling, his face filled with light from the line of dazzling candles at the edge of the stage, I felt the strangest fleeting bond pass between us, as if everything before that night had merely led up to this moment – that my life here had only just begun.

He suddenly leaned down and kissed me on both cheeks. Blushing furiously, I bowed and thanked him and bounced back to the refuge of the screen while he finished his speech, excusing the players, the play, the plot, the performances and the prologue, then joined us behind the screen as the audience hushed itself into an air of expectancy.

Juan had continued to refuse to accompany Lucia's dancing of The Creation of the World on his guitar, so Beryl had brought down an old wind-up gramophone she'd unearthed in the storeroom under the hall, together with the only record she could find – the last two sides of *Swan Lake* – which luckily Lucia had danced at her ballet school. As the audience settled down, Beryl wound up the gramophone and too hurriedly tip-tilted the heavy chromium head with its steel needle onto the edge of the record, scratching it. 'Oh, *blast!*' she could be heard swearing as she tried again, more carefully. A cobra-like hiss and a *clunk* were followed by the opening strains of the music (*clunk*), which acted like a magnet on Lucia (*clunk*) as she was drawn, as if against her will (*clunk*), from out of the darkness at the back and onto the empty stage.

I watched entranced through a gap in our screen as she tiptoed the first steps on her pointes, her hair tied back, her face made up and completely absorbed in what she was doing, arms gracefully crossed against her chest, the skirt of her blue tutu shimmering as though she were trembling with suppressed excitement. She had never looked so beautiful.

Then, half way through her dance, I sensed that something was wrong. The music was getting slower! Still keeping perfect time with her feet, Lucia seemed to wake up from her trance and looked around desperately. 'Wind it up, mother!' she yelled. '*Quickly*—'

Beryl, who had been completely engrossed in the performance, rushed to the gramophone and frantically wound it up, at which the music began to speed up again – too fast! – and yet Lucia still didn't miss a single step, dancing at several times the speed Tchaikovsky had intended and earning herself a standing ovation from the audience. With a huge and un-classical grin on her face, she took her curtsey.

The rest of the first scene passed off more or less without incident, apart from my mother (wearing a pair of Robert's long johns to represent nudity, with three huge fig leaves attached to her with knicker elastic) losing her voice completely. The act ended in total silence, with her and Alston entwined around a startled Karl, groping for the mushroom they were meant to eat, but which I'd forgotten to give him. Alston pretended that the mushroom was

119

concealed in Karl's outstretched armpit and tickled him until he toppled over backwards, his sandaled feet drumming helplessly inside the tree trunk as he wept and wailed. In desperation, I bowled the mushroom along the ground to them, but my mother trod on it.

Robert had to declare an impromptu interval while there was a frenzied argument behind the screens about who should take over my mother's part. Beryl and Lucia flatly refused, and for once even Selwyn was silent.

'Oh, *I'll* play her, for Christ's sake!'

Everyone turned to stare at Ruthven in stunned amazement.

'But you're a *man!*' cried an outraged Selwyn. 'And besides, you're *drunk*—'

'So what?' demanded Ruthven belligerently. 'At least I know the bloody words – I bloody wrote them, after all! And guess who *you'll* be playing, you pompous bloody ass!'

So Beryl ran up to the house for another pair of long johns into which Ruthven was eventually squeezed and over which my mother's elasticated fig leaves were strategically stretched. In a vain attempt to make him look less indecent, the skirt of Lucia's tutu, which only just covered his front when it was opened out, was tied round his waist with yards of twine. Selwyn, to everyone's unspoken fury, stepped smugly into the shoes of God (which he'd learnt by heart), and a quivering Estéban was told to play the Cherubim with the Fiery Sword, even though his shoulders were twitching so badly from stage fright that he looked more like a punch drunk boxer reliving an old fight.

Scene two finally opened (and very nearly closed again) with me sitting on a stool and writing a brief letter to God, ending 'Your Humble Obedient Serpent'. Unknown to me, though, Estéban was standing in the wings behind me trying to light his paraffin-soaked sword with a match while at the same time clutching his script and the skirts of his costume. Sword, script and costume suddenly burst into flames and the stage became a stampede of actors and actresses in varying stages of undress knocking him to the ground, rolling him over, and trampling his script to smother the flames. The play continued, however, with Estéban milking the applause as he strutted triumphantly along the footlights looking like a burnt out mud hut and waving his now hairless right arm at the audience.

Of all the performances, though, Ruthven's was the most outrageous. Bespectacled, pouring with sweat, and for reasons known only to himself speaking in a high-pitched Australian accent, he minced and stumbled around the stage ad-libbing appalling puns and failing completely to give Alston his correct cues. Alston took his revenge during a cuddle in the nightclub scene by furtively unbuttoning the bomb flap of Ruthven's long johns, which drove the audience up the scale of hysteria to such a point that Robert had to stop the play again and do him up. Then, towards the end, an increasingly puce Ruthven suddenly keeled over, gasping 'Tight... tight...!'

'*You're always bloody tight!*' hissed Selwyn from behind the screen.

'No, my *tutu*, you damn fool... Too tight...' He was plucking ineffectually at his waistband.

One look, and we could all see what had happened: the twine around his waist had become so sweat-soaked that it had started to shrink, digging more and more tightly into his stomach. Alston, who'd been dicing apples to put in Cain's *sangría,* leaned down from his barstool and brandished Castor's pruning knife in front of Ruthven's bulging eyes.

'Will you say your lines properly from now on?' he murmured.

'Yes!'

'Promise?'

'I promise!'

'No – I mean *really* promise!'

'For Christ's sake! I *promise, I promise—*'

With wonderful coolness Alston slipped his pruning knife under the waistband of Ruthven's tutu and sliced through it. Ruthven giggled, then farted horribly, to the delight of the audience.

In the last scene, the fight between Cain and Abel was so realistic that a breathless hush fell over everyone as Alastair and Robert grappled with each other, crashing around the stage, knocking over tables and chairs in their fight to the death. Then Alastair turned the tables on Robert, grabbing him round the neck and stabbing him repeatedly in the back, trying to puncture the bag of tomato ketchup that was strapped under Robert's waistcoat. The scene, in the stark up-light of the candles, suddenly took on a frightening, murderous aspect, made even more dramatic as Lucia rushed on stage and flung herself on top of Alastair, her fists flailing. 'Stop it! Stop it, you brute—'

'It's all right, darling,' gasped Robert, 'it's only in fun—'

As soon as Lucia had been dragged away by Beryl, Alastair managed to pierce the bag and Robert fell to the ground, covered in gore. Panic-stricken, Cain covered his body with one of the stinking groundsheets from the compost, when from the back of the stage, as if he were saying the lines from another play in another time, came Selwyn's schoolmasterly falsetto, *'Cain! Where is Abel, thy brother?'*

Still panting from exertion, Alastair turned to God with a theatrical shrug. "I know not!' he cried. *'Am I my brother's keeper?"*

Selwyn's precious last lines were completely lost as the audience burst into wild applause and the screens crashed to the ground as actors and actresses toppled over each other in their hurry to take their bows and reach among their friends in the audience for any dregs of wine that were left.

Quite unrehearsed (but dramatically very effective, I thought, even as I thanked my lucky stars that I'd had nothing to do with it) were the bucketfuls of donkey droppings and compost that Juan emptied from the top of the overhang, covering as many of the audience as he could reach with slime and muck.

I'd been wondering where he'd got to.

HIATUS

Seven days left, counting today and my last day – and it was raining.

The weather had broken at last, as it always did, apparently, after All Saints' Day, high winds rushing down from Europe dragging behind them huge heavy clouds which tore their bellies open on the jagged mountain-tops in relentless downpours all along the coast. Once-silent watercourses had become raging torrents again, their dignity restored at last as they carried rubbish and dead sheep and branches down to an angry sea – which nothing seemed able to pacify.

Juan and I were sheltering in the old sheep-hut below Canellun, having first gone to take a quick look at the *cala* from the top of the cliffs. But the scene below us had been inhuman, chilling, the once clear sea now milky-green with envious waves tearing at the rocks and crashing onto the little stone-covered beach as though to destroy it forever. The fishing boats had all been dragged up the slipways into the shelter of their sheds, the doors lashed shut against the storm. Even the café was nothing more than a concrete platform now, battered by the breakers, the chairs and tables gone, the canopy of palm fronds washed away by the thundering waves.

It was a bleak and desolate scene, and we turned for home feeling betrayed and resentful that our one certain plaything was subject to moods as foul as ours.

Half way back to Canellun and we were caught by another downpour which soaked us to the skin so quickly that we laughed and leapt around in it as if we were having a shower together. Neither of us wanted to go back to the house yet, to board games in the dining room, or to reading on our beds – or to quarrelling with each other out of boredom – so we took a shortcut through the increasingly misty groves to shelter in the hut.

I looked around me. The door was low and narrow, the window no more than a gap, high up, between the inward sloping rock face that formed the roof of the hut and the top of the wall which enclosed it. We sat opposite each other on the hard earth floor in semi-darkness, listening to the sounds of water surrounding us, to the pouring rain and the closer dripping of the trees and rocks, and to the nearby roar of the torrent.

The hut stood in the sort of grove I liked best, where a part of the mountain had burst through the polite earth, forcing Man to work round it and follow its dramatic outcrops and contours with respect. A few yards beyond the sheep hut was a huge landslide which had left a perfect semi-circle in the cliff face. In front of it a great outcrop of rock fell sheer into the groves below.

This was a wild place, which seemed to me to be more ancient and full of mystery than anywhere else. The sounds of all the different kinds of water falling around us only intensified the feeling of isolation. For all we knew, we might have been the only ones left alive in the mist-shrouded landscape.

Sitting opposite each other in the gloom, our eyes suddenly met by accident. But then I realised that Juan's weren't seeing me at all, that he was staring blankly ahead, his lips moving slightly. I quickly lowered my gaze, and then slowly looked up again, pretending to stare at the wall behind him so as not to disturb whatever was going on in his head.

I wondered what was. My own world seethed inside mine – seethed to bursting in what felt like a prison yard compared to the endless freedom he was allowed, with a mother and father who allowed him. For a moment, shockingly, I wished that Robert and Beryl were my parents, too – Robert so affectionate, always interested in what I had to say, explaining anything I didn't understand; Beryl so kind to children, preferring them to grown ups on the whole, always smiling when she saw me—

Was I jealous of Juan, I wondered? No. I just wanted to be a part of him, a brotherly part, so that I could know, if only once, what it must feel like to wake up in the morning and feel safe, like him, and reach out and pick anything, *everything*, until my arms were too full to carry anymore; to be alive and kicking until the instant I fell asleep!

I smiled to myself for a moment as I toyed with the thought of Juan in my place, at Beachborough, unable even to speak English properly – and then the endless beatings, the system of three black marks to a stripe, followed by six of the best, the dreaded work sheets – he wouldn't last a day in that unforgiving place. My smile faded. It wasn't even funny.

Sitting as we were, like mirrored reflections of each other, it was as though I suddenly heard in the silent movements of his lips the future expression of us both, revealed but unspoken, as if each of us were waiting for something still to come – something fated, but as yet unfathomable.

An even heavier downpour swept over us with a growing roar, startling us both out of our thoughts as we looked up through the narrow window at the darkening sky.

Seven days left.

And it was raining…

THE FALL

Within two days, the broken weather that everyone talked about had mended, with Robert already complaining that not enough rain had fallen. Having spent a week in bed with her lost voice, my mother found it, then promptly wore it out again from calling for me. Lucia sang in her bedroom, Tomás smiled and kicked excitedly in his cot on the terrace. It was a sharp, hot morning when Alastair arrived unexpectedly from Fornalutx brandishing a large cheque for an article he'd written for *The New Yorker* and suggesting that we all went to the *cala* for lunch to celebrate. Beryl happily took the saucepans off the Aga and closed the heavy lids with a bang.

There was no Isabella, as Castor had ridden off on her to check the olive trees, so Beryl decided that we'd better take the longer, easier path to the *cala,* through the gorge below the house.

Juan was in a particularly manic mood, weaving in and out of the straggling group as we went down, arms outstretched (he was an aeroplane that day), whining and howling and firing an imaginary machine gun into the convoy until my mother's patience began to wear thin. 'Juan, darling, I'm an unarmed plane from the Red Cross trying not to lose my patients—'

He was just starting to rake her with bullets when Robert's massive bulk skidded to a halt, like an obstinate mule, as he turned on him. 'For God's sake, Juan, you're driving us all mad! Either stop it, or go and be an aeroplane somewhere else! You're unnerving Diana, and I'm trying to talk to Alastair!'

'You're a *pest*, Juan!' shouted Lucia. 'And look, you've woken Tomás!' Furiously, she began rocking the baby's basket on her hip until Tomás obligingly woke up and started yelling.

Faced with this barrage of enemy fire, Juan was already fleeing, his rear gunner letting off raspberries at us as he disappeared round the bend.

I flew after him like the Righteous Wind after Iniquity, my Spitfire quickly gaining on his Messerschmidt, finally catching him up and engaging him in a dogfight which lasted until we both crash-landed among the rocks of the *cala,* breathless and happy.

'Listen, Simon—' he panted.

'Yes?'

'After lunch, when they're having their boring siesta, I want you to come with me somewhere and do the most exciting thing—'

I turned my head sharply to look at him.

'What?' I asked suspiciously.

'I'd tell you, but it's a secret, so I can't.'

'If it's another hole with nothing in it, or another bomb—'

'It isn't, I promise!'

'I'm not sure… I might…' Something about him looked peculiar. 'Where are your specs?' We began to search among the rocks. 'How cross will they be if we don't find them?' I asked.

He stretched out his arms as wide as he could. '*This* cross! They were my last emergency spare reserve ones,' he said mournfully. He darted a look over his shoulder. 'When Father comes, I'll hide in the *servicios*! That's a secret, too, so you mustn't tell. It's where I always go—'

I was shocked. 'But they're disgusting!' The only lavatory on the beach was a flimsy bamboo hut opposite the café, swarming with flies and consisting of nothing more than a stinking, bottomless hole in the ground, about the width of a ten-year-old boy.

'That's why I go there! Almost nobody ever comes because they all do *caca* in the sea! Except the fishermen, and they don't mind.

I can see what's going on outside through the bamboos. I watch everyone looking for me and shouting, but they never look in there.'

I found his specs, but with one lens missing. Sticking his thumb through the hole to make certain it had gone, he put them on, covering up the empty socket with his palm as we both searched for the other lens, but so much old rubbish and seaweed had been thrown up onto the beach by the storm that I began to doubt that we'd ever find it. Already I could hear the others' voices approaching.

'Quick!' I said urgently. 'You'd better hide—'

Juan raced off, across the bridge over the torrent which was still swollen with reddish brown water and rubbish from the mountains.

'What have you lost?' Robert and Alastair had rounded the bend.

'Well...' I struggled with the truth, and compromised. 'It's a bit difficult to describe... it's about this big—' I made an 'O' with my middle finger and my thumb, 'and it's made of glass – sort of like a magnifying glass, but without the handle!' There – perfectly truthful!

A few minutes later the others filed onto the beach and came across to us. Robert described what I was looking for.

'I don't remember you having a magnifying glass, Simon,' said my mother suspiciously. My heart sank. She sounded grumpy, probably from having to walk at the back of the column with Beryl and Lucia and Tomás, instead of with Robert and Alastair, who wanted to talk to each other.

'It doesn't matter – really,' I said airily, 'I can look for it after lunch.'

My mother eyed me as if I were the lunch she badly needed. She was always at her worst when she was hungry. 'I smell a rat,' she muttered.

'The torrent's full of them, Diana,' said Beryl lightly. My mother laughed, but her eyes were beginning to glint dangerously. I tried to will her to be quiet with a pleading look, but she brushed it aside.

'I don't think this one's in the torrent,' said my mother carefully, 'I think I'm looking at it. *What* magnifying glass? And where did you get it? Hmm?'

I felt the energy beginning to drain out of me, and a sort of paralysis set in from my brain downwards. Hanging my head, I kept searching the ground, but without hope, as three people suddenly spoke up at once,

'That's enough, Diana—' Robert began.

'Robert, take Simon—' Beryl started to say.

'—Is *this* what you're looking for?' asked Alastair, holding up Juan's lens.

There was a moment's stunned silence as we all looked at it.

'But that's a lens from Juan's spectacles!' cried Lucia.

'Nonsense, darling,' said Robert innocently, 'it's a magnifying glass without a handle!'

Beryl was grinning at me. 'Why didn't Juan help you look for it?'

'He couldn't see properly—' I turned towards my mother, but she was already striding away.

Alastair set off in pursuit, calling after her. When he'd caught up with her, he said something as he caught her arm. She stopped and turned on him, her calf-length skirt swirling. 'Then why couldn't he have said so in the first place, instead of making me feel a perfect fool?' Alastair put an arm around her shoulders and turned her away from us, towards the café.

'Oh *dear*,' said Beryl. 'Robert, what's to be done for the best do you think?'

'*Honi soit qui mal y pense!*' he replied, grinning at me. 'Rise above it. It's just love in a bad mood.' He stared after Alastair and my mother, clearing his sinuses with his fingertips before giving me a sidelong look. 'Love for you, I mean! Put it behind you. She's probably just hungry – I know *I* am!' And with a laugh he began to bound across the rocks towards the café.

132

Beryl pulled a face at me. 'I think you and I should go up slowly, and let Robert and Alastair calm her down. Better still, perhaps you could go to the *servicios* and tell Juan he can come out!'

I gaped at her.

'*Well...*' she grinned.

My mother was standing in wait for me as I ran down from the lavatory to the café, which had been miraculously restored after the storm. Putting her arm around my shoulder, like Alastair, she drew me away from the others. They were all sitting at the table talking quietly, pretending not to watch us, except Juan, who was staring at me and pretending to strangle himself. Silently, I wished him luck.

The terrace narrowed at the far end, to where there was only room for two of us to stand together against the pine rails. From there I could look straight down into the sea, as if from the flying bridge of a ship. Staring between the rails (I didn't want to hear what she was going to say), I saw that the effects of the storm could still be measured in the dark blueness of the sea, tinged with violet. Choppy braille-fingered waves in white gloves brushed against the rocks at either side of the cove, blindly searching—

'... *will you listen to me!*'

'Sorry—'

'I asked if you understood why I was so quick to accuse you? I know I was wrong, that you were covering up for Juan, but do you know why I didn't trust you?'

I looked away, towards the jetty. 'Because I pinched that money from your purse in London—'

My answer seemed to take her by surprise.

'Yes,' she said feebly.

'I would have told you, but you were asleep! And then I just forgot...'

Liar!

I squinted up at her against the dazzling blue sky.

'Did you tell Alastair?'

She glanced quickly over her shoulder to where he was sitting.

'No, of course not—'

Liar!

Lunch was awkward, the harmony gone, as if everyone's thoughts were off key. Even the *arroz con pescado* didn't taste quite as good, apparently because the fishermen hadn't been able to get out beyond the point since the storm, and had caught very little that morning.

As usual, Lucia and Juan squabbled about everything in furious undertones, punctuated by vicious little kicks under the table. We were sitting together at the far end, slightly removed from the others, Juan already sticking fish heads and octopus legs from the soup up his nostrils and wiggling his nose so that they appeared to be alive, which I found wonderfully disgusting. I did my best to hide him from the others by leaning across the table, but then he jammed one of the tentacles so far up his nose that he started to sneeze uncontrollably. The fish head in one nostril sailed harmlessly past Lucia, but the octopus leg shot into her soup, and she screamed and leapt to her feet, knocking over her soup and her chair as she frantically tried to brush off the bits of saffron rice and snot that had splashed over the front of her swimming costume.

'*Bless you!*' Robert shouted down the table, at which Juan collapsed on all fours beneath it, sneezing and laughing until he choked. I'd gone down with him, as if we'd both been torpedoed, laughing so helplessly that I couldn't even thump him on the back and Beryl had to reach under the table and drag him out and beat him between the shoulder blades to stop him from choking to death. Finally he let out the longest and most revolting sick-belch I'd ever heard, and even Lucia burst into disgusted giggles.

'Simon?' I heard my mother's sharp voice. 'Where's Simon?'

Lucia astonished me: 'Simon's *here*, Diana,' she called out with a slight tremor in her voice. 'Juan's lens fell out again, under the table—' All at once she folded in half, clutching her middle.

I crawled out from under the table, not daring to look at my mother, and saw Beryl instead, her shoulders shaking uncontrollably, and had to crawl straight back, only to come face to face with Lucia, clutching her stomach as though she'd been shot, her eyes pleading with me to put her out of her agony as she kept mouthing the words *'Bless you! Bless you!'* And then we saw that most dreaded of all sights – a steady stream of yellow liquid splashing down from the table onto the concrete. The three of us stared at each other in disbelief, Juan's eyes popping out of his head as he stared at the edge of the plastic tablecloth and the stream of spilled saffron-coloured soup that was pouring from it, forming a puddle on the concrete.

'Father's pissing on the table—!'

The three of us bolted, with Beryl stumbling after us like someone with food poisoning as we ran towards the steps, our helpless wails already leaking from us as we tumbled down onto the beach.

Beryl and Lucia managed to pull themselves together quite quickly, but Juan and I took an awful lot longer, stamping round and round in pointless, keening circles, like rag dolls, until Beryl got fed up and told us to throw ourselves into the sea and shock ourselves out of it – which worked. The water was much colder than it had been before the storm, acting on us like a sort of baptism, so that when we came out we were free of the unbearable tickling that had writhed around in the pits of our stomachs.

As we dried ourselves in the sun, Beryl sent Lucia back to the café to reassure the others and to see that Tomás was all right. But the further Lucia got from us, the more slowly she moved and the more she burst into spurts of giggles, which turned into hiccoughs as she tried to say 'Bless you—!'

Beryl shook her head in despair. 'She might as well go into the sea, too, and wash out her bathing dress. Now, you two! I think it would be best if you just went off for a while and played. You got away with it once, but I don't think you'll get away with it again, especially *you*, Simon, *eh*? Diana's just not in the *mood*! So I'd make yourselves scarce if I were you!'

Juan nudged me pointedly in the ribs as he nodded meekly at Beryl. Then he nudged me again, more sharply, and I caught on, and nodded too.

As soon as she was out of earshot, Juan grabbed my arm. 'Now we can do it! Come!' He pulled me to my feet excitedly. 'First, we go up the donkey steps, so they think we're going home—!'

The cove shrank beneath us as we climbed, until it looked just as it had when Alastair had first shown it to me; secret again, and silent, timeless…

Instead of turning right when we got to the top, and going towards the square tower, we turned left, out towards the headland on the opposite side of the cove from the café.

'Keep out of eyesight!' Juan called as he began to race ahead.

Whether it was too much wine or too much laughter, I felt completely lightheaded as I chased after him past stunted pines tilting crazily inland, then through a grove of asphodels, blackened from being eaten by the dead in the dead of night, according to Juan, as they scratched feebly at our bare legs. The grove ended in a sheer wall, which we scrambled down, onto a beaten track that led steeply downwards, the surface so worn that we had to slide down on our stomachs, clutching onto dead roots.

It was only as we crawled round the base of a massive rock, and looked down, that I realised where we were – back above the bay, diagonally opposite the café but a hundred feet up, with nothing but a narrow ledge sticking out below us to prevent us from falling straight into the distant sea below.

Horrified, I slammed the whole length of my body against the earth, like a magnet, clinging to the iron-filled rock beneath—

No!

I heard Juan slithering to a halt below me.

'Simon?'

'*No!* I can't—'

'But it's *easy!*' I heard him scrambling back up to me, then felt his hand tugging my ankle. 'Come!'

'I *can't!* I've got...' I struggled to remember the word – '*vertigo!*'

'Give me some!' he demanded.

'No, you idiot! Vertigo's a *feeling* – when you can't look down without falling—'

'But we're *going* to fall, that's the whole point!'

'*What—?*'

He climbed back up and lay down next to me, peering into my face. 'Listen! You know the rock at the *cala*, the big one that we all jump off – you like that feeling, don't you?'

'*Yes,* but—'

'Well, this rock is ten times higher, that's all, and the feeling is ten times more exciting!'

I said nothing – thought nothing—

'And anyway, I dared you, so if you don't, you're a cowardly custard!'

Fighting my fear, I started to pull myself out of the ground, except for my eyes, which I kept fixed to it. 'I'm not a coward, I've just got vertigo, that's all. When I look down—'

'Then don't look down, idiot! Look up at the sky—'

'That's worse—'

'*Why?* You can't fall into the sky—'

Shaking my head dismally, I eased myself onto all fours, clutching at a root beside me, and began to move down backwards, feet first, staring only at the earth, sweating with funk, the dust from the path sticking to my front like a skin, *like cowardice*! I needed to wash it off, before he realised—

At last I felt my feet touch the level surface of the outcrop and I wobbled upright, like a tightrope walker, my arms still reaching out for the safety of the earth. Stealing a look over my shoulder at Juan, I saw him teetering on the very edge of the plank of rock – Peter Pan – completely fearless—

'You see?' he grinned. 'It's easy!' Whipping off his specs, he tucked them through the side of his swimming slip and knotted the laces round one of the arms. 'This is how I lost my last pair, so now I tie them to me,' he said virtuously. 'Ready? Just don't look down—'

I slowly stood up, arms crossed against my scrawny chest as though clutching myself to myself, hands clasping my shoulders, willing them to be the hands of God—

I couldn't move—

'Here—' he stretched out an arm towards me.

I wanted to throw myself at him, to cling to him, but instead I clutched at his steady gaze and took his hand lightly, edging towards him until we stood side by side, our bodies pressed against each other, mine to his for courage, his to mine for balance.

For a moment I looked back, and upwards, sickeningly, at the almost vertical path leading down from the safety of the terraces above to this sudden and unnecessary confrontation with death—

And then Juan, like the fiend that he was, turned towards the café where I could see them all still sitting at the long table, and waved his arms before cupping his hands to his mouth and yelling out: '*Everyone! He's going to jump—!*'

With a wild grin he gripped my hand and pulled me suddenly out into space. For a frozen second I managed to look across the cove, in panic, to see my mother slowly rise from her seat in horror as I slowly, endlessly…

fell… .

THE SACRIFICE

Neither the sea nor I were ready, and I hit its unforgiving surface on my side with such force that everything exploded into drowning darkness.

When the pain in my head and lungs forced me conscious at last, I struggled to find somewhere to breathe in the chaotic, groaning maelstrom I'd created deep under the water. Even as I fought to rise upwards, my body seemed still to be trying to sink, all colour draining from my vision. Sleeping and waking, I thrashed my way towards the light until at the instant of letting go I burst through the surface of the sea, choking and retching for life, and yet pursued from the depths by the strangest feeling of regret.

Alastair was the first to reach me, having apparently dived fully clothed straight off the café terrace into the sea, followed by Robert.

Vaguely, I heard Juan's shouted protests of innocence and saw him swimming frantically away from his father, while Alastair caught hold of me in his huge grip and kept telling me that I was safe...

My mother stood on the jetty below the café with Beryl and Lucia, surrounded by a few sunbathers from the beach, weeping and trying not to show she was weeping as she called out constantly to Alastair to make sure I was alive, to keep my head above water, to give me artificial respiration, to *hurry, for Christ's sake!* until finally he delivered me to the foot of the slipway where I could reach out shakily for one of the palings. With the others she stood in the water up to her knees, her skirt soaking, and pulled me from the sea, swamping me with towels as she fell on me at last, hugging and kissing and blubbing all over me as she rubbed my skin until it burned. I'd been expecting an avalanche of anger and had all the wrong words at the ready, none of them usable now, except 'Where's Juan?'

'Done a bunk!' An exasperated Robert had joined us and was stripping off his wet clothes. 'He threatened to swim out into the currents! I had to let him go—'

'But it wasn't his *fault*—' I shouted through a towel, 'I just fell badly—'

'You shouldn't have fallen at all!' cried my mother. 'It was very *wicked* of him to take you there! I'm sorry, Uncle Robert, but it was *unforgivable*—' She suddenly let out a low, dramatic cry and clutched at her throat as she stared down at one of the towels. We all froze.

'*Blood!*' groaned Lady Macbeth.

A bright red smear (rather cheerful, I thought) dusted the towel she was clutching.

'It's only a *little*, Diana—' began Beryl.

'There's more on this towel!' said Lucia sharply.

My mother tore all the towels from my body, frantically searching for the leak, though when she tried to undo the lace of my swimming slip, I jerked away from her, outraged.

'Diana, it's his ear!' said Alastair in the nick of time, pointing at my right ear.

Wiping it with my hand, I looked, in a detached sort of way, at the red streak across my palm.

'Probably just a cut,' said Robert in the sudden silence.

My mother had turned to stone, so Beryl had a look. 'No, it's from *inside* – sort of watery—'

'Dear God, it's his brain fluid!' gasped my mother.

'His *what?*' demanded Lucia.

'*Dura mater*,' said Robert knowledgeably, 'it cushions the brain.'

'He hasn't *got* a brain,' she muttered under her breath.

My mother took a swing at her, but missed. Trying not to laugh, Beryl pushed Lucia away.

In the end, Robert decided that he and Alastair should take it in turns to carry me up to Canellun, my mother following behind, panting and wheezing, but uncomplaining. Like a Stoic, Robert said.

By seven o'clock that evening both my ears were hurting badly enough for Beryl to pour warm olive oil into them and send me to bed with an aspirin.

I was vaguely aware at one point of the light being switched on, painfully, as she put Juan to bed, and of his whispering and laughing in the darkness once she'd gone... and then nothing until my dreams became so violent with pain that I woke up in a tangle of nightmares and earache and a wet pillowcase. More aspirin... kitchen—

As I padded down the tiled stairs into the moonlit hall I heard the sound of my mother's laughter coming from the dining room beyond, and opened the door to find her sitting at the table with Beryl, having their coffees. She knocked over her cup as she hurried round the table, sinking to her knees, her hands gripping my shoulders. 'Darling, you look awful—' She turned anxiously to Beryl, who came and felt my forehead.

'Yes... *well!* Now where do you suppose I've put the thermometer? You give him some more aspirin, Diana, and make him a bed on the sofa, and I'll go and look in the bathroom—'

As soon as she'd gone, my mother fussed around me, her face curiously split in half, with desperate eyes staring out from the top, and a terrible forced smile curving up from below. I swallowed the pills she gave me, then lay on the sofa while she covered me with a rug.

'Juan's going to pay dearly for this!' she whispered savagely. I knew it wasn't me she was promising, though, but herself, and that I must somehow distract her.

I started to shiver as the fever began to take hold, and thought it might be an idea to shiver even more. She looked down at me in alarm. 'Well, we won't worry about him now,' she said quickly.

Beryl came back into the room, shaking the thermometer.

'He's shivering,' said my mother in a strained voice.

'We'll take it under his arm, then. We don't want him biting it in half—' Pulling back the blanket, she tucked the thermometer into my armpit. 'He *is* quite hot—' She peered down into my face. 'Would you like some lemon squash, Simon? I think it would *help*—'

While she went into the kitchen, my mother got to her feet and began pacing up and down, hands behind her back, pausing every now and then to stare down at the thermometer under my arm as though it were a snake about to strike her.

'Don't take it out yet, Diana!' called Beryl from the kitchen, and we both managed a weak smile. Finally, she couldn't bear the suspense any longer and snatched the thermometer from under my arm by its neck, holding it away from her as if it might still bite her. When she held it up under the dim light from the chandelier, her hand suddenly flew to her mouth. 'Dear God!' she gasped, and started to run for the kitchen, 'it's ony just over forty degrees!' she cried. 'And normal is 98.4!'

'For heaven's *sake*, Diana!' laughed Beryl as she came back into the room with my drink. 'It's *centigrade* here, not Fahrenheit! Give it to me—' Taking the thermometer, she handed the lemon juice to my mother, who drank it. Beryl stared at her as if she were a child. 'That was *Simon's*!' She grinned at me. 'Go and get him another one while I look at this in peace.' She held the thermometer under the light. 'Well, it's about 102° – quite high enough, I should have thought—' She looked at me over her shoulder and pulled a face. 'I suppose I'd better go and tell your grand-uncle. Diana!' she called. 'I'm just going to tell Robert, and then we'll have a Council of *War*.'

I strained to hear their muffled conversation from his study, but my mother chose that moment to come back with my drink. A few moments later the house started to shake slightly as Robert strode towards us across the hall and burst into the room in front of Beryl, his spectacles thrown back onto the top of his head, a relief-nib pen still clutched between his fingers. 'What's all this? Simon's got a fever? Well, that's all right, we'll send for the vet—'

My mother spun round furiously. 'He needs a *doctor*, Uncle, not a fucking *vet*—' She clapped a hand over her mouth. 'Oh, I'm so sorry! I'm overwrought—'

Robert threw an arm round her shoulders, laughing. 'No, no, it's quite all right! The vet in Valldemosa looks after us all at night, you see, otherwise we have to send to Soller or to Palma. It's much quicker to get García—'

'He's very good, Diana, I promise,' said Beryl reassuringly. 'In fact he's much better with humans than he is with animals. Isabella won't let him anywhere near her. Now then! It's after ten, so the telephone exchange will have shut down, so I'll just nip over to Valldemosa. I shan't be long—'

Once Beryl was gone, Robert took charge, sitting my mother down and giving her a brandy to steady her nerves, then thundering off to his study again to find something to distract me. Together we pored over box after box of ancient objects which had been given to him by admiring explorers and archaeologists, some of them from Agatha Christie's husband, Max Mallowan – ushabti figures and scarabs and signet stones from Egypt, iron figurines and fetishes from the Cameroon which my cousin Sally Chilver, an anthropologist, had given him, Greek and Roman coins, and seals covered in mystical symbols. Many of the things he showed me had magic powers, apparently, some of which only he could invoke, while others, like the circle of figurines, would obey whoever called on their powers provided the ritual sacrifice of blood-letting was observed.

The aspirin – or Robert's history lesson – began to work, covering the pain in my ears like an incoming tide.

Meanwhile my mother paced restlessly up and down, faster and faster, as if her pacing could bring Beryl back sooner. At one point she stopped and stared at us in disbelief. 'You're like a pair of schoolboys! Surely you've got work to do, Uncle Robert?'

He looked at her as if she were mad. 'Nonsense, I'm enjoying myself! All I've done tonight is answer letters from complete strangers who address me as "Dear Mr Graves" and expect an autograph by return – which they'll probably sell on for a guinea!'

Beryl finally returned with the vet, a tall, kind-looking man with a drooping moustache and sad brown eyes, carrying his medical case in front of him as though it contained a vicious animal. The tiled room echoed with a sudden torrent of Spanish, and whether it was the noise, or simply fear of what was to come, the tide of aspirin seemed suddenly to go out, exposing the pain in my ears again. At last he came over to the sofa and pulled back the rug that covered me with a look of mild astonishment on his face, as though expecting my bottom half to look like a sheep or a goat. Having shone a light into my ears, he softly prodded and probed and took my temperature and listened through his stethoscope as he talked continually in a low voice, with Beryl translating as he went along.

'You're *hot!* No, you're *very hot!* Much fever! And *debilitations!* Oh, God, not another one!' I could see her trying not to laugh as she looked at me. 'You have a *grand infection* of the ears! Mastoiditis, and perhaps a burst eardrum. He thinks your right ear is very inflamed, and there's *discharge*—'

'Honourable, I hope,' joked Robert, and was told to be quiet.

Finally, Señor García got up, and the three of them rattled away in Spanish for a moment before Beryl turned back to me. 'He says he's going to try giving you a penicillin injection, which might do the trick. If it gets any worse... well, we'll worry about that when it happens—'

Señor García sat beside me on the sofa and began to take some nightmarish equipment out of his case: what looked like a horse syringe, and a tin box full of gleaming needles, many of them longer than his hand, and some glass ampoules full of thick yellow liquid. He started talking quietly to Beryl again.

'*Right*,' she said bracingly. 'Senor García wants you over on your left side. He says it'll probably hurt a bit – maybe even a lot – because penicillin is very *dense* and it may take some minutes to get it all in. So he wants you to grip Uncle Robert's hand, and not be ashamed of crying because most people do, even grown men.'

Everyone got into position as I turned onto my left side, Robert leaning over the end of the sofa and gripping both my hands, my mother, ashen-faced, undoing my pyjama trousers and pulling them down, and Beryl behind me somewhere, talking to the vet.

Suddenly there was a cold swab of liquid on the cheek of my bottom, followed by a white streak of pain as the needle went in. I cried out in shock and clutched at Robert's hands.

'Hold on,' called Beryl, 'he's had to use a very big needle because the stuff's so thick—'

And then came the most appalling explosion of pain, flowering and expanding, and against my promise to myself I screamed and twisted violently away.

'Don't move, Simon!' shouted Beryl. '*Drat!* The needle's snapped – oh God, Robert, Diana's fainting – *catch her!*'

There was total confusion as Beryl jumped forward to catch my mother while Robert tried to break away from my grip which had somehow become locked to his hand.

I twisted round, staring across the bare cheek of my bottom where the stub of the needle stuck out from a rivulet of blood.

My mother looked like a knitted doll, floppy and useless, until she started to come round and sit up, saying she felt sick. All three of them helped her out into the kitchen, leaving me alone. I started to shiver again.

Robert came back and pulled a face at me. 'What a kerfuffle! She's just being sick. Beryl says don't move, but you haven't, so that's all right!' He began pacing up and down in front of the fireplace, stopping every now and then to rearrange the objects on the mantelpiece. 'I've always found that the thing to do with pain is to try and detach yourself from it – leave it plenty of room instead of crowding round it.' His huge hand suddenly appeared above my head. 'If you can raise your spirits to about here, you'll find that it hurts much less next time. That's my trick, anyway – sort of pack up and move out of your body until it's over. Try it. It works, I promise.'

Beryl and the vet came back into the room, deep in conversation. '*Right*, Simon,' she began, as though she were going to tell me about a wonderful treat, '*this is what we're going to do—*'

Like an automaton I did as I was told, turning onto my front and letting Uncle Robert lie across me so that I couldn't move. The broken needle was out before I realised it. Señor García spoke quietly to Robert as he searched for another needle in his tin.

'He says it's very important that you should relax the muscles in your bottom so that the penicillin can disperse more easily. If you tighten them it'll hurt much more. So relax, and start leaving yourself *now*. Here we go!'

Icy swab, blazing needle, and again the hideous, aching agony tearing into my brain. I tried to do what Robert said, tried to reach upwards in my head to where his hand had been, but the leaden pain seemed to overwhelm me under its weight, until I groaned and wept into the cushion beneath me.

At last I heard Beryl's voice, as though from another world, saying '*There!* It's over—'

Señor García finally left, in his own car, after a couple of gins and a parting suggestion that the best remedy for earache was to listen to music.

'I could sing him a German lullaby my mother taught me,' offered Robert helpfully when the doctor had gone.

'We want him to get better, not *worse!*' said Beryl firmly. 'Go and get me the gramophone, Robert, it's in the Press Room—'

When he and Beryl had gone up to bed, to the strains of the Dying Swan, my mother helped herself to a drink and came and sat down beside me on the edge of the sofa. Without asking me, she reached down and lifted the head off the gramophone record.

'Poor darling,' she murmured into the sudden silence, 'what a rotten end to your holidays!'

I let my head roll away from her so that I was staring at the grey linen cushions beside me. One of them was streaked with my snot, as though a slug had crawled over it. I tried to wipe it away.

'We must think of a treat to make up for it,' she added bracingly.

'—live here—' I chose at once.

'What—?'

'Sorry.' I hadn't realised that the words had overflowed, that I was so full of longing—

'What did you say?'

'I want to live here,' I told the cushions.

'Well, we can't!'

I didn't say we—

'Why not?'

'Because we live in London!' she said firmly. 'That's where I have to be for my work, for my friends—'

'Leave me behind, then!'

'Darling, don't do this to me!' she begged. 'I've had enough! I've had enough of this *bloody* place! We live in *England*, you go to school in *England*, and on Friday we go back to *England*, and that's *that*.'

'But I hate Beachborough, and Juan says I can go to school with him here, stay in his room—'

'*That's enough.*' She sprang to her feet, spilling her drink as she went over to make sure the door was closed properly 'You don't know what you're saying. You're still feverish. For one thing, it's not *up* to Juan, it's not even up to Uncle Robert or Beryl, it's up to *me*! I am your mother, and I say we're going back to England, and I don't want to hear another word! Understood?' She turned on me.

'Yes.'

She took another gulp at her drink, put it down on the mantelpiece, and began to pace up and down. 'I couldn't bear to live here, anyway,' she went on, in her 'trying to be reasonable' voice. 'The heat, the lotus-eaters, the drunks and layabouts... the thought of becoming like them—'

'But Uncle Robert isn't—'

'I don't mean Uncle Robert – he's remarkable, although how he can work in this climate defeats me – and surrounded by all these so-called writers and artists who never sell a word or a picture and live off private incomes and drink themselves into a stupor every night. They *disgust* me! I can't wait to get back to real people – alive and witty and interesting! There's no question of my leaving you here. I don't care how much you hate school – no, that's not true, of course I care, and I'm very sorry you hate it – but everyone goes through a period of hating their school, your grand-uncle included. He had a perfectly miserable time at Charterhouse, but look at him now – a world famous writer and poet, and *respected* – because he saw it through! What sort of respect have these people earned?'

'But I like them—' I stared at her in disbelief. 'I thought *you* liked them—'

'*Bah!*' She went back to her drink on the mantelpiece, picking it up then putting it down again as she caught sight of herself in the mirror and began rearranging her hair, lost in her reflection. 'You've no idea what it's like, staying here – never being able to say what you really think, always having to put on a face... if it hadn't been for Alastair I think I'd have gone mad... and there's another marriage on the rocks,' she murmured to her reflection. 'It's so *unhealthy* here! It saps you—' she shuddered. 'I swear I'm more exhausted than when I arrived, and I came here to get stronger—' she looked at me quickly '—and to give you a holiday, of course!' She tried to smile, but it died on the blade of my accusing glare. 'And don't look at me like that! You only like it here because you want to escape from reality like the rest of these deadbeats! Well, I won't let you!' Her voice hardened. 'Thanks to Juan, you've done nothing but get into trouble since you arrived – he's taught you to disobey, to lie, to answer back – look at you now! If it weren't for Juan, none of this would have happened! And yet Beryl allows it, and I can do nothing. Well, let me tell you, my fine cockalorum, Juan's in for a rude awakening though he doesn't know it yet – *and you are not to tell him* – but he's going to school in Palma soon, and then to school in England, where, God willing, they'll knock some sense into him – so your wanting to live here is completely out of the question anyway!'

Infuriatingly, I felt tears begin to well up into my eyes, and turned away from her again.

So this was the end for Juan and me, the whispered plots we'd hatched late into the night gone up in smoke. I'd probably never come back. All the promises made by the earth to me and by me to the earth and to myself were to be broken, not by me – by her. I *hated her*!

I stopped short, pulling myself back from the brink of blasphemy—

She was my mother...

I knew that. It was just that sometimes I wished she weren't. I understood my duty to her. If the worst came to the worst, I supposed we'd both die in defence of each other, but out of instinct, not love—

I'd have to pay for these thoughts, I knew—

But Truth was Truth – not like a lie; you couldn't take it back—

She was still talking, but I knew what she was saying now without even listening. She was in the middle of what my father used to call her 'fucking litany', the same words and phrases she clung to whenever she was frightened or tired. There was no danger in them – she was just winding down, like the gramophone in the grotto, like the dying swan... she'd go to bed in a minute. 'I have a perfect right... working-my-fingers-to-the-bone... I *will* not be treated... you have no idea of the sacrifice... you know I hate... love... you *must*... *will*...'

A sacrifice! That was it! Not just to *her*, but to *here* – to this place, this island, something that would tie me to it, something powerful enough for me to leave it here, knowing that when it was time for me to return I'd be brought back—

But how? And where? Where was there a place magical enough to do it? And when?

And sacrifice *what?*

I felt the heat of fever and excitement rising from my face and body into the heat of the room, inspiring me, burning me free—

Already I began to see how, and with what – but *where*—?

Alone, high up, close to the sun – spell cast into energy—

'... darling?' Her glass-cold hand on my forehead, bringing me back. 'You're so hot...'

Quick – what was she saying?

'Darling...? Are you perhaps I should sleep with you here get Beryl...'

NO—

Make sense of it! It's your only hope! Wake up!

'No – thank you... please could you leave me an aspirin? I'll wake you, I promise... and please could you put the record on again? The other side, without the scratch...'

'Are you sure?'

'Yes…'

Yes… yes…

The heavy needle grazing the dark outer rim of the gramophone record… *hiss… hisss… hissss…*

'Kiss—'

Kiss, kissss—

'Goodnight, darling…'

At last—

And then darkness, and the music stealing like God into the void she'd left behind, filling the sudden night with everything I longed for—

—everything but *where*—

The music finished, its beauty and tragedy released into the rhythmic hiss of its beginning as the needle circled the polished emptiness at the centre of the record… round and round, the hiss and the returning *thump* of the sea, of waves crashing against rocks – beyond anywhere I knew, beyond the *cala*, to where the sea swept past the entrance to the cove, high above it, on the farthest point of land, at the very tip of the most distant outstretched finger of my world – at the Martello tower—

—*there!*

TO THE TOWER

My last day—

My last chance!

The tower lay at the very end of the headland to the west of the *cala*, the path to it rising steeply behind the café and the boatsheds. When I turned to look back after a few minutes they lay dwarfed below me, so still and perfect that I felt I could have stuck a stamp on the back of what I saw and sent it to my father—

Glad you're not here— He wouldn't have understood.

I looked across the cove, to the ledge of rock from which Juan and I had jumped into the sea. Even from this distance the drop looked hair-raising. My ears started to throb again at the memory, and I turned away from the past and continued to climb towards a future which probably none of them would understand or could even imagine—

Beryl might, actually… and Uncle Robert… he knew about magic, believed in it—

As casually as I could, I'd asked him about the Martello tower. He'd looked vaguely out of the window above the sofa, even though it faced in quite the wrong direction. 'I haven't been there for years. It's an *atalaya*, really – an old watchtower – pre-Napoleonic, so not strictly speaking a *Martello* tower, which is a Corsican invention – late eighteenth century. It's pretty much a ruin, now, and dangerous. If you went there alone, and something happened, no one would ever know, so keep away from it. I've told Juan it's haunted—'

Good!

Once at the top of the steep path I turned right, onto a track which had almost disappeared under a carpet of brown pine needles. Apart from the ecstatic screeching of cicadas it was strangely still and silent – until I realised that it was the constant murmuring of the sea that I could no longer hear. The sun burned down through the thin cover of the struggling pines which seemed somehow to trap the heat beneath them, the air heavy and pungent with resin. I was sweating so much that even my hair had begun to drip—

Brilliant! This would be part of it—

I stopped and looked around, to make certain I was completely alone, then struggled out of Robert's old army knapsack.

That morning, in search of all the things I'd need if my plan were to work, I'd waited until I knew Robert was busy with the compost before slipping into his study like a wraith, quickly ransacking it with my eyes, choosing from among the charms on his mantelpiece some of the objects he'd shown me after the injection. Taking my pick, I'd hastily bundled them into the knapsack I'd unearthed in the store room under the cellar stairs. The drawers and the top of his desk I left strictly alone, terrified that by removing anything from them he would somehow 'see' me and burst into his study like a sorcerer. With a bit of luck he wouldn't miss the stuff on the mantelpiece, which I was only going to borrow for a few hours anyway. Laying the stiff knapsack carefully on the pine needles, I unbuckled the flaps and took out his water bottle, pouring some over my head and drinking a little, rolling it round my parched mouth. Famished, I took out the matchbox containing pieces of dried-up mushrooms from the jar on the mantelpiece in his study. After the play, he's shown them to me, saying that it was mushrooms like these which had surrounded the Tree of Knowledge – though much stronger, giving powerful insight and wisdom. Putting some in my mouth, I bit into them hungrily, and into the insides of my cheeks, to make more spit, until they softened at last, like the skin of old blisters, tasting of earth. I should have brought some biscuits—

Then I undressed, until I was naked except for my school belt, with Juan's sheath knife threaded through it by its scabbard. At once the sensation I felt was more than nakedness, more than freedom. In taking off my clothes I'd somehow revealed an invisible mantle of power, of savagery, and my cock began to harden as proof of it.

Squatting down, I stuffed my damp clothes and water bottle into the knapsack, revelling in the feeling of nothingness between myself and the vision of myself, in the heat of bare skin touching bare skin, like love – or friendship, anyway – as we both stood up, erect, stock-still, listening...

Still no one—

With a thrill of premonition I drew in the deepest breath I could, and held it—

Then let myself out – no longer *me*, now, but

him – a moving part of the earth and the rocks and the air around him, his hand swooping down to gather up the knapsack before he loped on through the ancient scrawny pine wood, among the great-great-grand-trees of trees that had grown here since the beginning of time, his sense of purpose filling him with such power that the invisible curtain of heat seemed to part before him and close behind him, hiding him—

Naked and sweating he ran on, eyes glazed with intent, fixed on such a distance that he would have run on forever if the sun-baked tower hadn't risen out of the ground in his path and stunned his palms against its warm stone—

Jarring me out of my trance—

A couple of ancient bronze cannon lay at the foot of the tower, flung down from the battlements by vandals and lying among the rocks like soldiers in the chaos of their own death. Panting for breath, I circled the *atalaya*, shielding my eyes against the sun as I craned my neck to look up its sheer walls. The only way into the tower seemed to be a rotten wooden staircase that led to a single entrance, some fifteen feet above me. Most of the treads were missing, which meant that I'd have to cling to the one handrail that was left, and which looked none too safe—

My fears and doubts became like children, left safely on the ground with the child I'd once been, while I swarmed up the broken staircase and in through the doorless opening—

The door itself had long gone, leaving only a dark tunnel that stretched through the massive thickness of the walls. Edging my way warily through the rubble towards a ghostly greenish light at the far end, I finally emerged into the shadowy emptiness of the inside of the tower and stared round in wonder, dwarfed by the vast, windowless void around me. Everything had gone: rooms, internal walls, ceilings had all collapsed into the cellars far below, and perhaps into the sea caves below them. Tendrils of ivy and brambles snaked among the debris as though endlessly devouring it in the half light. A spindly tree yearned upwards to where a beam of sunlight slammed a dazzling shaft high up against the far wall. I looked to my left, to where a flight of stone steps, embedded in the inner wall of the tower, led upwards to the source of light, to a doorless opening in the roof.

The sweat was drying on my body, brushed by phantom draughts rising from the vegetation below, their faintly putrid scent provoking thoughts of death. Robert was right – no one knew I was here. If I were to fall into that midden I might not be found for years – perhaps not until my flesh had been eaten by rats, and brambles had grown through my eye sockets, my ribs—

Something shifted beneath my feet, and I stared down fearfully at the tangled undergrowth. It was as though the floor of the tower had begun to turn slightly, to sink—

My heart in my mouth, I leapt for the stone steps, keeping as close to the wall as I could, my eyes fixed on the dazzling square of light in the roof. One of the stair treads sank beneath me, its root stirring somewhere in the depths of the wall with a faint heavy thud and a loose rattling of stones. Groaning with fear, I took the rest of the steps at a lightfooted run, like the wind, until I burst through the doorless opening in the roof—

Only to be struck senseless yet again by the heat and glare of the sun, my hands trying desperately to shade my eyes as I turned away from it. After a few moments I could feel it burning into my shoulders and quickly took off the knapsack in case she saw the telltale marks of the straps. My belt followed, Juan's knife falling out of its sheath and pointing towards me, fatefully, the blade dazzling with reflected sunlight. I squinted down at it for a moment, hypnotised—

No – that was all right—

With an excitement I could hardly control, I began to bask in the power of the sun, kicking off my espadrilles so that I could be completely naked. The soles of my feet burned against the hot stone, but I could endure anything. I was a pagan, a warrior, standing at the centre of the roof where it swelled upwards slightly as though being pushed from beneath, before crossing to the battlements and staring across the sea at all the small bays and inlets that stretched towards Soller and the distant, barren cone of the *Puig Mayor—*

Yes! The ancient volcano rising four thousand feet through the haze – then looking inland, towards Deya, to where a pale three-quarter moon hung, weightless above the wall of the mountains—

Yes!

Then further to my right, towards Valldemosa, gasping in disbelief as I found myself staring straight into the eye of the *Foradada,* a primaeval rock rising out of the sea which I'd only ever seen at a distance, from the coast road, the gaping hole of its all-seeing eye staring wildly back at me—

Yes!

An ecstatic feeling of inevitability overwhelmed me. These weren't things that I'd made up or conjured; they'd been here for ever, like an audience of ghosts waiting for this moment. I mustn't fail them—

I sank down onto the roof to think. My bottom, still black and blue from the injections, ached against the hot stone, even as it cooled in my shadow—

Think!

Sun, Moon, Mountains, Sky, Heat – and behind me the Sea, stretching away from me on three sides. All present – my witnesses – all witnessed in turn by the all-seeing Cyclops of the *Foradada*.

Everything I could see could see me. Everything I felt and did would be left here, like an indelible stain in time, as a charm to bring me back.

I reached for the knapsack and pulled out my clothes, laying them on the ground as a cushion for everything as I emptied the sack carefully through my spread fingers so that nothing broke: water, matches, oil, three of Robert's coins, in gold, silver and bronze, the feather of an albatross, the black magic figurines from the Cameroon, the dried corpse of a lizard, a bag of earth and small stones from the garden, and then the most vital thing of all, the jam jar with a live scorpion in it – the biggest I'd ever seen – caught that morning in the grotto. I unscrewed the lid. Still trapped by the glass walls of the jar, the scorpion scuttled round and round the bottom as I stared down at it, sweating and trembling as if already stung. It had all been so clear in my fever, when I had stared into the Truth and laboriously copied it into my memory. Six Towers – that was it! And then a Seventh—

Think!

Opening the bag of stones, I found a white one, soft enough to draw with, and began laboriously to copy what I'd seen in my fever onto the surface of the roof: three huge circles, with arrows pointing clockwise, the innermost circle indented like a cogwheel. Within this circle I drew a circle of six towers, with a seventh tower, upside down, between the Sixth and the First. The Seventh Tower was the Tower of Return, the crucible into which the energy of the other Towers would flow. Under the battlements of the six towers I wrote their headings: Sun, Moon, Earth, Air, Fire, Water, and filled each tower with the things that belonged to it. Then I joined the towers together with their corresponding number of arrows, all pointing in the direction of the Seventh Tower, whose seven arrows pierced the side of the first tower, to give it the energy I needed to move the circle.

The crenellations of the Towers pointed outwards, gripping the cogs of the Wheel of Time as it circled them.

Lastly, I drew a circle at the centre of the ring of towers for me to stand in, with a spoke reaching outwards to each of the towers, so that they'd become a moving part of me.

The one thing I lacked was a Serpent, not only to symbolise the contents of each of the Seven Towers but to represent More than Temptation, More than Knowledge. The dead lizard was a poor substitute, although its deadness was important. I was about to draw a serpent on the roof when I saw my elasticated school belt slithering like mercury past the corner of my eye, and grabbed it by its buckle with a shout of triumph. The buckle was a silver snake, 'S'-shaped, with scales and a head – worn by every schoolboy in England, and I'd ignored its significance! Feverishly, I fastened it round my waist again, tightening it until I could feel its coils gripping me. Taking a deep breath, as deep as when I'd let the coward in me out, I held it in my chest…

Time to do it—
now!

I let all my breath out, until I was even lighter than before, and stood up slowly, almost floating. Brushing the dust and grit from the cheeks of my bottom I wiped my hands on the pile of clothes until my palms were clean, then took the bottle of oil and went across to the Seventh Tower, the Tower of Return, standing with my feet between its walls as I emptied the oil gradually over my face and body, rubbing it in, quickly at first, then more slowly, forbiddenly, lingering in guilty surprise at the strange sensation of my hands sliding the warm silky oil over the warm silky skin of my body – no longer naked suddenly, but nude. The sense of power that surged through me was all-consuming. Nothing human could grip me now – I could slip through Time like an eel!

When I was completely covered except for the soles of my feet (which had to stay in touch with the earth, with the tower and landscape I had to return to), I wiped the palms of my hands on my clothes again, so that when I grasped the knife it wouldn't slip.

With my legs apart, and flexed, I raised my hands to the sky and stretched, as mightily as I could, until every muscle in my body juddered, joints cracking, my cock hard and glistening from being oiled, straining upwards cobra-like, spitting as I threw back my head and faced directly into the sun, eyes closed but dazzled, burning – and then into the moon, letting it float in the writhing black imprint of the sun. Clockwise, I turned back to the sun, and then towards the moon again, slowly at first, then slowly quicker, then more and more quickly, round and round, faster and faster, willing the circles to turn with me – sun, moon, sun, moon, sun–moon, sunmoon, summon, summon, summon the spirits of this place, my witnesses, to reach into my future and bring me back through the narrow waist of time, grain by grain through the hourglass of past, present, future, my body rotating, spinning, until something happened in my head, as if my brain had begun to overtake itself before bursting into a kaleidoscope not of colour but of energy, and my momentum became unconscious, detached, and I was whirling, whirling, in complete stillness—

—and it was the tower that was turning now, the circles spinning so fast they hovered around me—

It was working – on and on – round and round—

Until I fell to my knees in dizzying darkness, sobbing, clutching the roof as the stones beneath me sank, my body shaking uncontrollably until I was violently sick, and yet my mind calm, serene, because nothing mattered now; I was in another Time, my body in the past, the present non-existent, my spirit in the future of myself, unreachable by anyone but me and the Fates who would one day bring me back—

Juan had told me the most frightening thing about scorpions was the speed at which they struck.

As soon as the trance and the nausea had passed, I lit the candle with shaking hands and tilted it downwards over the middle of my circle, at the centre of all the circles, letting it drip freely onto the hot stone. The longer the wick became, the quicker the candle burned and the bigger the pool of melted wax beneath it. When the pool was big enough, I quickly rolled the still-lighted candle towards the fifth Tower—

Heart racing, I grabbed the jam jar and carefully tipped the angry scorpion, right-side-up, on top of the topmost wax, which was still molten. A second's struggle, and it was stuck fast as the wax began to harden. Reaching for Juan's knife from the Third Tower, I placed the tip of the blade between the scorpion's rearing tail and its body. *It mustn't kill itself!* As I struck the scorpion lightly on its back, I could see the drop of venom on the curved thorn of its sting as it struck the blade twice, with incredible speed.

I could hardly control my hands as I withdrew the knife and squinted at the tip—

Yes!

A smear of poison, right on the point—

Laying my left hand palm upwards in the middle of my circle, I held the point of the knife to the tip of my little finger, to the farthest and outermost headland of my body, to where I squatted on the rooftop of the tower, screwing my eyes tight shut as I arched my body over it, and fell on the hilt with all my weight, and with a thin, high scream, stabbed it—

—*home*—

PART TWO

THE WHITE GODDESS

[1989]

TURMOIL

At S'Esgleità, on the featureless plain between Palma and the mountains to the north, I stood at the crossroads, staring one by one into the vanishing points of the four empty roads that stretched away from it.

I'd left my jacket with my bags in the taxi, and left the surly, middle-aged taxi driver in the cool darkness of the bar in front of a sweating *tubo* of beer.

Nothing stirred in the breathless heat – no sound except the slight crunch of my shoes on the hot tarmac and the frenzied shrilling of cicadas.

Apart from the widened road, little had changed since I'd stopped here for a beer with Margot on our way back to Deya so long ago; the small church still glaring at my faithlessness from the other side of the road, the stucco still peeling from the square pillars outside the bar, the plants on the veranda above still hanging in drought-limp festoons over the entrance. Except for the church and the bar and a few ramshackle houses, there was nothing but the crossroads and the endless olive groves on which the village somehow managed to survive.

The taxi ride from the vast new airport, still stinking of wet cement, had been nightmarish, racing along the new motorway that now circled Palma, its sprawling suburbs stretching away to my left with only occasional glimpses, now, of the sea. I could have been anywhere in the Mediterranean. And yet what did I expect? It had been thirty years since I'd last been here – thirty years of frantic development to keep up with the demands of tourism.

When I'd asked the driver to take me to the Bar Formentor, he'd told me that our old haunt was long gone, turned into an expensive shoe shop.

—Forget Palma, then – drive straight to Deya—

A shrug of indifference...

Only when we'd turned off the motorway onto the familiar Valldemosa road did it feel as though there might yet be hope, that the past might still exist somewhere on the island, however concealed the entrance to it.

—Had Deya changed?— I asked the driver anxiously. Again he shrugged. The whole island had changed in his opinion. It had become a whore for the bankers and tourists and politicians, and it was in the nature of whores, the older they got, to attract a cheaper clientelle who expected more for their money. Deya? On the one hand there was talk of turning the whole north coast into a National Park so that nothing could be changed, and on the other there was talk of a motorway to be driven straight through it, from Valldemosa to Soller – perhaps even to Pollensa—

I was surprised by how much Spanish I remembered from my time at university in Madrid, even as I shook my head despairingly. If I could only reach back through this turmoil in my head and somehow grip the hand of that 'myself' who had returned here for the first time so long ago—

I shouldn't have come by plane – perhaps that was my mistake. It was too sudden, too abrupt. I should have followed in my own footsteps and come by boat, as I had that summer in 1960 – the night ferry from Barcelona steaming through the darkness—

That night, at sea, I remembered being forced awake from the discomfort of sleeping in a hard, plastic-covered chair and making my way to the upper deck into a bracing, unexpected wind, huddling over the ship's rail as I stared out into the paling darkness ahead.

Something had distracted me on the boat deck... the sound of quiet singing, that was it! A circle of strangely dressed people, mostly young, was sheltering in the lee of the ship's funnel. Under the glare of the floodlights they looked gaunt and surreal as they sang *Barbara Allen*, one girl with a high, clear voice singing the solo verses while the others joined in the chorus.

I remembered thinking that these people must be 'beats' or 'beatniks', or whatever they called themselves. At Barcelona I'd watched them board just before midnight, when the last gangplank had been on the point of being pulled away from the ship. Everyone had stared down at them in astonishment, at the bearded men and at the long, unkempt hair of the women, and they had stared back at us as though it were we who were mad – to be punctual, to be dressed in dreary clothes, *not* to have flowers in our hair. In London I'd noticed others like them and had simply dismissed them as a fad, as did most people I knew.

After a while they stopped singing and began to talk in low voices, looking over their shoulders as they started to make handrolled cigarettes. A couple of them nodded at me, but I didn't want to be drawn in, so I'd just nodded back—

—and turned away to look out to sea—

—*straight into a new and breathtaking world being born before my eyes as the ship crept like a child through the curtain of night and into the first dawn of its life, orange–pink, the colour of watered blood gleaming on the mountaintops of the island ahead, running down their slopes like molten lava, spilling onto the rocks before rushing towards us across the flat, calm sea and striking the ship to sudden cries of astonishment, then commotion, as passengers struggled from sleep to the rails of the ship, calling, exclaiming—*

—*oh, why could they not just say nothing, since nothing they said made any sense of this night in the dazzling armour of dawn lancing the sun, spilling blood-orange light as it sped past the ship towards Spain down the ploughed-up road of our wake—*

He was here! Even from this distance of years I could still summon him, my young remembered self, porphyry-prosed, passionate, moody—

I waited for more—

Nothing.

I looked at my watch. Just after two o'clock. Having left the ship that morning in 1960, I'd have kicked my heels in Palma until the bus left for Deya at two; about now, in fact. The timing was perfect. I asked the driver if the Deya bus still came along this road.

'Claro!' He stared round at me as if I were mad. How else would it get there—?

Perhaps if I were to let the bus overtake us! The old charabanc was bound to have been replaced by some air-conditioned monstrosity which would remind me of nothing, and yet if I were to let it pass us—

I knew it was ridiculous to put such faith in omens, but no sooner had I imagined the possibility of myself overtaking myself and then leading the way – his way – back into the past—

I asked if there was there still a café at the side of the road in S'Esgleità, at the crossroads.

'Claro!'

Perhaps we could pull in and have a cold beer – at my expense of course—

Slowly, as the invitation began to sink in, the car began to pick up speed.

Once we'd arrived in S'Esgleità I'd asked the driver to park in the shade behind the bar so that the sight of his modern taxi wouldn't interfere with my memories. He laughed, a little uneasily – was I being followed—?

I hoped so.

Having ordered our beers in the otherwise deserted bar, I quickly finished mine and told him I was going out for a little stroll.

Mopping at the sweat as it began to run down my face and neck, I shaded my eyes to look back again down the gleaming road towards Palma.

Still no sign…

What had he been doing in Majorca anyway? No! Perhaps that was my mistake – thinking of him in the third person, making him even more remote. What had I been doing here?

Already that felt better somehow.

Robert and Beryl had invited me to spend a month or so in Deya on my way to university in Madrid – my mother's last hope of a respectable future for me. The invitation had seemed spontaneous at the time, although I hadn't reckoned on her hidden agenda, her little betrayal, setting me up under the microscope of grand-avuncular scrutiny, a lamb to his well-meant slaughter—

—*diving through his unspeakable words into the deafening sea at Ca'n Floquet*—

There!

Again—

I stood at the crossroads between nothing and nowhere, an anvil for the hammer blows of the sun, holding my face up to it, willing it to smite me, willing for a sign, a revelation, for a fifth choice of road, for the retinal stone of the sun to be rolled away from the mouth of the past—

At first there was only a whine, persistent, mosquito-like until it deepened to a drone, and then into the beginnings of a roar, and I quickly turned and looked back down the road we'd come on, trying to see through the blot of the sun in the centre of my vision, as out of my blindness the leviathan emerged, horn blaring as it approached the crossroads, my eyes disbelieving, denying the apparition, the monstrous old caramel charabanc blasting me aside in the familiar dust and wind of its passing—

My heart soaring, blinking wildly from the smuts, I stared after it as it diminished in a swirl of dust and black smoke among the mirage pools in the road, its clamour fading, dwarfed by perspective and the vast silence of the mountains beyond it.

In the returning stillness I heard the clatter of the plastic fly curtain over the entrance to the bar. The taxi driver stood in the shade of the verandah, watching me, waiting.

I called over to him— 'The Deya Bus—!' I couldn't hide my excitement.

'Claro...' he shrugged.

—No, the real bus, the old brown one—!

He ambled out of the shadows – nothing strange about that; the new bus was too wide for these roads anyway. It was always crashing into things. They used the old bus whenever they had to wait for parts from the mainland—

I asked if we could go now, knowing that we'd catch up with it before it reached the mountains.

Again he shrugged. 'Claro.'

In spite of my growing allergy to the man, I sat in the front passenger seat this time so that I could see clearly as we sped on through the olive groves and into the foothills.

It wasn't long before we ran into the trail of dust left behind by the charabanc. The taxi driver shook his head, muttering sulkily that he'd washed his car only that morning, but I ignored him, staring around me with the same wonder that I'd felt as a child whenever we entered this gorge, the narrow pass into Shangri La, only wide enough for the road and the deep bed of a torrent next to it, bone dry and silent now, but in winter swollen and raging with melted snow from the surrounding mountains.

Moments later, as we rounded a hairpin bend, we saw the bus grinding its way up the steep road ahead, smoke belching from its exhaust, steam already leaking from its radiator. The nearer we got to it, the slower time seemed to move and the closer we seemed to be drawn towards the past—

—Don't overtake! I yelled. He was already changing down and moving out to his left. With a gasp of impatience he pulled back, striking the wheel with his hand – but I didn't care. I only knew that we had to hang back now, that there was something about the taxi driver's impatience and ignorance that was triggering an inexplicable crisis, that if we passed the bus everything would be lost—

We continued up the winding gorge. The beautiful, secret valley lay before us, green and fertile, completely contained within its circle of mountains. Valldemosa itself was perched on the steep saddle of rock at the far end, like an ascending army, spears of cypresses piercing the sky, dark umbrella pines like unmoving clouds of cannon fire suspended over the town, the chain mail of yellow tiled roofs tilting upwards, gleaming in the sunlight—

As the bus slowed down to go into a lower gear, I saw to my horror that instead of approaching the town along the old road across the valley floor, a new highway had been cut into the side of the mountain to our right, a bleeding gash where the weathered grey limestone had been sliced through to expose the red and orange veins of rock beneath, the new road bypassing the old town completely before circling back at the very top, towards the *Cartuja*, the monastery—

—Where was the old road—? I could hear the panic in my voice as I searched for the turning. The car became suddenly filled with fumes and smoke from the bus as we went round another bend, the taxi driver trying to wind up his window as he steered.

—Somewhere on the left—? There!

Just beyond the bus I could see the dark blue metal arrow, rusted now and tilting towards the ground – 'Valldemosa 0.5km' – Left! Turn left – I found myself shouting over the noise, my fear – Now—

He pulled out angrily, just as a lorry appeared round the bend above us, coming flat out down the hill, horn blaring, braking frantically in the face of this makeshift death as we swerved and skidded and the taxi driver, at the last moment, wrenched his wheel to the left—

PAST IMPERFECT

For the umpteenth time since we'd left Palma the bus driver leaned over the gears and poked me in the left leg, jolting me out of my thoughts as he gestured ahead. Although the windscreen was smeared with dust and oily steam from the radiator, I could still make out the unforgettable sight of Valldemosa rising above us like the Promised Land, glittering in the midsummer sun, the bell tower of the *Cartuja* still pointing like a dark finger to heaven. I couldn't look at it without thinking of Chopin and George Sand and the miserable winter they'd spent here. As a child, Beryl had taken me—

As a child? For Christ's sake, it had only been six years ago, and yet already it seemed a lifetime away, my boyhood a mere embarrassment to me now—

I shifted superstitiously in my seat. To even think like this was a betrayal of the promises I'd once made to myself in this very gorge. To disown my own childhood for the sake of appearances was wrong; I owed it too much. That child in me was my only guide to what lay ahead—

The driver forced the bus like a giant brown cork through the bottlenecks of narrow Valldemosan streets, so steep that there were moments when we hardly seemed to be moving at all as he fought his way through lower and lower gears to keep some sort of grip on the cobbles. The sheer racket of our progress, echoing back from the houses on either side, made conversation impossible, although he threw me a grin now and then, pointing to the temperature gauge on the radiator cap, the needle jammed far into the red, or stabbing his fingers up at the shuttered windows of the houses—

'*Siesta!*' he bellowed, and roared with laughter as he stuck a finger in his ear.

Eventually we made it to the top of the hill and into the square, where a line of brimming pails outside a bar marked our watering hole. There was an almighty backfire as the driver switched off the engine, the women passengers screaming and crossing themselves, the pig in its cage on the roof squealing in terror, the driver roaring with laughter as he slapped me on the thigh.

Half an hour later we were off again, the engine watered, the windscreen washed, and about a ton lighter without the Valldemosa passengers and their supplies. The needle on the radiator was firmly back in the black as we headed out of town, past a corner—

I stared at it in disbelief. A new development had been started where once there had been nothing but rocks and wild scrub – only a few houses and a restaurant as yet, but with land cleared for more. Garish signs on the pavement offered '*Pork Chopins*', '*Georges Sand-wiches*', '*Pollo-naise*'—

How could they?

And yet, as Beryl would have said, what business was it of mine? It was their country after all. If it weren't for that henge of childhood, those immovable stones of memory set in a landscape which I'd always imagined to be my private world, I probably wouldn't even have noticed. But the natural beauty which had once flourished on that corner had once been a part of me, and its obliteration hurt as much as if the bulldozers were in my head, uprooting those sacred standing stones of nostalgia to make way for a different world.

We roared on, through what was left of the tunnel of plane trees, through dappled sunlight, the breeze refreshing at last as it blew in from the wild north coast through the open windows.

I sneaked a look behind me, down the aisle of the bus, self-conscious of my place at the front, where the driver had firmly told me to sit when he'd looked at my luggage labels. A soft guitar chord drew my eye to the beatniks at the back of the bus. Still with us. What on earth did they expect to find in Deya?

Suddenly, change seemed to be everywhere, as though someone had quietly planted it after I'd left as a boy, and all at once it was bursting out of the ground in concrete beanstalks, dripping tendrils of new roads and building sites – a poisonous plant, with tourists for flowers. But then this was 1960, not 1953—

I looked out through the window again as we turned onto the coast road—

Where everything was as I remembered it at last! In taking that sharp right turn we'd somehow managed to return to the picture-past of memories, the time between my leaving and returning a mere illusion.

Again the driver's fingers stabbing at my leg and pointing down urgently to his left. Obligingly, knowing perfectly well what he was pointing at, I stood up and leaned over the hum of his old sweat, holding my breath as I stared down at the rooftops and belvedere of *Son Marroig* perched above the sea. The summer palace of the long dead Hapsburg Archduke nestling among its cypresses, half hidden from the road above. What must Robert have thought, walking down this road for the first time in 1929 to find the wild and savage landscape giving way to a sudden and mysterious civilisation – grand villas, formal gardens, a system of irrigation, and new roads carved out of the mountainsides, their massive retaining walls built almost a century ago with Aztec-like precision to hold back winter landslides.—

The thought of seeing my grand-uncle and Beryl again in a matter of minutes filled me with the same excitement and happiness as being back on the coast road. Since my first visit here, my mother and I had often seen them in London, when they came to stay with the Chilvers, or their friends the Simons, to pick up yet another prize or attend his latest book launch, or return to Oxford. Every time I'd seen them I'd longed for them to ask when I was coming back to stay with them in Deya, and here I was at last, returning to what I'd always thought of, ineradicably, as the heart of my family.

We crested the last hill, perhaps a thousand feet above the sea, and tilted downwards at last, suddenly, into the hollow of my own remembered world, the jagged coast stretching away in sharp-fingered headlands, dominated by the distant cone of the *Puig Mayor* gleaming sullenly through the haze.

The eyes of the bus swept round the last bend at downhill speed, and there was Deya—

home—

—the village rising on a crag out of the deep gorge below us, its drama overwhelmed at first by the spectacular theatre of mountains which had suddenly reappeared, falling sheer into a vast auditorium of terraces, the highest clinging to the barren cliff faces before spreading outwards and downwards in restraining, civilised rows – a countless audience of olive trees, each as different as human beings, curving in ever-widening tiers around the mountain flanks.

As we continued to descend the steep side of the hill, the village in turn rose more and more steeply out of the gorge beside us, as if to emphasise the power it had over the landscape.

I glanced quickly across the valley, searching for the bright green awning over the kitchen window at Canellun—

Still there—

I could hardly wait to stand on the drive again—

The bus stood empty, tilting towards the kerb, doors lolling open like dogs' tongues in the heat.

The other passengers had vanished, either into the cars or vans which had been waiting for them, or on foot, disappearing into doorways along the village street or, like the beatniks who had been met by a couple just like them, down the dusty track into the *Clot*, the hottest and smelliest part of the village in summer, where the rubbish was left to rot in the dry bed of the torrent.

But there'd been no one waiting for me.

I felt foolish, standing alone on the pavement with my very English suitcase and briefcase, but the driver had made urgent signs for me to stay there, shouting '*Espera! Espara!*' Did that mean 'hope? Or 'wait'? The sooner I learned the language the better.

Well, I'd hope or wait for a couple of minutes more, and then I'd start walking. He'd gone round the other side of the bus, into the middle of the road, sorting out the ropes which had tied the animals' cages and luggage to the roof-rack. Now and then he'd throw one back up onto the rack, neatly coiled and knotted.

Again I looked back up the street in the direction of Canellun, but still no cavalry appeared to rescue me. The heat was relentless, the silence of *siesta* unbroken except for the endless tinnitus of cicadas and the gentle hiss of steam escaping from the radiator of the bus.

At last the driver came round again, slamming the back door as he came, taking off his sweat-stained cap and chucking it onto the dashboard as he climbed up into his seat and heaved the door shut behind him. As he reached for the rag to mop himself, he winked down at me as he pressed the starter and kicked the engine into life with a roar and a furnace blast of fumes. Something in my face must have betrayed my uncertainty because he gestured to me again, emphatically, to stay where I was.

With a painful groaning and grinding of gears he began to reverse down the street, away from me, until he reached the rough ground at the top of the *Clot*, where he deftly spun the wheel round, slewing the tail of the bus straight across the main road and into the cave-like mouth of its garage opposite, the manoeuvre so practiced and effortless that it was astonishing to watch. A moment later, the bus had vanished completely into the deep shadows. From within, the huge grey doors were slowly pushed shut by unseen hands until they looked as if they hadn't been opened for years. The muffled roar of the engine was abruptly cut off, and it was as if the bus and our journey had never existed – as if I'd appeared on the deserted street out of nowhere.

The sudden silence expanded unbearably into the heat.

I stared up and down the blind, shuttered street. Nothing moved.

With no one left to witness what I did, I took of my jacket and threw it over my cases. It wasn't enough; the feeling of such sudden freedom was addictive, and I loosened my tie and undid the button of my collar. The relief was so instant that I could almost see my sweat vapourising. All at once I was sickened by my Englishness, by my slavish obedience to old-fashioned rules – especially my mother's – *always look your best when you travel – it keeps petty officials in their place—*

I didn't *want* to keep petty officials in their place!

With a flourish, I undid my cufflinks, wiped my dripping face on the sleeves of my shirt, and rolled them up.

Perhaps by going to Madrid I'd be free of her at last—

From somewhere at the bottom of the village came the sound of a car trying to start. Time to go; it was pointless waiting here like a twerp for nothing to happen. I picked up my jacket and cases and began to head on up the hill. I would walk to Canellun. The winding coast road was beautiful, and if I left my cases at the telegraph office, where the blue enamel sign still stuck out from the wall, I could pick them up later—

The car I'd heard before was now grinding its way up the street behind me, drawing abreast.

The sudden blare of its horn made me jump out of my skin, and I looked round angrily

'Olà, Señor!' The bus driver grinned up at me from under a different peaked cap, this one with *Taxi* embroidered on it in mildewed silver letters. In a tirade of Majorcan he seemed to be reproaching me as he got out of the car and picked up my cases.

He'd even put on a grubby grey linen jacket over his sweaty shirt. Slinging my cases into the boot, he beckoned me round to the front passenger door, and in a manoeuvre as practised as reversing the bus into the garage he put one hand through the open window to grip something, turned the outside handle with the other, and lifted the door clean off its hinges before standing aside like a bullfighter with his cape as he gestured me into the naked-looking seat. I quickly finished putting on my own jacket and climbed in, retying my tie as he replaced the door on its hinges.

A moment later he threw himself behind the wheel in a familiar explosion of sweat and garlic crying '*Vamonos, hombre!*' and pressing the starter relentlessly until he finally coaxed the wheezy old engine back into life.

We'd hardly left the village behind us before he was poking me in the thigh again and pointing out of his window at the wedge of sea which stretched away from the invisible *cala* far below us.

'*Miras!*' he bellowed.

'*I know!*' I wanted to shout back. '*I was born here—*'

FULL CIRCLE

Returning to Canellun was like returning to a part of myself that I'd lost, the memory of it so clear that when the taxi pulled up at the gates and the driver got out to open them, I could have told him precisely what would happen, and in what order, not only because I'd lived this moment a thousand times in my dreams, but because although I had grown in the meantime, everything I'd left behind so vividly had grown too, *so nothing had changed!* The huge palm tree, the Norfolk Island pine, the *algarrobas*, the giant cacti had all kept pace with my memory of them, so that the moment the driver drew the iron bolt on the gates with its familiar clang, I was poised for the dogs to start barking in the house, their warning yaps already floating down to us as the gates screeched open. Jumping quickly back into the car, he slammed the door as the two poodles hared out of the kitchen and onto the drive, barking hysterically now, bringing Beryl out after them, shouting at them to be quiet as we got half way up the drive and stalled, at the very moment when Robert burst through the kitchen doorway after her, scattering the fly curtain, looking the image of my memory of him, a cross between a prize fighter and a Roman emperor – same old shorts, blue Aertex shirt, down-at-heel espadrilles, storming past Beryl—

'For heaven's *sake*, Robert, he's *arriving*, not *leaving*—!'

'It's Simon, darling—!'

'I *know* it's Simon—!'

The three of us grinning fit to burst as everything came full circle at last, the driver lifting my door off its hinges to let me out to receive Robert's embrace. Gripping me by the shoulders, he kissed me on both cheeks – 'Welcome! Welcome!' He kissed me a third time: '*Thrice* welcome I bid you, grand-nephew!'

Slightly astonished, I glanced at Beryl, who pulled a comical face. 'Third time lucky, I suppose! Hello, Simon. You look awfully *hot!*'

Laughing, I went over to kiss her. She was unchanged apart from her greying hair and a slight stoop. With a gasp of relief I threw off my jacket and let it fall, symbolically, onto the drive.

'There's a drought, you know,' said Robert, turning to look up balefully at the parched mountains above us. 'I own half the water in Deya, apparently, but we're always the last to get any—'

'Oh, *Robert!* Simon doesn't want to hear about the dratted *drought*—!'

Robert ignored her and went straight into his usual 'what I've been doing today' routine: 'I've just had a cable from Sam Spiegel in Switzerland – he's asked me to collaborate on a film about T.E. Lawrence. I told him to come here and help peel the potatoes. He wants someone called Albert Finney to play Lawrence. Have you heard of him?'

'Yes, of course,' I answered. 'He's very good—'

'Ah, here's Juan,' sighed Beryl with relief, '—and Lucia—'

I looked in amazement – an amazement I struggled to hide – at the boy almost my age who was walking towards us down the drive. Like me he had grown, but out of all recognition. He was nearly as tall as Robert now, but his sun-bleached hair had turned dark, and he approached us with the strangely awkward, diffident air of someone who knew they were being watched, and hated it, leaning to one side in embarrassment as he held out his hand.

'Hey, Simon... cool!' I stared at him in disbelief. He'd become an American!

'Juan!' I gasped. 'How wonderful to see you – and Lucia—'

Lucia I'd have known anywhere, her toes turned out in the same dancer's walk, the same dark hair (though down to her shoulders now), the same serious, demure little mouth parting in a guarded smile as she came up and held out her hand— 'Hello, Simon,' she said, as though that were the end of the matter.

'I'm so sorry we couldn't come and meet you—' began Beryl hurriedly—

'I had to go to the doctor in Soller,' Robert interrupted. 'I've got the collywobbles – too much gas – and I don't mean the stuff Americans put in their cars!'

'Yes, well, we won't go into *that*, if it's all the same to you,' said Beryl firmly, 'but it's made us late, so we're still in the middle of lunch.' She beamed at me. 'We've kept yours hot for you, in case you were hungry. Come on up to the house.'

'Yes, there's someone I want you to meet!' exclaimed Robert. 'She must have held back – very properly – family reunion and all that—!'

'I'll just pay the driver—' I reached down for my jacket—

'No, no, we have an account – and it's nothing, anyway. Juan will bring your bags – come on, come and meet Margot – you'll like her!'

I glanced round and pulled a doubtful face at Beryl. 'It's all right,' she laughed, 'she's very *nice*!'

Robert was already half way up the drive as I set off after him, past the low wall of the terrace towards the kitchen doorway where he held aside the fly curtain impatiently.

I hurried the last few yards and ducked under his arm, forgetting the step and stumbling, with a curse, from dazzling sunlight into the cool darkness of the familiar kitchen – aware of Robert barging past me—'Don't worry, you'll soon get the hang of it again – come on!'

I followed him blindly, his bulk blocking out the light coming through the doorway of the dining room, then stepping from darkness back into streaming light—

'*Margot – Simon! Simon – Margot!*' he cried triumphantly, like a magician – and for an instant it was as though I'd been taken in by nothing more than the illusion of someone standing against the window on the far side of the dining table, her slender body molten in the sunlight. Blundering towards her past Robert's chair, I tried to adjust to the glare as I held out my hand, but her white shirt was ablaze, and the closer I got to the window the more dazzling she became—

She held out her hand just as I raised mine to shield my eyes, so we missed completely the first time.

'I'm so sorry,' I stammered, 'I can't quite see you—'

Dark hair, clouds of it—

I dropped my hand again, to shake hers, just as she raised hers to shield her extraordinary grey eyes, 'I'm so sorry,' she mimicked, and started to laugh, a low, happy sound, so spontaneous and infectious that I didn't even realise I'd joined in at first as I tried to make out her face, which she tilted this way and that, almost convulsed now as she offered me her stunning profiles, then threw back her head—

Robert was staring at us in astonishment, laughing, but seeming unsure why, and disliking it— '*I say, have you two met before?*' he yelled suddenly.

Behind him, the others had crowded into the dining room, bemused by our behaviour at first, then somehow swept up in our weird intoxication, even the dogs, who began to bark hysterically. I glanced round at my grand-uncle, no longer happy now, but increasingly desperate, eyes suddenly violent with a strange inner panic—

'No, that's *enough – stop it!*' he shouted. '*Stop it, I say!*'

As I helped Juan carry my bags upstairs we could still hear the recriminations wafting faintly from the dining room and across the hall below us—

'For heaven's sake, Robert, it's time you got over this stupid thing about *noise*—!'

'No, I know, I'm sorry—'

'We were only laughing—' Margot's voice, low and impatient—

'No, I know—'

'—you should have gone outside if you couldn't bear it—'

I'd never heard anyone except Beryl or Karl argue with Robert.

'She's extraordinary!' I hissed at Juan. 'Who is she?'

'Margot? She's father's… "muse" – you know – his inspiration.' He stopped and glanced back at me, as if to gauge my reaction. 'He writes poems to her—'

'Oh… yes…' I thought back. 'Wasn't there someone before, when I was last here?'

His eyes widened dramatically 'Judith!' he exclaimed in a triumphant whisper, as if he'd answered a $64,000 question.

'That's it—'

'Margot's completely different – unique—' He looked extraordinary, like an evangelist.

'You're not kidding.' We grinned at each other, then went on up the stairs. 'Not that I ever met Judith. It's funny, but I always thought muses were meant to be ancient Greek or Roman, not American—'

'Margot's half Greek,' he exclaimed. 'Or half Italian… I can't remember. Her last name's "Callas". The rest of her is Canadian. She's cool, man! And I mean… *cool*!'

'She certainly is,' I breathed. 'How old is she?'

'Twenty-four…? I think.'

To my surprise, he led me into his elder brother William's room at the top of the stairs, where my mother had slept last time. 'Aren't I sleeping in your room?' I asked.

Slinging my case onto the narrow bed, he smiled sheepishly. 'Mother thought it would be best… I don't sleep very well at the moment…'

'No, of course—!' I said quickly, relieved in a way. 'Where's William?'

185

'He's staying in England this summer.'

'Oh.' Although William was my mother's favourite, we'd never really seemed to hit it off for some reason. Someone else was missing, I realised. 'What about Tomás?' I asked. 'Where's he?'

Juan grinned, his eyes widening again. 'He's staying with his *Papás del Clot* this summer – his sort of adopted Majorcan family, down in the *Clot*. He loves it there—'

'Don't Robert and Beryl mind?'

'No, not at all! He's happy there. Here, it's too frantic in summer – hey! It's really good to see you again!' he burst out suddenly, clenching his fists and see-sawing them backwards and forwards in little bopping movements before looking away again, unable quite to meet my eyes.

'You too!' I exclaimed, relieved to recognise something of the old Juan at last. I was about to ask him about his American accent when Lucia called up from downstairs that my lunch was on the table.

The old Juan vanished as fleetingly as he'd appeared.

'Go!' he said urgently. 'You first!'

But by the time I'd reached the hall he still hadn't come down.

As I entered the dining room the strained atmosphere felt like bad weather until Lucia suddenly breezed in from the kitchen, humming, either uncaring or simply oblivious. 'Father's very sorry,' she said matter-of-factly as she plonked a fruit bowl onto the table, 'he didn't mean to *shout* – did you, Father?'

The tension in the room eased at once.

'No, it's loud noises, you see—' Robert began.

'I know,' I said at once, 'I remember – I'm sorry—'

He was standing by his chair at the head of the table, his huge fingers pushing agitatedly against his sinuses as he tried to clear them—'and there's something about hysteria – people out of control—'

'Simon, go and sit over there, between Margot and Father,' interrupted Lucia.

I dared myself to look at Margot, if only to confirm my first impression of her – and quickly looked away from her sudden, radiant smile, the forgotten worm of laughter in the pit of my stomach already wriggling again.

As Robert sucked in his stomach to let me through, he inadvertently let off both barrels of a pent-up fart. 'Blasted wind!' he muttered irritably as I slipped past in front of him. 'Sorry—'

Not daring to look at Margot, I sat down too quickly, forgetting the cornerpost of the table and barking my knee on it – a familiar pain – but at least it cured me of my longing to laugh. As I picked up my knife and fork I realised that steaming lamb stew and vegetables were the last things I wanted to eat.

'My new medicine might help,' Robert muttered hopefully, 'although he said the whole thing was probably psychosomatic—'

'I'm not surprised!' said Beryl tartly. 'If you didn't get in such a *state* about things...' She was sitting next to Lucia, who was eating an orange with her mouth open. I looked away.

'No, I know,' Robert interrupted hurriedly, then fixed me with a smile. 'How's my favourite niece-your-mother?'

'Fine, thank you. She sent tons of love—' I knew he'd sent her a cheque just before I came.

'And my brother Dick?'

'Not very well.' My grandfather had been coughing a lot recently, and losing weight.

'Oh, I'm sorry!' He sounded genuinely concerned. 'I'll write to him. He saved my bacon once, in Cairo. Did you know that?'

'Yes—'

He switched his glance to Margot. 'When I first went there he was Labour Adviser – to King Faroukh, I think – or was it us – the British, I mean? Anyway, I was flat broke and he got me a job teaching English. Did you know that I was probably single-handedly responsible for the Suez Crisis?'

When Margot said nothing, I glanced round at her. She was shaking her head, her smile glued politely to the corners of her mouth.

'One of my brightest pupils was a charming young fellow called Gamal Abdul Nasser—' He paused dramatically.

'*No!*' she exclaimed mockingly. 'Not *the* Gamal Abdul Nasser—!'

'Yes!' – he didn't seem to notice – 'which just goes to show that there's a lot to be said for keeping people in ignorance. I mean, if I hadn't taught Nasser to speak English—'

'—*he might never have come to power, and the Suez crisis might never have happened!*' Margot finished for him – too quickly, too loudly.

'Yes...' Robert stared at her, looking deflated. 'You're still cross—'

She stared back at him, her face immutable.

Robert pulled a stricken face at me, then suddenly lumbered to his feet, grabbed the salt cellar from the table, and balanced it on top of his head.

'*I'm very sorry I shouted at everyone!*' he declared, like child forced to apologise publicly.

Lucia laughed, then choked on her mouthful of orange.

'For heaven's *sake*, Robert,' groaned Beryl, grinning across at me as she thumped Lucia on the back. 'Sit down! You'll spill the salt, and then you'll have bad luck on top of everything *else*—'

'I shan't sit down until you've all forgiven me!'

We forgave him as one – even Margot – and he removed the salt cellar from his head as he sat down again with a smirk at me. 'Would you care for some salt? You seem to be making heavy weather of your lunch—'

'No, it's fine – really—' I protested. 'It's just the heat.'

The conversation moved on to my life on *The Manchester Guardian*, where I'd worked for almost two years.

'Will they let you go on writing bits and pieces when you're in Madrid?' asked Robert. He was trying to sound casual, but my instincts told me that the question was loaded in some way.

'So they said,' I answered carefully. Since I'd been promoted from general dogsbody to the honorary title of sub-secretary to Gerard Fay, the London Editor, I'd been allowed to try my hand at writing. 'As long as I know enough about the subject—' I could feel the jaws of a trap closing around me and tried to distract him by putting my knife and fork together and throwing Beryl an apologetic look. 'I'm sorry,' I smiled, 'I'm afraid I'm full up. It was delicious – I've only left the bones, really—'

'Oh, *good*!' she exclaimed. 'I was hoping you would – the dogs can have them for supper—'

But far from losing his thread, Robert used it to truss me like a Christmas turkey. 'Talking of bones,' he murmured triumphantly as his hand darted to my plate to help himself to the one nearest him, 'I have one to pick with you!' His pale blue eyes stared at me intently as he sucked on it.

'Robert, that's all over and done with!' interrupted Beryl sharply. 'There was no harm done—'

'No, but there might have been—' Robert insisted.

The first piece I'd been allowed to write for the paper, for the *London Letter* column, had been about the sale of some of his manuscripts to the University of Texas. Robert had given me the scoop on condition that I didn't disclose the staggering sum he'd been paid for them.

I was suddenly aware that he'd fixed me with his 'scolding' look, his mouth turned down, his under lip jutting out like a crabby old schoolmaster's. 'Hold out your hand, boy!' he demanded half-jokingly, raising his right arm.

In the spirit of the joke I held out my hand, palm up, at which he brought down his huge bunch of fives like bludgeon, in a stinging slap which barked my knuckles on the table. Then he burst out laughing.

'*Ouch!*' I gasped.

'Robert, how *could* you?' exclaimed Beryl.

'*Father*—!' Even Lucia was shocked.

'It's all right—' I said quickly. 'It's fine – honestly—'

'Sorry,' he pulled a face, 'I only meant it in fun! I forget my own strength sometimes. But you did deserve it—' He glanced uneasily at Margot. She was looking down, fiddling with the fork on my plate, her face concealed by a wild thicket of her hair—

Did I deserve it?

Apart from the fact that he'd written to me at the time, blowing me up (which made me think the subject was closed), I hadn't actually said anything in my original article about the money he'd received. When I'd filed the piece, I'd written '*for an undisclosed sum*', as he'd asked me to. But later that day Michael Wall, one of the Leader Writers who'd been asked to approve it, asked me casually, when we were having a pee, how much Robert had actually got for his manuscripts, and like a fool I'd told him – thirty thousand pounds—

So yes, I suppose I did deserve it.

Robert was under attack from all sides, Lucia demanding to know how he could do such a thing on my first day, Beryl repeating that no harm had been done by the article – on the contrary, his standing had shot up in the eyes of the Inland Revenue, quite apart from public opinion, while Margot—

I looked round – she still hadn't said a word—

She was sprawled over the table next to me, cheek resting on her hand as she toyed with my plate. I looked at the food I'd left and saw that she'd turned it into a landscape – the burnt mashed potato forming the cliffs of a narrow bay, lapped by a sea of gravy, the cliffs sprinkled with chopped greens to represent trees, the lumps of meat and bone piled up against them at one end to form a rocky beach—

'The *cala*!' I exclaimed delightedly.

'*What on earth are you doing, Margot?*' cried Lucia, staring indignantly at the plate. '*That's perfectly good food!*'

Margot was on her feet in a single fluid movement, scraping her hair back with her fingers, painfully, as if she'd like to pull it out by the roots. 'Who's for a swim?' she demanded, her voice tight with claustrophobia.

MARGOT

The Land Rover bounced and yawed down the dusty track to Son Bujosa, the farmhouse at the top of the endless path that led down to the *cala*. Margot was handling it with an assurance that was wonderful to watch, not fighting the uneven rocks beneath us as a man might have done, but allowing the wheels to find their own way over the rough ground, making small corrections only when necessary.

Expecting a rough ride, I'd jammed myself against the passenger door, one arm sticking out through the sliding window beside me so I could grip the gutter on the roof, but my fingers were already limp with trust.

She'd hardly said a word since we'd roared away from the gates of Canellun.

In the end, I was the only one who'd been able to go and swim with her, and I wondered uneasily if she was already regretting her offer.

'Is Juan *all right*?' The words were jolted out of me as the Land Rover bounced on down the track. We were coming into the clearing, and I was unnerved by her continued silence. Ahead of us stretched the shallow terraces which I'd once been convinced were haunted.

'Why do you ask?' she frowned, racing across the dried red earth of the clearing and pulling up in the shade of two *algarroba* trees. She switched off the engine and turned to me.

Her gaze, in the sudden, intense silence, was luminous. I had to nerve myself to go on. 'He's just so... *different*,' I began tentatively, trying to feel my way with her. 'I mean, he seems to be allergic to the sun now, which is crazy, because he used to love it – he was always half naked, completely wild, getting into one scrape after another... but just now I found him lying on his bed with the shutters drawn, strumming his guitar, fully dressed, and when I asked him to come with us he said the sun made his brain swell...'

I turned to look at her again. '*Does* it?'

She shrugged vaguely and stared out through the windscreen. 'I don't know... if he says so, then I suppose it must... it's just Robert,' she added, almost as an afterthought.

'What do you mean?'

'Juan can't live up to him...' She looked around us slowly, her gaze distracted. 'Not many people can...' Her voice faded away. She seemed lost in thought. 'Do you think there's something strange about this place?' she asked quietly.

I glanced at her sharply, to see if she was pulling my leg, but she was still staring out through the window.

'Yes,' I answered, in a voice as quiet as hers, my heart leaping at the thought that she could feel it too. 'I was thinking about it just now, as we came down the track. When I was here before I remember being convinced it was haunted – not by ghosts—' I broke off suddenly, self-consciously—

'By what, then?' she asked.

I pulled a dismissive sort of face. 'Oh, nothing really – I was probably just being childish—'

'Oh, come on!' Again that frown. 'We've all thought silly things when we were kids – and maybe some things weren't so silly. If they weren't ghosts, what were they?'

Her impatient stare was hypnotic, draining my will—

'Gods,' I croaked, and quickly cleared my throat. I expected her to laugh, but she just looked surprised. 'Not dead things, like ghosts,' I went on hurriedly, 'but *living* things... like ideas, if you see what I mean? I mean, I know gods aren't supposed to exist, that they're only myths, but we still think about them, don't we, so they *must* exist... if only in our heads,' I finished lamely.

She gave me a quirky sort of look. 'Why not?' she said lightly. 'I mean, who knows...? Perhaps we should ask your great-uncle—'

'*Grand*-uncle,' I said automatically, and quoted Robert as nearly as I could remember: '*Great is for ships and railway lines; grand is for fathers, uncles—!*'

'It's too hot in here,' she cut in suddenly, grabbing her basket and getting out. 'Come on, let's go swim—'

Numbly, I reached for my towel as she slammed her door, and then realised, with a stab of despair, that I'd left my swimming trunks behind. In the distraction of talking to Juan, I'd forgotten them.

'Come on!' she called impatiently, already half way across the clearing.

Grabbing my empty towel, I ran after her.

'So tell me about *you*,' she said as I fell in beside her.

An abyss of insignificance opened instantly inside my head. 'There's nothing to tell—'

'Oh, don't be an ass,' she said irritably, 'of course there's something to tell! Things must have happened to you – in fact I know they have – and you obviously feel things. Loosen up! Let's start again. How old are you? No one seems quite sure—'

'Seventeen. Eighteen in August—'

'You sound impatient – to be older, I mean. Well, don't worry, you soon will be, and then you'll wish you weren't—'

'I just think age is utterly irrelevant – an anachronism!' I burst out (was that what I meant—?)

'My, what big words you've got, Grandma!' she teased.

'No, I mean it!' I blundered on. 'I think it's how you behave that counts, not your age. For instance, I know that you're twenty-four, but you could be—'

195

'My, what big ears you've got, too!' She looked at me sharply. 'Who's been gossiping? Oh – Juan…'

'He wasn't gossiping,' I assured her quickly, 'I just asked him, and he told me.'

She snorted – with amusement? 'What else did he say?'

I was instantly tongue-tied. It was all very well for her, but I'd only just arrived and didn't know the rules yet – how far I could go—

'That bad, huh?'

'*No*,' I protested, 'nothing bad at all! He really likes you—'

She walked on, staring straight ahead as though I were no longer there. I couldn't bear it, even for a few seconds. 'Look, all he said was that you were Robert's… muse…' I waited anxiously for her reaction.

'Aaaah…!' she said at last, with the hint of a smile.

'Do you mind if I ask you something?' I began, encouraged by her smile.

She stopped dead and turned on me. '*Don't do that!* How can I possibly say if I mind when I don't know the question? I hate it when people do that! Just ask the question – don't *ask* if you can ask it!'

I felt the sweat on my face and neck go cold with shock. 'I'm sorry—'

The tension suddenly went out of her, and she shook her head wearily. 'No, *I'm* sorry,' she said. 'I'm in a bate…' she gave me a sidelong look. 'Is that the right word?'

'Yes.' I so wanted her to know that I was aware, that I understood. 'When we were in the dining room at lunch, when you suddenly got up—'

Her eyes narrowed again, warningly. 'What was your question?' she asked.

'It doesn't matter—'

'Oh, just ask it, for Christ sake!'

'All I wanted to know…' I took a deep breath, 'was what a muse… *does*, exactly?' I stared at her intently, poised for anything.

But she just stood there, her smile slowly fading into a different beauty, serious, downcast—

I found myself wishing I hadn't asked. 'It doesn't matter—'

'No—' she looked away. 'I just wish I could give you a straight answer...' Her voice was barely audible. She screwed up her eyes against the sun. 'But the rules are strict – complicated... secret... you must promise not to tell anyone...'

'Of course! I promise—!'

'No, I mean *really* promise – bindingly. You have to tie two things together in a knot, and they have to be yours – I can't give you anything of mine—'

I looked down at myself frantically – towel, T-shirt, shorts, socks, plimsolls—

'My laces!' I cried.

'Perfect...' she seemed to go into a trance, '...left to right, yin to yang, good to evil,' she intoned. *Crikey—!*

'Just don't forget you've tied them together.'

'I won't—!' I squatted down and quickly pulled at my laces.

'In fact, shoelaces make the most powerful knots of all,' she went on, still trance-like, as I tied them. 'Has Robert ever told you about the little *cordonnier*, the shoemaker in French folklore?'

'No.' I looked up at her enquiringly; her French accent was perfect. But she seemed to have lost interest.

'Doesn't matter... OK, when you're ready, take the knot in your right hand and swear after me: *I promise not to reveal what Margot tells me, not even to Robert!*'

Uneasily, I did as she asked, then stood up.

'What was your question again?' she asked vaguely.

'What does a muse *do*, exactly?' I repeated, as nearly as I could remember.

Her face burst into a triumphant grin. 'Why, she a-*muses* herself, of course!' she cried—

And she was gone, racing down the path as my unbelieving brain caught up with her words and sent me after her with a cry of outrage – only to crash face down onto the path because I'd forgotten my laces were tied together.

Winded, cursing myself for falling for the oldest trick in the book, I stared up from the painful ruts and stones in the path to where she was stamping round in circles twenty yards away, her head thrown back so far that her face was parallel to the sky as she laughed, with such abandon that I found myself joining in, agonisingly, because what I longed to do was beat myself to death.

I did what I could to save face, easing my feet out of my plimsolls, clutching them together by their still-joined laces, then picking myself up as painfully as I could, looking as injured as possible, delighted to discover a cut on my knee which was bleeding impressively—

'Hey, you're hurt—!' She'd come to a standstill, no longer laughing now.

'Not really—' I faked a feeble groan and straightened up, exaggerating my limp as I moved towards her. But something in my expression must have given me away, because she suddenly turned tail again with a cry, and bolted, just as I broke into a run.

I chased after her, yelling with frustration, not only because she ran like the wind, even with her basket clutched to her side – *but because even if I caught her I knew I couldn't lay hands on her*—

She raced into the avenue of pine trees, my nostrils suddenly filled with their hot, familiar scent as I woke up to where we were – by the square stone tower where Juan and I—

For a moment I thought that Juan must have shown Margot his rubble, his secret of the existence of nothing, because instead of running on down the path she was heading straight for the arch of stone steps which led up to the roof, laughing again now – and I soon realised why. Although I'd almost halved the distance between us, the moment I left the path and tried to follow her in my stockinged feet I began to skid around helplessly on the carpet of pine needles which covered the bare rock, my socks and feet pierced again and again, until I was dragged to a halt by the growing pain of trying to reach her.

'*Pax?*' She was half way up the stone steps, leaning on one knee, grinning down at me.

'*Pax?*' I howled, '*Look at me*—!' I felt like the victim of some mythic curse. A few moments ago I'd been walking along the path, all neat and tidy and trying to appear intelligent, and here I was panting and sweating, covered in blood and filth, my feet turned into porcupines—

Still grinning, she turned away to climb the rest of the steps to the roof. 'Come on up!' she called.

I hobbled towards the tower and followed her up the steps, leaning forward so that I could climb with my hands as well; there was no handrail, and if I looked to my left I knew that there was nothing but a sheer drop falling hundreds of feet into the gorge below. I'd never got over my fear of heights—

'Have you been up here before?' she called down. 'I suppose you must have—'

'No. It was out of bounds when we were children.'

When my eyes came level with the roof, the shock of what I saw almost paralysed me – Margot standing on top of the low crumbling parapet at the farthest corner, on the brink of death—

'*Don't – please*—!' the words were out before I could stop them.

Staring fixedly at the steps beneath me, I crawled onto the roof and slumped down with my back against the parapet on the landward side, as if my weight might somehow counterbalance hers and restore the equilibrium – prevent her from falling—

She'd turned back to me with a puzzled frown. 'What's up?'

'I'm sorry – I hate heights—' I tried to look up at her again, but couldn't.

There was a hollow tremor beneath me as she jumped lightly down onto the roof. '*Hate* them,' she asked, 'or *fear* them? There's a difference—'

199

Surprised, I opened my eyes and squinted up at her, but she was standing in front of the sun and I couldn't make out her expression. 'All right,' I said grudgingly, 'I suppose I'm afraid of them—'

'Even though you're nowhere near the edge?' She sounded disbelieving.

'That's not the point – in fact it's almost worse, because then you imagine the worst. I thought I was you, looking down – falling – ugh!' I covered my eyes with my hand.

'Well, if it makes you feel any better, I can't stand being shut in—'

'Really?' I was surprised. 'I love it!' I started to pull at the knot on my plimsolls. 'When I was a kid, we stayed with a cousin on Sark. She was the only one with the key to the tiny prison there. I used to lock myself up in it all day. Just the feeling of iron bars, of being caged... at least bars keep you safe—'

'Not me they don't!' She murmured.

I pulled off my socks and began to pick the pine needles out of them as she sat down on the parapet next to me. 'Why don't you just chuck 'em?' she asked.

I looked round at her, startled. She gestured at my socks, and I stared down at them, frowning – and past them, at my bare white legs, at the faint dark hairs which made them look grey and slug-like. I lowered them furtively, then crossed them, covering as much of them as I could with my arms.

'Don't worry,' she said casually, 'you'll soon get a tan—'

'Why?' I asked, pretending not to have heard her. 'I mean, why chuck my socks away?'

'Well, they must be stifling – and besides, if you don't mind my saying so, you look just a little out of place in those clothes. Did you buy them specially? I mean, are they *de rigeur* in England?'

'No, of course not!' I looked down at them in sudden hatred. 'They're just my old games clothes from school—'

'Ah! and you wish you were still at school—!'

'*No bloody fear—!*'

'Then chuck the lot of them! Your socks will do for now – I don't want to get you arrested. Here, give them to me—' she whipped them out of my hands and began rolling them up.

I made a grab for them, fearing they might smell, but she simply jumped up and moved away. 'You're not a schoolboy any more, you said so yourself. Hang on—' She found a lump of broken stucco in the corner and stuffed it into the ball of my socks. 'Here—' she held them out to me, 'you have to throw them as far as you can—'

'I can't—!'

'Yes you can. You won't fall, I promise.' She reached down to me. I took her hand instantly and suddenly found myself standing in front of her without the least memory of rising to my feet – just my heart thundering in my chest—

With a grin of daring she dumped the socks in my hand like a grenade. 'Chuck 'em,' she commanded, 'as far as you can! Into the gorge—!'

Mesmerised, I clutched the ball of my socks and then, incredibly, found myself running across the roof shouting '*Into the sun—!*', flinging it with all my might into the blindingness. '*Burn—!*'

With my knees pressed fearlessly against the parapet, shading my eyes with both hands, I watched as the migrainous blot arched through the sky—

'Keep watching—!' She was already standing beside me, her hand on my shoulder, the ball falling in front of the wall of mountains, seeming to come closer and closer as it fell, until it disappeared into the gorge below without a sound.

'There!' she murmured triumphantly, and began to chant 'No more Latin, no more French,' as she swept up her basket and made a run for the stairs, '—no more sitting on a hard school bench—!'

We ran like the wind, laughing, shouting at each other every stupid school rhyme we could think of, through the tunnelled shade of the Italian pines to where the donkey steps zigzagged down the steep hillside to the *cala*.

My spirit soared at the memory of her hand on my shoulder, at the sudden freedom I felt. It was as if, magically, she'd smashed some link in a chain that had shackled me to my childhood. I couldn't explain what she'd done, even to myself, nor how she'd done it, but something dark within me had vanished – some weight or pain that I'd lived with for so long that I'd mistaken it for a part of me. Gone! And in its place a sense of freedom that sent me flying after her, past her, bounding from rock to rock as I took almost sheer short cuts, like a goat, revelling in the danger – her presence, her closeness—

At the foot of the hill we were neck-and-neck as we raced round the last bend and onto the stony beach – so suddenly that I reeled to a halt as it raced towards us – the café, the fishing boats, the limpid blue sea – and found myself teetering, like Margot on the parapet, on the brink of a view that was so startling for the speed we'd come upon it that I had to pull back and stare at it again, if only to believe that it was still there, that it wasn't simply a trick of memory—

—*that nothing had changed*—!

'It's just the same!' I panted, laughing in disbelief, clutching my knees, fighting for breath. 'It hasn't even shrunk!' I glanced round at her. She was trying to catch her breath too, staring at me with her lips parted in a smile that yet again seemed to dare me to say more.

I looked back at the cove. 'It's not too late, you see! Usually when you go back somewhere, it's too late – everything's changed. You can never finish what you started. I mean, I always wanted to dive from that jetty over there—' I pointed to the far side of the cove, to where a boat house and slipway clung to the rocks, 'and it's still there! I can't remember why I was forbidden, but I can do it now—'

At that moment we heard the sound of voices above us, from the terrace of the café. A group of men and women were coming down, clutching the crude wooden handrails as they descended the steep cement steps – Americans by the sound of them, the women mostly middle-aged and over-made-up, with lengths of gaily-coloured material tied over their swimming costumes, gold bangles glinting on their wrists. Even from here I could see their painted fingernails, blood-red against the bleached railings.

One of the men, nut-brown, tall and balding, with a beard like a toupée, suddenly waved at us and called out Margot's name. *'How's Robert?'* he shouted.

'Fine, Fred… he's fine,' she called back, waving casually as she turned away.

'Who's that?' I asked, picking my way over the rocks.

'Fred Grunfeld,' she murmured. 'Don't you remember him? He's been here for years—'

I glanced back. They were crossing the bridge over the dry torrent, the man talking to the boy next to him now, about my age, wearing an American basketball vest over his black shorts, and specs. Something about him—

My gym shoes skidded on a rock, and I went sprawling. Margot burst out laughing.

Fuck! 'Who's that boy?' I asked, pretending nothing had happened, but she just laughed louder.

'Foster Grunfeld,' she said finally. 'Do you remember him?'

'Vaguely…'

We'd only taken a few paces onto the beach before she suddenly turned back to me. 'Too many people, goddammit!' she said under her breath. 'It gets worse every day—' Already the sunbathers were beginning to notice her. *'Hi, Margot—!'* *'Hey –Margot—!'* *'Margot, how lovely to see you!'* Murmuring their names, she raised a hand in acknowledgement, then turned to look over my shoulder. I glanced back. The party of Americans was following us onto the beach, threatening to hem us in. 'You said you always wanted to dive off the jetty, right—?'

Quickly making our way along the foot of the cliffs, behind the sunbathers who were all facing the sun out to sea, no longer noticing us, we reached the jetty at last, far enough away from the beach to make us indistinct to them. Margot led the way to the middle, to where a bastion of rock formed a kind of layby where the cement had been extended to incorporate it into the jetty.

Kicking off her espadrilles, she dropped her basket and started to unbutton her shirt and jeans. I looked at her askance, transfixed, as she took them off. Underneath she was wearing a simple black swimsuit – not the kind that I'd seen my mother and her friends wearing, with modesty panels and built-in corsets and leg bands like tourniquets – but like a dancer's leotard, of such thin material, like stretched silk, that it seemed to be part of her body, and yet so demure—

She reached down into her basket, bending effortlessly from the waist like a dancer, rummaging for something, her slender arms moving languidly, fluently, as if to music, before she found what she wanted – a red ribbon – and straightened up, her body stretching backwards like a drawn bow, arms raised, elbows out, one hand slipping the ribbon between her teeth before joining the fingers of her other hand as they buried themselves in the dark hair at the nape of her neck, pulling it upwards and back from her face, emphasising her cheekbones, her slanting grey eyes, her long slender neck now suddenly bare and vulnerable—

'My, what big eyes you've got, Grandma!' she grated between her clenched teeth.

'Sorry!' I looked away, flushing as I got to my feet, yet still aware, out of the corner of my eye, of her mocking gaze following me.

I moved to the end of the jetty, where I stood with my back to her, fuming at myself.

'*Last one in's a sissy*—!' I was blown aside by the speed of her passing, feet hissing on the concrete, her body leaping, arching through the air in a dive so fast and shallow that she slit open the still sea like an arrow and vanished, as if into another dimension.

The silence that rushed in after her was profound, uncanny, smoothing her wake, its eyes turned back on me watchfully as the shimmering streak of her body began to merge upwards towards the surface of the sea, farther away, no longer transparent there, her arms and legs blurred until the moment when she broke through the surface in a crawl already formed and powerful, carrying her to the far side of the cove.

Still deaf to everything, I stared after her, awestruck, until at last my ears 'popped', and the sounds of the cove became suddenly too clear, amplified by a return to consciousness, by the sheer cliffs that hemmed it in – the cries and splashes of children playing among the rocks, the clink of glasses on the terrace of the café on the far side of the cove. It was like Breughel's painting of *The Fall of Icarus* – none of them had witnessed what I'd seen or felt—

I took a deep breath and dived in after her, into the deafening embrace of the warm, familiar sea – back into my remembered world at last – and yet no longer mine, I realised with a jolt as I forced myself deeper and deeper. From the moment I'd stepped onto the *cala* it had become Margot's world – and yet not even hers, because we'd been driven to the farthest corner by people she could hardly bring herself to acknowledge. It belonged to neither of us any more. If it belonged to anyone, it was to the last person to stumble upon it for the first time and make it theirs.

Under water, out of sight and sound of the beach, I felt a sudden rush of 'place', of joy at returning to where had once been mine, and when my aching lungs forced me back to the surface, it was as that eleven-year-old who had dived his last dive into the timeless waters of the cove and now re-emerged as a man at last. Even so, my eyes were drawn instinctively to my left, to the ledge of rock far above the sea, where Juan had dared me... to the terrace of the café where Alastair had dived in after me, fully-dressed—

'Simon—?'

Margot was standing on the end of the jetty, where a moment before there had been no one—

I choked on some sea water and turned away from her to cough it up. Had she simply conjured herself? Or had I been so immersed in the past, before Margot had existed to us—?

I struggled to regain buoyancy, my rhythm haywire suddenly. With a grunt of frustration I launched myself into a sidestroke which brought me up to the jetty so fast that I had to back-paddle to stop myself colliding with it.

Margot looked unimpressed. 'What on earth were you doing out there?' she demanded. 'I thought you'd seen a *medusa* or something!'

'Just ghosts—' I spluttered, picking my way carefully among the minefield of black sea urchins under the water. 'Can you make yourself invisible?'

'Don't *you* start—!' She reached down and offered me her hand.

'What do you mean?' I looked up at her in surprise. 'And what's a *medusa*?'

'A jellyfish—' She waggled her hand impatiently and I took it, even though it would have been easier not to. 'Mind the sea urchins,' she said as I pulled myself out of the sea, in such a rush, to dazzle her, that my thin running shorts were dragged down my thighs.

'Fuck—!' I gasped, letting go and throwing myself back into the water. 'Sorry—'

'Oh, just kick the damn things off!' She was grinning, but irritated. 'You look as if you're wearing swimming trunks underneath anyway. I mean, who cares?'

'Nobody wears white swimming trunks!' I protested.

'So start a fashion! *Jesus—!*'

Goaded by her impatience, I struggled out of my shorts, half drowning in the process, and slung them up onto the jetty. Scooping them up, she flung them as far as she could across the cove where they hit the water with the cold wet slap of finality, and melted away.

'At this rate you'll be stark naked by the time we get back to Canellun! Here—' she held out her hand again, laughing.

This time I came out of the sea more carefully. I couldn't afford to lose anything else. Once on the jetty I turned away from her, looking down at the front of my briefs to make sure they were clean—

Later, after exploring the rocks and caves of the bay, beyond where I'd been allowed to swim as a boy, we sat on the jetty for an hour or so, side by side, close enough to feel each other's heat, elbows resting on knees, our backs propped against the rock, soaking up the sun. Self-conscious, yet basking in my near nakedness (imposed and therefore legitimate – yet unfamiliar and disturbing, my eyes flying open now and then, as if I were drunk, to stop my thoughts from falling – to make sure we were still alone—)

I squinted across the cove at the beach, and at the sun... going down... not sunset yet, but sinking, the café already in shadow, tucked into the dusk of the huge rocks that sheltered it...

I glanced round at Margot, still facing into the sun, eyes closed...

My glance became a gaze, my gaze a hunger, my hunger theft as I stole from her everything I could lay my eyes on, cramming my head with images which I could pore over later—

What was I doing? I looked away guiltily, the image of her body so imprinted on my brain that it took a moment to register the flotilla of faces bobbing towards us – Fred Grunfeld and his friends, to judge from the sun gleaming on his balding brown pate. No Foster, though. I looked round at Margot. She looked as if she were asleep—

'I think we're about to be invaded,' I said quietly, so as not to alarm her. Her eyes flew open, like a bird of prey's.

'Oh, well...' she sighed. 'Time to go anyway—' In a single lithe movement she was on her feet, stretching languidly and looking me up and down with a faint grin.

'What—?' I asked.

'Nothing...' She looked over to where Fred and the others were swimming towards us. 'Why, oh why,' she murmured under her breath, 'can't you fucking well leave me alone?'

Fred waved to her from the water, and shouted: 'You looked so idyllic, we thought we'd come and call on you!'

'Oh, that's too bad, Fred!' she called back like a regretful hostess. 'We're just on our way out, but do ring for tea!'

He was good natured enough to laugh, albeit uneasily.

Another man in the group, a huge fellow with matted black hair and a beard, flashed a gleaming smile at her. 'Just now I thought you had a girl with you,' he yelled in an American accent, 'in little white panties and no bra—!'

Margot lazily pointed a finger at him, like a gun, and pulled the trigger. 'Maybe that explains why your wife left you, Nathan!'

As she blew the smoke from her fingertip, there was a chorus of astonished gasps, and even a couple of American-style cheers from the women. The man stopped swimming and punched the water with his fist. '*Goddamit*, Margot, if you were a man—!'

'Oh, shut up, Nathan!' commanded Fred. 'You asked for it—' Treading water now, he looked up at me with an apologetic smile. 'I'm sorry about that. He didn't mean anything—'

'I forgot my swimming trunks,' I replied woodenly, wishing they'd all drown and take the memory of my pale body and skimpy underwear to their graves.

But they were treading water now, watching Margot, wary of coming any nearer until she'd signalled her intentions.

She played up to them wonderfully, outstaring them with a faint smile as she adjusted the ribbon round her hair.

'Won't you introduce us?' Fred called over politely.

Margot took her time. I thought she wasn't going to say anything, and was on the point, reluctantly, of introducing myself, when she drawled: 'This is Simon – Robert's grand-nephew—'

'Oh, shit,' muttered one of the women under her breath. I took an instant liking to her.

'Simon!' Fred beamed hugely. 'Do you remember me? I'm Fred Grunfeld, and this is Lady June, and Annie, Jackie, Nathan – it's been quite a while—'

'Yes. How do you do?' I said coolly but politely.

With a lopsided grin, he gestured surrender with his palms. 'Look, we'll just leave both you to it, OK? See you around—'

He turned back for the shore, the others following with a barbed chorus of goodbyes – all except the black-bearded Nathan, who floated away on his back, leering at Margot over the gleaming mound of his hairy brown belly. Something distracted him suddenly, up on the cliffs above us.

'Hey, *Vern!*' he yelled. 'What's that stickin' out of your shorts?'

'*Oh, Jesus, Nathan—!*' A thin, reedy voice from behind the boathouse—'You damn well know what it is—!'

'Did you get any shots yet?'

There was no answer from the man behind the boat house, but he must have signalled something because the fat man hooted with laughter. 'If you've got any of Margot, just you make sure you let me see 'em, Vern!' He aimed his finger lazily at Margot and fired off a round— '*Peeehooo* to you too!'

With a grin, he blew the smoke from his fingertip, rolled onto his stomach, and headed after the others in a messy, frenzied crawl.

Without a word, Margot turned and reached down into her basket to take out her shirt. 'That was Nathan Mazzini,' she murmured, 'local crook and drug pusher. Vern pretends to be a photographer, although he's nothing more than a peeping Tom. He uses his money to buy people, so they tolerate him, scratch his back – *Hey, Vern!*' she yelled suddenly towards the boathouse. 'You can come out now – I'm nearly dressed!'

There was an embarrassed silence.

'Hey, no, that's OK—!' His weedy voice drifted down to us as he appeared round the corner of the boathouse, ducking slightly as if expecting a hail of stones, a tall, scrawny man with a pot belly and long tartan shorts and the sort of trimmed beard I'd only ever seen on Greek coins.

'Hi!' he called down feebly. Reassured that we weren't going to attack him, he pulled out the camera that he'd been shielding with his body and which hung from a long strap round his neck. 'I was just trying out my new telephoto lens—'

'How long have you been up there, Vern?' Margot called up to him casually.

'Hey, I just got here—!'

'Liar!' she said under her breath. She looked up at him knowingly. 'Have you been taking pictures of me, Vern?'

'No!' He looked towards the *cala*. 'Hey, maybe a couple – you know—' he mumbled. 'I was just trying out my new lens – it's amazing—!'

Margot turned away, tearing the ribbon out of her hair and stuffing it into her basket, muttering, 'I *hate* being photographed!'

'Me too,' I agreed – but too glibly for her. She glared at me, and I struggled to justify myself. 'I mean, it's a kind of theft—' She gave a brusque nod as I looked away, trying to blot out the memory of stealing images of her body while her eyes were closed. 'Do you want me to do something? I could accidentally smash his camera on purpose—'

'Christ, you sound like Robert! No. There are enough feuds here without starting another one.'

An image from the past, of my father once dealing with a hostile photographer, galvanised me into shining armour. 'Look, just do what I ask, OK? No matter what. Trust me—!'

I ran along the jetty before she could say anything, and started to climb towards Vern.

'Hey—!' he called down in alarm, his hands closing protectively over the enormous cock-like lens of his camera.

'Hello—!' I called up brightly. 'I'm Simon—'

'Oh. Hi. I'm Vern,' he said grudgingly.

'I know.' I was panting as I reached him, 'Look, the thing is, Margot hates having her picture taken—'

'Hey, I don't just take pictures of *her*, you know!'

'No, of course not, but it's very difficult for her, being so beautiful and everything, and I just wondered—' I paused meaningfully.

'Yeah?'

'Well, I just wondered – if I were to take a picture of you and Margot... *together*... then maybe you could lay off her for a while – for a week, say—'

'Well, I don't know about that...' but I could see the fantasy was already catching fire.

'I mean, it would be one in the eye for that Nathan chap, wouldn't it?'

'Hey! Oh boy!' His face burst into hideous triumph. 'Oh, wouldn't it just!'

In a growing fever of excitement he disentangled himself from the strap and put it over my head. 'Hey, you'll be real careful, won't you? I mean, that lens alone cost me two hundred bucks—'

'*Simon—!*' Margot's warning voice from below me—

'*It's OK!*' I called back as Vern began to totter towards her down the slipway, his arms waving around frantically for balance. 'I'm just going to take a picture of you and Vern together—'

'You're *what*—?' she demanded, eyeing his approach with revulsion.

'—and in return he's promised not to take photographs of you for a week!' Desperate to get her to cooperate, I nodded at her frantically.

As Vern reached the jetty I raised the heavy camera and peered through the viewfinder – only to jerk back in shock as Margot's eyes glared back at me, her face close enough to touch. Vern's view of her sunbathing must have been even more graphic than mine.

I imagined his stolen images of her, tightly rolled on their dark spool – a scroll of wet dreams—

'Can I put my arm round you?' I heard him ask, and her emphatic 'No, *goddamn* it!'

So he had to content himself with standing next to her, sucking in his stomach so suddenly that his tartan Bermuda shorts slid perilously down his hips. 'Hey!' he screeched as he made a grab for them, 'Let's not start a fashion—!'

The bastard! '*Say cheese!*' I called down through gritted teeth. Margot stuck out her tongue, while Vern leered revoltingly as I laid the cross hairs of the viewfinder over his face, wishing the button were a trigger. The camera came alive as I pressed it, the shutter opening and closing with the quick, expensive sound of mechanical ejaculation—

'*Did you get it—?*' he yelled.

'Yes!'

As he wobbled back towards me up the slipway I examined the camera admiringly. 'This is quite something, Vern!' I exclaimed as I pointed to a red button on the front. 'What's this for?'

'That's the lens release,' he panted. 'You press it in with your thumb and turn the lens like a bayonet – don't do it, though—!'

'Of course not!' I shook my head impatiently. 'And what about this?' I pressed a catch on the side of the camera and the back flew open. 'Oh, dear—'

'*No, don't do that—!*' he yelled, missing his step as he reached up frantically for the camera.

Clumsily, I held it out towards him, lens up. One of the spools fell out, unravelling the film onto the rocks and into a puddle of sea water.

'*Oh, Jesus, you're exposing the film!*' he screamed.

'I'm so sorry—' I grabbed for the film, and the second reel fell out. 'Oh, dear—'

'Oh, *man!*' he wailed. 'There were some really cool pictures on that reel—!'

'I'm terribly sorry,' I said, sounding genuinely penitent, 'I'll buy you another film, of course—'

I glanced down at Margot, but her face was expressionless as she turned away.

'You came very close to the edge,' she murmured as we made our way back up the steep path from the *cala*, the sun warm on our backs again. Below us, the bay was almost deserted, sunk in shadow. 'I can look after myself—'

'I know,' I mumbled, hanging my head so she wouldn't see the huge grin on my face.

We were half way to the top when I saw a small group of latecomers making their way down, a family by the look of them – an older man, a slender blonde woman and a little girl, naked except for an enormous straw hat. The man saw us and stopped in his tracks, shielding his eyes against the sun.

'*Margot*—?' he bellowed suddenly, her name echoing among the rocks.

Margot waved up at him, laughing, and he bounded down the hill towards us, squat and powerful-looking, leaping from rock to rock, ignoring the well-worn track.

'It's Jacov,' said Margot, still smiling, 'coming down for his evening swim. You must have met him before – Jacov Lind – Austrian writer, very *avant garde*—?'

'I don't remember—' I fell back a pace, tying my towel round my waist.

'Maybe he was away when you were last here... or out of favour,' she added sardonically.

That rang a bell at least. He appeared to be in his forties, with a greying moustache that reminded me of Einstein – or was it Schweitzer—? his baggy blue shorts patched and dusty, his shirt held together by a single button over his big brown belly. He wasn't even out of breath as he came up to us, ignoring me completely – he had eyes only for Margot, laughing eyes, full of mischief. 'I came looking for you to the *Posada* earlier,' he rumbled in a voice like a landslide, 'but you weren't there!' Taking her hands, he kissed her on both cheeks. His glance, as it fell on me over each of her shoulders, was hooded, possessive.

'*Claro, hombre!*' she laughed, 'I was here, with Simon. He had some unfinished business down at the *cala*.' She turned to introduce me. 'Do you know each other? Simon was here a few years ago – he's Robert's grand-nephew, and this is Jacov Lind, chess grand-master of Deya, writer, and general hellraiser—'

He took my hand grudgingly. 'What "unfinished business"?' he demanded.

'For some reason his mother wouldn't let him go near the jetty when he was a kid—'

'Sea urchins!' he said abruptly. 'I won't let Oona go either, not till she's bigger—' he turned back to Margot, his faint glimmer of interest in me extinguished. 'So!' he rumbled. 'I come to the Posada to invite you to my party tonight! It's sudden, I know, a "*Happening*", they tell me, but this morning I get a letter saying my latest book will be published in England – maybe even an American edition—!'

'Jacov, that's wond—'

'*Yerch!*' he spat, beating off her congratulations with both arms, as though he were being attacked by a wasp, '*Say nothing!*' he shouted. 'Half of me doesn't give a fuck, the other half just wants to have a party! Will you come? I nearly called in to Canellun just now, to ask Robert—' he shook his head in a helpless gesture. 'You ask him if you like—'

'Ask him yourself,' she retorted, 'but he won't come—'

'You would think writers stick together,' he grumbled. Then he brightened up at her expression. 'You come, though?'

She put her head on one side, still smiling. 'Maybe – if Simon can come too...'

I was startled – touched—

Jacov rounded on me, frowning ferociously. '*Him*? Do I like him?'

'You might, if you give him a chance,' she said lightly. 'He's a bit of a hellraiser himself—'

'Wait a minute—' he glared at me through narrowed eyes, 'Simon... are you the boy made explosions with Juan once? Tried to blow up his old man—?'

'No!' I protested. 'I mean yes – but we didn't mean to blow—'

He threw back his head and roared with laughter, the sound so infectious that we joined in.

'What else you did?' he demanded, his dancing eyes greedy for more fuel.

'He tried to blow up his school—' Margot began, and he was off again, throwing back his head and punching the air with delight.

I stared at her in astonishment. 'How on earth did you know—?'

'There are no secrets here,' she grinned. 'You'll see—'

'Oh, there are secrets, all right!' Jacov suddenly stopped laughing, though his eyes still glittered mischievously. 'They just don't always belong to the people who are trying to keep them...' He fixed a strange basilisk stare on Margot, and then slowly dragged it, like a spider's thread, onto me. 'Trust no one here! Yourself less—'

'I meant that there were no secrets at Canellun,' Margot broke in sharply, 'I didn't mean Deya itself—'

Jacov shrugged lazily, his big grey moustache spreading across his face. 'All right, maybe Canellun's another country,' he conceded, 'but even so—'

'Hi, Margot—'

Jacov's wife had finally caught up with him, their little girl clinging happily to one hip, her shoulder basket swinging against the other.

'*Liebling!*' cried Jacov, throwing out his arm in a sweeping gesture. 'This is the boy who—'

215

'I know, Jacov,' she said calmly, 'I should think the whole of Deya knows by now. You're so *noisy*!' She turned and smiled at me. 'Hello, Simon. You won't remember me, but I was on the beach that day you fell off the cliff with Juan. How's your mother? She was so upset, but she still made everyone laugh—'

'She's fine – thank you,' I stammered, trying frantically to remember her. How could I possibly have forgotten someone so beautiful?

She turned to Jacov, who'd gone surprisingly quiet. 'Jacov, we must get on, or there'll be no party tonight. Will you carry Oona for me?'

Jacov swept his little girl into the air, knocking her huge hat off as he blew a raspberry on her tummy and made her scream with laughter. Then he settled her on his shoulders, naked and happy, staring down at us arrogantly from under her wild dark curls. For just an instant I found myself envying her unbearably.

'We'll see you both tonight, then,' said Jacov's wife as she stooped to pick up the dropped hat.

'Of course—!' we assured her at once.

She smiled back at me over her shoulder. 'And don't mind Jacov, Simon, he's just an old bear. Margot will tell you—'

'I'm a *bull*!' bellowed Jacov, affronted, before glancing at Margot almost shamefacedly, 'in china shop,' he murmured, his theatrical accent even more exaggerated, as if he were blaming his broken English for some misunderstanding between them. He looked quickly down at his daughter, squeezing her until her pips squeaked. '*Qué soy?*' he demanded.

'*Un toro!*' she yelled, forming her little fists into horns on either side of her head.

'*Toro!*' he roared, and he was gone, charging down the path in a cloud of dust and childish shrieks

Once they'd gone, I glanced round at Margot – but she'd vanished again, not physically this time – she was palpably standing there, facing into the sun from the step above me – but her face was sphinx-like, still, and so suffused with evening sunlight that the source of it appeared to be buried deep within her. Some trick of the light had turned her eyes into liquid gold, their moltenness overflowing, not as tears, but as a tegument, a golden mask, set forever in that instant—

The instant passed, realised only by me. Still in her own half dream, she turned away and began to climb the steps.

I stayed where I was, stock-still, trying to cling to the moment before she had moved, to that image of her, already irretrievable—

Whoever she was, or said she was, and wherever she said she came from, the face I'd just witnessed belonged to another time and to another world. Whether or not it had been a trick of the light, I knew that I could never see her in the same light again; there was more than one of her... and sometimes there was none.

THE HAPPENING

Racing along the upstairs corridor that night in a haze of bathroom
steam and soap and shaving cream, still knotting my tie as I ran
down the stairs—

'Ah, there you are, good, I wanted to talk to you—!' Robert,
half way across the hall below, glancing up at me over his shoulder,
looking like Beethoven's Ninth, hair standing on end, relief nib pen
jammed behind his ear— 'I thought you'd gone, and I wanted a
word with you before you went – I *say*,' feigning dazzlement, 'you
look awfully smart! Come into the study. Don't worry, I won't keep
you – I know Margot's waiting, but it's important—'

I hurried round beneath the stairs to his study as he barged
through the narrow double doors, setting them rattling and
quivering on their hinges. As I followed him in I was instantly
caught unawares by the remembered smell of his cigars, of books
and dust and of something else, indefinable, which was probably
him.

'Shut-the-Divil-out-and-take-a-pew, as *my* dear grand-uncle
used to say—' his Irish accent as atrocious as ever. He flung himself
into his chair behind the desk, '—your *great*-grand-uncle, Charles
Graves, Bishop of Limerick – the best-loved Protestant in all of
Oirland! Did you know that?'

'No—' Having closed the doors, I went and sat down opposite
him. The room was in darkness apart from his desk lamp, the
downcast pool of light cutting him off at the forehead like the
brim of a fedora, changing his appearance from Mad Composer to
Mobster, his broken nose—

'No, the thing is, Margot came to see me after your swim – what do you think – isn't she wonderful?'

'She's extraordinary—' I began.

His face was already alight as he anticipated my answer. 'I'm so glad you think so! And she's taken to you, too, which makes me very happy – you'll be company for her now that Alastair's gone back to Madrid – Alastair Reid – you remember him? No, of course you do! You're going to stay with him and Mary when you start university—'

'Yes—'

'Good! You'll be in safe hands—' He broke off, frowning fiercely. 'Where was I?'

For a moment I was as lost as he was, out of practice when it came to having a conversation with him, his quick mind going off at tangents—

'Oh, yes – he's been working on a libretto with me, and on a film script of *The White Goddess*. Now that he's gone, Margot's more or less on her own, you see – apart from us, and I'm not much good to her at the moment—' he gestured at the sea of papers in front of him. 'Quite apart from the film script, I've got a libretto to revise and three articles to finish by the end of the month, and the Lawrence thing for Sam Spiegel, and countless letters to answer – but that's all right, too – verse and prose are easy—' he dismissed them with a gesture. '*Poems* are another matter, though, and that's the trouble – they're becoming more and more urgent thanks to Margot, and quite rightly! I'm a poet, after all, first, last, and foremost. But it's hell sometimes, trying to fit it all in—'

He leaned forward into the light suddenly, no longer a Composer or a Mobster, but a Poet now, as he swept up his spectacles from his desk to his nose, dislodging the pen from behind his ear, catching it deftly, stretching out automatically to dip it in his ink-well while with his other hand he began rummaging through his papers. 'Where is it? Ah, here we are—!' With the tips of his fleshy fingers

220

he deftly pulled out a sheet of paper by its corner, scratched a title on it with his pen, and launched it towards me on its own current of air. 'I was searching for a title. See what you think—'

In spite of my need to get away I was flattered he should ask my opinion as I plucked the sheet of paper out of the air, nervous of the still-wet ink of the title – relieved to see that the poem was short—

'It's only a fragment, as I've said,' he shifted restlessly in his chair. 'But the rules still apply – no half measures—'

As I read the brief poem I was aware of him getting up and absentmindedly straightening the spines in the bookcase beside his desk, his mind clearly on the words I was reading.

'It's wonderful,' I said finally – which it was – but my response sounded utterly inadequate. How on earth did one criticise something which seemed so perfect? I struggled on manfully. 'It's Margot—?'

'Of course it's Margot!' he laughed. 'No, that's unfair—' he threw himself back into his chair, 'you've only just arrived, after all. I'll put you in the picture properly when there's time – about Margot – Beryl – it's complicated but simple, if you see what I mean – complicated to those who don't understand, simple to those who do. And Simons are supposed to be simple, aren't they?' Again he laughed at his own joke, then closed his eyes, his eyebrows raised as he marshalled his thoughts. 'No, seriously, what I said before, about Margot needing friends – she's a loner, you see – doesn't take to people easily, which is why I'm so pleased she likes you. Most of the people in the village are pretty awful, frankly—' he suddenly swivelled his chair round to face me. 'Oh, yes—! That's the point – what I wanted to see you about before you left. The thing is, you're a guest here, which is fine – we're delighted to have you – but you're more than a guest, if you see what I mean – you're *family*, and that means you have an added responsibility – to us. I mean, you're going to a party in the village tonight, with Margot, and that's fine too – you can look after her, and she's promised to do likewise – but the thing is, you go from *here,* if you follow me – as an ambassador, if you like Are you with me?'

'Yes—' No, not quite—

'I mean, Jacov's *"all right"*,' he mimed inverted commas with the forefingers of both hands, 'I'm quite fond of him in fact, and he works hard, which is more than can be said for the people he mixes with. They're dregs, most of them – beats, hipsters, whatever they call themselves. They're all into LSD and pot and God knows what else – it's the Deya disease,' he stared at me unwaveringly from under the brim of his fedora, 'and I don't want you to catch it!' Again he shifted uncomfortably in his chair. 'There's no cure for it, you see. And it's not that I'm a prig,' he added, 'I've tried most things myself, including "pot", not to mention mescalin and psyllocyabin – powerful hallucinogens which have had a deeply religious and poetic significance over the centuries. But my experiments were always strictly controlled, usually by my old friend Gordon Wasson – he's the world expert on mushrooms, so he knows what he's doing—' He broke off, as if suddenly aware that he was glowering at me. With a sigh he relaxed, and became my grand-uncle again. 'Look, I just need your assurance that you'll behave, as I'm sure you will, like one of *us!*'

'Of course—!'

'*Good!*' He threw me a sweet smile. 'That's settled, then! Off you go – have a good time! Look after Margot – oh, I tell you what, you might ask her if she could pop over with her accounts tomorrow. She'll know what I mean. It's the end of the month, and Karl's chasing me for figures—' he broke off, his mind clearly elsewhere. 'No, on second thoughts, I'll ask her myself… it's just that she might be short of money… No, forget it, she might be offended if it came from you – but listen, if my light's still on when you get back, come and tell me how it all went—'

Racing down the drive, already late, and yet elated, like a boy let out of school into this sub-tropical night, the dim light over the garage only emphasising the beauty around me, dashing for the gates, dragging them open, clanging them shut behind me, slamming the bolt home to the muffled sound of the dogs barking in the distant drawing room – sorry, Beryl—!

Running on down the dark road towards the village – and yet enough starlight to see by—

Elated, too, by my conversation with Robert, even though I'd said practically nothing, his words and meanings still racing through my brain, his high tenor voice and precise diction re-awakening memories of my childhood when he'd talk to me, even then, as an equal. The way he'd casually tossed his poem at me, asking my opinion (though admittedly not waiting for it) – still haunted by what I'd read – a 'fragment', he'd called it, so daylight-simple that I could almost remember every word after merely glancing at it. If that was a fragment, then what must the rest of his poems be like? To my shame, I'd never read them – too much like hard work. And what must Margot be truly like, to have inspired them? It wasn't just me, either; everyone seemed to fall under her spell. She was astonishing—!

And I was late.

By the time I reached the Posada I was in a muck sweat, gasping for breath, my legs trembling uncontrollably from running up the steep hairpin bends through the village. If only I were allowed to drive! All I could remember for certain was that the house had once been an inn, and now belonged to Robert, that it was next to the church and that the church was the highest point in the village, but I'd forgotten how high that point was, and the final flight of donkey steps threatened to bring on an asthma attack. By the dim light of a street lamp on the wall I could make out the Posada at last, as ancient as the church it was attached to—

No sign of life, though, its windows shuttered, dark, the doorway deep in shadow—

Gone—?

I slumped against the heavy wooden doors and banged on them with my fist. The hollow echo from the darkness within only emphasised the sudden emptiness I felt in my heart—

She hadn't waited—

I'd no idea where the party was, and even if I went down every street I still might not find it. The village was much larger than I remembered—

'You're late—'

Her voice so faint that for a moment I thought it was the sound of my own wheezing playing tricks on me. I looked back down the steps towards the little square, to where I thought the sound had come from – to where she was standing at the foot of the steps now, in the glimmer of a street lamp, hip-shot, hands behind her back, wearing a thin summer frock that must have cost a fortune – or nothing. Even in the breathless night the skirt wafted round her knees. She must have stepped out from the shadows—

'I hate waiting for people!' she called up.

'I know – I'm sorry,' I gasped, running down the steps, 'Robert wanted to talk to me – ' I was seized by a sudden coughing fit, made worse by trying to hold it in. 'I couldn't refuse—'

'For Christ's sake!' She started to grin in an appalled sort of way. 'Have you got asthma?'

'A bit—'

'Well, take off your tie for a start! No one wears a tie here, unless they're leaving the island – or dead!' I did as she told me. 'And unbutton your shirt collar—' The relief was instant. She looked me over again, shaking her head sadly. 'We've got to do something about your clothes...'

We—!

Setting off across the square side by side, I felt a moment of panic, casting about for something to say. Robert had said she liked me, but she was hard to please – hated chit chat and gossip—

'So what did Robert want to talk to you about?' she asked casually.

Relief flooded through me. 'About you, mostly – nice things!' I added hurriedly, with a quick glance at her. She didn't seem to care one way or the other. 'And about the party – the people here—'

'*Ah*,' she laughed, 'the drug-crazed down-and-outs, the beatnicks, lotus eaters—!'

'Yes—!'

'Well, they're not! Some of them are fine. The trouble is, Robert feels responsible for what's happened to Deya, but it's not his fault – not all of it. I mean, all right, maybe he started the gold rush when he wrote *Goodbye To All That* here, but you can't beat yourself up forever. Places like this just *happen*—'

Once we'd crossed the square we turned left, down a track on the other side of the hill, facing the deep valley overlooking the road to Valldemosa. Pinpoints of light glimmered like fireflies in the darkness of the hill opposite, until there was nothing but the sheer curtain of mountains, blacker than night against the starlit sky, walling us in. The sight thrilled me unaccountably as we jolted our way downwards in silence. She glanced round at me. 'You remember Alastair—?'

'Yes of course!'

'Well, he thinks Deya's getting more and more interesting, because of the very things that Robert hates – the beats, the down-and-outs, the so-called artists, the idle rich and the busy poor, all living here side by side in what he calls a strange symbiosis, a shared envy of each other which keeps them all on their toes. They feed off each other without actually killing each other. It's weird, but I think he's right—'

'Don't you hate all that, though?' I asked, remembering her reaction to Fred Grunfeld and his friends.

'In a way,' she said lightly, 'but then I'm just passing through. Paradise can become a prison after a while, which is why I prefer cities.'

'How could you?' It was unimaginable to me, for someone so wild and carefree – and yet she was so stylish, too, sophisticated – even her scent was unique, bewitching—

'Because you can disappear in cities. Here, someone's always watching.'

I thought of Vern, and was forced to agree.

The track had become a road, with dimly lit houses on either side. From one of them leaked the muffled sound of music – a heavy, repetitive beat—

'We're there,' she said distractedly. To my surprise she slowly came to a halt, as if reluctant to go in. 'Listen, Simon… I'm meant to warn you—' her eyes glittering in the half light, engulfing me—

I was mesmerised by her look. 'Warn me of what?' I asked faintly.

We out-stared each other for a moment, before she turned away with an exasperated sigh. 'Oh, the hell with it – you're old enough to make your own mistakes.'

As she pushed open the heavy door, we stepped from one darkness into another, from the darkness of the quiet night outside into a jungle darkness of heat and strange-smelling incense and bodies slick with sweat swaying to the deep bass rhythm of a music I'd never heard before blasting from a record player in the corner surrounded by candles throwing stark shadowed light upwards beneath the faces of the dancers, their eyes cast up or down in seeming oblivion, their movements macabre, sinister, like corpses dancing with the living dead—

Was this what Margot had meant? She was already several paces ahead of me, people calling out, trying to stop her, but she kept going, smiling back at them, waving—

I looked back at the dancers in a new light. They were just people after all, enjoying themselves – the men mostly in black, the girls in dark diaphanous dresses dripping with beads, their strange make-up hollowing their cheeks and eye sockets. Small children were dancing among them—

'*Hey, man*—*!*'

I jerked round. A girl was leaning against the wall behind me, sideways on, as though trying to sleep in an upright bed. She had a bottle of beer in one hand and a cigarette in the other. She raised her bottle arm and gestured vaguely across the room. 'She wants you,' she said with a sickly smile.

Margot was pointing impatiently at a pair of open doors and what appeared to be a tunnel beyond.

'Thank you,' I said hurriedly to the girl.

'Nothin' to me—' she shrugged, closing her eyes and giggling as I eased past.

Having caught up with her, Margot led me through the doorway and into a gloomy makeshift passage of screens, with blankets stretched over them to form a roof. From behind them came the sound of laughter and conversation and glimmers of light—

'*I see Margot – Moon Queen – Queen of Tides – tides ebbing, surging—!*'

It was only when Margot stepped aside, as though to avoid a dog turd, that I saw where the chanting, ghost-like voice was coming from. A girl was sitting cross-legged on a cushion in the middle of the passage, a lighted candle in front of her, her hair in pigtails, fists clutched to the side of her head, forefingers pointing ceiling-wards like antennae, staring up at Margot through a pair of granny glasses – one of the beats who'd been on the bus—!

'Hi, Gill,' said Margot distractedly, moving on quickly down the passage. I was about to sidestep the girl, too, when she fixed me with her eyes and forefingers. 'I see a stranger – Sun sign... Leo?'

'Yes!' I stopped and stared down at her in surprise.

'I see the pride of lions, I see danger – beware the Scorpion – beware The Stranger—!'

I was taken aback for a moment. 'I thought *I* was the stranger,' I joked uncomfortably—

'There's another one,' she said matter-of-factly in a precise English voice, 'someone you've just met... are about to meet...' She closed her eyes, frowning fiercely. 'Fuck! I saw it a moment ago – who are you anyway?'

'You tell *me!*'

'No... wait... I'm getting conflicting vibes—'

Whatever *they* were, but I was off, down the rest of the tunnel, like Alice in Wonderland, until I rounded the last screen and came into the light of a long, open room which gave onto a terrace at the end. A cold buffet had been arranged on trestle tables down the centre of the room where a number of people, older for the most part, were lounging on sofas and in armchairs or standing around with their drinks, talking and laughing – more like the cocktail parties I was used to in London. Margot was surrounded already, her back to me, until someone in her group touched her elbow and nodded in my direction. She broke away and came across. 'Sorry I deserted you, but Gill gives me the creeps when she's on one of her psychic kicks.' Her eyes widening dramatically. 'Are you going to fall in love with a tall dark stranger?'

Her words threw me for a moment— 'There was a stranger, yes—'

Someone thrust a glass of wine into my hand as she started to introduce me to the people she'd been with, but I was still distracted, until I heard myself saying 'How do you do?' to Jacov.

'How do I do what?' he demanded grumpily, before turning to the man beside him, tall and striking with a completely bald head. 'Mati, this is nephew of Robert Graves. Tried to blow him up!'

The man raised his eyebrows – or at least he would if he'd had any, but they were as bald as his head. 'Really?' he asked politely. 'When was that?'

'It was an accident,' I protested, already fed up with the story. 'I was ten—'

Jacov slammed his glass against mine, splashing us both. 'To anarchy!' he exclaimed, as large as life as ever, his wild eyes daring me on.

'To anarchy!' I laughed suddenly, no longer caring if this great bear of a man wanted to make me out to be more interesting than I was. After all, people who tried to live up to their reputations were a damn sight more fun than people who tried to live them down.

'Robert knows you come to my party tonight?' he asked as he refilled our glasses.

'Yes, of course,' I replied, amused by the sudden look of surprise on his face.

Almost at once the look dissolved into shrewdness. 'I bet he warn you against us!'

Caught off my guard, I grasped for straws, 'Not against you,' I said quickly, 'he likes you—'

A deep frown darkened his features. Uncertain of his next move, I clutched at the straw of the bald man's gaze. He was looking at me with his head on one side, smiling slightly. 'Things must have changed quite a bit since you were last here,' he drawled.

'In a way,' I answered with relief, 'and yet so much is still the same—' I glanced round the room. Behind me was another group of people, among them two nubile girls in tiny chamois shorts, and a man dressed like Buffalo Bill, complete with six guns— 'it's like nowhere else – another world—'

'Is Brave New World!' shouted Jacov, fixing me with his fiery eyes. 'Except not very brave yet,' he grunted, 'still crawling out from under stone, still very young, maybe ten-years-old, like you, once. How you behave when you was ten? Badly, I think! Asking *why* everything – why school, why boring master, why stupid rules?' Again, he waved expansively at the room. 'They too! And me? Ten years ago was in Paris, existentialist, giving birth to self all over again – first *néant*, nothingness, then pain, then hunger – for freedom – but different freedom! – of soul – freedom to *be*, to express self! Fuck State, fuck nationalism, no more borders—!' he waved at the room again. 'They too! So we choose exile! And where we come? Here! Paradise! And what we find? English poet is patriarch of village! Hates what we hate! Exile like us! Wonderful—!' He drained his glass, then shook his head lugubriously. 'Except Robert different than us. Stuck in mud, like in First World War. Great poet, maybe, but arrogant, old fashioned, look down on us – even though village higher than Canellun—!'

'Oh, come on – Robert's OK,' said the bald man lazily.

Jacov glowered at him. 'Is different for you, Mati! You are painter – no threat to him—!'

'—and nor are you, Jacov!' interrupted Margot impatiently. You're talking crap and you know it. He only hates people who behave badly and upset the villagers. You hate them too, you old hypocrite! Now can we change the subject, it's boring—'

I drifted away, riveted by the younger women, some of them clearly naked under their gauzy dresses, their skin gleaming elusively among the moving folds of their skirts, their nipples brazenly—

Christ—! I was gawping like a schoolboy, with the stirrings of an erection already. Looking up, I wandered over to where the buffet sagged under the weight of exotic Majorcan dishes. The music in the hallway came to an abrupt end as someone shouted '*Supper!*' and I was soon surrounded by over-heated dancers, by sweating skin and strange musky scents which caught in the back of my throat. Unable to pull back for the throng behind me, I eased my way along the edge of the table to the end. I'd already eaten, but the sight of so many dishes that we never had at Canellun was too much for me. Taking a plate, I began to help myself, reaching across the table for a slice of the dark serrano ham, only to find that it was attached to someone else – to Gill-the-Psychic – by her finger and thumb. 'I'm so sorry!' We both let go at once, and it flopped onto the table.

'Ah!' she recognised me. 'The Lion stranger—! Is this coincidence, I ask myself, or Fate—?'

'Greed, probably. I've already eaten—'

'Then it's Fate,' she decided, reaching for two more slices and putting one on each of our plates, her eyes still absorbed in my face. 'So who *are* you?' she asked casually, coming round the end of the table and standing next to me. 'You came with Margot, so I suppose you must be hers – everyone else is...' she helped herself to a spoonful of everything in reach, 'even the ones she doesn't want—'

Objecting to the thought of being lumped together with the Great Unwanted, I told her I was from Canellun.

'Ah!' she said brightly. 'Then you're Robert's!'

'Yes,' I said unthinkingly, and then, '*No*, actually – I'm *mine!*'

'Are you indeed?' she grinned up at me. 'Lucky you!'

Her flash of humour was unexpected. 'What do you do?' I asked politely.

'I'm a poet.'

As we eased out of the throng and began to eat, I found her admission almost embarrassing. When Robert said he was a poet one believed him without question – there was something Olympian about him after all – but for this peculiar girl in granny glasses to claim that she was a poet—

'How do you know?' I challenged her.

She stared at me, startled. '*Ah!*' her eyes magnifying behind her glasses. 'Unbeliever—!'

'It's just that most people who call themselves poets—'

'—aren't really poets at all,' she finished for me.

'No.'

She smiled faintly, then shrugged. 'I suppose you have to read one to know one.'

I warmed to her. At least she hadn't got on her high horse. 'No, you're right – I'm sorry—'

Again she smiled at me. 'All the same, there are days when I'm not, and they hurt.' She tilted her head to one side. 'Are you a poet?'

'God no!' I changed the subject. She was surprisingly easy to talk to, calm and almost strangely serene, so the next time she asked me a personal question I found myself replying honestly.

Once we'd eaten, she re-lit her bedraggled cigarette and inhaled deeply, with a curious look of relief on her face. Then, with a little choke, she held out the cigarette to me. 'Sorry—'

'Thanks—' I took the crude cigarette, relieved that the end she'd had in her mouth was dry, and puffed on it, choking slightly, like her, as I inhaled the acrid smoke. 'Bloody hell!' I rasped. 'Is it herbal?' For a while, at school, I'd tried herbal cigarettes to deceive the masters, but I'd still been rumbled and beaten. I took another puff, which tasted of burnt grass cuttings—

All at once, Margot had joined us, pressing lightly against my elbow. 'Gill, do you mind if I have a word with Simon—?' A sudden rush of pleasure to feel her beside me—

'I'm cool—!' With a little nod and a smile, Gill wandered away.

Staring at me intently, Margot gestured at my cigarette. 'You know what that is?'

'It's a cigarette!' I answered, slightly taken aback. 'I do know how to smoke, you know.'

'It's a *joint*,' she said quietly, emphatically.

'A joint what?' I couldn't quite see her point.

'A *joint*, for Christ's sake,' eyes wide with disbelief. 'Dope! Pot! Marijuana – what I was meant to warn you against—'

I looked at the cigarette with new respect, not unmixed with alarm. 'What will it do?'

'*Jesus*! Don't you know?' She let out a sigh of exasperation, then relaxed suddenly, smiling and shaking her head – at my ignorance? 'Just don't smoke too much the first time, OK? It can make you sick.' She started to turn away—

'About Robert—' I began.

232

She turned back sharply. I'd been about to ask her not to tell him, but realised I was on a hiding to nothing. 'I mean... he tried it, didn't he?' I demanded with an assumed bravado. 'He told me...'

With a shrug she walked off, leaving me feeling stupid. I took another puff, exhilarated by the thought that she'd been watching over me.

Gill was talking to the girl I'd first seen by the door, propped up against the wall – freestanding now, but still unfocussed. Was it from drink or marijuana? If it was marijuana, would that be me in a few minutes, or in half an hour – or in the middle of the night, perhaps? Already searching myself for symptoms, unsure of what to look for. All I felt at the moment was a slight hollowness in the pit of my stomach. How many puffs had I had? Two? Three? How many puffs did it take – and to do what?

I went up to the two of them, holding out the remains of the cigarette to Gill, but the girl snatched it out of my fingers with a predatory deftness and sucked at it until the tip glowed angrily.

'*Oh, man!*' she gasped, dragging the smoke into her lungs. Gill didn't seem to mind.

'What will it do to me?' I asked her quietly, my face a careful mask.

Gill looked at me through narrowed eyes. 'You mean you've never smoked before?'

'Yes, of course – but not a *joint*—'

'So that's why Margot—' She bit her bottom lip as she stared at me. 'Oh shit, I didn't realise, I'm sorry. Look, you'll be fine, you've hardly toked at all—'

'Hey!' The teetering girl swayed towards me, her eyes disjointed. 'Is this your first time?'

'Yes—'

Her eyes focussed briefly on my single word, then lost touch with each other completely as she thought about it. 'Toooo much... oh, but that is *toooo much*—' and suddenly she was throwing her arms in the air, shrilling 'Hey, everyone – *everyone!*' she shouted. The room started to fall silent. 'It's a *Happening*—! Gill's deflowered him! It's his first time with weed—!'

'Are you OK?'

I was out on the terrace, at one with the world, looking up at the dark mountains that surrounded us. Somewhere behind the house, unseen, the moon was rising.

Margot's question was as soft and dense as the sky, as much a part of what I was seeing as what I was hearing. I was overcome with happiness to feel her beside me again.

'I'm *cooool!*' I answered, and started giggling helplessly.

I heard her quiet laugh, and then she was leaning over the balcony and peering back into my face, her teeth glinting in the starlight. 'You're high, aren't you?'

'Six foot precisely in my stockinged feet,' I hiccupped. 'I have a certificate—'

'Shall we go in?'

The music was softer now as we went through into the darkness of the hall, easing our way through weaving, shimmering bodies as they swayed to it, adding with the freedom of their expression a new dimension to what had seemed to me unalterable. Already I felt as though I was on their wavelength, and I liked that. I liked everything, especially this growing sense of timelessness that was suffusing me, making me happily aware of it as it was happening. A *Happening...* was that what it meant – an extension of the present, of time being stretched as it materialised—?

There was a sudden disturbance as the front door was flung open to the sound of raised voices and harsh laughter, Mazzini and Vern and their cronies bursting into the room clutching bottles of beer and wine, whooping and guffawing.

'The bar must have closed early—' Gill had materialised beside us, swaying to the music. The atmosphere in the hall turned wary suddenly, as if raising its hackles, and yet the two girls in tiny shorts seemed unaware, gravitating at once towards Mazzini, the cowboy shambling after them.

'Who's the cowboy?' I asked Gill as conversation began to pick up again.

'That's Wes, from Texas. His father's in oil. Those are his daughters, Debbie and Pammy. His guns are named after them – they're real, and so are the bullets He's a bad trip—'

A moment later there was another influx of people, mostly drunk and spoiling for fun, and all at once the room was bursting with noise and brash laughter and the sound of a glass breaking. Jacov's voice could be heard bellowing *'Who are all these people? I do not invite them! Fuck off—!'*

'Time to go,' said Margot, breaking away.

'Do we have to?' I asked. 'It's such fun!'

She shrugged and made for the door. Saying a quick goodnight to Gill, I forced my way after her through the crowd, only to find Mazzini blocking her way, looking like a modern day Samson, hairy and sweating, a bottle of beer in each hand, his arms draped around the necks of the two nubile girls who were supporting him like pillars on either side.

'Hey, Margoooo!' I heard him drawl. 'What say you and me have a little dance?' Raising his arms from the girls' shoulders he made a drunken lunge for her. With a flash of anger she sidestepped and slipped behind him through the doorway. While he was still off-balance I barged into him with all my might, apologising profusely as he went sprawling across the floor in a trail of spilled beer.

Pursued by his oaths and threats, I made it out through the front door, slamming it triumphantly behind me and leaping up the steps into the street.

If to be 'high' was to feel this sense of exultation, of bursting happiness, then I was as high as the glaring moon – lightheaded, weightless—

Margot spun round at the sound of the door slamming, but once she saw it was me, she waited in the middle of the road, silhouetted in moonlight.

'Got him!' I cried, bounding up to her. 'I knocked him down and he's grovelling around on the floor – God, what a party! You've no idea—' I took a huge breath of scented night air—

'No idea of what?' She was smiling.

'Of what it's like...' I shook my head in disbelief. 'Yesterday morning I was in London – grey and raining, cold, dreading the idea of going to Spain, to university—' I stretched out my arms, embracing the blood-warm night and the moonlit landscape. 'And now I'm here, under the same moon, but *here—!' With you,* I almost said, but shied away. 'Those beats or whatever they're called – the children running around – everyone so free, so natural!'

'Most of them were stoned,' she grinned. 'Or drunk—'

'But they were *free*! Gill, Jacov, the children, those crazy dancers...'

I looked across the rooftops of the sleeping village again, to the mountains towering above us. 'The world beyond those mountains can't touch them here! This is another world – Shangri La, Eden—'

'*Whoah!*' she laughed. 'Slow down! How much did you smoke?'

I shook my head impatiently. 'It's not that, I promise. It's just that I've realised that *I'm* free too! Not even Robert can tell me what to do – not tonight—' I turned on her, taking her hands in mine, 'and it's all your fault! I was perfectly miserable until you came along, and now I'm *happy*!' I kissed her hands, laughing. 'I'm *happy*,' I whispered. 'You're extraordinary! I can't explain it—'

Still smiling, she pressed her fingers against my lips. 'Sssh,' she murmured.

A sudden silence surrounded us, dense and watchful. Then, from further down the street, the faint sound of a piano playing, the swift velvet notes stealing towards us like the overture to a new awareness. 'Listen!' I breathed. We began to walk towards the sound. It was Chopin – a Mazurka that I'd once tried (and failed) to learn at school. The soloist was wonderfully bold, assured—

'It's Marie-Lorre,' said Margot. 'She used to be a concert pianist—'

I turned to her in astonishment. 'You mean it's real – not a record?'

As we passed the window where the music was coming from, I was suddenly swept up in a fantasy. 'I say,' I said (the perfect gentleman), 'would you care to dance?'

Laughing, she gave me her hand, resting the other round my shoulder as I held her firmly by the waist and launched into a Mazurka. 'Now this I *can* do!' I cried. 'Not like that zombie stuff at the party!'

And so could she, as though born to it, down the hill and onto the coast road, stretching like a silver moonlit river towards Canellun, the power I felt as I held her in my arms overwhelming, the lightness of her feet, her dizzying scent—

When we could no longer hear the piano, we waltzed, to get our breath back, then hummed a tango, then a foxtrot, then a quickstep too quick for me— 'I say,' she gasped politely, 'do you know you're treading on my toes?'

'You hum it, I'll dance it!' I answered, quick as a flash.

'I say, that's awfully good!' she squawked like a duchess, tripping me up, sending me sprawling onto the road while she ran on ahead.

I chased after her round the last bend and we arrived at Canellun neck-and-neck, breathless and laughing as we slammed into the gates, setting them clanking in protest.

'It's lucky Isabella's not here,' I panted. 'She'd have woken the whole village!'

'Who's Isabella?'

'Robert's donkey.'

'Oh, she died! Robert wrote her an ode: *Isabella, or the Pot of Glue*—'
I burst out laughing. 'Poor Isabella!'

'Poor Keats!'

The light on the garage wall halfway up the drive appeared to wink at us, a dark palm frond stirring in the night breeze blowing back and forth across it, beckoning us on.

Reluctantly, not wanting this new and strange intimacy to end, I put my hand through the gate and pulled back the bolt. 'Robert said to go and see him if he was still awake—'

'OK,' she shrugged lightly.

Revelling in this renewed lease of her, I led the way up the drive. Once outside the kitchen door we could see the light from his study window.

'Leave the talking to me, all right?' Margot murmured as we crossed the terrace to the side door of his study. Without even knocking, she opened the door and led the way in.

Robert looked up from his work, his face suddenly incandescent with pleasure. '*How nice!*' he exclaimed. 'My two favourite people – after Beryl and the children, of course—!' He pushed his specs onto the top of his head as Margot went round and kissed him on the cheek. 'How was your party?'

'Fine,' said Margot casually, 'but then Mazzini and that lot arrived, so we left. Simon knocked him down—'

'Accidentally-on-purpose,' I interrupted. My actions hadn't been exactly courageous—

'Good for you!' Robert burst out. 'He's a dreadful man – a dope pedlar, a thief—'

'What are you working on?' asked Margot, distracting him.

'Another poem – for you—' he handed it to her. 'I've been trying to get shot of it for days, but it's still not cooked. Or is it? You be the judge—'

As Margot began to read, my eye fell on the poem I'd read earlier, still lying where I'd put it on top of the row of books on his desk. I re-read it, learning it instantly by heart.

'Were there any drugs at the party?' he asked me casually. My heart missed a beat—

'Too dark—' cut in Margot. She was frowning down at the poem. 'Is this a threat?' she asked.

'No! God, no!' Almost in panic he reached for a cigar and lit it. 'No, there's a *caveat* – you can see – no, the thing is, it came out of a moment between us – nothing to do with now, and even if it had been, it's long gone... you only have to smile, you know that! I was simply acknowledging the moment between us. That's my job after all—' he laughed uneasily, 'as your poet laureate. It's my duty to record things, to warn – oh, don't be cross – it's so nice to see you smiling again—'

'I still think it should go back in the oven,' said Margot, leaning over the desk and dropping the poem in front of him, her hair briefly touching his face. I breathed in sharply, in spite of myself. She looked eerily beautiful in the dim reflected light from his downcast desk lamp.

Robert pulled a face at me. '*Tant pis...*' He squirmed restlessly in his chair.

'I must go,' she said. 'I have to be up early—'

'Oh, don't go,' he said plaintively, 'I'll think it's my fault—'

'Shall I dance you back to the Posada?' I asked, trying to break the atmosphere between them.

Robert looked from one to the other of us, startled. 'Dance? What—?'

For a moment she even seemed to consider it, a half smile forming at the corners of her mouth. Then she slowly shook her head. 'No... then I'd have to dance you back to Canellun. We'd be coming and going all night. We'd get footsore—'

'Fancy-free—'

'Actually, you'd probably get run over,' grunted Robert with a dismissive sniff.

Standing above him, at opposite ends of the room, Margot and I grinned at each other. 'I'll walk you to the gate, at least,' I offered.

'Spoken like a gentleman, sir!' cried my grand-uncle happily. 'How nice – that you both get on!' He glanced up at Margot. 'Well, goodnight, then, since you choose to leave me. I'll keep going for a bit – turn up the oven, open the flue – try a new draft—' he laughed at his own pun.

Margot kissed him briefly and made for the door.

'Oh, and darling—' Robert called after her, 'no threat intended – truly!'

Opening the door, Margot threw him with a dazzling smile. 'None taken!' And she was gone.

Robert beamed up at me. 'I'm so glad she's happy again! It's thanks to you, you know—'

Caught off guard, I mumbled something inane, like 'thank you for having me'.

'*De nada!* Breakfast's at eight. Goodnight!'

And he was back at work before I'd left the room, his well-trained spectacles falling back onto his nose as he leaned forward.

I caught up with her at the bottom of the drive, and unbolted the gate again.

'Are you sure you don't want me to walk you home?' I asked as she slipped through. 'We don't have to dance—'

She turned back to me with a smile that Robert would have killed for. 'I'm sure.'

'Well… goodnight, then,' I said awkwardly, leaning over the gate to kiss her cheek. But in my awkwardness I misjudged the movement of her head towards me and found my lips accidentally pressed against hers. I drew back, as though stung. 'I'm so sorry—!'

She looked surprised. With a quiet, low laugh she leaned over the gate and placed her lips on mine, neither politely nor lingeringly, but unforgettably.

'So sorry—!' she murmured, and walked away.

Later, lying in bed, staring up into the writhing darkness above me, the words of his poem ran through and through my head as I lived and re-lived each moment at the gate, conjured and re-conjured her kiss again and again – the indescribable feel of the chiselled softness of her lips, her exotic scent, her murmured words—

All right, I was still 'high' in every sense, but who could she be that she had the power of lightning to strike you dead and alive in the same instant? And what had she meant by her kiss…?

To call it a signal would be to attach too much importance to it; to call it nothing would be a travesty—

It had been *meant*—!

It had been meant.

But meant as *what*—?

> *Are you shaken, are you stirred*
> *By a whisper of love?*
> *Spell-bound to a word*
> *Does time cease to move,*
> *Till her calm grey eye*
> *Expands to a sky*
> *And the clouds of her hair*
> *Like storms go by?*

[1989]

BERYL ALONE

Even now, after so many years, lying in that same bed staring up into what might have been the same writhing darkness above me, my memory of that night was as vivid as if she'd kissed me half an hour before, the reason for the kiss as unfathomable now as then. For all the years between, for all my maturity, I was still no closer to the truth of it. The best I could come up with was that it had been a kiss of mutual awareness, an unspoken seal of affinity between us – a conspiracy, almost.

I stirred uncomfortably in my bed, then turned over onto my side, to try and break the spell.

Arriving that afternoon at Canellun – a Canellun in which Robert no longer existed – had felt strange and unsettling. Having paid off the sullen taxi driver (who'd stood there like a mule until I'd piled enough tip into his hands for a car-wash and a week's holiday in Alicante), I headed up the drive with my suitcase, past the garage where a battered old Renault now skulked. In spite of myself, I still half expected Robert to burst through the fly curtain over the kitchen door, calling, waving—

But there was only silence and stillness. And longing.

I found Beryl in the far corner of the garden watering her fruit trees. Lying in the shade, a different dog, a collie, on its last legs by the look of it, warning her of my presence with a single exhausted bark. '*There* you are!' she exclaimed, as though she'd been searching for me for hours. She looked smaller and greyer and even more

243

stooped, and yet behind her spectacles her eyes, when she looked up, were as all-embracing as ever. I kissed her soundly on both cheeks. 'That's all very well,' she grumbled, 'but there's a dratted drought, and half the garden's stone dead!'

It seemed we were to carry on from where we'd left off.

After inspecting the damage we went up to the house, where she showed me an extension that had been built onto the dining room, with a spiral staircase outside, leading up to a new terrace above, which in turn lead into what had once been Juan's room but was now hers since Robert's death. 'It's much nicer,' she confessed. 'There's so much more room. And I have a terrace to myself now, and the last of the sun...'

Once back in the dining room, though, everything seemed the same apart from the extension which had been turned into a sitting room, most of the old furniture exactly as it was when I'd last seen it, containing little more than two large sofas, one of which I recognised as the old grey one on which I'd endured the injections of the vet – still stained, I could have sworn, with a smear of my snot.

On the wall hung a gleaming black phone. 'Good God!' I exclaimed.

'I know, it's a curse! It always rings when I'm not in the room. I'm sure it knows. I've put you in your old room, but you're very welcome to *our* old room if you like—' Instantly I had visions of Robert thundering down the hill from his resting place in the churchyard and turfing me out of his bed—

'No, William's room's fine, thank you—'

Later, while she was preparing supper, I asked if I could go and look at Robert's study.

'You can look at anything you like,' she laughed, 'but it's no different. Nothing's changed—'

Except for the aching void which Robert had once filled. Only the scent of him remained, the smell of old books and the faint mnemonic of cigars. I stood by the fireplace, looking down at the clutter of charms and talismans on the mantelpiece, among them the remains of the circle of black iron figurines.

I looked away, round the rest of the room – everything was in its place, never to be moved by him again—

His absence was almost as tangible as his presence, seeming to conjure him. In the sudden air of suspense I found myself holding my breath, expecting him at any moment to come crashing through the double doors, eyes staring, words half-formed, muttering to himself as he strode to his desk and grabbed his relief-nib pen, dipped it in the ink well and start to write while still in the act of sitting down—

I slowly exhaled, my fantasy futile. It was as if, without physical proof of his existence, my own existence seemed to diminish, falling through me like vertigo. Had they truly happened, those extraordinary events of almost thirty years ago, or were they nothing more than an aberration of memory distorted by time, and by my fear of exhuming them?

No. They had happened. Somewhere there was still my account of them, which I'd written at the time. If I could only remember what I'd done with it—

The room felt like a Pharaoh's burial chamber, with everything in place for his journey into the next world except for the mummified body of the Pharaoh himself. But then, for the last ten years Robert's mind had wandered in a wilderness of anxiety and bewilderment. It was as if he'd strayed out of his study one morning, forgetting what it was for.

At supper that night, while we were having coffee (Beryl and I in our old places, sitting diagonally on opposite sides of the dining table), she suddenly go up, went into the hall, and came back with a thin, buff-coloured folder which she plopped onto the table beside my cup.

In some surprise, I saw my name written down the side of it in her very individual capital letters, like the sign outside a cheap hotel, or a side-street cinema.

'What's this?' I asked, picking it up.

'Your letters to Robert,' she said simply. 'I put them aside for you. You can either take them away, or leave them here – whichever you like. If you leave them, they'll go into the archive. But at least I've given you the choice. And you're not the first person I've done this to, if that's any comfort. I'll leave you alone for a bit, to look through them. I'll be in the Press Room.'

Once she'd gone, I picked up the file – in some trepidation. What would I find? Childish scrawls? Immortal prose—? With my heart thundering in my chest, I started to read through the twenty-odd letters.

Some time later, she came quietly back, on the way to the kitchen with her empty cup. I threw down the file in disgust. 'I've never read anything so boring in my life!' I exclaimed. 'I can't even be bothered to finish them—'

She laughed. 'They're not *that* bad—'

'Yes they are. When you think how wonderful his letters to me were, they're a travesty. I'm astonished he even bothered to write back. All right, I was trying not to give things away, but even so—' I shook my head dismally.

'Cheer up!' She sat back in her chair. 'You were very young when you wrote most of them. What do you want to do with them?

'Leave them,' I said, hardly thinking. 'For a start I don't want them, and secondly, if I leave them here, for "posterity" as they laughingly call it, they'll serve as a permanent irritation to me, and a warning to others – rather like the slave muttering in the Emperor's ear during Roman Triumphs: "Remember you are mortal!" It's the sort of shame one should learn to live with.' I pushed the file towards her. 'But thank you very much for offering me the choice. It was very—'

She waved my words away, and asked after my cancer, as if it were already member of the family, and I answered in the same vein, 'Very well, thank you.'

'Will you live?' she demanded with a huge smile.

'I'll do my best,' I grinned back. Rather belatedly, I thanked her for suggesting to Foster that I buy his father's library.

'Don't thank me yet,' she insisted. 'You haven't even seen it. All I can remember is that there were an awful lot of books. And even if you buy them, how will you get them back to England?'

'I've got a pantechnicon coming out from Southampton. It'll be here next week.'

'Won't that be awfully expensive?'

'About £5000.' I laughed at her expression.

'Oh my giddy aunt!' She gazed at me anxiously. 'Will there be any profit left?'

'There'd better be! And talking of Foster, he asked if I'd go and have a drink with him at Las Palmeras tonight, to arrange about viewing the books tomorrow. Would you like to come?'

Beryl shook her head emphatically. 'No. Thanks all the same. I've still got some work to do on Robert's poems. Do you want to take the car? The keys are in it.'

I glanced out of the window behind me. There was no moon, but the sky was packed with stars. 'I think I'd rather walk, if that's all right? It's so wonderful to be back.'

Up at the house, the dog gave another solitary bark as I let myself out through the gates and onto the gleaming, starlit road.

The memory of my letters still rankled, although I knew that my decision had been right. Not that anyone would ever read them anyway.

My thoughts wandered to Robert, to his inimitable letters to me – and then straight into a further shame: where had I been during those years of his degeneration? Not here was the brutal answer. Oh, I'd made half-hearted offers to come out and help, but had always been told that there were plenty of 'carers'—that he wouldn't even recognise me anyway. I'd met one of the carers once, and hadn't cared for him much, and the thought that I'd be told what I could or couldn't do or say to my own grand-uncle was so unsettling that I'd felt nothing but relief when I was told that my services weren't needed – and nothing but regret now, for failing him. So what if he might or might not have 'known' me? I knew *him*, instinctively – that was the important thing – knew what he would have wanted from me – the songs he'd like sung to him, the practical jokes – but I'd simply convinced myself that he'd become nothing more than a husk – that the grand-uncle I'd known and loved was long gone – dead but indecently unburied—

It was a relief to be distracted from my miserable bloody thoughts by the chorus of belching frogs in the village deposito and to see, moments later, the flickering lights of Las Palmeras at the bottom of the street, an oasis in this desert of dark, shuttered houses.

As I passed below the terrace of the café I could make out a few desultory figures sitting at the huge white-painted iron tables – Jacov! – old and shrunk, hunched in his chair as he played chess with someone under the light of one of the bulbs which were strung through the trellis above the terrace. He glanced down at me through the railings as I passed below him, but didn't seem to recognise me. Even so, I nodded to him, murmuring his name.

Climbing the stairs to the café, I pushed open the rattling door and went in.

The bar had always reminded me of a Russian railway carriage, long and narrow, panelled to waist height with dark wood, a number of dim, fly-blown electric lamps hanging from the ceiling, stirring slightly in the draught of an old ceiling fan. The night was still hot enough to warrant it.

Glancing round, I spotted Vern sitting in the corner with some cronies. Although his beard was as trim as ever, he, too, looked old and sunken, staring at me blankly as I entered, before going back to his conversation.

I felt the same unease I'd felt in Robert's study. Did I no longer exist except as anonymous footsteps in the street, or as the stranger who pushed open the rattling bar-room door? Thirty years was a long time, admittedly, and yet I'd recognised Jacov and Vern instantly. Had I changed so much? All right, Jacov's moustache and Vern's beard made them more recognisable, and my own face was covered by stubble now, but even so—

I ordered a cortado and a Fundador from the same sullen barman of those days, his once good looks gone to wine-rack and ruin. He looked straight through me, like the others. Only when I asked for six packets of sugar for my coffee did his eyes narrow in a frown of faint recollection. I didn't wait for his reaction, but took my drinks onto the terrace where I chose an empty table in the shadow of the palm tree.

Some twenty minutes later there was a commotion in the bar, a sudden influx of people, and I heard someone call out Foster's name.

Then suddenly he was on the terrace, looking round eagerly, the same old Foster, chubby-faced, bespectacled, his curly hair receding, but still unquestionably the Foster of my youth – all of fifty now—

He spotted Jacov at once and offered him and his companion a drink, then did the rounds of the terrace, clapping friends on the back, shaking hands, insisting on buying a round—

Having failed to see me in the shadows of the palm tree, he disappeared back into the bar.

It just wasn't my night, and I gave up on it. Smiling ruefully at myself, I left a 25-peseta note under my glass, and slowly walked off the terrace and back onto the road to Canellun.

It seemed that I no longer belonged here. It wasn't simply greying hair or weight-loss – I no longer mattered, that was the point. It was like a foretaste of my own death. I must hurry if I were to write the story down. Even though logic dictated that death was the end, the memories of the dead lived on, like Robert, as ghosts among the living, just as the past lived on to haunt the living dead whose lives were unresolved. It was the ghost of my youth, after all, that I was pursuing now. I must stay alive somehow, if only to run that past to earth.

When I finally reached Canellun I felt so fired up, so certain of my existence at last – if only of my past existence – that I flung back the bolt on the gate without thinking.

Up at the house the dog barked, once, and I loved him for it. *Latrat Canis, ergo sum!*

Bolting the gate quietly behind me, I found myself looking back over it, into that night so long ago – yet now – into the memory of Margot's smile after she'd kissed me—

Restlessly I turned over onto my back again and stared up into the still-writhing darkness.

Whatever she had meant by that kiss, it had sealed my fate – and brought havoc in its wake—

[1960]

ON THE JETTY AT *CA'N FLOQUET*

The sound of Lucia's voice, calling up to me as if in a dream—
'*Simon, you must wake up! It's half past eight—!*'

Christ, I'd overslept—!

I leapt from sleep to wakefulness, from bed to window across the cool tiles of the floor, throwing open the shutters and leaning out into yet another beautiful morning. Below my window, everyone was at breakfast on the terrace.

'I said breakfast was at eight!' Robert smiling up at me impatiently. 'Come on, I want to go for a bathe! You can keep me company—'

'Robert, for heavens *sake*,' cried Beryl, 'he's still half asleep! At least let him have some breakfast!'

Lucia threw her father an anxious look and then squinted up at me. 'You can come down in your pyjamas if you like,' she called, 'nobody will mind.'

Stark naked, I grinned down at her. 'I'll put some on, then.'

By the time I'd washed and dressed and got downstairs, breakfast had been cleared away.

I found them all in the kitchen, Lucia and Juan washing up, Beryl feeding scraps to the poodles, and Robert, in a straw hat, busy with something on the kitchen table. Beryl poured me a cup of coffee as I apologised for being so late.

'It's *you* I feel sorry for,' she laughed, 'your grand-uncle's making you *Pa amb oli*—'

As I piled sugar into my coffee and stirred it I watched as Robert poured olive oil over a wedge of local bread, then rubbed garlic and a ripe tomato into the mess and added salt and pepper.

'Here—' he said cheerfully, slapping it into my hand, 'you can eat it on the way—'

Once through the gates we turned right and headed along the coast road, his pace falling quickly into step with mine, as if we were soldiers. Was this a throwback to the First World War, I wondered, or was he trying to keep my mind in step with his? I took a bite from the slab of bread-and-sick he'd given me – greasy and sour and not at all my idea of breakfast.

'How could you eat this stuff?' I muttered, more to myself than to him.

'*Pa amb oli?*' He sounded surprised. 'The Roman army marched on it for centuries—'

'I can taste their feet,' I grumbled.

Like a bird of prey he plucked the bread out of my hand and stuffed it into his mouth. 'Waste not, want not!' he exclaimed primly.

A couple of minutes later we strode past the turning down to the *cala*.

'Where are we going?' I asked.

'To *Ca'n Floquet*. Don't you remember? It's a bit further but it's private – part of the old Archduke's estate, although they let me bathe there, thank God, I can't bear the *cala* in summer – all those people—'

We walked on in silence for a while, Robert looking around now and then, clearing his sinuses, turning his head to spit against the wall behind us, grunting, clearing his throat as though he were on the point of saying something. But nothing came out and my mind wandered down to my bare legs, pleased to see that they'd already caught the sun from yesterday.

'The thing is, I wanted to talk to you,' he said suddenly with heavy intent, before staring distractedly out to sea.

Oh, God! Had he heard about last night – the 'joint'—?

But he said nothing more as we strode along, finally turning left down a wide track towards the rooftops of a huddle of houses. An old wooden sign said *Lluch-Alcari*, a name I remembered but couldn't for the life of me remember why. Once we reached the hamlet, though, it all fell into place – the pretty little square surrounded by a dozen or so houses—

'Ricardo and Betty Sicré lived here,' I exclaimed, remembering at last. 'They had a drawing room that reached out over the sea—'

'They still do,' said Robert absently. He was standing in front of a heavy iron gate, frowning, patting his pockets, turning them inside out—

'Blast!' he exclaimed finally, 'I seem to have left the key behind—'

I looked at him in slight astonishment. 'What's that hanging round your neck?'

Getting the hang of him again—

Once through the iron gate, we marched on down the steep, wild path towards the sea.

'No, I was thinking about Margot,' he said suddenly, as though in the middle of a conversation with himself. 'Sometimes she puts a spell on me and I forget everything. She's been thinking about me ever since we left Canellun. I can always tell. We have this sort of extra-sensory dependency—'

'What's she thinking?' I asked politely.

'About something quite else now,' he laughed, 'which is why I can talk to you.' He nudged me in the ribs with his elbow. 'Don't worry, I'm not *med*, as my dear mother used to say!'

She must have said it an awful lot, I thought to myself.

The path narrowed and he led the way at breakneck speed, as if to prove his fitness, down flights of stone steps and along the edges of terraces until we suddenly came to a clearing shaded by Italian pines. In the centre stood a huge round table, an old mill wheel, surrounded by stone seats—

'Sunday picnics!' I called out. 'We used to come here—'

'That's right!' He stopped and turned back to me, a shambolic figure, his towel dragging through the pine needles.

In the sudden silence between us I could hear the sound of trickling water, and looked towards an alcove which had been sunk into the terrace above us to contain a natural spring which overflowed a small stone trough. Instinctively, I looked up to the top of the terrace, above the spring—

'This is where Juan peed on my mother!'

She'd been lamenting the fact that the spring had dried up that year, so Juan had climbed to the top of the wall and obliged her with a fountain of his own—

Robert grunted, and abruptly turned away. 'Come on!'

I followed him reluctantly, revelling in the silence of the clearing, in the resinous scent of the pine trees, like a warm drug on the senses. If I remembered rightly, there had been statues surrounding the clearing when I was last here – a circle of nymphs and satyrs – though all that remained were a couple of broken pediments, one toppled onto its side—

'*Simon, come on! I want to bathe—!*'

I hurried after him, down a treacherous path where I finally skidded headlong on the pine needles, straight into my grand-uncle (it was like hitting a rock), and into the memory of the perfect little cove below us, with its own lagoon, a circle of rocks beyond the jetty protecting it from the bigger waves which rolled slowly past the inlet on the way to the headlands of the *cala*, a mile or so further along the coast. A curious Moorish-looking fishing hut with a domed roof stood on the jetty, a reminder of the island's early history. It was as if, no matter what we did here, nothing would alter it. Once we'd gone, and our wet footprints had dried, it would return to itself, into another time from ours.

Robert plonked himself down on a rock and began to undress, taking off his straw hat, removing the key on its leather thong from around his neck, then taking off his shirt, exposing the sudden shock of a scar which ran like a huge shark's bite around the side of his ribs. I looked away, not out of tact, but of revulsion, almost – and was instantly ashamed of myself. This was the wound he'd received in Mametz Wood, for God's sake, for King and Country! How dared I be so squeamish? And I must have seen it before, surely, when I'd last been here... memory played the oddest tricks... I looked back, deliberately, but having replaced his straw hat, he began to pull off his khaki shorts and drawers before reaching for his baggy bathing shorts. Unable to take this second shock, I hurriedly turned my back and began to undress down to my brief swimming trunks (which drew a fleeting look of surprise from him), and squatted self-consciously on the warm concrete, waiting for him to finish.

A moment later he strode past me, still in a world of his own, clearing his sinuses again, looking abstractedly round him until he reached the end of the jetty. Was Margot having another word with him, I wondered. I wished she'd talk to *me* like that—

All at once he doffed his straw hat and whipped it, like a flat stone, into the middle of the lagoon where it sat bobbing gently on the water. With an almighty and ungainly splash, he dived in, reappearing a few moments later under his dripping hat, raising it out of the water, perfectly positioned on his head. We both laughed. It was obviously an old trick, but a good one. I dived in after him, letting myself sink to the bottom of the lagoon, immersing myself in the amniotic embrace of the sea, in its sunlit depths, green and darker green, silent shoals of fish darting this way and that in perfect harmony.

Above me, Robert's pale legs and arms were dancing weirdly as he trod water, his black bathing shorts ballooning round his hips. There was a faint vibration from above, as if he were calling me. Kicking down against the rocks beneath me, I shot upwards, bursting through the surface behind him.

'—blast the boy – oh, there you are—! You gave me a fright—'

'It's so beautiful down there!'

'No, I know – look, I wanted to talk to you about your mother's letter—'

'What letter?' It was if a cloud had passed across the sun.

'She wrote to me before you came. She's worried—' He spun his hat back onto the jetty.

'*What?*' I stopped swimming and started to sink. Angrily, I turned on my side and swam round to face him. 'What do you mean?'

'This going to Madrid – to university – what-have-you—' He was panting from the effort of dog-paddling. 'Even though she and my brother Dick arranged it, she thinks you may be running away—'

'I'm not running away!' I protested furiously. 'If anything, I'm running *towards*!'

He grinned at me suddenly, delighted. 'Do you know, that's exactly what I said when I first came here – when people accused me of deserting England—'

'*I mean it!*' I glared at him.

'No, I'm sure you do – or rather, I *want* to be sure that you do. But the thing is, university's just another glorified school, really, and you haven't had much luck with schools. Trying to blow them up may be all very well in England, but in Franco's Spain they won't just expel you, they'll either shoot you out of hand or chuck you in prison and throw away the key—'

'That was years ago!' I protested.

'Only two years ago, according to your mother, but that's not the point; the point is that school, and even university, can do a great deal of harm to some people – lasting harm – and I want to prevent that if I can, not just for your mother's sake—' he spat out a mouthful of sea water, 'for yours. Look, let's get onto the rocks for a minute – it's tiring, treading water and trying to talk at the same time.' He rolled onto his stomach and struck out with a stately breaststroke for the rocks that surrounded the lagoon. I followed slowly, rehearsing the tongue-lashing I'd give my mother when I wrote to her.

Robert heaved himself onto the rocks, then turned and stretched down his hand towards me.

'It's all right, I can manage… thanks,' I grated through gritted teeth.

'Watch out for sea urchins—'

As I clambered rather inelegantly onto the reef, (my eyes peering down into the depths, looking for the telltale black smudges), Robert turned away from me and blew his nose through his fingers. I followed suit, imagining that it was my mother I was spattering all over the rocks—

'I mean, I had the most god-awful time at Charterhouse,' Robert went on. 'Not only was my mother German, but my middle name was "von Ranke" – not at all the thing in those days, just before the outbreak of the First War. I was bullied mercilessly. And that wasn't all… but the thing is, the only way I could get through was by pretending to be mad. If people think you're mad, they tend to leave you alone – have you noticed that? Although with hindsight I do sometimes wonder if I *wasn't* off my head… because there was Dick, you see…'

'My grandfather?' I prompted him after a moment.

'No – and he wasn't really called Dick – that was just the name I used to disguise his identity in *Goodbye To All That*. I called him "Peter" at Charterhouse—' he laughed suddenly, 'although *that* wasn't his name, either! His real name was George…' He stared unseeingly at the jetty opposite us. 'Isn't it odd – I haven't talked about this for ages—' he shot me an amused glance, 'and yet the older I get, the easier it gets – the less it matters, I suppose… and it might be of help to you. At the time, though, it was a matter of life or death. No, the thing is, your mother mentioned something about you and another boy at school—'

It was as though he'd punched me. I was speechless with shock—

Robert looked round, his expression changing as he saw my face. He was saying something, but I couldn't hear him for the roaring in my ears.

'*It was nothing!*' I shouted, rising to my feet in fury. 'How *could* she – it was just a *pash*—!' And before I even realised what I was doing I'd dived through his unspeakable words, deafening myself as the water thundered in my ears, powering deeper and deeper, down to the seabed—

In my haste to drown him out I'd almost drowned myself, having forgotten to take a proper breath, until I was forced, fuming, back to the surface – as far away from him as I could get.

He was still standing on the rock, his fists on his hips. 'Look, come back here, will you?' he called irritably. 'I'm trying to help, and I don't want to have to shout!'

I was trapped – not just by the rocks that surrounded the lagoon but by courtesy. To turn my back and swim away from him was unthinkable—

'The point is that you're not alone,' he said quietly as I swam towards him, 'that's what I'm trying to say. Look at me, will you?'

My eyes dragged themselves from the water onto the rocks and up his legs. It was like staring up at the Colossus of Rhodes. I met his eyes finally, and he smiled. 'You know, we're very alike in some ways,' he went on, 'and I don't just mean blood – I seem to remember we're both Leos for one thing, with all that implies – passion and loyalty, a sense of honour – and an instinct to love which is unstoppable once it's let loose. And a need to be loved, too. And yet we're both loners – am I right? In our heads at least, so when we finally let someone in from the outside world it's pretty shattering. In my case, with Dick as I still think of him, it was like a dam bursting, all my pent up feelings and passions sweeping everything before them. But those feelings were pure, poetic – and that's important. There was nothing physical. We never even kissed. Did you?'

'No—!'

'There you are, then!' he cried triumphantly. 'Just like me! Hang on, I'm coming in—'

He hit the surface like a depth-charge, the percussion sending shockwaves through the water. A moment later I was jolted violently as he swam between my legs before surfacing in front of me, laughing and spluttering. 'I thought I'd pay you back for giving me a fright!'

I glowered at him and he looked away, embarrassed, clearing his sinuses into the sea. 'No, seriously,' he said, 'it's not that I have anything against homosexuals *per se*, but on the whole they're flawed—' he rolled onto his back and floated beside me, '—morally, I mean. They have no real sense of honour. Men like Siegfried Sassoon, T.E. Lawrence – and others – fine in their way, and close friends once, but I had to let them go. It was either that or be dragged down to their level – mixing with their friends and so on, which became anathema to me—' He suddenly turned onto his front and swam up to me, until his face was only inches from mine. I noticed that he'd only shaved half his face that morning. 'Look,' he said, with an air of finality, *'you're not queer, are you?'*

'No I'm not!' Again.

'Good!' he exclaimed. 'That's all I wanted to hear!' With a cheerful grin he swam off.

I stared after him, frowning deeply, as much at my thoughts as at him. I'd told him the truth; I wasn't 'queer' in the sense which that dreadful word conjured in my mind – men in grubby raincoats slinking into the seat beside me in half empty cinemas or on buses, or mincing queens who behaved like women, or even seemingly

259

'straight' men like my two godfathers, and other close friends of my parents'—

And yet if Sherringham had wanted me to kiss him, I'd have kissed him. If he'd wanted me to make love to him, I'd have done it like a shot. I'd have done anything if he'd only asked. But he'd been in love himself, with a younger boy—

It had nothing to do with being 'queer' – that was the point. As boys, it was the only love we knew, apart from love for our parents – such as it was—

A strange medley of voices suddenly disturbed the idyll of the cove, and a moment later a fishing boat appeared beyond the outer rocks of the lagoon with half a dozen people on board, tourists by the look of them, laden down with cameras and binoculars. American tourists from the sound of their voices. I looked back at the jetty, wondering how Robert would react to this sudden intrusion. He was staring at them with a fierce frown. 'I say!' he called out imperiously, 'I'm afraid it's private here—' He broke into Majorcan, obviously chiding the two fishermen for bringing tourists to the cove, but they'd clearly been well bribed, looking away from him, shamefaced.

As it turned out, though, the tourists were members of a Kansas literary circle who made pilgrimages to Europe once a year to 'beard literary lions in their dens'. This year they'd chosen Lawrence Durrell, but were rudely rebuffed when they'd turned up at his house in Provence. Undaunted, they'd decided to find the nearest great writer to the South of France, and had come to Majorca. Had Mr Graves not received their telegram?

I pulled myself inconspicuously back onto the rock and watched in utter disbelief as Robert's whole attitude to them changed in reaction to their fawning and flattery, inviting them into the lagoon and onto the jetty, where they took endless snaps of him with his towel draped around him like a toga – and of each other, standing beside him. Once they'd exhausted their film, it was out with the autograph books, one of the women, her diamonds glinting cruelly in the sun, asking him to sign her handkerchief.

If this was fame, I thought, then you could keep it! And yet, to my slight self-disgust, I felt a sense of superiority, of exclusiveness, since the object of these peoples' long and uncomfortable journey (and of their hero worship), was my grand-uncle, who appeared to have become world famous while my back was turned. What I couldn't understand, though, was the way he pandered to them. My sympathies were entirely with Lawrence Durrell.

And then they were gone at last, still calling and waving as their boat slipped out of the lagoon and began to breast the bigger waves beyond.

I slowly stood up. The movement caught Robert's eye. 'Oh, there you are!' he exclaimed, then pulled a face. 'What about all *that?*'

'*How could you do it?*' I demanded hotly, at once regretting my tone of voice and diving into the sea to cool off.

When I surfaced, he was pacing up and down the jetty. 'How could I what?' he asked defensively.

'Toady' was too strong a word, though I longed to use it. 'Pander to those people like that—'

'Oh, they're all *right* – quite nice, really! They came all the way from Kansas—'

'I know,' I interrupted, 'I heard.'

'—and it's nice to know that they read my books, even in Kansas. They're my public. The least I can do is thank them – don't you think?'

'I suppose so,' I said grudgingly.

He came to a halt above me, staring out to sea. 'What you have to understand is that my American royalties are very important. They're the jam on our bread-and-scrape.' He looked down at me and laughed. 'I bet you anything you like my sales double in Kansas when they get home!'

'But they were using you!'

'Oh, it doesn't matter about *that*!' he protested, slightly hurt now. 'I'm just a native to them – chap in a loincloth living on a desert island. They'll go back with a good story and with pictures and autographs to prove it. No, they came a long way, looking for what might have been impossible, and I made it possible: good fairy,' he tapped the air with his magic wand, 'granting wishes!' His laugh was uncertain. 'Come on, I've got to get back. Here—' He reached down to me, just as Margot had reached down to me at the *cala* the day before, and an awful thought suddenly struck me. 'My mother's letter – you didn't show it to Margot—'

'What?' His eyes shifted away in confusion. 'I'm not sure... I may have done—' He gripped my hand and pulled suddenly, almost angrily, so that I lost my footing under the water and had to thrash about for a foothold. I felt a sudden, needle-like pain in my foot as I heaved myself up.

A moment later I was standing in front of him, dripping with his betrayal of me. Neither of us could bring ourselves to look at the other.

'But it was *private*!' I heard my voice breaking.

'No, I know! No, I just thought perhaps she could help...' He stared around, at anything but me. 'Listen, it's important that you understand something while you're here. There are no secrets – between any of us. I won't have it. Those are my terms, if you like. We're a family, and I include Margot. She's as much a part of us as you or Beryl or the children, though in a different way of course. I trust her completely. That said, I admit I was wrong – you've grown up faster than I'd thought. But I'd still have told Margot. She has a knack with young people; you only have to look at Juan – a month ago he wouldn't even come out of his room—'

'What's wrong with him?' I was surprised by the sincerity of his apology, and the mention of Juan. 'He's so different.' Margot had blamed Robert to some extent, but I wondered who Robert blamed.

'Yes, I know. Or rather, I don't know. Nobody knows really – adolescence, school, something inherited? Anyway, she'll get to the bottom of it... look, we'd better get on—' He suddenly tilted towards me, jabbing me in the ribs with his elbow. 'Are we still friends?'

I was taken aback that he should even ask – that he should care. When I met his pale blue eyes, though, they looked almost pleading. He really *did* care. 'Yes, of course! Always—'

'That's all right, then!' he exclaimed happily. 'Come on—!'

But no sooner had I started to walk up the jetty than I felt a stabbing pain through my right big toe and the ball of my foot. I hobbled the rest of the way.

'What's wrong?' he asked. 'Why are you limping?'

I plonked myself down on a rock and studied the sole of my foot. 'There are some black things... they look like holes—'

'Oh, blast!' he muttered, then laughed dryly. 'Either you've stepped on my feelings, or a sea urchin's! Let me look—' Gripping my ankle, he ran his fingers ungently along my sole, snagging a couple of spines. I wrenched my foot out of his grasp.

'*Jesus*—!' I gasped.

'Nasty. What we need is some olive oil and a pair of tweezers. Just get dressed while I think. The sooner we get them out, the better. Try not to put your weight on that foot.'

It was easier said than done as I struggled up the precipitous path from the cove, using the curled-in side of my foot to support me. By the time we'd reached the clearing my calf muscles were protesting violently at the contortions I was forcing on them. 'Look, you go on ahead. I'll make my own way—'

'No, I don't want to leave you – let me see – the Sicrés are in Paris... I know.! We'll call on the girls! I wanted you to meet them anyway, and if we go round the headland—'

'Girls?'

'Stella and Yancy. You'll like them. They're about your age – a bit older – and very pretty. They'll have everything we need. Right! How much do you weigh?'

I was non-plussed. 'I haven't a clue... nine stone something?'

'I can manage that. Jump up on the seat and I'll give you a piggyback—'

Moments later I was jolting across the clearing on his back, trying to make myself weightless, trying not to strangle him—

Instead of climbing up to Lluch Alcari, we kept to the wild coast path. He appeared to be inexhaustible, pausing only occasionally to heave me up with a giant shrug.

'Do you want me to walk for a bit?' I asked.

'Not yet... It's funny to think that I used to do this for a living – well, for the dying...'

'What do you mean?'

'At night, in the trenches, getting the dead and wounded out of No Man's Land. Even funnier to think that I used to curse the moon in those days...'

After a couple of breathers along the way, we finally breasted a rise in the path and I was suddenly pitched headlong back into my own familiar world, at the top of the donkey steps down to the *cala*. Robert went straight on upwards, though, towards the square tower, then suddenly surprised me by turning left, through a narrow gap in the wall, and up a steep flight of stone steps.

'Mind your head—'

I had to duck beneath an arching creeper, partially concealing a gate leading onto a terrace, bordered on one side by a pair of ancient stone-built cottages with massive wooden doors and donkey's-eye windows, tightly shuttered. 'These belong to the fishermen at the *cala*,' murmured Robert, letting me slide to the ground. A washing line weighed down with drab fishermen's clothes stretched across the terrace beneath a vine trellis. 'They live in the first cottage. I rent the far one from them and give it to people I like. Stella and Yancy have it at the moment—'

He pushed his way through the washing, holding a pair of trousers aside so that I could follow him, and we were faced at once with a second washing line, startlingly different, this one covered in gaily coloured girls' underwear and T-shirts and shorts. Robert looked round at me and pulled an amused face. 'I wonder what the fishermen make of *that!*' Ducking beneath the clothes, he looked up at the shuttered windows of the second cottage. 'Asleep...? Or out...?' he wondered. Cupping his hands to his mouth, he called up. '*Stella! Yancy!* It's me – Robert – with a walking wounded—!'

For a moment the silence dragged on. Then suddenly there were sounds like chickens being disturbed by a fox, shrieks and squawks of alarm, and finally laughter as the shutters on the first floor were thrown open with a crash and a beautiful girl with tousled blonde hair and the most extraordinary all-embracing smile leaned out of the window and grinned down at us through the trellis.

'*Hello!* What a lovely surprise—!' She put her head on one side as she looked at me, frowning slightly but still smiling. 'Oh...! Hello – wait – I know—' her face cleared, 'you must be Simon! We've heard all about you. I'm Stella. What's the time? We didn't get back till five. Look, come in, come in – the door's not locked. I'll come down!' And she was gone.

I looked at Robert, his face alight with pleasure. 'Isn't she lovely?' he said. 'It's so nice when people wake up happy! Come on—!'

STELLA

No sooner had we entered the darkened room than Robert went round throwing open all the shutters as if he owned the place – which I suppose he did in a way.

Sunlight poured in, dancing and glinting on the old polished furniture, on empty bottles of wine and the remains of a supper laid for three. What I'd imagined to be a hallway was in fact a hall-cum-dining-room-cum-sitting-room-cum-kitchen.

'God, what a mess!' muttered Robert, shaking his head but smiling indulgently. 'Here – help me clear up a bit, would you?'

'*Don't touch anything!*' A muffled cry from upstairs.

'I can't help it!' Robert shouted back. 'I have a compulsion for order—!'

As we carried the dishes and glasses to the sink, I asked him who Stella was.

'She's the daughter of my old friend James Reeves, one of the last true poets left in England. And of Mary, of course. James is one of my severest critics,' he pulled a face, 'but I still love him in spite of that. No, Stella's wonderful – always helpful and smiling—'

'And Yancy?' The name was so curious that it had stuck in my mind.

'Yancy's the daughter of another old friend, Len Lye, a New Zealander. He's a brilliant filmmaker who lived here for a while in the thirties – designed all the book jackets for the Seizin Press, that sort of thing. Yancy was brought up in America—'

'*You're not to clear up!*' Stella running down the stone stairs, laughing, golden, wearing nothing but a T-shirt over a pair of pink gingham bikini briefs. 'I mean it! We didn't know you were coming—' Taking a loaf of bread from Robert, she reached up to kiss his cheek before putting the bread in an earthenware crock, then taking it out again and putting it back on the table. '*Breakfast!*' she exclaimed with a laugh, looking directly at me. 'So you're Simon!' Fixing me with her bright blue eyes, still vulnerable with sleep, 'We heard all about you from Gill last night – hang on a minute—' she turned and shouted up the stairs. 'Yancy, come down and help, you idle slut!' Her voice sounded hoarse from the night before.

There was a muffled expletive among all the commotion above us. 'I'm coming, for Chrissake! Stop screaming! I've got a hangover and I can't find my skivvies—'

With another laugh, Stella turned back to me. 'Where was I? Oh yes – Gill! Apparently you two had a defining moment—'

'I didn't see you there,' I interrupted hurriedly, a yawning gulf opening suddenly between Robert and my feet. I glanced across at him. He had his back to us, washing up at the sink. I looked back at Stella, putting my finger frantically to my lips, willing her to understand. Her eyes widened in surprise. A moment later her mouth dawned into a mischievous smile.

'We arrived later,' she explained, 'after you and Margot had gone—'

'Margot?' Robert turned round from the sink. 'What's that—?'

'Nothing, Robert!' said Stella firmly, her dancing eyes still fixed on me, 'Just that we missed Simon and Margot at Jacov's party. Could you fill the kettle? I'll make some coffee.'

'I'll do it,' I offered, hobbling over to the stove.

'Why are you limping?' she asked.

'Oh yes!' cried Robert, turning from the washing up and drying his hands on the front of his shirt, 'that's why we came – Simon trod on a sea urchin—'

'Oh, poor you! Let's have a look. We'll need some olive oil and some tweezers – *Yancy!*' she yelled up the stairs again, 'bring your tweezers down!' To me, laughing, 'She's got eyebrows like hedges – she's always plucking them. Sit down here—' She pulled out a chair from the table.

Yancy appeared at last, in a man's shirt and a pair of cut-off jeans, attempting to float down the stairs, clutching her head with one hand and the handrail with the other. She was tall and attractive in a horsey sort of way, but a bit green around the gills.

'Hi, everyone,' she said faintly, holding out a pair of tweezers as she went over to Robert and kissed him gingerly on the stubbly side of his face. 'Jesus!' she gasped, rubbing her mouth.

Noisily, Stella pulled out a chair from the table and plonked herself down opposite me.

'Please don't do anything *loud*,' begged Yancy, sinking into another chair. 'Aspirin and coffee,' she whispered, 'then I'll be fine...'

'Well, the coffee's on,' said Robert brightly. 'Where are the aspirin?'

'In my room, I think,' she murmured vaguely.

'I'll go and get them if you like—' Robert made for the stairs.

'*No*—!' Yancy lurched to her feet, jarring her brain horribly.

'No, Robert—!' Stella, who had picked up my foot, dropped it with a painful thud as she jumped up. 'I'll go! You've seen quite enough chaos for one visit, and upstairs is even worse!'

Yancy waved her away and began to crawl back up the stairs.

'Don't worry, Robert,' said Stella hurriedly, 'she'll be fine once she's had some aspirin. Could you bring me the olive oil, d'you think?' She reached down for my foot again.

I was suddenly distracted by conflicting sounds from upstairs. Yancy, I could see, had just made it to the landing and yet, directly overhead, I could hear the sound of bare feet padding hurriedly across the floor. Stella froze as we exchanged glances in the same instant. Then she darted a fleeting glance behind her, at Robert, but he was busily clinking his way through the bottles, looking

269

for olive oil. By the time she turned back to me I'd fixed my face into a silent mask of astonishment, my mouth hanging open, breath drawn in as though I were about to betray her. She burst out laughing.

'What—?' asked Robert. 'What's so funny?'

'Nothing!' exclaimed Stella, as firmly as before. She didn't seem to be remotely in awe of him. 'Simon's face, if you *must* know!'

'Really?' Robert smirked at her. 'I can't say I've ever become hysterical at the sight of it, curious as it is. Margot did, mind you, as soon as she saw him—'

'Well there you are—' Stella said dryly, 'it *must* be funny!'

Her back still to Robert, she looked up at me from under her eyebrows and pressed her fingers to her lips, just as I had earlier. Her mouth was seriously beautiful, I realised, the upper lip unusually long and made for laughter, her teeth perfectly white and even.

Robert lumbered over with a saucer of olive oil and laid it down on the table. 'Can you get them out?' he asked impatiently.

'I don't know yet – and anyway, you're standing in the light—'

'Sorry.' He wandered off on another tour of inspection, staring round, straightening things. Stella grinned at me cheekily and went back to inspecting the base of my foot. 'Well, you've got five,' she announced cheerfully. 'I can get two out – maybe three, but the trouble is, if you grip them too hard, they shatter like glass.' Frowning with concentration, she reached for the tweezers and gently began to explore the pad of my big toe. 'This may take quite a while, Robert,' she said suddenly, loudly, flashing me a conspiratorial wink.

Sitting opposite her, I was in a state of bliss, my gaze resting at the juncture of her spread legs where the hem of her T-shirt failed quite to cover the thin pink gingham stretched tautly over the swell of her—

'*Ouch—!*'

With one hand she'd pressed agonisingly against the sea urchin spines, a frown of outrage darkening her face as she pulled at the hem of her T-shirt with her other hand. 'In fact, it could take a *very* long time and be *very* painful!' she exclaimed, glaring at me.

'Oh, blast!' muttered Robert, striding over to the table. 'I really ought to be getting back. Margot said she might drop by later this morning—'

'That's fine,' said Stella airily, 'leave Simon here. We'll look after him.'

'Well, if you're sure—' Robert dithered by the table, his eyes darting between me and the door.

'Of course I'm sure! We're going down to the *cala* later, for lunch. We'll take him with us. You'd like that, wouldn't you?' she asked, turning on me and squeezing my toe again—

'*Yes*! Wonderful!'

'Well, I'll be off, then.' He bent to kiss Stella on the cheek. 'I hope Yancy feels better soon.' Cramming his hat onto his head, he turned back to her. 'Look, why don't you both come to supper – on Saturday night, say? We'll celebrate Simon's arrival properly.'

'We'd love to, thanks.' She looked up at me with a snort that sounded suspiciously like a giggle. 'I'll tell Beryl, shall I?'

'Oh, yes, I suppose you'd better. Although I suppose I *might* remember,' said Robert doubtfully. 'Until Saturday, then. Look after Simon, won't you?' And he was gone, his heavy footsteps making the terrace quake.

Strangely, in the silence that followed, I felt no awkwardness at being left alone with the two girls. There was something so engaging and un-self-conscious about them (to say nothing of Stella's beauty and near-nakedness) that I didn't feel a moment's loss at his leaving me.

Yancy reappeared at the top of the stairs, peering nervously down at us. 'Has he gone?' she whispered urgently. 'Po's dying to go to the loo—'

The deeply tanned figure of a boy of about my age, wearing nothing but a towel round his waist, materialised suddenly on the landing behind her. Brushing past her unceremoniously, he vaulted down the stairs two at a time. '*Je vous jure que je vais m'enmerder!*' he gasped. Propelled across the hall by his predicament, he shot through door and ran along the front of the cottage.

'That was Po!' laughed Stella. 'The phantom footsteps! He's Yancy's. I think he ate something that didn't agree with him last night, and the loo's outside.' She looked up from my foot. 'The thing is, Robert feels rather protective towards us. He wouldn't *approve* – of Po. Or of us, come to that, letting him stay the night. So we don't tell him. *Do we?*' Again she squeezed my toe, like a vice.

'*No!*' I gasped, pulling my foot away. 'But I don't understand,' I said with an innocent smile, 'Robert said there were no secrets here—'

'Oh, *that!*' she exclaimed scornfully, as if she'd heard the claim a thousand times before. 'That's rubbish! We all have secrets! The only one who doesn't is Robert!'

'And Margot?' I asked.

'Margot?' She looked astonished. 'Margot has more secrets than the rest of us put together!'

'*God that's good!*' Stella slurping a mouthful of ripe peach soaked in white wine.

We were sitting at a table for four on the terrace of the café. Yancy and Po had deserted us for a swim, leaving behind the chaos of their lunch – oily shells of langoustines, broken bread and spilled wine.

'Here, try some.' Stella pronged a slice with her fork and jammed it into my wine glass to soak.

Above our heads a zephyr rustled through the palm fronds of the makeshift roof; below us, wavelets lapped and gurgled among the fissures in the rocks; all around us cicadas shrilled ecstatically in the heat. The sounds of paradise—

My gaze fell between the pine rails beside us, bleached with age and winter storms, at the flat-calm sea that filled the cove, greeny-blue, translucent, dotted with swimmers unaware of the wild underwater landscape of caves and canyons they were swimming above, so clearly visible from where we sat.

'Here—'

I slowly looked back at her as she held out her fork with its dripping mouthful of peach. Was it her golden face, smiling with anticipation, or her proffered fork, fresh from her lips that caused a sudden stirring of awareness? My gaze fell to her breasts, small yet perfectly filling the underwired bra of her bikini, her nipples straining against the pink gingham. I leaned towards her, Adam towards Eve, and took the dripping chunk of peach into my mouth. The sweetness of the fruit and the cool sourness of the wine were a perfect fusion, taking me back in an instant to boyhood picnics in Rome and Portofino, when such dunkings had been illicit treats. But I said nothing, grunting appreciatively.

'Isn't that just the best thing?' she demanded.

Her voice was quite unlike anyone else's. What I'd at first taken for morning hoarseness after a heavy night out seemed to be her normal way of speaking. I reached for the last of the wine and emptied the bottle equally between our two glasses.

She put her head on one side and smiled at me. 'You've no idea what a relief it is to be sitting opposite a new face. I get so bored listening to the same people, the same dreary little secrets. I mean, who cares if so-and-so's cheating with so-and-so, or thingummy-jig's having it off with a sheep!' She giggled into her wine glass. 'I'm sorry, I didn't mean to be "coarse" as my granny would say. I don't think I've got over last night yet.' She looked up at me suddenly. 'That's not to say that I won't listen to *your* secrets if you want me to. Or that yours are dreary,' she added, laughing.

'I don't think I've got any.'

'Don't be silly!' she snorted, as if I were a dim schoolboy, 'of course you have! Last night, for instance – smoking your first joint – remember?' Her eyebrows rose theatrically. 'Are you going to tell Robert about that?'

'Christ no!'

'There you are, then, you have a secret – already!' She took another sip from her glass.

I was suitably chastened. 'I hadn't thought of it like that.'

'Oh, don't worry,' she said brightly, 'it happens to all of us sooner or later. The *secret* is to keep your secrets to yourself. Or tell them to me if you're desperate,' she laughed, 'and I'll keep them for you!' Her smile faded and she looked at me earnestly. 'What you have to realise is that Deya isn't just any old village, it's a mirage – a fantasy. Nothing's truly real here… apart from Robert, perhaps – and Beryl… Canellun…' She frowned suddenly, turning her head to one side as if she'd just realised something. 'Canellun – that's it! *"Curiouser and curiouser"*, if you see what I mean. It's the rabbit hole into the fantasy – not that everyone falls down it, and not that everyone comes out of it – except Beryl. You'll have to take your chances…' She flashed me a huge grin. 'I'm a bit sloshed, I know, but I think that's what I mean. You're lucky, though, you're "family" so Robert will protect you – at both ends of the tunnel. If *you* fall from grace you'll be forgiven. He'll put it down to your youth, or to an aberration. Not that you'll ever fall out with him,' she added cheerfully, 'but all the same, it's best to be on your guard.'

'Thank you. I'll remember.' But I was watching a tiny rivulet of sweat as it trickled down between her breasts and under the wire of her bra. She wiped it away absently with her thumb.

'You were going to tell me about Margot.'

'Was I?' She looked surprised. 'Oh, yes—!'

I'd asked her on the way down, but she'd brushed the question aside with a brusque 'Later'.

She stared thoughtfully into her wine glass. 'Well, Margot's different.' She paused.

'In what way?'

'She's a one off, if you see what I mean. She *belongs* – in both worlds. A bit like Alice, I suppose. And she's lived on islands before, so she knows how things work. The trouble is, everyone wants to be her best friend, to be near her—' She looked up and grinned at me sardonically. 'Do *you*?'

Thrown, I groped for a suitable reaction. 'Give me a chance,' I laughed uneasily, 'I only met her yesterday!'

She pulled a face, shrugging off my answer. 'Bet you a pound you will! Everyone does – except for my father, that is. He doesn't trust her an inch – keeps warning Robert about her. They nearly fell out last time he was here—' I must have shown my surprise. 'It's just that he has an instinct about people—'

'Do *you* like her?' I interrupted. Inexplicably, her answer was important to me.

'Yes, actually,' she looked surprised, 'very much! Which is odd. I usually agree with my father. What's more to the point, though, is that Beryl likes her, and I've never known her to be wrong. And then there are Robert's poems to Margot. Have you read them?'

'Only one so far,' I admitted.

'Read them. They're extraordinary!'

Perhaps emboldened by the wine, I leaned towards her across the table. 'Stella, please don't get me wrong, but might your father be a bit jealous of Robert – as another poet, I mean?' I regretted the question instantly. 'I'm sorry – that sounds rude—'

She shook her head impatiently. 'No, it's all right – I'm sure most people think that, but more fool them! If you knew him you'd understand. He hasn't got a jealous bone in his body. That's what I love about him – about all real poets – they live so deeply in their own worlds, among their own obsessions, that what goes on in other poets' worlds is of no interest at all except as poetry. Rivalry simply doesn't exist at that level because they're all unique. He's just an honest man who speaks his mind. Robert respects that, which is why they're still friends, in spite of Margot.'

I found myself completely disarmed by Stella's frankness, and by her unaffected (perhaps unrealised) beauty. Something of what I felt must have shown in my eyes because she turned away slightly, her face colouring under her tan. '*Anyway!*' she said firmly. 'Margot. To tell you the truth, I hardly know anything about her. Nobody does. I mean, talk about secretive… I know she was married once, to an American painter, I think, called Carrick. They lived on a Greek island, but then something went wrong and she divorced him, and that's when Alastair met her. Do you know Alastair Reid?'

'Yes. I'm going to stay with him in Madrid—'

'Lucky you! Do you know his wife, Mary?'

I shook my head.

'You'll like her.' She gave me a deliberately arch look. 'She's from Boston. Very pretty. They have a baby son called Jasper…' She frowned. 'Where was I? Oh, yes – Margot. Well, Alastair met her on the *Leonardo da Vinci* – on her maiden voyage. He was covering it for some American magazine, all expenses paid. Anyway, he and Margot obviously hit it off because as soon as they came back to Europe he brought her to Deya and introduced her to Robert. And that was that – *boom!*' She made an explosive gesture, spilling wine on her forearm. Giggling helplessly, she began to lap it up. 'Sorry! Well, according to Robert, his hair stood on end and he felt as though he were having a heart attack or a stroke or something, because shards of words – that's how he described it – and fragments of poems he'd already written in the future – I think that's what he said – started to flash through his brain like missiles. He said that his head was full of chaos, as if he'd broken through into a new universe, or some such rubbish – *no!* I don't mean that, it's not rubbish, I just make it sound like rubbish—' She looked away suddenly, thoughtfully, running her hand unselfconsciously through her straight blonde hair, sweeping it off her face. She had good hands, slender and brown, her pale fingernails unpainted—

And yet in that instant of distraction her mouth looked sad, her long, expressive upper lip resting forlornly on the soft cushion of her lower lip.

'What about Margot?' I asked quietly, wanting her to go on. 'How did she feel, do you think?'

'Who knows?' she said vaguely, before suddenly focussing on the question. 'And that's the whole *point* – nobody does! She'll talk about anything except herself.' Stella turned back to me, fixing me with her clear blue eyes. 'But you can imagine what it must have been like for her, can't you? I mean, you know what Robert's like when he's really taken with someone – especially a beautiful woman – he's like a child! I was there at supper one night, quite early on, and he kept dashing off to his study, in the middle of a mouthful, and coming back with his toys – you know – all that stuff in his study, gold coins and rings and magic charms, boasting about the famous people who had given them to him – so desperate to impress her when he simply didn't need to. He even tried to give her some of them, but she wouldn't take them – which endeared her to Beryl, as you can imagine. The thing is, she came out of her divorce with practically nothing apparently, so now Robert gives her money – has to force it on her, more or less – and quite right too, in my opinion; if it weren't for him, she could be in Paris earning a fortune as a model, or whatever. I mean, you should see her clothes!' Stella's eyes widened in awe. 'She's got one of those old-fashioned cabin trunks at the Posada, stuffed with the most beautiful dresses and things, from when she was married – Balenciaga, Dior, Chanel. Her dowry, she calls it. And her *shoes*—! Ferragamo, Courrèges—'

'Stella,' I interrupted, 'for someone who knows nothing, you seem to know an awful lot!'

'But I don't!' she insisted. 'All right, I know about her clothes because she showed them to me one day, when it was pouring with rain, but everything else I know is from Robert. He's completely open about it—'

'And yet you say that Margot couldn't be more secretive.'

'Aaah, but that's different,' she said slowly, her face becoming serious again, her eyes seeming to focus inwards, 'part of her mystery, I suppose. Her spell. Part of Robert's fatal enchantment—'

I was taken aback. 'Fatal?'

'Of course!' She paused for a moment, still deep in thought. 'The Muse is always fatal to poets, Robert knows that. And I've seen it before, with my father, with other poets... Muses are sirens, whether they like it or not, just as all true poets are "Odyssians", as my father calls them, endlessly searching for undiscovered truths in a world that's...' she sighed, '...diminishing, somehow. And since we're on a mythical kick, and I'm a bit sloshed,' she grinned, 'I'll tell you what else I think: that Robert's right – Margot isn't really Margot at all – she's the reincarnation of some ancient goddess – or possessed by her at least. She's somehow doomed to be here whether she likes it or not. Trapped. But one day something will happen that releases her and she'll just vanish, as suddenly as she came...'

I was gripped by the suspense of her imagination, my mind racing through classical analogies. 'And then what,' I asked, 'if she *were* to vanish?'

'*Chaos!*' she erupted again, splashing less of her wine over herself this time because her glass was almost empty. Wiping abstractedly at the splashes, she seemed to stare through me into a future which only her long familiarity with Robert allowed her to foresee. 'No more poems – not real ones anyway. He'd go out of his mind, probably, which is why he tries so hard to weave his spell around her now, with love and poems, money...' She shook her head distractedly, as though at her thoughts. '"*All the wolves of the forest howl for Lyceia*",' she murmured. 'Do you know that poem of his? No, of course not.' She suddenly lurched towards me across the table. *'Margot doesn't need anyone!'* She stared at me intently, 'which makes her more powerful than any of us, Robert included.'

'Hey, Stella!' A sharp cry from below us. We looked down through the railings. Yancy was treading water by the rocks, straining to look up at us. *'Guardias!'* she called softly. 'On the beach!'

'Oh fuck!' breathed Stella, looking towards the *cala*.

Two *guardias* in full uniform, with their rifles slung over their shoulders, were making their way among the sunbathers along the narrow strip of beach, their hobnail boots skidding on the rocks. 'Looking for smugglers?' I speculated.

'No bloody fear!' growled Stella. 'They're looking for bikinis! Sodding Franco.' Raising her bottom from her chair, she pulled out the folded T-shirt she'd been sitting on and began to struggle into it.

I stared at her in astonishment as she began to pull it down over her bra.

'Bikinis are against the law in Spain,' she spat. 'I mean, how pathetic is that? Bloody fascists!' Sure enough, the *guardias* had picked on a pair of girls in bikinis and had begun to harangue them as they scrambled for their clothes.

Stella scanned the *cala* and the surrounding rocks. As her gaze swept round, she paused suddenly, her eyes alight with a new interest. 'Isn't that Margot over there, on the jetty?'

I jerked round hungrily. It was Margot all right, sitting with her basket in her now familiar position, her back against the rock, legs drawn up, reading what looked like a letter, so absorbed in what she was reading that for an insane moment I longed to be the subject of her intense scrutiny—

'Let's swim over and surprise her!' cried Stella, reaching for the hem of her T-shirt.

I looked at her doubtfully. 'I don't know. Perhaps she'd rather be left alone—'

'Nonsense!' exclaimed Stella, pulling her T-shirt over her head. 'Besides, she likes you – Gill told me. Come on—'

'What about the *guardias*?' I protested, half rising to follow her.

'Oh, pooh! We'll be hidden from them in the water, and if they see me on the jetty, what are they going to do? Swim out in their uniforms? Shoot me? Come *on*!' She slipped between the rails at the end of the terrace and vanished down the cliff.

It was only when I went after her that the remaining sea urchin spines in my foot reminded me painfully of their presence, and I was forced to follow her at an undignified hobble. 'Stella, I'm really not sure about this,' I called out, remembering Margot's need for privacy.

'Oh, balls!' laughed Stella, and dived in from the rock.

Reluctantly, I dived in after her. If nothing else, at least my foot didn't hurt in the water. Stella was half way across when she turned towards me, treading water as she put a finger to her lips. By the time she'd breaststroked her way quietly to the palings beyond the jetty I was relieved to see that at least Margot had finished reading her letter, or whatever it was. Although it still rested on her thighs, she was hunched over it, clasping her knees as she stared unseeingly towards the *cala*. Suddenly she sensed our presence, her head jerking round like a falcon's, fixing Stella with a glare, just as I climbed after her onto the slipway.

'Stella. Hi.' Her voice was flat, unwelcoming. Cursing myself for being there, I hung back as Margot stuffed the letter into her basket.

'We thought we'd surprise you!' Stella's cheerfulness sounded forced already.

'Simon…' murmured Margot vaguely, not looking at me.

I raised my hand feebly.

'Letter from home?' asked Stella.

'That sort of thing.'

'Robert thought you were going to Canellun.'

'Did he.'

Stella stared down at her, her head on one side. 'You're in a bad mood,' she said.

'I was fine...' Margot's voice trailed off into a dead silence.

'Aaah. Right. We'll bugger off, then.' In high-buttocked dudgeon she stomped past Margot towards the end of the jetty. 'Coming, Simon?'

But I needed to apologise first – and then she dived in anyway, without waiting for me.

I glanced at Margot in the sudden vacuum left by Stella, but she was staring at the *cala* again.

'*Guardias!*' She sounded surprised. 'Does Stella know?'

At that moment a faint breeze snatched at the envelope of her letter from wherever she'd put it and blew it past me along the jetty. I chased after it, careless of the pain in my foot, and managed to trap it under my heel. As I stooped to pick it up, I thought I recognised the handwriting from somewhere, although I couldn't quite place it. Not wishing to seem inquisitive, I deliberately looked away from it as I headed back to Margot.

'Why are you limping?' she asked incuriously.

'Sea urchin.'

She stared at me as she took the envelope. 'You should be more careful where you tread.'

Her words slipped between my ribs like cold steel. 'I wanted to say I was sorry—'

'Oh, stop apologising, for Christ's sake! You're always *apologising!*'

I stared down a her, shocked. In the sudden silence she glanced up at me, her grey eyes fierce beneath their dark brows. She looked away. 'It's just that it makes you sound weak... immature...'

'Well, I'm not!' I answered angrily. 'It's not *weak* to apologise – it's polite! I don't mean 'I'm sorry squirm-squirm-grovel—''

'I should hope not, in those swimming trunks—!'

The impulse which took me past her without a word to the end of the jetty and straight into the sea was childish, I knew, and I regretted it before I even hit the water.

The boy who dragged himself out of the sea and back onto the rocks below the café was still the same boy who had dived in from them, I realised with despair. Or was he?

Somewhere between, *something* had happened, something that had more to do with oracles than with a stupid attempt to surprise someone who didn't want to be disturbed. Stella had been no more than the unwitting catalyst. I'd been warned – that was the point – not just by Margot but by my own behaviour reflected in her anger.

The memory of it was almost unbearable.

When we left the café finally, I turned to wave to Margot, to show her that I understood, but the jetty was empty.

PARTY PIECES

That Saturday night Robert was as good as his word (passed on to a surprised but amenable Beryl by Stella), and threw a small party to welcome me, with cocktails on the terrace at sunset, to be followed by supper.

I'd passed him late that morning on his way to the study, when he'd suddenly punched me affectionately on the shoulder and told me that Margot had agreed to come. 'You should be honoured!' he exclaimed. 'I usually have to wheedle and beg her to eat with us—'

I stood where he'd left me, overcome by a growing excitement. I'd only seen Margot once since the incident on the jetty, waving to me from a passing car on the village street. If she'd agreed to come tonight, it must mean everything was all right between us again.

Beryl decided it was too hot to eat inside that evening, so we were to dine on the terrace, with candles for when night fell.

Everyone was caught up in a sudden party atmosphere as we heaved the heavy iron table that lived under the awning over the kitchen window out into the middle of the terrace and fetched the white wrought iron chairs, as cumbersome and aggressive as old drunks, from the breakfast terrace below my window, barking our shins and elbows as we manoeuvred them through the house. From the back of the airing cupboard Lucia, who knew the precise whereabouts of everything, unearthed a long damask tablecloth and matching napkins which Beryl hadn't seen for years. Robert busied himself concocting cocktails from the dregs of bottles of Stone's ginger wine, vermouth, and angostura bitters mixed with cognac and lemonade, while

Stella and Yancy laid the table with the best cutlery and glasses and candelabra.

Once everything was ready, we all sat down on the low wall of the terrace with our revolting drinks and surveyed what we'd created with something approaching awe. Even Robert was impressed. 'Am I dreaming this?' he asked of no one in particular.

'It's surreal—' breathed Yancy.

'—as if it had just fallen out of the sky,' added Stella.

'I think it's *fantastic!*' enthused Juan, his eyes alight at last. '*Wild!*'

'Oh, *Juan!*' snorted Lucia disapprovingly.

'Well, I don't know about *that*,' said Beryl matter-of-factly, 'but I think it looks very *nice*. We should do it more often.'

I agreed with all of them, although my first reaction to the table, with its dazzling white cloth and napery, gleaming cutlery and glasses, and the candelabras glinting silver-red in the sunset, was that we might have been sitting with our cocktails on the deck of a luxury liner, anticipating a fine supper.

'I feel we should make some extra effort,' said Robert. 'Dress for dinner or something—'

'I'm far too hot to drag myself back upstairs now,' said Beryl firmly.

'Wait – I know!' cried Lucia. 'We could all wear one of your scarves, father!'

'I don't think I've got one long enough—' quipped Robert.

'I meant one *each!*' snapped Lucia. 'You know I did.'

'For heaven's *sake*, Robert,' groaned Beryl wearily, 'it's a perfectly nice idea. Just go and get some scarves! It's bound to cool down after sunset—'

Robert dragged himself off like a martyr. A few minutes later there was a series of ghost-like groans from the kitchen, followed by hysterical barking from the dogs as Robert suddenly reappeared at the corner of the terrace, arms stretched out before him, his legs splayed wide apart, swathed from head to foot, like a technicoloured Egyptian mummy, in every scarf he could lay his hands on.

The effect of them, once we'd all chosen or been given the scarves that would best suit us, was surprisingly stylish, especially on the girls, who chose to wear them as stoles. But once this small excitement had been milked of its novelty the conversation began to flag and a strange hiatus descended on us all; a feeling emphasised by the sun at last sinking behind us.

Robert became increasingly restless. Finally he jerked to his feet as if he'd been sitting on an ants' nest and began pacing the terrace as he glared around him. 'Perhaps she's forgotten,' he said suddenly, as though finishing a conversation with himself. He turned to Beryl, agitatedly clearing his sinuses.

'*Well...* if she has, she has,' murmured Beryl, not ungently.

'All the more for us!' cried Lucia. But no one cheered.

Beryl was still looking up at Robert. 'I think we should eat soon, though, don't you? It's nearly dark, and the *gaspacho* will be getting warm...'

'Yes... no, of course... do you think I should go and look for her?'

'No.'

They stared at each other intently, as if communicating in a language of their own. Then Robert turned and strode from the terrace. 'I'll be in my study. Call me when it's on the table—'

After a moment, Beryl looked round at the rest of us and got to her feet. 'Right!' she said briskly. 'Lucia, we'll need some ice cubes for the soup – Juan, you'd better stir the *paella* again – Simon, light the candles, would you, and Stella and Yancy, perhaps you could give me a hand in the kitchen—'

I was alone on the terrace, my spirits sunk without trace as I began to light the candles, when Margot emerged out of the dusk on the drive, no more than a figment of my longing at first, angrily dismissed as candle-conjuring. I looked away, then back to where she'd been in my imagination – still there, but nearer now, standing at the entrance to the terrace, eyes wide with wonder, a smile of genuine astonishment on her lips—

'*How beautiful!*' she murmured as she approached.

Her quiet words precisely echoed my thoughts as I stared at her through the candlelight.

'Hi Si,' she grinned. I stared at her in astonishment. Nobody but my closest family had ever called me by the diminutive of my name. How did she know? I was still tongue-tied as we both, at the same instant, leaned across the table to kiss each other's cheeks—

Again, her *scent* – so stirring that I could hardly breathe out for breathing it in. 'I didn't hear the gate,' I heard myself mumbling inanely as I drew back.

'I'm not surprised!' She glanced towards the open kitchen window behind me from where the sounds of laughter and conversation were leaking out on a stream of electric light. And yet I'd been unaware of the noise until that moment.

'I'll go and tell Robert you're here – he'll be so pleased – he thought you weren't coming.' My breath caused the candles to gutter, throwing restless shadows up her face, at once concealing and revealing her sleight-of-beauty, her full, half-open lips, high cheekbones emphasised by the upcast shadows, calm grey eyes dilating hypnotically as the candle steadied again.

She shrugged, as if to say that I could do as I liked.

'About the other day... on the quay,' I began haltingly. 'Oh, the hell with it! No more apologies, I promise—'

She looked at me in exaggerated disbelief, just as Juan appeared suddenly at the entrance to the terrace carrying a pile of soup bowls. 'Hey, Margot! Cool—!'

'Hi, Juan!'

'Father will be so pleased you've come! But you'll need a scarf – here, have mine.'

Robert's tormented face glared up at me from what he was writing as I barged through the doors of his study (knocking was forbidden – he had nothing to hide—)

'Margot's here!' I cried triumphantly.

His naked vulnerability startled me – the change on his face from grim despair to almost unholy joy as he threw off his specs and towered to his feet. 'Where is she? Where—?'

'On the terrace,' I said faintly.

Rounding his desk, he flung open the side door of his study and strode out into the dusk.

As 'guest of honour', Robert insisted that I should sit at the head of the table with my back to the sea, Beryl on my right and Stella (again at Robert's insistence), on my left. As the others took their places, though, I realised that in fact I was sitting at the foot of the table, with Robert presiding at the other end, Margot beside him, their backs to the mountains.

I'd just made Beryl laugh – something I found it increasingly easy to do, and looked at her with a mixture of affection and curiosity. She didn't seem in the least to mind Robert sitting next to Margot at the head (or foot) of the table, or anything else about their relationship, come to that. Stella had been right: Beryl and Margot behaved more like close friends than two women vying for Robert's affections, and I found it puzzling. Perhaps it was time for me to wake up to what was going on around me and question things more, to look outwards rather than inwards—

The arrival in front of me of my bowl of *gaspacho* was a welcome distraction. Never having tried it before, however, I was suspicious at once of the two purblind cubes of ice, smeary with oil, staring up at me from a dark red sea of gelid-looking breadcrumbs with the consistency of winter slush... but once I'd put the first spoonful in my mouth and tasted the sudden rich cool rush of flavours, of ripe tomatoes and cucumber, raw onion, garlic, and the zest of indefinable 'other things', I became a slave to it, my face beginning to sweat with pleasure as I gulped it down. I was in the presence, I realised with relief, of something far more engrossing than my thoughts.

Half way through our second helpings, Robert suddenly clapped his hands and raised his voice above the hubbub of conversation and laughter. 'Listen everyone!' he called out. 'I've decided that as it's such a beautiful night, and as we're having such a wonderful supper, thanks to Beryl—' (heartfelt cheers and applause) '—you shall all sing for it when we've finished!'

Groans all round, except from Beryl. 'Oh, *good*!' she exclaimed. 'We haven't done this for ages! As long as nobody expects *me* to do anything.'

'Or me!' Margot sided with her at once.

'Coward!' Robert upbraided her, then quickly forced a laugh to show he was joking.

'Nor me,' chipped in Stella hurriedly. 'I mean, I *really* can't. My voice is disgusting.'

'Me neither,' said Juan quietly, pronouncing it 'neether', and held up his hand. 'Father—' he shook his head emphatically.

Surprisingly, Robert gave in at once. 'All right, Juan – although I wish you'd play for us—'

'He *has* to!' cried Lucia. 'I need him to accompany me—' She turned to look across at her brother and asked him, with surprising courtesy, to go and get his guitar. 'You won't have to play for long, but I can't do you-know-what without you, and I want to surprise Father!'

Juan got to his feet. 'OK,' he murmured with a trance-like smile, and left the table.

'Those who can't sing or play will have to recite something,' decided Robert, staring imperiously at Stella down the table. Then he turned back to Margot with a look of sudden intimacy, as if gathering her up in his fantasy. 'You could read one of my poems if you liked—'

'No.'

'Oh, won't you – please—?'

'*No*.' She outstared him. 'I mean it.'

'You can't *force* people, Robert!' Beryl called down the table.

Robert looked like a deflated balloon, and yet I could see how much he was enjoying the evening, sitting next to Margot in the candlelight as if on an island of their own. My heart went out to him for being so transparent. 'Oh, very well, then,' he grumbled with grudging good grace, 'Margot and Beryl are officially excused – but everyone else has to do *something*, however mere—'

'Don't be so patronising!' Margot frowning at him—

Robert pulled another face. 'I can't seem to say anything right tonight,' he lamented plaintively.

'Then best to say nothing!' Beryl called down the table, before turning to me with a huge, infectious grin. 'Poor Robert! It really *isn't* his night – and he does so love party pieces. His father used to make them all do it when they lived in North Wales, when they were young. Robert and your grandfather were best at it, apparently – they both had good voices, although Robert liked to show off more. What will *you* sing, d'you think?' she asked quietly, 'or haven't you made up your mind yet?'

'Actually, I was going to sing a folk song, but what you said just now, about North Wales, made me think of something else completely – a poem – though whether I can remember it, or find the nerve to recite it—'

'What *fun!*' she exclaimed. 'Is it rude?'

'God, no!' I protested, laughing. 'But it's very difficult, more like chanting than reciting.'

'Like Edith Sitwell, you mean?'

'Not quite – unless she were black, I suppose.'

The *paella* arrived in a waft of shellfish and saffron. By the time I'd put the first forkful in my mouth my taste buds were rioting again, even as I tried to remember the poem word for word. At first, the words were buried under memories of the night I'd first heard it recited by Richard ('Diccon') Hughes at Mor Edrin, the wind from Snowdon howling round the huge, sharp-cornered house. In the dining room, pitch darkness except for the embers of an enormous fire and a single candle casting sinister shadows up Diccon's face as he towered over the long dinner table looking like the ghost of Joseph Conrad, glaring round at the assembled company – at his family, at the Clough Williams-Ellis's, the Vaughans, Polly and John Hope, me – and launched into *The Congo* as Vachel Lindsay had taught him to recite it, roaring, bellowing, his face twisted in fury, then evil with cunning, now smashing his fist down on the table, now swaying, eyes closed as if in a trance—

My eyes flew open as I looked down the table at the sudden lodestone of all my energy. Even at that distance Margot filled my vision, as if my pupils had binocular powers. She was talking to Robert happily now, smiling, he basking in her smile, I basking in both their smiles as I nerved myself—

Did I dare do it? Had I the courage to risk her disappointment?

If I could only remember the words! Later, Diccon had taught them to me, together with all the intonations and gestures, just as he'd been taught by Vachel Lindsay—

I closed my eyes again and the poem began to emerge at last, word for word. This would be my offering to Margot, from the core of my one and only talent – an ability to convey passion through other peoples' words—

'Have you fallen asleep?' laughed Stella, poking me in the ribs.

As supper drew to a close there were none of the usual signs of winding down, of desultory conversation and inward regrets that the evening was coming to an end – a thing I hated above all else at mealtimes. Instead, there was a sense of anticipation, of excitement, as cheese gave way to fruit, and fruit to a tapering, expectant silence. Finally, Robert put down his paring knife with a clatter and glanced round in feigned surprise.

'Oh!' he exclaimed, his gas-blue eyes lighting up as if the shilling had finally dropped. 'I was having such a lovely time that I quite forgot!' (Derisive laughter as he got to his feet) 'All right, all right! But since I was the one to suggest this, I'll go first—' he launched into his terrible brogue again '—and put me song where me mouth is, as they say in dear old Oirland, and sing you *Father O'Flynn*, since sure it was one of the most popular songs of these last fifty years! It was written by my faither, an innocent unworldly man who sold it to his old school friend Charles Stanford for little more than a guinea. Stanford made tousands out of it, and never gave me faither a penny more – but then we Graveses are a bit naïve about money – like Father O'Flynn, as you'll hear—'

And in his high tenor voice he launched into the song:

> *'Of priests we can offer a charmin' variety*
> *Far renowned for larnin' and piety;*
> *Still, I'd advance you widout impropriety*
> *Father O'Flynn as the flower of them all—'*

—and so on and on, verse after verse, Robert's performance almost upstaging the song as he wriggled and shuffled, his huge body becoming more and more disjointed until it seemed inevitable that one of his arms or legs would suddenly fly off and come whizzing over our heads. Then, at a particularly awkward combination of words he nearly lost his false teeth, at which Beryl became helpless with silent laughter. The rest of us, having finally mastered the chorus, bellowed it out for the last time and burst into rousing applause. Glancing happily at Margot, still hooting with laughter, he threw himself back into his chair.

'Bravo, father!' cried Lucia finally. 'Right – *next!* – or we'll be here all night—'

Robert was instantly himself again, taking command. 'All right, everyone, calm down! Who's it to be? *Stella!*' he declared finally.

'Oh, fiddlesticks!' she groaned, before grudgingly getting to her feet and launching straight into the most ludicrous tuneless chant about a Chinaman who lived in Japan whose name was Chinerakka Chu Chin Chan.

As she collapsed back into her seat to a roar of applause, Robert fixed her with a look of baffled amazement. 'You astonish me, Stella!' he cried. 'As the daughter of one of the best poets in England, and one of my closest friends to boot, to allow your head to be filled with such oriental gibberish—!'

'It was my father who taught it to me!' she countered triumphantly.

In contrast to the previous two songs, Yancy's rendering of a New Zealand drover's song was curiously touching. As she rose to her full six feet, carelessly flinging the end of her blue stole over her shoulder, she sang it as if it were her National Anthem, her voice clear and steady, staring straight ahead of her as if at her nation's flag, her face growing increasingly puce under her tan, not with embarrassment it seemed to me, but with suppressed nostalgia. No sooner had she come to the end of her song than she, too, slumped back into her chair, covering her face with her stole as we all cheered her.

Earlier, I'd reserved the right to go last, if only because my offering required a certain amount of stage management, so now it was Lucia's turn. Her song was not only sad but beautiful, and what was more, I remembered most of it, having been taught it by Davina Dundas when I'd worked for her briefly at her bizarre folk song *crêperie* on the New King's Road, before joining *The Manchester Guardian*.

It was an ancient French ballad whose haunting melody was belied by the horror of its story:

'Sur la marche du Palais,
Sur la marche du Palais…
L'est une femme si tendre, allons-là.
L'est une femme si tendre—.

Elle est tant enamouré,
Elle est tant enamouré,
Qu'elle ne sait lequel prendre, allons-là,
Qu'elle ne sait lequel prendre.

C'est le p'tit cordonnier!
C'est le p'tit cordonnier!
Qu'a eu la préférence, allons-là,
Qu'a eu la preference…'

Juan accompanied her quietly, effortlessly, hardly looking at his guitar as he played, his dream-filled eyes fixed on the table in front of him. As Lucia sang, my attention was caught by Robert at the far end of the table, now shifting restlessly in his chair, eyes glittering with a new urgency, his gaze darting from Lucia – or perhaps from the words she was singing – to Margot, who seemed deliberately to be ignoring him, her head turned away as she listened, looking up at the night sky.

I followed her gaze, the sight of Robert fidgeting too distracting, but when Lucia started to sing about the *p'tit cordonnier*, I found myself distracted again. I'd heard the words recently—

And then it struck me: Margot, on the way down to the *cala* on my first day— *'Has Robert told you about the little shoemaker in French folklore?'* Disturbed by my thoughts, and by the words of the song, I found myself looking away, upwards again, my gaze sharing the same star-pricked sky as Margot's.

And yet what she couldn't see, with her back to the mountains, was a strange, refulgent glow, silver-white, that was spreading along the peaks behind where she and Robert were sitting, forming a halo above them. In my naivety I found myself wondering, wildly, if this were some kind of poetic manifestation – or if someone had exploded an atom bomb and we'd all be hit by the shockwave—

But nothing happened. The suspense dragged on and on to the sound of nothing more than Juan's muted guitar and Lucia's voice, more impassioned now as she came to the climax of her song.

And then slowly, in a eurekan moment that both dwarfed and dazzled me with the simplicity of its truth, the moon rose from behind the mountains in the nimbus of its own light, spellbinding, baffling, as Stella turned to me, her eye caught by the sudden glare on my face, on my white shirt, and the trail of moonlight racing down the white tablecloth towards Robert and Margot as Lucia sang the last verse of her ballad:

> '… *Et là vous dormiriez,*
> *Et là vous dormiriez,*
> *Jusqu'à la fin du monde allons là,*
> *Jusqu'à la fin du monde.'*

Only when she finally chose to release us from the song were we free to applaud at last, every eye smarting, even Beryl's, who must have heard it countless times. 'Why did you sing *that*?' she asked delightedly. 'You haven't sung it for years!'

'Everyone's been getting at Father tonight,' Lucia laughed self-deprecatingly, 'so I thought I'd give him a present.'

'*And you have!*' cried Robert over the applause, his glance darting from Lucia to Margot, who was still clapping. 'But thankfully I'm true to the White Goddess, or I'd be trembling in my shoes! No, it's a very powerful song – *La Belle Dame sans Merci* – Keats knew what he was on about – I included it in *The White Goddess*, you know—'

'Not *now*, Robert, for heaven's *sake*,' begged Beryl, 'we don't need a lecture *now*! Lucia, that was lovely, and Juan, you played *very well*! Now it's Simon's turn. I want to hear his poem.'

'It's not *my* poem,' I corrected her hastily, 'it's Vachel Lindsay's.'

'I say, what an extraordinary choice!' cried Robert. 'I knew him, you know, at Oxford – good poet!'

Beryl turned on him. '*Oh, be quiet, Robert!*'

Juan, who had vanished into his seat again once he'd played his part, suddenly burst into irrepressible laughter at the ticked-off look on Robert's face, mimicking him so brilliantly that for a moment they looked like reflections of each other.

This small diversion gave me time to prepare for the poem, slipping behind Stella and Yancy to close the kitchen shutters and block out the light. Stella turned to me with a puzzled frown. 'Could you blow out the candles?' I whispered urgently. 'All except the one in front of my place—'

She did as I asked, ignoring murmurs of protest from the others. 'Simon said to blow them out,' she said firmly.

In the sudden gloom and acrid stench from the smoking wicks, the terrace seemed to surrender itself to the moonlight, and to an expectant hush as I stood behind my single guttering candle, inching forward until I could feel the upthrust heat and light touching my chin, casting my face into stark shadow as I allowed the primeval curse and fury of the poem to well up inside me—

'*The Congo*,' I announced finally, and threw myself into the poem as if it were the vast river itself, choked with the bloated black corpses of its horrific past, allowing it to sweep me down the moonlit tablecloth towards her—

REVELATIONS

Later that night, long after we'd all gone to bed, I found myself unable to sleep, kept awake not only by the burn on the palm of my right hand where I'd slammed it down onto the lighted candle, but by the mnemonic it triggered, endlessly, of reciting the poem, of its effect on the others – on Margot – her inner being quite suddenly exposed, if only for an instant, transforming her somehow into even more than I'd imagined her to be—

Finally, my blood fizzing with restlessness, I got out of bed and pulled on my shorts and a T-shirt before creeping out into the corridor and down the stairs, stopping mid-step as I suddenly heard the desultory murmur of conversation from Robert and Beryl's room—

Had I woken them? Motionless, one hand on the banister, the other resting like a stethoscope against the wall of their room, I strained with all my senses to listen in the darkness to the echoes of the past few minutes, but in the playback of what I heard in my head there had been no sudden exclamation, no rude awakening; they must have been talking for some time, Robert sounding anxious, Beryl grudgingly awake, calming him—

No denser than the shadow of myself, I crept on down the stairs and across the moonlit hall, through the dining room and into the kitchen. I didn't need to turn on the light to find the key to the door hanging from its hook on the end of the wooden drainer above the sink, letting myself out into the velvet stillness of the night, the silence broken only by the drowsy chirring of cicadas and the soft clunking of sheep bells in the olive groves above the house.

Padding barefoot onto the moonlit terrace, I suddenly felt like a guilty man returning to the scene of his crime – and yet what crime? Unless it was a crime to fall in love – to stumble into it as if I'd missed my footing and pitched forward into another dimension of the senses, a seventh sense, beyond even the sorcery of insight.

I looked around in desperation. Somehow I had to sort out what had happened—

Although all traces of the party had gone, the iron table pushed back against the kitchen wall, the memories and echoes of the evening still haunted the terrace.

Grasping one of the heavy iron chairs by its arms, I heaved it across to the centre, to where we'd all sat, and let it down quietly, facing the moon, an anchor to my wild thoughts. I was still too restless, too excited to sit down yet, and began to pace around the chair, touching it occasionally as I passed, as though to earth the power-surge that was coursing through me—

So what had happened? Think—!

Nothing! Nothing that anyone would have noticed, at least – except for Margot...

I'd recited *The Congo*, yes – but I'd finally done it as it was truly meant to be done, and yet better, better even than Diccon Hughes had done it, because the poem had been *mine* tonight, my instrument, the expression of myself, more powerful than myself because of the spell of words not mine yet *mine* tonight – I the magician, empowered by God only knew what – by Vachel Lindsay himself, perhaps – to convince her of my worth, of the power of my sudden naked love for her—

And yet it wasn't as if it had been a love poem – on the contrary, it was a poem about hatred and revenge, which was at once both strange and explicable, since to turn hatred into a declaration of love required a suspension of disbelief that only a magician could conjure and only she could allow—

And the words, the shouting and banging and the sheer syncopated rhythm of the poem had all had their shocking effect, so that when, at the end, I'd fixed my gaze on Margot and screamed out the last word while at the same time bringing down my hand on the lighted candle in front of me, the sudden darkness and silence became demonic, my ears filled with the echo of her triumphant shout, my brain seared with that last sight of her before darkness, her look of wonder and enthralment, that sudden, blinding flash of reciprocated love—

I was hardly aware of the cries of shock in the darkness, of the applause, of Robert thundering towards me in the returning moonlight and embracing me, insisting that I should follow in my parents' footsteps and go on the stage – it was only when the candles were being re-lit and I slowly returned to the present and looked around that I realised that everyone at the table was seeing me in a new light, as someone who had pulled off something lasting, worthwhile—

But I had eyes only for Margot, still applauding (more slowly than the others) smiling ineffably as she stared down the table at me, her eyes still glistening with a shared passion, looking back at me hypnotically, her gaze a lowered drawbridge to her power—

It was as if we had *met* at last, on equal ground.

I stopped pacing and flung myself into the heavy iron chair, the moment of euphoria suddenly swept aside by confusion – panic, almost. I was out of my depth. She wasn't mine, and never could be. She was Robert's – *no!* – that wasn't true, not quite. Already I'd seen them together enough to realise that she was his only when she wanted to be. When she didn't, she was hers alone.

And yet she *was* Robert's – in the sense that Gill had meant it, at least. Whatever it was he took from her – her power, his inspiration – she was his muse. So how was it that I, too, could feel that same inspiration, that same longing to cast spells into words to express my feelings for her?

Thou shalt not covet—

But I didn't! Not in that sense. Surely it was possible for two men to fall in love with the same woman without wanting to possess her for themselves alone?

A familiar vertigo rushed through me, making me cling to the arms of the chair. All at once I was in a darker, emptier place than I'd ever known, as if condemned to solitude for life. If it weren't for Margot's existence...

The kitchen light was turned on suddenly, startling me as it lit up the terrace. Screwing up my eyes against the glare, I saw Robert shambling past the Aga to the shelves by the window where he started to rummage among the tins and packets that Beryl used for cooking.

'Hello!' I called out, in case he should see me and take me for an intruder – or a ghost.

He spun round, his hands still at shelf height, and pressed his face to the mosquito-netting. 'Who's there?' he called sharply.

'It's me – Simon—'

'How nice! Hang on, I'm just getting some bicarbonate of soda—'

'Shall I come in?'

'No, I'll come out.'

Moments later he strode onto the terrace stirring his glass of fizzing bicarb with his huge finger, then downing it in one, standing stock still for a few seconds before letting out a strangled belch. 'Blasted stomach!' he gasped. 'It's our weakest point, you know – Leos. Couldn't you sleep either?'

'No. Nothing to do with my stomach, though – I just couldn't get tonight out of my head.'

'Yes! No, it was great fun – party pieces always are. We do it too seldom. And you were terrific, by the way – quite got my hackles going – and Margot's!' His face clouded over. 'But there was something else—' He started to pace up and down in front of me, his thoughts driving his feet. 'Did you feel it? A sort of foreboding—'

I knew instinctively what he wanted me to say. 'She did seem a bit... distracted.'

He turned on me, his eyes igniting. 'Exactly! But it's more than distraction, you see. She's got something on her mind, I know she has, but she won't tell me what it is, which makes me powerless to help. I mean, I know I exhaust her sometimes – my demands on her... but it's more than that.' He frowned down at me suddenly, intently, as if actually aware of me for the first time. 'It must be difficult for you to understand all this – Margot – Beryl—'

'No!' I insisted at once. 'I *do* understand. I may not know very much, but I still understand!'

After a piercing look, he gave an abrupt nod. 'Good! That's instinct – your mother's blood, I shouldn't wonder. But the point is, you're my grand-nephew, and you have a right to know. I trust you completely, and besides, *not* knowing something makes a secret of it, which I won't have—'

He went back to pacing, his heavy footfalls sounding strangely hollow on the tiles of the terrace, reminding me that it also served as the roof of the vaulted *deposito* below, echoing from lack of water.

At the corner of the terrace he stopped for a moment and looked up at the moon, the moonlight turning his silver hair into a halo of incandescent light. When finally he turned back to me and spoke, it was in a different voice, almost another man's, firmer and lower, as though coming from a deeper place inside him. 'Look – I am a poet. Agreed?'

'Yes—!' The words – his intensity – took me completely by surprise.

'What's more, I am a true poet,' he went on. 'Of course, I write prose as well – books and articles and what-have-you – but that's simply to please people, to make money. I'm not ashamed of that; the more people I please and the more books I sell, the better I can support my family and the more time I can spend on poems, which is the whole point. The thing is, though, that none of this diminishes my poetic powers – on the contrary, it heightens them because all my energy is moving in the same direction – towards poetry.'

He towered over me again, staring down as if willing me to understand. 'What you have to realise, though, is that the older one gets as a poet, the more fanatic one gets – time running out, the search for perfection – whatever – and you have to remember that one's dealing with a language of great antiquity, enormous range, and strict internal rules of what can go with what. In the poetic trance one has to keep a thousand things in mind and make them *agree* – which happens when one's service to the Goddess is complete,' he sighed theatrically, 'and-doesn't-when-it-isn't! Are you with me so far?'

'Yes—' He was speaking as simply as he could, I realised, to help me understand.

'Very occasionally – only three times in my experience – the Triple Goddess takes possession of a mortal – a woman – who becomes The Muse – rather like in the Bible when you read of people being "possessed" by the Holy Spirit. Margot is possessed, to an extraordinary degree, more so than any of the others in fact, and of course I am possessed by her. All of which proves that the longer and harder I work in the service of the Goddess, the more urgently and clearly she needs to communicate with me. It's quite frightening, sometimes, the intensity – her demands—'

He fell silent for a moment, staring at the ground as he paced, his footsteps adjusting themselves automatically to the dark lines formed between the moonlit tiles, as though walking a tight rope. 'And then sometimes, like tonight – *nothing!*' He turned to me again, his arms outspread, as if offering himself. 'I mean here I am, her poet, ready, pen poised, waiting for a sign, for that single flash that will spark a poem – my tribute to her – which she *needs!* She has no reality except what I reveal of her in my poems. Margot and I have a duty to each other, she knows that.

Hers is to be the oracle of the Goddess, to inspire me to ever greater feats of worship, of poetry, while mine is to love her with words that reflect the magic she bestows on me... and yet I've been sitting next to her all evening—' again he held out his arms, helplessly, '—and... *nothing!*'

I felt he expected something of me, something that I was more than willing to give in spite of the risk of making a fool of myself. 'Perhaps you... demand too much of her?' I suggested tentatively.

'Of course I do, and she of me! That's all part of it! This isn't a game for mortals, don't forget – no cries of *pax!* No quarter given! We're both in deadly earnest of each other, of ourselves... so that when she vanishes, like tonight, I feel... betrayed, I suppose – bereft of words, at least, and there's nothing more awful for a poet than to be denied inspiration – except to be robbed of it, of course—' He turned on me suddenly, his pale eyes huge, hypnotic. 'But when she's "At Home", as it were, when I knock on her door in the dead of night and the passage light comes on upstairs, the sheer ecstasy of the door being opened by her, of following her into the house in a trance on an indescribable upsurge of words and feelings—' He broke off to stare ruefully up at the moon again. 'But not tonight... not for too long, now,' he murmured to himself, 'and it hurts...' He glanced round at me. 'It makes my stomach ache, more and more, and the more it aches the more it distracts me, and the less use I am to her, and the more it aches!' he laughed bitterly. 'Anyway... Beryl's arranged for me to see a specialist in Madrid next week, a top man who'll find out what's wrong, hopefully, and make me better. And tonight Margot told me that she needs a break for a while, so I'm going to take her with me – leave her with Alastair and Mary, come back alone—'

But I was already half deaf with shock, my heart beating so thunderously in my ears that I had to struggle to take in what he was saying.

'They'll find her a flat somewhere, just for a while. Beryl thinks it's for the best—' He broke off suddenly, frowning at me. 'What is it? What's wrong?'

'Nothing!'

'Yes there is!' He stared at me intently, and while half of me longed to sink into the ground with grief, the other half longed for him to acknowledge this sudden agony.

'It's Margot, isn't it?' he demanded. 'Of course it is. You've become attached to her – and she to you – which just goes to show how powerful she can be when she chooses. I mean, you've only just arrived, and yet you're in thrall to her already – which is fine, because you're a part of me, a part of all this, and you really *do* seem to understand, which makes me very happy.' He stared down at me. 'Oh, don't be downhearted! Look, I know it's awful, her going, but imagine what it's like for me! At least you'll be in Madrid yourself soon… And listen, I tell you what – you could keep an eye on her for me while you're there – will you do that? Help her find a flat, make sure she's got enough money, that sort of thing—'

'Of course,' I said faintly, before finally nerving myself to ask 'How long will she be gone?'

He shrugged helplessly. 'Who knows? A month or two… or three… I'll introduce her to some friends of mine in the movie business there. They're making a film at the moment, about the life of *El Cid*, and I might be able to get her some work…' He looked away distractedly, pressing at his cheekbones. 'I mean, oh, God, I don't know – perhaps it'll do us both good to have a break from each other… that's what I have to believe, at least – because she believes it. The thing is, one can't always fathom the workings of the Goddess. Her effect on me is as powerful as the moon's effect on the earth – beautiful and intriguing in some ways, and yet ruthless, capricious, cruel – the power she wields, the tides she pulls, the violent waves… and the end, the climax, can be an absolute bloodbath – for the poet. But this isn't the end, I know it isn't. It can't be. I have to be patient, that's all...'

He wandered off to the corner of the terrace again, where all at once he let rip a series of cathartic farts. *'Aahhh!'* he gasped. 'That's better! I'll be able to sleep now—' He headed towards the entrance of the terrace. 'We mustn't despair, either of us! We'll talk more tomorrow.' He glanced back briefly at the moon, then at me, grinning. 'I think you've had enough illumination for one night!' And with that he pulled an imaginary light cord and strode off the terrace, then back into the house through the kitchen door, turning off the light—

A moment later, the moon went out.

I looked up, astonished, to where I'd last seen it, to where a diagonal bank of cloud now obscured it completely.

Robert's delighted laughter floated out from inside the darkened kitchen.

Over the next few days, as the realisation that she was leaving sank in like a slow poison, my life appeared to continue as usual only when Margot and I were together, falling apart completely whenever I was alone. Except, of course, that there was nothing 'as usual' about anything any more; everything had changed, if only in my own mind, and nothing I could do would change it back. Worst of all, I could tell no one about my love for her; not only would I look a fool if I did, but she wasn't mine to love. I had to hold my tongue – to behave and seem the same as ever. If I wanted to be with her more often than I actually was, then it had to be at one remove, through Robert, whose nature was to tell me anything I asked, or even to volunteer what I needed to know without my asking at all. In me he had the near perfect partner in his eternal card game, someone to whom he could deal out his thoughts at any time, then shuffle and re-deal them until they suited that day's perception of her; a game of patience to him, of impatience to me, my thirst for knowledge of her unslakeable.

As the day of their departure drew closer, Robert grew more and more uneasy, fearful not only of the effect Madrid might have on her, but of his own ability to survive in the void of her absence. What if he couldn't endure it, if his poetic inspiration dried up, as it had once or twice in the past apparently, and driven him almost mad? Like everyone else, I did everything I could to reassure him because that was what he needed most – to be convinced, despite his worst fears, that this was nothing more than a temporary separation, that far from suffering, his work might actually benefit from a period without the distraction of her presence. As for me, the realisation that at least I'd soon be with her in Madrid somehow kept me going, despite my instinctive dread of the place. Nothing I'd heard about the city was in the slightest bit reassuring.

In spite of Robert's anxieties and stomach troubles, life went on as usual at Canellun – as hectically as ever. His use of time was phenomenal, his ability to expand the day until he'd crammed it full of everything he'd decided to do at breakfast, was astonishing. The morning post, bundles of letters tied up with string, would be quickly and ruthlessly sorted by Karl (who dealt with the time wasters), leaving Robert a pile of correspondence sometimes a foot high, to answer himself. Once this was done, there was the serious matter of work-in-hand, whatever books or articles or poems he was working on, the whole day peppered with the arrival of children on bicycles from the telegraph office in the village bearing often indecipherable handwritten cables on cheap blue paper, neatly folded and sealed, from filmmakers, scholars, publishers, all to be discussed with Beryl, who replied to many of them in the Press Room on her grey ex-US Navy typewriter with its CAPS key permanently jammed down. After lunch, a short siesta, a quick swim – an hour there and back, sometimes fifty minutes, depending on pressure of work. He almost never wore a watch, convinced that the combination of his own magnetic force and the iron lode in the mountains around Deya always played havoc with them, so he timed his walks punctiliously by the electric kitchen clock, trying to beat his own record whenever he swam alone. Afternoon tea was followed by more poems, general work, more telegrams, correspondence again, until nightfall. After supper, more of anything outstanding until his relief nib pen was thrown down with more relief than nib.

On our last night before they left for Madrid, Margot invited us all to supper at the Posada, where the atmosphere was uncomfortable, almost feverish, all evening, at one moment everyone speaking at once, the next an uneasy silence. It was as if some mischievous spirit were switching the light of conversation on and off at random. Robert was up and down like a yo-yo, offering to help, then firmly told to sit down; one minute talking whatever gibberish came into his head, to lighten the atmosphere, the next slumped in his chair, brooding and restless.

As chameleon to his mercurial emotions I found myself empathising with each of his chains of thought as they linked themselves to the slightest casual slip of the tongue from anyone who reminded him of his departure, or of Margot's not returning with him. Not that Margot was much help; I'd never seen her so happy and carefree – like a prisoner on the verge of being released – nor so oblivious of the torment which Robert (and I, desperately straining to keep my true feelings reined in) were going through. By the end of supper I felt as drained as he looked.

Juan, when I occasionally glanced at him, seemed equally affected, like some minor disciple at The Last Supper, following Margot with his eyes, not fawningly as one might expect of a smitten sixteen-year-old, but with a quiet intensity which betrayed his feelings far more poignantly than Robert's histrionics. I felt almost sorrier for Juan, who seemed to depend for his life on Margot's presence here. I knew that Robert's self-discipline and sense of purpose would see him through, but Juan seemed to have no purpose at all, stuck between a strange school in Switzerland and a home which had somehow sapped him of his very identity.

Finally, in an attempt to distract everyone (and in some cryptic, demented way demonstrate my own love for Margot) I announced that I was going to pierce my own earlobe, having secretly admired one of the beats in the village, Phil Shepherd, an artist who had just impaled his on a knitting needle. Robert's attention was gripped at once as he insisted that I should pierce my left earlobe, since among Spanish gypsies it signified bachelorhood, while a ring in both ears indicated a married man, and a ring in the right ear a widower. But once Margot had supplied a bodkin, for which he made a pommel out of a champagne cork so that I could grip it firmly enough to pierce the gristle, gouts of blood began to pour down my neck as I tried to ram it through. What with Lucia screaming at me to stop, Juan screaming with laughter, Margot cheering me on and Beryl looking like a grieving widow on a war memorial, head bowed, hands shielding her eyes, groaning, the noise became too much for Robert, and yet again he ended up in the dog house for shouting at us all to be quiet. Not even when I passed him the salt cellar could I raise a smile from him.

In fact, my only consolation for mutilating myself was a gold sleeper from one of Lucia's ears (which she begged me never to return to her), and the knowledge that I would bear this stigmata of my love for Margot for the rest of my life – if I didn't die from blood poisoning first.

ALONE WITH BERYL

The next morning, the day of their departure, was the most beautiful yet – a betrayal by Nature of my innermost despair, and I cursed her for it.

Earlobe throbbing like a second heart, I waited outside with the others in the freshly-minted morning sunlight to say goodbye as Robert blundered in and out of the house in search of things he thought he'd forgotten – and didn't need anyway according to Beryl, who had packed for him. She sat on the low wall of the terrace dressed in a smart linen bolero coat and skirt, her handbag on her lap, shaking her head and grinning round at me every time he vanished back into the house.

'Is he always like this when he goes away?' I asked disbelievingly.

'*Yes*. All he's doing is casting spells for his safe return and saying goodbye to everything in case his plane crashes. He hates flying.' She twisted round to speak to Margot, shielding her eyes against the sun. 'I'm sorry, but there's nothing I can *do*! If he misses something out, we'll only have to come back.' I forced myself to look round as well, trying to shield not only my eyes but my heart from the vision of Margot in a stylish summer frock quietly playing hopscotch with a fir cone on the square tiles of the terrace, purse clutched behind her back, dark hair jouncing softly to her movements.

'It's fine!' she said lightly, throwing Beryl a ravishing smile as she went on with her game.

How *could* someone as radiant and beautiful as the morning itself cause such unhappiness? Not that it was her fault, any more than it was the sun's fault for shining, or mine for being in love with her. The fault was Love's alone – this human contagion that had infected my entire body, inflaming every thought and nerve-ending until my soul itself seemed to burn with fever. Not that I was alone in my feelings, I realised, with Robert and perhaps even Juan struck down as well. Where Robert was so lucky, though, was in being able to channel the infection, to bleed himself of the constant fever of his love for her with words that contained her very essence, that actually *smelt* of her as I read them, while all I could do was endure the infection silently, without expression of any kind. Even as I longed for a cure, in the same breath I realised that I'd rather die of what I felt for her than live and feel nothing.

'What will he think he's forgotten next?' she asked casually.

'His *passport*,' said Beryl firmly, and they laughed together, just as Robert charged out through the fly curtain over the kitchen door clutching his stylish black sombrero to his head – an extraordinary sight if you weren't expecting it, pale blue linen suit already crumpled and creased, the trousers held up with string, his favourite coloured waistcoat bursting open across his chest.

'How nice to hear you both laughing!' he exclaimed.

'We're laughing at *you*!' declared Beryl bluntly. 'Now is there anything *else* you think you've forgotten, or can we go at last?'

'Yes, no, of course! All done—! No – wait – I haven't said goodbye to the children—'

'We're here, Father!' called Lucia. She and Juan had been propping up the back of the waiting Land Rover having a discussion about some jam they were going to make that night on the far side of the island. As she came out from behind the Land Rover, Lucia took one look at Robert and shook her head despairingly. 'Haven't you got a belt, father? What on earth will they think of you in Madrid?'

'Couldn't find it – and they can think what they like!' He tucked the knot into the waistband of his trousers and pulled his waistcoat over it. 'I know who I am and I've got a passport to prove it!' he suddenly clapped his hands over his pockets. '*Christ*, my passport! I haven't got my passport!'

'For heaven's *sake*, Robert,' burst out Beryl, laughing at Margot and me as she opened the driver's door, 'Majorca's *Spanish*! You're going to *Spain*! You don't *need* a dratted passport! Now say your goodbyes and get in, or we'll miss the plane.'

Embracing his children, he turned to me and kissed me soundly on both cheeks, brutally crushing my left ear. 'You're the man of the house while I'm away. Look after Beryl for me – help her as much as you can.'

'Of course,' I was slightly baffled. What about Juan—?

'We'll talk more when I get back.'

His shambolic presence was suddenly replaced by Margot's – poised, beautiful, her smile throttling me. 'Hi Si!' She kissed me briefly on the lips. 'Bye, Si!' Then on my cheeks—

'How did you know I was called "Si"?' I asked her, grasping at any straw to keep her there.

'Alastair,' she murmured, grinning, before kissing me again, briefly. 'See you in Madrid.'

I nodded fiercely, smiling back, and a moment later they were all aboard, the engine roaring, gears grinding into reverse as Beryl started to back down the drive, Juan and Lucia keeping pace on either side of the Land Rover to open and close the gates—

'No, wait! *Wait!*' Robert's cry through the open window as he groped for the door handle. 'My spectacles! I've left my spectacles behind—'

From the seat behind him, Margot leaned forward and raised his sombrero, revealing his glasses perched on top of his head. Released from their forced captivity, they tumbled onto his nose.

A last sight of them both grinning at me, and they were gone, like triumphant bride and groom, dragging my useless, clattering heart behind them.

Beryl and I sat at our usual places that night, the two of us alone among the ghosts of the others. It felt odd at first, sitting diagonally opposite her, like strangers on a train, but then I began to rather like the fact that we didn't have to look directly at each other, that she had the window behind my right shoulder to look through, and I had the doorway into the kitchen and the front door beyond, so that I could see anyone coming in. It also meant that we weren't forced into conversation, that we could sit in companionable silence in a room that was usually loud with talk and laughter.

'It's so quiet,' I said at last, wondering if I'd let the silence drag on too long.

'I *know*,' she looked up from her soup, beaming at me, 'it's *wonderful*! Robert in Madrid, the children on the other side of the island—'

'I don't quite understand why they had to go to Andraitx to make jam,' I puzzled. 'Why couldn't they make it here?'

Her head sank towards her soup as she let out a noise like an asthmatic dragging in her last breath.

'It's a *jam session*, you fool!' she laughed. 'They're making *music*, not marmalade!' She got up to clear the bowls, leaving me slightly stunned by my naivety. 'What did you do today?' she asked.

'Nothing much, really,' I answered.

(Apart from fleeing the terrace while Juan and Lucia were still closing the gates behind the Land Rover and racing down the steps to the grotto, eyes already blinded by tears, out onto the coast road and into the olive groves, leaping like a suicide over the edges of the terraces onto the terraces below until I fell badly, knees and ankles cut, sobbing like a child at the intolerable loss of Margot, at the gaping chasm of her no-longer-thereness—)

'I called in on Stella,' I said, trying to sound normal.

(Blundering through the door of her cottage a couple of hours later, parched, bloody, with nowhere else to go, Stella jumping up in alarm at the sight of me, then laughing as I told her that I'd tumbled all the way down the mountain from Canellun, filling the washing up bowl with water, standing me in it, agreeing to divide my legs between us, she washing down the left one, I the right—)

'—she's quite extraordinary,' I went on as I took our things to the kitchen.

(Stella laughing up at me as she reached the brief leg of Juan's old shorts with her sponge, my cock suddenly heavy with awareness, the closeness of her hand, her perfect smile – the shock of my betrayal completely throwing me, turning away, squatting down in shame to hide my growing erection, pretending to wash my feet—)

'*Yes*,' said Beryl firmly. 'She makes a *very nice change* – from everyone else, I mean.'

My sense of isolation increased as we ploughed through our chicken, beans and potatoes. Never one for idle gossip, Beryl seemed content to eat in silence, which was fine, except that I'd been longing to ask her something when we were alone together, and this was the first real chance since that night on the terrace when Robert had offered to tell me about her relationship with Margot, before switching off the moon and going to bed. When I should have asked him later, I kept forgetting, and now that she and I were alone together I was tongue-tied by her silence. As a matter of principle she almost never asked a leading question (except of a child or an animal) in case she trespassed on peoples' privacy – which was all very well until the boot was on the other foot and one needed to ask *her* a leading question.

The silence between us ticked inaudibly away. I stole a glance at my great-aunt, absently feeding titbits to the dogs while staring dreamily at the sunset out of the window behind me, a sudden, perfect still life of self-containment, quite remote from me.

'I've been wanting to ask you something, but I don't quite know how to,' I said finally, in a rush. 'I mean, I don't want to put my foot in it, or offend you...'

'Good grief!' she breathed, her eyes huge with astonishment. 'Ask me *what*? It must be very important!'

'Not at all! Or at least, only to me. The thing is,' I finally grasped the nettle, 'Robert said the other night that he wanted to tell me about you and Margot, but he never got round to it. I mean, I know it's none of my business, except that he said he wanted to explain—'

'Explain *what*?' she was grinning now, clearly enjoying my discomfort.

'Well...' I groped for a way in. 'You seem very *fond* of her – of Margot, I mean—'

'*Certainly* I'm fond of her! She'd hardly keep coming here if I weren't.'

'No, of course! It's just that it's quite difficult to understand...' I finished lamely.

'For heaven's sake, *what's* difficult to understand?'

'Well, both of you...' I groped for some subtle way to express myself, 'being part of Robert—'

'Oh, I *see*—' Her smile became almost uncontrollable. 'As in ruby and amethyst!'

'I'm sorry?'

Still smiling, she shook her head in despair. '*Ruby and Amethyst*,' she said at last. 'It's a poem of Robert's.'

She took off her glasses and dried her eyes. 'Oh dear,' she gasped, 'your *face*!' Replacing her specs, she pulled herself together. 'Look, it's really very *simple*; there's certainly no mystery about it, in spite of what people might think – not that it's any of their business anyway. But if you say he wanted to tell you, then I'm sure he did. The thing is, Robert's a *poet*, first and foremost, which is what's always attracted me to him, but in order for him to write at his best, he needs a *muse* – he always has, ever since Laura Riding, who was the first, I suppose.' She frowned to herself briefly. 'Well, there's nothing I can do about *that*! Not many wives can fulfil everything a poet needs – not

314

forever. Luckily, I've liked almost all his muses — although to be truthful, I suppose I like Margot the best.'

'Why?' I asked, delighted that she did.

'Well, for one thing, she makes me laugh. Perhaps not so much in the past few weeks, but then Robert can be very demanding sometimes, especially when he works himself into a state about something. At the moment I'm not sure whether his fears are real or imagined, but what I *can* say is that he's had a wonderful run with his poems lately, and he owes it all to Margot. Without her, things would be very different, which is why she's so much a part of us — as all his muses have been.' She raised her eyebrows enquiringly. 'Will that do? I think it'll have to, for the moment.'

'Of course,' I answered hurriedly, although I wished she'd go on. Most importantly, I longed to know (not out of prurience but out of a need to balance equations in my head) if he and Margot had ever made love, which he'd seemed to imply. Beryl was the last person I could ask, though. Besides, she'd just lit her evening cigarette and vanished again, even deeper into her thoughts. I lit one of my own and stared unseeingly ahead of me, into the kitchen, realising how little I actually knew about her, apart from the fact that her father had been Sir Somebody Something, a high-powered solicitor, or Solicitor General — a most unlikely father-in-law to Robert. His first father-in-law had been Sir William Nicholson, who'd at least had Art in common with him. I knew that Beryl had done brilliantly at Oxford, and yet her whole life seemed to be devoted to protecting Robert, as much from himself as from others, her sharp eye fixed on the future, wary of danger and omens. Perhaps because she'd lived with his genius for so long, with his superstitions and spells, she'd acquired an almost mystical power of her own, as a matriarch, foreseeing, defending—

'Now that I've answered your question,' she said suddenly, 'perhaps you wouldn't mind answering one of mine?'

I looked at her, startled. 'Of course — anything!'

'It's just that I've always wondered about something that happened when you were last here, as a boy, with Diana.' She got to her feet. 'Come through to the Press Room for a moment.'

Puzzled, I scraped back my chair and followed her as she crossed the hall in her slow, unhurried way, slightly stooped, one hand resting against the front of her thigh as though to support her back, the poodles dancing round her feet.

'Why's it called the Press Room?' I asked. 'Someone told me once, but I've forgotten.'

'Because that's where Robert and Laura kept the printing press – a great brute of a thing—'

'Of *course* – the Seizin Press!'

'*Yes.*'

Once inside the room it seemed almost inconceivable that a bloody great printing press, with all the typefaces and paraphernalia that went with it, could have fitted in, let alone the printer himself. As Beryl's study now, sparsely furnished as it was with a chaise-longue under the window, a desk and a chair, it still seemed quite small, although one had to take into account the packed bookshelves that lined the walls with Robert's dog-eared reference books, many of them huge and in almost countless volumes.

'Now where was I?' she mused, looking above her desk at a long row of quarto Lett's diaries stretching back to the thirties, the dates pasted carelessly onto the foot of each spine. 'The thing is, I always look through these when people haven't been back for a while – just to remind myself – ah, here we are, 1953...' She took down the volume and plonked it on her typewriter. 'I'm sure I left a marker... *yes.*' The diary fell open at an old envelope. 'It was soon after the play we did to celebrate Robert's and your birthdays, do you remember – *Am I My Brother's Keeper?* It was one of the best plays we ever did! The Moreheads were there, and the Metcalfs – do you remember them?' She turned to me, smiling.

'No... I remember the play, of course, and Alan's book about the two Niles, but I don't remember them *then*, if you see what I mean. There's so much that I don't remember, even though it was only a few years ago. And so much has happened since then.' I shrugged helplessly. It was as if I'd deliberately tried to forget – perhaps out of fear that I'd never return.

'Well, see if you can remember this—' She stared at me intently, as if she were trying to wheedle some sort of confession from me, before she looked down at her diary. 'It was your last day, and you'd disappeared again – without Juan for once, thank goodness. Your mother had worked herself up into one of her *states*, when you finally came up out of the olive grove below the house, in a frightful mess, covered in blood, and Diana slapped you – for frightening her. So of course you vanished again. Juan and I found you in the end, in the old sheep hut below Canellun, half naked, covered in sick, clutching Robert's old army knapsack. The top of your little finger was almost severed...' She glanced up enquiringly as I looked down at the deep scar round the little finger of my left hand. She nodded, satisfied. 'You were quite delirious – shouting something about a scorpion, and cutting your finger to get the poison out, so I got you up to Canellun and stuffed you with what was left of the aspirins and put you in the bath. You were sunburned in places you shouldn't have been,' she grinned up at me, 'but asking you about it only made you more upset. Like a fool, I said that you'd feel better once you were back in England the next day, and you started yelling that you didn't want to go home, that you hated England, and that you'd done something to bring you back, and that no one could stop it – and then Diana burst into the bathroom and shouted at you to stop shouting, and that was the end of that!' She shook her head ruefully. 'Poor Diana... she tried so hard, but I don't think she was really cut out to be a mother... not then, at least. How are things between you now?'

'Much better – we still drive each other mad sometimes, but we laugh a lot, too.'

'Oh, *good*, I'm so pleased. We're very fond of her, you know.' She looked back at her diary. 'Anyway, later, when I'd got you to bed and went back to the bathroom to clear up, I found Robert's knapsack, and of course I opened it – *well!*' she exclaimed, looking up at me, her eyes wide with conjecture. 'What *had* you been up to?'

Without waiting for an answer she held the diary open against her chest. 'Now we have to go through to the study—' Again, she led the way. 'Isn't this *exciting!*'

I wasn't so sure. The walls that seemed to separate me from some of my childhood memories were still impenetrable. These things had obviously happened, and yet I found that I could only imagine them—

Beryl pushed open the doors of the study and switched on the light. The instant I followed her in I was struck by Robert's presence, even though he was in Madrid – the smell of cigars—

'It's as if he were still here, isn't it?' laughed Beryl. 'That's why I keep the doors shut.'

'To keep him in, you mean?'

'Good heavens no! To keep him *out*! It's impossible to work in my room with him breathing down my neck. Now, have a look at the things on the mantelpiece – tell me if you recognise anything—'

I went over to the fireplace, an ugly, suburban thing of brick and cement with a mean little grate. Staring down at the jumbled collection of artefacts on the mantelpiece, my eye was caught at once by the circle of malevolent-looking black iron figurines—

'The tower!' I heard myself gasp, even as I began to search for other mementos of that day, the mists clearing as if at the sudden revelation to an arcane riddle— 'The Martello Tower, on the point—'

'The *atalaya*—'

'Yes—' Christ! How could I have forgotten?

'What reminded you?' she asked urgently.

'These—' I pointed to the circle of iron men.

'*Yes!*' She was looking at her diary again. 'What else?'

'Some of these—' I pointed at a neat pile of ancient coins. I turned to her. 'Did you ever tell Robert?'

'Yes,' she grinned, 'but not until after you and Diana had gone back to England. I told him what little I knew, then gave him the knap-sack, still covered in blood. He emptied it out onto his desk – there were other bits and pieces as well, all very odd. He stared down at them for a while with a deep frown, and then the penny dropped. "*He's been casting spells!*" he said.' She looked up at me. 'Is that true?'

I nodded. 'To bring me back—'

'*Well.*' She smiled. 'They seem to have *worked*.'

'They've taken their bloody time,' I grunted.

'Perhaps you weren't *meant* to come back till now. Perhaps there's a reason.'

Margot! But I said nothing.

'So Robert was right...' She stared at me intently. 'There's just one more question – the thing I most wanted to know, to tell you the truth—' She reached out and lifted the lid of a small, ancient looking clay pot. 'Did you take any of *these* to the *atalaya?*'

I leaned forward and looked inside, at what appeared to be scraps of dried-up old leather. 'What are they?' I asked.

'Well, these aren't actually the ones that used to be here. These are dried Mexican mushrooms, given to Robert by Gordon Wasson – hallucinogenic mushrooms... very *powerful*! But when you were here, Robert had some English ones, "magic" mushrooms, he called them – tiny little dried-up things...' She looked at me expectantly, but I could only shrug.

'I'm not sure...'

'It's just that it would have explained your being delirious. Scorpion stings don't have that effect really, not here – and besides, you probably got most of the poison out when you cut your finger...' She looked at me enquiringly, but again I could only shrug and shake my head. She sighed regretfully. 'I didn't say anything to Robert at the time because I wasn't sure, but I made him put them away, just in case... I mean, imagine if Juan had got hold of them!' With a laugh she replaced the pot lid and closed her diary. 'I'll go and put the coffee on... don't forget to shut the doors behind you.'

No sooner had she left the room than a dense silence descended, seeming to muffle my ears as Robert's presence overwhelmed me again. I found myself pressed against the mantelpiece, my head drooping forward against the chimney breast as I looked down through half closed eyes at the jumble of artefacts, breathing in deeply through my nose, inhaling not only the scent of his room, but the presence of Robert himself, sitting at his desk behind me in another time, unaware of my presence, fidgeting, straightening his pens, reaching for a sheet of paper—

I would probably never know what made me open the pot again, dip my fingers in and take a pinch of half a dozen or so fragments of mushroom and put them in my pocket – only that it wasn't me who did it but someone I'd once known in another existence, while Robert looked on from behind his desk, unseeing—

Without looking back I hurriedly turned out the light and left, closing the doors of the study, leaving the secret of what had happened in the past, as if with the child I'd once been.

Over the next few days while we waited for Robert to return, Beryl and I became closer than ever. With a few exceptions I'd always found it easier to get on with women than with men – perhaps because they were more forgiving on the whole. They were certainly more amenable to the needs of others, so that when I asked if she could teach me to drive properly, she agreed at once – before doing a slight double take. 'What do you mean *properly*?' she asked. 'Have you driven before, or not?'

'Yes, of course, in North Wales. Diccon and Frances used to let me drive the Jeep as far as the Harlech road, and Robert Hughes let me drive his DUKW across the estuary once, to Portmeirion—'

'Hmmm,' she grunted doubtfully. However, it was agreed that I would drive her as far as the outskirts of Palma the next day to do the weekly shop – or as far as her nerve would take her, at least.

In the event, I'd hardly scraped my way backwards out of the garage before she was reaching for her door handle.

'Everything's on the wrong side!' I shouted over the roaring engine. 'I should be sitting where you are!'

'I couldn't agree more!' she shouted back. 'Mind the dratted *dogs*!'

They were racing around us in circles, yapping hysterically, snapping at the wheels.

Juan and Lucia, standing at the gates to cut them off, were keeping an eye open for oncoming traffic as my foot slipped off the brake pedal and onto the accelerator, sending the leviathan hurtling towards them in a hail of gravel. As I roared through the gates Beryl shrieked, Juan flung himself headlong into the ditch, and Lucia vanished over the wall on the far side of the road. With great presence of mind I flung the wheel to the left and headed towards Deya in first gear.

'*Change down!*' yelled Beryl.

'*Down what?*'

'*Go into second!*'

My eyes were everywhere at once, my hands shaking uncontrollably as I wrenched at the gear stick, forgetting the clutch, and got what felt like a severe electric shock. I tried again, using the clutch, and got it right.

'*Right!*' she shrieked.

'Right!'

'*No – keep to the right, you fool!* We're in *Spain*—!'

With an oath, I swerved across to the right-hand side of the road before glancing briefly in the rearview mirror. We were being chased by the dogs, chased by Juan and Lucia, followed by the cats. I raised my hand briefly to reassure them.

'*Who are you waving at?*' Beryl, panic-stricken, looking straight ahead, 'there's nobody *there*! Keep your hands on the wheel and don't let go! I must be *mad*!'

'Don't worry, I'm getting the hang of it. What happens if we're stopped by the *guardias?*'

'I'll pretend I'm ill. I won't even have to *pretend!*'

'Don't I need a driving license or something?' it suddenly occurred to me.

'Nobody worries about that here – unless you kill someone.'

It was as if the village had been warned of my coming, the main street empty, not even a dog to be seen, and I went down it like a tank commander expecting trouble, the engine howling in second gear.

'*Go into third!*'

I went into fourth, and the Land Rover bolted, Beryl screaming '*Brake!*', my feet playing the pedals like a demented organist until I struck lucky and hit the brake and the clutch at the same time and dragged the gear-lever into second as I skidded round the hair-raising bend at the bottom of the street.

'It's as if it were wagging its tail!' I shouted happily.

'It's called *skidding*—'

But by the time we reached the top of the pass I felt that I was in complete control, changing gears as if I'd been changing them all my life, sticking like glue to the right-hand side of the road, recalling every fleeting moment of my past experience behind the wheel, darting occasional glances at Beryl who had rammed herself against her door like a tinned sardine, her face set in a rictus of terror.

'Don't worry!' I called out. 'I really *am* getting the hang of it. I know it sounds strange, but it's as if it *wants* to be driven well—'

'It *does* want to be driven well!'

'No, I mean it's as if it were helping me—'

The feeling was even better than smoking 'pot', and I turned to Beryl, my heart bursting as I shouted over the roar of the engine. 'I can't tell you how wonderful it is, driving a Land Rover! We're completely at one with each other.'

'Oh my giddy aunt,' she groaned.

I glanced up into the rearview mirror, imagining that Margot was sitting beside me. Strangely, she and the Land Rover had become interchangeable in my thoughts – her litheness and delicacy, the Land Rover's indestructible power – which might have sounded slightly mad and illogical, but wasn't; I was discovering that love had a logic all its own, irrational to anyone not love-struck, but perfect sense to those who were, those who moved at a different speed through the same time as others.

The intensity of my feelings kept shocking me, but then I wasn't simply in love with a woman but with a myth more acceptable to me than God or Christ or the Holy Ghost because she *existed*, her very existence proof of Robert's conviction that she was indeed the White Goddess in mortal form – which I accepted without question because I, too, had seen and sensed both her mortal and immortal guises.

He's gone... yet again; although I still feel his presence, and remember enough of this part of the story to carry on without him. It's towards the end that I foresee trouble, when the maze-like complications of events remain impenetrable still. And yet I remember so clearly writing it all down that night, towards the end, in a sweat of terror, convinced that I'd be killed at any moment, while Robert, half mad with anger and fear for his sanity prowled the night between his study and his bed.

'To Be Opened Only In The Event Of My Death' – that much I remembered clearly. All very dramatic, the dozen or so pages of confession which I'd left... where? I still hadn't the faintest idea. Perhaps it was lost forever. Or perhaps, if I persevere, he'll lead me to it.

A strange day today, torn between the worlds of past and future as I headed towards Son Rullan for my meeting with Foster to view his father's library.

The drive up the mountain was hair-raising, the boulder-strewn track so steep that the only way to take it was ventre-à-terre, the accelerator flat on the floor as I wrenched the wheel of Beryl's battered old Renault to right and left to avoid the rocks. I longed for the Land Rover. One single loss of nerve and I felt that the car would hurtle boot over bonnet back to the bottom and explode in a pillar of flame – a not uncommon occurrence in these mountains. Above me, like Mount Athos, Son Rullan clung spectacularly to its cliff top.

When I finally made it to the gates of the courtyard I was so shaking with nerves that I couldn't even get out until I'd lit a cigar.

It was while I sat there, my heart still thundering in my ears, that I became aware of the sound of a piano playing. It was Chopin. Again. Did no one play anything else here? This time it was the prelude that sounded like raindrops, the one (if I remembered rightly) that he'd composed during the wet and miserable winter he'd spent in Valldemosa with George Sand. If someone were actually playing, then they were playing extraordinarily well. Foster? It seemed inconceivable.

This sudden and unexpected encounter with classical music fifteen hundred feet above the sea in a wild, deserted landscape was surreal, my curiosity drawing me out of the car like a magnet, leaving the door hanging open for fear of interrupting the music. Moving soundlessly across the courtyard in my espadrilles I approached the heavy open doors of the house, spread wide as if to welcome me, the glass-panelled doors beyond opening inwards, as though beckoning me towards the source of the music.

Standing on the threshold looking in, I had to let my eyes get used to the gloom before I could make out what appeared to be a huge entrance hall, entirely whitewashed apart from the flagstoned floor. In the middle of the room, beneath a massive iron chandelier, stood a grand piano, as black as the room was white. Sitting at the keyboard with her back to me was a young woman—

Margot—?

I was stunned for a moment, my brain in free-fall until common sense tumbled out of bed and told me not to be so stupid. That had all been thirty years ago – Margot would be fifty-five now, and the girl at the piano could hardly be out of her teens, her flawless shoulders and arms golden brown against the thin cotton shift she wore, her thick mane of black hair rippling and swaying to the slight movements of a body lost in the emotion of what she was playing.

And then, too soon, the plaintive piece was finished, the final chord merging into a thickening silence as the girl's bare feet softly released the pedals.

'You've come to look at the books.' A plain statement of fact, spoken quietly.

I was taken aback. 'Yes,' I answered at once, hardly recognising my own voice. 'How did you know I was here?'

'Your shadow. And the smell of your cigar.'

I flicked it away impatiently. 'I'm sorry—'

'I don't mind—' She got to her feet, a girl of twenty or so, startlingly beautiful, her full red lips a dramatic contrast to her black hair and ankle-length white shift. She was clearly naked beneath it, the gauzy material falling sheer from her hard dark nipples, skimming the neat smudge of her pubic hair.

I wanted to tell her how beautiful she was, as beautiful as her playing, but I said nothing – out of respect for her near-nakedness, I suppose. Not that she seemed in the least abashed. It was as much a statement of fact as her first comment to me. And this was Deya after all—

I told her my name in an attempt to keep her there, but she just smiled slightly.

'I know. Foster's in the study. Up the stairs and straight through.'

And she was gone. One last glimpse of her as she stepped out into the dazzling courtyard, her thin shift seemingly incinerated by the first stroke of the sun, leaving her quite naked for an instant before she passed out of sight.

'Ffffuck!' I gasped to myself.

Foster, when I found him at last (the house had been cunningly built on its crag, with steps and passages following the contours of the giant rock it had been built on) came round his desk to greet me with hand outstretched, an all-American beam on his cherubic face, spectacles flashing like strobe lights in the rays of the morning sun. I hoped I wouldn't get a migraine. 'Simon – it was you!'

'Of course—'

'No – I mean last night, when I came to meet you at Las Palmeras – I didn't recognise you—'

'Nor I you – I'm sorry. But I got your message this morning.'

The firm handclasp ended, the squeezing hand on my right shoulder, as if testing my strength, withdrawn inconclusively. I asked him about the apparition I'd just seen downstairs.

'Oh, La Sylphide!' he laughed. 'That's what I call her. Isn't she something? She's Mati Klarwein's. I let her play whenever she likes. She even has a key. Now, the thing is,' he threw his arm around my back and squeezed my other shoulder as he led me towards one of the many rooms that led off the study, 'I've had quite a bit of interest in these books since I spoke to you. I've been put in touch with booksellers in New York and Chicago—'

The creaking seesaw of business jolted up and down in its usual predictable fashion, each of us politely taking it in turns to get the upper hand as he led me through the ground floor—

God almighty!

Around the walls and in double-sided aisles, from floor to ceiling, were books… in their thousands… we wandered into the next room, and the next… in their tens of thousands…!

In the past I'd bought more than my fair share of private collections and even medium-sized libraries, but this was bookselling on an industrial scale; mythic, almost, when one considered that they'd all have to be carried down from this eerie in the mountains of an island in the Mediterranean, sixty miles by forty miles – no larger than my home county, and somehow got back to the little town of Holt, in Norfolk. Did I truly want them, though? In my head I was already set on a different course in which my professional future played little part. I could just as happily do without the stultifying work of having to collate and catalogue every volume, every pamphlet, every sheet of music—

I found myself sweating, and not simply from the heat; this was like a night sweat, common to lymphomaniacs, drenching

328

me, running down my face like rain, down my neck and chest. Discreetly, I mopped at myself with my shirt sleeves: Foster would mistake my sweating for greed, and hike the price.

I looked round again at the claustrophobic shelves towering around me. What did I know about art and music? Not enough, that was for sure. And yet it was this library that had brought me back to Majorca, returning me to a past I'd fled so long ago. At whatever level, this must be 'meant', and the seesaw finally stopped in mid-air as we stared at each other on level terms at last, and the deal was struck.

ROBERT'S RETURN

The weather broke at last. Leaden clouds massed amongst the mountain tops before spilling over like silent landslides, engulfing the high olive groves and lesser peaks and finally the entire village in a silent, rolling mist.

On the streets, people suddenly emerged out of the fog and as suddenly vanished again, and yet the sound of their voices and footsteps seemed to last forever, unnaturally loud under the low ceiling of cloud; not the weather for telling secrets out loud.

On the morning of Robert's return, Beryl dropped me in the village to get our lunch and supper while she drove off to the airport to pick him up, not in the least daunted by the weather.

With Juan and Beryl's help, my anorexic Spanish had put on weight, so that I could now count up to infinity and understand much of what was said to me, even managing the occasional conversation, though I was still inclined to burst into Italian or French when Spanish words failed me. By simply reading signs in the shops, and instructions on the sides of packets, I managed to hoover up whole chunks of vocabulary. This was not like the dead lessons of school, after all, but an urgent and practical necessity if I were to get on in Madrid.

The walk back to Canellun through the tumbling clouds was almost like a foretaste of death, cut off from everyone and everything except when the fickle mist was blown apart by some unfelt draught, exposing crags and small ravines and sudden cascades of vegetation that were so unfamiliar to me in their isolation that I became completely disoriented, the road beneath my feet the only certainty of my whereabouts. It came as a surprising relief to see the twin gates of Ca'n Torrent and Canellun emerging through the whorls of mist, and then the Land Rover, safely back in its garage, the house emerging weirdly out of the clouds as I approached.

Ducking through the fly curtain into the kitchen, eyes tight shut against the flailing cords—

'Ah. *There* you are! Hello!' Robert washing up at the sink in his black sombrero and waistcoat, shaking the water from his hands and gripping me by the shoulders before planting two stubbly kisses on my cheeks—

'I'm so glad you're home!' I gasped.

'So am I,' he turned back to the sink. 'In some ways, at least. I say, grab a dishcloth, would you, and give me a hand. Beryl's got a headache and she's gone to lie down for a bit.'

'I'm sorry... what's all this washing up? I did it before we left.'

'I just finished your leftovers from last night, that's all,' he laughed, 'I was feeling peckish.'

'I thought you wouldn't be back for hours, what with shopping in Palma, and the mist—'

'No, no!' he shook his head impatiently, 'The mist's only in Deya – there's bright sunshine as soon as you get to *Son Marroig* – clear as a bell. No, Deya has its own micro climate you see – the mountains here are so full of iron that it even affects the weather. As for shopping, I couldn't face it. I wanted to get home. I know it sounds stupid, but for some reason I was convinced that Margot was here, waiting—'

'How is she?'

'*Euphoric!* There's no other word for it.' He glanced up from the sink, his eyes haunted. 'The moment we arrived in Madrid she was off, like a greyhound from the slips. I could hardly keep up with her. Thank God for Alastair and Mary – they distracted her while I had my siestas – much needed, I can tell you – and they have such a huge circle of friends that there were parties almost every night.

Extraordinary, the pace they live at. Oh, and Margot sent her love, by the way, lots of it, as did Alastair.' He picked up a ceramic salad bowl with remnants of salad still in it, swooshed them round with his huge fingers and stuffed them into his mouth before plunging the bowl into the water. 'Which reminds me – slight change of plan – Mary's up all night with Jasper teething, so Alastair thought it might be best if you went straight to a *pensión* when you got to Madrid – throw you in at the deep end, so to speak. He seems to think you'll just rot about if you stay with them—'

I tried to hide my shock, but it must have shown.

'Cheer up! It's the best way to learn Spanish, after all – to mix with Spaniards – and they'll all be there if you need them. Anyway, he's found you a *pensión*, in the centre of town – or rather, we found it together. It's not too bad, and it's very cheap – only ten shillings a week—' he handed me the dripping salad bowl, 'so I took the liberty of paying your first month's rent on the spot—'

'Thank you,' I said faintly, my manners wrestling with the dread of what lay ahead.

'*De nada*! Oh, and apparently you have to sign on at the university next Wednesday.'

Whether it was the added shock of hearing this, or because the salad bowl was still greasy, it suddenly skidded through my fingers and onto the tiled floor, shattering – shattering everything, it seemed – our mood, my happiness at seeing him again— 'Oh, *Christ*,' I groaned, squatting down and instinctively trying to piece it together again, to make it never have happened—

'Blast it!' exclaimed Robert angrily as he stared down at the mess. 'That was eighteenth century – we've had it since we first came here—'

'I'm so sorry!' Head bowed, I stared down helplessly at the shards as if they were tea leaves, trying to make sense of them.

'Oh well,' he tried valiantly to shrug it off, 'can't be helped, I suppose. We choose to use it, we chance to break it. The thing is, though, you've also broken its *baraka*. You have to apologise to it now.'

'Its *what*?'

'Its *baraka*. My friend Idries Shah introduced me to it. It's a Sufi word, from *bárak* – lightning. There's no equivalent in English, really. *Baraka* encompasses the whole experience of that bowl, from the life of the man who made it, to its place in our lives – which is over now. Its virtue, if you like – no! – its *soul*, that's better – which is why you have to ask its forgiveness.'

I glanced up at him, to see if he was joking, but he wasn't. I looked down at the smashed bowl again, half of it unbroken, the other half in fragments. 'I apologise profusely for destroying your *baraka*,' I told it, with genuine feeling.

Robert nodded briskly, satisfied. 'Right, you can sweep it up now.'

'Shouldn't I put it in a box or something? Someone might be able to mend it one day.'

'No. It would only snag at my sight whenever I saw it. No, chuck it away—' He reached under the sink for the dustpan and brush. 'Here—'

As I swept up the remains he started pacing restlessly round the kitchen, grunting to himself.

'No, there was something else...' He stopped dead, pressing his bunched fingertips to his lips, frowning. 'Oh yes!' he brightened up. 'I know—! Look, leave all that and come through to the study – there's something I wanted to give you.'

Hurriedly emptying the dustpan into the non-compost-meantis bin, I caught up with him just as he was barging through the already open doors to the study. Crossing to his desk, he rummaged through the piles of post that Karl had opened and laid out for him. 'Lots of lovely cheques!' he exclaimed. 'Oh, and I've been put up for another prize! That'll put the cat among the Stygians – my critics,' he laughed. 'But where the devil are they? I can't have dreamt them.' He looked down at the floor behind his desk. 'Ah, here we are!' Grabbing his glasses, he flung himself into his chair and heaved a parcel onto his lap, still tied up with string but with the wrapping paper partially torn off at one end.

'Have you ever read *The White Goddess*?' he asked.

'No, I don't think so.'

'Well, Faber's have just sent me some copies of the new paperback edition—' he started to pick at the knot on the parcel. 'I know it must seem odd in these days of plenty, but having been through two world wars I can't bear to waste anything, not even string... where was I? Oh yes! Your mother tells me you write plays and short stories and things. Do you write poetry at all?'

Again I was caught off-balance. 'Well... sometimes... but nothing like yours—'

'I should hope not! One of me is quite enough. No, but seriously, it's important to speak with your own voice. Poems in the style of other people are seldom any good. In order to write poetry at all, though, you'll need this book – ah! There we are—' The string, suddenly lifeless, fell away from the parcel as Robert tipped it on its open end and pulled out a clutch of half a dozen identical pale blue and white paperbacks. Taking one of them, he opened it, reached for his relief nib pen, jammed it in the inkwell, and began writing on the endpaper. 'Do you have any of your poems with you?' he asked casually.

'I'm afraid not,' I lied.

'Pity. I'd like to have seen some. There we are!' He closed the book and lobbed it at me. It was surprisingly heavy and densely printed, his inscription, when I turned to it, brief but affectionate, and already smudged.

'Thank you,' I said warmly. 'Is it a novel?'

'God, no!' he cried, pretending to be affronted. 'It's a grammar. Of poetry and poetic myth – a Book of Rules, if you like. Ignore them at your peril! No, seriously, it's probably the most important thing I've ever written – apart from poems themselves, of course. It came out of a sort of dream-trance during the last war. I don't think I've ever written anything so quickly – three weeks for the first draft – rather like Coleridge's Kubla Khan, except that unlike him I finished what I started. Do you know that poem of mine – *The Person from Porlock?*' Without waiting for a reply, he began to quote:

> *"Unkind fate sent the Porlock person*
> *To collect fivepence from a poet's house;*
> *Pocketing which old debt he rode away,*
> *Heedless and gay, homeward bound for Porlock.*

> *O Porlock person, habitual scapegoat,*
> *should any masterpiece be marred or scotched,*
> *I wish your burly fist on the front door*
> *Had banged yet oftener in literature!"*

'Brilliant!' I cried.

'It's good, isn't it?' he beamed with almost childlike pleasure. Then his smile faded suddenly. 'Although with hindsight I think I may have published *The White Goddess* too soon – but needs musted in those days. There were still mysteries unsolved, though, and I got a pelting from some of my critics – archaeologists and academics for the most part. But the joke is that almost everything I said at the time – and which they refuted – has proved to be right over the years, so yah-boo to them.' He stirred restlessly in his seat. 'No, the point of the book is that it's the Truth – not just *my* truth, but *Her* truth, which I can see and they can't.'

'Has Margot read it?' I asked.

'Of course.' At the mention of her name he got restlessly to his feet, grabbing the other five copies of the book and trying to stuff them into the overcrowded shelves of his own works. Since he clearly wasn't concentrating on what he was doing, I got up to help him, patiently making a space for them between *Count Belisarius* and *Wife to Mr Milton* while he flung himself back into his chair.

'It was uncanny, her intuition,' he went on, lighting a cigarette from an old packet of *Celtas*, 'she even solved some of the puzzles that had baffled me – which will call for a new edition at some point. She's truly extraordinary.' I went back to my seat, to find him frowning fiercely across the desk, his eyes seeming to burn through me. 'I miss her dreadfully, you know, even though I was with her only this morning.' A piece of coarse black tobacco had got stuck to his lips. Picking it off with his fingers he popped it into his mouth and bit down on it fiercely. 'I keep thinking about that bowl you broke.'

'Oh God!'

'No, no—' He held up his hand. 'That's forgotten! What I mean is…' the piece of tobacco got in the way of his speech and he spat it out impatiently towards the bookshelves, 'What I mean is that it's like a migraine, the memory of it – a stain on the vision – but I think there was a point to your dropping it. It was "meant", if you like – as if I had to sacrifice the bowl in order to see things more clearly. You see, Margot and I, when we're together, invoke a *baraka*. In poets and their muses, *baraka* is virtue, as I said – something more, and deeper, than chivalry – a positive force field as impregnable as it is potent. But when we're apart, she's vulnerable; the *baraka* isn't simply divided between us equally – it only truly works if we're together. On her own, it becomes mutable, unpredictable, like her moods lately. Now, one half of the bowl was still intact – did you notice? – but the other half was in smithereens. My half – the half nearest to me – was intact… but the thing is, if one of us breaks the *baraka*, the other is dragged down… the bowl becomes useless…'

'In what way?' I urged him on, concentrating hard, determined not to lose him.

'Oh, there are countless ways... mostly dishonourable – hence the "code" of *baraka*. The most fatal thing, though, would be the sudden appearance of a 'Twin', a dark mirror image of oneself – in my case, another poet. The Twin is evil; he drains the life, the magic, from the sacred partnership. What's even worse, though – unendurable, in fact – is that it's *she* who invites *him* – remember that.' He took another puff of his cigarette and effortlessly blew a perfect triple smoke ring. As the chimeral circles hovered and expanded towards me, he suddenly stabbed them through with his forefinger. '*Die!*' he murmured, then caught my eye and laughed. 'Not *you* – the evil Twin!'

'But Margot loves you! She'd never hurt you.'

'Not consciously, no. But in Madrid she was *gone*, as I say – I've never seen her so radiant, so beautiful – or so callous, I suppose – no pun intended! All right, it's to be expected after being cooped up here for so long, and yet she was dangerous somehow... there were moments when my life seemed to hang by a thread... I can't describe it really... but she chose to spare me.' He grinned suddenly, ruefully. 'It's all right – you don't have to believe me.'

'But I do,' I protested. 'That's just it – I can see how it must have been – imagine it—' I stared at him fiercely, willing him to accept my word even though I realised that I was being reckless, exposing my feelings too blatantly—

He stared back at me, the heat of his gaze matching mine. 'Yes...' he said at last, 'I believe you do. Perhaps you're a little in love with her yourself.'

For a moment I was lost for words. 'She casts a spell,' I managed finally.

'—a *glamour*! No, that's right – she demands it. It's not your fault,' he smiled kindly, 'or mine, come to that. No, when she's possessed, I am possessed by her – in the same instant. We always know...' He covered his forehead and eyes with his hand, rubbing them wearily. 'Sometimes it lasts for days... and nights... and I drown myself in her midnight wastes of sea and hold my breath for as long as we're joined together, without once coming up for air...' He focussed on me again, his brow clearing as he smiled, almost bleakly. 'It's hard, you know... being a poet.'

We stared at each other across the desk, my thoughts spellbound by his words which so exactly mirrored my feelings for Margot and yet were inexpressible as mine.

'You know, I'm very glad you're here,' he said unexpectedly. 'Perhaps it's because you feel so strongly about her that I find it so easy to talk to you. And you care. It's a great help—'

The door behind me opened suddenly, Beryl popping her head round, looking for me, a huge grin on her face. 'Well, I've searched the pantry and the fridge and the Aga, Simon, but I *still* can't find our dratted lunch!'

'Oh Christ, I'm so sorry—' I delved into my basket and grabbed the neck of the chicken I'd been sent to buy. Underneath were the crushed remains of our cold lunch, bursting soggily out of their brown wrapping paper.

LAST DAYS

As the clouds of my departure for Madrid loomed ever closer and more threatening, so the diminishing clear sky of what was left of my time in Deya grew ever more radiant.

Apart from his endless work, I seemed to become Robert's chief distraction. Beryl was worn out from listening to his fears about Margot, repeating herself time and again as she insisted that he should leave her alone to settle in. With no one else around to unburden himself upon, he sought me out whenever the need took him, even in mid-sentence of his work, to run his latest thoughts and poems past me, his thoughts feverish, his poems astonishingly evocative yet full of disquiet and foreboding. I did my best to measure up to his increasing faith in me by trying to appear intelligent, but a lot of what he said and wrote went straight over my head. Only when it came to his feelings was I of any real use. His chief worry as the days passed, was that although he'd heard from Alastair that he'd found her a flat, he still hadn't heard from Margot herself, in spite of her promises to write as often as she could.

'I just can't understand it!' he exclaimed as he paced the terrace restlessly after tea one day. 'I've written to her five times since I left her—'

'For heaven's *sake*, Robert!' Beryl wearily raised her cup of tea to her lips in one hand, her afternoon cigarette held stylishly in the other. 'I'm not *surprised* she hasn't written. It takes a week to decipher *one* of your letters, never mind *five*. Give her room to breathe. She's having a break from you; let her enjoy it in peace – I know *I* would!' She grinned round at me.

'Perhaps she's busy doing up her new flat,' I offered helpfully.

'Yes – no, you're right, both of you. I expect too much, I suppose. I just can't bear being out of touch with her like this.'

'Well, if you *must* write to her every day, then do so,' said Beryl briskly, 'just don't post the letters.'

'It's not just the letters,' he insisted, 'I need to read my latest poems to her.'

'Doesn't mean that *she* needs to read them,' Beryl retorted, rather brutally.

But Robert seemed to take it on the chin. 'No, I suppose not,' he said glumly.

Listening to their conversation I couldn't help feeling sympathy for both of them. Beryl had had to endure years of Robert's muses and must have become exhausted by his constant demands and mood swings. What I found odd, though, was that she treated him more like a lovelorn teenage son than her 64-year-old poet–husband, who was a genius to boot. And yet Robert seemed to find it perfectly acceptable – necessary, even. Since his love for Margot was as youthful and passionate as mine, perhaps he deserved to be treated like someone my age. And as long as he was inspired to write, I didn't see that it mattered much how he behaved privately.

An hour later, while I was helping Beryl with the watering, one of the children from the telegraph office cycled up the drive with a cable for him. Within moments he was shouting for me from the terrace, waving the cable triumphantly. It was from Margot, apologising for her silence, promising to write soon, disliking the tone of his new poems but sending her love all the same – on condition that he wrote to her a little less often as she was frantically trying to do up her new apartment.

Minutes later we were striding along the coast road with our swimming things as he quickly adjusted his pace to mine and launched into a jubilant monologue about the electric shock he'd felt when he'd been given the telegram, how he'd tipped the girl fifty pesetas for bearing good news, how happy he was to be united with Margot again, if only through telegraphy, how he'd sleep like a baby tonight—

By the time we passed the square tower and the fishermen's cottages, though, he'd lapsed into a telltale silence before the gramophone needle of his fears came down on the same groove of his complaint that she still hadn't actually *written* to him – for which he in no way condemned her, only that he wished, like an animal in pain, to be put out of his misery—

'She *will* write!' I assured him fervently. 'By Monday,' I predicted wildly, 'I bet you.'

'How much?' he asked, cheering up a little.

'A hundred pesetas,' I wagered, even more rashly.

'I warn you, I'll hold you to it,' he said, 'and a gentleman always pays his debts! Have you even *got* a hundred pesetas?'

I pulled a hopeful face to myself as we stopped for a moment on the cliff top overlooking the *cala* far below. The sun had already abandoned it, the last stragglers dragging their way up the donkey steps towards us.

'This is the best time to swim,' announced Robert, 'especially when it's so hot, when the sun's setting behind the hill, and everyone's gone except the people who belong here.'

Passing the breathless climbers on our way down, Robert greeted the people he knew and liked, and as usual ignored those he didn't know or actively disliked.

Once we'd rounded the bend at the bottom of the hill and been confronted once again by the beauty of the cove and the darkening sea, I suddenly saw what he meant. I'd always imagined that the fishermen lived in Deya itself, or in the cottage next to Stella and Yancy, or in the huts and stone cottages scattered along the torrent, but as we came out onto the *cala* it was as if we'd walked onto the stage set of an Italian opera. All the boat house doors were open, exposing not the boats that I'd expected, but the fishermens' living quarters, complete with tables and chairs, cooking stoves, the walls covered with old photographs and garish religious pictures, the beds made up to look like divans, everything neat and tidy and with space down the middle to accommodate their fishing boats during violent storms.

As for the fisher-folk, they were all sitting on the wooden palings of the slipways in the cool of the evening, mending their nets or trimming and polishing the huge lanterns that hung over the sterns of their tethered fishing boats. I half expected them to burst into a Verdi chorus acknowledging their simple fate, but instead they all looked up smiling to greet Robert as we passed. He returned their greetings in his atrocious accent, raising his straw hat to the women among them.

'I had no idea they actually lived here!' I murmured.

'Of course they do – most of them, at least. This is the start of their day. In an hour or so, at dusk, the men will put out to sea, then fish all night, attracting the fish with their lanterns, and come back at dawn to sort their catch and sell it. Then they sleep in their sheds through the heat of the day and start all over again in the evening.'

'But what about winter? Or when it's stormy?'

'Oh, the money they make from smuggling tides them over the bad times,' he said blithely, 'cigarettes, cognac, that sort of thing. Not drugs, though – they won't touch them.'

Reaching the far end of the deserted beach, where he preferred to swim, we changed with our backs to each other, hidden from the fishermen by a stump of rock.

After our swim – Robert as competitive as ever, outdistancing me, holding his breath under water for twice as long as I could in spite of having half a lung less than me – we sat on rocks next to each other, slowly drying ourselves. For once he appeared not to be in a hurry, staring out to sea with an intense frown, half-naked, like Caliban conjuring shipwrecks – which in a way he was doing, I realised, weaving spells, willing Margot to be cast up again on the shores of his island...

The sound and movement of the sea became hypnotic, sinking me into an almost dreamlike state as I listened to the rise and fall of its breathing, ever quieter and more drawn out, as though preparing itself for sleep…

Robert snorted suddenly and turned away to blow his nose, nostril by nostril, into the rocks, then began to dress, the spell – this spell, at least – broken.

But no sooner had we come in sight of the fishermen again, already heaving their boats down the slipways to rest at the water's edge, than the spell of the place returned to where we'd left it.

'It's like another world now,' I said, almost to myself.

'What?' Robert cleared his throat and looked around, as if for the first time. 'Yes,' he agreed, 'although it's more like Time within Time, if you see what I mean. During the day it's a twentieth century picture postcard, colourful, glossy, full of sunlight and holidaymakers and yachts coming and going… but in the evening they all vanish as if they'd never existed, and the true spirit of the place – the fishing community that's been here for centuries – comes into its own. And yet once or twice every hundred years or so there's a god-awful storm and the whole lot is swept away by the sea – houses, people, boats – and it's as if *they'd* never existed. So between the picture postcard and this, which is the dream – which the reality?'

'*This*—' I said firmly, gesturing at the fishermen, 'is reality.'

'Quite!' he laughed. 'Everyone else can just fuck off – including us!'

Leaving the strange duality of the world below us in the gathering gloom, we climbed slowly towards the square tower, still golden in the last rays of the sun. To our right, the distant mountains glowed like lava, pink and red and black, as though visibly exuding the absorbed heat of the day.

We climbed side by side where we could, in single file when we couldn't, Robert leading, still worrying the subject of Margot like a dog – now trying to fathom her more recent behaviour. Was she hiding something from him? And if she were, was it something personal – her family, that sort of thing – or something more serious, which might threaten their *baraka*? What did I think? I'd been with her the most during her last days here – did I know anything he didn't—?

'Honestly, Robert,' I insisted yet again, 'I really think she just needed a break. She was claustrophobic. Perhaps you just love her too much, sometimes… smother her.'

'Yes… no, I know…' But he seemed to be only half listening. 'Have *you* ever been in love?' he asked suddenly.

'Of course!'

'There's no "of course" about it! It's rare. I mean *truly* in love.'

'Yes.' I looked away, not wanting to be reminded of it, then looked back at him intently, willing him to believe me. 'I have.'

'All right,' he said, nodding briefly, 'I'll take your word for it.'

Although I'd been flattered at the beginning to be singled out as his confidant, the feeling had soon faded, replaced by a more meaningful sense of duty to him. His love for Margot had to come first, not only because he'd found her first but because his love for her was more valuable than mine, his poems proof of it. My job was to listen to him, to calm him down – a job I took seriously, since I not only enjoyed the mental exercise of trying to keep up with him, but the distraction kept my thoughts off Madrid. In spite of the huge disparity in our ages, there were times when he even made me feel quite wise – until I realised that this was only because he'd stooped to my age to make it possible for me to understand him.

One evening, when Beryl had just received a telegram from the Sillitoes asking if they could come and stay, he was quite his old self, bright-eyed, smiling, pouncing on the slightest chance for a good point or a bad pun. Alan was a good listener, apparently, and would take over from me as Robert's confidant, while Ruth, who was a close friend of Beryl's, would be like a breath of fresh air to her. To my surprise, I felt only the slightest pang of jealousy; I liked Alan, a quiet, thoughtful, pipe-puffing man who would probably put everything into a more philosophical perspective for Robert than I could – and besides, we'd grown so mutually dependent lately that I'd begun to see why Beryl had become drained by his obsessiveness. There were only so many answers one could give to the same questions. At least with the promise of Alan's arrival, Robert could wind down his reliance on me and in an odd way lessen the wrench, for me, of being torn from him.

And yet, looking around the happy table, the thought of having to leave all this, perhaps forever, suddenly overwhelmed me, to the point where I had to slip away and go outside.

Which was worse.

Standing on the terrace under the starlit sky, letting my senses adjust to the sounds and smells of night, I felt the sudden heartbreak of leaving – the sickening void, almost of bereavement. Between the trees I could make out the wedge of dark glinting sea, and far out the twinkling lights of the fishing boats reflecting the stars. Somewhere out there, on the farthest point, was the *atalaya* where as a boy I'd performed my bizarre Rite of Return. Did the effect of such a thing last forever, I wondered, or did I have to renew it every time I came here? I renewed it now, just in case, imagining myself back on the curved stone roof of the tower in blinding sunlight, re-inhabiting the naked body of the boy I'd been then, standing among the symbols of an invented mystery, arms stretched out in supplication to the sun and moon in the same sky, begging to be brought back—

'Hey… Simon!'

Juan—! I turned round, letting my arms fall awkwardly to my sides—

'You OK?'

'Fine,' I insisted. 'Just stretching.'

'Ah… Mother sent me to look for you – you know… see if you were OK—'

347

'I just needed some air,' I said lamely.

He nodded in his peculiar way, eyes widening as his head went up, then stayed there; more an acknowledgement than a nod. With his hands still in his pockets, he looked up further, at the stars. 'Beautiful night,' he murmured.

'Yes.' To my surprise, I didn't mind his company, even at a moment like this. His presence was actually comforting in a way. He was so easygoing these days that if I'd asked to be left alone he'd have gone without the slightest ill-feeling. But I didn't want him to go. He may have become odd, with his curious take on life and his American accent caught from *Écolint* in Switzerland, but he was never dull. He looked down from the stars, his eyes fleetingly catching mine before wandering off again, into the darkness.

'You don't want to leave.' A statement, not a question.

'No.'

'Nor me – mostly. But then, when I've gone, sometimes I don't want to come back. Until I'm back – and then I don't want to leave.' He grinned, infectiously. 'Crazy, eh?'

'Crazy,' I nodded.

'I mean, it's hard here – like the rocks. You have to be hard to live here. To leave here, too...'

Again I was surprised by how right he was.

'I mean, I used to be pretty wild, right? I didn't respect anything except Mother and Father. Without them I'd probably be dead by now. Without Father I'd probably be alive by now.' He burst out laughing, a slightly demented laugh. 'Only kidding! But that's OK. He's hard, too. He has to be. But I knew this place was harder than me, so I stopped fighting it. I just belong here now – like a tree. I mean, I've grown here all my life, watching people coming and going— "Who's that?" they say. "Oh, that's Juan, Robert Graves' son." "Is he at Oxford, too?" "No, he's a tree!"' He laughed again. 'Which is fine, because I don't have to *be* anything! Like Margot. She just *is*.' His eyes grazed mine. 'You have a thing for her – right?'

My eyes homed in on him like gun barrels, hot and wary. His hands came up, as if to ward them off. 'No, it's OK! I do too, even though she belongs to Father. There's nothing I can do about it, though – I'm a tree, right? All I can do is watch her – hate it when she's gone. But the point is, it's Deya that made her happen, that brought her here, just as it brought Father here. And you, maybe. Father says these mountains are magnetic, which is why we're all dragged back, even against our will, even though we're not made of metal. Maybe it's our belt buckles!' The laughter squirted out of him again, the sound so infectious that I couldn't help laughing too. And yet a moment later he was staring at me in deadly earnest. 'But the thing is, we can't stop it. No one can, unless they anger this place, and then the rocks here break anyone who doesn't show respect. Either they kill them or banish them – a bit like Father. I've seen it happen – people falling onto the rocks and dying, or drowning, or just vanishing, as if they'd never been. Once you've been chosen, though, once you've been *pulled* here… you've felt it, haven't you?'

'I suppose I must have, or it wouldn't hurt so much to leave.'

'Then you'll come back, I promise! Meanwhile, at least you'll be near Margot.' He punched me playfully on the shoulder, like an all-American kid. 'I'd better go in, or Mother will send someone else – maybe we'll *all* end up out here!' Again, he could hardly suppress his amusement. 'Listen, I'll just tell them you're "communing with nature", like Aunt Clarissa – taking the longest piss in history—'

His laughter trailed after him like the wild child he'd once been as he left the terrace. I looked up, smiling now, at the dark wall of mountains which I would soon have to cross into that other world, free of despair suddenly, the void I'd felt earlier now filled with a surge of hope.

On Monday I won my bet. As I was on my way down to breakfast, Robert suddenly erupted from his study, calling my name several times in his excitement. 'Oh, there you are!' he cried, waving a letter at me. 'Look! You were right after all! I shall pay you at once! Come on—'

Still slightly dazed from sleep, I traipsed after him into the study, where he flung himself into his chair and pulled open one of the drawers of his desk. Taking a fat wad of money from it, he peeled off a five thousand peseta banknote and held it out to me.

Helplessly, I patted the pockets of my shorts. 'I'm afraid I haven't got any change—'

'Neither have I!' he laughed. 'This is simply the hundred pesetas I owe you – the rest is a present, to thank you. I don't know what I'd have done without you lately – or what I'll do when you've gone – drive poor Beryl mad, I suppose – although Alan will help for a bit. Take it! I insist.'

Flushed with confusion, I did so, staring down at the huge banknote, too embarrassed to put it in my pocket.

'And besides,' he went on, 'you'll need taxis and things to visit Margot. She's quite a way from the centre of town. I shall rely on you to keep me informed – you understand...'

'Yes, of course,' I assured him, though not quite certain what he meant. Did he want me to spy on her? Surely not—

'Don't intrude on her, though – you know what she's like... oh, for God's sake!' he growled impatiently. 'Just tell me she's all right – that I have nothing to fear—' He slung the wad of money back into his drawer and picked up her letter again, staring at it fiercely, as if it contained a riddle of some kind.

'How does she sound?' I asked.

'I can't really tell... still no address, except care of Alastair and Mary. I mean, it's affectionate and all that, but it doesn't seem to actually *say* anything.' He pulled a face at me as he turned the page. 'But at least its in her handwriting – oh! She says that they'll all meet you at the airport tomorrow evening. What time do you arrive? I'll cable her, that's it! I'll do it now – give me an excuse to thank her for her letter—'

The morning of my departure, and yet again I was betrayed by the weather. It was raining.

Everyone was ecstatic, except me – though I tried hard not to show it.

Chucking my cases into the back of the Land Rover, I turned to stare up through the misty groves towards the cloud-covered mountains, the trunks and branches of the olive trees already black with rain, their foliage silver-green as if with age and wisdom. I was reminded, painfully, of Robert's poem *Turn of the Moon*. There was no wind, the drizzle falling straight down, quietly, evenly, stirring nothing as it fell. It was so very beautiful. After the slam of the Land Rover's back door, the dense peace returned, filled only with the soft skiffle of rain on the truck's tin roof and the faint gurgling of down pipes from the gutters filling the *deposito* under the terrace – sounds that meant so much to Robert and Beryl.

I walked round to the passenger door and climbed in next to her. For once I didn't want to drive, wanted only to look at what I was leaving behind. Beryl stared at me owlishly through her spectacles, well aware of what I was feeling.

'You're soaked!' she laughed suddenly.

I looked down at the hoar of rain on my jacket and began to brush it off. 'It'll dry.'

'Isn't it *wonderful*?' She was thinking of her flowers and fruit trees.

A sudden violent banging at my window almost frightened the life out of me. Robert, looking like a wild crone, his head covered with a mackintosh, opened the door and thrust a letter into my hand. 'I forgot – this is for Margot!'

'Oh *Robert*,' groaned Beryl, 'you'll let all the animals out—'

'No, it's all right, I shut the door.' He stared at me, frowning intently. 'Look, I know we've said our goodbyes and all that, but come back soon. I mean it. Bring Margot if you can! Just for a short visit, if she prefers.'

'I'll do my best,' I promised.

'Can we go now?' Beryl asked him, turning the key in the ignition and pressing the starter. The engine roared at once, drowning his reply. Blowing me a kiss with his fingertips, he slammed my door and stepped aside as we pulled away.

Halfway down the drive I looked back, in anguish, but he was already gone.

Never forget who brings the rain
In swarthy goatskin bags from a far sea:
It is the Moon as she turns, repairing
Damages of long drought and sunstroke.
Never count upon rain, never foretell it,
For no power can bring rain
Except the Moon as she turns; and who can rule her?

She is prone to delay the necessary floods,
Lest such a gift might become obligation,
A month, or two, or three; then suddenly
Not relenting but by way of whim
Will perhaps conjure from the cloudless west
A single raindrop to surprise with hope
Each haggard, upturned face.

Were the Moon a Sun, we would count upon her
To bring rain seasonably, as she turned;
Yet no one thinks to thank the regular Sun
For shining fierce in Summer, mild in winter—
Why should the Moon so drudge?

But if one night she brings us, as she turns,
Soft, steady, even, copious rain
That harms no leaf nor flower, but gently falls,
Hour after hour, sinking to the tap roots,
And the sodden earth exhales at dawn
A long sigh scented with pure gratitude,
Such rain — the first rain of our lives, it seems,
Neither foretold, cajoled, nor counted on—
Is woman giving as she loves.

PART THREE

MADRID

MADREAD

There was no one to meet me at the airport. Minute by minute, everything I'd hoped and longed for died death after death as I waited in vain for Margot to come.

'The Flying Coffin' as it was called, with its passenger door removed yet again for repairs, had flown unpressurised at five thousand feet from Palma to Madrid, landing its deaf and frozen passengers at sunset.

Still waiting for someone to come, I thawed out at a bar on the concourse of a new and brutal building – *Welcome to Franco's Spain!* – staring up at a ceiling so high that the human beings it had been built to dwarf were reduced to the insignificance of insects beneath its cavernous roof.

Knocking back my cognac, as much for courage as warmth, I soon realised that if I were to become absorbed into life here I'd have to buy a hat. Apart from a few foreigners, everyone seemed to be wearing them, the women's hats sharp and spiteful with the feathers of game birds – and how awful they all looked in the deathly neon light – grey and drawn, their clothes straight out of the thirties and forties, the men mostly in cheap double-breasted suits in horrible shades of brown and grey, the square-shouldered women hardly better, their tailored skirts reaching unflatteringly to mid-calf—

Still no one…

I had no address or telephone number for Margot or Alastair – nothing but the cheap printed card of the *pensión*, which Robert had insisted I hang onto.

At half past nine I gave up in despair.

Outside the airport, shockingly, it was night. The taxi driver, on being handed the card with my address, was clearly unimpressed, chucking my cases casually into the boot.

Numb with a loneliness which I refused to acknowledge even to myself, I sat wedged into the corner of the back seat as we drove towards Madrid along a road full of potholes, lined with hoardings and the occasional makeshift hovel in the squalor of the verge, its occupants eating together outside by the light of a single low-watt bulb or a neon tube suspended on lethal-looking wires from the electricity cables overhead—

'*Gitanos!*' grunted the driver to himself, and spat pointedly out of the open window. I'd read enough George Borrow to know that he meant gypsies. Guiltily I reached for my still tender left earlobe, having been told to take out my new gold earring in case the *guardias* here should mistake me for one.

The dark countryside gave way to the outskirts of the city, the streets lined with huge concrete blocks of flats, their occupants seemingly driven out onto the litter-strewn pavements by the oppressive heat, looking as grey as death in the cast-out light from neon-lit shopfronts. I'd always thought the gas-filled tubes a loathsome invention, a light to lighten the dead, as in a mortuary. The effect was so bleak that I had to fight back a renewed despair.

Concrete blocks finally gave way to the older part of the city, but everything was still lit by the same fluorescence. Even streets which might have been picturesque during the day looked sordid and poverty stricken by night. Whenever we were forced to a stop at traffic lights, the stench of sewers wafted in through the windows of the cab, each intersection alive with its own congregation of beggars, some standing hunched over crutches, legless or one-legged, others blind or one-armed, rattling their tin cups, with signs round their necks saying they'd been maimed in the war – the Spanish Civil War, I presumed. Had they truly begged for more than twenty years?

I found myself comparing this city with Rome, but it was like comparing hell to heaven. And yet this was where I was doomed to live for the next three years. I couldn't afford to hate it so violently at first sight. Surely I'd find *something* beautiful (or at least hopeful) to cling to—

The cab lurched to the right, the driver plunging us into a maze of ever-narrowing cobbled streets, our headlights and the occasional street lamp only emphasising the dilapidated state of the buildings on either side, some of the oldest and poorest houses seemingly held up only by the inch-thick succession of bullfighting posters stuck to their walls. No beggars here; no one to beg from except each other.

We began to speed downhill over the cobbles, a wider street, dark and deserted, with grander houses, their massive coaching doors set deep into the walls, when the driver suddenly pulled up on our right, wrenched on the handbrake, and twisted round, demanding double what it said on the clock. His hand followed his foul breath over the back of his seat, gesturing to me impatiently.

Incapable of arguing with him, I reached dumbly for my wallet and gave him what he asked to the nearest peseta. I was damned if I'd tip him! But then, perhaps trips to the airport were always charged *aller-retour*, as in France. I relented, and gave him a *duro*.

With a grudging '*Gracias, Señor*', he got out of the cab and went round to the boot, where I joined him on the cobbles as he dumped my cases before getting back into his cab and slamming the door.

'*Gracias!*' I called out sarcastically. He raised a hand vaguely as he began to pocket my money.

In the light of a wall-mounted gas lamp I stared up at the dark five-storied building, then at the dwarfing pair of huge carriage doors facing me, with a wicket gate in the middle. No bell, no knocker, only an iron ring bolt. I turned it. The latch rose out of its keep on the other side of the door, but the door still wouldn't budge. By the faint light of the street lamp I searched through the numerous aluminium and plastic name-plates screwed to the stone portico. *Pensión Illiturgi. Primera Piso.* At a loss to know what to do, I walked backwards into the street, and looked up again, but all the shutters were closed, no chinks of light anywhere, the tall stone façade melting into the heat and darkness of the night sky.

The cab still hadn't moved. I bent down to look inside, to where the driver sat with his interior light still on, staring out at me as though I were a lunatic. I stretched out my arms and shrugged helplessly.

In a single violent movement he was out of the cab again and advancing on me. I took a step back, driven as much by the reek of old garlic as by his threatening approach.

'*Hombre! No sabes nada?*' With a contemptuous shake of his head he turned and strode out into the middle of the road and clapped his hands three times, like pistol shots.

Moments later, from further up the street, came the sound of running feet and the clink of metal.

The driver turned back to me, his stare no less contemptuous. '*El sereno!*' he growled, before throwing himself back into his cab, gunning the engine and screeching away down the cobbled hill.

Bewildered, I turned back, to see a strange apparition heading towards me at a shuffling run down the far side of the street, and felt a momentary stab of fear. It was as if Marley's ghost, complete with clanking chains, had come to life in the form of a fleeing soldier wearing a peaked cap, a long grey army greatcoat and heavy boots. A game larder of huge keys jangled from rings on his belt.

As he ran across the cobbles towards me, though, I realised there was nothing to fear: beneath his outsize cap and within his voluminous army greatcoat he was hardly more than the skeleton of a man, his neck no thicker than a vulture's, his anxious face yellow and sweating in the faint light of the gas lamp. Panting with exertion, he saluted me briefly.

'*Pensión Illiturgi?*' I enquired.

'*Si, Señor!*' He pulled one of the rings of iron keys from his belt, selected one, and rammed it home in the wicket gate, turned it quickly, and flung open the door before reaching for my suitcases and heaving them over the footplate. With a murmur of thanks, I followed him through, fumbling for a tip.

Suddenly there was light as he pressed the plunger of a metal time switch on the wall – a single dusty bulb hanging from the cavernous ceiling bringing us into startling closeness to each other. Perhaps it was my expression of shock at his gaunt and starved appearance that caused the *sereno* to look away, as if ashamed. Distressed, I pulled out half a pocketful of change and thrust it into his hand. But he wasn't expecting so much, and most of the coins fell onto the cobbles. Imagining that I'd dropped them accidentally, he scrabbled around for them, then offered them back to me. I shook my head and gestured for him to keep them. '*Para Usted*—' I managed to say.

He looked down at the money in disbelief before coming to attention suddenly and saluting me – with the hand that held the coins, unfortunately, so they flew all over the cobbles again.

The light went out.

With a muttered oath he flung himself at the wall and groped for the plunger. For the second time we both grovelled on the ground for the coins. Pocketing them at last, he ran out into the dark cobbled courtyard beyond and looked up at the back of the building before tiptoeing back to me, his finger pressed to his lips. Pointing upwards, he clasped his hands together and laid his head on them. '*Dormiendo!*' he mouthed, before grabbing my cases and hauling them towards a narrow iron fire escape. He hadn't climbed three steps before he and the cases became wedged immovably between the railings.

The light went out.

With a curse, I groped my way back to the wall of the portico and fumbled for the lethal-looking metal plunger which fizzed and sparked as I rammed it home, before returning to the fire escape where the *serreno* was in the throes of ejecting himself backwards from the grip of my cases. With nothing to hold them against the railings, they tumbled after him, knocking him to the cobbles. I helped him up as he apologised in a hoarse whisper, then grasped the handles of the suitcases again and began to climb the stairs sideways, panting and sweating and giving off a strong odour of old dirt with his every move.

The light went out.

Cursing wearily, we both stopped dead in our tracks.

Fuck it! I thought, and pointed on upwards. We could just see each other in the reflected light of the city from the square of sky above us. So on we went, to the first landing, where he put down my cases and jabbed his finger at the top of the next flight of steps, to where a wider landing ended at a pair of darkened glass-panelled doors. '*Pensión Illiturgi!*' he whispered, then pointed to himself. '*Prohibido!*' He wasn't allowed up. He pointed to himself again, then to the courtyard below. '*Me voy!*' I'm off! Then he tapped me on the shoulder and pointed upwards at the doorway with one hand, while with the other he pretended to knock, then quickly put a finger to his lips. '*Sssh!*' He did it again, just in case I'd missed the point. Then he took my hand and bowed over it. '*Gracias, Señor! Gracias—!*' he whispered vehemently, turned away, tripped over my briefcase, yet somehow managed to grip the railings on either side and steady himself. With a reassuring wave, he was gone.

I didn't want him to go, my sense of loneliness flooding back as I continued up the steps on tiptoe, to the iron stairhead which appeared to have been turned into a *terrazza*, with pots of geraniums, and knocked softly on one of the rattling glass panels of the door...

Nothing. I tapped again, cupping my face in my hands and peering into the darkness through the door pane. Dimly I could make out some kind of hallway, with heavy lumps of furniture. I was about to knock a third time, when to my horror something pale and ghostly rose out of the darkness at the back of the hall and expanded, flapping its wings like a giant spectral bat as it flew towards the door. A moment later the brutish, staring-eyed face of a dead girl was pressed against the inside of the door pane.

Fear rooted me to the spot. Even in the gloom of the stairwell my face must have reflected my horror, which was then reflected in hers as she drew back in equal terror. '*Quien es?*' she demanded faintly, and I let out a gasp of relief.

'*Señor Gough*,' I called out quietly, cursing a name that was unpronounceable to foreigners.

'*Momentito, por favor*,' her voice quavering as she vanished. A moment later the lights in the hall came on and she returned to the door – some kind of servant girl in a thin cotton shift with a threadbare blanket clutched round her shoulders, and not at all deformed; it was the pane of cheap glass I'd looked through that had distorted her features. Behind her, on the floor at the back of the hall, I saw the straw palliasse she'd been sleeping on. Reassured by my smile of relief, she unbolted the door to let me in. One by one I heaved my cases over the threshold.

'*Ssssh!*' she whispered urgently, miming that everyone was asleep. Picking up my briefcase, she signalled me to follow her down a dingy passage smelling of old fish and quaking slightly with the muffled snores of other residents. Grimly, I followed her with my suitcases, but only as far as the first door on the right, which she unlocked and opened, switching on the light before gesturing me to enter. Heaving my suitcases inside, I was astonished to see my grandfather's zinc-panelled trunk standing in the middle of the room like a member of my family waiting patiently to be reunited with me. I turned back to thank her. Pointing along the corridor to her left, she mouthed '*Servicios*' – lavatory – then whispered '*Buenas noches, señor*', closing the door behind her without a sound.

I looked around, at a room so small and dreary that my gaze flew back to the trunk as if to cling to something familiar. My mother had sent it on to me by rail as soon as Beryl had telegraphed her my address in Madrid. Its very familiarity made my eyes prickle dangerously—

I mustn't give in—!

I looked round the room again, but nothing had improved, its awfulness confirmed now, unchangeable. More like a monk's cell than a bedroom, it was long and narrow and painted a vile shade of pale yellow diarrhoea. All it contained was a single bed, a chair, a rickety desk, a deal wardrobe with drawers, and a small washbasin beside a high window which was almost the worst feature of all, with frosted panes instead of plain glass. When I turned the handle and opened them, I realised why: my room overlooked the cast iron 'terrace' at the top of the fire escape, which in turn looked into my room.

What was that sudden dreadful smell? I turned back, my nose seeking it out. The basin! I leaned over the grimy bowl for an instant before recoiling in revulsion from the stench of raw sewage seeping out of it. Jesus Christ! This was actually fucking unbearable! *Everything* was fucking unbearable—! Holding my nose and trying not to retch, I groped for the plug among the calcified aluminium taps, my glance falling accidentally, fatally, onto the tiny plug hole no more than half an inch across which was bunged solid with wads of old hair and what looked like pale animal fat. My gorge rising, I rammed the small plug into its hole and turned away despairingly to get my toothbrush and toothpaste, kneeling on the grimy rag rug by my bed, springing the latches of my case, opening the lid—

A note from Beryl lay on top of my clothes like a *memento mori* of Deya, together with a thin sheaf of papers. *Dear Simon – I thought you might like these to keep you company. Good luck in Madrid! Come back soon! Love, Beryl.* Beneath her letter was Robert's *Symptoms of Love* and half a dozen other new poems which she must have typed out for me and slipped into my suitcase while it stood in the hall on my last day.

I didn't even realise I was crying until my tears hit the thin blue paper, darkening it in great splodges. Uncaring, I riffled through the poems, the nightmare of the present contrasted brutally against a gilded past which had ended only a few hours ago at Canellun, in the gentle rain—

Clutching the sheaf of poems, I dragged myself to my feet, slammed out the light, and in the sudden anonymity of darkness threw myself weeping onto the bed, stifling my groans of despair in the pillow, bellowing at Margot, begging for sleep, for oblivion, to know why she'd broken her promise, why she hadn't come to meet me – why? Why? *Why?*

Eventually, mercifully, sleep put me to death.

> *Love is a universal migraine,*
> *A bright stain on the vision,*
> *Blotting out reason.*
> *Symptoms of true love*
> *Are leanness, jealousy,*
> *Laggard dawns;*
> *Are omens and nightmares,*
> *Listening for a knock—*

—hearing it in my dreams,
a soft tapping at my door,
the door opening—

> *Waiting for a sign—*

—smelling her scent,
even in my sleep,
feeling the weight of her knee on the side of my bed—

> *For the touch of her fingers*
> *In a darkened room,*
> *for a searching look—*

—shaking me gently by the shoulder—

'Si? Wake up!'

Turning towards her, eyes flying open in disbelief, meeting hers in the faint light from the passage—

—rising like Lazarus from sleep into her arms, clasping her to me, sobbing her name, kissing her face, her lips through my tears, burying my head in her neck, under her hair, among the memories of all my love for her—

Take courage, lover!
Could you endure such grief
At any hand but hers?

ALASTAIR

'*Sssh—!*'

She drew back with a tremulous smile, her eyes glittering in the dim light from the passage. Stretching across me, she turned on the bedside lamp before looking back, her eyes widening in mock surprise, whispering 'Is that what you usually wear in bed?' trying to lighten the atmosphere between us. But nothing could diminish the intensity of that first embrace—

'Of course not!' I whispered back shakily.

She stared at me, knowing everything, saying nothing. 'Well, at least you don't have to get dressed – come on!' Effortlessly, she slid from the bed to her feet. 'Alastair's waiting outside with a cab—' She looked briefly round the room. 'Jesus, what a dump! I can't believe he put you here – or perhaps I can. We'll find you somewhere else—'

'What time is it?' I asked, turning away furtively to wipe my face with the coverlet.

'Nearly midnight. Leave all that—'

'*Midnight?*'

'It's *early*, Si! You're in *Madrid*! Come on—'

Outside in the passage the assortment of snores had got worse, as though a competition were in progress. 'Lock your door,' she whispered. 'I could have been anybody.'

Oh no you bloody couldn't! Just the same, I did as she said and pocketed the key.

She was already in the hall when I caught up with her, pressing a small banknote into the servant girl's hand, causing her to let go of her blanket in astonishment. As I came up to them, the girl blushed furiously as she stooped to pick it up, but I reached it first, draping it over her shoulders again.

'*Gracias, Señor!*' she whispered shyly, but her eyes were only for Margot, as were mine, from her snappy patent leather high heels with severe little straps over the arches of her feet, to her stylish silk dress, open at the throat, and her immortal face, like Nephertiti's, skeletally beautiful yet perfect beyond belief, her eyes all-embracing as she smiled at the girl. '*Gracias, Maria, hasta luego*—'

The girl's whispered thanks followed us like zephyrs as we tiptoed down the stairwell.

'How did you know her name?' I marvelled.

'I asked her, you fool!' Laughing quietly, she reached back and took my hand. 'Listen, Si, Alastair's a bit drunk – there's nothing he doesn't know tonight, if you see what I mean. Mary got fed up with him, so they had a row and she went home – which is why we didn't meet you at the airport. Just don't rise to his bait, OK? He's not mean-drunk or anything, just... a bit drunk!'

'Right!'

The light came on.

Below us, the *sereno* had flung himself against the wall like a martyred saint in an attitude of terminal ecstatic shock, his hands jammed against the fizzing metal plunger of the light. The moment we reached him, he waved us towards the wicket gate like royalty, bowing so low as we passed that he knocked himself in the eye with one of the keys dangling from his belt.

'*Muchisimas gracias, Pedro,*' she murmured, slipping him some change and a dazzling smile.

The taxi was waiting on the street, engine running, the back door wide open, the interior light spilling out onto the gleaming cobbles. Lolling in the back seat was Alastair, his familiar granite face wreathed in smiles as we approached.

'*You see?*' he called out to Margot in his faintly Scottish burr. 'What did I tell you?'

Margot stooped gracefully into the cab. 'Budge over, you great lump!'

I followed her in, barely managing to shut the door before Alastair sprawled across her and reached out his huge hand to me. 'Si! Good to see you again.'

I took his hand, laughing. 'And you.'

'There!' he exclaimed, flinging himself back into his corner. 'I said he'd be fine, and he is.'

'No thanks to you,' breathed Margot.

'*Señor?*' demanded the driver.

'*Momentito*—' Alastair lurched forward again, steadying himself against the dickey seat to look round at me. 'Have you eaten yet?'

'No, actually—'

'Nor have we. *Tapas*, then!' And to the driver, '*Plaza Mayor, hombre! Vamonos!*'

At last – somewhere beautiful!

As we sat at a café table under one of the arcades on the Plaza Mayor, I looked hungrily across the huge square lined with gaslit arcades identical to this one, interspersed with occasional *flambeaux*. Parading round the middle of the cobbled square whole families were still making their after dinner *paseos* in the half-darkness, stopping now and then to greet other families—

'I can't believe so many people are still up,' I exclaimed, 'even children!'

'That's Madrid for you,' said Alastair as he finished ordering from the waiter, '"*the city of dreadful and endless night!*" Most people here don't eat till ten or eleven – or until half past midnight, like us. Madrid never sleeps. Whatever they miss out on at night they make up for with a three-hour *siesta*. It's civilised here! The *Madrillenos* concentrate on the most important things in life – conversation, food, wine, bullfights and *frontón*. For everything else – *mañana!* How are you liking it so far?'

'Well, this is great – beautiful! But when I first arrived I thought it was the most god-awful place I'd ever been to – the stench, the poverty, beggars everywhere. I mean, compared with Rome—'

'*Don't!*' he said abruptly, leaning heavily over the table to make his point. 'Don't compare it with anywhere. This is Madrid, and you're *here*, and that's *it*.'

'Hey!' protested Margot.

But Alastair wasn't to be deflected. 'No, no,' he went on, trying to sound reasonable, 'I just want him to realise where he is. Spain's a hard country – not like Italy, or even Majorca – and Madrid is its hard heart, slap bang in the middle, burning in summer, freezing in winter, and hundreds of miles from bloody anywhere. It's hard because it's full of people who've survived – survived distance and poverty and the Inquisition, and then one of the bloodiest civil wars in history – hence the beggars everywhere—'

My lesson was interrupted by the arrival of the waiter with our drinks – an unlabelled bottle of what looked like white wine, and three narrow schooners, followed by saucers of plump olives and toasted almonds. 'This is *Manzanilla*,' Alastair went on, like a schoolmaster, as he began pouring with exaggerated care into the glasses. 'I prefer it to *fino*. It's still made in Jerez, but by the sea, so it's saltier – perfect with *tapas*. Also, because the mouth of the glass is so narrow, it's difficult to get drunk on it—'

Margot let out a scarcely suppressed grunt of disbelief.

'I'm *fine!*' he protested. 'A little tipsy, perhaps, but only because I haven't eaten yet.' He raised his glass to me. 'Here's to you, Si. See what you think.'

I took a sip from the narrow mouth of the glass, wishing my nose were smaller, and was instantly surprised by the cool, clean taste of the sherry, the hint of saltiness – not of brine, but of haars and sea air – the alcohol flowering in my nasal passages, gently warming my eyes—'I say!'

Smiling, he reached over and thumped me on the shoulder. 'We'll make a Spaniard of you yet!'

'Sherry doesn't taste like this in England,' I mused.

'Of course it bloody doesn't! Those heathens serve it out of prissy drinks cupboards at room temperature! Pale sherries have to be cellar cold. For that reason, you should always pick up your glass by its stem, then hold it by its foot. Never touch the sides – it warms the sherry.'

'Is there *nothing* you don't know?' asked Margot sardonically.

'Tonight? *Nothing*,' he beamed as Margot and I exchanged a brief smile of conspiracy, 'and it's up to me to teach Simon everything I know. I promised Diana—'

'Christ, we'll be here all night! You know so much!'

The waiter returned, his tray piled high with steaming *tapas*, galvanising Alastair into clearing the decks and arranging the little oval dishes on the table. 'The idea is to try a little of everything,' he explained, handing me a small metal fork with a flat-sided edge to cut with, 'but try these first. You've got *gambas pil-pil, revoltillos, croquetas, criadillas*—' He refilled our glasses. 'I've chosen some of my favourites, but you can make up your own mind—'

We all set to, Margot gracefully, Alastair wolfishly, and I ravenous suddenly, the smells of the piping hot dishes as stimulating as the sherry. Stuffing a forkful of little prawns into my mouth, still sizzling in oil and garlic and tiny red squares of something-or-other, I groaned with pleasure, my mouth burning at first from the heat of the oil, and then from something quite else as my tongue and the inside of my lips were set on fire— '*Fuck*—!' I exploded, poking my fork at the little red things. 'What are *these*?'

Alastair feigned surprise. 'Chillies,' he chided me. 'Have you never eaten chillies before?'

'No—' I reached urgently for my glass of cold sherry and tried to quench the fire.

'Try eating some bread,' Margot suggested, 'it helps.'

Glaring at Alastair, I chewed on some bread and fanned my mouth. 'You could have warned me,' I grumbled, unable even to close my lips.

'No I couldn't,' he said casually, stabbing his fork into my gambas and stuffing them into his mouth. 'It's up to you to find out. I'll help you of course – warn you about things that are actually dangerous – but not about chillies. I'm not your fucking nursemaid, Si.' He stared me out as I looked up at him, shocked at the casual violence of his words. 'I made that clear to your mother when I agreed to help settle you in here, and I made it clear to Robert when he came. You're not a kid any more, you're a man.'

'*Jesus* Alastair,' Margot interrupted, 'give him a break – he's only just arrived.'

He held up his hand, stopping her. 'So did I, once, in an awful lot of places, and there was no one there to help *me*. Si and I go back a long way—' His eyes narrowed. 'Isn't that so?'

'Yes,' I answered, wishing he'd change the subject. 'It's all right. I understand—'

'I know him – all his dark little corners…' His stared me out. 'Am I right?'

I refused to answer. What did he know, in fact? Only what my mother had told him, and she knew only as much as I told her. Why was it that adults always presumed that they knew you better than you knew yourself? All they saw was what little you chose to show them; all they knew was what little you chose to disclose. Alastair had survived a lot, I knew, but at almost half his age so had I, if only half as many dreads and fears. I glanced at Margot, meeting her smouldering look with a twin-like complicity. I was closer to Alastair's ideal of survival than he realised, and she knew it. I also knew the value of silence, that by saying nothing I was making a point, which slowly sank in. When he sneaked a look at Margot he seemed to realise that he was on a losing wicket and declared his innings. 'Anyway...' he mumbled, reaching for his glass, 'Madrid could be the making of you if look on it as a challenge and measure up to it —'

Margot began to clap slowly, like a bored audience. 'I'm sure we'd all like to thank Mr Reid for his interesting little talk,' she drawled. With a grin at Alastair's discomfiture, I joined in.

A passing waiter, presuming he was being summoned, paused to ask what we wanted. Laughing in spite of himself, Alastair waved him away and turned back to the table and threw up his hands. 'All right, all right – no more lectures. Now come on, let's eat while everything's still hot. Si, why don't you try a slice of that—' He pointed to what looked like part of a huge sliced egg in gravy. I jabbed at it with my fork and stuck it in my mouth without realising how hot it was. I quickly sucked in some air. The consistency was rubbery, a bit like squid, but the gravy was powerful, meaty, setting off my salivary glands again. '*Hmm!*' I hummed appreciatively.

'What is it?' asked Margot, reaching out with her fork and pronging a slice.

Alastair waited until it was almost in her mouth. 'Bull's testicle,' he said, dead pan.

Margot lowered her fork and turned on him. 'What's *wrong* with you tonight?' she demanded angrily. 'You get drunk, you fight with Mary, you snipe at Simon, and then you start on me—'

'Eat it,' said Alastair, his smile stuck, apparently unmovable. 'I dare you.'

'*You* eat it!' she retaliated, stabbing the fork at his mouth, so quickly that he had to open up or be impaled on the tines. 'You don't get it, do you?' she went on while he chewed frantically. 'I don't *want* to eat bull's balls! If I'd wanted them, I'd have ordered them. I don't need to be *macho*, or play silly games!'

'*Whoa!*' Again, Alastair raised his hands in surrender '*Pax!* OK?' But his eyes were still fixed on me. 'Listen, Si, I'm only trying to help, truly. I mean, look at these *tapas*—' His hand swept over them in the gesture of a salesman. 'The whole lot cost less than a shilling! You need never starve here, that's the point. *Tapas* are the best and freshest food in Madrid, and nothing's wasted. Look—' he began pointing to the dishes, 'here we have sweetbreads, tripe, intestines, testicles, all in different sauces, and it's the same with the seafood – these are sea slugs, for instance. Can you imagine anyone in England eating them? Try one. It's not a trick, I promise. I've told you what they are—'

'I know what they are,' I said, suddenly remembering Selwyn Jepson's reaction to them at the café on the *cala*. Lacking Margot's courage to refuse, I did as he asked, my natural revulsion overcome by the strong garlic and tomato sauce that covered it. I nodded at Alastair. 'Actually, they're rather good.'

'They're usually pregnant,' he said airily, 'so you get three or four for the price of one—'

'*Don't eat it, Si!*' Margot turned on him again, but he was already helpless with laughter, his granite face breaking up, crumbling into a landslide, as if he were weeping, turning away from Margot as she rained blows onto his shoulder and then his back.

'*Are they really pregnant?*' she demanded.

'I don't know!' he hooted. 'He'll have to spit it out so we can all look!' He bent over double, slapping his thigh, his body wracked with laughter – laughter so infectious that Margot and I were both caught up in it in spite of ourselves. Around us, people began to turn and stare and then to join in. Suddenly conscious of them, Alastair got a grip on himself, gasping painfully as he put on the brakes, taking out his handkerchief and wiping his eyes and face.

'Are they really pregnant?' Margot persisted, snatching the hanky from him and dabbing under her eyes before passing it to me. I took it, more out of a sense that it would link me to them in a kind of tear-brotherhood than because I actually needed it. Wiping my eyes briefly, I handed it back to Alastair.

'I don't know, honestly,' he snorted. 'It just appealed to my sense of thrift.'

Margot shook her head in disbelief. 'Was it your sense of thrift that made you choose Simon's room in that *pensión*? I wouldn't put a dog in it.'

'Hey, now hang on a minute!' he retorted, still half laughing, but indignant. 'Mary and I spent bloody days trying to find him somewhere to stay, and when Robert came, *he* tried! It had to be somewhere central, somewhere he could afford—'

'It's fine,' I interrupted quickly, 'really!'

'It's *not* fine,' Margot insisted. 'It's a dump!'

'Listen!' Staring at Margot, Alastair pointed at me like a prosecuting barrister. 'He gets two guineas a week from his grandfather and that's *it* – about four hundred pesetas. His digs cost him 12/6d a week, with breakfast, which leaves him thirty shillings a week to live on – about two hundred and fifty pesetas, out of which he has to feed and clothe himself, pay his fares to university, take taxis sometimes – I did the fucking sums! Madrid may be the cheapest city in Europe, thank God, but it's not free – *nothing's* free!'

'I'm very grateful to you and Mary,' I began politely.

'Oh, balls! I just want you to know that we didn't just stick a pin in a phone book. I may be hard on you, but I'm not a bastard – *à propos* of which I might as well tell you – because if I don't Mary will – she's a toffee-nosed Bostonian and she went off in a huff about it – the reason we didn't come to meet you at the airport was because I forbade it. I wanted to see if you could hack it on your own – which you did, and good for you.' He looked at his watch, trying to focus on it. 'Now, the night is yet young – I think – so let's finish up here and go and paint the town a delicate shade of knicker-pink! Time to introduce you to flamenco, Si – and I mean *real flamenco*, not the crap they play to tourists.'

We sat in the back of a taxi, Margot between us, our arms linked through hers on either side as I puzzled over my feelings for Alastair.

He'd been pretty aggressive admittedly, but then he'd been drinking all evening – and he was a Scot after all. Even so, I didn't actually know him as well as I thought, which took me by surprise. When I'd first got to truly know him, that summer in Deya with my mother, I'd thought of him even then as what Robert called a 'loner', as someone who could look after himself no matter what, and I remembered wondering vaguely if he might become my new father now that my mother was divorced. I'd always liked him, and he'd seemed to go out of his way to be kind to me in a paternal sort of way—

I was suddenly distracted by a waft of Margot's haunting perfume, blown towards me by some chance cross-breeze through the open windows of the cab, and looked at her perfect profile in the light from passing streetlamps, safe to do so because she was laughing at something Alastair had said, and not looking at me. I had to take a sharp breath inwards simply to remind myself to breathe, my heart racing in response. The way she'd defended me against Alastair, her eyes like raptors, sharp with the prey of him—

And yet he hadn't seemed to mind her defending me – provoked her, even. They were obviously close, but not in the serious way that he and my mother were close. This friendship was far more relaxed and carefree. Drink was probably a part of it, too, but then perhaps he'd got drunk because he'd had something difficult to say to me – laying down the rules – and he'd got a bit pissed so that he could use it as an excuse for appearing to be hard. Tomorrow, when he was sober again, he'd probably apologise and become just as I remembered him, a bit stern and thoughtful, but with occasional flashes of unexpected humour—

'I forgot to ask you, Si,' he said suddenly, 'how are Robert and Beryl?'

Christ! Robert's letter—

'They're fine, thanks.' Reluctantly disengaging my arm from Margot's, I dug it out of my inside pocket. 'I'm so sorry, I forgot – I was meant to give you this—' I held the letter out to her.

'Thanks,' she murmured, taking it with a slight frown and slipping it into her purse.

'He said to tell you that he needs letters. From everyone,' I lied.

'Then letters he shall have!' Alastair proclaimed like a Shakespearean actor. 'I'll write to him tomorrow – tell him that you're in good fettle—'

Margot seemed not to hear, still frowning as she stared out through the driver's window.

EL CORDOBEZ

From the outside, the bar we arrived at in a narrow back street looked like all the other bars in Madrid I'd seen through taxi windows at night – neon-lit, uninviting, the few tables on the pavement occupied only by men.

Inside, though, the place was heaving, the sound of conversation deafening, the acrid smoke and jungle-like heat almost impenetrable at first. Undaunted, Alastair plunged straight into the throng, towering above everyone, Margot following, with me bringing up the rear, looking around in wonder at the swarthy animated men bellowing at each other at the tops of their voices, smoking, drinking, gesticulating violently, occasionally bending their heads forward to hawk and spit gobs of phlegm carefully between their feet onto the sawdust-strewn floor, too engrossed in their conversations to use the brass spittoons by the bar.

As we made our way deeper into the room, I began to hear snatches of guitar music and the urgent clatter of castanets. A moment later we entered another room through a pair of heavy curtains, Alastair having signalled that there were three of us, and paid an entrance fee. The inner room was much wider than the bar, and dark, filled with people either sitting at tables or standing against the walls, all staring spellbound at a small floodlit stage where a man and woman were dancing surrounded by a semi-circle of half a dozen other dancers and musicians sitting on chairs.

Wordlessly, Alastair reached back for Margot and me and arranged us at the back of the crowd, against the wall. Since we were all of us at least a head taller than the people in front of us, we could clearly see the woman dancer in her blood-red tiered dress reach down and begin sensuously to raise her skirts at either side, her body swaying, the stout heels of her shoes stamping out a rhythm, faster and faster as she revealed first her slender ankles, then her calves, as pale as marble, her knees – before angrily releasing her skirt and whirling away from the approaching male dancer, her castanets chirring their warning with incredible speed, like the tails of rattlesnakes. With an unwavering glare the male dancer, in tight black trousers and cummerbund and white ruffled shirt, continued to approach her in a controlled frenzy of desire, it seemed – or was it hatred? – heels smashing faster and faster into the wooden floor, his body erect in every gesture and intention, eyes flashing, her eyes flashing, the two of them caught up in a formal ecstasy that brimmed over the stage and into the packed room where hoarse cries of 'Olé!' spurred on the dancers to their approaching climax. On stage, the growing hysteria seemed to sweep through the semi-circle of musicians and dancers, the huge guitars strummed and thumped with increasing fury, the seated dancers clapping in double time, then in syncopated rhythm, one against the other at the percussive speed of machine gun fire, all in perfect time, every eye entranced, fixed unblinking on the dancers as the tempo rose again, the dancers sweeping past each other, round each other, drawn into an increasing vortex of passion without so much as touching, the electric charge of their closeness sparking feats of such pagan feeling that the audience began to roar their approval, and the end, when it came, abrupt and stunning – the dancers back to back, arms raised like matadors at the kill and yet the bull un-felled, a figment of our imaginations, the music suddenly dead and gone, sucked into the past, the dance done to the death, the room filled with the sound of stamping feet and shouts for more – and more—! Never in my life had I witnessed such raw emotions crammed into so short a time, or so small a space, a vivid dream come and gone in the blink of an eye—

Barely acknowledging the rapturous audience, the dancers, chests heaving from their exertions, unfroze from their final positions and strode off to opposite sides of the stage, the musicians following the man, the dancers the woman as they stepped down from the edge of the stage and broke open their fans in the half-darkness of the wings—

'Bloody hell!' I found myself exclaiming to Margot and Alastair. 'I mean *bloody hell!*'

'Quite something, eh?' Alastair grinned at me. Even though she'd seen them before, apparently, Margot was equally affected, her eyes still alight with what she'd seen as she shook her head slowly – in disbelief? – in empathy, perhaps?

'I'll get us all a drink,' offered Alastair.

'No, no, let me,' I delved into my pocket for money. 'Please! It's the least I can do—'

He shrugged. 'Fine with me. Margot? Beer's the only thing to drink in this heat—'

'I'll have a Coke,' she said impassively, 'with ice and lemon.'

I grinned at her. *Touché!*

'I'd better come with you,' Alastair glanced at me, shrugging off the slight. 'I need to ask the barman something, and you might need help—'

'I can speak enough Spanish to ask for two beers and a Coke,' I retorted irritably.

'Of course you can! But you might need help with the glasses.'

Touché to him.

Once through the curtain and into the bar we could hardly hear ourselves speak.

Alastair's height drew the barman's attention almost at once, but instead of ordering, he pointed at me. The harassed barman then pointed at me, impatiently.

'*Dos cervezas y un Coca-Cola con hielo y limón, por favor!*' I bellowed at him, at which he fired off some incomprehensible question.

'*Tubos!*' shouted Alastair, before turning to me. 'If you ask for *cervezas*, they'll ask you which kind of bottle you want! *Tubos* come out of a tap. They're just as good, and half the price!'

I handed him a fifty peseta note. 'You'd better do it,' I said resignedly.

'Haven't you got anything smaller?' he demanded. 'I only need a few—'

I took back the note and offered him what was left of the change from my pocket.

When the barman returned with our drinks, Alastair paid for them and asked him an involved question which I couldn't get the hang of at all. I *had* to learn this language – fast. I might as well be deaf and dumb, not knowing what people were saying, not knowing how to say it myself—

Whatever the barman said to him, Alastair seemed pleased, handing me back my change, and a couple of glasses to carry as he shepherded me towards the curtain again. 'Good news—' he yelled. 'We were just in time! The man I wanted you to hear is coming up next – the last act—'

There was no sign of Margot where we'd left her. Our eyes swept the room anxiously, until I saw her waving from a table near the stage. We made our way to her through the crowd.

'One of the men at this table just came over and offered it to me,' she said, slightly mystified.

'Good for him,' grunted Alastair. 'I'd have done the same myself.'

Margot snorted, as Alastair raised his glass in my direction. 'You've got a good accent,' he conceded grudgingly.

'Why, Rhett!' exclaimed Margot in a deep Southern drawl. 'That's the nicest thing you've said to him all night!'

'No, I mean it. It's better than mine, and I'm a bad loser.' He took a swig of his beer and turned to Margot. 'Your admirer's on next,' he murmured. She frowned at him blankly. '*El Cordobez.*'

'Oh, don't be an ass,' she laughed. 'You imagined all that.'

'Mary didn't!' He leaned over the table to explain to me. 'When we all came here last week, there was this old bastard, *El Cordobez*, singing. He must have been seventy or eighty, but one look at Margot and he was knocked for six – did his whole bloody act staring at her, which put Mary's nose out of joint, I can tell you – as a blonde she's always the centre of attention in Madrid. Anyway, the point is, he's one of the finest singers of *cante hondo* in Spain – that's the true *flamenco* I was talking about—' he glanced around the room. 'Almost everyone here is from Andalucia, where it comes from. The *Madrillenos* despise the Andalucians, but even they worship this man.'

Judging from the way the room was filling up, he was right, the crowds at the back overflowing amongst the tables now so that those sitting half way into the room had to stand up to see, all eyes anticipating the singer's entrance. On stage, a solitary chair had been set to the right of centre.

A few moments later a single figure detached himself from the shadowy performers in the wings and climbed up into the spotlights on stage. At once the audience began to roar and applaud as he walked calmly to the middle, smiling as if in doubt of the reason for their applause, followed at a distance by the tall, bent figure of his guitarist, who seemed to use the thunderous applause as camouflage to slip unnoticed onto the chair, cradling his guitar across his thighs as if it were a woman, hunching over the instrument as he began softly to tune it. After a moment, the two men exchanged a few words as the applause continued, until *El Cordobez* turned to face us, his hands gently appealing for quiet.

Alastair had wildly exaggerated his age. He appeared to be in his late sixties, perhaps, a short, powerful-looking man, oiled grey hair swept back, his eyes dark and piercing, set deep into his head, face deeply lined – though whether by sun or laughter or life itself was anyone's guess. Standing there in a sleeveless cardigan over a white shirt open at the throat, I would have mistaken him for a peasant from his gnarled hands and thick, claw-like nails.

The audience hushed itself, allowing his guitarist to listen as he fine-tuned his instrument. From around the room there was a sudden, audible drawing in of breath.

From God alone knew where in his body, *El Cordobez* suddenly produced the most unearthly sound, impossibly high for an open-throated voice, half musical, half cry of grief, sustained, *muezzim*-like, for an incredible length of time, rising and falling, rising again, then tumbling into an avalanche of staccato words to embrace the first huge entrance of the guitar, a magical chord that seemed to contain the echo of every note he'd sung.

I was convinced that my hair must be standing on end. Around us, there were quiet, deep throated cries of '*olé!*' and '*hombre!*' egging him on, in a trance, it seemed. I had no idea what the song was about – a grievance over some unattainable woman, or the massacre of his entire family, but the sense of lament was so stirring that my imagination ran as wild as his voice among the wild landscape of his homeland. With strangely stiff and primitive gestures he occasionally laid his clawed fingertips, like the prongs of a pitchfork, against his breastbone or his heart, or awkwardly half spread his arms at waist level, palms upwards as though to offer the injustice or the horrors of his song to his judges among the audience who growled or bayed their support for him. As his passion grew, so the guitarist hit the notes and chords and sound box of his guitar with increasing fervour, each of them inciting the other to greater and greater urgency, the barrel chest and diaphragm of *El Cordobez* providing endless power to the inhuman sound that came out of his mouth, his face contorted with a growing anguish. The guitar I could recognise as a guitar, but his voice was incomparable with any I'd ever heard, the primal sound of a creature in pain, and yet more beautiful, more expressive than any sound in nature.

The climax was sudden and brief, his words and gestures once again staccato with revenge and fury, as if to say '*this is what was done to me; this is what I did in return*—' and with a final unearthly cry, a final chord, the song was sung.

At once the room erupted into a roar of approval and yells and stamping feet, not simply expressions of delight at hearing a song sung from the heart and soul of a master, it seemed to me, but the catharsis of a homesick people for the land of the song he'd sung, for the bond that united them all.

I glanced at Margot, her eyes haunted, fixed unwaveringly on the small bull-like figure of *El Cordobez* as he slowly came out of his trance and smiled again. Making a sign to his accompanist to join him, he walked to the front of the stage and bowed once, stiffly. The guitarist merely stood up and gestured with his hand to the old man, at which the applause redoubled. *El Cordobez* bowed once again, briefly, before peering out into the audience, shielding his eyes against the spotlight until he saw Margot – not by accident, I was convinced, but because he'd somehow arranged for her to be given this table. A slight tremor passed through him as their eyes met, his searching glance a sudden embrace as he stiffly held out his arms to her. The applause faltered and died, replaced by an air of buzzing expectancy as the audience craned their necks to find the cause of this sudden gesture.

Unwilling – or unable – to break the shared gaze that joined them together, he half turned his head to growl urgently to his guitarist, taking him by surprise for a moment, but only for a moment, before he grunted acknowledgement and instantly changed his fingering on the strings as the old man shyly murmured to Margot, his hands gently gesturing for her to rise. Without the slightest hesitation she stood up, smiling back into the smile of the old man as if no one else in the room existed.

And he began to sing – not to the hot packed room of his admirers, but to her alone.

Like a wily serpent, Alastair carefully slid his torso along the edge of the table, one hand gripping the edge for support, the other grasping my head and dragging it towards him. 'This is an extraordinary honour!' he whispered savagely into my ear. 'The old bastard's in love with her!'

Who isn't? I wanted to shout back at him.

Having listened to a few words of the song, he pulled my ear even closer to his mouth. 'It's a fucking love song!' he hissed. I didn't need to be told that – I could see it from the expression on *El Cordobez*'s face, from his intonation, from the way his eyes were locked into hers – 'I think he's written it for her—!' He listened again. 'I'll try and translate it for you—' I wished he wouldn't – the sound I was hearing was so extraordinary, heart-wrenching – but Alastair was unstoppable. '"*I looked into your face and saw that it was the face of my duende*"'—that's a sort of spectre of destiny for Andalucians... '"*Now I am blind to all other faces...*"' I stared at the old man as he sang, his eyes burning into Margot's, his gestures as stilted as before, but more impassioned, his whole body, his very soul trying to convey the meaning of his song to her. I didn't dare look up to see her expression; I could see it in my head anyway, rapt and still, her eyes hypnotic, daring him on— '"*My woman asks me why I no longer look at her*—'" Alastair hissed in my ear. '"*She has no cause to be jealous... a man who has seen his duende is already dead*". Christ!' he gasped. 'He's not pulling his punches!'

Once again the room shook and heaved to the thunder of stamping feet and roars of acclaim as he ended his song, everyone sitting at tables leaping spontaneously to their feet, Alastair and I following suit, flanking Margot on either side, applauding with the rest. I sneaked a quick look at her, but she was still mesmerised, lost in the immediate past of his song, her eyes haunted with sadness as she stared at *El Cordobez* taking a reluctant bow, her hands held together in front of her mouth as if frozen in the act of clapping, forefingers lightly touching the centre of her full, parted lips – then suddenly aware that she was the centre of everyone's attention and slipping out of vision into her seat like a vanishing trick. Alastair and I sat down at once, instinctively pulling our chairs closer, as though to conceal her from the curious and admiring looks.

Alastair's look was no less admiring, but more cynical. 'You do seem to have the most extraordinary effect on people,' he observed, smiling crookedly.

Margot turned on him, a dangerous look in her eyes. '*Don't*... spoil it,' she said.

It was as if she'd slapped him. 'No... I'm sorry.'

By the time we left, Margot was her old self again, spinning away down the middle of the empty street in perfect imitation of the *flamenco* dancers, skirt swirling round her knees, stamping her feet, arms raised sinuously above her head. Once we'd caught up, we fell into step on either side of her.

'I like being sung to!' she cried happily.

At once Alastair launched into a lusty, tuneless rendering of '*Speed, Bonny Boat*'—

'Not like that!' she protested. 'Jesus! Stick to poems – leave the singing to *El Cordobez*!'

'I didn't know you wrote poetry too,' I said, surprised.

'When he's not being a hack,' said Margot mockingly. 'Which is most of the time.'

'Nothing wrong with being a hack!' insisted Alastair defensively. 'At least it keeps my bread buttered.'

'Since when did you need butter?' asked Margot half teasingly. 'You've got Mary—'

'That's neither here nor there,' he said curtly. 'Let's cut through to the *Avenidas* – we can pick up a cab.'

More than a little drunk myself by this time, I was still looking down at the cobbles, absorbed by the sight of Margot's elegantly shod feet between Alastair's polished brogues and my scuffed black lace-ups, imagining that Alastair and I were her bodyguards (and liking the fantasy) when we suddenly emerged out of the dark alleyway and onto a broad, tree-lined boulevard with traffic still racing in both directions, even at this hour.

The contrast between what we'd left behind us and the wide pavements we now trod was astonishing. Even though it must have been after two in the morning they were still thronged with people, most of them well dressed as they emerged from smart restaurants or ice cream parlours, or browsed in expensive-looking shop windows. Moving among them, almost invisibly, were the night vendors – waif-like boys with trays of sweets and pastries hanging from cords round their necks, lottery ticket sellers with their monotonous cries of '*Para hoy! Para Hoy!*' And beggars, of course, but different here, as if intimidated by their rich surroundings (or by the *guardias*), standing respectfully in the deep gutter between parked cars every twenty yards or so, as if each had his own clearly defined patch, the eyes of the un-blind downcast, the eyes of the blind defiant, those with hands dejectedly reaching out for alms, those without hands or arms relying on their wives or children or dogs to beg on their behalf.

I was vaguely aware of Alastair detaching himself from us to wave down a taxi, and of Margot telling him not to, that she didn't feel like going to bed yet, so we continued to walk along the *Avenida* arm-in-arm, Margot occasionally stamping her feet in fast, *flamenco*-like movements as she hummed to herself, dragging us across the pavement occasionally to look at something that had caught her eye in the discreetly lit windows of the best shops.

But while they were engrossed in the shoes and gloves and handbags displayed in the vast plate glass window of one of the few truly modern shops, with the unpronounceable name of Loewe, it was the people around us who gripped my attention, the contrast between the rich and the poor so stark as to be almost unbelievable. If I weren't seeing it with my own eyes, I'd have found it impossible to imagine that these prosperous, well-fed people could parade so blatantly and obliviously in front of their maimed and impoverished audience of vagrants and street vendors – who seemed themselves (to give the rich their due), equally oblivious of *them*, except as providers. This was survival of the fittest carried to almost unacceptable extremes of inhumanity. Perhaps the well-off Spaniards were so used to the sight of beggars that they no longer saw them, in spite of the fact that they were their fellow countrymen, and yet no one, so far as I could see, had given the poor wretches a single *centimo*. Well, that might be the Spanish way of doing things, but it wasn't the English way!

Slipping my arm out of Margot's, I rummaged for coins in my pockets, regretting that I'd given so much to the *sereno*, and to Alastair, to pay for the drinks. The *centimos* were easily separated from the *pesetas* because they were bigger and lighter, made of aluminium. Ambling slowly along the edge of the pavement, I began to dole out the coins based on the severity of each beggar's injuries, or whether or not he had children with him. I didn't want to be thanked (or asked for more), but let the coins fall into their hats as I passed, as though I'd dropped them accidentally.

By the time I'd given to three of them, though, it was as if some signal had been passed ahead of me, because the fourth beggar was anxiously watching out for me, mounting the curb on his crutches, eyes staring, hand outstretched, already talking before I could even hear what he was saying. Realising that I was hoist by the petard of my own largesse, I brushed past the man irritably, almost sending him flying, then felt guilt stricken and chucked him a peseta, then felt worse because he had to grovel for it.

Enough! Stuffing my hand back in my pocket, I searched out Margot and Alastair who were about twenty yards ahead, parallel with the next beggar—

It was as I quickened my pace, looking around watchfully, that my eye was caught by an extraordinary sight on the far side of the *avenida*. Moving swiftly with the traffic, a homemade cart on bicycle wheels was being pulled along by two guttersnipes with ropes over their shoulders. A third boy ran behind, a rope around his waist, acting as brakeman. But it was the contents of the cart that filled me with a kind of fascinated horror – a huge bearded beggar with only stumps for legs and a black patch over his right eye was leaning forward, ape-like, on his knuckles, his head moving watchfully from side to side. Now and then, with an angry gesture, he would wave at the cars behind to give him a wider birth when suddenly, in spite of the six lanes of traffic that separated us, something on my side of the avenue caught his eye. I glanced back down the pavement at the beggar on crutches who was signalling urgently to him, like a bookie, making gestures above his head, then pointing up the street towards me.

I realised at once that my height and hatlessness had betrayed me as the villainous-looking beggar picked me out of the crowd in an instant and fixed me with a demonic glare. Leaning even further forward on his knuckles, he shouted at the boys pulling him, and over his shoulder at the boy behind. One after the other they threw out their left arms and began to move into the traffic, gliding across the three lanes so determinedly, the man's gestures so violent, that cars and taxis at once gave way to them.

I'd come to a complete standstill, so engrossed in their manoeuvres that I didn't for a moment consider my own safety as they swung across the central reservation at full speed, like a nightmarish *calèche*, the 'ponies' choosing their moment to perfection as they began to thread their way at high speed through the oncoming traffic on my side of the avenue, ignoring the screeching brakes and hooting as they finally reached the inside lane and hurtled towards me. I was paralysed by indecision. If I turned and ran, Margot and Alastair would think me a coward; if I cried out for help, they'd think I couldn't cope—

So I stood my ground, not like a hero but like a rabbit caught in the beam of headlights as the two slum kids in front finally swung their tumbril round into a vacant space between the parked cars, ramming it against the kerb, shortening their ropes expertly and straining to keep it there so that their gruesome cargo, now level with the pavement, could swing himself out of the cart on his stumps and knuckles and scuttle towards me along the pavement like a mutant. He moved with astonishing speed, his stumps thrusting him forward, his knuckles, wrapped round with strips of old leather to protect them, dragging his huge torso behind him. In action he looked less like an ape now and more like a hyena, hindquarters sloped back, baring his blackened teeth at me in a grimace of feral greed, his one bloodshot eye grasping hold of me like a third hand, pinning me to the spot.

No more than a couple of feet from me, he suddenly pulled up and sank back onto his haunches, his stumps pointed towards me like the barrels of a sawn-off shotgun, sweeping his hand over them in the same gesture that Alastair had used to draw my attention to the cheapness of the *tapas*. His huge, filthy claw shot out to within an inch of my face, gesturing urgently for money. I must have failed to react quickly enough because he suddenly grabbed at the black patch over his right eye and raised it, exposing what appeared to be a jellyfish slithering milkily around in the deeply scarred socket. As I recoiled in disgust he shouted with laughter, reaching up to clutch the lapel of my jacket and shake me. Without thinking twice, I gave him everything I had in my pocket, including the fifty peseta note I'd offered Alastair earlier. With a grunt of greed he grabbed at the money with both hands, so violently that some of the coins scattered over the pavement in a jingling shower. Stuffing what he had into his greasy leather waistcoat, he was on the point of scraping up the rest when something behind me caught his eye. Dimly, I was aware of the sound of feet running towards me as he suddenly spun round on his stumps and bolted for his trolley, shouting to his boys as he flung himself onto it. With the same extraordinary agility as before they swung the trolley round, judged their moment to perfection again, and slipped effortlessly into the traffic, just as Alastair, bellowing '*Oi! Coño!*' raced past me and after them, into the street. But they were already whirling away on their silent wheels, the beggar facing the brake boy now, yelling taunts at Alastair, waving my banknote and spitting at him until they were swept away in the traffic.

Margot reached me, breathless, staring anxiously into my face, asking if I was all right – how much was stolen—

'He didn't steal anything,' I said, coming out of my trance. 'I sort of gave it to him—'

'You *what*?'

I squatted down to retrieve some of the coins he'd dropped. A couple of passers-by, who must have seen what had happened, did the same, handing the coins down to me as if I were the beggar. For a ridiculous moment I felt a flash of sympathy for him.

'It's just that he was so *revolting*!' I gasped. 'It's fine, honestly – I only lost fifty or sixty pesetas—' Thank God the five thousand peseta note that Robert had given me was still safe in my inside pocket.

It wasn't fine with Alastair, though. He came running back, demanding to know what had happened, and when Margot told him he stared at me in disbelief. 'You must be out of your fucking mind!' he shouted. 'What were you thinking of?' His eyes narrowed. 'Tell me the truth – were you giving him money, or paying him to go away?'

'I don't know,' I mumbled. 'A bit of both, I suppose—'

'Don't you understand *anything* I've told you?' he exploded. 'These are the leftover dregs of the Civil War – soldiers, most of them, who fought on the wrong side, which is why they're beggars now – as a lesson to others. If the State can't afford to feed them, you *certainly* bloody can't!'

'That's enough, Alastair,' Margot interrupted.

'*No!* He's got to learn! He's *got* to. This is a dictatorship, not some fucking limp-wristed democracy! To survive here you have to detach yourself from reality—'

'Pretend it isn't happening, you mean?' I retorted angrily.

'Yes! There's no point doling out money to beggars – in a few years they'll all be dead anyway, from cold and starvation and disease. That's Franco's plan – much less contentious than rounding them all up and gassing them, like Hitler. You're in Spain! Don't interfere in what doesn't concern you. Quite apart from anything else, you could bugger it up for the rest of us. We're all here under sufferance. You go on about Rome – well, learn a lesson from it: "*When in Rome—*"'

'Your laces are undone,' murmured Margot, squatting down like a well-oiled spring to retie them.

'Thanks,' he said vaguely. 'Listen, Si, I really don't mean to give you a hard time, but you've got to hit the ground running here. There are no second chances.'

Margot rose up in front of him and dropped him a graceful curtsy. 'We're obliged to you for your lecture, Mr Darcy,' she declared in a perfect imitation of an English accent, 'but gosh, is that the time? Mother's waiting up—' Slipping her arm through mine, she turned on her heel with me in tow and began to walk us smartly away in the direction we'd come.

'Brilliant!' I gasped, squeezing her arm.

'*Hey!*' shouted Alastair behind us. We looked back over our shoulders, laughing at his stunned expression. Taking a sudden step forward, to follow us, he crashed full-length onto the pavement.

'I do believe Darcy's tipsy!' Margot gasped. 'Someone should call a constable!'

Alastair, still struggling to stand up, toppled over again. Passers-by, scandalised, were giving him a wide berth. One old gentleman even poked him in the ribs with his cane and gave him a piece of his mind.

With a shouted oath, Alastair began to pull off his shoes. '*Quick!*' cried Margot, grabbing my hand and pulling me after her between the parked cars and out into the road where she flagged down a passing cab. Bundling me into the back, she followed me in, still holding my hand, slamming the door. '*Vamonos, hombre!*' she shouted at the driver. We both turned to look out of the back window as we pulled away. Alastair, in his socks, with his shoes slung round his neck, was already waving down another green-lighted taxi and pointing after us.

Margot leant forward to speak to the driver. 'What's your address?' she asked me.

No! I didn't want to go there – not yet!

'*Calle de las Huertas, 14,*' I answered faintly, wishing instantly that I'd thought up a wrong address so that I could spend the rest of the night with her – the rest of my life with her—

When we finally pulled up with a jolt outside my *pensión* I leapt out of the taxi, as we'd agreed. Margot leaned out of the open window. 'Be good, Si!' she murmured quickly. 'Be safe.'

Darting a quick look down the street, I leaned down and kissed her, our lips touching briefly. 'Of course!' I laughed. 'And thank you. For everything!' I sensed the other cab turning into the bottom of the hill below us, and looked back. 'I think he's coming—'

'I'll ring you!' she cried as she turned back to the driver. '*Guadalquivir—!*'

But I couldn't hear the number of her street – which I'd thought was a river, anyway – as the cab roared away. My last sight of her, framed in the back window of the taxi, was of her face against the glass, smiling, waving, the image burning itself into my memory.

Moments later the street was flooded with light as Alastair's cab, headlamps blazing, thundered up the steep, cobbled hill and screeched to a halt as it came level with me. Alastair leaned out of the open window, gripping the leather strap to steady himself. 'You snake in the bloody grass!' he growled. There was the faintest smile on his craggy face. 'Where'd she go?' he demanded.

'To some river—'

With a bark of laughter, he shook his head ruefully, producing his shoes in his other hand, still joined together, the knot of his laces dark with spit. 'I can't undo the fucking things! Listen, Si, I'm sorry we didn't meet you at the airport – all right? I was wrong.'

'It doesn't matter,' I said lightly. 'It's different here, I understand that. But I'm a quick learner.'

'We'll see,' he grinned back at me. 'Look, you'd better come to supper – meet Mary. This week's hopeless. Next Wednesday, say. Come early – six thirty – you can meet Jasper before we put him to bed.' He reached into one of his waistcoat pockets and held out a visiting card. 'I hate interruptions, so only telephone if it's important – don't if it isn't.' He turned to the driver. '*Oria 25, El Viso—*'

The taxi pulled away, and a moment later I was alone again.

And yet no longer alone. We were *together*, in the same city—

I looked up at the dark, forbidding façade of my new home. So what if it was a shit hole? Nothing else mattered!

On a raw surge of happiness I clapped my hands three times, loudly, confidently, and heard in the distance the footsteps of my jangling gaoler hurrying to let me back into my cell.

MARY

The following morning I slept until ten, having ignored a couple of calls to breakfast and gone back to sleep. There was nothing to wake up for, after all, unless Margot telephoned.

Dragging myself out of bed finally, I went to the basin to brush my teeth – without removing the plug, and leaving my spat out water as an added stench-stopper while I looked underneath the basin to try and work out what was wrong with the plumbing. A quick glance was enough: it lacked an 'S' bend – rather like me at the moment – no natural trap to prevent my raw emotions from overwhelming me. But while caustic soda and bleach might cure the drain of its problems, I could think of nothing that could cure mine – not (if the truth were told) that I was in hurry to cure them; I was in love, which empowered me to allow everything else to vanish into the sharp perspective of its true insignificance.

Even so, I could at least try to make my room more habitable, particularly if Margot were to visit me again. I could start with the pictures, perhaps; at the moment there were only a couple of crude oleographs, one of improbable flowers, the other, above my bed, of Christ's head bleeding under his crown of thorns, eyes rolled up to heaven in an expression of '*Oh God, not again!*' as though he'd caught the previous occupant of the room masturbating beneath him for the umpteenth time. He had to go. I had no intention of curbing my own bestial ecstasies, after all (provided they were in no way related to Margot). Reaching up, I unhooked the surprisingly light picture and shoved it face down under the bed, where I doubted anyone would find it.

I made a list: caustic soda, pictures, bleach – and a hat, of course. Looking them all up in my Spanish dictionary, I went down the hall in search of breakfast.

Minutes later I was out on the streets, still in search of breakfast.

My first impressions of Madrid by daylight were no rosier than the night before; less, if anything, since everything that had been either shrouded or softened by darkness was now blatant reality, the general air of poverty and neglect as I walked through the maze of narrow streets more reminiscent of the ruined Europe of my boyhood than the Europe that existed today beyond the frontiers of this impoverished country. I felt strangely alien and out-of-synch, as if I didn't actually exist among the stony-faced crowds on the pavements, to the drivers of the battered cars and bicycles and mule-drawn carts lumbering over the cobbles. It wasn't exactly that I was invisible to them, simply that I was ignored – resented, perhaps – the living proof of a future world that had no place here – not yet, at least.

I came to a pleasant, tree-lined square on my right, the Plaza Santa Anna, sat down outside the nearest reasonable-looking café, and clapped for a waiter.

As the last person in to breakfast that morning at the *pensión*, I'd been given a bowl of stewed, lukewarm coffee, a crust of bread and a slice of what looked and smelt like the sole of someone's old shoe, which turned out to be cured ham, though what it had been cured of was unclear. Of life, certainly; I'd never seen anything so long dead yet still unburied. On my way back past the kitchen to the front door, I'd inadvertently glanced in, to see the slattern of a cook sitting in the window picking clean the slimy bones of last night's fish, her shocking steel teeth so closely packed together that I could almost hear them screeching against each other as she fed them scraps of fish from her greasy fingers. Catching sight of me, she gave me a huge grin, her mouth opening like the jaws of a mechanical digger. '*Holá!*' she cried, spraying her mangled mouthful across the room.

Even though breakfast was included, I decided to have it elsewhere in future

The waiter appeared with an unexpected smile of welcome on his face and a flourish of his napkin, wiping the aluminium tabletop until it gleamed like a new dawn—

—What could he bring the *señor* on this beautiful morning—?

From now on, I decided happily, this would be my watering hole.

Empty days were torn from my life like the diary pages in old black-and-white films, complete with wind-blown leaves – not of Autumn, but of heat and drought. Still no word from Margot. In the end I rang Alastair, once, briefly, in the evening, when I imagined he must have stopped work, to make sure that I was still expected to supper on Wednesday. Of course. Was Margot all right? Of course – she was in Barcelona for a few days. Was *I* all right? Of course. Until Wednesday, then—

Stop bothering me—!

When the day came to sign-on at the university I made my way to the outskirts of Madrid, to a campus of monolithic and hideous concrete and red brick buildings and queued up with hundreds of others in the vast central hall of the largest building, sick with the urge to make a run for it. And yet this was the whole point of my coming to Madrid, my grandfather coughing up nobly to send me here. To let him down was unthinkable, just as it was unthinkable to break my promise to Gerard Fay and Joan McCulloch and my friends at *The Manchester Guardian* that I'd come back with a degree and work my way up through the paper – not that any of them would actually give a damn if I didn't, so why should I?

Because I'd promised. Myself.

This was not what I'd imagined, though, even in nightmares – no dreaming spires, no ivy clad quads, no force-feeding of the intellect and imagination by great minds. Yet again I'd be trapped in the vicious circle of classroom life, of punctuality, attendance, of boredom and inevitable rebellion. Like a refugee I continued to stand in line clutching my papers and passport photographs until, after a wait of hours, I was finally given an identity card (which confirmed nothing more than that I was me) and told to present myself in Room 313 on Monday morning at nine o'clock for my first lesson.

Increasingly throughout the endless dreary process I'd clung to a single thought: Margot. If I wanted to be near her then I'd have to remain in Madrid, and if I wanted to remain in Madrid then I had to attend university or my grandfather would cut me off and I'd have to go home. It was as simple as that.

My taxi drew up outside Alastair's house at precisely six thirty that Wednesday evening.

Remembering my unfamiliar hat at the last moment, I rammed it back on my head, still clutching a wilting bunch of flowers I'd bought that morning at Atocha station, paid the driver his six pesetas and watched as he pulled quietly away down the comfortable tree lined street, as though in deference to its well-heeled occupants. *El Viso* had turned out to be a welcome surprise.

Apart from its roof tiles and shutters, Oria 25 could almost have been mistaken for a townhouse in Chelsea, with its front garden, white stucco walls, and stone steps leading up to a pillared portico. I rang the bell and waited – interminably it seemed – until finally the door was flung open by a slender blonde woman with an expensive-looking urchin's haircut and a dazzling smile. I whipped off my hat and stuck out my flowers. 'Hi!' she exclaimed. 'You must be Simon! I'm sorry, we were all upstairs. I'm Mary – oh, how sweet!' She accepted my flowers as if they might be sticky.

'How do you do?' I asked as we shook hands.

Over her shoulder she was clutching a bulging blue blanket which suddenly wriggled at the sound of my voice and then

400

produced a head, cherubic, blue-eyed, staring gravely out at me. 'And this is Jasper,' she added by way of introduction.

Small children usually cried when they saw me, which was odd, because I liked them on the whole. I waited, resigned, for Jasper to start bawling, but he didn't, continuing to study me with a serious frown. 'How d'you don't?' I asked him politely. 'I'm Simon.'

'Simon,' he repeated after a moment, then buried his grinning face in his mother's neck.

'He likes you!' Mary sounded surprised. I was astonished. 'Alastair's waiting upstairs. Come on in. I warn you, it's quite a climb.'

I followed them through the dark, gloomy hall and up flight after narrowing flight of stairs, my attention divided between guiltily admiring Mary's boyish, all-American bottom sheathed in tight blue jeans, and innocently returning Jasper's broad (and widening) grin as he looked down at me. 'How old are you?' I asked him, dragging my gaze upwards from his mother's behind. He repeated my question, almost word for word.

'Eighteen,' I replied.

'Nearly two,' said Mary.

'He seems remarkably intelligent,' I said, without explaining my reasons for thinking so.

'He's pretty bright. Too bright, sometimes. Nearly there—'

The last flight of stairs led directly and strikingly into a huge attic room, so high and so overwhelmingly white that for a moment I imagined we'd entered a Utopian world fifty years from now, the low walls, the steep sloping ceilings, rafters, sofas, rugs, lamps, all white. Only the floor was of varnished wood, and even that was half covered by a vast shaggy white rug hemmed in on three sides by deep white sofas. I stared round, speechless.

'*Si! Good to see you!*' I turned instinctively to my left, where Alastair's voice had come from, to discover that the room continued behind me, to the left, but on a raised dais – Alastair's open-plan study by the look of it, with a dazzling white desk, book-lined walls, white filing cabinets, and Alastair himself stepping down into the room—

'Simon's brought us these lovely flowers,' said Mary vaguely, looking round – for a bin? Alastair shook my hand warmly. It was strangely reassuring to see his tight, parsimonious smile again, and I think my pleasure must have shown because untypically he threw an arm round my shoulders.

'What an extraordinary room,' I exclaimed, no longer tongue-tied by it.

'We both designed it,' said Mary proudly, laying my flowers carefully on the white coffee table. 'Then we came to an arrangement with the landlord, and *hey presto* it was built – a whole new floor in the roof space!' A dazzling smile. 'We love it! It's Alastair's study, really, but we entertain in it too.'

'The rest of the house is like a mausoleum to Spanish bad taste,' explained Alastair dourly. 'Impossible to work in. This suits me just fine.'

For someone so fastidious, I imagined that it did, the whiteness and light and space allowing him a freedom that lent his movements an almost feline air for such a big man, his gestures relaxed, graceful, as he began pouring from the chilled bottle of sherry on the coffee table. As always, he was neatly dressed in old clothes, beautifully laundered and ironed, the sheer whiteness of the room accentuating the pale khakiness of his trousers, the gleam of his old belt, the washed out blue denim of his shirt. Even his face added subtle colour to the room, slightly tanned, his lips surprisingly red, his eyes surprisingly blue.

'It's like a newly primed canvas,' I observed at last, 'the slightest colour has a dramatic effect.' Even a huge sand painting of Bill Waldren's, almost filling the end wall, looked startling.

'Precisely!' He handed me a glass of sherry. 'Well seen. It has the same effect on conversation, I've found. People are calmer, more thoughtful—' This was the Alastair I knew and recognised – deliberate, precise, slightly severe, a far cry from the Alastair of my first night here. I glanced at Mary, smiling up at him as he offered her a bowl of almonds, her smile like the finest porcelain, beautiful but with a hint of brittleness that had less to do with Alastair's effect on her, I felt, than with her upbringing.

'Thank you, dear—'

Whoops, I thought to myself – but perhaps that was how they addressed each other in the rarified Bostonian circles she apparently came from. She had all the hallmarks of a perfect East Coast upbringing – charm, poise, a quiet, attractive voice, and that most telling hallmark of all, the absence of visible hallmarks of any kind – no jewellery apart from a simple wedding ring, no labels, not even on her jeans, no vulgar display. One just took it for granted that her background was 24-carat gold. I liked her style, and the way she played with Jasper, who became the centre of all our attention for the next half-hour, hung squealing in the air and dropped like a bright blue bomb onto the deep white sofas. What I'd mistaken for a blanket turned out to be his 'sleep suit' as Mary called it, a fluffy all-in-one affair from America with legs and arms that seemed far too big for him. Only his head seemed to be in proportion to it. Gathering up all the loose material at the back I carried him face-down, like a handbag, round and round the room, faster and faster, until he was flying and yelling with delight.

'Simon, he'll be sick!' laughed Mary. Just in case, I crash landed him gently onto her lap and slumped giddily onto the sofa next to hers. Unsurprisingly, he was down her legs and back up mine like a rat up a drain, so the three of us took it in turn to fly him round the room until Mary finally and firmly declared that it was bedtime. At first, Jasper disagreed loudly and tearfully, but Mary was adamant. Did he want to go to bed crying, or did he want to kiss everyone and go happily to bed? Realising he was on a hiding to nothing, he chose the kissing option and held up his arms to us. I was impressed, gladly enduring the smears of snot as he embraced first me and then Alastair, who hugged him with surprising warmth.

'I'll tell Consuelo fifteen minutes,' said Mary brightly as Alastair handed Jasper back to her.

It was only after they'd both gone that I realised she'd removed the one jarring note in the room – my half dead flowers—

—only to present them a little later, like a firework display, in the middle of the massive dining table on the ground floor. 'How on earth did you revive them?' I asked in amazement.

'Oh, it's an old trick I learned at home,' she said casually, yet clearly flattered that I'd noticed. 'First I cut off an inch or so from their stems, and crush them, then I douse them completely in cold water for five minutes, shake them out gently, upside down, then put them in a vase of fresh water with half an aspirin and a teaspoon of sugar. It always seems to work. Now, what have you two been talking about upstairs?'

She was sitting at the head of the ornate dining table, with Alastair on her right, against the window, and me on her left. Crystal and silverware gleamed in the candlelight.

'Very little, to be honest,' I said as Alastair filled our glasses with frosty white wine – although I'd asked after Margot at one point, to be told that she'd arrived back in Madrid that morning, which had made my spirits soar in silence. Apart from that, we'd talked mostly about his new room, and the pleasure it gave him. I focussed on Mary again, and smiled apologetically. 'Forgive me, but after two weeks of speaking hardly a word of English – except to myself – I keep trying to translate what I want to say into Spanish without knowing half the words – like a stroke victim, I imagine, learning how to speak again—' The wine was as elegant as Mary's smile, so I drank some more. 'But my feelings are returning like a tide – or do I mean receding? Are one's feelings like sand or sea—?'

'What's the Spanish for "recede"?' asked Alastair in his schoolmaster's guise. 'The verb—'

'*Receder*,' I answered instinctively, rolling the pebbles of the 'r's over my tongue, pronouncing the 'c' as 'th', as I'd been taught. They both looked surprised. 'Am I right?'

'I've no idea,' he grinned, 'I've never had to use the word. I'll look it up—'

'Alastair, you *fraud*!' cried Mary. 'I thought you were being serious!'

He ignored her completely. 'You have a very good accent,' he conceded.

So he'd said before, but he'd obviously forgotten.

'That's what I like about Spanish,' I said to Mary at once, trying to soften Alastair's put-down, 'it's so logical, and much closer to Latin even than Italian, which makes it easier to learn, especially the verbs.' I felt lightheaded. Was it the sudden speaking of English again, or the sherry we'd had upstairs? The bottle had been almost empty when we'd come down. 'I'm sorry,' I said, 'I'm talking too much—'

'Not at all!' said Mary brightly, picking up an incongruous little hand bell – incongruous because it was unpolished and made of brass – and ringing it. Alastair's surprise seemed exaggerated.

Someone entered the room behind me and shuffled towards us. I turned slightly, to see that it was the cook, a fat middle-aged woman with a sour moustachioed mouth and dark rims round her gleaming, olive-black eyes, wearing bedroom slippers and carrying a tureen. As she approached Mary she forced an ingratiating smile, as threadbare as old knicker elastic.

'*Mi gaspacho, Señora!*' she cried triumphantly in a mannish voice as she set down the tureen.

'*Qué bueno!*' Mary exclaimed, clapping her hands together. '*Gracias, Consuelo!*'

I was slightly taken aback. With a name ending in an 'o', I'd presumed Consuelo was a man. I could almost hear the elastic snap

405

as the woman's smile perished utterly once she'd turned away from Mary and shuffled past me to the kitchen.

'*God almighty!*' breathed Alastair. 'She must have cooked for the Borgias.'

'Don't be nasty, dear,' said Mary as she began to ladle out the cold soup. 'She's highly recommended by the agency.'

'So were the last two, and they were a disaster.'

'Perhaps if you'd been nicer to them—'

'I liked *Maria!* ' he protested. 'All right, she drank us out of house and home, but at least she could cook! And laugh. And surely a year should stand for something—'

'It stood for longer than *she* could! She spent most of her last month unconscious on the kitchen floor, with no dinner for anyone. Now, if you don't like Consuelo, fine, but let's discuss it later. We have a guest—' She turned to me with her bright, brittle smile. 'Do start, Simon – and tell us about university life. I know Alastair's dying to hear.'

I glanced across at Alastair, who was clearly dying for nothing of the sort. I wondered what was going on between the two of them.

'Don't mind him,' said Mary brightly, 'he's just in a glump because he's had an article returned by *Holiday Magazine* with acres of suggested revisions. He's not very good at imagining what we Americans want to know about foreign parts, are you, dear?'

'And care less, frankly,' he grunted. 'This *gaspacho*'s too thin; and there are no breadcrumbs in it—' He reached for his glass. While Mary and I had more or less sipped at our wine, he was knocking his back like water. He gave me a wintry smile. 'I'm sorry, Si, I didn't mean to be rude – tell me about university.'

As a third party, it was clearly up to me to distract them from each other. 'Well, there's not a lot to tell, really,' I began hesitantly. 'I've only been to a couple of classes so far, and it's like going back to kindergarten – you know: '*Tengo mucho calor; me llama Simón; el catto sat on the matto*', that sort of thing. To be honest, I learn far more at the *pensión* than I do at university, where everyone's held up by the slowest learner. Although there's the occasional jolly moment, I suppose,' I added rather desperately. 'I mean, one of my professors owns twenty-two pairs of white high-heeled shoes, all numbered.'

'He should be bloody arrested!' exclaimed Alastair, animated at last.

'No, no, she's a woman!' I reassured him hurriedly. 'Today she was wearing pair number fourteen. She takes them off and shows us at the beginning of each class... It's something to do with Princess Fabiola, I think... Although I may have got that wrong.'

'She's must have a footish!' exclaimed Alastair, deadpan. Even Mary laughed, in spite of herself.

The rest of the *gaspacho* slipped down relatively peacefully, until she tinkled her bell again. Alastair winced theatrically. 'Look, why don't you just *call* her?' he protested. 'And what *is* that bloody thing anyway?'

'*Sssh!*' Mary hissed under her breath. 'Wait till she's finished—'

Consuelo shuffled back into the room, accepting Mary's fulsome thanks and praises with the merest grimace this time, ignoring Alastair and me completely as she took away the dishes.

'*Well?*' demanded Alastair sharply as she finally left the room. '*What's with the bell?*'

Mary turned on him. 'It's Consuelo's!' she said forcefully. 'She takes it wherever she works, apparently. She says she's used to it.'

'Jesus Christ, that's all we need – a Pavlovian cook! Perhaps if I barked at her she'd cook better!' He began to bark, noisily, making me laugh.

'*Alastair, stop it.*' Mary's cheeks were flushed as she showed her temper at last.

He pulled a face as he refilled our glasses. Mary had still hardly touched hers. 'And what's with the bedroom slippers?' he persisted. 'Is she sleeping in the kitchen?'

'No, she is not! She's got bad ankles, that's all.'

'They're not just bad, they're horrific!' He took a pull at his glass as he looked at Mary through narrowed eyes, spoiling for a fight. 'You're terrified of her,' he observed suddenly, as if he'd finally managed to open a stubborn oyster.

'I am not so!' she said defiantly.

'Yes you are – "*Si Consuelo, no Consuelo—!*"' Consuelo strode back into the room, unsummoned, bearing a large metal *paella* pan by its two handles, plonking it down as if it were the accursed remains of a mortal enemy, and stalked out.

'She's changed into her shoes!' I whispered theatrically.

'Great!' Alastair's face lit up. 'Perhaps she's leaving.'

'Oh, for Christ's sake, Alastair,' grated Mary, 'grow up!' She turned to me, her smile now painfully forced. 'Would you hand me your plate, Simon?'

'Yes, of course.' I did as she asked. 'I say, it smells wonderful!'

'Doesn't it just!' She threw me a grateful look as she heaped my plate with glossy, still-smoking rice, coloured peppers, onions and chunks of juicy-looking meat on the bone.

'And how are you enjoying Madrid?' she asked, handing me back my plate.

'Nice weather for the time of year,' snorted Alastair, guffawing into his napkin. Mary ignored him, filling his plate and handing it to him without a glance.

'Well, I like it much more than when I first arrived,' I answered hurriedly, reminding myself not to make comparisons with Rome – or anywhere else. 'It seems incredibly poor, though, which is fine in a way, because everything's so cheap, but at the same time the poor seem to have a pretty grim time of it—'

'Franco!' grunted Alastair. 'I told you, he likes to keep it that way.'

We'd all started to eat the *paella*, which was as good as it looked and smelt, when Alastair suddenly flung down his fork and spat out a mouthful of bony meat onto his plate. 'It's fucking *rabbit*!' he shouted. 'I *hate* fucking rabbit!'

'It's fucking *chicken*!' Mary yelled back, all manners fled. 'I bought it myself this morning!'

'Then she's swapped them! It's the oldest trick in the book – *Jesus*!'

Mary turned to me, her eyes blazing. 'Simon, is it chicken or rabbit?' she demanded.

'It's delicious, whatever it is!' I said diplomatically.

Mary snatched the bell and rang its tinkling neck. Consuelo erupted into the room.

Mary took a supreme grip on herself, even trying to smile. *'Perdonna me, Consuelo,'* she said in her halting Spanish, *'pero este paella, es de pollo, ó es de coño?'*

Alastair choked so violently on his glass of wine that he sprayed it over the table before emitting a scream of laughter that stunned even Consuelo.

'Conejo,' I corrected Mary gently. 'Rabbit is *conejo* in Spanish – my professor keeps pet rabbits. *Coño* means—'

'Cunt!' shrieked Alastair, completely hysterical now, slapping his thighs, rocking back and forth like a madman, helpless with laughter. 'No one accused her of putting pussy in the *paella*!'

Pandemonium—

'Alastair, you're *disgusting*—'

Unable to help myself any longer, I burst into uncontrollable schoolboy giggles while Consuelo cursed her way back to the kitchen and Alastair, incapable of speech now, tears rolling down his face, rocked back and forth under a hail of profanity from Mary until Consuelo burst back into the room clutching in one hand her hat and coat and a handbag the size of a large turkey, and in the other the blood-soaked head and neck of a chicken. *'Es de pollo!'* she roared, flinging it down on the table, before demanding, in stentorian tones, to be paid. Alastair refused point blank, Mary couldn't find her purse, I could only come up with twenty-four pesetas, so Consuelo threatened to call the police. Alastair leapt to his feet and circled the table towards her, threatening to look in her handbag, at which Consuelo finally cut her losses, snatched up her bell and bag, and fled from the house—

Followed moments later by Alastair and me as the front door slammed like a bomb-blast behind us.

It wasn't until we got to the bottom of the steps that Alastair looked at me in slight amazement. 'How the fuck did we get here?' he asked.

'I'm not quite sure. It was awfully quick.' I glanced back at the house. 'Have you got your keys?'

He slapped at his pockets as he followed my glance. 'It's all right – the dining room windows are still open—'

They slammed shut before he'd even finished speaking.

'Well?' he demanded as we turned into the street. 'Which was it? Chicken or rabbit?'

'Rabbit!' I said instantly. 'Very *good* rabbit.'

'Ha! The chicken's head was just a blind – the rest of it was in her bag.'

'Do you mind if I ask you something?'

'Ask away—'

'Why were you in such a bad mood at supper? I mean, you were fine in the attic.'

'It had nothing to do with *Holiday Magazine*, believe me – it was that pretentious bloody table, the best china, best silver, candles – for Christ's sake, I just wanted a cosy kitchen supper, not dinner in a funeral parlour! And as for that bloody bell! It's just not my style, that sort of crap—'

It was almost dark, the street lamps lighting us beneath the trees, the heat still glove-like.

'What will you do now?' he asked.

I shrugged. 'Go and find some *tapas*, I suppose—'

Alastair began rummaging in his pockets. 'Here, let me – it's my fault, after all.'

'No, no!' I protested. 'I'll be fine – it just seemed such a waste of good *paella*. I hope Mary won't think I was rude, laughing like that.'

'Don't worry,' he reassured me, 'you were sickeningly polite – she loved it.'

He suddenly came to a halt on the corner and gestured to his right. 'Well, I'm going this way – see if Margot's still up… nightcap…' His words petered out.

At the sound of her name I spun round on him, my eyes imploring him to let me come too—

He frowned awkwardly, clearly wishing he'd said nothing. 'She's probably asleep,' he mumbled, 'or she'll throw me out for being a bit pissed… you know what she's like.' He scratched his head abstractedly. 'Look, we'll do something together, soon… all of us… OK?' He held out his hand.

'Yes, of course,' I said faintly, shaking his hand. 'Please give her my love.' Mentally, I knocked myself out cold. 'Goodnight.. and thank you—'

'Night, Si – sorry about the supper!' He turned away and began to walk up the hill, slightly unsteadily, hands deep in his pockets. I stared after him, bereft suddenly. A moment later I heard him talking out loud to himself – '*Consuelo, este paella, es de pollo, ó es de coño—?*' throwing back his head, stamping his feet on the pavement, laughing hysterically as he vanished under the trees.

ON MARGOT'S TERRACE

The next three days were spent crammed between the book ends of misery, claustrophobic with heat and crushing helplessness, unable to ring Margot because I had no number for her, unwilling to disturb Alastair to ask for it. I skipped my course, ate in and tried to study, but always with one ear listening out for the telephone. It rang often, but never for me. My study target was to learn thirty useful words a day and three verbs, two regular and one irregular, but time hung so heavy on my hands that I doubled my quota even though it seemed to halve my comprehension.

A letter came from Robert – his second since I'd arrived, wondering politely how I was, but in fact far more interested in Margot's state of mind and whereabouts; he still hadn't had a proper letter from her. He sounded a bit jagged, so I wrote back at once to say that she was still doing up her flat, apparently, that she hadn't yet got a telephone, and that I didn't want to impose on her until she was ready. I was struck by the dullness of my letter to him, but in fact there was nothing to say, really, and I seemed to lack the energy to say so interestingly.

In the evenings I had supper in the *pensión* with my new friend Manolo, a law student at the university. His huge head sat, neckless, upon his massive shoulders like an artillery shell, pointed at the top, his shoulders and torso hunched around it like the barrel of a squat howitzer. His legs, however, were like a stork's, supporting the heavy field-piece of his body and carrying him around with surprising nimbleness. The food was dreadful, and I ate it without troubling my taste buds, trying not to think of the steel-fanged cook who had concocted whichever dish it was. Although Manolo was a couple of years older than me, he treated me as an equal – even with deference at first; foreigners were uncommon in Madrid and uncensored news from the outside world was hard to come by. Even though his chances of ever going to England (still less to America) were apparently remote, my presence at least gave him a chance to air his schoolboy English while at the same time allowing me to exercise my stable of newly-learned Spanish vocabulary. Whenever I came a cropper he patiently corrected me, and heaved me back into the saddle, teaching me useful colloquial phrases as he did so.

The nights I spent back in my room, either going over what I'd learned that day or hacking my way through the dense forest of *The White Goddess*, losing my way, going back to the beginning, losing my way again among the Welsh trees and folklore and bards whose names I couldn't even pronounce. If this was a grammar of poetry, then poetry (as I'd always suspected) was a thousand times more difficult to master than mere Spanish.

Then sleep – or an attempt to sleep at least, staring up into the half-darkness of my city bedroom, listening to the distant traffic and the comings and goings of residents clattering up and down the iron fire escape outside my open window, or exaggeratedly tiptoeing past my door.

Then silence, apart from the barefoot pattering of Maria, making up her bed in the hall.

Would Margot come to me again? Her presence in the room was still as palpable as the heat. I lay naked on the bed, my sheet thrown back, sweating at her closeness, even reaching out my arm sometimes to touch her, whispering her name into the darkness, my cock lying like a lead pipe against my stomach, as aching as my heart for the touch of her hand, but denied even the touch of mine so long as thoughts of her filled the inner sanctum of my mind, for fear of defiling her.

How could Alastair, at thirty-five, be so sure of himself that he could wander off to her flat after our abortive supper and just presume that she'd let him in? Not that he seemed to care much one way or another. Would I have as much self-confidence at his age? All right, he'd been a bit drunk...

Although come to think of it, people did the same thing to my mother sometimes, dropping in after supper or after seeing a show on the off-chance that she'd invite them in for a drink and a late night chat – clever, lonely people, mostly, who hated to go home. But not Alastair, surely; his life was as full as an egg with Mary (however volatile their relationship), and with Jasper and his work, and unlike me, he wasn't in love with Margot, which seemed to make his simplest demands on her (and her refusals) a matter of casual indifference to both of them. They could take or leave each other as they liked, while I, who needed more than either of them could give, had nothing even to take or leave.

Finally, somewhere between silence and sleep, would come the nightly anaesthetic tumble into unfathomable mind-worlds, no longer master of my thoughts but once more the plaything of forebodings and fantasy until I sank into unconsciousness.

On the third morning (when I'd given up hope), she rang, sounding bright and happy, demanding to know why I hadn't telephoned.

'I don't have your number,' I said, hardly able to speak for the speed at which I'd left my room, snatching the earpiece of the phone from Maria, the blood racing through my throat and ears—

'Alastair has it—'

'I didn't like to disturb him.'

'For Christ's sake! Listen, Si, do you want to come over and sunbathe?'

'*Sunbathe?*' Either I was going deaf or she was off her head—

'*Sunbathe!* Lie in the sun and get a tan. I have a roof – do you want to come?'

'Of course – where?'

'*Here!* Oh, sorry, I see what you mean – Guadalquivir 16. Top bell. I'm *bored*! Half an hour!'

I sagged against the wall-mounted telephone, clinging to the dialling tone as if to her voice, then slowly replaced the earpiece on it's hook. *Take off my clothes in the middle of a city?* The idea was utterly bizarre – and yet so typical of Margot—

Diving into the bathroom for a shower, thankful that my body was still suntanned from Deya, yelling for Maria to bring me freshly-laundered clothes—

The taxi took me back up the endless Castellana which I was getting to know intimately, having walked all the way back down it to the city after saying goodnight to Alastair on the street corner three nights before. Driving past the end of his street, the taxi turned left a few streets up the hill and drew up outside her apartment block. I hadn't realised they lived so close.

The street was deserted, the sun brutal as I got out of the cab and headed for the shade of her building, the plate glass door buzzing me through within moments of pressing her bell, the lift in the hall out of order, leaving me flight after flight of marble stairs to climb, round and round the lift shaft, the intensity of my longing driving me upwards at dizzying speed, ninety-nine steps until I reached her door under the roof of the building – open – I pushed it wider, knocking as I entered, drenched with sweat—

She was waiting for me, dressed in a towelling robe, a sudden masterpiece as yet unpainted, every remembered detail of her alive with the genius of her reality. No memory of her could ever do her justice, I realised – one had to be *here* to see and feel and scent that effortless beauty, to laugh as we were laughing now as we rushed into an embrace, fusing together as if it were the most natural thing in the world, then holding each other away at arm's length, still laughing—

She suddenly tore off my hat and flung it across the room. 'You're late!'

'I had to have a shower—'

'You could have showered here.'

'—and change my clothes—'

'You're only going to take them off!' She began to wrestle with my jacket and tie. 'How can you bear to wear all this crap?' she demanded. 'You look *stewed*.'

'I am!' I gasped, helping her. 'Women are so lucky – they only need to put on a dress! Look, you're not serious about this are you – sunbathing, I mean—?'

'Of course!' Grinning at me as she slung my jacket and tie over the back of a chair. 'Finish undressing and come outside—' She headed back through the French windows.

'But I didn't bring any swimming trunks—'

'No – really?' she glanced back at me in mock surprise. 'So what?' she called from the terrace. 'We're not overlooked. Listen, there's a bottle of wine in the ice box and glasses on the sink—'

I undressed down to my freshly laundered briefs, looking round the room. It was a good room, big and light, with sloping ceilings, a heavy old refectory table stretching between the door and a far passage, an old, carved sideboard along the wall on the other side of the room, and in the far corner, against the wall of glass which gave onto her terrace and a panoramic view of Madrid, a low divan with richly coloured cushions strewn along the back.

I glanced through the windows. She was standing by a pair of canvas covered mattresses on the leads, slipping out of her towelling robe to reveal herself in a black bikini, stark and simple, her skin honey coloured – even the bits that had been covered by a swimsuit in Deya. With effortless grace she sank down onto her mattress—

I looked away in confusion, kicking off my shoes and socks then padding across the room and down the passage, past a small

417

bathroom on the right, and then the kitchen – peeking guiltily through the open door of her bedroom opposite—

Her double bed was unmade, the top sheet tumbled like a frozen waterfall onto the floor. Under the window, which shared the same view as the sitting room, stood her cabin trunk, its curved lid thrown back, a lilac polka dot dress spilling out of it. I longed to go in—

No! I had no right – not yet – conscious still of the 'almostness' of her embrace just now, her welcome so much more than I'd expected, yet so overwhelming that I'd been too caught up in it to take advantage of the moment, to kiss her properly—

I turned back to the kitchen in a quick fury of regret.

There was an opened bottle of wine in the fridge and a solid block of ice in the compartment above, which I treated to a frenzy of ice-picking, as if it were Trotsky himself, filling a bowl with the smithereens, grabbing two glasses and a tray and a pair of her stylish dark glasses which I'd found on the kitchen table. Putting them on (as much to hide my self-consciousness as for effect), I tinkled my way like a near-naked Egyptian slave back though the dining room and out onto the terrace, where once again the blazing sun struck me a stunning blow. 'God, it's hot!' I gasped.

Margot looked up from her mattress and burst out laughing. 'How *louche!*' she cried. 'If Cecil Beaton could see you now!' She sat up effortlessly and patted the space between the two mattresses. 'Put it down here—'

The lead roof burned under my feet, and musical tinkle turned to cacophonous jangle as I raced for my mattress with the tray. Once on it, I collapsed like a deckchair, my knees round my ears as I carefully laid the quivering tray between us. 'This is insane!' I breathed. 'It must be against the law—'

'So what?' she demanded as she started to fill our glasses. 'No one can see us.'

'All the same,' I peered round, her dark glasses lending an eerie, devilish red glow to everything I looked at. 'I feel depraved!'

'You look it,' she laughed. 'Remember Mazzini, at the *cala*, mistaking you for a girl?'

'How could I forget?' I said ruefully. 'He needs an oculist!'

'He just sees what he wants to see,' she shrugged. 'Nubile girls are his passion.'

'Talk about depraved.'

'Look, do you mind doing your back first, so I can do my front?'

'Of course not!' I drank some wine, gasping at its coldness. 'God, that's good!' I smiled at her happily. She was looking at me with a slight frown, unmoving, both arms behind her back. 'Is that a yoga position?' I was curious. Yoga had become all the rage among the hipsters in Deya that summer.

She remained motionless. 'I'm waiting for you to lie on your front, Si.'

'Oh.' And then the penny dropped. 'Oh, God. I'm sorry!' Clutching my glass, I hurriedly stretched out and turned onto my stomach, cursing my stupidity.

I heard her chuckle quietly to herself. 'If it's depravity you want—'

A moment later, her bra plopped over my wine glass. 'Crikey!' I breathed, swivelling the dark glasses round to the back of my head and waggling them at her as I panted like a dog.

'Eat your heart out, buster!' she cried, snatching them out of my hand.

'Oh, I do,' I assured her quietly, 'I do...'

I contemplated her bra before lifting it off my glass and folding the cups into each other, holding them gently in one hand while I tried to drink with the other. It was almost impossible at this angle.

'You can be pretty naive sometimes,' she murmured. 'Just like Robert—'

Oh, *great*!

'—perhaps it's a family thing—'

'Is it so bad to be naive?' I asked.

'I didn't say that.'

'I'd rather be naive than cynical!' I said emphatically.

'I'd rather you were too,' she murmured after a moment, deflating the conversation.

We lay there in silence for a while, melting into the merciless heat. I longed to look round at her, but instead made do with sending out 'vibrations' as Gill called them – hot pulses of thought-waves in an attempt to communicate with her psychically: *I love you, don't you understand? I need to be as much a part of your nakedness as you are of mine!* What did it matter that she'd taken off her bra? We were equally dressed now – or equally naked, if she preferred. But she didn't trust me yet – there was no other explanation. Unless, like me (but unbelievably), she was self-conscious, too.

I reached for my wine glass again and took another sip, and choked. 'I'm just going to sit up for a moment,' I said, quietly, not wanting to startle her. 'I can't drink on my front—' I sat up, still with my back to her, and drained my glass.

'More?' she asked.

'Please—' I reached back to her with my glass, making no attempt to turn round. *Trust me!*

'Not up there!' she laughed, gripping my wrist and forcing it down.

She held my hand steady as she poured, her slender fingers warm and firm against mine. The impulse to turn round, to fling the glass across the terrace and take her in my arms was like the beginning of a brainstorm, a lightning bolt streaking down my arm and into her hand as it held mine. *Surely she could feel it!* I began to shake with the aftershock—

'Steady! I'll just give you some ice—' And it was gone, the lightning earthed in her casual words.

'There.' She pushed my hand away with her fingertips and lay back on her creaking mattress.

'Thank you.' After taking a quick swig I lay down, too. It was only as I did so, and felt the discomfort of a fully-fledged erection lying like a lump of driftwood beneath me that I realised how aroused I was. *Christ!* One touch of her hand was all it took to wake the Kraken! And once awake, I felt it swell and swell beneath me, aching to be free—

How could I put it to sleep again? Drink some more wine? Might make it worse. Sing it a lullaby? I eased onto my right side, away from her, humming, trying not to look down at it. *Think of the worst thing that could happen!* I thought of my erection, which only engorged it more. *Think of death!* I thought of dying elephants, whose bulls apparently tried to fuck them back to life— Try again, *harder!* I thought of my erection – *softer*, then – Beethoven's *'Pastoral'*—!

I played what I remembered through my head until I must have dozed off.

Something hard – her heel? – nudged my bottom. 'Are you asleep, Si?' She sounded astonished.

'God – sorry – I must have dropped off—' I struggled to wake up. 'Did you say something?'

She sighed impatiently. 'I was telling you about going to France tomorrow.'

'What?' My head jerked up, like an animal scenting danger, turning to face her, shocked – shocked again by the sight of her breasts, dark-tipped, perfect, shimmering with oil. 'Why?' I demanded.

'*Hey!*' Her face turned towards me sharply, eyes invisible behind her dark glasses.

'Sorry—' I looked down again, bleakly, at the hot matt lead of the rooftop. 'I was asleep. I didn't hear what you were saying. Please?'

She seemed to relent, her body sinking back into her mattress. 'It's just that I'm going to Marseilles, that's all, to buy a car, an old Citroën – you'll love it! You know, like the ones the French gangsters use, with huge front tyre guards and running boards. It's impossible to buy a car here in Spain unless it's Spanish, and who wants a Spanish car anyway? This one's really cheap, only five hundred dollars through a friend... it's beautiful!'

'May I look at you?' I asked.

There was the slightest pause. 'All right.'

I sat up urgently, cross-legged, staring at her but careful to keep my eyes fixed on hers. 'How long will you be gone?' I asked

'For Christ's sake.' With lightning speed she reached over and grabbed her bra, sat up and swivelled round on her mattress, away from me, fastening the clasp in front of her, sliding it round her back, tying the halter-neck. 'Stop questioning me, Si!' she snapped. 'You have no right – *no one* has the right! I'm going to France to buy a car, and that's *it* – that's *IT,* god*dammit*—!'

'Is that why you asked me here – to tell me?' My petulant words were out before I could stop them.

'What?' She swung round to face me again, frowning fiercely. 'Don't be stupid! I invited you to come because I wanted to see you – because I like seeing you! I thought you'd be pleased about the car. It means we can get out of this god-awful city sometimes.'

'I'm sorry!' I held up both my hands, almost in panic, 'Truly! I take it back. I didn't mean to question you, and I won't do it again... I'm sorry.'

'In Deya you said you'd never say "sorry" again.'

'I'm *sorr*—!' I cut myself off as if I'd slammed down a phone.

She stared at me impassively, eyes unreadable behind her dark glasses.

'I can't see your eyes,' I muttered.

She snatched her glasses off. 'Listen, Si, you're young—' I opened my mouth to protest. 'No, *listen!* It's because you're young and because I'm fond of you that I give you more leeway than anyone else. More than you know. Don't become like the others, OK? Never question me!'

'I won't,' I assured her desperately. 'I promise.'

It was as if she were tasting my promise, for truth, before briefly nodding at last. 'I just wanted to ask you to do something, that's all – or rather, to *not* do something—'

I leapt at the chance of her words. 'Of course – anything.'

'I'd just rather you didn't tell Robert, that's all.'

'Then I won't!' Shaking my head emphatically, smiling at her. 'Simple.'

She smiled back, fleetingly. 'I'm going to do my back now, so you can do your front—' As lithe as a cat she stretched out on her stomach, adjusting her briefs so that they covered her bottom, then reaching up to unfasten her bra again. 'Wake me at five if I fall asleep, OK? I have to go out tonight.'

Who with—?

Where—?

Why?

I clenched my teeth till they juddered.

It must have been the sun dipping behind the distant hills, cooling me down, that woke me. Jolting upright, I looked round at Margot—

Gone! Her mattress empty. *Christ!* I looked at my watch. Five thirty. Couldn't I get *anything* right?

I padded into the sitting room, already full of dusk and shadows. The passage light was on, the sound of a shower running in the bathroom. I stood outside and knocked. 'I'm so sorry!' I shouted through the door. 'I overslept!' The shower stopped.

'So did I, but it's OK – just! Could you let yourself out, Si? I'm in a rush. I'll see you in a few days. Be good!'

'You too!' I called back inanely. 'Drive safely!'

Going back into the even darker sitting room, I turned on the light and began to dress, hurriedly, so I'd be gone before she came out and had to say goodbye all over again. Already my skin felt tender to my clothes. As I dragged my jacket and tie from the back of the chair where she'd thrown them, I disturbed a pile of papers on the seat, toppling them—

With a quick dive I caught them just in time. It was only then that I realised that they were all letters from Robert, sent care of Alastair, most of them unopened. My eye was caught by one she *had* opened, by the words '*My darling—*' and quickly looked away as I replaced them on the table.

How remote he seemed suddenly.

How remote everything seemed.

Numbly, I let myself out.

NIGHTMARES

Feeling strangely out of sorts that evening, I ate in on my own, early, and went to bed.

And yet sleep seemed miles away, my skin burning from too much sun, my brain sandpapered raw by self-recriminations which hadn't stopped since I'd left her flat. Would I ever grow up in her eyes? I was at her mercy in everything – too young, too immature (that *fucking* word!), to have any sway over her. It was as if being young were my fault. To hell with it! I was doing everything I could to grow up faster. Short of going to a clinic and being put to sleep for ten years, I didn't see what more I could do – and even that would be pointless, I realised, since I wasn't a bottle of claret; I could hardly mature in my sleep.

Why hadn't she woken me up on the terrace, so that we could have said goodbye properly? What did I lack that she could simply leave me there to fry and wake up without her? My skin burned at the memory of failing her, of waking up alone – and at dusk, too, that fatal moment when the volume and energy of life were turned down with the setting sun. I shivered with revulsion.

I was too anxious to please, that was the trouble – still too unsure of myself. I despised it in others, so others would inevitably despise it in me. I thought of Alastair's sophistication, of my utter lack of it when it came to love. But what could I do? Look pale and interesting? Play hard to get? She didn't *want* to get me, for Christ's sake – not yet, at least. And anyway, she hated games – hated still more the people who played them. Honesty was all she cared about, and yet if I were to remain honest then I had to remain *me* – too

425

young. But this was now and I was here and she had *happened*, not at a time of my choosing, or of Robert's, or even of hers! Fate had thrown us together, I was convinced of it, as convinced as I was that somewhere ahead of us a course was being charted from which none of us could escape. Well, wherever it was leading, I had nothing to lose but my life, and it was hers for the asking.

Meanwhile, all I could do was play out my part, close my eyes and trust her, trust in myself to be myself, learn not to make demands on her – *to grow up!*

I shivered again, in spite of the heat of the room, and of sunburn. Was I coming down with something?

Yes. Incurably.

I stood on the corner of Alastair's street, my body stolen from me, no longer in my hands but in the hands of warmongers fighting to the death through every inch of it, the cold sweat of my own defeat coursing down my body, filling my shoes, leaking out through the holes into the pavement—

I tried to steady myself by leaning against a lamppost at the corner of the street – but the only little lady in sight was old and bourgeois and sour, pushing a tartan plastic shopping trolley towards me, like a weapon – and I hated George Formby anyway.

'*Boracho!*' she spat as she gave me a wide berth, her trolley pointing at me all the while, so that when she passed on down the *avenida*, looking back at me in disgust, she was pulling it behind her.

Her little husband peeked out at me anxiously from under the black-rimmed lid of the trolley, as trapped as I was, bought and paid for. '*No soy boracho*,' I whispered to him breathlessly, recognising in his expression the fear I felt in mine. '*Soy infermo!*'

My slightest resistance to what was going on inside me was met with a punishing counter-resistance, so that my head ached and swam with the effort of trying to explain myself, my stomach heaving until eventually I had to push myself away from the lamp post and make a stumbling dash for it down Alastair's street, my feet squelching, the sick rising like sour magma in my throat. As I leaned, retching, over the low wall of someone's garden, a horrid little pied terrier, half bald with mange, came yapping hysterically towards me across the lawn, fangs bared as my stomach erupted in a gush of projectile vomit, spattering the dog's hindquarters as it tried to dodge with a yelp of surprise.

Spasm after spasm wracked me until my legs gave way as I clung to the wall, head splitting, unable to move. The dog and I stared at each other, its fangs bared as if in a smile now, sniffing the air. Then the revolting creature began to lap at its hindquarters, ignoring me, its eyes turned inwards with pleasure: I was a friend, come to feed it—

What had possessed me last night?

Still sleepless and burning, and yet in a kind of dream, I'd finally got out of bed, pulled out my suitcase of holiday clothes from underneath it, and begun to rummage through them. What if they'd been washed? Perhaps it wouldn't matter. What had I been wearing that night at Canellun, with Beryl? Shorts? No – trousers, I was sure of it; I'd made an effort that night. Robert had left me in charge—

There – my blue trousers – which I couldn't wear in Madrid because only labourers wore blue trousers here. In the first pocket, nothing. I delved into the second pocket – yes! Deep down among the fluff, the desiccated pieces of Robert's mushrooms – half a dozen of them. All I wanted was to feel different, to stop this endless drone of thoughts going round and round in my head. I wanted a new perspective – a new maturity – to be able to see further – deeper!

So I'd carefully disentangled two of the bits of mushroom from the fluff and put them in my mouth, chewing them back to life, biting my tongue to make more saliva to soften them. A memory from somewhere tried to struggle to the surface, and gave up.

The reaction I'd hoped for failed to materialise, and I'd finally fallen asleep with the pieces of mushroom still lodged soggily between my teeth.

By morning they'd gone – swallowed in my sleep, perhaps.

I'd almost forgotten about them until after breakfast in my usual café. On the way to the bank to pick up my weekly allowance, strange feelings of physical and mental uncertainty began to distort normality, my stomach to shift, the tops of the buildings on the banking street to lean in towards each other, gossiping about money matters way over my head.

Inside the bank it got worse. As I approached Captain Hewson, the Chief Cashier at Drummond's in Trafalgar Square, he was suddenly supplanted by a swarthy individual who didn't speak a word of English and treated me with ill-concealed contempt once he'd stared through the mahogany counter at the holes in my shoes, refusing to pass my chit to the cashier until I'd underlined my signature – that was the law in Spain – no underlining, no pertaters, mate! I threw him a fascist salute which he ignored because I'd thrown it in my head, mindful of Alastair's warnings. I could still think, at least—

My stomach moved again, with the feeling of boulders being disturbed by an unfamiliar force, and I fled the bank for fear of disgracing myself, out into the burning street where I somehow managed to hail three cabs at once. Choosing the driver with the kindest face, I gave him Alastair's address.

Sweltering in the confines of the taxi, my anxiety began to turn to panic as I clung frantically to the leather hand grip and to the dwindling memory of the self that I still recognised, slipping through me as fast as I clutched at him, vanishing through my fingers, through the floor into the road—

Finally, on the brink of throwing up, I begged the driver to stop, paid him off, and began to walk on up the hill like a drunkard, using trees and walls for support, breathing heavily through my nose as the waves of nausea came and went—

In a moment of sudden clarity I looked down at myself sprawled over the low wall of the garden staring down into the messy and incomprehensible omens of my own stomach. I looked for the dog, but it had vanished into the pied vomit, wagging its tail. I threw up again, started to vanish again, like the dog, my shoes filling with the wet cement of the pavement as it poured in through the holes in my downers, my uppers polished to reflection with wetness—

Oh, Christ—! Was this death?

Floundering across the street of wet cement – what street? Oria—? Or 'ere—? Or 'ere—?

What's meant anyway—?

I searched for everything I couldn't remember until number 25 rang a bell with my finger as I fell against the door, my head bursting open like a watermelon—

Apparently it was Mary, alone, who found me on the doorstep, dragged me into the house, forced me to help her get me up the stairs, into the bathroom, stripped and washed me, then dragged me across the tiled hallway and into the spare bedroom where she left me on the floor while she went off to telephone their doctor. All this she told me later, because I remembered nothing – nothing until the violent nightmares in Goya's etchings slid down from their frames on the walls and into my splitting skull, too weak to defend myself when I was manhandled by two of the bastards and flung face-up on the cell mattress, Franco leaning over me, rimless specs glinting, a migrainous double-tailed snake slithering out of his ears and into his hand, their fangs stabbing coldly into my chest, shrinking away from them but still bitten, *here* and *here* and *here*, the bites cold and sharp so that I cried out in fear, struggled—

'*Calma te! Calma te—!*'

Snatching the snake by its neck, I tore it from him, flinging it under the bed, leaning head first over the side to watch as it slithered across the dark tiles and into the shadowy bole of the mushroom tree in the corner before their hands were all over me again, lifting me, throwing me onto my stomach—

Upon thy belly shalt thou go—

No, not that – never! You fuckers!

Fighting for my honour as they piled on top of me, holding me down, stabbing me in the arse for resisting them—

I left my body, to the height of Robert's hand, and all pain and pressure were gone suddenly. Murmurings and whisperings around me, and the sound of an enamel bowl scraping in the marble sink at Canellun for my mother to be sick in. Where was Beryl—?

Darkness—

But that was all right, because my eyes were dark, too, so I could see perfectly as I raised my head from the moonlit desert and stared down into Margot's marble face lying beneath me, covered in sand, blowing it away from her wide open lifeless eyes, her half open mouth filled with volcanic dust as I sank my tongue into it, between her parted lips, my body writhing against hers, knowing that with one thrust she would return to life within her marbled body, my parched tongue searching, searching for her secret as I squirmed against her, cock turning to marble, sperm to dust—

—and dust shalt thou eat—

I had been a serpent once, my fate already sealed, still lurking within me, poised to strike—

Strike whom? Strike Margot? Robert?

I drew back in fear – too fast! – my dry tongue pulled out by its roots from between her teeth. *I could never harm them!* And besides, Robert was immune, already bitten by a viper in the heel while walking in the Pyrenees past the volcanic cone of the *Puig Mayor* erupting from her mouth into a vast flock of black words blotting out of the sun in endless poems distorting into impenetrable equations as they flew towards me in the growing darkness of tunnels and streets, the legless beggar hurtling out of the night on the spinning wheels of his tumbril, fixing me with his slithering eye, sweeping me up in the stench of his grasp and racing me down the infinite perspective of deserted, lamp-lit *avenidas,* flaunting back at me the triumph of my fear and weakness until the roar of his laughter was sucked into the silence of wheels vanishing into infinity...

It turned out that Alastair had been away, covering a story for *The New Yorker* when I'd collapsed on his doorstep. Once I'd finally come through, though, and returned to sanity, Mary couldn't have been kinder, waving aside my embarrassment, assuring me that it was no worse than when Jasper came down with gastric flu – just more of it. And besides, any friend of Alastair's—! She threw me a wry smile. She'd spoken to him on the phone and he'd insisted, together with their doctor (the Franco of my dreams), that I should stay where I was till he returned. So I did my best to help Mary with Jasper as much as I could, which was far from a chore, in spite of the bouts of weakness and disorientation I continued to feel. For some reason known only to himself (and therefore inexpressible except as laughter or sinking his teeth into my calves), Jasper took a liking to me, which I returned in spades (and any other weapon I could chase him round the house with), bashing his bum through six inches of all-American nappy from the PX, his bottom as deaf to my blows as Quasimodo to the bells of Notre Dame as he whirled through the house, overflowing with helpless giggles and screams and yells of '*Pax!*' as I'd taught him to do, and which I respected instantly, even as he ignored my own cries and sank his teeth into me yet again.

At first, Mary watched us both with an air of startled bemusement, but within a day of witnessing our idiotic games

431

she almost visibly shucked off her Bostonian Mortimer Maddox bringings-up and joined in, becoming once again, I was convinced, the tow-haired girl of her past, bright and carefree and increasingly enchanting. At night, once the exhausted Jasper was in bed, we'd sit in the kitchen eating whatever she knocked up (the domestic agency having struck them from their books), and discuss the next day's nannying. It was as if some inner light had been turned on deep inside her, and it became increasingly difficult to look at her without being dazzled by it.

When Alastair returned at last, he was as merry as a grig, laden down with presents for Jasper, with scent for Mary, and a fountain pen for me 'to improve your shambolic handwriting'.

Alastair's handwriting, I'd noticed as I'd helped Mary tidy the attic, was as remarkable and perfectly formed as mine was illegible. He wrote on foolscap paper using wide margins at either side, as if each page of manuscript were a poem, even if it was prose, the words only committed to paper, it seemed, when they were precisely formed in his head. I hadn't noticed a single correction or crossing out. Something about his handwriting rang a bell from somewhere – perhaps from letters to my mother? But wherever I'd seen it, it seemed to reveal a side of him that he might not realise he was exposing: deliberate and precise, yes, but also, in a curious way, vulnerable for its very perfection.

When he finally took me up to his study 'for a little chat' and thanked me warmly for the help I'd given Mary, he wanted to know everything he didn't already know about my illness – especially about my dreams, most of which (those that I remembered) were not the telling kind, so I kept quiet about them. Even so, when I'd finished, he stared down at me from his desk, his eyes narrowed. 'Franco thought you'd had sunstroke, or gastroenteritis, but if I didn't know you better, Si, I'd say you'd been tripping on LSD or something.'

I was shocked by his insight. 'But I've never touched the stuff!' I insisted, blushing furiously.

'No, no, I'm sure you haven't! It just reminded me, when you described the colours of violence, the vividness... I've known people... Anyway, you've come through, that's the important thing.'

To my astonishment, he invited me to stay on for a week or so, until I was fully recovered. Mary and Jasper had taken to me, apparently, although Jasper seemed to have turned into a fully-fledged cannibal in Alastair's absence. Perhaps I could invent some kind of gag or gobstopper which would curb his appetite for human flesh – he scowled down at a savage bite mark on his forearm. Also, I'd clearly worked hard at my Spanish. Mary had overheard my conversations with their charlady and was deeply impressed.

The temptation to accept was almost overpowering, and yet I knew that I'd have to return to my *pensión* in the end, and the longer I left it the harder it would be to leave. Perhaps if I left tomorrow?

He looked surprised for a moment, then nodded shrewdly. 'If you're sure you're well enough?'

'I'm fine, honestly! It was just a bug.'

THE CITROËN

And yet the next day, as I made my way back to the *pensión*, I regretted my decision to leave so soon. Waves of nausea interspersed with vivid, unbearable snatches of the nightmares I'd had when I was ill had left me feeling distinctly shaken and unsure of myself.

I tried to put it down to the effect of leaving a safe port in an uncertain sea, even though in saying goodbye to Jasper I knew I'd made the right decision. Judas himself must have had an easier time of it, the tears and tantrums at what Jasper saw as my betrayal of him echoing round and round the house like a haunted train as he was carried farther and farther away from me. If it was like this after five days, what would it have been like after ten? My feelings for him went beyond mere affection, into a region of my own childhood that I couldn't quite bring myself to address except as an unexpected empathy for a small person leading such a happy, uncomplicated life. Envy had nothing to do with it – at eighteen it was too late for all that to matter now. Children deserved happy childhoods, that was all, and I hated the thought that I'd burst his bubble. So I'd ended up almost fleeing the house, my eyes smarting at the thought of what I was leaving behind, picking up a cab on the Castellana and going back to my *pensión* with the same dread I'd felt when I used to be sent back to school.

But it was no better at the *pensión*; Manolo was at university, the place deserted except for Maria, my room inert with heat and silence, so I fled there, too, grabbing another letter from Robert which had arrived in my absence, intending to answer it at the café.

Half an hour later, having read the letter and the rest of my post, but lacking the energy to answer any of them, I dragged myself back down the hill, deciding that sleep, even in the stifling heat of my room, was preferable to being awake.

Lost in thought, staring down at the cobblestones, it wasn't until the last moment that I finally looked up and saw a gleaming black Citroën parked outside the carriage doors of the *pensión*, its massive mudguards and headlights bulging towards me, the silver double chevron gleaming on its radiator grille. It was another moment before the significance of what I was looking at sank in—

Margot!

Joy and adrenalin flooded through me as I ran under the arch and up the fire escape three steps at a time, into the sudden familiar sound of her laughter above my head, low and intimate—

I looked up, to where she was leaning out over the windowsill of my room staring down at me, her face reflecting my happiness as I raced up the rest of the stairs and through the rattling doors, down the passage, through the open door of my room, Margot still standing by the window, a mere silhouette against the brightness until I took her in my arms and embraced her at last, breathed her in—

'You're back!' I gasped.

'I'm back,' she pushed me away, playfully driving me towards the door, 'but what's all this I hear about you being ill – close to death? I expected to find you lying in bed, limp and sweating—' She laid her palm against my forehead. 'You are – how revolting – lie down at once!' A neat trip, and I ended up flat on my back on the bed. 'You have! How wise!'

I lay there panting and laughing. 'God, it's hot! Will it never end?'

'They say there's a change coming.'

'How did you get in?' I asked breathlessly.

'Maria, of course! She thinks I'm your *novia*.' My heart stopped dead at the thought of her being taken for my girlfriend. 'Do you mind – that she let me in?'

'Of course not!' I struggled to ignore the pain of her words. 'It's so wonderful to see you again. Is that your car outside? It is, isn't it? Can we go for a drive?'

She glanced at her watch. 'Not now – I'm already late. I was just leaving you a note.'

Something was rustling under my shoulders. Reaching beneath me, I pulled out a sheaf of Robert's letters to me, written on the onion-skin paper he used. I hadn't put them there—

I looked up at her, startled. 'Have you been reading my letters?'

'Of course!' She looked at me in exaggerated surprise, as if it were the most natural thing to do. 'They're about me, after all. Do you mind?'

'No—' I frowned, exasperated by my feelings. The question was too rooted in how I'd been brought up never to read other peoples' letters or diaries – 'I mean yes, I suppose I do in a way, and yet you're right, they *are* about you. But at least now you've read them you'll know that I've said nothing, as I promised. I have no secrets from you, you know that—'

She suddenly jolted the bed with her knee. '*Whoa!*' she cried, her eyes widening dangerously. 'That sounds just a little *too* like Robert!'

'Sorry!' I couldn't help grinning at her. 'But you did say we were alike.' I looked at her more thoughtfully. 'Don't you trust me? Is that it?'

'Hey, they were just lying on your desk, Si – anyone could have read them! I was bored waiting for you, that's all. And besides, you read mine!'

I stared at her, bewildered. '*What?*'

'When you came to sunbathe – I don't know – while I was in the shower?'

I sat up abruptly, stung to the quick. 'How can you even *think* that?' I demanded. 'I wanted to leave quickly, so that you wouldn't have to say goodbye again. I just grabbed my jacket from the chair and knocked the letters over. I saw they were from Robert, mostly unopened, but that's *all* I saw! I put them, on the table.'

She frowned down at me intently, then suddenly relaxed. 'All right, I believe you, OK? I'm sorry. I'm just not sure who to trust at the moment. Maybe you *should* read them, then we'd be quits.'

'Maybe *you* should read them,' I said without thinking. 'They might not be as bad—' I quickly held up my hands, as if to show I was unarmed, and smiled at her. 'I wouldn't dream of reading them. If only you—'

'If only I what?'

I stared up at her, lost in her gaze, my head spinning with unsayable words, all badly timed for this moment. If she could only *trust* me! I tore my eyes from her, breaking the spell, and delved into my jacket pocket. 'Look!' I pulled out Robert's last letter. 'This was waiting for me when I got back from Alastair and Mary's.' I took it out of its air mail envelope. 'Listen—' I started to read out loud:

'*Dearest Simon—*
I'm so grateful to you for your letters; Margot sends hers by invisible gusts of air and never puts her address on them. I swam again – the water boiled… Idries Shah would like to call on Margot when in Madrid, but I have no address, I repeat… Needest thou cash?—'

'There!' I said triumphantly, handing her the letter. 'I've told him *nothing,* not even your address!' I suddenly tripped over my conscience. 'And I should have.'

'Why?'

'Because he loves you.' I looked away, unable quite to meet her eyes. 'And because he asked me to.'

'Aaah…'

'But I *haven't,*' I insisted.

She smiled faintly, and ruffled my hair. 'Poor Si… divided loyalties are hell. In the end you always have to choose, though.'

'I know.' But I didn't want to think about that. Also, something was puzzling me: 'Why doesn't *Alastair* give him your address? He knows you both better than I do.' My voice sounded plaintive. 'No, wait!' I exclaimed, taking her hand quickly. 'I didn't mean it to sound like that – forget I asked.'

Margot sat down beside me, still holding my hand. 'Listen, Si, for one thing, Alastair isn't "family". He feels under no obligation to tell Robert anything if he doesn't want to – he's made that clear to him from the beginning, I promise you. Secondly, Alastair has a *thing* about privacy, not just his own, but everyone's. Peoples' private lives are no one else's business. *No one's.* If anyone tries to pry into his, or betrays his trust, they're as good as dead as far as he's concerned.' She grinned at me ruefully. 'In fact, I don't know which of them's worse in that sense – Alastair or Robert.'

'*I* do,' I said quietly, emphatically, remembering moments of Robert's wrath in the past.

'All right, so do I,' she acknowledged after a moment. 'So let's not tempt fate, OK?' For the briefest moment she looked haunted, then suddenly sprang to her feet. 'I must go—'

We rose from the bed like twins, before I turned away, breaking the link that bound us, unable to bear the thought of her going. I put Robert's letters back on my desk. As I did so, my eyes fell on a flamboyant note lying in the middle of the desk. '*Hi, Si!*' it began. I turned to her. 'What's this? Oh – your note!' I read it quickly. Did I want to drive up to Toledo with her and Alastair tomorrow? There was a church there with some El Grecos that he wanted us to see, and catacombs, full of dead bodies—

'Want to come?' she asked brightly.

'You bet!'

'Oh, and Alastair said we should bring overcoats; apparently it's freezing in the catacombs.'

'What bliss – to be cold at last!'

'Until tomorrow, then.' Her smile was hypnotic.

'Until tomorrow.' We kissed each other's cheeks in turn, slowly, almost formally – a mere ritual to an outsider, but to me an arcane seal of our commitment to each other, like an exchange of vows.

THE STANDING DEAD

The drive to Toledo, in the foothills of` the mountains to the south of Madrid, was exhilarating. To drive anywhere with Margot was exciting enough, but at the wheel of her own car she seemed as much a part of its character as the leather upholstery and the humming wheels under the long black bonnet, animating everything with her presence, as she did with people, making them her own. She drove beautifully – fast, but taking only calculated risks, as if she were on a winning streak that always paid off.

Sitting beside her, Alastair seemed increasingly uncomfortable with her speed and manoeuvres, making phantom grasps at the dashboard occasionally, or pinning himself back in his seat with his brake foot, swearing under his breath. A welcome breeze blew through our open windows, catching at Margot's hair as it poured behind her from the red bandanna which kept it off her face.

Lying next to me on the seat, like an ominous prophecy, was a long green canvas games bag with two tennis racquets sticking out of it. They were going to play tennis after we'd been to Toledo. The thought smarted, and I looked away.

Once out of Madrid, we crossed the arid plain in a swirl of dust, not a blade of living grass to be seen, just parched scrub and olive trees, with the occasional cluster of cypresses marking the presence of *haciendas* and small farms to our distant left and right. Everything was baked dry, shadowless under today's strangely brassy sun.

We sped through straggling roadside villages, the dilapidated houses sinking back, in our wake, into a past from which it seemed nothing was expected any longer, and nothing would come. The farther we went, the more it felt as though we were driving into that past, the traffic thinning to almost nothing, the few buses and lorries we encountered all ramshackle with age, built long before the war and held together with little more than wire and welding and blind faith. The further we went, the worse the surface of the road became, exposing the cobbled bones of its foundations; the further we went, the more mule-drawn carts and heavily laden donkeys became the norm, cars the exception, as we climbed into the foothills.

'I know we're driving forwards,' I said at last, dreamily, 'but we seem to be going backwards.'

Alastair turned round sharply in his seat. 'Are you feeling all right?' he asked.

'In *time*, he means, you idiot!' said Margot, swerving round a pothole. 'And he's right. We must look like something from the future to these people.'

Alastair shrugged. 'If you think it's backward here, you should see the poorest parts of Spain.'

But Margot wasn't listening. 'Do you think if I drove to Toledo in reverse we'd go back through the centuries?' she wondered – half jokingly, I presumed, to humour me.

But Alastair didn't seem to be in the mood for fantasy – too distracted by her driving, perhaps. 'Don't be ridiculous, of course you couldn't!'

'Why not?'

'Oh, for Christ's sake,' he said irritably, 'you must see that even if you turned round and went backwards you'd still be travelling *towards* Toledo – towards the future—'

'*You* might be,' she countered, 'but what if Simon's right? I can do it in my head, after all – I can imagine, like him, that we're driving into the past – why not in reality?'

'Because reality is *now* – the present!'

'So what's the future?'

'Hypothetical.'

'And the past?'

'Hearsay.'

I wished I could think at his speed—

'What about Toledo, then?' She was clearly baiting him. 'Does it really exist, or is it just a figment of your imagination? Not that you seem to have one today.'

'I can only say that it existed when I last saw it,' he said pedantically. 'Whether or not it still exists we won't know until we have visual proof. Whether or not it will exist tomorrow—'

'God, you're so *boring!*' she shouted suddenly, tossing her head and stamping on the accelerator in revenge. 'You take everything so literally! Loosen up! None of this is what you really think – I've read your poems, remember?'

He stared round at her. 'You know, you're quite unnerving behind a wheel. I don't know what it is – you're still you, and it suits you in a strange kind of way, but you're a different person somehow.'

'I agree!' I agreed (though not in the way that I imagined Alastair meant). I caught her eye in the mirror. 'Is it because driving makes you happy?'

'Clever Si!' She grinned at me in the rear view mirror. 'Driving makes me happy because I'm good at it. Dancing makes me happy because I'm good at it. People like doing what they're good at—'

'So what else are you good at?' asked Alastair with a hint of condescension in his voice.

I knew at once that he'd gone too far. Margot turned to him, her face expressionless behind her dark glasses. 'Playing "chicken",' she said, taking her hands off the wheel. She continued to stare at him, as though the road no longer existed. We slowly picked up speed as we strayed across it towards the deep ditch on the left. Fascinated, I jammed myself deep into the corner, ready to crash at any moment, but not giving a damn if we did. Alastair squirmed restlessly in his seat, his eyes darting nervously to right and left. We hit another pothole, the car swerving— *'Christ!'* he shouted, grabbing the wheel—

Still without taking her eyes off him, she folded her arms across her chest, leaving Alastair to steer as she slowly, mercilessly accelerated.

'All right, all right, I take it back!' he screeched. *'I was being facetious – brake, for fuck's sake! Brake! You're good at everything!'* Margot's face slowly broke into a superior smile as she took her foot off the accelerator and noisily laid an egg. We both burst out laughing.

'—especially at scaring the shit out of people!' he growled.

Her eyes found mine again in her mirror. 'You OK, Si?'

'Fine,' I waved casually, 'couldn't be happier!'

'You're both off your heads!' he shouted. 'We could have been killed—'

'*Could* have,' she emphasised. 'That's the point.'

Alastair suggested that we made a slight detour as we approached Toledo so that our first sight of it would be as spectacular as possible. Even he kept his thoughts to himself as we pulled in off the road on the far side of Tagus gorge and gazed across at the ancient hill town, once the capital of Spain, seemingly poised between heaven and earth, rising like a sombre myth out of its Roman foundations, more ancient – and far more beautiful – than Madrid, crowned with the unmistakeable symbols of Church and State – the Cathedral with its triple crowns of thorns slotted like wedding rings over its pointed spire on one side, and the imposing fortress of the Alcázar on the other, glaring across the plain from which we'd come, towards the Guardarama mountains to the west, the Guadalajaras to the east—

We finally crossed the river over one of the old stone bridges into the fortified town, lightly hooting our way through lines of pack mules, carts, donkeys, townspeople, shepherds driving their small, startled flocks of walking mutton to the abattoir. Below the vertiginous arches of the bridge, the mighty Tagus had dwindled in the endless heat of summer to a turgid trickle, half choked with evil-smelling rubbish and dead trees. When I pointed this out to Alastair, he merely shrugged. 'It'll probably be a raging torrent again in a day or so – apparently there's a storm on the way. You only have to look at the sky—'

I looked up at the sun, now almost obscured by an advancing army of ominous cloud, and longed for rain; in spite of being almost two thousand feet above Madrid, the heat reflected from the narrow winding streets of ochre stone and brick was suffocating, even with the car windows wide open.

With over an hour to kill before our guided tour of the catacombs, we had a cold beer in a little square under the shade of some plane trees, their frazzled leaves rustling with drought, before going off in search of Alastair's El Grecos.

Traipsing from one gloomy church to another, I found it increasingly difficult to appreciate the old master's works, not simply because they weren't really to my taste (the gaunt, elongated figures more evocative of death than life), or because the paintings were all framed within the wider yet more claustrophobic constraints of a religion which I thought of as steeped in blood and hypocrisy, but because I became increasingly engrossed in watching Margot's face as she looked up at them.

Her red bandanna had been converted, almost magically, into a carmine headscarf, her genuflection on entering each church a graceful mark of respect for the religion of this country – and for the beliefs of her own childhood, perhaps. She seemed to kneel as a Catholic child and rise as a woman, a pagan, so startlingly beautiful that she eclipsed El Greco every time – even in the church of Santo Tomé, as she looked up at the arched canvas of his masterpiece, *The Burial of the Count of Orgaz,* at which she stared and stared, moving towards it like a sleepwalker, her eyes luminous with the strange reflected light from it, the light of passing souls reflected from the faces of long dead noblemen bearing witness to the burial, the figure of Christ high above preparing to welcome the Count in an unearthly blaze of sixteenth century neon light.

Margot stared up at the painting with a naked, unguarded intensity which provoked the strangest envy in me – not jealousy of earthly rivals, but envy of the old genius who now commanded her attention and respect. Only once had I received such a look from her.

Alastair, his eyes also fixed on the painting, had moved silently up behind her in a way that I almost resented, bearing in mind what I was thinking, the murmur of his voice echoing strangely in the vault of the church. 'El Greco was paid twelve hundred ducats for that painting – a fortune in those days.'

'*So what*?' she whispered sharply, her eyes still glued to the painting. 'Who *cares*?'

He was clearly taken aback by her vehemence, his shoulders rising in a slow shrug of defeat before he turned away. 'Just me, I suppose,' he muttered.

Our last port of call was to the church where we were to join the tour of the catacombs. Again, I wasn't paying much attention at first, puzzling over Margot's change of mood since we'd left Santo Tomé, her brow darkening like the sky, her eyes now barred against intruders. I knew better than to rattle at those bars with stupid comments or questions – as did Alastair, it seemed, who kept his thoughts to himself.

We stopped by the car for our overcoats. 'Will we really need them?' she asked him with a frown.

'The last time we came we were frozen stiff,' he answered cautiously. 'Mary vowed never again. I'll carry yours, if you like—'

But with an impatient shake of her head she turned away.

Alastair glanced at me, his eyebrows raised in baffled enquiry. Equally baffled, I shrugged at him. Whatever was going on in her head, it was more than some casual remark he'd made.

446

She turned on him suddenly. 'Are we actually going to *enjoy* this?' she demanded.

'I don't know about *enjoy*,' he said after a moment, 'but it's fascinating. I don't want to tell you what to expect because that'd spoil it. I mean, it's not like looking at paintings, but it's still thought-provoking in a very Spanish sort of way.'

'I'm not sure I like the sound of that...' She stared at him fixedly. 'Is it all *death*?' Her eyes narrowed as she studied him, her hands gripping her folded coat behind her like a schoolgirl. The belt of the coat was trailing in the dust, so I lifted it up, getting a quick frown for my trouble.

'Well,' Alastair let out an exasperated sigh, 'it's a *catacomb*, for Christ's sake! There are dead bodies, but they're long dead – they don't *smell* or anything! What I wanted to show you was the other side of the Spanish way of life. Death. Once you've seen how people treat their dead, you have a fair idea of how they treat the living, and how the living expect to be treated when they die. To the Spaniards, their mortal remains mean nothing compared with their immortal souls. To them a dead body's nothing more than a warning to the living. It's the reality that counts, not fairytales and fancies. Which I admire.' His frown cleared. 'Look, I just wanted to share it with you; you don't even have to agree. If you don't like it, we'll leave. Simple as that.'

'Promise?'

'I promise.'

He reached out and touched her arm, almost diffidently, and she seemed to relax at last, releasing her locked hands from behind her back, winding her light woollen coat round her wrists at the front, like a muff, leaving two gaps at her elbows through which we both obediently threaded our arms, the three of us marching off in line abreast, each putting our best foot forward at the same moment—

'*Left!*' commanded Alastair, grinning, mimicking Robert. '*Left!* Left, right, *left!*'

We entered the church through a side door somewhere in the maze of backstreets. A sandwich board outside, advertising tours of the catacombs, was the only clue to their existence. The use of cameras was forbidden, apparently.

Inside, in the cool vaulted gloom of the church, a huddle of some dozen people, men and women, waited restlessly around an ancient stone font, shuffling their feet, eyes mostly cast downwards, as though guilty of some secret perversion which might be mistaken for necrophilia.

Again, the heady, all-pervading smell of incense, that clever drug of Catholicism, once inhaled never forgotten, a universal reminder of the One True Faith – so much more evocative than the smell of dry rot and bad breath that pervaded the Anglican church of my boyhood.

We approached the silent group, some of them already wearing overcoats. Without actually joining them, Alastair stopped and began to put his on, motioning to us to do the same. The air in the church was dank, as if the sun had never warmed its stones. I helped Margot into her coat and then put mine on. We stood apart from the others, in a huddle of our own, turned inwards, like a cabal.

Unusually lost for words, Alastair stared at us both expectantly, an imbecilic smile starting to spread over his face like a wintry sun rising over the Cairngorms. '*When shall we three meet again,*' he suddenly growled under his breath, in his broadest Scots accent, '*in thunder, lightning, or in rain?*'

'*When the hurly-burly's done,*' I continued delightedly, '*when the battle's lost and won!*'

At which Margot got the giggles, more out of nervousness than amusement, perhaps, but it was still highly infectious. Alastair hushed us, frowning, which only spurred me on. I *wanted* her to laugh—

'I played Lady Macbeth at school,' I whispered to her. 'On the first night I walked up the inside of my nightie in the sleepwalking scene and set fire to one of my pigtails with the candle—'

A heavy door at the far end of the nave was suddenly opened and slammed shut with a crash that reverberated through the church, startling us all. A moment later we could hear the echo of brisk footsteps and the sound of heavy keys being jangled, reminding me of the *sereno*. Then, out of the gloom of the nave emerged the short, brutish figure of our guide, his tattered grey uniform bursting its buttons, a too-small peaked cap jammed on the back of his head as if glued there with hair oil. Hawking and spitting noisily into an old rag, he strutted towards us up the centre of the aisle, swinging his keys in a gross parody of St Peter, his gaze sweeping in judgement over the small group awaiting him, and clearly finding us wanting – until he saw Margot. For a moment his eyes swelled with lechery before heading for the others.

'*Y entonces!*' he shouted, without the slightest respect for church's sanctity. '*Estamos todos aquí?*'

There was an uneasy murmur of assent from around the font.

'*Bueno! Y nadie lleva una camera fotográfica?*' Everyone shook their heads as he increased his pace, charging the group like a bull as he dragged a jingling leather satchel from his side onto his enormous belly. '*Pues, vamos a pagar—!*'

While they got their money out and began to pay him he started to crack jokes, his Spanish too rough and quick for my ears, but not for his fellow Spaniards in the group, who laughed uneasily.

'"*The dead are looking forward to our visit*",' Alastair translated, '"*so don't fall behind*". He's certainly not the guide we had before.'

Margot shrugged. 'Maybe he'll brighten things up.'

Having fleeced the people round the font, he turned and came over to us, beating his satchel like a drum, his eyes once again fixed on Margot as he barged into our circle. Close up, he was even more unsavoury than his manner, giving off a reek of sour sweat and Macassar oil that reminded me of a decomposing animal, driving us all back a pace, which he took as a sign of welcome, and moved in closer. His Mexican moustache, straggling and untrimmed, spread across the dark stubble of his face in a leer of complicity as Margot struggled to smile at him.

'*Ay, guapa!*' he exclaimed, his mouth opening like an oven door to expel a furnaceful of stale garlic and cheap brandy. '*De donde vienes?*'

'*De Canada*,' she answered politely.

He feigned astonishment that she could have come so far just to see him! Alastair quickly held out a twenty-five peseta note and asking for three tickets.

Barely aware of him, the guide's bloodshot gaze continued to absorb Margot like a surgical swab, visibly draining the energy from her. She turned away, trying to hide her disgust. Handing back the change, he promised to reserve all the best views in the crypt for Alastair's beautiful wife. The three of us exchanged startled looks as he slammed his satchel shut and strutted away, shouting for everyone to follow him closely. Stragglers would be abandoned—!

Macabre as he was, there was something about his graveyard humour that seemed to appeal to Alastair, who stared after him with a lopsided smile on his face. But when we looked round at Margot she was clutching the cuffs of her coat sleeves to her mouth, her eyes wide with disgust.

'He's *revolting*,' she hissed. '*Jesus!*'

Alastair quickly went over and put his hand on her arm. 'Hey, he's not so bad – really! He's just a peasant doing and un-peasant job,' he smirked. 'And he's a classic, if you think about it – like the gravedigger in Hamlet; you can't work among the dead day after day without having a ghoulish sense of humour. Besides, he's all we've got. It's crazy to have come all this way and not see it through – isn't it?'

I admired the way she pulled herself together. 'Just don't let him touch me!' she warned.

Deep in the back of the church the guide had thrown open another heavy oak door, switched on a dim electric light, and begun to lead the way down a spiral staircase into the crypt. The air grew colder and colder as we descended behind the others, the stone walls of the stairwell, our only support in the absence of a rail, deathly cold to the touch, the smell down here unfamiliar, with a musty sting to it, like stale snuff.

We finally emerged into a wide passageway, again dimly lit, with cells on either side, their stuccoed walls reaching to only a third the height of what appeared to be an enormous natural cavern, its vaulted ceiling some forty feet above us. Into the walls were set heavy doors with iron bolts and barred spy holes – more like the doors to prison cells than the store rooms of a church.

The guide was standing with his back to the first door on the right, calling to everyone to hurry. The dead were impatient to meet us, he shouted, but they wouldn't wait forever—

No sooner had we joined the semi-circle that had formed around him, than his rat-like eyes found Margot's. Brusquely pushing people out of the way, he made a grab for her hand. With a low cry of disgust she wrenched it away, and Alastair had to impose himself between them, insisting that the guide shouldn't touch her – she was nervous, and disliked being touched by anyone but him.

'*Qué suerte para ti!*' the guide congratulated him, laughing, not in the least fazed, taking Alastair and me by the arm instead and forcing us to pull Margot through the others towards the door of the cell. '*Veng' acquí – veng' acquí!*' he begged us urgently, on a blast of foul breath. '*Para ustedes, hay un sitio mejor!*' Lining us up in front of the other sightseers, as if to face a firing squad, he finally released us and backed away to the door of the first cell. '*Acquí, en estas celdas,*' he began pontificating his well-worn patter, '*están las mommias de martires españoles del siglo dieciseis—!*'

Alastair turned to murmur in Margot's ear. 'He's trying to tell us that what we're going to see are the mummified remains of sixteenth century Spanish martyrs, but they're not. According to a friend of mine, they're Jews, massacred during one of the pogroms—'

The guide had turned to unbolt the door, glancing theatrically over his shoulder at us as he did so. '*Es para prevenir que se escapan!*' he explained hoarsely, before peering on tiptoe through the spy hole, his body suddenly tense, motionless. Again he looked back at us, a finger to his lips. '*Sssh!*' He laid his head on his hands, '*Estan dormiendo!*' Carefully selecting one of the heavy keys from his ring, he slipped it into the lock and slowly turned it before heaving open the door, still on tiptoe, like a pantomime villain.

We all stared into the impenetrable darkness of the cell.

'*Esperan!*' he grunted. Wait! Tiptoeing into the cell, he suddenly veered to his left and vanished into the darkness, a strange crackling sound accompanying his progress.

A moment later, a light came on like a physical blow, and we found ourselves staring aghast at the stuff of nightmares – a standing crowd of some thirty or forty mummified corpses stacked like firewood against the far wall, eyes seemingly blinded by the light, jaws agape, leaning back as if in terror, their skeletons still half-covered in desiccated yellow skin and fragments of cloth. Around them, and across the floor, were scattered the dismembered remains of some of their limbs—

The guide's face suddenly appeared round the doorway, grinning like a madman. One look at our faces mirroring the horror of what we were witnessing, and he bellowed with laughter.

Margot was the first to recoil, forcing her way back through the people crowded behind us, Alastair following. Staying only to glare at the guide as though marking him for death, I went after them, pursued by his sneering guffaws.

Margot leant against the far wall, shaking her head in disbelief. She turned to Alastair, her eyes stark with outrage. 'How *could* he?' she demanded. 'He's *disgusting!* How could *you*—?'

Still clearly shocked by the guide's behaviour, and her reaction to it, Alastair made a feeble attempt to take her hands, as if to prevent a 'scene'. 'I know, I know. I'm sorry – I had no idea he'd take the piss out of them. He wasn't here before – he's an animal!'

Margot wrenched her hand away. 'We have to *do* something!' she begged, stamping her foot. 'We have to free them—!' She looked at both of us, her eyes haunted by what she'd seen, her face haggard under the feeble light of an overhanging bulb.

'Margot, they're dead,' said Alastair gently.

'But you've only got to look at them to see *how* they died!' she burst out. 'They died in terror!' Tears welled in her eyes, making them huge with grief. Angrily, she turned away from us. Alastair pressed his handkerchief into her hand, which she accepted with a gesture of helplessness, not looking at him. '—And then to have no *peace*,' she went on quietly, her voice trembling, 'to be turned into a freak show by that disgusting little man... we have to *do* something!'

'There's nothing any of us can do,' Alastair murmured. 'If we tried, we'd be arrested—'

She glanced round at me briefly, eyes brimming with mute appeal, wrenching at my heart as she turned away again, as if to hide her shame of us. In spite of the cold, my body burned in sympathy, every instinct raw with the need to champion her, to redeem this moment in some way—

I watched as the other visitors took it in turns to crowd into the doorway of the cell with expressions of astonishment or disgust, one woman with a small scream of fright. Staring over their heads I could see the guide take one of the corpses' hands and shake it. There was the sound of uneasy laughter.

'Look, let's go!' said Alastair decisively. 'I promised if you didn't like it—'

'*Like* it?' She turned on him like a Fury, her face alive with anger now, so beautiful that her anger was all that existed to me. '*How could I like it*? It's *revolting!*'

Alastair forced himself to meet her eyes. 'I just hoped you'd see... what *I* see!'

They outstared each other, somehow excluding me. 'Well, I *don't!*' she said at last in a low, angry voice, and he looked away with his familiar shrug, hands held palms upwards, as though to show her that he had nothing left to defend himself with. 'You just don't get it, do you?' she demanded fiercely 'I'm *damned* if I'll leave and let that creep think I'm a coward! We'll stay – I'll look at everything!' She suddenly turned to me. 'If that's OK with you, Si?'

'Yes, of course!' I said once. 'Whatever you want – it's just that I've got a bit of a gippy tummy and I need to go to the loo. I'll be as quick as I can—'

I approached the guide just as he'd turned back to switch off the light in the cell.

'*Hay servicios, por favor?*' I asked, clutching my stomach and bending forward slightly.

'*Ayee, joven!*' he sneered gleefully. '*Tienes miedo?*' he leaned towards me, his eyes dancing with spite, '*O mierda!*' He waved scornfully towards the stairs. '*Escaleras arriba, y después, la segunda a la izquierda! Vamos!*' Turning away, he marched to the head of his troupe, leaving the cell door ajar behind him.

I waved reassuringly to Alastair and Margot and shuffled quickly towards the stairs as if my sphincter were already leaking.

Why hadn't he locked and bolted the door? Had I simply distracted him, or had he got tired of his feeble joke about the corpses escaping? Whatever the reason it was a godsend. I'd envisaged having to use the old buckets and paint tins piled around the bottom of the stairs to help me scale the wall—

Hurrying noisily up the steps until I was out of sight, I slumped against the cold stones, hearing his voice slowly fading away down the passage below. He must have taken a sudden turn somewhere, because all at once his voice faded into silence.

Like an animal, I listened with all my might before finally pushing myself away from the wall and creeping back down the steps.

The passage was deserted, cold with haloed light – and yet I could feel a host of eyes on me, watching my every move from the far side of death. *Did I have to do this?*

The memory of Margot's grief-stricken face—

Yes!

Moving as silently as I could, I crossed to the cell door and heaved it open wide enough to slip through. Once inside, the darkness seemed to come alive. Something rustled among the corpses. In rising panic I moved to the left, as the guide had done, groping for the light switch. There was a sharp crack under my foot. With a gasp of relief I found the switch and turned on the light—

Even though I'd seen them before, and had tried to harden myself to what I knew I'd see now, the sight was as shocking now as then, the collective terror on the faces of the corpses even more spine-chilling, since I was closer to them now, and alone—

I mustn't funk it!

My heart beating sickeningly in my throat, I moved towards the mummified bodies who seemed, in my fear of them, to draw back still further as I approached. Again the cracking underfoot. Looking down briefly – as frightened of taking my eyes from them as of looking into their sightless stares – I saw that I was crushing a human hand, and swore with fright.

Gasping for breath, sweating in spite of the cold, I stood in front of the standing dead, my eyes darting from one to another, choosing which of them to free. The corpse at the very end – a woman, perhaps – was shorter than the others, with strands of long lank hair still attached to her skull.

My hands shaking uncontrollably, I reached out for her skull, the colour of saffron, and took hold of it gently on either side, as if she were someone I cherished, and tried to pull it towards me, hoping that the ligaments, or whatever it was that held the skull to the neck, had rotted, or been eaten through. To smuggle out a whole skeleton would be impossible, a mere arm or a leg meaningless to Margot. Only the head, the essence of their beings, would do—

But it wouldn't budge. It wasn't vertebrae or ligaments that were fastening her skull to her neck, I realised, but her leathery, desiccated skin. *'Oh, forgive me – please!'* I groaned, pulling her suddenly, violently towards me, trying to detach her from her companions as they creaked and cracked in protest and began to rear forward, as if to hold her back. Panic-stricken, I wrenched at her skull even more brutally, bending it forward and back like a murderer, twisting it, sobbing with fear as the whole mass shifted towards me in protest. Something in their midst collapsed, sending up a cloud of sulphurous, choking dust, like mustard gas. A rat raced out between my feet—

Through the madness of panic I heard a far-off rumble of what sounded like thunder, followed almost instantly by the distant sound of the guide's insane laughter approaching—

Frantically, I raised my knee and rammed it into the corpse's chest, moaning with disgust as my knee sank through her ribcage before I finally managed to tear her skull from her body, the rest of her crashing back, headless, among the others in a cloud of yellow dust and disintegration.

Christ, what had I done?

For a brief moment I stared down, appalled, at the head I'd ripped from its body, before stuffing it feverishly through the folds in my coat, manoeuvring it against my stomach, clutching it to me through my coat pockets as I stumbled desperately for the door, switched off the light, and peered out—

Nothing – except for the sound of the guide's voice getting nearer, keys jangling—

Streaking across the passage, I lowered my head and bent forward over my enlarged belly, as if from stomach ache, clinging to the precious trophy with both hands deep in my coat pockets now, reaching the corner just as the guide came round it, keys swinging, glancing at me with unconcealed contempt as he led his crocodile of sightseers back towards the stairs.

Margot and Alastair were still at the tail end of the line, her face a mask of cold indifference until she saw me. 'Si, are you all right?'

'I'm fine – fine!' I gabbled under my breath.

Alastair fixed me with a frown. 'What's that all over your face?' he demanded.

With one hand clutching the head under my coat, I wiped at my forehead. 'Just sweat—'

'No, here—' Margot reached out for my chin and began wiping my face with Alastair's handkerchief, then showed it to me, smeared with saffron-coloured dust.

'From the stairwell—' I said quickly.

'No it's not,' said Alastair looking down at his own hands. His eyes narrowed in suspicion. 'It's on your coat, too – what have you been up to?'

'Nothing!' Clasping the head to me with one hand, I dusted off my coat. 'It must have been in the loo, then—'

'*Ayeee! Qué passa por acqui?*' The dreaded cry of alarm from the guide, paralysing me, turning my heart to ice. '*Alto!*' He'd halted abruptly near the half open door of the cell, arms outstretched to hold back the others.

'*What have you done?*' hissed Alastair.

Unable to speak, I could only shake my head in furious denial. *He understood nothing!*

Grabbing us both us by the arm, he hurried us towards the others as they spread out across the passage, everyone craning forward to see what was happening. The guide herded us back, shouting that something was wrong – the cell was not as he'd left it – we were not to move until he'd investigated!

Faint with fear, wondering what clue I'd left behind for the mad bastard, I watched him advance on the cell, throwing open the door and rushing into the darkness with a shout of bravado.

The light came on suddenly, followed by the sounds of a scuffle, then more shouts – of alarm this time, cries for help— *'Ayuda me! Ayuda me—!'*

Then throttling sounds. Then silence.

The light went out.

A moment later he toppled out of the cell, mouth agape, clawing at his throat where the hand of a skeleton appeared to be strangling the life out of him, forcing him to his knees. Eyes bulging as he stared up at us, he suddenly threw back his head and began to laugh hysterically, tears pouring down his cheeks as he pointed at our terrified faces. Struggling back to his feet, he slung the hand back into the darkened cell, slammed and bolted the door, and headed for the stairs, the cavern echoing with demonic laughter.

The guide stood in the open door of the church, holding out his upturned cap for tips, exchanging banter with someone invisible to me in the street outside as one by one the queue filed past him, dropping the occasional coin into his hat.

Suddenly a young *guardia*, rifle slung over his shoulder, appeared in the sunlight beyond the doors, looking into the church as though something the guide had said to him had sparked his interest, scanning the faces of the sightseers as they filed past. He was joined a moment later by a second, older *guardia*, thumb under his rifle strap, standing on tiptoe to see past the people blocking his eye-line—

Christ! Would this never end—?

Margot was in front of me, Alastair in front of her, his bulk concealing us. I clutched at her elbow. *'Guardias!'* I whispered urgently. 'Can you distract the guide?'

She turned round sharply, eyes questioning yet instantly aware. 'Of course!' She nudged Alastair sharply in the back. 'Give the guide all your loose change!' she hissed. 'He'll think it's Christmas—'

458

'*What?*' He turned on her as if she were mad.

'*Just do it!*'

Rummaging in his pocket, Alastair hauled out a fistful of coins just as we came level with the guide, dropping them in his hat before stepping down into the street and finally exposing Margot to the gaze of the two *guardias* who stared at her for a moment, dumb-struck—

It was Margot they'd been waiting to see – not me—!

A flood of relief, watching them suddenly lower their eyes in confusion, as if dazzled, the guide so distracted as he counted Alastair's bounty that he ignored me completely as I slipped past him.

'We really need to get the hell out of here!' I panted as we caught up with Alastair. '*Now!*'

THE STORM

Alastair insisted on taking the wheel this time, to draw less attention to ourselves, and for once Margot didn't question him as she threw me a fleeting, worried look.

Driving swiftly but carefully though the narrow streets of the town, he fired a barrage of questions at me through the rear view mirror: *what had I done? The truth! What was he to expect? Police sirens – the sound of an explosion? Smoke? Would I never grow up—?*

I was almost flattered that he should think me capable of creating a bomb from nothing, and for a moment wished I had – it would have been a much more fitting end for the poor murdered Jews. 'It's nothing like that, honestly,' I protested feebly, the reaction to what I'd done taking hold at last in a kind of nervous exhaustion. 'It's just a memento, really, for Margot—'

She turned round in the passenger seat, surprised, smiling—

'You mean you've *stolen* something?' he demanded.

'No! Not stolen – *liberated*!'

'For the love of Christ, are you *insane*?' He glanced round furiously. '*What* have you "liberated"?'

'Wait till we're out of Toledo—'

'*Well?*' he demanded as we turned back onto the road to Madrid at last.

I glanced through the rear window, to make sure we weren't being followed, and began to unbutton my coat.

Margot knelt up excitedly on her seat and leaned over the back as I reached into the folds of my coat and lifted out the mummified head, like a child from my womb. 'I think it's a "she",' I murmured, 'she was smaller than the rest—'

Her involuntary cry of shock, low and harrowing, was far more affecting than I'd expected – or hoped for. Mesmerised, I stared into her eyes as they brimmed with a compassion that was more real and beautiful than in any painting of El Greco's. A single tear plopped onto the dead face, seeming to hiss as it dissolved into the parchment-like skin, leaving only the faintest dark stain where it had fallen. I waited, stupidly, as if for something to grow out of it, and although nothing did, the look that grew between us when she met my gaze at last was so powerful, so secret that I was caught like a hind in the sudden thicket of her love, unable to move.

'She's beautiful!' she murmured, leaning even further over the back of her seat, grasping the sides of my head, as I had grasped the girl's in the catacomb, pulling me towards her to kiss me tenderly on the mouth, then taking the head from my lap and kissing it too—

'*What is it?*' shouted Alastair frenziedly. '*What's he stolen?*'

Touching my stunned lips with her fingertips, Margot swivelled back and down into her seat, holding up her strange trophy for Alastair to see—

The car slewed across the road as he stamped on all three pedals at once, gears whizzing, tyres screeching, throttle roaring as he fought for control—

'*Are you out of your fucking mind?*' he screamed, mounting the verge and stalling the engine before turning on me. '*You just don't get it, do you?* When you first arrived I made it clear to you that this was a *dictatorship*, that you must *never* compromise my position here or we'd all be thrown out. We're here on sufferance, for Christ's sake! One word from Franco and we're gone! And yet you steal a sacred relic from a tomb belonging to the Holy Roman Catholic Church of Spain and to hell with the rest of us – the years of work!'

'*I'm sorry!*' I shouted, taken aback by his ferocity, yet stirred by a defensive anger of my own. 'But Margot was right – you know she was!'

'Alastair, if it was anyone's fault it was mine—!'

'No, god*dammit*!' He turned on her as fiercely as he'd turned on me, 'I won't have you defending him! He's a bloody liability and always has been, and without exception there's always some woman trying to protect him, whether it's his mother, his godmother, Beryl, Mary, you—!'

Margot rounded on him, but I interrupted before she could say a word. 'Alastair, I'm sorry, truly! I didn't think—'

'*You never do!* You never have! You just jump in and then wonder why you're drowning, why everyone's risking their lives to pull you out—'

A sudden vivid memory of him diving into the sea from the café terrace at the *cala*—

Perhaps he'd been struck by the same memory, because all at once he seemed to calm down a little, letting out his pent up breath in an exasperated sigh, shaking his head wearily. 'Oh, Christ! We've got to dump it!' he said decisively. 'Here – now!' He looked out at the wild rocks and scrub of the hillside, bleak against the threatening sky.

'*No!*' Margot's was outraged. 'It would make the whole thing pointless – and besides, she's mine, not yours! She's part of our lives now.'

'Exactly!' I chipped in eagerly. 'The only thing that worries me is her *baraka*—'

'*Oh, for the love of Christ*—' Alastair threw himself violently backwards in his seat, clutching his hair as if to tear it out. 'You don't believe in all that fucking *crap*, do you?'

'*Yes!*' we both exclaimed at once.

'—because it's true!' I insisted. 'It's obvious! But I've disturbed it, not just by taking her head, but taking her from the people she died with, even though I meant it for the best. But just to chuck her away on this hillside—' I shook my head furiously. 'We *can't*! Look, if you'd rather, I'll get out and hitch my way back to Madrid – take her with me—'

'*Oh, brilliant!*' he cried sarcastically, his voice rising to a higher and higher pitch of disbelief. 'With her head under your arm? That'll stop the fucking traffic!' He turned on me again, his eyes wild, almost out of control. 'Have you any idea what the penalty is for grave-robbing in Spain? *Have you?*'

'No,' I answered fearfully.

He sat there shaking his head furiously, looking increasingly bewildered as the strangest noise of hysteria began to build up in his throat. '*Well, neither have I!*'

Later, as we approached the outskirts of Madrid (the last half hour having passed in the silence of a Mexican stand-off between the two of them, each seeming to dare the other to speak first and re-ignite their quarrel), Alastair finally seemed to relax a little, cutting his breakneck speed as he entered the suburbs, as though suddenly conscious of limits of every kind.

I was still smarting from his attack, my opinion of myself turned upside down yet again – not from the injustice of what he'd said, but from the truth of it.

They'd finally started talking again, in a desultory, polite sort of way, Margot fanning her face with both hands, to little effect apart from wafting the occasional faint breath of her scent towards me in the back seat, where I inhaled myself into a kind of stupor.

'I don't know if I can stand Madrid much longer,' she gasped. 'It's *stifling*! Do we have to play tennis?'

Alastair shrugged. 'I've booked the court – I'll have to pay for it—'

'Oh, God forbid that you should lose five *duros*!' she exclaimed.

'Actually, it's more than that, but the showers make it worth every penny. I bet you'd like a shower now,' he coaxed her, 'a cool stinging deluge, like rain—'

'You bastard!' she gasped, punching him in the shoulder. 'But what about Si?'

'I'm going to drop him off at his *pensión* – him and that *thing*.'

'But it's mine!' she flared up again.

Alastair turned on her. '*Just think for a minute* – imagine if we were stopped by the police for some reason—'

'It's OK,' I said quickly, not wanting another row, 'I'll look after her for you. I don't mind.'

With a wide grin, Margot suddenly swivelled round in her seat. 'Listen, Si – why not come round for supper tonight – just the two of us? Haggis-face here has to go to a press thing at the Ministry of Lies—'

My world turned right-side-up at last, dizzyingly, the momentum from despair to ecstasy so sudden that I almost skidded past what she'd said—

'Yes—! Thank you!'

The clouds which we'd out-run after leaving the hills below Toledo were finally beginning to tower over the city as I jumped out of the cab outside her building that evening.

Looking up excitedly, I decided they were a favourable omen, and went flying up the stairs in spite of the oppressive heat. When I heard the first faint grumble of thunder over the Guadalajaras I flew even faster, galvanised by its energy—

This was the night! Tonight I would win or lose, live or die – or be damned!

Her door was jammed open slightly with leather cushions on either side, bringing me up short as effectively as if it had been shut. I called out as I knocked, incapable of just breezing in, as I longed

465

to. Pushing gently against the cushion on the far side, I leaned in, but she wasn't there – just her tennis shoes abandoned chaotically in the middle of the tiled floor—

A moment later she appeared at the open doors onto the terrace wearing a white Aertex shirt pulled out over the waistband of her brief tennis skirt, dark sweaty hair still tied back. The heat seemed to rise from the sheen of sweat running down her face and neck and into the open collar of her shirt, clinging limply to her body. I so longed to embrace her, to bury my face—

'Hi, Si!' She seemed flustered, distracted.

Behind her, to my chagrin, Alastair suddenly lumbered into view in full tennis whites, his shirt also pulled out over his shorts, dripping with sweat. I'd never seen him look so shambolic.

Supper for three, then! I had to turn away for a moment, pretending to fight for breath as I smothered the life out of my feelings before they betrayed me.

'It's so airless in here—' Margot gasped as I turned back, to see her swooping down gracefully to pick up her plimsolls. 'I jammed the door open on the off-chance we'd get a breeze, but no such luck.'

Alastair stepped into the room, hands in his shorts' pockets, giving me a friendly wink. 'Don't worry,' he drawled, 'The haggis is on his way out.'

Was I so transparent? 'Nonsense,' I protested. 'Aren't you staying?'

He shook his head with a lopsided grin as he passed me and reached down for his tennis bag. He smelled like a race horse fresh from the gallops, hot, clean, animal-like. Why hadn't they showered?

Straightening up, he turned to Margot on the far side of the room where she leaned against the door jamb, ankles crossed, arms folded almost defensively across her chest.

Again, as in the catacombs, they exchanged an unreadable look between them.

'Yes? No?' he asked impatiently.

After a split second she shook her head. 'No – I don't know…
maybe.'

Alastair shrugged slowly, his eyes closing automatically as his
shoulders came up.

'Have a lovely evening!' she said brightly.

He threw her a rueful smile. 'I doubt it.' Heading for the open
door, he waggled his fingers at us. "Bye, then! Have fun.' And
he was gone, taking the ninety-nine steps two at a time, his stout
calves bulging in my imagination at every downward leap.

And yet no sooner had he gone than I almost wished he'd stayed
– a moment of weakness on my part as I felt the disparity in our ages
suddenly. What if I lacked his guts to see this through? I glanced
back at Margot, still leaning thoughtfully against the door jamb.

Then suddenly, as if released from a spell, she grinned at me,
kicked the leather cushions out of the way, slammed the door and
leant against it, her eyes alight with mischief. '*There!*' she gasped.

And *there* we were, safely back in the world of 'us' again, the
door closed against outsiders, free to be anything we liked to each
other, however childish, in our walled playground. Grabbing my
hand, she pulled me after her towards the passage. 'Let me show
you what we've got – there's no way I was going to cook in this
heat, so I picked up a few things on the way home—'

Once in the kitchen, she flung open the door of the fridge and sank
down on her haunches. Draping myself over the open door, I watched
her, rapt, as she looked in, the cold light from the fridge spilling onto
her tense, tanned thighs, onto the hem of her pleated tennis skirt,
on her slender brown arms as they reached in to rummage among
the paper bags of what she'd bought. 'God, that's good!' she gasped,
fanning the cold air from the fridge towards her face and neck.

'Didn't you get your shower at the club?' I asked.

'Cut off! The drought's official, apparently – in public places, at
least. I'll have one in a minute. OK – so we've got cold chicken,
salad, avocados, endive, *flan*—'

467

'Mayonnaise?' I asked.

'With the *flan*?' she mused doubtfully.

'With the chicken.'

'No.'

'Have you got an egg?'

She pulled out the chicken and looked cautiously inside it. 'No—'

Laughing, I leaned over further, our hair touching. 'Are you sure you haven't got an egg?'

'Wait—' She reached into the back of the fridge and started clucking as she opened her hand and produced an egg in the flat of her palm. 'We'll call it Alastair!' she decided. She looked up at me, still smiling, but out of the game for a moment. 'What have you done with her?'

'I wrapped her in some old clothes and locked her in my suitcase.' I stared into her hypnotic grey eyes, startlingly pale in the blue-white light from the fridge as she frowned slightly, then nodded, satisfied. She looked back at the egg in her palm. 'Why do you need Alastair?'

'Mayonnaise. Wouldn't you like some – with the chicken?'

'If you promise to beat it hard enough.'

'What's he done?' I asked lightly.

'What Alastair does,' she grunted.

'Then I'll give him a damn good thrashing! Do you think we could warm him up a bit, though? Cold eggs are hopeless.'

Without a word she slipped it straight down the open neck of her tennis shirt and held it between her breasts, pressing it to her heart. 'Oh God!' she closed her eyes ecstatically, then opened them like an owl. 'Can you really make mayonnaise?' she asked.

'Yes. Theo Fitzgibbon taught me.'

'Who's he?' she asked casually.

'She. Theodora – serious cook – writes books. Whenever we stay with her she makes me help in the kitchen…' I stared down at

468

her teasing face, knowing she was about to take the piss out of me. 'I'd rather it wasn't hard-boiled,' I said pointedly.

With a quick laugh she reached into her shirt for the egg, rolled it up her neck and held it against her cheek. 'What else do you need? Olive oil?'

'Yes—' I ransacked my memory and reeled off a list. She was on her feet in a trice, slipping the egg carefully into the safekeeping of my palm, then flying round the kitchen like a girl playing hunt-the-thimble, opening cupboards, rummaging through drawers, piling up ingredients and implements on the sideboard, unendurable to watch in her sweat-soaked shirt and tiny skirt—

'God, you're quick!' I gasped – *God, you're beautiful—! God, I love you!*

Without thinking, I raised the egg to my nose, sniffing her elusive perfume on the shell—

'There's white wine in the ice box,' she said at last. 'Do you want to open it while I have a quick shower?'

Once she was in the bathroom I set to on the mayonnaise, separating the egg, plopping the yolk into the mixing bowl she'd left out for me, adding a good dollop of mustard (Dijon, worst luck – I preferred Colman's), and whisking them together into a glossy emulsion. The oil in the mustard would make it less likely that the yolk would separate when I added the olive oil in green drips and dribbles, beating Alastair to a pulp as I'd promised, marvelling at the vivid colours of nature fading into a compromise that favoured neither egg nor oil but married them perfectly into a firm, supple sauce which had taken an eternity to create – until a French naval chef had invented *Mahonnaise* for his Admiral one hot summer's night in Port Mahon, during the Napoleonic Wars. How *could* it have taken so long? Garlic peeled, crushed, finely-diced, added with a splash of vinegar, whisked fiercely to help evaporate the sinal tears of the vinegar, a squeeze of lemon, blanching and slightly thinning the emulsion, then a draught of the cold white wine –

for me – biting its way like a rabid dog down my throat, bringing cold tears to my eyes, strengthening my arm as I thrashed the sauce again, then finger-stripped the thyme leaves against the grain, chopped them coarse, chucked them in with a pinch of sugar to counteract the garlic, then salt and ground pepper to release the taste, tasted it, beat it, added more salt to sting the blandness of the chicken into life, and left it to infuse in the heat of the kitchen.

Even as I'd started on the mayonnaise I knew that the distraction was crucial to my sanity, like applying the brakes to a mind on the verge of lunacy, reining in the wildness of a passion that threatened to tip me into some cataclysmic gesture or remark that might destroy me if my timing were wrong. This wasn't playtime any more – I had to grow up – *now* – *tonight!* – control myself, stand back and give her room to breathe, like the mayonnaise—

Another distant rumble of thunder, more prolonged this time, and nearer, as if the night were being born at last, hot, exciting, young. Some would find the sound ominous; others would hear it with relief, imagining the end of drought and stifling heat, but to me it was an augury, a propitious sign that the Muse's mistress (now mine) was stirring among the elements, among her fellow deities, moving towards us above the battle of the storm to witness a private drama of her own making. This was the gods' night out, after all, an immortal pub crawl high above the city in search of mischief, of catalysis—!

And I was ready for them, the little shoemaker, charged with such energy that it was spitting from my brain in flashes, blinding me to my fate – indifferent—

Concentrate! *Chicken*—

Out of the fridge, where it should never have been put, a wiry bird, cornfed by the look of it, almost the same colour and weight as the girl's skull—

Swiftly dissecting it, as I'd been taught by my father, legs, thighs, breasts neatly sliced and laid out on an oval plate with a space in the middle for the bowl of mayonnaise, the meaty wishbone crooked over the edge of the bowl as a taster.

Thunder – again – about as far away as last time, but more ponderous, inevitable—

Concentrate! *Salad*—

A quick wash, then the avocado cut in half, twisted open like a Chinese puzzle, the stone – the heart – exposed, still living, split like a log and wedged out with the heavy knife blade, discarded, skin peeled away, flesh sliced, so perfectly firm, yellow-fading-to-green, like the egg yolk and the olive oil, the fat endive stemmed, outer leaves placed like a stockade around the inside of the small salad bowl she'd left out for me, the kernel and the rest of the salad diced, then tipped into the middle, sprinkled with what was left of the thyme and dressed simply with olive oil and lemon juice, a crack of pepper, a feathering of sugar and a good pinch of salt to sharpen the inside of the mouth, purifying the breath, the teeth—

Don't think! Don't stop!

Having played the chef in my weird manic fantasy, I now took the butler's part, piling everything neatly onto a tray and taking it through into the sitting room – the dining room now—

The sound of the shower stopped as I passed the bathroom door.

Unsure of where she wanted us to sit, I unloaded my tray onto the middle of the long oak table on my left, dropping a fork in my haste. Reaching down for it, I saw Robert's letters, back on the seat of the chair, all opened now, in a neat pile. I looked away. He had no business here tonight—

The bathroom door opened, flooding the passage with light as she flitted across to her room, wrapped in a short white towel which barely covered her, pushing open her bedroom door, squaring the hypotenuse of light between the kitchen, the bathroom, her bedroom—

'Was that thunder I heard?' she called out.

'Yes!' There'd been a note of anxiety in her voice. 'It's still miles away, though!'

'I *hate* thunderstorms!'

I wished I could strike it from the menu. And yet the storm would come. Whatever was to happen would *happen*!

Dusk had already fallen, earlier and more dramatically than usual, the first hot breath of the coming violence already skittering an old newspaper across the terrace, juggling it into the air before bursting it apart and mischievously flinging page after page over the rails – while I went on with my charade, playing chef and butler, weather forecaster, confidant, prepared to play any part she liked—

I waited for her out on the terrace, trying to calm down in the gathering darkness as I stared out over the rooftops of the city, when I heard a faint swishing sound and turned back into the room to see her approaching the table like an apparition from a past world, wearing an ankle-length silk kaftan, the patterns as vivid and abstract as my abstraction for her, brown feet bare, hair still wet from the shower, caught up with Spanish combs and left to hang in dripping coils down the back of her neck—

'Beautiful!' I managed to say, amazed that I could speak at all.

No startled look or coy denial, just a radiant smile before she turned away to pick up the wishbone from the side of the bowl and dipped it in the mayonnaise. Tasting it, she turned back to me, her eyes widening in surprise. 'Very *good!*' She skidded it back through the mayonnaise and tore off some meat with her teeth.

I bowed low, smiling the smug pretentious smile of a flattered chef. '*Je vous en pris, Ma'moiselle—*'

'*Mais non, Marcel, j'insiste! C'est formidable—!*' She turned away for another dip.

'*Marcel?*' I was outraged. 'Marcel's a queer hairdresser in Ealing – wears a toupée—'

'So you *do* know him!' she rounded on me angrily. 'He said you'd never met—!'

Laughing, carefree, I jumped down into the dining room, slipped the wishbone between my teeth, took her in my arms, and danced her back to the table. 'I wasn't sure where you wanted us to sit,' I said, glancing down at the plates and cutlery I'd piled up in the middle.

'One at each end, definitely. I've taken the trouble to dress up, after all. We'll imagine the servants—'

I held out the wishbone to her, my little finger crooked round one side, wishing with all my might as we snapped it between us – leaving me with my wish (this wish at least) granted.

We sat, baronially, at either end of the long table, lighted candles in saucers stretching between us, flickering in the slight breeze from the open glass doors onto the terrace, each with a plate of food and a sweating glass of white wine in front of us.

Perhaps because I hadn't worked up the same appetite by playing tennis, I was the first to look up from my plate into a world more private than the one I'd sat down to, when she'd seemed so far away at first. No sooner had she sat down herself, though, than she'd reached behind her and turned off the ceiling light, leaving only the candles and a standard lamp in the far corner of the room to eat by.

Just as my eyes had become accustomed to the candlelight (which seemed to draw us closer), my ears had become accustomed to the sullen rumbles of thunder as they, too, edged closer, sharpening my focus. 'This is what it must have felt like at Waterloo,' I said lightly, off the top of my imagination, wanting only to distract her from the approaching storm, 'listening to the distant cannon fire while we ate our supper—' I left the thought hanging in the air for her to catch or let fall, as she chose.

She looked up, smiling. 'And who would we have been?' she asked. 'English or French?'

'English, of course!'

'I'm not sure about that. In fact, I'd have had to be French.'

'All right,' I searched quickly for a solution, 'we could have been each other's hostage to fortune, until the battle was decided—'

A fork of lightning split the black sky in two, blindingly, as if the shell of night had burst open for a moment, exposing the day to come.

We both stared out at it, Margot tense, unmoving, while I simply counted the seconds: *eleven, twelve, thirteen*—

A much louder, more ominous peal of thunder, reaching behind us from left to right, reverberating on and on into the distance—

'Don't worry,' I reassured her, 'it's still thirteen miles away—'

Bolt upright, she turned to me, her eyes taut with strain. 'How do you know that?' she demanded.

'Simple – we used to do it at school – you just count the seconds between the lightning strike and the next roll of thunder; that gives you the miles between here and the heart of the storm. The closer they are together, the sooner the storm will pass over,' I added, to comfort her.

'What were you saying, before?'

'Just rubbish… Waterloo.'

'Oh, yes,' she said vaguely.

Another vivid display of forked lightning, this time like the root system of a monstrous tree, the dazzling tendrils of its roots stretching down from the dark heavens, earthing themselves into the foundations of the city, awe-inspiring, lighting up the whole sky, the room, the terrace—

Margot had counted up to nine when the next thunder clap went off.

'It's getting closer.'

Almost at once the lights flickered and went out and she was on her feet, running across the room to the dresser, reaching into a drawer for more candles, stamping her foot – 'God*dammit*, I hate this—!'

474

'I know—' I hurried to help her. 'Here – let me—'

She gave me half a dozen candles. 'Stick them anywhere – I don't care – I need *light!*'

I did as she asked, lighting them one by one, dripping wax onto anything they might stick to.

'You'll stay, won't you?' she asked sharply. 'Until it's over – till the lights come on, at least—'

'Of course!'

'All night if necessary—'

'Yes—' *Forever!*

Like a bad joke, the lights came on again, and she laughed with relief.

'I'd better be off, then,' I said ruefully, putting the candles down.

'Idiot! Don't stop – they're bound to go out again—'

I longed to take her in my arms, to comfort her, persuade her she was safe, and yet what I'd found so natural and easy when we were happy, when I'd danced her over to the table, was impossible to repeat when she was afraid, when I might add to her fear – be misunderstood—

'Say something!' she said urgently. 'Distract me—'

In my haste to help I came up with the first question that entered my head: 'How long will you stay in Madrid, do you think?' I held up my hands instantly at her expression. 'I'm not questioning you,' I added hurriedly, 'I just wondered how much you liked it here—'

'I don't – not tonight!' She relented suddenly, with a sigh. 'Oh, it's not that bad, I suppose – in fact I love it in some ways – but not like Alastair. He *really* loves it – the heat, the bullfights, the constant aggression, even when people are just talking to each other. He's as obsessed as they are – blood and death, *duende*, revenge—'

'But *why?*'

'Makes him feel alive, I suppose – gets his adrenalin going – inspires him. You know what poets are like; they're obsessive. I mean, he loved the catacombs, the gloom, the closeness to death.'

She threw me a quick smile. 'I think he was jealous of what you did, which is why he was so angry. You mustn't resent him, though; he cares about you – feels responsible—'

I busied myself with another candle. 'Yes, I know. Or at least I think I do. It's just that he's quite ruthless sometimes – a bit like Robert in a way – not that *he'd* have wanted me to chuck away the skull—'

'If it's any comfort, I think Robert would have done the same as you.' I must have looked surprised. 'Alastair thinks so, too.'

'Do you love him?' I asked suddenly, the question coming from nowhere, provoking an instant frown from her, eyes flaring. 'Robert, I mean—' already kicking myself for blurting out the question. Had I drunk too much already?

She let out a sharp sigh – of exasperation? 'Of course I love him,' she said distractedly.

'Yes, but are you *in* love with him?' I had to risk her anger if need be. 'I know, I know, I'm not meant to ask you personal things – it's just that I don't understand, and I need to.' Her frown deepened. 'Please?' After a brief moment she nodded, reluctantly. 'I mean, you have a kind of mystical power over him... *on* him... *in* him – oh, I don't know for Christ's sake, but whatever your power is, it causes him to write extraordinary poems to you, and I mean extraordinary by any standards, and yet you avoid him, you won't even write to him, and I don't understand. Isn't it worth everything to be the muse of such a poet? He needs you so badly – your love, your powers—'

'He needs *poems,* Si!' She was out of her chair, striding over to the window, arms folded protectively round her ribs. 'I just inspire them, that's all... and Robert's love is more than a need, it's a hunger – insatiable. He *devours* me! Even when I'm not there I can feel him taking great chunks out of me with his endless streams of letters carping on and on... and whenever I'm with him, I'm trapped... we only have to look at each other and I become...' she shuddered, 'paralysed… possessed… Whatever he wants from me he takes – no! – that's wrong – I *give*, and the poems pour out of him – but everything inside me just drains away.'

'But he gives back, surely?'

She turned on me, eyes hunted. 'That's the whole *point*, I don't know any more! He gives, yes – he gives his charms, his poems, money – blinding me, until I'm so full of him that I no longer know who I am. I'm terrified of waking up one day and finding I no longer exist, that there's nothing left! He gives me everything – everything he can afford to give… but not what he can't afford—'

'What do you mean?'

'My freedom.'

She said it so quietly and simply that it took a moment for the words to sink in. I stared at her, stunned by the implications. She returned to the table and took a drink from her glass, her eyes wild, unseeing. 'But if I have one instinct left, it's self-preservation,' she murmured to herself. 'If the only way I can break free is to change his perception of me – become repugnant to him—'

Another lightning strike, so close that I could have sworn I heard it hiss, followed a mere second later by a clap of thunder that frightened the life out of both of us as it rocked the whole building. Shaking, she stared out onto the terrace as if hypnotised. *'You've no idea what it's like to be needed by Robert!'* she shouted over the noise. *'I could almost believe this storm was* him, *for Christ's sake!'* She rounded on me. 'You may think I have powers, but believe me, Robert…' She shook her head furiously, whether to stop herself saying something she'd regret or to ward off what she thought was his presence in the room. 'And he's a powerful enemy, Si. He never forgives. You only have to look at the people who were once his closest friends – Laura, Sassoon, even Lawrence—'

'But the real ones still are!' I found myself protesting. 'Robert Frost, James Reeves, Idries Shah—'

'God, you sound just like him!' She turned back to me, with an almost pitying face. 'They're all *real*, Si. It's just that some are more human than others—'

I gazed back at her down the mist-filled tunnel of her words, the mist clearing, her words revealed in their ominous starkness. I stared at her in dread. 'Are you saying you won't go back?'

The pause was longer than the question, longer than truth, shorter than lies— 'I don't know,' she murmured finally, looking away. 'And yet I have to – I owe it to him.'

'But you're afraid?'

'No. Not this time.'

'Why not this time?'

She shook her head, looking down, then out through the windows, avoiding my gaze.

'Tell me – please!' I said urgently. 'You can trust me, you know you can!'

'But I *can't!*' she cried, tearing herself away again, as if he were haunting her wherever she stood. 'Don't you *understand*? You're part of him – *family*, blood – his messenger, his spy—'

The shock of her words dragged me violently to my feet, my chair crashing to the floor. '*I am not his spy!*' I shouted. 'I'm *not!*' engulfing her in my innocence, my voice, my heart, breaking – 'I'm *not...*' tears burning with rage—

She flew towards me, a streak of iridescent silk, face stricken, taking my hands in hers. 'No, I didn't mean that, Si, I'm sorry, it's *wrong*, I know it's wrong! You're not his spy, you're *loyal*, that's all I meant—' she pressed my clenched fists to her lips, softening them, and yet her eyes still fixed unblinking on mine, '—but he asked you to watch me.'

'*Not like that*—' I was appalled. 'To watch *over* you, to look after you—'

'But you *can't*,' she flung my hands back at me and turned away. 'You can't! I know you try to, and I love you for it, but you come too close – you want to know too much: *why* everything – why I go to France, *why* I won't write to him, *why, why, WHY*? It's *stifling*! It's as if you were *him!*'

'*But I'm not him!*' I reached out for her, dragging her round to me, clutching at her to prevent myself from falling into the unbearable void of her mistrust— '*I'm me!* I love him – I'd – *kill* for him—'

'*There!*' she cried accusingly—

'*But I'd kill for you, too,*' I cried, '*don't you understand?* I'd – give my *soul* for you. I'd – *die* for you—' My words torn from me in the agony of their revelation, pressing her hands to my lips, to the sides of my streaming face, my heart freed at last. '*I'm – in love with you!* Oh, can't you *see*—?'

Strobes of lightning – vivid, blinding, fusing my words to the naked shock in her eyes, followed instantly by a peal of thunder so shattering that it seemed to burst through the open windows, filling the room with its terrifying din, dousing the light, something crashing to the floor in the guttering darkness, Margot's body driven into mine with a cry of fear—

'*He can't hear us in this!*' I shouted exultantly, my arms crushing her to the safety of my body. '*He can't see us—!*' I buried my face in the hot sheen of her neck, beneath her dark hair, the trail of her indescribable scent dragging my lips upwards to the smooth secret place behind her ear where she hid it, the delicate cartilage of her ear pressing back like a kiss against my lips as I slid from there to her eyebrows, to her closed eyes, to the hollow of her cheek, to her full soft lips at last opening to the urgency of mine, into the deepest mystery of my life as the storm raged around us, jolting her body with every deafening peal of thunder, the palms of my hands huge with passion, kneading her back, pressing her to me, sliding downwards over her nakedness beneath the thin smooth silk of her kaftan, drawing her hips towards me, her vulva hard against my equal hardness – huger, hungrier than I'd ever known it, the pliant willow of her body drawn to the solid oak of mine, a love-battle of the trees among the storm around us, parched for love, for rain, for the shelter that would grow over us, conceal us from him as we kissed so deeply, secretly that only we would know – would ever know— '*I love you,*' I groaned, '*I love you, I love you—*' with unspoken vows and promises of all I possessed – until with a violent sob she tore her mouth from mine, her head thrown back, my lips instantly at her neck, at the pulse of her arching throat—

'*Can't!*' Her cry strangled by emotion, by the impossible angle of her neck. '*No—*'

Her arms, which had clung to me so hungrily, now falling almost lifeless to my waist before rising gently between us, her palms flat against my chest, my hard nipples screeching to their touch as the shock of her words finally reached my heart, beating to a halt beneath her pressing palms, her eyes staring not at me, but as if I were no longer there, upwards, through the ceiling into the storm that surrounded us, into some mystery of her own – '*I can't!*'

'*We can!*' despairingly, searching her unseeing eyes for some proof of my existence to her—

'I can't, I can't—' Her low voice resigned, fatalistic, frightening me – and then her dazed eyes looking back at me at last, slowly filling with tortured pity – a dreaded look, a death sentence – the agony I felt reflected in her eyes as she slowly reached up and took my face between her hands and gently kissed my cheek, my tears – 'I'm so sorry,' she whispered.

'But *why*?' I sobbed. '*I love you.*' Unable to meet her eyes any longer, my head falling blindly against the dark heat of her neck, in shame—

'Chaos,' she murmured, the word sounding as if she'd said it in Greek – oracular, fatal—

'Is it me?' my face sinking back against her shoulder. 'It is, isn't it?'
'*No—*'

'It is, it must be!' My voice breaking—

'*No!*' her arms around me as my legs gave way in despair, my face sliding down the sheer silk of her dress from her shoulder

to her breasts, and downwards, my arms still around her, hands
slipping over the torture of her nakedness under the slithering
silk, further and further down, unchecked by her, unstopped,
until I sank to the floor, Margot on her knees now, folded over
me, her arms stretched along my back, still holding me as I fell
onto my side, knees drawn into my chest, weeping without a
sound, without a sound—

The battle of the clouds had moved on, my fate now sealed, inescapable.

In their wake came a hot marauding wind, a crazed band of
looters blasting everything before them, rampaging round the
room, tilting the pictures, storming through the flat, breaking
glasses in the kitchen, extinguishing half the candles – and then
torrential rain, dinning so violently onto the terrace and the awning
outside that for a while it was impossible to hear or speak.

And yet neither of us made a move from where we lay; the
consolation of rain, its tumult, its promise of relief becoming sacred
to the moment, more quick and relevant than any reaction of ours
to the agony of this tragedy of errors – my delusions—

As she knew, drawing me quietly, patiently towards her.

I lay on my back on the tiled floor among the desolation of my
love for her, Margot alongside me, head propped up on one hand so
that she could stare down at me, I up at her, willing myself to die—

She reached for a fallen candle, still burning, and set it upright
on the floor.

Chaos. Although I didn't yet understand, I knew instinctively
that whatever it was she'd seen at that moment when she'd stared
into the storm above us had been meant for her alone.

Whom the gods love, they first make mad – but although I might
be mad, I was only mortal-mad as yet, neither loved enough – nor
truly mad enough – to contradict her, to force myself on her as
others might have done. A sign of weakness on my part? No – but

nor a sign of strength. The tune and words of love were hers – my task to dance to them, nothing more.

With a growing consciousness I realised that I'd lain there speechless for too long, numb with loss, staring up into her strangely patient, watchful eyes, so beautiful, bewitching—

'I love you,' I managed to whisper at last, tears of honest grief blurring my vision of her.

She leant over me until her face was directly above mine in the candlelight, her eyes luminous. 'You love what you *see*, Si – what you think you see.' Her eyes searching mine, willing me to understand.

'No!' I turned my face away from her, tears dashing onto the tiles beneath my head. 'I love what I *know*!'

She cupped my cheek, drawing my face back towards hers. 'Look at me,' she whispered.

'—and what I don't know…' I stared up at her defiantly.

She frowned, her eyes unblinking, still willing me to understand. 'But I'm Janus, Si,' she murmured at last. 'What you see… is not what you get…'

I opened my mouth to protest, but she laid a finger over my lips and shook her head almost imperceptibly.

Without a word we stared on at each other until I became lost in the maze of her infinite grey eyes, sucked into the vortex of her powers – over Robert, over me, over everyone she touched – the rest of my life draining into the tiles beneath me.

> *Who calls her two-faced? Faces she has three:*
> *The first inscrutable, for the outer world;*
> *The second shrouded in self-contemplation;*
> *The third, her face of love,*
> *Once for an endless moment turned on me.*

THE MATADOR

At dawn I let myself out, silently, having spent the night, at her insistence, on the pallet in the far corner of the drawing room – like a dog (though not beside her on her bed, where I belonged, or even across her feet, but at a room's remove from her, staring upwards, sightless, into the impenetrable enigma of myself – *what was the point of me—?*)

There was no point.

The only refuge for a mind unable to deal with what had happened was self-imposed amnesia – an almost surgical numbing of those parts of the brain which would otherwise have screamed in agony all the way back through the sodden, deserted streets of Madrid. And yet to indulge such misery publicly was pointless – as pointless as trying to unburden myself to a friend, since I knew no one here who could begin to understand – not even Alastair, who's face would inevitably mirror the scorn I felt for myself. My despair was mine alone; inexpressible, speechless.

Was I a coward? The recurring thought was unendurable, which meant that there must be more than a hint of truth in it. Had I simply lacked the manliness to impose my will on her? Perhaps; but then, I'd never wanted to impose my will on her in the first place. The choice had been hers, and hers alone.

Once I'd let myself into my room, I flung myself fully-dressed onto the bed and gave up the ghosts of all my dreams and fantasies before my head had even hit the pillow.

After almost two days buried deep in my bed, I finally got up, unable to sleep any longer. No sooner had my bare feet hit the cold tiles of the floor, though, than the awful reality of my plight returned with shocking vividness.

Things didn't improve much after I'd left the *pensión*: on my way to the café on the Plaza Santa Anna I intervened angrily when I saw a group of street urchins trying to stone to death a three-legged dog on a bombsite left over from the Civil War. The dog, badly injured and not even trusting its saviour, crawled into a drain under the rubble. Nothing I could say or do would bring him out, and in the end I had to leave him, promising to bring him back something to eat from the café.

But I forgot, walking downhill by another route to the Retiro park, and when I did remember, I could only add the omission to the litany of other omissions until their combined weight forced me down onto the grass, covering my face with my arms.

The sun was blazing down again with its usual Spanish cruelty (a cruelty I was fast adopting, it seemed – I hadn't even 'noticed' a beggar lately), evaporating the muggy air, drawing the scent of rain from the earth and trees, filling my spirits with new hope as I picked myself up and walked on across the park, my face to the sun—

This was not the end of us! Far from it! Yes, I had bared my very soul to Margot, but so had she bared hers to me for an instant, unforgettably. Now, at last, she knew what I was – an honourable man, in love with her – and not a spy. I could never betray her, fail her, force myself upon her. We were as close, if not closer in our instincts for each other as blood brother and sister – or as unrequited lovers in chivalry. She had lain with me patiently for hours that night, when she could have sent me away. The bond between us, however inexplicable, was as powerful as ever. Nothing had truly changed between us. If anything our honesty, like the sudden reappearance of the sun, had cleared the air and taken us to a higher plane of understanding than before. It was up to me to acclimatise myself to this new altitude, to prove myself still worthy of her, to start again, but from a new maturity learned from the harsh lesson of that night.

Another dreaded sunset, this one the bloodiest I'd seen yet, like a silent Cecil B. deMille replay of the imagined battle that had raged over the city two nights before. From the canyons of the city streets it would probably have gone unnoticed, but from the park below the Prado it was an awe-inspiring sight, the distant west-facing windows of the city blazing with a reflected fire so realistic that I began to doubt my eyes, my ears for their inability to hear the frantic sound of approaching sirens. Guts and viscera, orange and yellow fat, the unlikely brilliant greens and yellows of bile, were swiftly sucked from the sky through a filter of dark clouds and into the blood-clotted drain of the setting sun until it finally sank beneath the city.

I walked back to the *pensión* through a twilight luminous with peace. Tomorrow, I would take some food to the dog, a libation of sorts – or later tonight, perhaps, after supper. I would have to eat in – my monthly allowance was nearly gone and I still had almost a week to go before the next. Supper at the *pensión* would be on tick, after all – like my unkept promises to the dog.

Once back in my room, I found my afternoon post slipped under the door: another letter from Robert, and one in Alastair's distinctive handwriting. I tore it open at once. Wrapped in a single sheet of paper was a ticket to the bullfight tomorrow, on the sheet of paper a single word: '*Coming?*' Even as my heart leapt with pleasure I laughed at his obsession with economy which seemed to stretch even to his use of ink and words. *Coming?* You bet I was coming! Two days without a word from either of them had been torture enough.

Later, in high spirits, I went in to dinner. Manolo, looking like The Fat Controller, was sitting at his usual table playing with a train of crusts, snowing salt on them, then dunking them one by

485

one into a saucer of olive oil before popping them into his mouth, his eyes lighting up when I came in. Abruptly, he kicked out the chair next to him, extending his hand to it as if about to introduce his mother, his mouth so full that he could only snort a greeting.

'Tonight, happy!' he managed to spit out in English at last, stabbing his finger at me.

'Very happy!' I'd been unable even to answer his anxious knocks on my door the night before.

'*Mi allegre!*'

'Me too—' I took my ticket to the bullfight out of my pocket and waved it under his nose. Eyes bursting from his head, he snatched the ticket and showered it with oily kisses. I snatched it back, wiping it on my trousers.

'Ay, *qué suerte tienes!*' he gasped. '*Dominguín!*'

'*Dominguín*—!' The finest bullfighter in Spain, the vivid posters for his fight plastered all over Madrid.

Maria came to the table with two bowls of hot, greasy dishwater, commenting at once on the suntan I'd picked up in the park. Manolo inspected it for the first time, shaking his head sadly. I had clearly not been to university that day (I hadn't been for two weeks).

On the point of returning to the kitchen, Maria suddenly turned back, her face alight with memory. She had seen my *novia* that afternoon—

Margot—?

On her return from the shops, she'd seen her parked outside in her black Citröen. Presuming she was waiting for me, Maria had told her that I'd gone out earlier. She had driven away, looking troubled.

Cursing myself for not being there, ecstatic at the thought that she'd come at all, I puzzled over it for the rest of supper, trying to ignore Manolo as he turned from Fat Controller into Poirot, proposing and discarding a dozen theories to explain her strange behaviour, all of them preposterous.

I was late for the bullfight. I hadn't realised it was *fiesta* and that there wouldn't be a taxi to be had for love or money, so I'd had to walk half way across the city through almost deserted streets under a burning sun.

Once admitted to the monumental building, I hurried through the grimy vaulted passageways and arches, the floors littered with filth, searching for my seat number at every tunnelled entrance into the stands, disorientated by wave after wave of inexplicable sound, like torrential rain that poured through each succeeding tunnel I passed until I finally realised that the sound was the distant drawn-out roar of '*Olé*' from the vast crowds above me. Finding my staircase at last, I began to climb out of the relative cool and darkness of the galleries and into the crushing heat and full-throated bellowing of thousand upon thousand *aficionados*. I stood at the top of the steps, stunned by the atmosphere of the packed arena, by the hot animal stench rising from the bullring and the sweltering, shouting people above and below, reaching up tier upon tier almost to the eaves of the stadium.

A moment later I was pounced on by a petty functionary demanding to see my ticket. Tearing off the stub, he grudgingly led me down the steps to the front of the second tier where I spotted Alastair at once, alone between two empty seats, staring fixedly into the bullring where a pair of frightened horses were being spurred on to drag the hog-tied carcass of a bull by its hind legs towards an opening gate. Deliberately under-tipping the usher, I made my way politely past the other spectators in the row, just as Alastair looked round, his face lighting up almost with astonishment at seeing me. 'So you came!' He rose to shake my hand warmly. 'Good for you!'

I flopped into the seat next to him, taking off my hat to fan my face, shoving my jacket under the seat. 'Thank God we're in the shade,' I gasped, 'I didn't realise it was *fiesta,* so I had to walk—'

'Never mind that – you came, that's the main thing! I didn't think you would.'

'Of course I came – I wouldn't miss this for anything.' Or the chance to see Margot again.

'Your first big fight! I almost envy you – and you're going to see the best there is. The young fellow who just fought wasn't bad – plenty of guts and a clean kill, but wait till you see Dominguín! God I love it! Even the bad fights. It's so *quick* – in the old-fashioned sense – the quick and the dead. This is as close as you'll ever come to human sacrifice, to ancient Rome, the Colosseum – I bet you didn't know that Julius Caesar was a bullfighter?'

'No!'

'It was his favourite sport when he was Governor of Spain. All right, he did it on horseback in those days, like a *picador*, but even so...' He looked round at me, grinning excitedly. 'So you're OK then? You understand what's happening?'

'Don't worry, I'm fine. I'll pick it up as we go along—'

He looked at me quizzically, as though he didn't quite have faith in my ability to catch on.

At that moment the row of people on the far side of him began to get to their feet to allow an old man to get through, the front of his trousers soaked with what looked like piss. No sooner had he sat down in the empty seat next to Alastair than his wife started haranguing him under her breath, thumping her black handbag over his lap to cover him as he plaintively explained that he hadn't been able to wait to get back to see the kill.

Something was wrong—

'Where's Margot?' I asked Alastair. 'I thought she'd be here—'

But my words were drowned by a fanfare blaring from loudspeakers all around the stadium as a group of tumblers – dwarves in garish eighteenth century costumes – dashed into the ring with a bull's head crudely nailed to a wooden frame on wheels and began reliving the last fight, to roars of '*Olé!*' from the laughing crowd. Even I was amused for a moment, before I turned back to the distracted Alastair. '*Margot!*' I had to shout over the noise. '*Where is she?*'

He turned to me with a frown of irritation. 'Don't be silly, you know where she is! She's in France—'

I stared at him blankly. '*In France?*'

His frown faded to stone as he turned to look back at me. 'She came to see you – yesterday!'

'No! I mean yes – she came, apparently, Maria saw her, but I was out, and in the end she just drove off—'

He stared at me in disbelief. '*For Christ's sake!*' he exploded. '*You mean she hasn't told you?*'

'Told me *what?*' All at once I could hardly breathe for dread.

He slammed his fist into his palm. '*She was meant to tell you – before she left!*'

'Tell me *what?*' I stared at him, transfixed by the sudden panic in his eyes, panic which turned suddenly to grim purpose. I stared down the length of it, as if down the blade of a matador's sword poised for the kill, as he plunged it home—

'*Everything!*' He suddenly clutched at his head, gripping fistfuls of hair. 'About *us*—! *Margot and me, for Christ's sake!* The Camargue... *living together*! I'm leaving Mary—'

The blade of his words piercing me to the quick, paralysing me—

'I wanted her to tell you after Toledo, but she kept putting it off – didn't want to hurt you!'

My life pouring out of me, so stunned by what he'd said that it took moments to form words of any kind – words for myself, not for him: 'Oh, God...' I gasped. 'I'm so stupid... so fucking stupid... I think I'm going to be sick—'

Stumbling blindly to my feet, forcing my way along the row of people to the gangway, staggering up the stairs to the exit, my hand over my mouth, jeered by the under-tipped usher, retching as I clung to the rail and half fell down the concrete steps into the godsent gloom of the passageway below where I flung myself behind one of the arches and threw up my heart in wave after wave of self-revulsion—

489

'*Simon!*' Alastair's feet clattering down the steps and into the gloom of the gallery, slowing, searching, finding me just as I vomited again. 'Oh, Jesus!' He recoiled from the mess—

'Go away,' I gasped. 'Please.'

'Can I help?'

I shook my head, my brain still spinning from the shock of his words repeating themselves over and over again until I had to say something out loud simply to drown them. 'I've been so *blind!*' I shouted through the sour sick dripping from my nose. 'So *stupid!* So fucking stupid.'

'No!' His voice was emphatic, close behind me. '*You weren't to know.* You weren't *meant* to know, Si – not until yesterday! It was a secret – it still is – a deathly secret – *nobody knows yet* – not even Mary—' He dared to put his hand on my back. I shook it off angrily. What about Jasper? But I knew better than to ask him—

'Have you finished being sick?' he asked. I must have nodded. 'Come away, then, there's a drinking fountain over here – wash your mouth out. Sick rots your teeth—'

Revolted by the sight and smell of my own vomit, I backed away from the arch and staggered over to the drinking fountain on the far side of the passage, refusing to look at him as I slumped against the wall and pressed the spigot, my hands shaking uncontrollably, rinsing my mouth out with the weak dribble of lukewarm water, splashing my face, then sobbing suddenly, violently, like a wild animal—

'Are you ill again, is that it?' He sounded genuinely concerned.

I shook my head dazedly. *Was it possible that he was as stupid as me? That he didn't know?*

'So this is just... Margot?' He gasped incredulously.

'*Who else?*' I yelled at him, tears spurting out of my eyes, to my shame, my fury – 'Who else has the power to do this?' I spread my arms, willing him to witness my degradation. '*Who else?*'

'Oh shit,' he groaned, turning away as he suddenly slammed his fist into his palm again. 'Shit, shit, *shit!*'

The sound of another fanfare echoed through the tunnels and into the passageways. Alastair's head jerked up, listening, his eyes alive with what he saw in his imagination. 'It's starting!'

'Just go!' I shouted. '*Go!* Leave me alone—'

He turned back to me, his face suddenly set, as if he'd come to a decision. 'I can't. This is more important.' His eyes narrowed. 'It looks as though you're not the only one who's been blind and stupid. Listen, Si, honestly, I thought it was nothing more than a schoolboy pash – like Juan's—'

'Alastair, I'm *eighteen,* for Christ's sake! I lived with—'

'All right, all right!' He threw up his hands. 'I was wrong. It's just that you're still so young in some ways—'

'Oh, *fuck off.*'

'I *can't*—' He glared at me fiercely, then looked away for a moment as he took a slow, deep breath. 'Because that's not all... there's more—'

Again the sense of vertigo, of falling into an abyss. 'What do you mean?'

His eyes skidded away from mine, as if searching for inspiration before he stamped his foot angrily into the filth of the passage. 'For fuck's sake, I'm no *good* at this!' he shouted. '*Margot was meant to do it!*' Rubbing his mouth fiercely against the back of his hand, he seemed to pull himself together, taking a step towards me, gripping me by both arms – to prevent me from lashing out? '*Listen Si,*' his eyes pinning me to the wall, '*she needs you.* She needs your help – we both do...'

I stared at him in disbelief.

'You may not give a damn about me, and I understand that,' he hurried on, 'but you obviously still care for Margot. Am I right? *Am I right, Si?*'

Perhaps I said something, because he nodded fiercely. Gripping my arms even tighter, he shook me slightly. '*Listen*! On Friday she's flying from Marseilles to Majorca, to see Robert... to tell him...

to ask him to let her go! Can you understand that? God knows why, but she has to – she feels she owes it to him. I wanted to be with her, but I've got Mary to deal with… Jasper… packing up – and I'd only make things worse anyway. I – *we*,' he corrected himself instantly, then took a deep breath, 'wanted you to be there – in Deya – to help her—'

I stared at him, stupefied.

'*You're the only one she trusts,* do you hear? Apart from me,' he added, 'and I can't go.' He shook me again. 'I need you there to look after her, to get her out if necessary. Listen, Si!' He shook his head violently, as if to clear it. 'Robert's out of his mind at the moment, believe me.' Angrily, I broke away from his grip on my arms. 'No, *wait*,' he went on urgently, 'she can't even read his letters any more – I've been reading them for her, and they're frightening – full of threats and dire warnings – he's *unstable*, Si, like nitro-bloody-glycerine, sweating, just waiting for a last blow to set him off!'

'He's in love!' I cut in angrily.

'*So am I, for Christ's sake!*' he cried desperately, then stared at me, his eyebrows raised. 'So are you.'

With a furious shake of my head I ignored his patronising tone. 'But it'll kill him!' I cried. 'She's his muse, his *life!*'

'*As she is mine!*' He stared wildly around again, still searching for words, looking hunted suddenly. 'Listen, Si, I can't force you to help us, I know that, but you must realise that I'm fond of you, that I'd never hurt you deliberately. You're Diana's son – I've known you most of your life… for God's sake, we're not *enemies!* None of us are enemies unless Robert makes us so.'

The appeal in his voice, his unexpected sincerity, his oddly quaint turn of phrase took me by surprise. For the first time, I felt for him, all at once seeing him not as a rival but as someone on the same road as me, but further along it, leaving me behind, beaten fair and square—

He seemed to sense my sudden uncertainty. 'Look,' he went on hurriedly, 'if Robert goes off his head, which he well might, I want Margot out of there – fast. I need to know she's safe, that you'll be there – *because that's what she wants*—' He stared at me urgently. 'Robert threatened to come to Madrid, to have it out with her, but Margot telegraphed him, telling him to wait, that she was coming to him. Will you go? Please… for her.'

I tried to think, frantically, not knowing what to say, seeing only a future that was dark and frightening for its sheer uncertainty – I'd have to lie to Robert and Beryl, deceive, pretend – *Christ!* I looked at Alastair directly, for the first time. 'But what if Robert thinks that I've—' I couldn't even bring myself to speak the word—

'*What?*' he demanded, seeming to stare into my mind – '*Betrayed* him – is that what you mean?' I could only stare back at him. 'Oh, *balls!* As far as he or anyone else is concerned, you know nothing – and you *did* know nothing – until now! Robert loves you – he trusts you – he says so in his letters – it's the one thing he says that still makes any sense! Si, listen to me: it's half-term at university—'

'Is it?' I asked, astonished that he should know.

'Who *cares*? That's your story. Margot needed you to bring her cabin trunk to Deya – which is the other thing she was meant to have bloody well asked you – she couldn't get it into the boot of her car, and I'll be flying to France, so the only way to get it there is by train and boat – with you. You know what she's like – she can't be without it, and once Robert sees it he'll think she's come back for good, which will give her time to confront him…' His voice trailed off, as if that was as far as he could see into the future.

I stared at him, my imagination racing ahead faster than his words.

'You don't have to lie, you don't have to betray anyone, least of all Robert. Margot will do all the talking – you're just there for the ride; unless things turn nasty, of course – but Margot knows what to do if that happens. Robert would *approve*, Si – surely you can see that – it's what he'd have done himself if your roles were reversed. He'd want to protect her! Yes?'

'From himself?' I snorted derisively.

'That's not what I meant.'

'Oh, Christ, I don't *know*...' The horror of knowing what I now knew still sinking in, the longing to be with her rising through the horror to the surface, like a swimmer fighting for his life. However grudgingly, I could see the logic of what he'd said – but 'What about Beryl?' I demanded suddenly.

'*Beryl?*' He looked at me in astonishment. 'All Beryl wants is peace and quiet! She's fed to the teeth with him at the moment, his mood-swings, obsessions – for God's sake, it isn't as if this is the first time this has happened – his muses come and go like storms, and another one will come, I promise you—'

Not like Margot, they wouldn't!

'As long as Robert's all right, Beryl's all right. And he'll get over it, believe me – he always does. *I know him!* If Margot can only convince him to release her... peacefully... Will you go, Si?'

What choice did I have? Stay on in Madrid and never see her again? Or keep my promise to myself and go to her, knowing she needed me? Not to see her again would be unbearable even now, knowing that she'd chosen Alastair from among the three of us. But there was still time, I realised suddenly. If I went to her, managed to persuade her to stay with Robert, without betraying him myself – on the contrary—!

'All right,' I answered faintly, 'I'll go.'

'*Excellent!* Good man!' He had the sense not to embrace me or slap me on the back, and yet he still held out his hand, forcing me by default to shake it, warm and firm, a promise sealed by his standards. 'That's a weight off my mind, I don't mind telling you!' His relief was almost touching—

A sudden roar from the crowd above us, wild, ecstatic, reverberating round and round through the arched passageways, Alastair's gaze dragged upwards towards the sound. '*Domingu*í*n!*'

he cried. 'He's in the ring—!' He turned on me urgently. 'What do you want to do now?' he asked. 'Why not stay, eh? Till the end?' He looked at me quizzically, frowning. 'Where's your jacket, anyway – and your hat?'

'Oh, Christ, I've left them under my seat—'

'Don't worry,' he reassured me quickly. 'They'll be safe. *Madrillenos* don't steal. Come on!'

I followed him up the stairs, until an awful thought stopped me dead in my tracks. '*Alastair!*' I shouted up, above the roar of the crowd. '*I can't go!*'

A few steps above me, he spun round—

'I haven't got any money! My allowance doesn't come through till next week, and I'm spent out—'

'Oh, for fuck's sake!' he yelled back at me, grinning with relief. 'Don't worry about that – I'll lend you some. You can pay it back to Margot when you see her – just your fare, I mean, not the trunk – we'll pay for that. Now come *on!*'

I was in my seat again, everything safe beneath me, leaning over the rail, staring down into the ring, hardly aware of what was happening in spite of Alastair's running commentary in between wild moments of his bellowing '*Olé!*' at each pass of the bull, each hair's-breadth escape of Dominguín as he swayed like a stalk of wheat away from the lethal horns of the charging beast, his feet rooted to the sand, using only the sinuous movements of his body and his cape to avert a dreadful death—

And yet in spite of the fatal beauty of the scene, in my head I was already with Margot, speeding to her rescue, defending her to Robert, lessening the danger, drawing her closer and closer to me—

Robert's last letter had contained elements of what Alastair had described—darker than the others, curt, suspicious... by going back I could cheer him up, reason with him – and with Margot—

There was everything to play for still, and I would play this last act with all my might, prove to her that my love was the equal of Alastair's – *no!* – greater, truer – because I'd be *there*, beside her. Even though I could never compete with Robert's poems, I had the rest of my life to triumph in some equal way.

I hadn't cared that she'd been Robert's lover, so why should I care if she were Alastair's, so long as that part of her that I so loved remained *ours* and ours alone, walled in forever. So what if Alastair was using me? I didn't care! Margot still needed me – that was all that mattered.

It was the sudden, uncanny hush in the stadium that returned me to the present with a jolt. What had I missed?

The bull, finally exhausted by the fight, tormented by the *picas* and *banderillas* hanging from deep wounds in its back, had come to a standstill in front of Dominguín, frothing bloodily at nostrils and mouth, ribs heaving, forelegs slightly splayed, head sinking with each outward snort, seeming to accept its fate as Dominguín approached him in a series of infinitesimal, almost invisible footsteps, sideways on, his sword unsheathed, steadying the blade on his left forearm, slowly raising it by its hilt above his head, his body drawn like a ritual bow in an instant of motionless time, tense, poised perfectly for the kill, before loosing his sword with bewildering speed and deftness between the shoulders of the bull, with such force that the matador's feet were lifted from the ground, the blade passing straight through the bloody forequarters of the beast, downwards, piercing its heart—

For an endless moment the dying bull, like the vast crowd which had risen to its feet, remained standing, gasping, groaning, until its forelegs at last gave way beneath it and it sank slowly to its knees.

As the crowd erupted into a spontaneous, deafening roar of acclaim, Alastair suddenly turned to me, his eyes still gorged with what he'd witnessed. '*What I said earlier, Si*—' he bellowed above the roar, focussing my attention on him, '—*about all this being a deathly secret... I meant it! If you breathe a word to anyone, especially to Robert, I'll kill you*—'

[1989]

THE PERSON FROM PORLOCK

—and I'd believed him.

Even from this distance I could remember the chill his words had sent through me at the time. And yet I hadn't been afraid – that came later – I simply accepted his threat as the price of failure on my part; but since I had no intention of failing, it was only the unfamiliar violence of his expression, of his words, that had chilled me. He wasn't given to histrionics – I knew him well enough to know that – so his sudden outburst must have come from some unfamiliar part of his psyche, unfamiliar even to him; it could only have come from his being truly in love, perhaps for the first time in his life.

How was it possible that I could have been so blind to their affair to have had not the slightest inkling in spite (in retrospect) of all the clues and hints that I must have missed or ignored – and yet still couldn't recall clearly enough to be able to say 'there! – something wrong there—!' How was it possible to have been so naive? My youth – again? Always looking inwards first, unaware until too late of the world beyond *me* and *I*. In my defence, though, the world in those days was equally naïve and uncynical – one only had to look at Robert's trustingness to realise that.

And it wasn't as if I were alone; Robert and I had both been 'had'.

All right, they hadn't meant for me to know – it had been 'a deathly secret' – but even so, Alastair's self-control, in my company at least, had been phenomenal; in his place I'd never have been able to keep it up. Only the forbiddenness of my love for Margot had forced me to observe the curfew of my own feelings unless we were alone – and even then I hadn't dared express my true feelings until the last moment, under cover of the storm—

And Margot? Not by a single look had she given herself away – not that I'd noticed, at least. If anything, she'd been quite hard on Alastair, taking my side more often than not. But then, I'd always found it impossible to see past her, past the incandescent mirror she held up – and my own reflection in it.

I turned onto my left side, hoping to break the spell of the past, opening my eyes to the luminous face of my alarm clock. Ten to five in the morning, and I had to be up at seven, back at Foster's at eight to finish the packing we'd been doing for a week now, four of us, filling the hundreds of huge cardboard boxes which White's agent in Palma had dropped off at the foot of the mountain, and which were now piled into a vast pyramid in the front hall of Son Rullan, the grand piano sulking darkly under a blanket in the far corner, like a parrot with a cloth over its cage. And yet pyramids of any kind, whether of books or stone, were no more than reminders of mortality now.

During that week of packing up I'd found that my interest in the books themselves had waned as remorselessly as the moon, until there was nothing left to focus on, no tide by which to be pulled, nor even light to see by – and yet I seemed to have lumbered myself with a necropolis of the bloody things. But it was out of my hands now, the Bill of Sale signed (subject to collation), monies transferred, ten tons of books about which I knew virtually nothing wrapped round my neck like a ship's cable and ready to take me to the bottom, perhaps for the last time. Too late to pull out, though, the noose that tied me to it too tight. And besides, I'd need the money if I were to take that final leap – leave bookselling, sell the shop once I'd seen this through, and concentrate entirely on writing my way back into the past, racing against time to unearth it before it buried me forever.

Restlessly, I turned back onto my right side, looking for signs of dawn through the shutters. For once my trick hadn't worked – perhaps because I wasn't dreaming now, but awake and anxious. Suddenly to lose the meaning of one's working life at almost fifty-years-old was the equivalent, I imagined, of a messy divorce, the sense of solitude, of emptiness, recriminations, guilt, financial strain – awful, if that were all there was; but at least I had something else to fill the void—

Except that *he* seemed to have vanished again.

The past was so fugitive when one set out in search of it, as if the imperative to know what had happened were too invasive, too threatening, driving the primitive child of memory deeper and deeper into the forest as the compulsion of those attempting to unearth it drew ever closer. Only when I pulled back, or looked the other way, did he seem to feel safe enough to re-emerge from the surrounding darkness.

I gave up on sleep, fumbling for the switch beside me to turn on the bedside light, and found myself staring directly at the desk against the wall on my right. It wasn't a desk at all really, just a heavy old olive wood table with a single drawer which my cousin William had used as his desk. It was there that I'd finally sat down that night, so many years ago, in a muck sweat of heat and fear, to write my account of what had happened, so that when Alastair came to kill me there'd at least be some sort of explanation left behind – for Beryl if for no one else.

God only knew what I'd done with the manuscript, that record of events which I'd sweated over – so melodramatically in retrospect. And yet at the time—

I'd first remembered its existence as I lay in the night-dark ward at Bart's after my first biopsy, my brain still swimming with anaesthetics and wild visionary fancies as I issued a call to arms to my every instinct to outwit the spectre of the Person from Porlock as he'd banged on the door of my life to cut it short. Only if I failed to repay him the debt of my wasted years could I hope to get rid of him, and only by finding the manuscript and the evidence it contained could I unearth the full truth of it. But having willed myself to forget for so long, the harder I struggled to remember what I'd done with it, the deeper it seemed to bury itself, until its contents and whereabouts had simply vanished from memory. Once I'd convinced myself that it held the key to my continued existence, though, I'd searched my house from attic to cellars on my return from Bart's – but never found it.

It wasn't that I'd forgotten the outcome – that was common knowledge to everyone involved – but that I'd forgotten the mechanics of it, the chronology, the vital thread of events which had led me into the deepest part of that labyrinthine story to confront, not the familiar Daedalus, as I'd expected, but the terrifying chimera, half beast, half man, who had gored me to the point of death that night.

Without the help of my younger self I couldn't reach back, couldn't finish – it was as simple as that; and if I couldn't finish, there was no point in going on. I was already lost—

Almost in panic, I threw back the sheet, got out of bed, and sat down again at the schoolboy chair in front of the desk, the same chair that I'd sat on thirty years before. Nothing changed at Canellun unless it was either borrowed or broken. Or dead.

I turned away from thinking about Robert's death; I needed to think beyond it, back to the days when it had been unthinkable, to when Beryl had been all that stood between me and annihilation.

Even now, the thought of returning to that bitter end was almost unbearable – to have to relive the horror, not as the adult I'd become, but as the callow youth that I'd been then, alone, completely out of my depth—

I stared down at the desk, straining to return to that night, back into the mind of my younger self as he in turn had tried so desperately to put everything in the right order, fighting against the temptation to exaggerate as he imagined himself to be Jonathan Harker—

That was it! How typical of me – how childish – the vampire slayer, feverishly writing down his account of Dracula as he waited for his inevitable death, then hiding his diary in the hope that whoever came after him would find it and follow his instructions to the letter. And yet I'd somehow managed to stick to facts, and only facts, writing far into the night, page after page... hadn't I—?

And then what? Re-reading it, perhaps? Being ashamed of what I'd written?

Why did I keep thinking that—?

Perhaps something within me had gone wrong... perhaps I'd questioned the point of what I was doing – and of what I'd done – realising that whoever killed me had a perfect right to do so, that to take revenge on them from beyond the grave was cowardly. Better to leave things as they were, take one's medicine—

—so as the dawn had broken outside my window like a gently-fried egg (to my exhausted imagination), spreading and spreading across the fading night sky, the yolk of sun congealing in the hot fat of yet another morning sputtering with birdsong, I had sealed the envelope, got out of the chair—

Yes! Oh Christ, yes—!

I rose quickly out of the chair, lifted the chair onto the table, climbed onto the table, then onto the chair and opened the door of the 'secret' passage in the wall that had once linked this room with Juan's.

Heart racing, I hauled myself up into the opening, fumbling instinctively for the light switch, finding it, turning it on, the bulb still working after all these years, fly blown and dusty like everything else there as I crouched along the passage on tiptoe so as not to wake Beryl, sleeping in Juan's room now. The passage was airless, stifling as I crept past old trunks and piles of boxes – band boxes, hat boxes, shoe boxes – all neatly stacked under their coating of dust, to where an opening on the left led up some steps into the vast roof space of the house, where—

There—!

Still there.

On the second step, half hidden by a fallen bird's nest, the envelope, so covered with dust and plaster that it was almost invisible. Snatching it wildly, I shook off the dust and bird shit of years before wiping at it frantically with my fingers so I could read what I'd written: 'To Whom It May Concern. To be opened only in the event of my death'. Clutching it to me, I hurried back down the tunnel and through the opening into my room, almost knocking the chair off the table as I groped for it with my dangling feet.

Moments later I was sitting at the desk again, staring at the envelope in my shaking hand.

What had I been thinking of – to have virtually buried it so that it might never be found? If I'd wanted it to be found, why hide it? If I'd been ashamed of it, why keep it at all? Was it too far-fetched to imagine that I'd left it there for myself in years to come? And yet that was how it felt, holding it in my hand again, the very essence of what I'd been, of everything I'd felt, half buried in the future in the hope that one day I'd stumble across it, and know—

I tore open the envelope, carefully unfolded the stiff, brittle manuscript, lay it on the table, in its original footprint, in the place where I'd written it so long ago, and began to read...

Like most people, I'd done things in my life which I truly regretted, things which I longed with all my heart to take back, to unsay, undo, to move back the hands of time if only for a moment so that I could withdraw words or actions which would be a cause of shame for the rest of my life.

No wonder I'd hidden the bloody thing! And thank Christ no one else had found it!

I should have been warned at once, from the first moment, by the fact that it wasn't even in my usual illegible handwriting but in the phoney copperplate that I'd adopted for exams at school, or for bread-and-butter letters – or for what I'd imagined had been Jonathan Harker's handwriting.

As I forced myself to read through the twelve closely-written pages, I realised that the document was a travesty of what had happened, expressing thoughts which weren't even my thoughts but thoughts I'd acquired, through fear – not even my own feelings, since my feelings had been ruthlessly self-censored, damning myself, damning Margot, damning Alastair. Even from this distance I could remember the fear I'd felt, the cowardice, even, and that in hiding it at the last moment I *had* been ashamed of it.

The feeling of being so let down, particularly by someone who had once been me, at the very moment I most needed him, was awful – so awful that I felt like giving up altogether. The words had been mine, after all, regardless of the pressure I'd been under at the time, their only usefulness the factual eyewitness account of what had happened, and yet even as I read the lies and half truths, the truth itself came flooding back, everything falling into its proper place at last in a sleight-of-hand that left me dazed and sweating with remembered fear.

Later – much later (perhaps out of sheer desperation to breathe life back into the vision I'd had at Bart's) – I felt a sudden crushing need to race to the rescue of my younger self, a prisoner of his own words expressed in panic deep within a maze of Robert's making, of terror and recrimination that had overwhelmed him at the time, to such a point that he'd let go the thread that had brought him here and run for his life through the pitch darkness – where he still remained in spirit, trapped, alone, unable to move for shame and fear.

However fantastical the idea, I became convinced that the manuscript had been his final cry for help, that all the help he'd given me had had but a single purpose: to draw me back into the past and find him, to untell the lies and half truths and finally set him free.

Now that I had everything I needed at last – a clear recollection of how the story ended – and someone besides my present self to fight for, I was ready to go back, unfettered by dread, and bring him out.

PART FOUR

—TO EXODUS

[1961]

THE RETURN

The night ferry berthed, as usual, at eight o'clock in the morning. Staring out at Palma from the upper deck, I'd never seen it look more serene, more freshly-minted, gleaming in the early morning sun.

A single car drove slowly along the *Paseo Maritimo*, the only visible sign of life, side windows blazing with reflected sunlight. The ship dropped anchor with a roar that reverberated round the port, as reliable as any alarm clock, and sure enough the cafés along the front began to raise their shutters, open their doors, bring out their aluminium chairs and tables, flashing their bright, welcoming semaphores at the passengers. Palma was a city after my own heart, slow to fall asleep, slow to wake up. Along the causeway that joined us to the *Paseo*, the engines of a fleet of taxis began to cough and wheeze into life one after the other and start their slow crawl towards the ship's gangplanks.

The sheer joy of being free of Madrid at last! To be back—

It was nearly an hour before Margot's trunk was brought up from the hold and strapped to the roof of a taxi which sped me through the almost deserted streets towards the road to Valldemosa, the driver friendly for once, my Spanish now fluent enough to discuss anything – the island, the weather – still no rain!

As we turned onto the coast road at last, beyond Valldemosa, I felt the sudden imminence of Margot, and at the same time a sudden dread of what might be lying in wait for us all. I'd telegraphed ahead to Beryl the night before, in the hope that it might in some way help to defuse things until I got there.

Looking sharply to left and right as we entered Deyá, eyes peeled for Margot, just in case, but the village still half asleep, still mostly in shadow; just Madame Coll outside her corner shop, massive in sleeveless black, putting out her display of yesterday's vegetables with bruising violence—

Jumping out of the taxi and into blazing sunlight at Canellun, opening the gates, the dogs racing down the drive barking frenziedly as they chased the wheels of the taxi towards the house, Beryl emerging through the fly curtain over the kitchen door with a huge smile, one arm holding the other behind her as she waited for me – '*There* you are!' she cried as I hurried towards her, her specs glinting the same semaphore of welcome that I'd seen in Palma. 'I thought you'd missed the dratted *boat*!'

'I had to wait till they got Margot's trunk out of the hold,' I explained, kissing her on both cheeks, almost overwhelmed by happiness at seeing her again (and relief that nothing catastrophic seemed to have happened yet). Once I'd paid the driver and helped him unload the trunk, I followed her into the house.

It might as well have been the same sheep's head she went back to chopping up on the kitchen table, the dogs whining with hunger, the cats smarming against her legs, tails erect, twitching—

'Has Margot arrived yet?' I asked at once.

'*Yes* – thank *goodness*! She arrived last night, rather late, so there wasn't time to talk much. It was fine at first, but then Robert took her off into his study and they *quarrelled*—' she sighed exhaustedly '—so she went back to the Posada. She was meant to come back this morning, to swim with him at Ca'n Floquet, but she didn't turn up. Then he waited for you, but you didn't turn up either, so he went off on his own. You've only just missed him.'

'How is he?' I asked.

'How do you *expect*,' she said tetchily, 'not hearing from Margot for so long? He's been living on his nerves. His stomach's playing him up again, he's on edge all the time, fighting with the new mayor about water – almost everything's *dead*.' She looked round at me with an expression I couldn't quite fathom – accusingly? 'Couldn't you have got her to write to him *somehow* – send him her address?'

The look on her face and the chiding tone of her voice were unbearable. 'Beryl, I tried to get her to write, honestly, but I could hardly *force* her. Robert wrote to her so often that I think she felt smothered. I couldn't send him her address because she didn't even want *me* to know it – until the end, when it was too late. All I could do was tell him that she was fine, that she loved him—'

'*Yes...*' she said, dispiritedly. 'He was grateful for that at least. We both were. He missed you too, you know – your walks together. He's only had Alan and Ruth since you left, and they're long gone. Thank heaven you're *back*.' She looked up from the sheep's head, an unrecognisable shambles of meat and bone now, with two weird eyes, unsliced, staring out of it mutantly, one at me, purblind, the other staring back into the mess of its fate. 'Why couldn't she have just *written* to him?' she murmured, looking back at the mishmash of meat and bone on the table. 'Why couldn't *Alastair* have persuaded her?'

'I don't know...' I answered faintly. 'You know what she's like...'

'Well, I *thought* I did! But I'm not so sure any more... she seems so distracted – not herself at all... I could hardly get anything out of her last night, and nor could Robert.'

'Perhaps she was just tired.'

'Perhaps.' She looked at me intently, frowning, as if trying to see inside my head. 'Do you think something *happened* in Madrid?'

My heart tripped over itself in its rush for innocence. 'What do you mean?' I asked tautly.

'Well, *I* don't know, I wasn't there! I'm not *psychic*—'

'No, of course not,' I said quickly, meaning that of course she wasn't psychic – but she seemed to take it as the answer to her question and looked away again, shrugging helplessly. 'It's all still such a *mess*! She was meant to go away for a break, but it doesn't seem to have done her much *good*—'

Although I'd realised that I'd have to face Beryl's questions in the end, I hadn't expected them to come so soon, or to be so sharp. As yet I hadn't had to tell a deliberate lie, but increasingly I dreaded the moment when I might. I needed to distract her somehow, to get out of the house *now*—

It took me a moment to realise that something about Canellun was different – and another moment to realise what was wrong. 'Where are the others?' I asked.

The distraction seemed to be a relief for her, too, because she shook her head, grinning. 'They're back at school, of course – Lucia at Oxford, Juan in Switzerland, and Tomás in Palma with the Seymour-Smiths—'

The distraction seemed to clear my mind: 'Look, I tell you what!' I exclaimed in a sudden flash of inspiration. 'Why don't I take Margot's trunk to her now, in the Land Rover. Perhaps she's just overslept. Then we could both drive to Lluch Alcari and find Robert.'

Beryl stared up at me, eyes wide with deliverance. '*Wonderful!*' she breathed. 'Margot doesn't even know you're here yet – your telegram didn't arrive till first thing this morning. And Robert would be so *pleased*.' She glanced at the clock above the fridge. 'You've plenty of time.' She looked down at the slavering poodles and ruffled their faces briefly. 'I mean, we don't want any *scenes*, do we?' she asked them. '*No!* We don't want any *complications*! *Eh?*'

A stranger walking into the kitchen at that moment might have mistaken her for just another dotty middle-aged expat who talked to her animals and probably shared their food, but I knew her well enough to know that this was Beryl at her happiest, when some nagging worry had been miraculously lifted off her shoulders so that she could get on with her life without it being complicated by the chaos of Robert's.

'Right!' she said excitedly. 'If you take your bags upstairs and get out of those awful city clothes, I'll find some rope for the roof-rack. You're in your old room—'

Free at last, and at one with the Land Rover again, I sped back along the coast road, Margot's trunk lashed to the roof like a triumphal offering, revelling in the thought that I was still guiltless, simply doing as I'd been bidden in perfect faith, roaring up the narrow bends towards the church in a single inhalation of breath, past the *Estanco*, the noise of the engine shattering the peace between the buildings, a vandal's symphony, driving me on and on up the hairpin bends like a Valkyrie on 'uppers', as high as I could go until finally I slewed the Land Rover side-on to the wide donkey steps that led up to the Posada and the church, bathed in sunlight, dragging on the handbrake, switching off the engine—

The sudden silence was more disquieting than the racket of my arrival, so crushing with its own suspense that I threw myself out of the cab as noisily as possible, slamming the door behind me before slumping against it, the comforting mechanical sounds of the Land Rover settling against my back as it cooled down—

I was in *now* again – reality – my heart thundering to make up for missed beats, for time gained, or whatever it was that I'd left in my wake as I'd roared up the hill. Turning round, I stared up the row of ancient stone houses, the Posada blank-faced, its heavy doors and shutters closed—

Gone? The house a magnet of misgivings suddenly, drawing me almost against my will up the shallow donkey steps, my hand trailing uncertainly along the top of the low wall on my right.

Standing opposite the Posada at last, staring up at its inscrutable façade, some inexplicable reluctance holding me back before I pulled myself together and strode across the cobbles, raising the heavy iron knocker, banging it down three times. Not, as Robert might have done, imperiously, alarming her, but (in measured Morse code); three quick dots for 'S'—

The hollow echo seemed endless, the imagined gloom and stillness within—

'*Margot?*' I called out, my voice sounding freakish to me.

Nothing. The windows on the first floor, I knew, gave onto a passage outside the bedrooms and bathroom, and her bedroom door would be shut – but even so...

I turned and walked back to the low stone wall. Across the valley I could see Canellun, the green canvas blinds, like wary, half closed eyelids over the dining room and kitchen windows, the shutters of my room open wide, the dark window watching me, as every window in Deya seemed to watch and wait—

All at once there was a faint, sharp cry, a crash, and the shutters above suddenly exploded outwards, screeching, slamming back against the wall—

And she was there, framed in the window against the darkness behind her, as radiant as the morning, smiling down at me a smile of such relief, such joy—

'You came!'

'Of course—' I could hardly speak for the happiness I'd brought her.

Our gazes locked, until finally she tilted her head to one side. 'Did you bring it?'

Wordlessly, I pointed back down the steps to the Land Rover – to my sudden vision of it – parked like Cinderella's pumpkin carriage at the foot of the steps, the gloss of her cabin trunk gleaming on the roof rack, invisible rats and mice (invisible to anyone but me), in the powdered periwigs and frock coats of footmen, already busy loosening the ropes that held it to the roof—

She must have seen them too, because she laughed delightedly as she leaned out to look, her hands curled under the inside of the windowsill, her inner forearms, facing me, pale and vulnerable as she looked down at me again, her eyes suddenly molten with gratitude. 'Thank you!'

Still spellbound, I could only shrug helplessly, unable to cope with what was happening in my head.

'I'll come down and let you in.'

By the time I'd carried her trunk from the Land Rover (the cords that held it strangely loose, the weight of it surprisingly lighter than when I'd heaved it up onto the roof at Canellun), Margot had unbolted and thrown open the double doors of the house and was heating up some coffee on the stove in the small kitchen, unable to join me outside for lack of trousers. As soon as my bulk blocked out the light through the front doors, though, she came running to help lower the trunk to the stone-flagged floor before flinging her arms round my neck and hugging me to her, my face buried at last in the dizzying remembered essence of her, aware yet uncaring that she was naked under the man's shirt that she wore – Alastair's? So what? She was here, in my arms, Alastair in Madrid—

'Are you all right, Si?' she asked, drawing back at last and fixing me with her luminous grey eyes, as if searching mine for signs of flight, 'Alastair cabled me – said he'd told you everything... I know I was meant to do it, and I'm sorry... Are you all right with it – with *us*? All of us?' she added, as if I were an ingredient that might make the difference between success and failure.

I nodded quickly, wordlessly, as I pulled out his letter to her from my shorts' pocket. 'He gave me this for you,' I managed to say finally.

She took the crushed envelope with a slight frown, as though what it contained had nothing to do with now. 'Come and have some coffee.'

I followed her through into the gloom of the shuttered kitchen, her silhouette pale and ghostly in the faint light from the closed shutters. 'Robert's on his way to Ca'n Floquet,' I said, the sound of my voice breaking the weird fallacy of her almost-thereness.

'Oh *God!*' She spun round, clutching her forehead. 'I was meant to swim with him this morning, and I've overslept—'

'It's all right – it's fine,' I said quickly, holding out my hands to calm her. 'It's just that Beryl thought it would be a good idea to drive down now – surprise him—' I looked at my watch. 'Even if he's walked fast he still won't have arrived yet.'

'Brilliant!' She smiled with relief. 'Let's do it! Now that you're here it'll be so much easier—' She stared at me intently. 'From now on, you're not to leave me alone with him, OK? Promise!'

'I promise.'

After downing our coffee, we went back into the hall where once again I heaved her trunk onto my shoulder and followed her to the stairs. 'You're sure you can manage, Si?' she asked anxiously. 'Just don't mark the walls or anything, OK? I want to leave the house immaculate—'

I faltered only slightly. 'You're still leaving, then?' I asked as casually as I could.

'Of course! It's just a matter of when – when to tell him—'

I looked up uneasily into the corners of the high ceiling, convinced that Robert was somehow there, listening, watching, his presence ghost-like, all-pervading...

Once outside her bedroom I lowered the trunk to the floor and we each took a handle to slide it through the door and across the tiled floor of the big, sparsely-furnished room – just a huge iron bedstead, a night table, dark wardrobe, marble-topped chest of drawers with mirror, faded pictures of Deya painted by previous occupants and left behind as tokens of gratitude.

'Under the window, Si,' she said, kicking a rug out of the way, then abandoning the handle at her end of the cabin trunk and throwing her weight next to mine, shoulder to shoulder, hip against hip as we accelerated across the floor tiles, faster and faster, laughing now, curving round at the last moment in a graceful sweep before berthing it, like a stately liner, in its waiting dock between the long shuttered windows.

Straightening up, she suddenly frowned with exasperation. 'Dammit – the key!'

She ran back across the room, calling out to me to open the shutters, her thin shirt tails floating around the tops of her thighs – Undine in the green half light of the room, her bare feet silent as they sped across the tiled floor before she vanished—

Oh, don't! I begged silently, the torment of her presence/absence both equally unbearable as I flung myself at the shutters, unlocking them, throwing them open but with my eyes still staring back into the room in the hope that by drenching it with light I might somehow break her spell, dispel this sudden, unexpected anguish of our reunion – more painful, I realised in disbelief, than being apart from her—

But this side of the house was still in shadow, the added light too diffused to change anything.

From downstairs, a sharp, echoing cry of frustration: *'Where did I put the damn things?'*

I didn't know. I was in a different time from hers, crossing in a dream to the wide bed and kneeling beside it, the top sheet thrown back, the impression of her head on the pillow, the slight weight of her naked body imprinted on the bottom sheet and the mattress beneath, stretching out my arms to embrace the spectre of her as she'd lain there before I'd woken her, my head sinking face down into the hollow of her pillow, inhaling her with all my might into the innermost darkness of my love for her—

'Found them!' From downstairs—

Suddenly aware that I was sobbing, for breath, for the will to go on – appalled at myself, dragging my head from the pillow—

Stop—! Stop now!

Coiling my body backwards in desperation, then striking like a snake in a blur of speed, smashing my head with the force of all my despair into the iron bedstead, sickeningly.

By the time she breezed back into the room I was crawling away on hand and knees, clutching the top of my head – but no longer sobbing, at least—

'What on earth are you doing?' she laughed, hurrying towards the trunk.

'I skidded,' I said faintly, 'banged my head.'

'Idiot!' She squatted down in front of the elaborate brass lock and inserted the key, her shirt tail riding up, the sleek line of muscle from the cheek of her bottom along her thigh to the side of her knee flexing as she balanced on the balls of her feet—

I looked away frantically.

'I'm just going to change, Si,' she said as she sprung the lock and stood up to raise the lid, the front of her shirt now pressed demurely between the tops of her thighs with her other hand. 'I'll be down in a sec, OK?'

'Yes, of course—' Coming to my senses at last—

Still clutching the top of my head, I crossed to the door, aware as I walked through it of a warm stickiness under my hand. Once out in the passage, I took my hand away and stared at my palm, thick with blood. Shocked, I turned back – to show it to Margot, perhaps – *look what you've made me do!* But I was already gone to her, forced to stare helplessly from my world in the passage into the world of her bedroom, a Peeping Tom, frozen to the spot as she stood against the open window with her back to me and took hold of the tails of her shirt and peeled it over her head in a moment of such shocking metamorphosis, the ambush of her sudden nudity so bewildering that I was rooted to the spot, even as my every instinct rose through the growing mist and begged me to *go – go now, before she sees you!*

I vanished like a wraith, one hand still clutching my head to prevent the blood dripping onto anything of Robert's, the other jammed over my mouth, gagging the agony of her.

Once downstairs, I raced to the huge china sink in the kitchen and flung on the cold tap that stuck out from the wall above it, holding my head under its obliterating deluge, stifling the wracking sounds I was making, the thunder of cold water numbing my head, my hands, my brain, as I willed everything to stop – *to stop now!*

Reaching above my head, I groped for the tap and turned it off, swilling away the streaks of blood from the sides of the sink, running my hands through my hair, over the bulging cut, stinging now as I looked up and suddenly chanced to catch sight of someone's face in the shard of shaving mirror that Robert must once have jammed behind the cold water pipe when he'd lived here, a face not recognisable as mine at first, nor Robert's, and yet expressing in its torment the horror of impending loss—

'*Ready, Si?*' Her carefree voice calling down to me—

THE CLASH

In complete contrast to my breakneck drive up to the Posada, Margot took the steep gradient back down the hill in second gear, hooting lightly at blind corners.

Although surprised by our measured progress, I found it a relief, giving me more time to recover the shreds of myself that I'd scraped together in panic at the sound of her voice from the landing above, mopping frantically at the cut with a rag as I'd watched her drop her espadrilles onto the stone flags before leaping barefoot from the stairs into the hall, slipping her feet into them, facing away from me towards the open front doors, clearly distracted, her mind on her meeting with Robert, I imagined, not looking back at me as I stuffed the blood-soaked rag back into my pocket.

By the time we'd roared past Canellun, I was able to speak at last without my voice betraying me. 'Beryl said it was all a bit grim last night—'

She frowned. 'Actually, it was OK at first – fine, in fact – the Prodigal returns, the fatted calf – fatted sheep, at least – Robert quite his old self, laughing, talking rubbish – you know what he's like when things go his way. But then he swept me off to his study...' she sighed heavily, 'and nothing had changed at all. If anything, it was worse – why hadn't I written to him, sent him my address? Had I any idea how hurtful it was to be ignored, to be unable to think or write, to be filled with despair day after day...' She darted a quick smile at me. 'He said that if it hadn't been for you, he wouldn't have known if I was dead or alive! But even you didn't know my address, apparently—' She took her foot off the accelerator and turned to me. 'I was wrong to say what I said to you that night. You're a *true* friend.'

I looked away quickly, out of my side window, words forming uselessly, unsayably: *Have you forgotten what else I said to you that night—?*

As if sensing my slide into darkness she hit the accelerator with a jolt, shaking us both up in our seats. 'Then he started laying into Alastair,' she went on, 'for refusing to give him my address, for telling him to leave me alone – so now *they've* fallen out, and when Robert wrote to Mary she didn't even reply, so *they've* fallen out.' She shook her head wearily. 'And then he began to behave like some crabby old schoolmaster, demanding to see my accounts of what I'd spent in Madrid. How *dared* he, on my first night? But I'd had enough by then, and went back to the Posada.' Her voice tailed off as she stared broodingly at the road ahead. 'I didn't mean to *torture* him by not writing – I just wanted him to *wake* up! To realise that I wouldn't be there forever... I mean, for Christ's *sake!*' she exploded, thumping the wheel. 'He's not a child, he's a grown man, a *poet!* He knows the score – things come to an end! Muses burn themselves out, like stars. It's happened to him before, it'll happen again.'

Alastair's words—

'But you're *different!*' I blurted out. 'Surely you can see that? You're not like the others – the implacable Laura, the chaotic Judith, and God knows who else... except for your accents, of course—'

'What do you mean?' she asked irritably. 'I'm not an American—'

'No, but you *could* be... you *fit*, if you see what I mean? You're all beautiful, all from the New World... it was just a thought,' I added quickly. 'But you're not like them!' *You're not like anyone!* 'Even Beryl says so. You were a godsend – a *goddess*-send, if you like.' I forced a wry smile. 'He was like a young poet again – passionate, inspired—'

'What – so you think I'm responsible for him?' She shot me an angry glance.

'No, of course not,' I said hurriedly – and yet I couldn't rid myself of the image of him that I'd conjured in the shard of his shaving mirror at the Posada, of the utter torment, the starvation for her that I'd seen in the face that stared back at me. 'Only for the poems… It's just that he must be so desperate, that's all. The thought of losing you must be killing him. I know it would kill me—'

'Well, he's going to have to get used to it,' she said grimly, ignoring my last comment as she turned off the coast road and bumped down the dusty track to Lluch Alcari before pulling up with another jolt in the middle of the tiny deserted square of stone houses and switching off the engine.

In the sudden oppressive heat and silence I stared straight ahead through the windscreen. 'Couldn't you give him one last chance?' I asked quietly.

'*No*, Si!' She turned to me sharply, frowning. 'For Christ's sake, you sound as if you're taking his side!' I opened my mouth to protest. 'Well, *don't*. That's not what I need you for! I know you're a part of Robert, but you're also a part of me! Alastair says I've paid for you to be here – oh, *shit!*' She suddenly banged her head on the wheel. '*Why did I say that?* I'm so sorry – I didn't even mean it—'

And yet she'd said it, and I could feel the pain of it draining the blood from my face. 'I'm paying you back as soon as my allowance arrives in Palma,' I said faintly. 'I told Alastair—'

But she'd already laid her hand gently on my bare arm, her eyes, when I turned to look into them, glistening. 'Forgive me. I panicked for a moment, that's all. You owe me nothing. I needed you, and you came—' She leaned towards me impulsively and kissed me. 'Forgiven?'

'Of course—' My lips roused, burning from the brief touch of hers. 'Always.' I could feel my eyes smarting as I stared back at her. 'What I said that night in Madrid, in the storm—'

Her fingertips were over my mouth before I could say another word. '*Sssh!* Not now, Si, please… things are complicated enough.'

She drew back suddenly, frowning, staring above my eyes. '*You're bleeding!*'

Once out of the Land Rover I mopped furiously at my head, cursing myself for my childish gesture of self-rage in her bedroom, stuffing the rag back in my pocket before she could see the bloody thing as I followed her across the square to the iron gate in the wall, almost hidden by ivy.

'What if he's locked it behind him?' I asked trying to sound normal.

'He never does,' she answered casually over her shoulder, 'in case he leaves the key on the jetty. And sometimes Beryl sends people down to see him. He likes company when he swims – to be admired,' she added, her voice cold. We pushed through the screeching iron gate and closed it behind us with a heavy clang. The track was as wild and beautiful as ever, the ancient stone wall on our right pocked with wild flowers and cacti, to our left the terraces falling steeply away to the sea – inscrutable today, flat calm, brooding. Margot's anxiety was infectious, and I ran to catch up with her, taking her hand to reassure her as we walked on side by side down the uneven path. 'Look!' I laughed, pointing to a discarded fig skin, and then, a few paces later, to the spat-out stone of an apricot gleaming wetly beside the path. 'It's like following the spoor of a wild animal!'

'Don't remind me!' she said irritably, pulling her hand out of mine.

'What is it?' I asked, exasperated. 'What's wrong? You're getting jumpier and jumpier—'

'You don't know what it's like, Si.' She stopped suddenly and turned on me. 'Look, somehow I have to tell him that I went to a party last night, after I left him – at Mazzini's—'

I stared at her, astonished. '*Mazzini's? Why*—?'

'*Why not?*' she demanded. 'I can do as I please.'

'Of course you can – but *Mazzini* – Christ!'

'Oh, for God's sake, he's just a man – a bit of an "asshole", as Juan would say. But after I'd left Canellun I bumped into Stella on her way up from her cottage, and she asked me to go with her to Mazzini's party, so I went... out of some stupid need for revenge, I suppose. Actually, it was all rather dull, to tell you the truth; Mazzini behaves better in his own house than he does in other people's. But you know Robert – he'll think of it as some kind of betrayal—'

'Then don't tell him!' I insisted.

'I can't *not*! If I don't, someone else will – or they'll tell Beryl, which is worse. And besides, he'll just *know*. He's spooky at the moment – second sight, third sight – he's got eyes everywhere—'

So I wasn't alone in imagining his omniscience. Her voice trailed off as we came to the clearing. In the great heat, the scent of resin from the Italian pines that shaded it was intoxicating, hemmed in beneath the canopy. We walked over the carpet of dead pine needles and fir cones in silence, as though we were crossing someone's drawing room, the circle of stone benches round the mill-wheel table adding to the illusion; I could almost imagine the ghosts of Archducal picnickers watching us from a century before and was tempted, superstitiously, to acknowledge their presence by raising my hat.

At the far edge of the clearing Margot quickly turned to me. 'Don't say anything from now on, OK?' she murmured. 'With the sea this calm he'll be able to hear every word.'

I found my heart beating faster with apprehension as we left the clearing and carried on down the steepening path, wondering what kind of reception I'd get from my grand-uncle. All right, I'd always written back to him from Madrid, usually by return, but I hadn't always told the truth – not the whole truth, at least—

Then suddenly he was there, below us, sitting on the jetty with his back towards us, staring out to sea, already dressed, his black swimming shorts beside him turned inside-out to dry, like a dead octopus, the horrible white mesh lining exposed to the sun, his towel laid out next to them.

'*I've been expecting you!*' he shouted suddenly from under his hat, without even turning round or looking up. '*Come on down!*'

Margot and I looked at each other in disbelief. '*Jesus!*' I gasped.

'I warned you,' she muttered under her breath.

He was waiting to greet us at the bottom, his arms stretched up to help Margot, his smile like a ripe fig, bursting with pleasure. 'How nice!' he cried, 'I knew you'd come!'

Margot ignored his offer of help, leaping past him from the rocks onto the concrete jetty, before relenting, turning back to kiss his unshaven cheeks while I scrambled down the rocks and waited my turn—

'Welcome back, grand-nephew!' he exclaimed as he turned to me at last, gripping me by the shoulders and planting two rough kisses on my cheeks. 'Thank you for your letters.' He turned to Margot and poked her playfully in the chest. 'Not for yours, though!' She jerked away from him irritably. 'No, I'm sorry – I didn't mean to bring it up again,' he said hurriedly. 'Do you want to bathe? I've had mine, but I don't mind waiting—'

'I'd love one,' I said at once, trying to cover for Margot. 'What's it like?'

'Perfect, I suppose,' he said glumly, looking up at the sky with a grimace as we walked down the jetty, 'if you like a calm sea, which I don't, and no wind, which I don't, and the blasted sun and the blasted drought, which I don't and don't! Did you see the garden at Canellun? It's like Mother Hubbard's cupboard! Poor Beryl, she's just about had enough.'

Margot and I went down to the edge of the jetty and began to undress, politely turning away from each other as we did so. Robert's presence, fully dressed, was oddly unsettling as he got up and began pacing restlessly across the jetty behind us, clearing his throat, darting looks at us—

'You know, it's all very queer,' he said abstractedly. 'I woke up this morning with terrible stomach cramps after last night, and yet the moment I unlocked the gate here, they vanished!'

Margot said nothing. I smiled back at him, trying to fill the chasm between them. 'Well, there you are – you must have known more than you knew, if you see what I mean—' I glanced at Margot, only to be caught off-balance yet again by the sight of her wearing the black bikini she'd worn in Madrid. Effortlessly, she reached down for her discarded jeans and pulled her dark red ribbon from one of the pockets before straightening up, running her hands through her wild black hair, back arching, elbows reaching upwards as she deftly tied her hair behind her head—

I risked a quick glance at Robert. His face, as he stared at her, was set into a mask, half tragic, half mad, eyes burning, teeth gritted, with a frown of such intensity that I knew he was willing himself on her with all his powers.

Completely unaware of the effect she was having, Margot came towards me with a smile that excluded him utterly, and together we went the edge of the jetty and looked down into the translucent blue-green sea, our toes curling over the edge of the jetty, ready to dive off.

'I thought you never wore a bikini in Deya,' I murmured.

'That's at the *cala*,' she said quietly. 'It's fine here.'

'*I say, do you know, it's quite uncanny!*' Robert called out to us from the top of the jetty, 'from behind, you could be mistaken for twins—'

From his viewpoint, I supposed we could – roughly the same height and build, the same coloured hair, both naked except for scraps of black cloth. His words were strangely thrilling, my arousal so swift that I only had time to gasp '*Go—!*' before I dived in, as fast and as far as I could, to hide it.

As I sank to the depths, I felt the shock of her entry and watched as she streaked past, grinning round at me as she headed towards the outcrops of rock that formed the lagoon. With a violent kick I shot to the surface, slicking back my hair over the stinging reminder of my cut. The sea would heal it—

Robert had come to the edge of the jetty to watch us, agitatedly clearing his sinuses, staring down at the surface of the sea. 'Where is she?' he demanded anxiously.

'I don't know—' I was the point of turning round to look for her when I felt a blow in the middle of my back – 'Christ!' – and felt her fingers under the waistband of my swimming trunks, at the back. With a yell, I tore myself from her grip and circled her, ready to pay her back.

Glancing at Robert, I saw him watching our horseplay, a growing frown on his face, almost of disapproval. I wondered, fleetingly, if he were jealous of our antics.

'Why not come in again?' I called up to him. 'It's wonderful!'

He shook his head irritably and glanced away. 'No – Margot, come closer!' he called out to her suddenly. 'I want to talk to you—'

Although taken aback for a moment, Margot did as he asked, reaching the jetty in a couple of crawl strokes, then treading water below him.

'I waited for you this morning, you know – for our bathe.' He looked at her sternly. 'As we agreed. I waited nearly an hour...'

'I'm sorry,' she squinted up at him, 'I overslept. Simon woke me.'

His face cleared at once 'Did you really? Oh well, that's all right, then! I couldn't sleep either – I lay awake most of the night, trying to find you. I'm so glad you're back!' He forced a smile. 'Part of you, at least... perhaps the rest of you will follow by another post!' His laughter was equally forced. 'Or perhaps you left it in Madrid, and Simon's brought it back with him.'

'He brought my trunk,' she said flatly.

Robert's face lit up. 'Oh, of course – I'd forgotten. Well, it's an important part of you.'

'But not all. Maybe there's something still missing.'

'Nonsense!' he exclaimed, his face clouding over again. 'I'd know at once if there were. Look, have you had enough? I want to go up—'

'But we've only just got in!' She sighed with exasperation. The current had pulled her away slightly, but with a single stroke she returned to the jetty.

Robert reached down to her. 'Here – take my hand—'

'I can manage,' she insisted, but Robert's hand was still outstretched, his face grimly determined. I saw her head sag for a moment before she finally reached up. 'Mind the sea urchins!' he grunted, and with his great strength coupled with her innate grace, he fished her bodily out of the water and let her down gently in front of him, gleaming like a mermaid. 'There!' he laughed triumphantly. 'I can still do it, you see, even at sixty-four!'

'I went to a party last night,' I heard her say suddenly, coldly, 'at Nathan Mazzini's.'

Oh, great! I groaned to myself – no Marquis of Queensberry rules here: just kick him in the crutch while he's pulling you out of the sea!

Robert looked stunned at her outburst. '*What*? No—!' His look turned to bewilderment as he shook his head, as if to clear it. 'Why?'

'To spite you, of course!' Her second jab seemed to glance off him as he stared at her.

'No! Don't be silly—'

'Could you get me my towel, please?' Her voice emotionless. 'It's in my basket.'

As Robert obediently turned away, I grabbed at the rocks under the jetty and began to heave myself up. Above me, Margot squatted on her haunches and reached down. 'Mind the sea urchins,' she mimicked Robert, grinning, her eyes glinting dangerously.

Robert came back with her towel, his gaze fixed on her implacably as she helped me up onto the jetty. 'No, you're teasing me!' he exclaimed. 'Mazzini's no good, you know that—'

'I said I went to his party,' she interrupted him. 'I didn't say I enjoyed it.'

'Oh, *well!*' Robert's face cleared again, as if by magic. 'That's different! Although I still wish you hadn't—' He rummaged in his shoulder basket and pulled out a fig, splitting it open with his thumbs. 'Here – share my fig.' He held one half up to her mouth.

Margot shook her head impatiently as she turned away to dry herself. 'Not hungry – thanks.'

Robert masked his rejection by pulling a face at me and offering the fig instead. I took it with what I hoped was an affectionate smile – I liked figs – loved Robert – hated to see him hurt—

Once we'd dressed and gathered up our things, we left the jetty without another word, Robert leading, taking the almost vertical path like a goat, calves straining, then Margot, with me bringing up the rear, conscious of the growing heat as we left the sea below us, conscious, too, of Margot's wet bikini bottom emerging like once-invisible ink through the seat of her jeans.

The continuing silence of our progress, apart from our slightly laboured breathing and Robert's constant sniffs and grunts, began to tighten the screw of suspense between them. It was so unlike him not to chatter away as we climbed that it finally dawned on me that perhaps he was working himself up into a rage. Whatever the reason, the tension continued to mount, Robert's weather seeming to cast a cloud over us all.

By the time we reached the shade of the clearing he was some ten yards ahead of us. I was on the point of saying something to her when he suddenly skidded to a halt on the pine needles and turned on her, his face set like stone. 'No, the thing is, you either belong to me or to them – to the Nathan Mazzinis of this world. You can't have it both ways.' His glance fixed on me alarmingly. 'That goes for you, too, Simon. I've spoken to you about it before.'

'Simon wasn't even there!' broke in Margot angrily.

'No, I know—'

'Robert, for Christ's sake!' she interrupted him again. 'It's all so simple for you – you see everything as black or white, light or dark, good or evil! Well I don't! For a start, things aren't always as they seem – there are shades of black and shades of white – and I don't mean fucking *grey* – and I have a right to see them as I see them. Mazzini's *nothing*. He's a bore and a bully—'

'No, he's more than that,' Robert cut in. 'He's a part of the cancer of Deyá – a big part, because he feeds the cancer with his filthy drugs and crooked deals – he's anathema!'

'But he *isn't*!' Margot insisted fiercely. 'He's just a creep! All right, so some people here take drugs – *you've* taken drugs—'

'Not like them!' he cried defensively. '—And only ever for pure reasons – poetic reasons – to explore myths, to open myself to the Muse. Not for self-gratification or oblivion, or whatever it is those bastards are searching for!'

'But they're not bastards, Robert, not all of them – not Gill or Mati or Phil Shepherd or George Sheridan, or the Grunfelds – and it isn't as if they force themselves on you, they just live here, with as much right as you – just as I have as much right to see them as you have to see the Sillitoes or the Shahs!'

'*Not when you live under my roof, you don't!*' he roared. '*Your loyalty is to me!*'

The shockwave of his words, of his almost biblical wrath, hit us both simultaneously. Glancing at Margot, I saw the colour drain from her face, as I felt it draining from mine. Without a word she stalked over to the mill-wheel table, chucking her basket onto it before slumping down on the nearest stone bench, hands thrust deep into the pockets of her jeans, legs splayed, glaring back at him with a strangely mixed expression of fright and reflected fury.

It sobered him at once. Although still angry, he looked away, eyes wild and staring, as if searching for less harmful words. 'No, I'm sorry,' he said at last as he began to pace restlessly up and down, still keeping his distance from us. 'I didn't mean to bellow... but what you're saying is not the point – or rather, it's only half the point. The other half is that you're not doing this of your own free will – you're being driven to it – by Her – to spite me – or to test me, perhaps. I know the signs. Well, I've been tested before, and I've always come through...' He stopped for a moment to stare up at the distant sunlit mountains, as though for inspiration. 'No, the only people who benefit from your behaviour are the enemy – the dregs and drug pushers. Your presence among them gives them clout – you must see that – and it's the last thing you'd want. Of course I see things as either good or evil – I was brought up to tell the difference, to embrace one and abominate the other. Ultimately, it's my one protection—'

'And mine?' she demanded, goading him.

'*I protect you!*' he shouted. 'That's my duty, as you know – the point of everything I do! I take both the mortal and the moral high ground because I defend us both – to the death! *You*—!' He suddenly turned and stabbed his finger at me, '—are family! And *you*—!' He pointed at Margot almost malevolently, 'are my muse! You're both a part of me, irrevocably. There can be no flag of convenience, no go-betweening, no compromise! Your loyalty is to me – as mine is to you – to the death!'

'Unquestioning loyalty?' demanded Margot angrily.

'No, not unquestioning,' he said, deflated suddenly, as though drained by the conversation, by her aggression, for which I knew the reason and he didn't. 'But you've questioned me before, and I've always been right, and you've agreed. By consorting with these people you're reneging on that agreement.'

She seemed to take strength from his sudden weakness. 'You mean I'm beating my wings against your bars! You're *stifling* me,

Robert!' I longed to be close enough to touch her, to somehow earth her to the ground of reason, to stop her hurting him for hurt's sake—

'No!' he contradicted her angrily. 'I surround you with my protection! You're wasting yourself, weakening your powers – your magical powers, given to you by the Goddess – as are mine, providing we're together, in every sense of the word! My only constraints on you are my warnings, my attempts to safeguard those powers—'

'To feed your poems!'

He shook his head, as if dazed, seemingly bewildered by her relentless attack on him. 'If you were to prevent me from writing poems, then you'd only spite yourself. You'd be as much the loser as I – more – because you'd become worthless! We both know our duty to each other. So long as we're together, we're the most powerful embodiment of poet and muse on earth! I fulfil my duty to you to the letter. If you fail to do the same, you'll pay the terrible—'

'Robert!' Her sharp cry stopped him in his tracks as he turned to her. She glanced at me, then back at him, frowning, her eyes full of unspoken meaning.

Robert stared at me dazedly for a moment, still steeped in the anger of his last remark. Then he seemed to catch on. 'No – no, I know—' he sighed, shaking his head. 'No, Simon's "all right"... he understands. Not everything, perhaps, but enough... I've talked to him... he's part of all this...' He was muttering now, almost to himself, not looking at us, but into a world of his own, his fingers pressed to the centre of his forehead, as though to a third eye. It was profoundly unsettling, because his eyes, still staring at me, seemed blind to my presence. 'Look, I'm going to go on ahead,' he said suddenly, decisively.

'But we've brought the Land Rover,' Margot protested. 'Beryl asked us to.'

'No. I'd rather walk up alone,' he insisted. 'Something's badly wrong... I have a sixth sense about these things. I need to think...' Her glanced up at the sky, beyond the canopy of trees. 'Perhaps it's the weather,' he joked feebly to himself. 'The papers talk of storms heading this way... I wish that's all it were...'

Nodding to us sternly, he walked away, pressing his fingers brutally to his cheek bones.

A hot blast of wind blew among the treetops, separating them for a moment to allow a shaft of sunlight to enter the no-man's-land between Robert and us, as if drawing a line between us. Not daring to cross it, I walked over to the stone bench next to Margot's and sank down on it.

She ignored me, her eyes haunted, her face drawn. 'He knows,' she murmured finally. 'He doesn't know what he knows... but he knows...'

A moment later we almost jumped out of our skins as a fir cone, as hard and dense as iron, ricocheted off the mill-wheel and whizzed viciously through the air between us. Robert stood on the path beyond the clearing, glaring at us balefully. '*It's a matter of honour!*' he shouted. 'In its true sense! Not just to me, but to yourself!'

MARES' TAILS

Early the following morning, as we'd arranged, I turned up at the Posada with the Land Rover. The last thing she wanted, she'd told me, was to come to Canellun where she'd inevitably be forced to face Robert again.

Not only was the morning as hot as ever, but the sudden breeze up here felt like the opening of an oven door, stifling, enervating. And yet somehow I had to re-energise myself, use my imagination cleverly enough to rescue them both. My conversation with Beryl the day before had finally convinced me of the urgency of the situation, but the *sirocco*, or whatever they called this wind in Majorca, seemed to have filled my head with nothing but doubt and uncertainty, made worse as I found that once again the doors of the Posada were locked, the shutters closed, the house, this time, hollow for lack of her. No amount of banging on the door or calling up to the windows could conjure her. She (and her word to me), were gone.

I searched the door and the steps in case she'd left a note which had been blown away, but found nothing. As I looked around for the last time, I felt a kind of sickness, not only for the void she'd left within me, but for the dread of exclusion from her.

She didn't need me any more. It was as simple as that.

In the end I returned to the Land Rover and drove off, choosing the narrow back road down to the village, my mind haunted by doubt and self-doubt as I replayed the scene in the clearing to myself – not just Robert's part in it, but afterwards, when he'd gone—

535

Once we were alone, Margot had insisted that we wait long enough for Robert to get back to Canellun before following him. The shock of their quarrel had clearly affected her deeply, and nothing I tried to say to reassure her was of the slightest use, so in the end I just kept quiet as she paced round and round the clearing, frowning fiercely, in a shroud of what I could only suppose was anger, indecision, hurt – revenge, perhaps – or perhaps something quite else, beyond me.

I only knew that for the first time I felt alone in her presence.

Wary of saying anything more out loud, I tried to make myself invisible, sitting stock still, staring at the ground, my very existence seemingly pointless to both of us at that moment, her bewildering reluctance to make use of the arsenal of my feelings for her draining me of purpose, until I must have dozed off in the heat...

'Right—! Let's go!' Her voice decisive, waking me as she grabbed the handles of her basket and slung it onto her shoulder.

And off we went at last, in single file, I following her, still without a word.

Only when we reached the gate and found that Robert had locked it behind him did she finally explode into a string of curses, damning him for his arrogance, his bullying behaviour, his pettiness—

In the end I got us both over the wall with a few scratches and bruises, but her temper was incandescent by now. If Robert had still been walking along the road as she raced the Land Rover back to Deya, she'd probably have run him down.

Once we'd passed Canellun, though, and climbed the hill to the Posada, most of her anger seemed to have burned off. Pulling on the handbrake at the foot of the steps, she reached for her basket, then paused for a moment to stare at me. Taking a deep breath, she let it out with a low growl, almost of self-disgust, her shoulders relaxing at last. 'I'm sorry, Si – I've been unbearable, I know.'

I stared back at her impotently. 'Do you want me to stay?'

She looked away. 'Actually, I need to be alone for a bit – if that's OK?'

'Of course,' I answered at once, minding horribly.

'What about you?' she asked, turning back to me. 'What will you do?'

I shrugged. 'The same, I suppose…'

She leaned over, embracing me at last. 'It's a pity we can't be alone together,' she drew back, smiling. 'Listen, why don't you come by tomorrow morning? Nine o'clock, say. Bring the Land Rover if you can. Maybe I'll have worked things out by then—'

When I returned to Canellun, I found Beryl collecting the last of the *algarrobas* by the garage, Joté and Ygrec, lying near her on the drive, seeming too stunned by the heat even to bark, merely raising their heads at my arrival, as if I'd finally become a member of the family and could be politely ignored.

'I don't think much of your efforts to cheer Robert up!' Beryl greeted me bluntly 'He was in a *dreadful* state when he got home.'

Taken aback by her sharp and unexpected reproof, I was speechless for a moment. I'd had enough criticism for one day. 'Beryl, I tried!' I insisted. 'Truly. But it was as if I wasn't even there most of the time. Where is he, by the way? Perhaps I should apologise—'

'No, not yet – he's upstairs, lying down.' Her voice and attitude still unrelenting. 'It's not like him at *all*.'

'Here, let me—' I gently took the squat basket from her and started filling it, wary of her mood, trying to imagine what Robert might have said to her when he got back from the clearing. My only chance lay in telling her the truth of what had happened. 'Look, it was like being caught between two planets about to collide. As far as they were concerned I might as well have been invisible. There was simply nothing I could do! I mean, all right, he was angry with me at one point, but I think he was simply using me to be angry with Margot – I don't know – as buffer between them, a sort of human sacrifice in a way... but Margot was angry too, that was the trouble, and they just...' I shrugged impotently, '*collided*. I know I should have done more, but they wouldn't have listened to me. They were too far gone—'

'All the same... ' She stared at me, still frowning. 'From what Robert said, you need to be very certain whose side you're on.'

Her words shocked me. 'But I am!' I protested fervently, 'I love them both – I'm on both their sides – and yours. The last thing in the world I want is for the whole thing to blow up—!'

After staring at me for a moment, she seemed to accept my word, nodding briefly before slumping down on the low wall with a heavy sigh. 'For heaven's sake, what *are* we going to do?' she asked, suddenly herself again. 'Margot won't tell us what's wrong, Robert feels ill and can't talk about anything except his forebodings – and they're always *right*! What *is* the matter with everyone? When Margot came back to Deya I thought they'd finally made it up, but things have got *worse*, not better.' She stared round at me, her eyes magnified, huge and helpless behind her spectacles.

Equally helpless, I shrugged again, wary of where the conversation was heading. *I could not lie to her!* 'It's up to them, I suppose,' I mumbled. 'Isn't it?' She looked unconvinced. 'It's just that everything about their importance to each other seems so complicated, so wrapped up in history and myth and magic, in things I can't even begin to understand—'

'If you ask me, it's not half as complicated as they both think,' said Beryl matter-of-factly. 'Robert wants too much, and Margot wants less and less – for whatever reason. I've warned him, goodness knows, but he's incapable of controlling his need for her – quite the opposite – the further she draws away from him, the harder he pursues her. If she could only make some move towards him, he'd back away, I know he would, but she won't give an inch. I don't understand it. She's always been so generous – as Robert has – or tried to be at least.' She pulled a face at me. 'All right, he's a poet, and poets are selfish almost by definition, and the greater the poet, the greedier he becomes, it seems – for inspiration. Once you take that away...' She sighed exhaustedly. 'For heavens' sake, he's nearly *sixty-five*, Simon!' she exclaimed. 'Most men are retired by his age, but his poems are still as good as they've ever been – better, some of them, which only makes everything worse. But if he goes on like this he'll burn himself out, which is the last thing any of us wants...' She shook her head defeatedly. 'It's all such a *mess!*'

'What if Margot *did* go?' I asked, instantly afraid that I'd gone too far.

She gave a weary shrug. 'It would be a *blow*, certainly – a *terrible blow!* – one I could do without, quite frankly. If only she weren't so vital to him...' She sighed. 'I don't know... perhaps if *I* were to talk to her...' She looked round at me, questioningly. 'But the trouble is, Robert doesn't want anyone to interfere in case it makes things worse. I do wish she'd pull herself together, though – make some sort of effort—' She stared unseeing into the cheerlessness of her drought-dead garden, at the panting dogs almost comatose in the heat, then back at me suddenly. 'I mean, she talks to *you*, doesn't she?'

I found myself turning away from her instinctively, searching the ground even though there were no *algarrobas* left to gather. 'Up to a point,' I admitted reluctantly, remembering how we'd just parted, 'but only up to a point. She said virtually nothing after their row—'

Beryl looked away, shaking her head, not at me but at her thoughts. 'What makes it even worse is that we're in October now,' she sighed.

'October?'

'It's the worst month for poets – for true poets, at least! October's the month of death, of human sacrifice—' She suddenly grinned at my expression. 'It doesn't matter what you or I think, it's what

Robert believes – that's the *thing.*' She looked away for a moment. 'Look, perhaps it would be best if you ate at *Jaimés* tonight. In his present mood, he's best left alone with me. Put your supper on our account.' She turned back to me with an apologetic smile. 'I'm sorry I doubted you just now. I know how much you care really. It's just that Robert sees betrayal everywhere at the moment, and I suppose it's catching.'

I stared down at the dogs, nodding gloomily, envying their uncomplicated loyalty.

Coming downstairs to breakfast the next morning, I heard Robert and Karl arguing in the study – or rather, I heard Karl arguing in his heavily-accented voice, and Robert's mostly monosyllabic replies. I thought I caught the sound of Margot's name as I crossed the hall towards the kitchen, where I found Beryl staring broodingly at the percolator as the coffee dripped through. 'Oh, *hello!*' she said, brightening up. 'Did you sleep well?'

'Fine, thanks,' I lied, 'did you?'

'On and off – it didn't help with the wind getting up.'

'And Robert?'

'Impossible. Karl's in with him at the moment, trying to talk some sense into him. Rather him than me,' she grinned.

I grimaced in sympathy. 'Do you need the Land Rover today?' I asked. 'Margot asked me to pick her up at nine, and I've no idea what she wants to do—'

'No, take it – just promise me that you'll try and talk some sense into *her.*'

So I'd set off in the Land Rover that morning trying desperately to think of ways to soften the blow to Robert if Margot stuck to her word and left him – and, selfishly, of ways to lessen my responsibility and sense of guilt. If I could only persuade Margot to compromise in some way, to return to him

– like Wendy to Peter Pan, once a year (or as often as it took to keep his poetic reason alive), then no matter how childish it might sound, it was worth a try. Perhaps if I simply floated it as an abstract idea, without mentioning Peter Pan, it might stand a chance. However I worded it, though, I'd have to be careful; if she thought for a moment that I was defending Robert, she'd simply 'vanish' again.

I put my foot down on the accelerator.

But vanish she had, without a single clue as to where she'd gone.

Jolting slowly down the uneven back road into the village, I tried to reason with myself. Perhaps she'd just gone to the bakery for *ensaimadas*, or to Las Palmeras for breakfast – or for a walk, or a swim, or for any of a thousand alternatives to my worst fears—

I drove down the village street in second gear, looking anxiously to right and left, but the street was almost deserted apart from the occasional Majorcan bustling to the bakery or to Madame Coll's. There were hardly any foreigners about—

Except for Stella—!

As I drove beneath the terrace of Las Palmeras, I saw her sitting alone at a table by the railings overlooking the road, having breakfast. At the familiar sound of the Land Rover she looked up at once, then jumped to her feet and gestured emphatically that I should join her.

Thank God! Someone my own age whom I could talk to – even though I could say nothing—

Circling round, I roared back up the street, pulling in just below her.

She was hanging over the railings now, laughing down at me, and for a brief moment I felt as though I didn't have a care in the world, enchanted yet again by her wonderful smile, her sheer vitality...

'I heard you were back!' she shouted down. 'Come and have breakfast with me!'

'Have you seen Margot this morning?' I called up, shielding my eyes from the sun.

'No, but I've only just got here. Come on up!' She turned away without waiting for a reply.

I gave in at once. The terrace was as good a vantage point as any—

'Margot said you were back in Deya – I'm so glad!' I said as soon as I'd sat down next to her with my coffee and *ensaimada*. 'What brought you?'

'Beryl – she needed someone to help her sort out Canellun before winter – at least that's our story! In fact I think she just needed company – someone to distract her from Robert—' she shook her head despairingly. 'He's been a bloody nightmare! He doesn't seem to mind having me around, though, which is why Beryl asked me, I suppose.'

'Thank God she did,' I grinned at her. 'How long are you staying?'

'I'm flying home tomorrow night, worst luck.'

'Sod it!' I couldn't hide my disappointment that she was leaving at the moment I needed her most.

'What about you? Aren't you meant to be in Madrid, at university?'

'I'm fed up with it, to tell you the truth. Imagine what it's like in this heat—'

'Not as bad as Sussex in the rain, I promise you! But there's a change coming. Have you seen the mares' tails?' I stared at her blankly. 'Not in my face, idiot – in the sky!'

I looked up, beyond the vine trellis that sheltered us from the sun. The sky was half filled with feathery clouds, like horses' tails, some of them seeming to stretch for miles. 'What do they mean?'

'They're omens – aeromancies, my father calls them. There's a violent wind coming, from the Sahara, full of sand—'

'Oh, great!' I grunted. 'Beryl needs *rain*, not bloody sand.'

A car came slowly up the street below, and I turned quickly to look down, just in case—

No...

Still looking into the street, it took a moment for Stella's words to penetrate: 'You've got it badly, haven't you?'

I jerked round. 'I'm sorry – what?'

'Margot.'

And all at once I felt the strangest rush of relief, the barriers of secrecy tumbling before her steady gaze – and more than relief – an almost perverse joy that I'd been found out by Stella, by a girl, my love acknowledged at last by someone more than an equal—

'I mean, look at you!' she was saying. 'You must have lost a stone since I last saw you. You look positively gaunt – you can't even say her name without going peculiar.'

'Yes I can!' I protested, suddenly irritated that my feelings should be so transparent. 'It's just that she's in a bit of a state, and she wanted me to be here.'

Stella outstared me. 'She's using you,' she said, in a strange, knowing monotone—

'*No* – Christ, Stella! I *offered* to come – to bring her trunk to her, stick around for a bit.'

'There must be more to it than that,' she said, her clear blue eyes piercing me through. 'Something's going on, isn't it?' I stared back at her, saying nothing. Her eyes narrowed suddenly. 'She's going to leave Robert – that's it! – and she needs your help. He listens to you... I'm right, aren't I?' I looked away, determined to reveal nothing. 'Well, that's hardly a secret!' she added scornfully. 'It's been going on for months! He's been driving everyone mad, complaining about not hearing from her. The only mystery is how Beryl has stayed sane. So unless there's something else—?'

I shook my head urgently. 'I can't say anything, so please don't ask. I promised.'

She weighed my words, perhaps wondering if I was being self-important. 'I'd do the same for you, don't you see?' I went on, determined to convince her that I wasn't. 'If *you* had a secret.'

She seemed to accept what I said, and yet she looked hurt – the last thing I'd intended—

'*Yearch!*' she burst out suddenly, disgustedly. 'I'm sick to death of secrets!'

'Me too, believe me!' I agreed grimly. 'Robert's right – they always lead to chaos.' I stared at her, trying to make amends. 'God, I envy you,' I said fervently, 'you're so alive, always happy!'

Far from pleasing her, she seemed almost to resent my words. Her expression hardened. 'It's better than moping around like a love-sick idiot,' she retorted. 'You're quite a pair, you and Robert, both pining after the same woman – sorry – *goddess*—! And look what she's done to you both! Thank God I'm not a muse, and never will be. They seem to spread nothing but misery.'

I was taken aback by her sudden anger. 'But you've always liked Margot, defended her—'

'Maybe I did,' she said petulantly, 'but now I'm not so sure. She's hurting people. Perhaps my father was right all along.'

'Stella, wait,' I reached out and touched her arm, to stop her before she went too far, 'you can't judge her – not yet. Things aren't what they seem, believe me. *Trust* me! The last thing she wants is to hurt anyone.'

She shook off my hand and leaned across the table, her eyes burning. 'Listen, Simon, perhaps there *is* something going on that I don't know about, but if you're the pig-in-the middle, between Margot and Robert, then God help you! Your life won't be worth a candle.'

Somehow we staggered through the rest of breakfast in an uneasy truce, neither of us having the stomach to squabble any more. We both knew Deya well enough to know that lethal feuds could grow from simple disagreements like ours, attracting the bored and idle spirits of the place to the sound of raised voices, drawing in the houses and olive groves and even the mountains that surrounded the village to form a claustrophobic circle, egging on protagonists to greater and greater enmity until tempers snapped, chairs were thrown back and friendships crushed between the unforgiving rocks of the unsayable and the unspeakable. Robert's history of quarrels alone was proof enough of how badly things could go wrong, and neither of us was fool enough to tempt fate.

Stella said that she'd come into Deya early so that she could catch the morning bus into Palma, where she had some last errands to run for Beryl.

'I'd drive you myself—' I began, as I walked her over to the queue at the bus stop.

'—but you have to find Margot,' she finished the sentence for me with a cynical sniff.

'I just promised, that's all,' I heard myself saying, as if from a great distance.

'You make an awful lot of promises,' she said accusingly.

'Which I keep!' I protested, damned if I'd let her get away with that. 'Or try to, at least—'

She dumped her basket on the wall, some way from the back of the queue, and looked up at me angrily. 'Honestly, Simon, you're as bad as Robert in some ways, trusting everyone, believing everything you're told.'

'What if I do? Is it so awful?'

'No,' she sighed at last, shaking her head as if tired of the argument. 'I suppose it's quite endearing in a way. And it's good to keep your promises.' She looked at me imploringly. 'Just don't expect others to keep theirs. Do you understand?' She outstared me. 'One last thing, before you go back to looking for her... if Margot's not where she said she'd be, then you won't find her, no matter how hard you try.'

What irritated me more than anything else that wasted day, more than the sirocco-like wind that grew ominously stronger and more stifling, more than our squabble at breakfast, was that she was right.

HAG-RIDDEN

That night at Canellun, as the wind thumped and buffeted the thick stone walls, Robert seemed hardly aware that he was at table, his eyes darting wildly round the room as though anticipating someone who failed to materialise, grunting and clearing his throat, on the point of addressing a ghost, it seemed, before thinking better of it – or being distracted by quite a different thought and subsiding for a moment before starting up again, grunting and clearing his throat.

His actions became almost comical, particularly when something got trapped under the top plate of his false teeth and he took it out with a grunted apology. 'Sorry – pips—' scratching the top of the denture with his nails before laying it on the table in front of him while he searched the corners of his mouth with his tongue for whatever was irritating him. Beryl and I happened to exchange glances, but while she could safely bury her head below the tabletop, shoulders quaking in silent laughter as she pretended to feed scraps to the dogs, I was left staring at the kitchen door until my eyes stung, breathing deeply, begging myself not to burst into a fit of giggles. 'Not at all,' I managed to say finally, as though it were the most natural thing in the world to take one's teeth out at table.

And yet the sight of his messy false teeth, still clogged with food, the pink plate so small compared to the size of his head, was oddly touching – not only the smallness of the unnaturally even semi-circle of teeth themselves, but his complete lack of self-consciousness in taking them out, his mouth an old man's now, a crumbling cavern, like the mouth of a tortoise.

The sight sobered me. For the first time that I could remember, he looked defenceless, and I turned away.

Perhaps it was the unrelenting sound of the wind outside, rattling the windows and thundering in the chimney that made conversation so difficult tonight, as if we were listening to unfamiliar music for the first time, a restless symphony of nature, all of us on tenterhooks for the sound of tiles being torn from the roof – or worse—

'Something's going to happen!' Robert proclaimed suddenly, out of nowhere and nothing

Beryl and I did the washing up as though destroying the evidence of a crime, quickly and methodically – for my part, the cold fatty lamb we'd eaten lying as uneasily on my stomach as the guilt on my conscience. She was putting the kettle on for coffee when a violent crash against the window almost made her drop it. 'Oh, *drat*,' she turned to me urgently. 'One of the shutters must have come loose – do you think you could go out and close it before it's blown to smithereens? I'll lock them from the inside—'

I fought my way out through the front door and the fly-curtain and into the teeth of the pitch-dark gale howling down from the mountains above, rushing me so fast round the corner of the house that I had to cling to the wildly swinging shutter to prevent myself from being blown across the terrace. Laughing out loud from sheer exhilaration, I reached for the far shutter and prized it from its catch, then found myself, bizarrely, staring into Beryl's grinning face as she opened the kitchen windows and reached out for the shutters as I flung my weight against them and she was able to lock them tight from inside.

Later, when she'd taken Robert's coffee to him in his study, we sat on either side of the alcove by the fireplace, she with her back against the wall which protected her from draughts in winter, me on the other side of the fireplace, both of us smoking companionably.

'So no sign of her, then?' she asked, continuing our snatched conversation from before supper, which Robert had interrupted with a brusque demand for something to eat.

I shook my head. 'No. I kept going back to the Posada till the last moment, but the only difference was that the message I'd jammed into the door had gone – probably blown away—'

She shrugged fatalistically. 'Well, there's nothing we can do tonight. We'll just have to wait and see what tomorrow brings.'

Later still, while she was working her way slowly through the pages of *El Diario de Mallorca*, I fell into a sort of daydream, my elbows on my knees, head in my hands, staring unseeingly into the empty fireplace as the wind roared in the chimney like an uncontrollable fire. From outside came the sound of tiles or flowerpots shattering on the terraces.

Which of them had summoned this unnatural wind? Was it my grand-uncle with his weird powers and magic charms, using it to scour the mountains and valleys for her? Or was it Margot, venting her frustration on the landscape which had imprisoned her for so long? Or had she invoked it as cover for her flight from the island, making it impossible for anyone to follow? To my mind they were both capable of supernatural feats, both unstable enough to use them to dash each other to pieces—

The lights dimmed, and Beryl looked up from her paper with a lopsided smile. 'Oh *dear*—!'

The lights dimmed again, and flickered, for longer this time. With an exaggerated sigh she put down her paper. 'I suppose we'd better light one of the candles, just in case—'

A moment later, Robert shambled into the room, a demented Prospero, his relief nib pen jammed behind his ear. 'The lights are going to go out!' he exclaimed.

'Well, they *might*,' said Beryl matter-of-factly, 'but then again, they might *not*! All the lamps are primed and you've got plenty of candles in the study—'

'I can't seem to settle to anything,' he said distractedly.

'Then it won't matter if the lights go out, will it?' she demanded, grinning down at me as she lit the candle on the mantelpiece. '*Honestly!*'

'Has anyone seen my teeth?' he asked, looking around vaguely.

She shook her head wearily. 'They're on the draining board! They'll probably taste of soap—'

'Doesn't matter,' he grunted, going into the kitchen.

'And I wish you wouldn't walk about with your pen behind your ear!' she called after him. 'Last time you did it, you stabbed yourself through the hand—'

Robert came back into the room, ramming his false teeth into his mouth. 'It was probably a bad poem!' he spluttered, trying to smile at me through his hand. 'I'm always made to pay one way or another—' His plate embedded itself comfortably against the roof of his mouth. I smiled back at him, glad that he seemed to have shaken off his supper gloom, but a moment later he was pacing the floor restlessly, peering out into the darkness through the window above the sofa while Beryl got out the oil lamps from the bottom of the dining room cupboard and began to line them up on the table.

'For heaven's *sake*, Robert!' she cried as their paths almost collided. 'If you can't think and you can't work, just go to bed! It'll all be better in the morning – at least we'll be able to *see!*'

'Yes – no, I know—' he mumbled distractedly, fidgeting with the candle on the mantelpiece now, straightening it, then staring into the flame as if hypnotised. 'She's somewhere, I know… I can feel her—'

'Of course she's *somewhere*,' gasped Beryl. 'Everyone's *somewhere!*'

We both sat down again, if only to keep out of his way as he went on pacing up and down.

'That's not what I meant—' he muttered.

A moment later there was an almighty crash as the kitchen door flew open against the sink and the raging wind howled into the dining room, rattling the pictures. Imagining that it was my fault for not closing the door properly, I was half out of my chair before I glanced up at Robert, already staring through the doorway into the kitchen as though he'd seen an apparition, eyes wild, hackles visibly rising, terrifyingly, like a cat's, his huge body seeming suddenly to expand—

The kitchen door slammed shut, violently, shaking the whole house – and he was gone, his movements concealed by the alcove wall. I leaned out urgently, in an attempt to see past it, and a second later caught the briefest spectral glimpse of Margot, hag-ridden, her face drained, eyes staring, wild dark hair flowing like storm clouds in her wake—

And then she, too, was gone.

I jumped out of my chair to see past the alcove wall. She was following Robert swiftly, without a word, across the dark hall and into his lighted study.

'It's Margot, isn't it?' asked Beryl, her eyes wide with foreboding as she stared up at me.

I sat down again, shakily. 'Yes… I don't think she saw us.'

'So he was right,' she murmured.

'Yes.' I felt sick, with the shock of her appearance, with dread—

'*Well*,' she said at last, heavily, 'we'd best leave them to it, I suppose.' And she picked up her newspaper again, as if to hide her thoughts behind it.

My thoughts were already racing down the slalom of panic, my heart thundering, expecting at any moment to hear cries of rage from the study – a shouted summons to account for my treachery – but all I could hear was the howling wind, like her co-conspirator, waiting to snatch her back from us.

Was she already confessing everything to Robert, even about Alastair, everything down to the smallest part – my part – in the affair? A small part to her, perhaps, but to Robert? He'd know at once that I'd deceived him. The least I could expect was that he'd knock me down – throw me out—

'Actually, I think I'll go to bed,' said Beryl wearily, folding her newspaper and getting to her feet. 'I can't concentrate, and there's no point staying up. How about you?'

I got to my feet. 'I'll hang on for a bit if that's all right?' I was glad she was going, that she wouldn't have to witness the fight. 'They might need something...'

'Well, if you're sure...' She reached up her face to be kissed. 'I'm very glad you're here,' she murmured, her remark wrenching at my conscience, my eyes smarting. 'So am I,' I managed to reply in a steady voice as she turned away, thankfully without looking up at me again, stooped with tiredness, her cardigan clutched to her.

'Don't forget to blow out the candles, will you?' she called back. 'If the lights go out, use the oil lamps – they can burn all night quite safely.'

I moved from the alcove, where it might look as though I were hiding from him, to my chair on the far side of the table, so that I could see the whole room and the door leading through into the hall. With the table between us, I'd at least have a chance to apologise before he came at me—

I sat there in the wretched suspense of guilt, waiting for the explosion from his study, for his thundering footsteps approaching the dining room, for the shouts of rage, the blows—

Waiting on and on, until sheer exhaustion forced me to cross my arms on the table and lay my head on them and close my eyes, just for a moment...

I was awoken violently, into near-darkness, by another crash. The lights had failed, the candle on the mantelpiece guttering wildly in the draught, not from the kitchen door this time, but from somewhere else. Hurriedly fumbling for my lighter, I lit one of the oil lamps and rammed home the glass chimney. As the light steadied and grew, there was another distant crash, this time of breaking glass—

What the hell was going on?

Taking the lamp in my left hand, I grabbed a poker from the fireplace and went through into the hall, where the wind was coming from—

'*Robert?*' Beryl calling down from the top of the stairs—

'*No, it's Simon,*' I shouted back. 'Don't come down until I know what's happening. There's broken glass—'

The doors to Robert's study were crashing open and shut as if at the will of some malevolent spirit inside. '*Margot?*' I shouted. '*Robert—?*' But no sooner had I rammed the doors open than I was almost thrown down the cellar steps opposite by the power of the wind roaring towards me out of the study. Chucking away the poker, I forced my way in – to a scene of devastation, of shrieking wind and flying manuscripts, the thin pages filling the air like phantoms, pictures and objects shattering on the tiled floor – no Margot, no Robert – the door onto the terrace wide open, allowing the maniacal wind to wreak its havoc—

Enraged by the destruction, I fought my way out onto the terrace, my lamp held high, shouting their names, my cries dashed from my mouth by the violence of the wind, the funnel of the lamp blown off and shattered, another tile crashing to the ground beside me as I warded off the debris from the olive groves above, my eyes half closed against flying sand—

'*Simon! Help me shut the door—!*' Beryl in her nightdress at the doorway, clinging to both sides, her dressing gown blown up to the ceiling behind her—

Between us, using all our strength, we finally managed to push the door shut, and lock it.

In the sudden, eerie quiet of the room, lit only by the base of my flickering lamp, we looked round in silence, and then at each other.

'Did you see them at all?' she demanded anxiously.

'No – nothing.'

She heaved a sigh, rubbing her hand back and forth across her forehead. 'What a *mess*,' she said exhaustedly. 'We'd better get some more lamps – try and clear up a bit.'

We did what we could by lamplight, sweeping up the broken glass, replacing everything that had been blown from the mantelpiece – one of the figurines broken in half, the clay pot of dried mushrooms shattered, gathering up his manuscripts and correspondence and leaving them in muddled piles on his desk to be sorted out tomorrow.

'What on earth happened, do you think?' I asked, my voice shaky from pent up emotion.

'I don't know,' she shook her head wearily, 'and to tell you the truth, I'm too tired to care.'

I offered to finish up, so that she could go to bed.

'No... we've both done enough for tonight. If you could just leave a lamp burning on the dining room table—'

'Do you think they're all right?' I asked, amazed by her coolness.

'I don't think they're *dead*, if that's what you mean.' She managed to smile faintly. '*Mad*, possibly, but not *dead*! He'll make his way back somehow... and there's nothing more we can do until he does.'

VERTIGO

I was awoken from nightmares by yet another crash – this time my bedroom door being flung open against the chest-of-drawers, and the sight of Robert bursting into the room, wild-eyed – not going for me, though, but straight to the window, throwing back the shutters—

'Sun's out – wind's gone!'

'*Christ, Robert!*' I gasped, finding myself already sitting bolt upright in bed, stark naked. 'You gave me a fright—'

'Sorry! I've been up for hours, tidying, and I need a break—' He turned to me without actually looking, like an officer and a gentlemen. 'I thought we'd go to the *cala* – have a swim if we can. I want to tell you what's happened. I've made us some *pa amb oli*. Don't dawdle—!' And he was gone.

I washed and dressed as quickly as I could, so bewildered by his unexpected mood that I couldn't even begin to imagine the cause of it. *Fact*: he wasn't angry; *fact*: he hadn't gone for me—

He was waiting in the kitchen as I hurried in, impatiently holding out my slab of bread dribbling with olive oil and crushed tomatoes. 'I've told Beryl to go back to sleep,' he grunted, 'she had a bad night. Come on, we'll take the short cut.'

As often happened when he wanted to talk about something important, he marshalled his thoughts first, clearing his throat, sniffing, poking his cheeks, so that we'd already passed through the wicket gate opposite Canellun before he finally blurted out the headline of what he wanted to say.

'No, the thing is – she's gone!' he announced dramatically.

Shocked to the core, I stopped dead. '*What?*'

'Margot!'

'Yes, I know—'

'No, it's all right!' he said hastily as he looked me in the face for the first time and registered my alarm, 'she's coming back. It's only for a bit – until she's better—'

'I'm sorry... *what?*' I couldn't seem to hear him—

'Margot!' he said impatiently, as though talking to a simpleton. 'She's gone – to the South of France – to the Camargue, actually. No, I know it's a blow – it's a blow to me, too, I can tell you! But she had to go, or I'd have devoured her – at least, that's how she saw it, and perhaps she's right. Beryl thinks it's for the best – let everything calm down – sort herself out. I mean, Margot was at the end of her tether last night, in a godawful state, and the worst part is that it's all my fault really. Being my muse has put enormous pressure on her, and she's still badly claustrophobic. Madrid was no good for her, in spite of Alastair and Mary doing their best to help. Cities are hell.' He barged me gently in the shoulder, like a herdsman trying to shift a reluctant bullock, and I walked on with him, my mind beginning to seethe – with despair, panic, with un-askable questions, with questions for Margot which were unanswerable now—

'So she's gone to some friends near Saintes Maries,' he went on, completely unaware of what I was going through, 'to a farmhouse, with wonderful skies, white horses... no address, so I've promised not to write to her until she's completely better – she'll tell me when that is—' As soon as we reached the track through the gorge he rearranged his pace to match mine, as if by doing so he could infect me with the same enthusiasm. 'So I'll just have to grin and bear it – again!'

'Did she leave a message at all?' I *had* to know – it was crucial. 'For me, I mean?' Some clue as to what the bloody hell I was meant to do now—

556

'Oh, yes!' He stopped in his tracks and turned to me. 'Of course she did! She said to thank you for everything – as do I. She couldn't have come back here without you, she said, so I'm doubly grateful. She told me to kiss you—' he gripped my shoulders and planted a whiskery kiss on both my cheeks, 'which I do with pleasure!'

What? Was that all—? 'Nothing else?' I was desperate for more—

'No, I don't think so,' he said vaguely, walking on. 'As I say, she was in a dreadful state—'

But I couldn't leave it at that – he'd told me nothing! 'What happened last night? Your study – where did you go?'

'Back to the Posada, of course! I couldn't let her go alone, the wind was terrific. If it hadn't been for me, she wouldn't have made it – and as for my study, I can't have closed the door properly, that's all.' He made his familiar gesture of tossing spilled salt over his shoulder. '*Tant pis!* Serve me right, I suppose – for trying to cage her. No real harm done, though – nothing that can't be mended at least. No, it was proof of the bond between us that she fought her way through that wind to come and see me. She even brought me her accounts! A lesser being in that state would have just done a bunk and left me to pick up the pieces. But she brought all her fears to me, and I blew them away – cleared the air between us completely. You only have to look at the sky—' He looked up at the perfect day, smiling, 'God's in his heaven, all's right with the world!' He frowned suddenly, deeply. 'Except that she's gone, of course.'

But I could find nothing inside me to echo the brilliance of the morning, or Robert's weird euphoria, so completely unfounded. Couldn't he *see* that he'd driven her away, with promises to return that she'd never keep? He was worse than naive – he was culpable! I found myself wanting to shout at him, to beg him not to make a fool of himself, to *wake up*, if only for a moment, and realise that she was gone forever – leaving us both alone—

But I could say nothing, on pain of death. I hadn't the slightest doubt that Alastair would keep his word to me if I broke mine to

557

him. He and Robert were both in love with Margot, each madly enough to revenge themselves instantly on a mere traitor—

The deeper we descended into the gorge the lower my spirits sank as my every nerve-ending began to screech at the pain of her leaving – disbelief that she'd left without a word to me – no last rites, no last kiss – just her sudden flight and the abandonment of all my love for her—

I must pull myself together! If Robert sensed my despair he'd worry at it until I'd told him everything— 'When did she leave?' I asked, grasping for something to distract him.

'She ordered a taxi for the airport just after dawn. She'll be in Marseilles by now.' Briefly, he searched the sky.

I could picture her instantly – impeccable, ravishing, running down the steps of the plane into Alastair's arms—

Look away—!

We were walking along the bank of the torrent now, in the deepest part of the gorge, the dry riverbed choked with elephant boulders and dead trees, strangely ominous in the silence of its violent past, the dripping limestone caves on the far bank leaking a deep rust-red trickle from oxidization, like menstrual blood seeping from the womb of the mountains behind us—

She was here – still – as she had always been! I had to believe it!

At once, like a soothsayer, I found myself overwhelmed by superstition and omens – the preternatural wind of the night before, the sacking of Robert's study, the broken figurine on his hearth, and now this: seeing a familiar sight and attributing to it a new and disturbing interpretation – all premonitions of tragedy, I was convinced – of a disaster still to come—

As if to emphasise my sense of foreboding, I became aware of a distant roaring sound as we continued along the bank of the torrent, to the point when I found myself looking up uneasily at the towering cliffs to our right, to the square tower poised so precariously above the gorge. No sign of a landslide, though, and yet the noise getting ominously louder. I glanced uneasily at Robert, but he seemed oblivious. I looked back, upstream, knowing that if there had been an unseen storm on the plateau behind the mountains two thousand feet above us, we could be swept to our deaths by a sudden surge in the torrent as it forced its way through this narrowest part of the ravine—

Moments later, as we came out of the gorge with its strangely conflicting echoes, the reality of what I was hearing began to dawn on me.

'Doesn't sound as though we'll get our bathe!' Robert declared with a look of sudden, hungry suspense in his eyes, and no sooner had we rounded the cliffs that guarded the entrance to the *cala* than we were confronted by the full fury of the sea, deafening, spectacular, the waves engulfing the beach utterly, to the point where it no longer existed as they crashed straight against the foot of the towering cliffs, dragging boulders and rocks from the alluvium. With an almighty *thump!* that shook the ground beneath us, a rogue wave struck the rock to which the café still clung, stripped to its bare poles by wind and waves, obliterating it completely under a vast sheet of water and spume which then dashed itself onto the roofs and slipways of the boat sheds below, the spray soaking us as we stood and marvelled.

'*Isn't it terrific?*' Robert bellowed at me, his eyes wild with excitement. '*It's like a difficult poem – the fight – the absolute need to overcome—!*'

'*What about the fishermen?*' I yelled back.

He pointed casually upwards, behind him. '*Long gone!*' he shouted. '*They've learned to leave nature to do its worst! Come on, we'll go back the other way – I want you to look down at it from the top—*'

No sooner had we returned to the shelter of the cliffs than we were able to talk normally again, the sound of the sea already a muffled roar.

'*Phew!*' he grinned hugely, transformed for a moment back into his youth. 'Quite something, isn't it? Now, don't look down again until we reach the top, all right? I want to show you something—'

We began climbing the crude donkey steps towards the square tower, my eyes fixed obediently on my feet. It wasn't long before his thoughts returned to Margot. 'The thing is, she wants me to send her trunk on to her in France, and of course I'll do it – I promised I would… and yet I'm loath to, somehow. It's comforting to know it's still here, that she'd have to come back for it. But there we are, I suppose – it's part of the vow of abstinence I've made to her – to return everything of hers while refusing to take back anything of mine – rings, jewellery, letters, poems… because they're no longer mine, of course – and that's the point! But at least she gave me the key to her trunk – entrusted it to me, rather – so I'll put in my last poems to her, as a charm – with a letter—'

'I thought you weren't meant to write to her.'

'No, that's different!' he said at once, as though he'd already reasoned it through. 'It's not like writing to her at an *address*, because I don't know it. It's more like drawing a bow at a venture, if you see what I mean – and my arrow will hit its mark, I promise you!'

Would she even read what he wrote? I doubted it.

We went on climbing, Robert leading, and when we finally reached the top he turned back and clutched my arm. 'Close your eyes!' he insisted. 'I'll guide you—'

I did as he asked, suddenly haunted by the memory of Alastair doing the same thing to me as a boy, feeling Robert's strong grip on my arm as he led me over the stony ground, his hand trembling slightly as he edged me forward, then suddenly clenching my arm with a grip of steel—

'*Stop!* Wait – you're right on the edge. I've got you. You can look down – *now!*'

I did as he said, but the instant I looked down at the chaos of the sea, my eyes seemed to fall out of my head like boulders, hurtling down the hundreds of feet into the violent maelstrom below, dragging my brain and body after them with sickening lightness, turning, spinning, nothing to cling to, nothing to hold, falling, Juan's manic laughter in my ears—

When I came to my senses again, it was to find that he'd dragged me back from the edge, forced me to the ground, and rammed my head between my knees.

'Why didn't you tell me you had vertigo?' he shouted, with the anger of someone who blamed himself as much as me.

'I forgot,' I gasped, 'I thought it had gone... I'm sorry—'

'You fainted – I nearly dropped you!'

'I'm sorry – just give me a minute—'

He began to circle round me, agitatedly, looking anywhere but at me. 'It must be awful – vertigo. I remember at Charterhouse, when Mallory took some of us off to climb in Snowdonia, a couple of boys simply couldn't take it—'

'Of course I can take it!' I protested, humiliated by my weakness. 'It's just that my eyes were closed and I didn't realise I was so close to the edge—'

'No, of course,' he agreed politely. 'Look, I tell you what, let's drop in on Stella if she's still there – have a glass of water. I could do with one myself, actually—'

The thought was heartening; it might give me a chance to make up for the day before – and upwards to anywhere was better than downwards.

Getting to my feet, I found that I was still shaken, not simply from the effects of vertigo but from another rush of guilt. Had he known what I knew, he'd probably have let me fall – or even pushed me – which perhaps I deserved in some ways... my first loyalty was to him, after all—

We'd turned through Stella's open gate and climbed the steps before I realised we were there, confronted at once by a number of the fishermen sitting on chairs lined up outside the wall of their cottage as they waited philosophically for the sea to subside and return to them what was left of their livelihood. They all greeted

Robert quietly, respectfully, as he commiserated with them on their losses in his atrocious *Mallorquín*, pointing up to the perfect sky like an old Indian chief, then down, behind him, over his shoulder again, at the ravages of the sea he'd witnessed.

They took his comments seriously, and when he assured them that all would be well tomorrow, they nodded in what seemed like time-honoured agreement: he was a famous poet after all, a sage who understood the workings of the moon and the winds and had bothered to come and look at the devastation they had suffered, before even the Mayor of Deya had bothered, a magician who would return time and again with his wealthy friends for catch after catch from their fishing boats, and lunch after lunch until they were on their feet again. He was a foreigner, but so had the Archduke been a foreigner, and yet they had both adopted Deya as their own—

Even as I watched and listened to the brief exchanges between them, utterly absorbed in the moments of their passing, a parallel streak of selfish thought still managed to identify the sudden chaos of their lives with mine, the very point and usefulness of my life swept away by a fate as cruel as theirs, yet worse than theirs, since I had no future here any more, only a fate which I longed to be without.

I needed to move away from them – *now!* – to be with Stella, to beg her help before I lost my nerve completely—

And suddenly she was there, laughing as she ran up to embrace us both, waving to the fishermen, pulling Robert away while he was still raising his straw hat to them, leading us back under the vine trellis through strobic shafts of sunlight.

'The thing is, Margot's gone!' exclaimed Robert, before he'd even crossed the threshold.

Stella turned back to him from the gloom of the kitchen, frowning, her eyes catching mine for a second. 'Oh, Robert, no! What – *forever?*'

'No, no!' He flung his hat onto the table. 'God, no! She's gone to France for a while. No, it's for the best, really – she wasn't ready to come back yet. I've been demanding too much of her, and Madrid was hopeless you see, too frantic, so she's gone to the Camargue, to friends – do her good! She's still badly shaken—'

He went on, as he always did, pouring out his news or his woes to anyone he came across in a stream of consciousness that was almost embarrassing to listen to – and slightly hurtful, since I'd presumed that everything he'd told me had been said in confidence. But not Robert; he'd cheerfully do his washing in public because nothing of his was ever truly dirty; it might smell of honest sweat, but he had nothing to be ashamed of – everything out in the open – no secrets—

No secrets! I looked away.

Stella busied herself as he talked, throwing open the shutters, flooding the room with light, clearing last night's supper (for one) from the table, throwing the occasional questioning glance at the desperation in my face as Robert paced up and down, addressing the kitchen range and the plate-rack with his problems, his back turned to us for a moment, allowing me to signal urgently to Stella to make sure that I stayed behind when he left. She caught on at once, nodding quickly before Robert turned back to us, his eyes almost messianic with inner light.

'No, I know it must sound strange, but in a way it's for the best. We've shifted a stifling weight, and we can both breathe again at last! And she's left me so full of energy, of determination to be prepared this time – for when she comes back... in fact, I must get to work – I need to revise some poems, write to her—' He frowned at me suddenly. 'What did we come for, anyway?' He turned quickly to Stella— 'Not that it isn't always lovely to see you, darling, but I must get on—'

'A drink of water,' I reminded him.

'Oh, yes!' He turned to the sink at once and filled two glasses, holding one out to me as he drained his. 'There!' He belched. 'Come along—'

'Actually, Robert,' Stella broke in, 'do you think you could leave Simon behind for a bit? I need someone to help me move the beds upstairs.'

'Yes, of course – keep him with my blessing – although I'll miss him, naturally! I'd stay and help you myself, but I've so much to do—'

Briefly kissing us both, he strode straight out through the door, clutching his shoulder basket to his side, his teeming mind already at work behind his desk.

We stood stock still, straining to listen as he bade farewell to the fishermen, then lumbered down the steps, slamming the gate behind him—

Whether it was the vertigo, or the cold water I'd knocked back too quickly, I found myself suddenly racing to the kitchen sink and vomiting into it, violently, waving Stella away frantically as she rushed forward, gasping apologies to her between each painful retch, throwing on the tap above my head, soaking my head, then rinsing my mouth again and again as the sickness began to pass. 'God, I'm so sorry!' I gasped, swilling the sink clean before turning off the tap at last, Stella already beside me, throwing a towel over my head—

'Nonsense! Poor you—' She began to rub my hair vigorously through the towel as I leaned over the sink, until I straightened up and took over from her, to disguise my shaking hands, my trembling body, everything that was letting me down—

'Is it something you've eaten?' she asked.

I shook my head again, trying to form words, tears suddenly stinging my eyes under cover of her towel, pressing it to my face, begging them to stop, shivering as the cold water ran down my back—

'What is it, then?' she asked urgently. 'Simon, what's *wrong*?'

Again I shook my head, with a futility I could no longer control. 'She's gone!' I groaned into the towel—

'I know!' She sounded impatient. 'Robert just said all that—'

'*No, you don't understand!*' I shouted, tearing the towel away in fury. 'She's *gone*—! *She's never coming back – never*—! *But he doesn't know!*' I rammed the towel against my mouth, so that only my eyes were visible to her, begging her to understand so that I didn't have to say the words myself – betray with words the three people I most loved—

Stella stared at me, her shocked face darkening into a tense frown of concentration as she struggled to understand. 'What are you saying? Tell me—!'

I shook my head helplessly. 'I *can't*, don't you see? I *swore*—!'

'Swore what?' she demanded at once. 'Who to?' She reached out and clasped my wrist, her eyes searching mine intently. 'Simon, I can't help if you don't tell me! Here—' She pulled me over to the table and sat us both down, taking my hands in hers. 'Simon, listen – do you trust me?' she asked intently.

'Of course I do!'

'Then tell me! Look, I know what it's like, living at Canellun – it's dangerous! You can get sucked in, lose all sense of proportion. It casts a sort of spell… Why do you think my father doesn't come here any more? Why do you think I choose to stay here, in the cottage? You have to be as strong as Beryl to survive up there. I won't tell anyone, I promise, cross my heart! And I'll be gone tonight anyway, so there'll be no one to tell. *What* have you sworn?'

'To tell no one—' I could say that much, surely?

'Who made you swear? Robert?' I shook my head furiously. 'Beryl, then…? Margot?'

I went on shaking my head, willing her to read my mind.

'But there *is* no one else!' She threw away my hands in disgust. 'Look, this is childish! If you won't tell me, then you obviously don't trust me. You'd better go—'

'*Alastair!*' I gasped, in sheer desperation – and his name was out, whirling into the dark corners of the room.

Stella looked stunned, disbelieving, her eyes searching mine for an explanation, for something more than a piece of jigsaw in a puzzle which had no space for it.

So I told her everything – almost everything – haltingly at first, but then more fluently as I realised that in speaking his name I'd somehow exorcised it, if only for the moment, of the power it had over me. Stella listened intently. By the end, her face was heavy with a sadness which only added to my sense of guilt.

Neither of us said anything for a moment. To my over-heated imagination the echoes of the story seemed to reverberate on and on, for years to come—

'God, what a mess!' she murmured at last. 'It'll probably kill him when he finds out.'

'If he doesn't kill me first!' I blurted out, before I could stop myself.

She looked me square in the face, pitilessly. 'Actually, I wouldn't put it past him,' she retorted. 'How can you have been so blind, not to realise that they were having an affair?'

'Because I was in love with her too!' I answered angrily, let down by her reaction. 'All right, I was blind, and deaf and stupid, but that was the perfect smokescreen, wasn't it – for Alastair? For me to be in love with Margot at the same time as him.'

'And Robert,' she said coldly. 'Like the blind leading the blind, the pair of you.'

'Have *you* ever been in love?' I countered angrily. 'To the very brink?'

She relented under my stare, sinking back into the person I recognised. 'All right, I'm sorry.' And yet she was still frowning unhappily. 'But how could Margot just leave you to face the music alone?'

'You still don't understand!' I cried. 'She was at her wits' end, exhausted, frightened – you know what Robert can be like – perhaps she just lost her nerve – perhaps she thought I could cope on my own – keep my mouth shut, which I must – I know I must – except to you—'

'Well, at least that explains what she was doing in Palma yesterday—'

'What do you mean?'

'I saw her coming out of *Viajes Marsans*, Robert and Beryl's travel agent. She didn't see me, but she was putting a ticket in her purse. It couldn't have been anything else—'

So she'd been in Palma all the time... I turned away, rubbing fiercely at my face with both hands, suddenly fearful of crying. 'What should I do?' I asked shakily.

Stella roused herself with a deep sigh. 'Well, you can't tell him, that's for sure,' she said. 'It's too late now anyway – the dice is cast—'

'Die,' I corrected her automatically, without thinking—

'*Oh, shut up, Simon!*' She shot out of her chair and began pacing up and down. 'Who bloody *cares* – die, dice, die—?' It was as though she were conjugating death, like a verb.

I held up my hands. 'I'm sorry – it just slipped out.' I turned to watch her as she strode up and down, taken aback by her anger and yet at the same time trying to make room for it, wishing I understood what was behind it. 'Why are you so cross?' I asked finally.

'Because you've been such a bloody fool!' she retorted. 'You've messed everything up – for Robert, for Beryl, for—' she shook her head furiously, '*everyone*! I warned you not to get involved— 'She glared at me. 'I suppose you expected me to just sit here and hold your hand and say '*there, there, poor Simon*'. Well, I won't! You got yourself into this mess – no one forced you!' Her eyes narrowed suddenly. 'Why did you come to me anyway?' she demanded.

I shrugged helplessly. 'Who else could I go to?'

'Oh, *great*! I suppose it hasn't occurred to you that you've dropped *me* in the shit now – that I'm as guilty as you if I say nothing.'

I looked round at her in alarm. 'Oh, don't worry,' she went on bitterly, 'I won't sneak. But Robert deserves better than this – from Margot, Alastair – especially from you! You're his family, for God's sake! And as for poor Beryl! How *could* you?' With an exasperated sigh she turned her back on me. 'If you really want my advice,' she said coldly, 'then say nothing – to anyone. Just leave, *now* – tomorrow – before he finds out from someone else – Mary, for instance.' She turned back to me. 'Where *is* Mary, anyway?'

'Christ!' I gasped, shocked by the thought. 'I don't know – in Madrid, I suppose—'

'In which case she'll know by now, won't she? And knowing Mary, she won't take it lying down. She'll want revenge.'

The pressure inside my head became suddenly unbearable. '*God, I hate secrets!* I'm no *good* at them! Why couldn't Margot have just told Robert the truth – asked him to release her, as she said she would, as Alastair said she would—?'

'Well, she didn't—' said Stella unhelpfully, 'and a moment ago you refused to blame her!'

'I don't,' I said wearily. 'I can't.' A new thought suddenly occurred to me. 'Perhaps she was trying to protect me! If she'd told Robert that I knew—'

Stella snorted disdainfully. 'Make any excuse you like for her – you're still on your own. Are *you* going to tell him? No – because he'll never forgive you.'

'*Exactly – so I can't!*' I stared at her in desperation. 'It all seemed so simple in Madrid, a secret-no-secret which I'd only have to keep for a few days, until Margot told him, and then I'd be free of it. But suddenly she's gone – *everyone's* gone – and I'm caught in a web of lies which yesterday were only secrets... and all the lies have promises attached to them, which I daren't break...' I found myself sobbing for breath— 'because I'm in love with her – I'm so in love with her!' It was as if my sanity snapped suddenly as I grabbed at my hair with both hands and tried to pull it out by its roots, and failed, and smashed my head down on the table again and again— 'and it hurts! It *hurts!* It *HURTS!*'

Stunned by my own violence, I let my head rest on the table finally, face down, circling it with my arms as I wept into the darkness I'd created. 'Because I'm so full of love, and it keeps growing and growing, and there's nowhere for it to go and it's got to die, but it's beautiful, and I don't want it to die.'

I'd been vaguely aware of Stella shouting at me as I'd smashed my head on the table, begging me to stop, then throwing her arms round my shoulders until my rage drove her away, now trying to pull me upright in my chair to ram a soaking cloth against my forehead—

I grabbed at it, dragging it through the pain, covering my eyes, its wetness and coldness shocking me back to reality – only to have to face the fool I'd made of myself.

I got up, turning away from her in shame. 'Stella, I'm so sorry... I didn't mean it to be like this – to drag you into it. I just needed to talk to someone...' I made for the door before forcing myself to turn back and beg one last favour of her. 'Look, you won't say anything will you – to anyone?'

She shook her head numbly.

'Promise?'

With that single word too many, the anger surged back into her eyes. '*Promise?* What good are promises? Which promises will *you* keep?'

THE MINOTAUR

It took me until evening to pull myself together enough to return to Canellun as if nothing had happened. Any sooner and Beryl would have seen through me at once and I'd probably have broken down and told her everything I knew in a suicidal bid to stop the unrelenting torment of love and loss and lies and lies and more lies.

Whether from smashing my head, or from Stella's savaging, or from the sudden unbearable emptiness within me which Margot had filled to the brim until now, my brain felt as if it might burst from the pressure inside.

I avoided the road for fear of running into someone I knew, knowing I'd be unable to make sense of anything they might say because everyone, now, was in a different world from mine. Instead, I walked through the endless olive groves which wound their way below the road, taken by surprise when I suddenly found myself in the grove below Canellun, with the landslide and sheep-hut framed like some idyllic painting in its own symmetry. Making straight for the cave-like mouth of the hut where Juan and I had once taken refuge, I vanished into the gloom, throwing myself down on the earth floor where I fell almost instantly into a sleep of exhaustion and flight from what I could no longer bear to think of.

I awoke at dusk, rested, strangely at peace, my eyes opening with growing excitement into an ongoing dream as I stared out through the entrance of the sheep-hut at the red earth of the terrace, now molten with the last rays of sunlight, the shadow of an *algarroba* tree lying felled by the setting sun across the rough ground outside—

The landslide – that was it – in my dream – the perfect place!

Stumbling to my feet, I ran out of the hut and back along the terrace, beneath the huge rocks which overhung it to where, some thirty of forty feet above me, a great chunk of the upper terrace had collapsed into this one, as if some mythic giant had used it as a foothold to reach the summit of the *Teix*, and the ground here had given way beneath the weight of his foot.

Staring up at it, my imagination's eye was already shaping the fallen rocks into row after row of stone seats, a hundred or more of them, reaching up from the ground to the narrow cave at the top of the landslide and along the top of the escarpment above, each seat with an uninterrupted view of the stage below which would reach out across the terrace I was standing on in a perfect semi-circle exactly reflecting, as if in a pool of still water, the convexity of the stage to the concavity of what would become the auditorium, obeying precisely the rule of physics in which nothing could be removed in space without being simultaneously replaced by an amount equal to its loss – or whatever the law was—

Apart from love, of course, to which no such law applied.

I smothered my feelings, and gazed up again at the landslide. Quite apart from the natural cave at the top, there were countless holes and fissures in the rocks that surrounded it to fill with a thousand nightlights and candles, so that at dusk the walls would blaze with the red reflected light of the limestone within, while on moonlit nights the audience would look down not simply at the performers on the stage but at the panoramic backdrop of falling hills and the deep wedge of moonlit sea beyond—

As hard as my earlier panic tried to swamp me again, I forced it back, concentrating feverishly on the future, on a time when this awfulness, like the terrace itself, would be buried under the

landslide of time, waiting to be transformed into a thing of beauty
– an atonement—

I would go back to the house through the grotto, clean myself up in the freshwater spring there, and get ready to face whatever music was to be played at Canellun that night.

By the time I'd climbed the spiral of stone steps out of the grotto, emerging like a ghost into the gloom of the garden at Canellun, it was almost dark, my earlier dread and panic returning in a surge of present fear that swept over me again, punishingly – how *dared* I ignore it – imagine that the past could be written off without penalties, without payment? This was the opposite of inspiration – this was *now* – reality – and no amount of fantasy, however well-intentioned, would get me off its hook.

Hurrying towards the kitchen, I barged my way through the fly-curtain just as Robert and Beryl came in through the doorway to the dining room, as if we had all come onstage at the same moment.

'Oh, there you are!' he cried. 'I was getting worried! Beryl's got a headache, so I was about to lay the table—'

'Don't worry, I'll do it,' I said. 'You go back to work.'

'What have you done to your forehead?' asked Beryl.

'I walked into a tree.'

'Are you sure it wasn't the other way round?' Robert's laugh was slightly forced. 'They tend to move around at night, taking revenge on their tormentors—'

'Oh, *Robert!*' Beryl shook her head irritably, then regretted it, holding her forehead. 'Just go back to work, would you? I'll call you when supper's ready.'

Pulling a comical face at me, he lumbered off.

'He seems so much happier,' I remarked as I stared after him.

'*Well...*' she crossed wearily to the Aga and stirred one of the pans on it. 'He's convinced himself that Margot's going to come back, that everything's all right... I only wish *I* could!'

'Do you want an aspirin?' I asked, anxious to change the subject.

'No. Thank you. I'll take one after supper if it hasn't gone away.' She went on fiddling with the pans, without turning round. 'What do *you* make of it all – Margot leaving like that? It's so unlike her not to say goodbye.'

I shook my head, grateful not to have to look her in the eye. 'I don't know what to make of it,' I mumbled, 'or of anything else, come to that. Shall I lay the table?'

Safely out of her sight in the dining room, I slumped over the tray of plates and glasses and cutlery, the weight of my love and duty to Margot heavier than I could bear. If it could only be over *now – everything –* so that we could all return to where we were—

I laid the table like an automaton, until at one point I almost lost control, grabbing one of the heavy green glasses and flinging it with all my might into the fireplace, yearning for the explosion that would end it all – and yet the glass still clutched in my hand, unthrown, glass and silence unbroken, taunting me for lack of courage.

I laid it down quietly beside Robert's place.

When supper was finally ready, and Beryl had called him to the table, it was like eating with someone in the manic phase of manic depression; he could hardly stop talking – about Sufism, about *baraka* again, about *The Hebrew Myths*, with Joshua Podro almost marginalised by Robert's seer's vision of the truth, and about his forthcoming inaugural speech, in Latin, when he took up his poetry professorship at Oxford. He'd delighted in taking Auden down a peg or two after he'd proposed his own 'ghost writer' in Latin, when Robert could write his own Latin speech standing on his head and still take off his trousers without missing a gerundive – and about Margot of course, sandwiching her between and among everything he said, sharpening the pain of her absence.

A stranger at the table might have thought him a braggart, but in fact it was nothing more than bravado on his part, a way of psyching himself up to cope with the loneliness facing him without Margot. Only by believing in himself and his powers could he bridge the abyss of her second flight from him, with work and work and still more work. She would come back, he was certain of it—

But the more he talked, and the more he justified himself to her (even though she wasn't there), the deeper my heart sank. Stella was right – I must go. Tomorrow.

Beryl seemed to have had enough of him that night. No sooner was supper out of the way than she rose from the table and said she was going to take a couple of aspirin after all, and go to bed. Without embracing either of us she shuffled off, looking tired and bent, calling out a faint goodnight.

I'd stood up as she left the table, but Robert stayed where he was, looking almost baffled until he seemed to feel the after-shock of her leaving, his eyes slowly focussing on the present, troubled, uncertain, then suddenly hauling himself to his feet at last and blundering to the doorway into the hall, calling up to ask if she was all right.

'Of *course* I'm all right!' she shouted down from the landing above. 'I've got a headache, that's all, and you're making it *worse*!'

'Oh...'

He came back to his chair looking even more bewildered until he'd sorted it out in his head. 'No, the thing is,' he said finally, 'your great-aunt feels things much more deeply than people realise. A lot of *baraka* was destroyed last night and it's upset her more than she lets on. A bit like being burgled, I suppose, but by the wind. Or by an evil spirit, perhaps – I'm not sure yet. What I *am* sure of, though, is that it was all *fated*.' He turned and stared at me suddenly, frowning. 'I say, are you all right? You're very quiet this evening.'

'I'm fine!' I insisted at once, sitting up from the slump I'd fallen into.

'It's Margot, isn't it? You miss her—'

I could almost hear the gears in my head changing down as I approached a potential hazard. 'Yes, of course,' I said, as neutrally as I could.

'Me too,' he muttered, looking around wildly. 'It's hell… like mislaying one's heart.' He took a pull at himself. 'But there it is – we have to get through somehow—' He glanced round at me. 'Did she give you any clue that she was so near the end of her tether? No, of course not – you'd have told me—'

I changed into an even lower gear, eyes peeled for danger. 'You know what she's like,' I said carefully, 'keeps everything to herself—'

'No, I know—'

'—although I think your quarrel at Lluch Alcari frightened her—' Was I *mad*? I jammed on the brake in panic. 'Not that she said anything much,' I added quickly.

'Oh God,' he muttered to himself, rubbing his face with his hands, then running them through his hair. 'I went too far, I know—' He closed his eyes wearily, 'but the fact is, all our nerves were shattered by then…' He stared fiercely into his memories of that morning, then shook his head angrily. 'It's no good – I can't think about that now – I've got to look forward…' He suddenly got to his feet. 'Let's get rid of all this.'

We cleared everything from the table and washed up in a weirdly muted frenzy, neither of us saying a word, and yet Robert expressing his agitation in his own peculiar percussionese, clanging the compost bin lids, banging the doors under the sink, noisily clunking the enamel washing up bowls together before filling them with water, cascading the plates into the soapy one, splashing the floor and the animals, ignoring them as they bolted for shelter under the table, clattering the cutlery into fistfuls and flinging them after the plates, punctuating the din with sniffs and grunts and the occasional '*Blast!*' or '*Fuck!*' as he washed up, fork after knife after plate slung into the rinsing bowl from where I took them and dried them, breaking off at one point to close the doors between us and the hall in an attempt to spare Beryl the worst of the racket.

'You ought to start a skiffle group,' I muttered as he finally emptied out the dirty dishwater and turned his bowl upsidedown, letting it drop with a deep reverberating clunk, like a huge sheepbell, onto the rim of the black marble sink.

'What?' he grunted.

'You know – Lonnie Donnegan—'

'Never met him,' his eyes tormented with inner thoughts.

And he was off again, in a trance, grabbing the empty coal scuttle, flinging open the kitchen door and striding out to the coal shed opposite to scare the shit out of the rats.

It was his way, like his previous boastfulness, of surrounding himself with yet more proof of his existence, losing himself in the noise of his chores like some primitive warding off wild animals at night by banging things together – his only defence against the omens and nightmares to come – of loss and loneliness, of Margot gone. Later, when he went to bed, he would talk to Beryl, whether or not she was awake, until he fell asleep at last—

It was also unnerving. Even though I recognised the effect it was having on him, I couldn't be certain of the cause for his sudden mania. Margot apart, was he having a premonition of some kind – of treachery, perhaps?

I went to the Aga and threw up the lid of the hotplate, suddenly infected by the violence of his noise-game, grasping the steel riddle and smashing it down on the planetary circles of the hotplate, using the notched end to raise the heavy iron bung from the centre of the furnace in a waft of sulphurous volcanic heat, holding my breath to prevent an asthma attack as I reached for the coal funnel and rammed it into the glowing hole, the poisonous gases rising out of it like the phantoms of my own fears—

Again the door crashed against the sink as Robert barged his way back through the fly curtain with a full coal-scuttle. 'Have you seen the moon?' he cried, smiling now, his mood completely changed. 'She's almost full… thanks for doing that – no, I think I know who you meant just now – *Last Train* to somewhere… *San Francisco*?'

'*San Fernando*,' I corrected him, my fears vanishing as swiftly as his change of mood.

'That's it!' He grabbed the steel rod from me, throwing open the bottom door of the Aga, springing open the black stoker's door inside and stabbing the rod into the dull glow within, riddling furiously until the glow became incandescent. 'Juan used to sing it with some boys from the village. Thimbles – that was it!' He slammed the doors shut, raised the coal-scuttle with both hands and began, deafeningly, to pour the coal into the funnel. '*For the wash boards!*' he shouted over the din. 'There wasn't a thimble or a washboard left in Deya. All the village women threatened to go on strike if they weren't returned!'

Having emptied the coal-scuttle, he put it down in its place, quietly at last, put the funnel away, dropping the bung back into its hole before closing the lid over the hotplate and hanging the steel riddle over the handrail. 'Look, let's go through to the study – cheer each other up.'

He led the way, leaving me to close the study doors behind us. When I turned round he was standing behind his desk, staring as though mesmerised through the side window that faced towards the grotto and the sea. 'Imagine—!' he said forcefully. 'If night were day, and if the world were flat – and if I had telescopic eyesight, of course—' he pointed out through the window, 'Margot and I could wave to each other. She's just over there – a hundred miles or so, at Saintes Maries – Aigues Mortes just to the left of it—' He waggled his fingers at her, laughing as he flung himself into his chair, his eyes challenging me to disbelieve him. 'Isn't that extraordinary?'

'Yes!' I exclaimed politely.

'It makes her feel very near… perhaps I'll hire a boat one day – surprise her—'

Don't—! 'You don't know her address,' I reminded him quickly.

He shrugged dismissively. 'That wouldn't matter.' He bunched his fingers together and tapped them against the middle of his forehead. 'She'd know I was there – she'd find me.' He began straightening the papers on his desk. 'Now then, what about you?' he asked brightly. 'How can we cheer *you* up?'

'I'm fine—'

'No you're not. All this has hit you badly – as it has me. We need to look after each other. Let's start at the beginning – how long will you stay, d'you think?'

I was thrown into confusion. Had he been reading my mind? 'Er... I could leave tomorrow—'

'No, you misunderstand me!' he protested, shaking his head. 'Stay as long as you like – I could do with the company. No, I just wondered if you shouldn't be back in Madrid. I know how easy it is to bunk off, but the discipline of university life is very important—'

'I'm sure it is, at Oxford,' I said, 'but Madrid's nothing more than a kindergarten. I do most of my work at the *pensión*.'

'Well, it's up to you, of course – I just don't want to get a cross letter from your mama demanding to know why you're here and not in Madrid! Anyway,' he waved the problem aside, 'so long as you *are* here, I think we should make a plan, don't you? I've always found that making a plan helps one get through. Starting with tomorrow, for instance: what will you do tomorrow?'

'Tomorrow...' I rummaged into the future, still at a loss for *time* – time to think clearly – he always went so fast – 'Oh, yes! I have to go into Palma, to pick up my allowance from *Banco March*—'

'Good!' he exclaimed, warming to his subject at once. 'We're getting somewhere already! If you have any problems there, just mention my name. Juan March is an old friend of mine – in spite of his dealings with Franco.' He broke off suddenly and threw me a beatific smile. 'I say, if you really *are* picking up your allowance, I wonder if you could let me have the twelve hundred pesetas Margot lent you? It was mine, you see.'

Again I must have misunderstood him. 'I'm sorry – what?'

'Twelve hundred pesetas – no? Apparently Margot lent you the money in Madrid, for your fare here.'

'*Wha-at?*' I felt myself falling through my own entrails, heart thundering—

Taken aback by my expression, Robert quickly raised his hand. 'No, don't worry,' he said hurriedly, 'it doesn't matter – perhaps she was mistaken.'

'*Margot – said – I – owed – her – money?*' I stared at him wildly, hardly able to get the words out for fear of throwing up, of breaking down—

'Yes – wait – I've got them here – her accounts—' He reached for his reading glasses and began to rifle through the pages in front of him, a long list in Margot's distinctive handwriting. 'I was going through them earlier, that's all… yes, here we are.' He stabbed his forefinger at the line. '*Lent Simon 1200 pesetas for fare to Majorca.*' He looked up at me with the same smile, shrugging, chucking his glasses back onto the desk. 'Who cares? It's only money! As I say, it doesn't matter, if you're short—'

'It *does* matter!' I shouted, fighting back tears of rage. '*It matters like hell – to me!*'

He stared at me, bewildered. 'What does?'

I took a deep breath, fixing him with a glare not meant for him, but for Margot. 'I was given three thousand pesetas in Madrid,' I insisted furiously, 'eighteen hundred to bring her trunk here, and twelve hundred for my fare – not in cash, but in tickets, because she wanted me to be with her!'

'Oh *well* – that explains it!' he interrupted at once, gesturing me to calm down—

'I told Alastair that I couldn't come, that last month's allowance had run out—'

580

'*Alastair?*' he frowned.

I shook my head furiously as I realised how close I was to the edge. 'I mean Margot,' I blundered on, 'Alastair just wanted to help, but she needed her trunk, and the deal was that she'd pay my fare if I brought it to her—'

'Well, there we are!' he cried. 'You owe me nothing! It's all right—'

'*No it's not all right!*' I seethed, her broken word crushing me with its sense of betrayal, its consequences— '*How could she do that?*' I cried, almost out of control. 'How could she say I owed her money when I didn't?'

The sheer intensity of my fury dragged Robert towards me across his desk, stretching his arms towards me as though to hold me back. 'No – stop! Look, she must have been confused, that's all. You know what she's like—' His eyes melted. 'Oh, don't be upset – please!'

But I was past hearing. 'And now I feel as though I *do* owe you money, even though I don't – but my allowance is only eight hundred pesetas, which has to last a month—'

'You owe me nothing! There! It's only filthy luchre, after all.' *So he still thought I owed him the money!* 'And besides, I'm flush at the moment – I gave her another five hundred dollars last night, to buy a car.'

'But she's already got a car!' I cried distractedly—

'What?'

'—a Citroën, like a French gangster's—'

Oh, *Christ! What had I done?* Having almost drowned in my own thoughts, I'd surfaced into his –

'*No* – that can't be right—!' He reached for his glasses again and began scrabbling through her accounts—

In that godawful moment, the silence of suspense as his finger moved down the list, I realised that I was finally lost – that I'd betrayed her in return—

'No!' he insisted emphatically. 'She couldn't have – it would be down here.' He looked at me severely, a headmaster suddenly, 'You're mistaken!'

His words maddened me. *'I've driven in it!'* I shouted.

'No!' He flung down his glasses again and stared at me balefully. *'You're lying!'*

With that hated, fateful word, I could feel the pent up fury rise into my face, forcing him to look away for an instant, wildly, to the window above my head, before his tormented eyes grazed mine again. 'I don't understand,' he said faintly, 'you must be ill… that's it! You've behaved strangely all evening – you'd better go to bed – *now!*' His voice rising— 'Before you say something you regret!'

'You've already paid for it – don't you see?'

To be called a liar when I'd told the truth was unbearable – though not as unbearable as the sight of the sudden, brutal shock in his face. 'What?' he gasped. 'What are you saying?'

And it was all too late – too far; too late for lies, too far to draw back—

I smashed my fist into the side of my head—

'Oh, God, Robert! Don't make me—!'

'What?' he shouted. *'Tell me at once!* What are you saying?'

'I *can't!*' Tears of remorse and despair already starting from my eyes, the horror of my betrayal racing towards me like Nemesis— 'I swore—!'

He stumbled to his feet, towering over the desk as he leaned towards me, his body huge with threat. *'Swore what?'* he demanded fiercely. *'To Margot?* You know something! Tell me what you know this minute, or by God—!' he flung himself round the edge of his desk—

'It's for *them!*' I shouted, 'the money – it's for *them!*'

He stopped dead in his tracks. *'Them?* Who's "them", for Christ's sake?'

'Margot… Alastair…' I could hardly speak – the truth, like vertigo, pulling me to my death— 'The Camargue—'

'*What*—?' He clutched at his head as though I'd hit him, his eyes unfocussed suddenly, staring inwards in panic at the horrors of revelation, as if into his own grave. 'You mean they're…' Unable to bring himself to say the unspeakable.

'Yes.'

He stared out at me from the nightmare in his head, uncomprehending. 'But he's *married*!'

'He's left Mary—'

'*What?*' He strode towards me. '*You're lying, you bastard! You're lying—!*'

'*Oh Robert, don't say that!*' I shouted through my tears. 'I beg you – I'm *not* lying! Why do you think I've said nothing? Because I *can't* lie, because I can't bear what I know! Margot was meant to tell you, not me – and she's gone!'

But he was on top of me now, towering, swelling as I'd seen him swell before but more terrifying than before, his body, face, fury filling the room with a menace I'd never seen, a mask of anger so obliterating – '*Tell me you're lying!*' he roared—

'Oh, I can't bear it!' he gasped—

—as he split in two before my eyes, between good and evil, rage and reason, fighting each of him to the death within himself and above me, through me, tearing me in half as I tried to protect myself from both of him with nothing but murderous truth to defend myself.

He suddenly covered his eyes with his hand, unable to look at me. 'You're saying… that Alastair has left Mary and Jasper—' he leaned over me threateningly, breathing into my face, 'that he's living with Margot in the Camargue – *as her lover?*'

'Yes—' I whispered.

He raised his hand from his eyes like a visor, warding off the blindingness of apocalypse all around him as I found myself staring into their growing wildness, my own fate forgotten now as I was swept up into the vortex of his—

'*And you knew!*' he bellowed, his monstrous dark forequarters twisting round in front of me as he grabbed the arms of my chair—

I nodded dumbly, paralysed by my awful vision of him, his huge head still twisting round, aligning the horns of his hatred, his fury, to my heart, my head—

'*You've known all along – and said nothing?*'

I could hardly hear him for my fear. His fist rose to the ceiling like an axe-head—

'*You've betrayed me! I'll kill you—!*'

'Oh, Christ, I could kill you—'

He recoiled from me in horror, flinging my chair away from him against the wall, my head crashing against it as he turned and strode to the doors of the study—

'*Beryl!*' he shouted as he flung them open—

But she was already there, hurrying into the room, her dressing gown clutched round her—

'Now then, now then!' The voice of lost causes, measured, calm— 'What's all this dreadful *yelling*? Robert, go and sit down—!'

Later—

Much later… the three of us sitting in exhausted silence at last, the clamour of accusations, denials, recriminations still echoing round the walls and round and round in our heads.

My own head reeled in the sudden peace of silence, even as I became aware how battered I felt, first from Robert's relentless verbal bludgeoning, but then, as Beryl managed slowly, outburst by outburst, to calm him down, from the even worse pain of his disgust for me, until that, too, was eclipsed by the growing weight of desolation that seemed to descend on him like an invisible landslide from the *Teix* high above us, burying him under an avalanche of sudden, unforeseen mortality—

Until I couldn't even look at him for the hurt I'd caused, nor he at me for causing it, nor Beryl at either of us, her eyes almost closed with tiredness as she stared down at the impenetrable dark floor between us, as if into the future.

'*Well*,' she murmured at last, 'there's nothing more we can do tonight… except sleep on it, I suppose… not that we'll get much sleep.' With a heavy sigh she raised her head and stared at Robert. 'Tomorrow, I think you should write to her.'

'I have no address—' his exhausted voice reaching out of the gloom beyond the reach of his desk lamp.

'Put it in her trunk… you were going to anyway.'

'She may not reply—'

'You should still write… it'll drive you mad if you don't, you know it will. Perhaps we should both write. If she can't face you, she might at least send *me* some explanation. But I think we should all go to bed now. It's late.' She turned to me with a look that caught me completely off-guard, a look of unexpected compassion.

I responded to it at once, like a schoolboy whose voice – and heart, and will – had been broken. 'I'm so very sorry for what I've done…' Even as I despised myself for the tone of my voice, for the need to say it—

'Yes, *well*.' She shook her head wearily. 'It's a bit late for that, isn't it?' And yet her eyes continued to relent. 'Still… it wasn't you who went off with her, or made her deceive us… you were just caught up in something far bigger and far worse than your part in it. You were just a pawn, I suppose, and even pawns have to sleep…'

I might as well have murdered him, I thought as I climbed the dark stairs to bed – like Cain – like Alastair in the birthday play, plunging his knife into Robert's back time and again—

I closed my bedroom door behind me as quietly as if I no longer existed here—

Coward! The word was out—

I'd hardly said a word in her defence! In the panic of trying to unburden myself of the lies and secrets I'd had to live with, I'd rushed like a coward into the confessional and given them up to Robert like sins. My one jot of comfort was that I hadn't asked for absolution, or begged for mercy. How brave was that?

In Robert's mind I'd committed an unforgivable treason against him and would have to pay for it, with part of my life at least – that most vital part, *belonging* – to my own family, which he alone could give or take away.

And even now not all the truth was out, the dark corners of my own traitorous intentions still upswept. He'd accepted my love for Margot as being as pure as homage to his goddess, but he still knew nothing of my bewitchment, the helpless thrall I felt in her presence, the profanity of my desire for her, the lengths to which I would have gone to take her from him if I'd only been man enough—

But I hadn't been man enough. Instead, I'd betrayed her, betrayed them all—and then betrayed myself, the least yet worst of all. And I would have to live with that.

Forever.

MALEDICTION

I slept late. No one called up to wake me. As I went downstairs, slowly, reluctantly, the house around me felt unnaturally still, abandoned, all the doors and windows wide open. Perhaps I was over-reacting to the sense of desolation, and yet I felt as though I were coming down stairs for the first time, as a stranger, not knowing who I might see, how I should behave—

As I crossed the hall past the open French windows on both sides of the house, I glanced instinctively towards Robert's study, but his doors were wide open, too. No sound of his voice—

The dining room – as still as a painting of itself—

The kitchen—

Beryl—! Sitting at the table with her back to the window, smoking a cigarette, a cup of coffee beside her, the dogs at her feet.

'Ah. There you are,' she murmured. 'I was about to call you.' The dogs half-heartedly wagging their tails in what looked uncomfortably like pity.

'I'm so sorry, I overslept.'

'I thought it best to leave you. Do you want breakfast?'

'I'll get it,' I offered hurriedly, going to the larder for cereal, to the fridge for milk, to the sink for a bowl and spoon, trying to fill the silence with seamless action and quiet noise because I didn't know what to say or how to say it, or even where to begin, except with breakfast.

No sooner had I covered my cereal with sugar than I realised that I'd have to sit and eat it now, crunch it revoltingly and interminably, mouthful after mouthful—

'Actually, I think I'll just have a cup of coffee if I may.'

Beryl merely nodded, and the silence between us stretched on. If I didn't break it soon, I felt it might harden like cement, that nothing would ever be said again. 'Is Robert here?' I asked finally, sounding as normal as I could.

'He's gone for a bathe.' She looked at the clock above the fridge. 'He'll be back soon.'

I was stranded in the middle of the kitchen floor. 'Would you rather I went to the village for breakfast?' I asked. She shook her head faintly, eyes closed. 'Or I could just leave if you'd rather – go and pack—'

'Oh, just sit down and have your breakfast!' she said, exasperated. 'As I say, he'll be back in a minute. It's up to him.'

Heart sinking, I took my coffee to the other side of the table, by the sink, and sat down, wedging myself in with my back to the window, like her. In the renewed silence I realised that she was leaving it to me to make the first move: pawn to great-aunt, with no help from her—

'Beryl, there's no excuse for what I've done, I know that—'

She looked strangely relieved by my outburst, as if she'd doubted the sincerity of my contrition the night before. '*No,*' she said firmly. 'There's no excuse… but there must have been a *reason,* surely?'

'Yes—' I was as relieved as she was that I seemed to have said what she needed me to say, that we were still speaking in spite of everything, and yet to confess to everything was almost impossible, even to her. I took a deep breath. 'Beryl, the thing is, it's not as simple as it seems.' I faltered, 'The reason for what I did—' I shook my head furiously, unable to find the right words—

'Oh, for heaven's sake, just *say* it!' she said impatiently. 'You've been in love with Margot from the beginning! Yes?'

I stared at her in shock. 'How did you know?'

She lowered her head, shaking it – in despair, I thought at first, until her shoulders heaved slightly with silent laughter. She looked up at me finally, eyes dancing behind her spectacles. 'I *was there*, you know – when you first met! The two of you laughing, then all of us, Robert getting crosser and crosser because he didn't understand what was happening—' She shook her head at the memory.

'You're extraordinary!' I muttered.

'Well, I don't know about *that*.' The smile faded from her face. 'And it doesn't alter the fact that you've hurt him very badly. He trusted you – we both trusted you – and you've let us down.'

Again I felt the blood drain from my face.

'How you make up for it I don't know… I don't even know if you *can* make up for it – to your grand-uncle. He's very angry – very angry indeed, especially with Alastair. It was a wicked thing to do, after all the help and friendship Robert's given him over the years. *Wicked*! He'll never forgive him… but where's it all going to end, that's what I'd like to know…' She rubbed at the strain on her forehead. 'Without Margot, there'll be no poems, and without poems there'll be no Robert as far as he's concerned. The whole point of his life has simply vanished. To be deserted by The White Goddess, to have his powers revoked – which is how he sees it – is a death sentence. He was in a *terrible state* this morning!' She stared at me, her eyes so deeply troubled that all the guilt and horror of the night before swept over me again.

'And it's my fault,' I said faintly, unable to look at her. 'Look, *do* you want me to leave?'

'Well, I can't *stop* you,' she replied, 'if that's what you want to do—'

'No, of course not!' I protested.

'*Good*… I'm very glad. I think that would be running away, don't you? – instead of facing up to what you've done and trying to make amends. This has all come as a terrible shock to him, and he's afraid it might drive him mad. I'd rather you stayed and did whatever he asks of you, no matter how difficult, or how painful. I think you owe him that, don't you?'

How could she even ask? 'Of course I owe it to him – I owe him everything!'

'Yes… well, I just wish you could have realised that before you were drawn into all this. But it's neither here nor there now – what's done is done. I think he'll want to go over it again with you, though, and it won't be pleasant, but I need you to be completely honest with him, to tell him *everything* – calmly – so he knows exactly where he stands, with nothing hidden from him. Then perhaps he can deal with it, put it all into some kind of perspective, because as things are at the moment I'm *very worried* for him!' She looked at me intently. 'The slightest thing could tip him over the edge—'

We heard the dreaded sound of the gates clanging together at the bottom of the drive, Beryl reaching down for the dogs' collars to hold them back as they started barking— '*Sit,* Joté!' she commanded as she got to her feet. 'Ygrec, *sit*! It's only the Master – *yes!* The *Master!* Now be quiet—!'

She peered round at me with a smile that was strangely conspiratorial, as if I were still eleven and she were still trying to defend me. 'The thing is, it's *not* your fault – not all of it… you didn't *cause* all this to happen, although you did conceal it, which was wrong. But I think you know that now.'

A moment later Robert burst through the fly curtain, clutching his straw hat.

Beryl was already there to greet him, a queen to her king, kissing his cheek – I'd never seen her kiss him before – hugging him, a diminutive figure against his huge bulk. 'Hello, darling!' she said warmly. 'Did you have a good bathe?'

'Thank you,' he murmured, doffing his hat to her, his eyes lighting on me suddenly, and turning to cold blue stone. I'd stood up the moment he came in, ready for whatever blow might fall.

'Good morning,' I said, unsure of what to say, what to do—

'Hello,' he grunted, as if to a stranger, himself a stranger to me now, piercing me with his withering gaze. 'Actually, it's not a good morning at all – it's one of the worst mornings I've ever had to endure, and you're the cause of it.'

Beryl looked up at him, frowning. 'Robert—'

'No – I know—' he held up his hand to her. 'Be that as it may, your great-aunt has spent most of the morning defending you, and in some ways I suppose she has a point – I'm not the only one to have been deceived – but in other ways I think what you've done is indefensible. Whether or not I'll ever be able to forgive you I can't say, not yet—' His face was terrible to look at, stone dead, loveless. 'I have to work now – I've a lot to do – but I want to talk to you later. I need to know everything – the *truth* – from the beginning. I want you to stay close to the house. Don't speak to anyone except Beryl. I'll send for you when I'm ready.'

The days that followed were a living hell, although at first the relief of not having to lie or evade any more was like an anaesthetic, numbing the pain of Robert's endless barrage of questions. By the second day, though, when I thought I'd told him everything I knew down to the smallest detail, (apart from my true feelings for Margot, which Beryl had hardly touched on), of what she'd worn, what she'd bought, how she'd looked at Alastair, he renewed his onslaught from the beginning, in part, perhaps, to catch me out in what I'd told him, but mostly to feed his anger and pain – a strange form of gluttony that could never be satisfied, no matter what I said, or how often I said it.

And I could have said anything; our shared naivety, which had so effortlessly drawn us together, laid him open time and again to any lie I might have chosen to tell, any story I might have made up to deflect the blame from myself, and yet I was incapable of taking advantage of him for fear of the bad luck which would inevitably catch up with me if I did.

The remorseless questioning went on, until my head reeled with a kind of shellshock. He was merciless. I was his only scapegoat, after all, and once his first incandescent rage had blown itself off, like flaming brandy over a Christmas pudding, the scorched holly of his anger still remained, as a warning to me. Even though I was occasionally allowed to pick at the charred and bitter currants round the edge, the invitation to help myself to a slice of him, which had once been my automatic right, never came.

On the third day of my inquisition we were back in his study again, but this time, once he'd started on the subject of Alastair, it wasn't long before he began pacing up and down like a caged animal, his eyes burning with hatred and revenge, seemingly unable to endure the claustrophobia of his room, until he could bear it no longer and suddenly flung open the door onto the terrace—

'Come on!' he commanded, 'we're going to do something! I'm damned if I'll sit here and do nothing. And besides, I need some air—'

But there was no air. The afternoon was sultry and still, the sun glazed over with high cloud, like the eye of an angry, dying year.

He strode off down the shadowless drive with me in tow, out onto the coast road where I drew level with him on his left-hand side, at which he instantly adjusted his pace to mine so that there could be no distraction to the rhythm of his thoughts as we marched along together. I was childishly reassured by the familiar ritual, and took care to keep in step.

'He's the Twin, you see,' he said finally, continuing to demolish Alastair, 'the fatal Twin who steals the Muse – the inspiration – from the one true poet, in the belief that he'll depose me – which he won't, of course, because he's not a true poet and never will be. I've decided to curse him – and Margot – and so shall you. Her powers were waning fast – did you notice that – how her powers were weakened by her own treachery?'

I had to admit that she'd seemed different towards the end – apprehensive, less sure of herself – and on the night of the violent wind, when she'd been blown, as if by her own chaos, from the Posada to Canellun, her eyes blind with a panic I'd never seen in them before – and yet who could blame her, faced with the fury she'd predicted that night in Madrid, and which I'd since witnessed for myself?

Even so, everything I'd told him seemed to fit into his reading of events, every fact, which he dissected like a surgeon and then handed back to me in the light of his greater intelligence and understanding of the significance of what I'd said, was proved right, time after time.

I was so engrossed in our thoughts as we marched on, my eyes staring intently at the ground, that when I finally looked up it was to see that we were approaching the square tower. I was astonished, with no memory at all of coming down this path. Robert, too, glanced up before stopping abruptly as we drew abreast of it, forcing me to an untidy halt.

He glared at the tower with fierce intent for a moment, then shook his head. 'No,' he muttered to himself, 'not close enough—' He frowned heavily, covering his eyes with his hand for a moment, as though clutching at some vision in his head. 'No, I know!' he exclaimed suddenly. 'Come on!'

We went on, much faster than before, down the treacherous zigzag path to the *cala* at almost breakneck speed.

Where on earth were we going? We neither of us had our swimming things—

When I finally reached the bottom, a good twenty yards behind him, Robert had already crossed the torrent and started to climb the hill behind the café.

'Come on!' he shouted back at me. 'We have to do this together!'

Do *what*? *Where*? But I said nothing, crossing the bridge after him.

Halfway up the hill I suddenly realised where he was leading me, and stumbled with apprehension. We were going back to the tower on the headland, to the *atalaya*.

As I went on climbing, my memories of it began to flood back, as though an amnesial dam had burst inside my head. overwhelming me with everything I thought I'd never have to face again—

'*Do we have to go there?*' I shouted up at Robert, already on the ridge of the headland.

He stopped and glared down at me, face grim with determination. 'Go *where*?' he challenged.

'To the *atalaya*—'

'How did you know?'

'I just knew, that's all. Wait – please!'

He waited impatiently until I reached him. 'I'm sorry,' I fought for breath, 'it's just that something happened there when I was a boy – I took some magic things from your study – cast a spell—'

His frown cleared suddenly. 'Oh, that – yes – Beryl told me. Something about a scorpion—' I nodded urgently. 'What was your spell?' His curiosity piqued at last.

'To bring me back—'

'Well, it worked, didn't it?' His frown returning, his tone forbidding again. 'I wish to God it hadn't!' He must have seen the hurt in my eyes. 'Even so… why are we going there?'

'Because it's the closest point to Margot and Alastair—'

His stare at last contained a grain of what we'd once shared for each other.

'Then it's doubly right! Come on.'

I followed him as he strode determinedly along the faint path, now strewn with seven more years of pine needles since I'd last raced along it, naked, the oppressive, heavy scent of the wild pines still seeming to suck the oxygen from the air. What with the heat and stillness around us, I felt as though I were being drawn back into an unfinished dream, my hackles rising in premonition – of *what?* I'd been a mere child then, and yet something had happened which had tied me to this moment, knowing that I'd be here, that I'd return, as I had begged to—

Well, I'd got what I'd asked for, as if in a fairytale – with consequences attached and a price to pay that were beyond my worst fears, and far beyond my means to pay them.

I followed Robert with a sudden fatalism which was almost a relief, since I had no choice now but to follow him, so that by the time we caught our first glimpse of the tower I was close behind, my heart racing as we came through the last of the trees to where the pale stone tower reared out of the ground, stark and massive against its backdrop of dark blue sea, as daunting as I remembered it, undiminished in any way by the years between. I shivered involuntarily as I looked up at it, and then down again from its giddy height.

'*Blast!*' Robert jolted to a halt. 'Where's the staircase—?'

I looked up again, astonished that I hadn't noticed it had gone, leaving nothing to connect the doorway of the tower, some fifteen feet above us, to the ground below. All the old cannon had gone, too, perhaps into the sea, or to be melted down for bronze—

'It must have rotted,' Robert muttered. Defiantly, he stared up at the tower, thwarted by its sheer impregnability, then walked off, looking around him – for a fallen tree, perhaps, to use as a ramp—

I expected to feel nothing but relief that we couldn't get in, that I wouldn't have to face whatever awaited me here, but instead I felt as baulked as Robert. '*Have you found anything?*' I called out as he disappeared round the far side of the tower, towards the point.

'*No!*' His voice echoed weirdly off the outside wall of the tower, skimming round it like a flat stone across the surface of the sea. '*Come here—!*'

When I found him, he was standing on the edge of the cliff, a hundred feet or so above the still-restless swell of the waves below. Fearing vertigo again, I fixed my gaze firmly on his face, a face which had once more become merciless, the face of a judge, suddenly – or an executioner.

'Here will do just as well,' he said, adapting as he went along. 'In fact, we're nearer, and the place is just as sacred in its way – to the dead. This is where the Fascists used to kill their prisoners during the Spanish Civil War – they tied their arms and legs and threw them into the sea... only twenty-five years ago. One day they'll have their revenge – as will I. Come and stand next to me here on the edge, never mind your vertigo – in fact, to hell with your vertigo!' He grabbed me by my arm and pulled me next to him. 'If you fall, you fall! It's your look out—'

With my heart thundering sickeningly in my chest, I did as he asked, and for a moment we stood in silence as he pressed agitatedly at his sinuses, snorting angrily, hawking and spitting into the sea below.

'I could so easily kill you, you know,' he said off-handedly. 'If it weren't for your mother—'

'I know,' I answered. *Do it, then!*

But he didn't seem to hear. 'I want you to stare straight out to sea – don't look down, because I won't save you this time – there—' he pointed, 'slightly east of north—' His finger moving to the right, like a gun barrel. '*There!* I'll tell you when to repeat what I say—'

With his arm still outstretched, his fingers deforming themselves into an imprecation of *malocchio* that I'd become so familiar with in Italy, he paused for a moment to take a huge breath before launching violently into his curse on Alastair.

At first it was nothing more than an onslaught of fury and abuse, but then his words somehow alchemised into something far more sinister and archaic, into the essence of malediction itself, making my blood run cold, and when he occasionally commanded me to repeat what he'd said (as proof of my loyalty I supposed), I found myself crossing my fingers behind my back in the hope that my denial would weigh down his curse and sink it in the sea long before it reached the coast of France, if for no other reason than that Alastair had saved my life when Juan had pulled me from the ledge of rock. I glanced at Robert once, out of the corner of my eye, but the sight of him radiating hatred, almost to the point of madness, was unbearable to watch, and I quickly looked away.

When he started on Margot, even though his curse on her was more qualified (promising that he would expunge it forever if she would only return to him), I swivelled my eyes deliberately to the right, and stared instead towards the distant barren cone of the *Puig Mayor*, unsaying his every word with a conviction as powerful as his in my last helpless, speechless defence of her.

Once he'd finished, once the violence of his words and feelings was finally absorbed into the stunned silence around us, we turned for home without a word.

By this time, the whole affair was beginning to drive me into a kind of madness of my own. Late that night I sat down at the table in my room by candlelight and wrote my account of everything that had happened, from beginning to end, convinced not only that Alastair, but Robert himself might kill me if something else were to snap in his mind.

I'd hardly written the first page, though, before I realised that what I was writing was a travesty, not of the facts themselves, but of the wild, deluded dreams and passions which had driven them – the handwriting not even my own, but in a copperplate I'd been taught at school, in the kind of hand that Jonathan Harker might have used in his diary as he awaited his fate at the mercy of Dracula. Perhaps in an attempt to repay my debt to him (or out of cowardice), I wrote it for Robert's eyes only, for Beryl's sake, so that if he were to kill me, no blame would attach itself to him from my confession – only to Alastair, in case he wanted it to look as though Alastair had done it. No mention of falling out with my grand-uncle, of his terrifying rage, or of my true feelings for Margot, which I'd still managed to conceal from him. And besides, I dared not return to those times, to those scenes, to that love, as I wrote my account of what had happened – I not only dared not, I could not. *I could not—!*

She was gone—

She was gone... leaving me not only alone, but in such darkness that if I were to look back from what I was writing, caught unawares by some sudden radiance of her memory, I would go insane—

So I neither dared nor questioned, but pressed on, covering twelve sides of paper, putting the date against the last full stop, signing it not as me but as the dregs of what I'd become, and when I read it through, in growing despair at my inability to fly into the sun of what I so longed to express, to find the courage to transcend myself and tell the story in all the violent colours of its truth, I wanted only to hide what I'd written. Having drained every drop of blood from my account – all love, all beauty, passion, I'd reduced it to nothing more than a mawkish tale told by a fucking idiot.

LAST RITES

Robert continued to brainwash us both (there was no other word for it) until I became as convinced as he that the woman I'd loved no longer existed except as some ineffable memory we'd once shared, however unequally. So that slowly, as the days dragged on and the weather finally broke, filling the sky with clouds and heavy-hearted, drenching rain, my love for Margot, like Robert's, began to rot for lack of her, and turn to hatred.

I couldn't bring myself to explore the reasons for this sea change any more deeply than that – except perhaps to put it down to a deliberate act of self-preservation, choosing to cling to what I knew and loved in the absence of what I no longer knew and no longer dared to love. She had betrayed me first – that was the point – cheapened my love for her with debt after saying I owed her nothing, and gone, without even saying goodbye, leaving me alone to face my grand-uncle's wrath, to deceive him, deceive Beryl—

And yet—

To hell with all that! I had to wall her up, whether or not my love for her still lived, and leave, and not look back no matter what, because it was all too late now anyway, my love for her condemned to the same death as Robert's.

Karl, too, was in disgrace, not only for championing her in the first place, but for calling Robert a fool for losing the source of his greatest inspiration. Apparently he'd warned him time and again that his overbearing obsession for Margot would eventually drive her away, or into someone else's arms. Typically of Karl, he spoke his mind without a thought (or care) for anyone's feelings, not even Robert's.

Their row had become a blazing one, with Robert accusing him of disloyalty and ingratitude, and Karl retaliating by telling Robert to grow up, to stop behaving like a child before it was too late, before he lost all credibility with his peers and his public.

After that, Karl was banished from the house except on twice-daily matters of business, he and Renee and the children keeping to their side of the torrent which now raged between the two properties like a reminder of Robert's implacability.

Quite apart from his mental torment, Robert's stomach pains had returned, to the point that whenever he sat down to write to Margot or Alastair he felt so sick that he had to break off after a few sentences. His excuse, to me, was that he couldn't finish writing to either of them until he was convinced that my account of what had happened was true and irrefutable, even though I'd given him my word of honour that it was—

'What honour?' he'd demanded angrily, forcing me to look away in despair.

And yet even now, in spite of all that had happened, despite my disloyalty, he seemed unable to let go of me, or to throw me out. I was still all he had, I supposed. Although Beryl was closer to him than anyone, she was too worn out by the unrelenting heat, by his need for her to answer unanswerable questions and by the need to reassure him endlessly with the same words, over and over again. For his part, though, Robert still needed to talk, to think out loud to someone who'd not only listen but who knew instinctively what he meant, as if the common bond of our once-love for Margot, for all the hatred that now covered it like a biting winter frost, might yet survive this winter of his despair and return to him in spring as proof of The Goddess's bounty, as proof that a poet's death need be no less (nor more) symbolic than the change of seasons. He hadn't the slightest fear of dying as a man, but to die as a poet while faithfully discharging his duty to Her at the height of his powers was unthinkable. There had to be hope, a chance to win back the grail of Her favours, by fair means or foul, a way through the catastrophe of what had happened and away from the unthinkable end he foresaw for himself.

As for me, in spite of everything, there was nowhere I would rather be than here, with him – for much the same reason that he needed to be with me. At least, as we talked about her, she still lived within us beneath the bitter frost of malice and jealousy, her absent glamour as vivid as a dream just woken from, bringing him not only necessary pain but the chance of vital inspiration. Given time, he might yet exploit her loss. Deep within himself he knew, as I did, that nothing he could do or say would ever lessen her thrall, the poems she'd inspired in him the very proof and promise of his love-now-hatred for her. For my part, I had nothing to show for it that was of the slightest use to anyone; broken hearts were two a penny.

Then, one morning, after yet another violent mood-swing the night before, he suddenly appeared on the terrace above where Beryl and I were working in the garden, his hair wild, his face distraught.

'*It's done!*' he cried.

'*What's* done?' demanded Beryl, staring up at him in alarm.

'My letters – to *them*! What I've said will destroy them! Simon can drive me to the Posada – I might need him—'

Beryl looked away with a deep sigh. 'Well, you'd better take my letter to Margot too, I suppose – not that it'll destroy anyone, but still… it's on my desk.'

'Do you mind if I run upstairs and get my swimming things?' I called up to him. 'I might go for a bathe afterwards—'

He frowned irritably. 'Just hurry up, will you? I want to get this over with.'

I ran upstairs to my room, my mind already teeming with demons that were mine, not his, with rage, with thoughts of my own revenge, driven to what I had to do by the shared hysteria for vengeance which had gripped the last few days at Canellun. This was my last chance to reach her, to express the murderous pain I felt – *how could she have done this to me?* And once I'd hit on the instrument of my revenge – *how could I do this to her?*

Duende—

I pulled out my suitcase from under the bed—

By the time I ran out onto the drive, Robert was already halfway to the gates. Ramming my shoulder basket under the back seat of the Land Rover, I jumped into the driving seat, started the engine, and slowly followed him as he walked ahead of me, like a mute at a funeral.

Once we were out on the road and he'd finally decided to open the door and climb in, I continued to drive slowly, out of respect for his brooding, restless silence. Was the beginning of a new poem going through his head at last? He sat with his basket on his lap, the three letters, in airmail envelopes, sticking out of it. Perhaps he was simply imagining the effect that his letters, at least, would have on Margot and Alastair. As a poet, his words would be far more lethal than blows. Feeling sick at the thought of what the envelopes contained, I slid open my window which had been closed against the rain.

The sky was overcast with the threat of more rain to come, the air hot and muggy, with a faint smell of putrefaction to it.

Still without a word between us, we reached the steps below the Posada and got out.

At first, as we climbed the shallow steps, I couldn't make out what was so different until I realised that the usual silence up here, at the top of the village, was now underscored by the distant roar of the swollen torrent snaking through the valley hundreds of feet below us, towards the *cala*. Although it was also, almost certainly, the source of the smell of decay, it was a wonderful sound, a moment of irrelevant beauty in a day that was already sullen with doom.

Robert seemed not to notice it, striding up the donkey steps, fumbling in his basket. Without even looking up at the shuttered house, he pulled out the heavy iron key and rammed it into the lock, turning it with the usual screech of protest as the bolt was drawn back. I felt that we were somehow trespassing on hallowed ground, but Robert simply flung open the door and strode in. This was his property after all, and he'd already turned himself into an aggrieved landlord repossessing it from a delinquent tenant – 'Look out for any damage!' he called out as he went from room to room on the ground floor. 'See if anything's broken or missing—'

Unwilling to join his witch hunt, I looked around, knowing I'd find nothing. All trace of her was gone. My gaze drifted upwards to the gallery above, to the door of her room.

From the kitchen I heard him throw open doors and cupboards, rifling, rummaging, snorting with irritation occasionally, working himself into another rage. The sweat on the back of my neck went cold at the memory of his fury, the beast within him capable of bursting out with nightmarish speed—

There was the sudden sound of a heavy glass shattering on the tiled floor, of Robert swearing, followed by a brief silence. I knew, without being there, that he was staring down at the glittering green shards, searching for omens.

Whatever he read into the breakage, he looked demented as he came through into the dining hall and headed straight for the stairs.

'*Come on*—!' he commanded, without looking at me.

Grabbing my basket, I followed him as he took the steps two at a time, as though he might still catch her on the premises – as he longed to – storming like an enraged bull along the gallery, throwing open the door of her room and walking straight onto the sword that awaited him in the gloom—

I was close behind him as he entered, close enough to hear the abysmal groan he let out, as if he'd been run through the heart—

'*Robert?*' I stared at him from the doorway of the shuttered room as he faltered, then dragged himself together and stumbled over to the windows. Following him in, I too was assailed by the miasma of her unforgettable scent haunting the lifeless air until Robert, like a drowning man, wrenched open the windows and flung the shutters outwards, throwing himself over the sill to breathe in any breath but hers.

'*I can't bear it!*' His voice broken with love for what he'd killed.

But *I* could bear it, inhaling the memory of her like an addict, faint from the effort of breathing her *in, and in, and in* – letting nothing out, until my brain reeled, staring at her trunk, as if at the ark of her covenant between us, still placed where the two of us had dragged it less than a week ago.

Apart from that, just her sheets and bedspread, neatly folded at the foot of the bare mattress, her pillows laid against them like standing stones—

Robert suddenly turned back from the window into the room, fumbling in his basket, grabbing the letters and thrusting them at me – 'Here – you do it!' He delved for the key to her trunk and flung it onto the tiles. 'Put my letter to her on top – but first, I want you to read it – it's not sealed – then seal it and put them in the trunk and lock it—'

I stared into the havoc in his eyes, not quite understanding.

'*Do as I tell you!*' he bellowed, striding to the door. 'I'm going to look through the rest of the house – make sure—'

I stood where he'd left me, dumb with shock, alone with all that was left of her – the anguish of her redolence, the neat pile of her sheets, the Pandora's box of everything she held most precious left behind her in panic, not realising that it would be returned to her as a coffin containing the corpse of Robert's love, of Beryl's, mine—

I put down my shoulder basket and the letters and picked up the key from where Robert had flung it – small but heavy, made of ornate brass.

'*Have you read it?*' he shouted from another room, as he threw open cupboard doors and drawers and slammed them shut—

'Give me a chance!' I croaked, grabbing the envelope addressed to Margot in his handwriting, pulling out the letter— *'Margot – Simon has told me everything—'*

Oh God, oh God, oh God!

I found it more and more unbearable to read as I imagined the effect it would have on her, until my eyes blurred over and I had to close them, smearing away the tears with my fingers.

'*Well?*' Robert glared in at me from the doorway.

'It's awful,' I stared at him in desperation. 'Do you really have to send it?'

'Of course I do! She has to know that she's forfeited everything – my love, the favours of the Goddess, her muse-hood – she's *nothing*, now – *nothing* – unless she returns to me. She's a mere mortal now – not even that – as I've told her! Get on with it, will you?'

And he was gone again, storming along the gallery and down the stairs.

I couldn't bring myself to finish the letter, the poisoned ink and words already sapping my energy as I sank to my knees in front of her cabin trunk and flung my arms over it as though over her body, begging her not to leave, to return us all to where we were, to Robert's forgiveness, whatever the price, to the dazzling light of our first meeting—

'*Have you done it?*' His voice echoing up from below as he swept up the shards of broken glass.

'*I'm doing it!*' I yelled back furiously.

'*Don't forget to seal the envelope!*'

Why? To add my poison to his?

Licking the gum, I sealed the envelope and reached for the others as I took the key and rammed it into the lock and turned it, heaving up the vaulted lid of the trunk –

—almost fainting from the sudden surfeit of her scent, the very essence of her, more intimate than ever for its confinement, lifting out the fitted tray to a sigh of relief from the trapped air within, her perfume more powerful still, my face and hands drawn into the body of the trunk, burying themselves among the memories of my love for her, sifting, searching through her finery for everything she'd been and still was to me – alive, triumphant, laughing—

And finding nothing but the sloughed-off skins of her incarnations, the treasured disguises that she would use to dazzle other men, until I was wracked with helpless sobs of grief, of love, of hatred, loss, which I dared not let Robert hear, smothering her name and my screams of 'Why?' and *'Why?'* and *'WHY?'* with armfuls of treacherous slithering clothes until a rage like madness burst through me and I began to tear them from their layers of rustling tissue paper and fling them across the floor with one hand as I reached for my basket with the other, dragging it towards me, pulling out my rolled-up towel, unfurling its unnatural weight across the floor until the leaden sound of a human head thudded out of it and continued to roll on across the tiles where it rocked for a moment on its side, facing me, mouth agape in the horror of her death, the saffron parchment of her skin drawn taut across the bones of her face—

'*Simon*—?'

'*Wait*—!' I yelled back, beyond caring now as I leapt to my feet and grabbed up her clothes, flinging them feverishly back into the trunk, then reaching for the mummified head with both hands before falling to my knees again, the skull held high above my head like an offering to the god of vengeance as I rammed it into the chaos of her clothes, face up, then jammed the letters brutally into her gaping mouth, transforming it into a surreal *shout* of words, of curses – before picking up the tray of trinkets by its handles and sliding it home and slamming the lid shut on the nightmare I'd improvised for her, slamming the hasp into its keep, locking it shut—

My eye flew from the key to the open window and I was on my feet in an instant, striding back into the room with the key grasped in my clenched fist as I turned and ran towards it, my arm drawn back to fling the key out across the rooftops below—

—when the memory of throwing-not-throwing the glass into the fireplace at Canellun flashed through my head and I clenched my fingers round the key, pressing it to my mouth—

Returning to Canellun in the Land Rover with Robert, as restless as before – worse than before – fidgeting with his basket, with his face, looking wildly around him, unseeing.

'Did you do as I asked?' he said at last.

'Yes.'

'I have your word? You locked the trunk?'

'Yes – and yes.'

He held out his hand. 'You'd better give me the key.'

'I threw it out of the window,' I lied, the key burning through my pocket against my thigh, 'as far as I could—'

He turned to me with a frown of anger, then suddenly clasped at his head, his eyes closing in despair – 'I've nowhere to send it anyway,' he gasped.

I said nothing. She had a second key, I was sure of it.

Once I'd driven to the top of the drive at Canellun I had to brake sharply as he started to get out while we were still moving. Without another word to me he slammed his door and strode straight past the kitchen towards his study, and I knew, with a sense of awful desolation, that this was the end between us.

Later, in the quiet of that afternoon, Beryl and I sat on the terrace under the awning over the kitchen window, sheltering from the sun.

For the past hour or so I'd felt the strangest sensations in my head, as if waking slowly from a familiar dream which I longed to be free of and yet longed to return to, the feeling of relief and regret almost unbearable.

I glanced round at her, sensing that this, too, might be our last chance to be alone together – a chance I must take if I were ever to unravel the knot which had bound me so helplessly to a course of events beyond my control. Only she, I was convinced, could help me make sense of it now.

Instinctively, I felt that something of what was going through my head was going through hers, the words unsayable as yet because they were still unformed; as always, she was waiting like an oracle for me to speak first, either to ask what I wanted to ask, or to say what I wanted to say – but if I didn't ask or say something soon, the moment would be lost.

I felt the sudden terrible claustrophobia of finality begin to close in on me, leaving me nowhere to go, going nowhere but leave—

I took a deep breath, as if it were my last. 'I think I should leave.' The words out before I could change them— 'Tomorrow.'

For a moment she frowned, then slowly nodded. 'Yes,' she said simply. 'It's probably for the best.'

'He's very angry,' I went on, unable to stop now, 'he can't even bring himself to look at me.'

'Well, what do you *expect*?' she asked quietly. 'You remind him of everything that's gone wrong... Are you *sure* though?' She stared at me, her eyes full of the sympathy she reserved only for children or animals in distress.

I looked away, nodding, not trusting myself to speak.

Perhaps aware of my difficulty she, too, looked away, towards the village, lost in thought.

'It was all *meant*, you know,' she murmured at last, glancing round at me as if to make sure that I was in a fit state to listen.

The quiet intensity of her voice sharpened my senses at once. 'What do you mean?' I asked, making a powerful effort to pull myself together. This was what I'd been waiting for, after all—

'Did you ever read that copy of *The White Goddess* that Robert gave you – before you went to Madrid?'

Yet again I was caught out. 'I tried, honestly – but it's a bit like fighting one's way through an impenetrable Welsh forest in pitch darkness—' I pulled a face, trying to make light of my failure. 'I'll keep trying, though—'

'I think you *should*,' she murmured, almost to herself. Then she cleared her throat. 'It's all in there, you see, if you know where to look for it – and last night I looked for it because there were simply too many bells ringing in my head. Robert foresaw all this when he first wrote it, almost twenty years ago – just after you were born, I suppose – the Goddess, the Muse – Margot – he the poet, Alastair the Twin, and even you, Llew Llaw, the little shoemaker – all as he predicted. Except that I don't think you'll die for your part in it – at least, I hope not. Perhaps you didn't go quite as far as you were meant to go—'

Infuriatingly I felt that I was concentrating too hard on what she was saying without properly grasping the point. 'What do you mean, exactly?' I asked

With a small sigh – of impatience? – she looked away again, back towards the mountains towering over Deya, already washed with the blood of the setting sun.

'Everything that's happened has been a self-fulfilling prophecy,' she said at last. 'By which I mean that no one could have done anything of their own free will, try as they might – not Robert, not Margot, not you, not even Alastair, though I hate to admit it… The vision – and it *was a vision* – was Robert's, and everyone has played their part in it, as he foresaw they would… I just can't believe I could have been so blind not to have seen it while it was happening – but perhaps that was *meant*, too. As I say, you were as helpless as the others, and if I'm to believe you – which I *do* – then you were as blind as I was until the end. Everyone was blind in their way – except Alastair of course – the Twin, the betrayer – but then his part was to see his chance and take it…'

609

We sat in silence as her words began to release themselves into my slow brain, and then to expand, filling it with a new awareness which I grasped at like a drowning man – but still said nothing, unsure of whether or not she was throwing me a lifeline, an absolution of some kind—

And yet in the instant I convinced myself that she had, my mind expanded into a deeper consciousness: that the oracular powers I'd so casually attributed to her were real, that she was more than my familiar great-aunt—

'Beryl—' my last chance to consult her – my last confession – 'I think I've done something wrong.'

'Oh *dear*—' She turned to stare at me intently, waiting. So I told her what I'd done with the skull, with their letters, about trying to throw away the key—

'But you didn't – throw the key away, I mean?'

'No. When Robert asked me for it, I lied – said I'd chucked it out of the window—'

'Does he know about the rest?'

'No. He was downstairs. He couldn't bear to do it himself—'

'So where's the key now?'

'In my pocket.'

She heaved a sigh and looked away again, her eye caught by one of the cats trying to catch a gecko as it slipped out from its crevice in the wall. 'Abyssinia, you *brute*!' she called out softly as the cat caught the gecko by its tail – which immediately detached itself, still twitching, while the stunted gecko made its escape. With feline embarrassment, the cat started to play with the still-twitching tail.

'Well, I don't know about *you*,' said Beryl at last, 'but I think there's been enough harm done already.'

She looked round at me again, her kindly eyes wide, enquiring.

Later still, I found myself wandering aimlessly, numbly, through the grotto, my childhood memory of it still haunting me, not simply because I'd been born into a new life and a new awareness here, but because nothing had truly changed at Canellun – except for my place there – so that the Eden into which I'd at last been born, though gone to me now, perhaps forever, still existed in my head, where it would remain for as long as I lived.

What had caused me to destroy myself so utterly? What had I done – or seen, or heard, or even tasted – that had proved so fatal? And why? Because I'd always, unwittingly, played the serpent?

And yet Beryl's simple explanation, that we'd all danced to the fatal tune of Robert's premonition of nearly twenty years before, unable to take a single step beyond the boundaries of his poetic choreography, was the only answer that made sense to me now. As poet laureate to his Goddess, he alone had the power to manipulate the dance to Her demands. If there were another explanation, perhaps I'd find it one day, but for the moment it shattered the blame between us all, like the salad bowl I'd broken on the kitchen floor, with Robert's shard the largest of them all.

Eventually I climbed up the grotto steps into the twilit garden, where I found Beryl staring down disconsolately at her bedraggled plants, the dogs lying at her feet.

'*There* you are!' she said quietly as I came up to her (Robert's study light, overlooking the steps, already switched on). 'I was looking for you.'

'Has the rain helped at all?' I asked.

'Too late, I'm afraid… sometimes I wonder why I even bother… where were you?'

'Saying goodbye to the grotto.'

'Oh *dear*—' She pulled a face of commiseration.

'Beryl, the thought of never coming back—' I shook my head angrily, my eyes already stinging.

'You *will* come back.' She laid a hand on my arm. 'I promise. Robert will forgive you—'

'*But he never forgives!*'

'*Sssh!*' She glanced up at his window. 'He *will*! Trust me. He's as much to blame as you, after all, in his way. Deep inside, I think he knows that already – he just can't face it yet.'

I nodded furiously, unable to speak.

'And at least you've learned something from all this – which is your punishment, I suppose – or your gift… depending on how you look at it.'

Again I nodded and tried to smile, but could only pull off a ghastly grimace.

'Now then,' she said more briskly, 'I was looking for you because I've put the key to the Posada on the front seat of the Land Rover. What you do with it is up to you.'

I looked at her blankly for a moment, then caught on. 'Right!' I stared into the challenge in her eyes, smiling suddenly. 'I'll go now!'

She grinned back at me, my fellow-conspirator again. 'I'll open the gates—'

As I reversed out of the drive, past where she stood, I looked down at her through the side window in sudden astonishment – 'You've forgiven her, haven't you?' I asked quietly.

'Perhaps I have.'

The sun still shone on the top of the hill, high above Canellun, as I climbed the wide steps up to the Posada, clutching the heavy key in one hand, my empty basket in the other.

The initial excitement I'd felt had begun to ebb away, the thought of what I had to do making me quake inwardly, even as my feet began to drag. This would take more courage than I'd realised.

In my growing apprehension, I slammed the key into the lock and turned it violently, as Robert had done, throwing open the door and marching into the house, crossing the almost-darkness of the shuttered hall and climbing the stairs two at a time, striding along the landing to her door which I'd slammed behind me earlier.

Grasping the handle, I threw it open again, as if still expecting to come face to face with her—

But the room was empty, filled only with sunset, her scent almost gone, the shutters and windows still wide open as I'd left them, her cabin trunk still on the floor between them, from where it had already gone in my head, vanished back to her as if she were still immortal.

The sheets of tissue paper that I'd torn from her clothes began skittering across the tiled floor towards me, stirred by the draught from the open door.

Taking the key from my pocket, I crossed over to the cabin trunk and slowly knelt down in front of it again, slipping the key into the lock, turning it, springing the hasp, raising the heavy lid, the scent of her recurring and recurring as I lifted out the tray, almost dropping it as I stared down again, in horror, at the horror I'd wished on her—

Tears welled in my eyes as I carefully prized the letters out of the girl's gaping mouth and laid them aside before lifting out her head and laying it down gently beside me on the floor.

All that was left now was the chaos of her clothes – her precious clothes – rammed and coiled and twisted among each other in the chaos of hatred. One by one I unravelled everything, took them out, folded them, laying the garments beside me in neat growing piles until the trunk was empty.

Staring down into its void, at the cloth lining, patterned with tiny periwinkles, I yearned for the courage to fill the emptiness with my self, to ease the tray onto its runnels above me and rock the trunk until the lid crashed down, imprisoning me, the heavy hasp falling into its keep, and be returned to her—

I struggled to my feet with a groan, my hand pressing back the sound I'd heard as I gathered up the sheets of tissue paper from the floor and like an old retainer began to re-pack her trunk, meticulously, layer after layer, line after line, as if it were a sonnet, saving the best till last, so that she might see it first—

Lifting the tray by its handles, I lined it up over the mouth of the trunk and let it fall softly into place with its almost human sigh, the final waft of her so harrowing that I had to stop breathing for a moment and turn away.

Without even looking at them for fear that I might fail to put them back – or put back only Beryl's letter to Margot and dispose of Robert's – burn them – I laid the three envelopes on the tray and slammed the lid shut, closed the hasp and locked it and leapt up before I could think again – or again and again and again – and ran for the window, throwing the key with all my might—

—*into the sun—!*

—already sinking behind the far hill, my gesture futile except as one lie less – my only lie – wracked by futile remorse as I turned away and scooped up the skull and the last sheet of tissue paper and wrapped it up tenderly on my lap, pressing her to me like the head of a child, to my stomach, my heart, to everywhere that hurt—

I sat and rocked her until the sounds of my grief became nothing more than distant echoes reverberating from dark to darker corners of the room, my face cracked with long-dried tears, the first stars glittering faintly through the open windows as I staggered to my feet at last and toppled full length onto her bed, next to where she'd lain.

Tomorrow—

Oh God, tomorrow...

I would return. Beryl had promised me, so I would return, like the fishermen to the *cala* after the storm, and somehow make amends.

But tomorrow...

I stared up at the darkening ceiling as if in a trance, my mind's eye like a silent camera staring not into the past of my life here, but into the void of that tomorrow, when I was gone—

—peering in through the doorway of my room at Canellun, empty of my belongings now, the bed stripped, the mattress bare except for a neat pile of Robert's letters to me, returned as a gesture of contrition, weighed down with a candlestick: '*Dearest grand-nephew*—' The edges of the onion-skin paper stirring and rustling slightly in the evening breeze—

—peering in through the window of the study at Robert and Beryl sitting on either side of his desk in silence, Beryl staring at the sheets of blank paper in front of him, Robert thrown back in his chair, grasping the back of his head, staring wildly through the side window of the study towards the Camargue—

—to the Posada, closed and shuttered now except in my mind's eye, in my mind's ear the murmur of Robert's quiet voice reciting as I stare, ghost-like, from the doorway back into the growing murk of Margot's empty bedroom, at the dark bulk of her cabin trunk barely discernible between the shuttered windows—

—at the impression of my body where it had lain beside hers at last—

Alas for obstinate doubt; the dread
of error in supposing my heart freed,
all care for her stone dead!
Ineffably will shine the hills and
radiant coast
of early morning when she is gone
indeed—
her divine elements disbanded,
disembodied,
and through the misty orchards in love
spread—
when she is gone indeed…

But still among them moves her restless ghost.

ACKNOWLEDGEMENTS

I am deeply indebted in every way (and will probably remain so for the rest of my life) to the following:

Joy Layle, Mark Shivas and Michael Wearing of BBC Television, Johnny and Sandy Byrne, Dr James and Martha Foght, Rollo Armstrong, Henrietta Gough, Sir John MacTaggart, Bart., Tristram Hull, Nicholas Kittoe, Hamish and Gita Riley-Smith, William and Carol Fuller, Robert Hardy, Rayne Kruger and Prue Leith, Rachel Gurney, Simon Finch, Lucy and Richard Devitt, Peter and Mati Harrington, Adrian and Hermione Harrington, David and Marina Clark, and Jeremy and Mary Brettingham.

I am also profoundly grateful to the following for their unfailing criticism, help and patience:

James and Caroline Layte, Stella Irwin, Jonathan and Nicky Gathorne-Hardy, Richard and Caroline Girling, Mike and Lisa Hooton, Jenny Agutter, Elma Cameron, Keith Schilling and Kathy Lewis, Delaval and Veronica Astley, Matthew Guinness, Henry Layte, Sam Jordison and Eloise Millar, Mary Sandys, Professor Andrew Lister and St Bartholomew's Hospital, Rahere, Dean Steven Corey and Dr John Hawk (of Special Collections, Gleeson Library, University of San Francisco), The Antiquarian Bookseller's Association, Oliver and Claire Riviere, Kit Martin (for striking the flint that set fire to the scaffolding which obscured the early drafts of the book) and Sally (for watching it burn so revealingly), Peter Davidson, Dr Andrew Biswell and Leslie Gardner (for their kind attempts to fan the flames), *Givenchy et Cie* for 'Le de...'.

I would also like to gratefully acknowledge Carcanet Press Limited for their kind permission to reproduce the poems included in this book, taken from *Robert Graves, The Complete Poems*, Vol. I (1995), II (1997) and III (1999).

Thanks to A.P. WATT Limited for their permission to use The White Goddess in the title, for granting e-book rights.

In particular, thanks to The Robert Graves Copyright Trust.

Galley Beggar is grateful to the following people for their generous sponsorship of *The White Goddess: An Encounter*.

Benefactors:

Ian Peter Macdonald
Vivian Tait
Peter Wilson MBE
Geoff Rowe
James Layte
Gillie Mussett
Mike and Lisa Hooton
Hugh Aldersey-Williams
Ray Giordano

Principal founding sponsor:

Charles Carey

We would also like extend thanks to Lucy Lyall-Grant and Ben Cracknell (and all at his studios) for their marvellous help with copy-editing and typesetting.